ONE STEP BEHIND

Henning Mankell has become a worldwide phenomenon with his crime writing, gripping thrillers and atmospheric novels set in Africa. His prizewinning and critically acclaimed Kurt Wallander thrillers are currently dominating bestseller lists all over the globe. His books have been translated into over forty languages and made into numerous international film and television adaptations: most recently the BAFTA-award-winning BBC television series *Wallander*, starring Kenneth Branagh. Mankell devotes much of his free time to working with Aids charities in Africa, where he is director of the Teatro Avenida in Maputo. In 2008 the University of St Andrews conferred on Henning Mankell an honorary degree of Doctor of Letters, in recognition of his major contribution to literature and to the practical exercise of conscience.

Ebba Segerberg teaches English at Washington University in St Louis, Missouri.

ALSO BY HENNING MANKELL

HENNING MANKELL

One Step Behind

TRANSLATED FROM THE SWEDISH BY

Ebba Segerberg

VINTAGE BOOKS
London

Published by Vintage 2012

4 6 8 10 9 7 5 3

Copyright © Henning Mankell, 1997
English translation copyright © The New Press 2000

Henning Mankell has asserted his right under the Copyright, Designs
and Patents Act 1988 to be identified as the author of this work

First published with the title *Steget Efter* in 1997 by Ordfronts
Förlag, Stockholm

First published in Great Britain in 2002 by
The Harvill Press

Vintage
Random House, 20 Vauxhall Bridge Road,
London SW1V 2SA

www.vintage-books.co.uk

Addresses for companies within The Random House Group Limited
can be found at: www.randomhouse.co.uk/offices.htm

The Random House Group Limited Reg. No. 954009

A CIP catalogue record for this book
is available from the British Library

ISBN 9780099571759

The Random House Group Limited supports The Forest
Stewardship Council (FSC®), the leading international forest
certification organisation. Our books carrying the FSC label are
printed on FSC® certified paper. FSC is the only forest certification
scheme endorsed by the leading environmental organisations,
including Greenpeace. Our paper procurement policy can be found
at www.randomhouse.co.uk/environment

Printed and bound by CPI Group Ltd, Croydon, CR0 4YY

There are always many more disordered than ordered systems
FROM THE SECOND LAW OF THERMODYNAMICS

The Overture to *Rigoletto*
GIUSEPPE VERDI

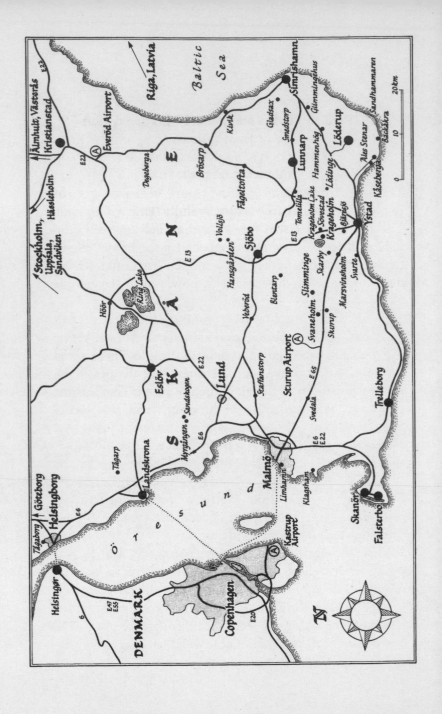

PROLOGUE

The rain stopped shortly after 5 p.m. The man crouching beside the thick tree trunk carefully removed his coat. The rain hadn't lasted for more than half an hour, and it hadn't been heavy, but damp had nonetheless seeped through his clothing. He felt a sudden flash of anger. He didn't want to catch a cold. Not now, not in the middle of summer.

He laid the raincoat on the ground and stood up. His legs were stiff. He started swaying back and forth gently to get his circulation going, at the same time looking around for any signs of movement. He knew that the people he was waiting for wouldn't arrive before 8 p.m. That was the plan. But there was a chance, however small, that someone else would come walking down one of the paths that snaked through the nature reserve. That was the only factor that lay beyond his control, the only thing he couldn't be sure of. Even so, he wasn't worried. It was Midsummer's Eve. There weren't any camping or picnic areas in the reserve, and the people had chosen the spot with care. They wanted to be alone.

They had decided on this place two weeks ago. At that point he had been following them closely for several months. He had even come to look at the spot after he learned of their decision. He had taken great pains not to let himself be seen as he wandered through the reserve. At one point an elderly couple came walking along one of the paths and he had hidden himself behind some trees until they passed.

Later, when he found the spot for their Midsummer festivities, he had immediately been struck by how ideal it was. It lay in a hollow with thick undergrowth all around. There were a few trees further up the hill. They couldn't have chosen a better spot – not for their purposes, nor his own.

The rain clouds were dispersing. The sun came out and it immediately became warmer. It had been a chilly June. Everyone had complained about the early summer in Skåne, and he had agreed. He always did. It's the only way to sidestep life's obstacles, he thought, to escape whatever crosses one's path. He had learned the art of agreeing.

He looked up at the sky. There would be no more rain. The spring and early summer had really been quite cold. But now, as evening approached on Midsummer's Eve, the sun came out at last. It will be a beautiful evening, he thought. As well as memorable.

The air smelt of wet grass. He heard the sound of flapping wings somewhere. To the left below the hill was a glimpse of the sea. He stood with his legs apart and spat out the wad of chewing tobacco that had started to dissolve in his mouth, then stamped it into the sand. He never left a single trace. He often thought that he should stop using tobacco. It was a bad habit, something that didn't suit him.

They had decided to meet in Hammar. That was the best place, since two of them were coming from Simrishamn and the others from Ystad. They would drive out to the nature reserve, park their cars, and walk to the spot they had chosen. They had not been able to agree upon anything for a long time. They had discussed various alternatives and sent the proposals back and forth. But when one of them finally suggested this place, the others had quickly assented, perhaps because they had run out of time. One of them took care of the food, while another went to Copenhagen and rented the clothes and wigs that were needed. Nothing would be left to chance. They even took the possibility of bad weather into account. At 2 p.m. on Midsummer's Eve, one of them put a big tarpaulin in his red duffel bag. He also included a roll of tape and some old aluminium tent pegs. If it rained, they would have shelter.

Everything was ready. There was only one thing that could not have been anticipated. One of them suddenly became ill. It was a young woman, the one who had perhaps been looking forward to the Midsummer's Eve plans most of all. She had met the others less than a year before. When she woke up that morning she had felt nauseated. At first she thought it was because she was nervous. But some hours later, when it was already midday, she had started vomiting and running a temperature. She still hoped it would pass. But when her lift arrived, she stood at the door on trembling legs and said that she was too ill to go.

Consequently, there were only three of them in Hammar shortly before 7.30 p.m on Midsummer's Eve. But they did not allow this to spoil the mood. They were experienced; they knew that these things happened. One could never guard against sudden illness.

They parked outside the nature reserve, took their baskets, and disappeared down one of the paths. One of them thought he heard an accordion in the distance. But otherwise there were just birds and the distant sound of the sea.

When they arrived at the selected spot they knew at once

that it had been the right choice. Here they would be undisturbed and free to await the dawn.

The sky was now completely free of clouds. The midsummer night would be clear and beautiful. They had made the plans for Midsummer's Eve at the beginning of February, when they had spoken of their longing for light summer nights. They had drunk large quantities of wine and quarrelled at length about the precise meaning of the word dusk. At what point did this particular moment between light and dark arrive? How could one really describe the landscape of twilight in words? How much could you actually still see when the light passed into this obscure state of transition, defined by a certain length of the shadows? They had not come to an agreement. The question of dusk had remained unsolved. But they had started planning their celebration that evening.

They arrived at the hollow and put down their baskets, then separated and changed behind some thick bushes. They wedged small make-up mirrors in the branches so they could check that their wigs were on straight.

None of them sensed the man who observed their careful preparations from a distance. Getting the wigs to sit straight turned out to be the easiest part. Putting on the corsets, padding and petticoats was more difficult, as was arranging the cravat and the ruffles, not to mention applying the thick layers of powder. They wanted every detail to be perfect. They were playing a game, but the game was in earnest.

At 8 p.m. they came out from behind their bushes and looked at each other. It was a breathtaking moment. Once more they had left their own time for another age. The age of Bellman, the bacchanalian 18th-century poet.

They drew closer and burst into laughter. But then they

4

regained their composure. They spread out a large table-cloth, unpacked their baskets and put on a tape with several renditions of the most famous songs from Bellman's work, *Fredman's Epistles.* Then the celebration began.

When winter comes, they said to each other, we will think back on this evening. They were creating yet another secret for themselves.

At midnight he had still not made up his mind. He knew he had plenty of time. They would be staying until dawn. Perhaps they would even stay and sleep all morning. He knew their plans down to the last detail. It gave him a feeling of unlimited power. Only he who had the upper hand would escape.

Just after 11 p.m., when he could tell that they were tipsy, he had carefully changed his position. He had picked out the starting point for his actions on his first visit. It was a dense thicket a bit higher up the hill. Here he had a full view of everything that was happening on the light-blue tablecloth. And he could approach them without being seen. From time to time they left the tablecloth in order to relieve themselves. He could see everything they did.

It was past midnight. Still he waited. He waited because he was hesitating. Something was wrong. There should have been four of them. One of them had not come. In his head he went through the possible reasons. There was no reason. Something unexpected must have happened. Had the girl changed her mind? Was she sick?

He listened to the music and the laughter. From time to time he imagined that he too sat down there on the light-blue tablecloth, a wineglass in his hand. Afterwards he would try on one of the wigs. Perhaps some of the clothes, too? There was so much he could do. There were no limits. He could not have had more power over them if he had been invisible.

He continued to wait. The laughter rose and fell. Somewhere above his head a night bird swooped by.

It was 3.10 a.m. He couldn't wait any longer. The moment was at hand, the hour he alone had appointed. He could barely remember the last time he had worn a watch. The hours and minutes ticked continuously within him. He had an inner clock that was always on time.

Down by the light-blue tablecloth everything was still. They lay with their arms wrapped around one another, listening to the music. He didn't know if they were sleeping, but they were lost in the moment, and did not sense that he was right behind them.

He picked up the revolver with the silencer that had been lying on his raincoat. He looked around quickly, then made his way stealthily to the tree located directly behind the group, and paused for a few seconds. No one had noticed anything. He looked around one last time. But there was no one else there. They were alone.

He stepped out and shot each of them once in the head. He couldn't help it that blood splattered onto the white wigs. It was over so quickly that he barely had time to register what he was doing. But now they lay dead at his feet, still wrapped around each other, just like a few seconds before.

He turned off the tape recorder that had been playing and listened. The birds were chirping. Once again he looked around. Of course there was no one there. He put his gun away and spread a napkin out on the cloth. He never left a trace.

He sat down on the napkin and looked at those who

had recently been laughing and who now were dead. The idyll hasn't been affected, he thought. The only difference is that we are now four. As the plan had been all along.

He poured himself a glass of red wine. He didn't really drink, but now he simply couldn't resist. Then he tried on one of the wigs. He ate a little of the food. He wasn't particularly hungry.

At 3.30 a.m. he got up. He still had much to do. The nature reserve was frequented by early risers. In the unlikely event that someone left the path and found their way into the hollow, they must not find any traces. At least not yet.

The last thing he did before he left the spot was look through their bags and clothes. He found what he was looking for. All three had been carrying their passports. Now he put them into his coat pocket. Later that day he would burn them.

He looked around one last time. He took a little camera out of his pocket and took a picture.

Only one. It was like looking at a painting of a picnic from the 18th century, except that someone had spilled blood on this painting.

It was the morning after Midsummer's Eve. Saturday, June 22. It was going to be a beautiful day. Summer had come to Skåne at last.

Part One

CHAPTER ONE

On Wednesday, 7 August 1996, Kurt Wallander came close to being killed in a traffic accident just east of Ystad. It happened early in the morning, shortly after 6 a.m. He had just driven through Nybrostrand on his way out to Österlen. Suddenly he had seen a truck looming in front of his Peugeot. He heard the truck's horn blaring as he wrenched the steering wheel to one side.

Afterwards he had pulled off the road. That was when the fear set in. His heart pounded in his chest. He felt nauseated and dizzy, and he thought he was about to faint. He kept his hands tightly clenched on the wheel. As he calmed down he realised what had happened. He had fallen asleep at the wheel. Nodded off just long enough for his old car to begin to drift into the opposite lane. One second longer and he would have been dead, crushed by the heavy truck.

The realisation made him feel suddenly empty. The only thing he could think of was the time, a few years earlier, when he had almost hit an elk outside Tingsryd. But then it had been dark and foggy. This time he had nodded off at the wheel.

The fatigue. He didn't understand it. It had come over him without warning, shortly before the start of his holiday at the beginning of June. This year he had taken his holiday early, but the whole holiday had been lost to rain. It was only when he returned to work shortly after

Midsummer that the warm and sunny weather had come to Skåne. The tiredness had been there all along. He fell asleep whenever he sat down. Even after a long night's undisturbed sleep, he had to force himself out of bed. Often when he was in the car he found himself needing to pull over to take a short nap.

His daughter Linda had asked him about his lack of energy during the week that they had spent sightseeing together in Gotland. It was on one of the last days, when they had stayed in an inn in Burgsvik. They had spent the day exploring the southern tip of Gotland, and had eaten dinner at a pizzeria before returning to the inn. The evening was particularly beautiful.

She had asked him point-blank about the fatigue. He had studied her face in the glow of the kerosene lamp and realised that her question had been thought out in advance, but he shrugged it off. There was nothing wrong with him. Surely the fact that he used part of his holiday to catch up on lost sleep was to be expected. Linda didn't ask any more questions. But he knew that she hadn't believed him.

Now he realised that he couldn't ignore it any longer. The fatigue wasn't natural. Something was wrong. He tried to think if he had other symptoms that could signal an illness. But apart from the fact that he sometimes woke in the middle of the night with leg cramps, he hadn't been able to think of anything. He knew how close to death he had been. He couldn't put it off any longer. He would make an appointment with the doctor that day.

He started the engine, rolling down the windows as he drove on. Although it was already August, the heat of summer showed no sign of easing. Wallander was on his way to his father's house in Löderup. No matter how many times he went down this road, he still found it hard to adjust to the fact that his father wouldn't be sitting there in his studio, wreathed in the ever-present smell of turpentine, before the easel on which he painted pictures with a recurring and unchanging subject: a landscape, with or without a grouse in the foreground, the sun hanging from invisible threads above the trees.

It had been close to two years now since Gertrud had called him at the police station in Ystad to tell him that his father was lying dead on the studio floor. He could still recall with photographic clarity his drive out to Löderup, unable to believe it could be true. But when he had seen Gertrud in the yard, he had known he could not deny it any longer. He had known what awaited him.

The two years had gone by quickly. As often as he could, but not often enough, he visited Gertrud, who still lived in his father's house. A year went by before they began to clean up the studio in earnest. They found a total of 32 finished paintings. One night in December of 1995, they sat down at Gertrud's kitchen table and made a list of the people who would receive these last paintings. Wallander kept two for himself, one with a grouse, the other without. Linda would get one, as would Mona, his ex-wife. Surprisingly, and to Wallander's disappointment, his sister Kristina hadn't wanted one. Gertrud already had several, and so they had 28 paintings to give away. After some hesitation, Wallander sent one to a detective in Kristianstad with whom he had sporadic contact. But after giving away 23 paintings, including one to each of Gertrud's relatives, there were five paintings remaining.

Wallander wondered what he should do with them. He knew that he would never be able to make himself burn them. Technically they belonged to Gertrud, but she had said that he and Kristina should have them. She had come into their father's life so late.

Wallander passed the turn-off to Kåseberga. He would be there soon. He thought about the task that lay before him. One evening in May, he and Gertrud had taken a long walk along the tractor paths that wound their way along the edges of the linseed fields. She had told him that she no longer wanted to live there. It was starting to get too lonely.

"I don't want to live there so long that he starts to haunt me," she had said.

Instinctively, he knew what she meant. He would probably have reacted the same way. They walked between the fields and she asked for his help in selling the house. There was no hurry; it could wait until the summer's end, but she wanted to move out before the autumn. Her sister was recently widowed and lived outside the town of Rynge, and she wanted to move there.

Now the time had come. Wallander had taken the day off. At 9 a.m. an estate agent would come out from Ystad, and together they would settle on a reasonable selling price. Before that, Wallander and Gertrud would go through the last few boxes of his father's belongings. They had finished packing the week before. Martinsson, one of his colleagues, came out with a trailer and they made several trips to the dump outside Hedeskoga. Wallander experienced a growing sense of unease. It seemed to him that the remnants of a person's life inevitably ended up at the nearest dump.

All that was left of his father now – aside from the memories – were some photographs, five paintings, and a few boxes of old letters and papers. Nothing more. His life was over and completely accounted for.

Wallander turned down the road leading to his father's house. He caught a glimpse of Gertrud waiting in the yard. To his surprise he saw that she was wearing the same dress she had worn at their wedding. He immediately felt a lump in his throat. For Gertrud, this was a moment of solemnity. She was leaving her home.

They drank coffee in the kitchen, where the doors to the cupboards stood ajar, revealing empty shelves. Gertrud's sister was coming to collect her today. Wallander would keep one key and give the other to the estate agent. Together they leafed through the contents of the two boxes. Among the old letters Wallander was surprised to find a pair of children's shoes that he seemed to remember from his childhood. Had his father saved them all these years?

He carried the boxes out to the car. When he closed the car door, he saw Gertrud on the steps. She smiled.

"There are five paintings left. You haven't forgotten about them, have you?"

Wallander shook his head. He walked towards his father's studio. The door was open. Although they had cleaned it, the smell of turpentine remained. The pot that his father had used for making his endless cups of coffee stood on the stove.

This may be the last time I am here, he thought. But unlike Gertrud, I haven't dressed up. I'm in my baggy old clothes. And if I hadn't been lucky I could be dead, like my father. Linda would have had to drive to the dump with what was left after me. And among my stuff she would find two paintings, one with a grouse painted in the foreground.

The place scared him. His father was still in there in the dark studio. The paintings were leaning against one wall. He carried them to the car. Then he laid them in the boot and spread a blanket over them. Gertrud remained on the steps.

"Is there anything else?" she asked.

Wallander shook his head. "There's nothing else," he answered. "Nothing."

At 9 a.m. the estate agent's car swung into the yard, and a man got out from behind the wheel. To his surprise, Wallander realised that he recognised him. His name was Robert Åkerblom. A few years earlier his wife had been brutally murdered and her body dumped in an old well. It had been one of the most difficult and grisly murder investigations that Wallander had ever been involved in.

He frowned. He had decided to contact a large estate agent with offices all over Sweden. Åkerblom's business did not belong to them, if it even still existed. Wallander thought he had heard that it had shut down shortly after Louise Åkerblom's murder.

He went out onto the steps. Robert Åkerblom looked exactly as Wallander remembered him. At their first meeting in Wallander's office he had wept. The man's worry and grief for his wife had been genuine. Wallander recalled that they had been active in a non-Lutheran church. He thought they were Methodists.

They shook hands. "We meet again," Robert Åkerblom said.

His voice sounded familiar. For a second Wallander felt confused. What was the right thing to say? But Robert Åkerblom beat him to it.

"I grieve for her as much now as I did then," he said slowly. "But it's even harder for the girls."

Wallander remembered the two girls. They had been so young then. They had been unable to fully understand what had happened.

"It must be hard," Wallander said. For a moment he was afraid that the events of the last meeting would repeat themselves; that Robert Åkerblom would start crying. But that didn't happen.

"I tried to keep the business going," Åkerblom said, "but I didn't have the energy. When I got the offer to join the firm of a competitor, I took it. I've never regretted it. I don't have the long nights of going over the books any more. I've been able to spend more time with the girls."

Gertrud joined them and they went through the house together. Åkerblom made notes and took some photographs. Afterwards they had a cup of coffee in the kitchen. The price that Åkerblom came up with seemed low to Wallander at first, but then he realised that it was three times what his father had paid for the place.

Åkerblom left a little after 11 a.m. Wallander thought he should stay until Gertrud's sister came to get her, but she seemed to sense his thoughts and told him she didn't mind being left alone.

"It's a beautiful day," she said. "Summer has come at last, even though it's almost over. I'll sit in the garden."

"I'll stay if you like. I'm off work today."

Gertrud shook her head. "Come and see me in Rynge," she said. "But wait a couple of weeks. I have to get settled in."

Wallander got in his car and drove back to Ystad. He was going straight home to make an appointment with his doctor. Then he would sign up to use the laundry and clean his flat. Since he wasn't in a hurry, he chose the longer way home. He liked driving, just looking at the landscape and letting his mind wander. He had just passed Valleberga when the phone rang. It was Martinsson. Wallander pulled over.

"I've been trying to get hold of you," Martinsson said. "Of course no one mentioned that you were off work today. And do you know that your answerphone is broken?"

Wallander knew the machine sometimes jammed. He also immediately knew that something had happened. Although he had been a policeman for a long time, the feeling was always the same. His stomach tensed up. He held his breath.

"I'm calling you from Hansson's office," Martinsson said. "Astrid Hillström's mother is here to see me."

"Who?"

"Astrid Hillström. One of the missing young people. Her mother."

Now Wallander knew who he meant.

"What does she want?"

"She's very upset. Her daughter sent her a postcard from Vienna."

Wallander frowned. "Isn't it good news that she's finally written?"

"She claims her daughter didn't write the postcard. She's upset that we're not doing anything."

"How can we do anything when a crime doesn't seem to have been committed, when all the evidence indicates that they left of their own accord?"

Martinsson paused for a moment before answering. "I don't know what it is," he said. "But I have a feeling that there's something to what she's saying. Maybe."

Wallander immediately grew more attentive. Over the years he had learned to take Martinsson's hunches seriously. More often than not, they were proved right.

"Do you want me to come in?"

"No, but I think you, me, and Svedberg should talk this over tomorrow morning."

"What time?"

"How about 8 a.m.? I'll tell Svedberg."

Wallander sat for a moment when the conversation was over, watching a tractor out on a field. He thought about what Martinsson had said. He had also met Astrid Hillström's mother on several occasions. He went over the events again in his mind. A few days after Midsummer's Eve some young people were reported missing. It happened right after he had returned from his rainy holiday. He had reviewed the case together with a couple of his colleagues. From the outset he had doubted that a crime had been committed and, as it turned out, a postcard arrived from Hamburg three days later, with a picture of the central railway station on the front. Wallander could recall its message word for word. *We are travelling around Europe. We may be gone until the middle of August.*

Today it was Wednesday, 7 August. They would be home soon. Now another postcard written by Astrid Hillström came from Vienna. The first card was signed by all three of them. Their parents recognised the signatures. Astrid Hillström's mother hesitated, but she allowed herself to be convinced by the others.

Wallander glanced in his rear-view mirror and drove out onto the main road. Perhaps Martinsson was right about his misgivings.

Wallander parked on Mariagatan and carried the boxes and five paintings up to his flat. Then he sat down by the phone. At his regular doctor's office he only reached an answerphone message telling him that the doctor wouldn't be back from holiday until August 12th. Wallander wondered if he should wait until then, but he couldn't shake the thought of how close to death he had come that morning. He called another doctor and made an appointment for 11 a.m. the following morning. He signed up to do his laundry, then started cleaning his flat. He was already completely exhausted after doing the bedroom. He ran the vacuum cleaner back and forth a few times over the living room floor, then put it away. He carried the boxes and paintings into the room that Linda used on her sporadic visits. He drank three glasses of water in the kitchen, wondering about his thirst and the fatigue. What was causing them?

It was already midday, and he realised he was hungry. A quick look in the refrigerator told him there wasn't much there. He put on his coat and went out. It was a nice day. As he walked to the centre of town, he looked at the properties for sale in the windows of three separate real estate offices, and realised that the price Robert Åkerblom had suggested was fair. They could hardly get more than 300,000 kronor for the house in Löderup.

He stopped at a takeaway restaurant, ate a hamburger and drank two bottles of mineral water. Then he went into a shoe shop where he knew the owner, and used the lavatory. When he came back out onto the street, he felt unsure of what to do next. He should have used his day off to do his shopping. He had no food in the house, but he didn't have the energy to go back for the car and drive to a supermarket.

Just past Hamngatan, he crossed the train tracks and turned down Spanienfararegatan. When he arrived down at the waterfront, he strolled along the pier and looked at the sailing boats, wondering what it would be like to sail. It was something he had never experienced. He realised he needed to pee again, and used the lavatories at the harbour café, drank another bottle of mineral water, and sat down on a bench outside the red coast guard building.

The last time he had been here it had been winter, the night Baiba left. It was already dark as he drove her to Sturup Airport, and the wind made whirls of snow dance in the headlights. They hadn't said a word. After he had watched her disappear past the checkpoint, he had returned to Ystad and sat on this bench. The wind had been very cold and he was freezing, but he sat here and realised that everything was over. He wouldn't see Baiba again. Their breakup was final.

She came to Ystad in December of 1994. His father had recently died and he had just finished one of the most challenging investigations of his career. But that autumn he had also, for the first time in many years, been making plans for the future. He decided to leave Mariagatan, move to the country, and get a dog. He had even visited a kennel and looked at Labrador puppies. He was going to make a fresh start. And above all, he wanted Baiba to come and live with him. She visited him over Christmas and Wallander could tell that she and Linda got along well. Then, on New Year's Eve 1995, the last few days before she was due to return to Riga, they talked seriously about the future. Maybe she would move to Sweden permanently as early as next summer. They looked at houses together. They looked at a house on a subdivision of an old farm outside Svenstorp several times. But then, one evening in March, when Wallander was already in bed, she called from Riga and told him she was having doubts. She didn't want to get married, didn't want to move to Sweden – at least not yet. He thought he would be able to get her to change her mind, but the conversation ended with an unpleasant

21

quarrel, their first, after which they didn't speak for more than a month. Finally, Wallander called her and they decided he would go to Riga that summer. They spent two weeks by the sea in a run-down old house that she had borrowed from one of her colleagues at the university.

They took long walks on the beach and Wallander made a point of waiting for her to broach the question of the future. But when she finally did, she was vague and noncommittal. Not now, not yet. Why couldn't things stay as they were?

When Wallander returned to Sweden, he felt dejected and unsure of where things stood. The autumn went by without another meeting. They had talked about it, made plans, and considered various alternatives, but nothing had eventuated. Wallander became jealous. Was there another man in Riga? Someone he didn't know anything about? On several occasions he called her in the middle of the night and although she insisted that she was alone, he had the distinct feeling that there was someone with her.

Baiba had come to Ystad for Christmas that year. Linda had been with them on Christmas Eve before leaving for Scotland with friends. And it was then, a couple of days into the new year, that Baiba had told him she could never move to Sweden. She had gone back and forth in her mind for a long time. But now she knew. She didn't want to lose her position at the university. What could she do in Sweden, especially in Ystad? She could perhaps become an interpreter, but what else? Wallander tried in vain to persuade her to change her mind. Without saying so explicitly, they knew it was over. After four years there was no longer any road leading into the future. Wallander spent the rest of that winter evening on the frozen bench, feeling more abandoned than ever before. But then another feeling had crept over him. Relief. At least he now knew where things stood.

A motorboat sped out of the harbour. Wallander got up. He needed to find a lavatory again.

They called each other from time to time, but gradually that had stopped too. Now they hadn't been in touch for over six months. One day when he and Linda were walking around Visby she had asked if things with Baiba were finally over.

"Yes," he replied. "It's over."

She had waited for him to continue.

"I don't think either of us really wanted to break it off," he had told her. "But it was inevitable."

When he got home, he lay down on the sofa to read the paper but fell asleep almost immediately. An hour later he woke up with a start in the middle of a dream. He had been in Rome with his father. Rydberg had also been with them, and some small, dwarf-like creatures who insisted on pinching their legs.

I'm dreaming about the dead, he thought. What does that mean? I dream about my father almost every night and he's dead. So is Rydberg, my old colleague and friend, the one who taught me everything I can claim to know. And he's been gone for almost five years.

He went out to the balcony. It was still warm and calm. Clouds were starting to pile up on the horizon. Suddenly it struck him how terribly lonely he was. Apart from Linda, who lived in Stockholm and whom he saw only occasionally, he had almost no friends. The people he spent time with were people from work. And he never saw them socially.

He went into the bathroom and washed his face. He looked in the mirror and saw that he had a tan, but the tiredness still shone through. His left eye was bloodshot. His hairline had receded further. He stepped on the scales, and noted that he weighed a couple of kilos less than he had at the start of the summer, but it was still too much.

The phone rang. It was Gertrud.

"I just wanted to let you know that I made it safely to Rynge. Everything went well."

"I've been thinking about you," Wallander told her. "I should have stayed there with you."

"I think I needed to be alone with all my memories. But things will be fine here. My sister and I get along well. We always have."

"I'll be out to see you in a week or so."

After he had hung up the phone rang again immediately. This time it was his colleague Ann-Britt Höglund.

"I just wanted to hear how it went," she said.

"How what went?"

"Weren't you supposed to meet with an estate agent today to discuss selling your father's house?"

Wallander recalled that he had mentioned it to her the day before.

"It went pretty well," he said. "You can buy it for 300,000 kronor if you like."

"I never even got to see it," she replied.

"It feels quite strange," he told her. "The house is so empty now. Getrud has moved and someone else will buy it. It'll probably be used as a summer house. Other people will live in it and not know anything about my father."

"All houses have ghosts," she said. "Except the newest ones."

"The smell of turpentine will linger for a while," Wallander said. "But when that's gone there will be nothing left of the people who once lived there."

"That's so sad."

"It's just the way it is. I'll see you tomorrow. Thanks for calling."

Wallander went to the kitchen and drank some water. Ann-Britt was a very thoughtful person. She remembered things. He would never have thought to do the same if the situation had been reversed.

It was already 7 p.m. He fried some Falu sausage and potatoes and ate in front of the TV. He flipped through the channels, but nothing seemed interesting. Afterwards he took his cup of coffee and went out onto the balcony. As soon as the sun went down, it grew cooler, and he went back in again.

He spent the rest of the evening going through the things he had brought back from Löderup earlier that day. At the bottom of one of the boxes there was a brown envelope. When he opened it he found a couple of old, faded photographs. He couldn't recall ever having seen them before. He was in one of them, aged four or five, perched on the hood of a big American car. His father was standing beside him so he wouldn't fall off.

Wallander took the photograph into the kitchen and got a magnifying glass from one of the kitchen drawers.

We're smiling, he thought. I'm looking straight into the camera and beaming with pride. I've been allowed to sit on one of the art dealer's cars, one of the men who used to buy my father's paintings for outrageous prices. My father is also smiling, but he's looking at me.

Wallander sat with the snapshot for a long time. It spoke to him from a distant and unreachable past. Once upon a time he and his father had been very close, but all that had changed when he decided to become a policeman. In the last few years of his father's life, they had slowly been retracing their steps back to the closeness that had been lost.

But we never made it this far, Wallander thought. Not all the way back to the smile I had as I sat on the hood of this gleaming Buick. We almost got there in Rome, but it still wasn't like this.

Wallander tacked the photo to his kitchen door. Then he went back out onto the balcony. The clouds had come closer. He sat down in front of the TV and watched the end of an old movie.

At midnight he went to bed. He had a meeting with Svedberg and Martinsson the next day, and he had to go to the doctor. He lay awake in the darkness for a long time. Two years ago he had thought about moving from the flat on Mariagatan. He had dreamed of getting a dog, of living with Baiba. But nothing had come of it. No Baiba, no house, no dog. Everything had stayed the same.

Something's got to happen, he thought. Something that makes it possible for me to start thinking about the future again.

It was almost 3 a.m. before he finally fell asleep.

CHAPTER TWO

The clouds started clearing during the early hours of the morning. Wallander was already awake at 6 a.m. He had been dreaming about his father again. Fragmented and unconnected images had flickered through his subconscious. In the dream he had been both a child and an adult. There had been no coherent story. Recalling the dream was like trying to follow a ship into fog.

He got up, showered, and drank some coffee. When he walked out onto the street he noticed that the warmth of summer still lingered and that it was unusually calm. He drove to the police station. It was not yet 7 a.m., and the corridors were empty. He got another cup of coffee and went into his office. For once his desk was virtually free of folders and he wondered when he'd last had so little to do. During the past few years Wallander had seen his workload increase in proportion to the diminishing resources of the police force. Investigations were rushed or ignored altogether. Often a preliminary report resulted in a suspected crime going uninvestigated. Wallander knew that this would not be the case if only they had more time, if only there were more of them.

Did crime pay? That age-old question was still open to debate. Even those who felt that crime now had the upper hand were hard-pressed to pinpoint the moment when the tables had turned. Wallander was convinced that the criminal element had a stronger hold in Sweden than ever before. Criminals engaged in sophisticated financial dealings seemed to live in a safe haven, and the judicial system seemed to have capitulated completely.

Wallander often discussed these problems with his colleagues. He noticed that civilian fears at these developments were growing. Gertrud talked about it. The neighbours he ran into in the laundry talked about it. Wallander knew their fears were justified. But he didn't see any signs of preventive measures being taken. On the contrary, the reduction of numbers within the police force and judicial personnel continued. He took off his coat, opened the window, and looked out at the old water tower.

During the last few years, vigilante groups had been on the rise in Sweden, groups like The Civilian Guard. Wallander had long feared this development. When the justice system started to break down, the lynching mentality of the mob took over. Taking justice into one's own hands came to seem normal.

As he stood there at the window, he wondered how many illegal weapons were floating around Sweden. And he wondered what the figures would be in a couple of years.

He sat down at his desk. His door was slightly ajar and he heard voices out in the corridor, and a woman's laugh. Wallander smiled. That was their chief of police, Lisa Holgersson. She had replaced Björk a few years ago. Many of Wallander's colleagues had resisted the idea of a woman in such a high position, but Wallander gained respect for her early on.

The phone rang. It was Ebba, the receptionist.

"Did it go well?" she asked.

Wallander realised she meant yesterday. "The house isn't sold yet, of course," he said. "But I'm sure it will go well."

"I'm calling to see if you have time to talk to some visitors at 10.30 this morning."

"Visitors at this time of year?"

"It's a group of retired marine officers who meet in Skåne every August. They have some sort of society. I think they call themselves 'The Sea Bears'."

Wallander thought about his doctor's appointment. "I think you'll have to ask someone else this time," he answered. "I'm going to be out between 10.30 and midday."

"Then I'll ask Ann-Britt. These old sea captains might enjoy talking to a woman police officer."

"Or else they'll think just the opposite," Wallander said.

By 8 a.m. Wallander had not managed to do anything more than rock back and forth in his chair and look out the window. Tiredness gnawed at his body, and he was worried about what the doctor would find. Were the fatigue and cramps signs of a serious illness?

He got up out of his chair and walked to one of the conference rooms. Martinsson was already there, looking clean-cut and tanned. Wallander thought about the time, two years earlier, when Martinsson had come very close to giving up his career. His daughter had been attacked in the playground because her father was a policeman. But he had stuck it out. To Wallander he would always be the young man who had just joined the force, despite the fact that he had worked in Ystad longer than most of them.

They sat down and talked about the weather. After five minutes Martinsson said, "Where the hell is Svedberg?"

His question was justified, since Svedberg was known for his punctuality.

"Did you talk to him?"

"He had already gone when I tried to reach him. But I left a message on his answerphone."

Wallander nodded in the direction of the telephone that stood on the table.

"You should probably give him another call."

Martinsson dialled the number.

"Where are you?" he asked. "We're waiting for you."

He put the receiver down. "I'm just getting the machine."

"He must be on his way," Wallander said. "Let's start without him."

Martinsson leafed through a stack of papers. Then he pushed a postcard over to Wallander. It was an aerial shot of central Vienna.

"This is the card that the Hillström family found in their letter box on Tuesday, 6 August. As you can see, Astrid Hillström says that they're thinking of staying a little longer than they had originally planned. But everything is fine and they all send their regards. She asks her mother to call around and tell everyone that they're well."

Wallander read the card. The handwriting reminded him of Linda's. It was the same round lettering. He put it back.

"Eva Hillström came here, you said."

"She literally burst into my office. We knew she was the nervous type, but this was something else. She's clearly terrified and convinced that she's right."

"What's she so sure of?"

"That something's happened to them. That her daughter didn't write that postcard."

Wallander thought for a moment. "Is it the handwriting? The signature?"

"It resembles Astrid Hillström's writing. But her mother claims it's a very easy style to copy, as is her signature. She's right about that."

Wallander pulled over a notebook and a pen. In less

than a minute he had perfected Astrid Hillström's hand-writing and signature.

"Eva Hillström is anxious about her daughter's welfare and turns to the police. That's understandable. But if it isn't the handwriting or the signature that's worrying her, then what is it?"

"She couldn't say."

"But you did ask her."

"I asked her about everything. Was there something about the choice of words? Or was there something in the way she put it? She didn't know. But she was certain that her daughter hadn't written the card."

Wallander made a face and shook his head. "It must have been something."

They looked at each other.

"Do you remember what you said to me yesterday?" Wallander asked. "That you were starting to get worried yourself?"

Martinsson nodded. "Something doesn't add up," he said. "I just can't put my finger on it."

"Let's put the question another way," Wallander said. "If they haven't left on this unplanned holiday, then what's happened? And who's writing these cards? We know that their cars and their passports are missing."

"I'm obviously mistaken," Martinsson answered. "I was probably influenced by Eva Hillström's anxiety."

"Parents always worry about their children," Wallander said. "If you only knew how many times I've wondered what Linda was up to. Especially when you get postcards from strange places all around the world."

"So what do we do?" Martinsson asked.

"We continue to keep the situation under surveillance," Wallander said. "But let's go over the facts from the beginning, just to make sure we haven't missed anything."

Martinsson summarised the events in his unfailingly clear fashion. Ann-Britt Höglund had once asked Wallander if he realised that Martinsson had learned how to make presentations by observing him. Wallander had scoffed at this, but Höglund had stood her ground. Wallander still didn't know if it was true.

The chain of events was simple enough. Three people, all between the ages of 20 and 23, decided to celebrate Midsummer's Eve together. One of them, Martin Boge, lived in Simrishamn, while the other two, Lena Norman and Astrid Hillström, came from the western part of Ystad. They were old friends and spent a lot of time together. Their parents were all wealthy. Lena Norman was studying at Lund University while the other two had temporary jobs. None of them had ever had any problems with the law or with drugs. Astrid Hillström and Martin Boge still lived at home; Lena Norman lived in halls of residence in Lund. They didn't tell anyone where they were planning to hold their Midsummer's Eve party. Their parents had talked to one another and to their friends but no one seemed to know anything. This was not unusual, since they were often secretive and never divulged their plans to outsiders. At the time of their disappearance, they had two cars at their disposal: a Volvo and a Toyota. These cars disappeared at the same time as their owners, on the afternoon of 21 June. After that no one had seen them again. The first postcard was sent on 26 June from Hamburg, stating their intention to travel through Europe. A couple of weeks later, Astrid Hillström had sent a second postcard from Paris in which she explained that they were on their way south. And now she had apparently sent a third postcard.

Martinsson stopped talking.

Wallander reflected on what he had said. "What could possibly have gone wrong?" he asked.

"I have no idea."

"Is there any indication of anything out of the ordinary in relation to their disappearance?"

"Not really."

Wallander leaned back in his chair. "The only thing we have is Eva Hillström's anxiety," he said. "A worried mother."

"She claims her daughter didn't write the cards."

Wallander nodded. "Does she want us to file a missing persons report?"

"No. She wanted us to do something. That was how she put it: 'You have to do something.'"

"What can we really do other than file the report? We've alerted Customs."

They fell silent. It was already 8.45 a.m. Wallander looked questioningly at Martinsson.

"Svedberg?"

Martinsson picked up the receiver and dialled Svedberg's number, then hung up.

"The answerphone again."

Wallander pushed the postcard back across the table to Martinsson. "I don't think we're going to get much further," he said. "But I think I'll have a talk with Eva Hillström. Then we'll evaluate what action to take from here. But we have no grounds for declaring this a missing persons case, at least not yet."

Martinsson wrote her number on a piece of paper. "She's an accountant."

"And the father?"

"They're divorced. I think he called once, just after Midsummer."

Wallander got up while Martinsson collected the

papers. They left the conference room together.

"Maybe Svedberg did the same thing I did and took a day off without us being told about it."

"He's already been on holiday," Martinsson said emphatically. "He hasn't got any holidays left."

Wallander looked at him with surprise. "How do you know that?"

"I asked him if he could switch one of his weeks with me. But he couldn't because for once he wanted an unbroken chunk of time."

"I don't think he's ever done that before," Wallander said.

They parted outside Martinsson's office and Wallander went to his office. He sat down at his desk and dialled the first phone number Martinsson had given him. Eva Hillström answered the phone. They agreed that she should come by the police station later that afternoon.

"Has anything happened?" she asked.

"No," Wallander answered. "I just think I should talk to you as well."

He hung up and was about to go and get a cup of coffee when Höglund appeared at his door. Although she had just returned from a holiday, she was as pale as ever. Wallander thought her pallor came from within. She still hadn't recovered from a serious gunshot wound of two years earlier. She was healed physically, but Wallander doubted how well she was emotionally. Sometimes he felt that she was still afraid. It didn't surprise him. Almost every day, he thought about the time that he had been stabbed. And that had happened more than 20 years ago.

"Is this a good time?"

Wallander gestured to the chair opposite his desk, and she sat down.

"Have you seen Svedberg?" he asked.

She shook her head.

"He was supposed to come to a meeting with me and Martinsson, but he didn't show up."

"He's not one to miss a meeting."

"You're right. But he did today."

"Have you called him at home? Is he sick?"

"Martinsson left several messages on his answerphone. And besides, Svedberg is never sick."

They contemplated Svedberg's absence for a while.

"What was it you wanted to talk to me about?" Wallander asked finally.

"Do you remember those Baltic car smugglers?"

"How could I forget? I worked on that miserable case for two years before we got them. At least the ones in Sweden."

"Well, it seems as though it's started up again."

"Even with the leaders in jail?"

"It looks like others have stepped in to fill their shoes. Only this time they aren't working out of Gothenburg. Their tracks point towards Lycksele, among other places."

Wallander was surprised. "Lapland?"

"With today's technology you can operate from virtu ally anywhere."

Wallander shook his head, but he knew that Höglund was right. Organised criminals always made use of the latest technology.

"I don't have the energy to start again," he said. "No more car smuggling for me."

"I'll take it on. Lisa asked me to. I think she realises how tired you are of stolen cars. But I'd like you to outline the situation for me, as well as give me a couple of pointers."

Wallander nodded. They set a time for the next day, then went and got some coffee and sat down by an open window in the canteen.

"How was your holiday?" he asked.

Her eyes suddenly filled with tears. Wallander went to say something but she stopped him with a gesture.

"It wasn't so great," she said when she had regained her composure. "But I don't want to talk about it."

She picked up her cup of coffee and got up quickly. Wallander watched her leave. He remained seated, thinking about her reaction.

We don't know very much, he thought. They don't know much about me and I don't know much about them. We work together, maybe over the course of an entire career, and what do we learn about each other? Nothing.

He looked down at his watch. He had plenty of time, but he decided to set off walking down to Kapellgatan, where the doctor's office was. He was filled with dread.

The doctor was young. He was called Göransson and came from somewhere up north. Wallander told him about his symptoms: the fatigue, the thirst, the increased urination. He also mentioned his leg cramps.

The doctor's diagnosis was swift, and surprised him.

"It sounds like too much sugar," he said.

"Sugar?"

"Diabetes."

For a split second Wallander was paralysed. The thought had never occurred to him.

"You look like you weigh a little too much," the doctor said. "We'll find out if that's the case. But I want to start off by listening to your heart. Do you know if you have high blood pressure?"

36

Wallander shook his head. Then he took off his shirt and lay down on the table.

His pulse was normal, but his blood pressure was too high. 170 over 105. He got on the scale: 92 kilos. The doctor sent him for a urinalysis and a blood test. The nurse smiled at him. Wallander thought she looked like his sister Kristina. After she had finished, he went back in to see the doctor.

"Normally you should have a blood-sugar level of between 2.5 and 6.4," Göransson said. "Yours is 15.3. That's much too high."

Wallander started to feel sick.

"This explains your fatigue," Göransson continued. "It explains your thirst and the leg cramps. It also explains why you need to urinate so often."

"Is there medication for this?" Wallander asked.

"First we'll try to control it by changing your diet," Göransson said. "We also have to reduce your blood pressure. Do you exercise frequently?"

"No."

"Then you'll have to start right away. Diet and exercise. If that doesn't help we'll have to go a step further. With this blood-sugar level you're wearing down your whole system."

I'm diabetic, Wallander thought. At that moment it struck him as something shameful.

Göransson seemed to sense his dismay. "This is something we can control," he said. "You won't die from it. At least not yet."

They took more blood tests, and Wallander was given dietary guidelines, and was told to come back on Monday morning.

He left the surgery at 11.30 a.m. He walked over to the cemetery and sat down on a bench. He still couldn't grasp what the doctor had told him. He found his glasses and started reading the meal plans.

He got back to the police station at 12.30. There were some phone messages for him, but nothing that couldn't wait. He bumped into Hansson in the corridor.

"Has Svedberg turned up?" Wallander asked.

"Why, isn't he in?"

Wallander didn't elaborate. Eva Hillström was supposed to come in shortly after 1 p.m. He knocked on Martinsson's half-open door, but the room was empty. The thin folder from their meeting that day was lying on the desk. Wallander took it and went into his office. He quickly leafed through the few papers there were and stared at the three postcards, but he was having trouble concentrating. He kept thinking about what the doctor had told him.

Finally Ebba called him from the reception desk and told him that Eva Hillström had arrived. Wallander walked out to meet her. A group of older, jovial men were on their way out. Wallander guessed they were the retired marine officers who had come for a tour.

Eva Hillström was tall and thin. Her expression was guarded. From the first time he met her, Wallander formed the impression that she was the kind of person who always expected the worst. He shook her hand and asked her to follow him to his office. On the way he asked her if she wanted a cup of coffee.

"I don't drink coffee," she said. "My stomach can't take it."

She sat down in the visitor's chair without taking her eyes off him.

She thinks I have news for her, Wallander thought. And she expects the news to be bad.

He sat down at his desk. "You spoke with my colleague yesterday," he said. "You brought by a postcard you received a couple of days earlier, signed by your daughter and sent from Vienna. But you claim it wasn't written by her. Is that correct?"

"Yes." Her answer was forceful.

"Martinsson said you couldn't explain why you felt this way."

"That's right, I can't."

Wallander took out the postcards and laid them in front of her.

"You said that your daughter's handwriting and signature are easy to forge."

"Try for yourself."

"I've already done that. And I agree with you; her handwriting isn't very hard to copy."

"Then why do you have to ask?"

Wallander looked at her for a moment. She was just as tense as Martinsson had described.

"I'm asking these questions in order to confirm certain statements," he said. "It's sometimes necessary."

She nodded impatiently.

"We have no real reason to believe that someone other than Astrid wrote these cards," Wallander said. "Can you think of anything else that makes you doubt their authenticity?"

"No, but I know I'm right."

"Right about what?"

"That she didn't write this card, or any of the others."

Suddenly, she stood up and started to scream at him. Wallander was completely unprepared for the violence of her reaction. She was leaning over his desk, and she grabbed his arms and shook him, screaming the whole time.

"Why don't you do anything? Something must have happened!"

Wallander freed himself from her grasp with some difficulty and stood up.

"I think you'd better calm down," he said.

But Eva Hillström kept screaming. Wallander wondered what people walking by his door were thinking. He went around his desk, grabbed her firmly by the shoulders, pushed her down in the chair and and held her there. Her outburst stopped as abruptly as it had begun. Wallander slowly loosened his grip and returned to his chair. Eva Hillström stared down at the floor. Wallander waited, thoroughly shaken. There was something about her reaction, something about her conviction, that was contagious.

"What is it that you think has happened?" he asked after a little while.

She shook her head. "I don't know."

"There is nothing to indicate an accident or anything else."

She looked at Wallander.

"Astrid and her friends have gone on trips before," he said. "Although perhaps not for as long as this one. They had cars, money, passports. My colleagues have gone over this before. What's more, they're of an age when you're inclined to act on impulse without having made prior plans. I have a daughter myself who is a couple of years older than Astrid. I know how it is."

"I just know," she said. "I know I tend to worry. But this time there's something that doesn't feel right."

"The other parents don't seem quite as worried as you do. What about Martin Boge's and Lena Norman's parents?"

"I don't understand them."

"We take your concern seriously," he said. "That's our job. I promise to review this case one more time."

His words seemed to reassure her momentarily, but then the anxiety returned. Her face was open and vulnerable. Wallander felt sorry for her.

The conversation was over. She got up, and he followed her out to the reception area.

"I'm sorry I lost control," she said.

"It's natural to be worried," Wallander said.

She shook his hand quickly, then disappeared through the glass doors.

Wallander went back to his room. Martinsson stuck his head out the door of his office and looked at him with curiosity.

"What were you doing in there?"

"She's genuinely frightened," Wallander said. "We have to acknowledge that; but I don't know what to do about it." Wallander looked thoughtfully at Martinsson. "I'd like to do a thorough review of this case tomorrow with everyone who has the time. We have to decide if we should declare them missing or not. Something about this whole thing worries me."

Martinsson nodded. "Have you seen Svedberg?" he asked.

"He still hasn't been in touch?"

"No. Just the same old answerphone message."

Wallander grimaced. "That's not like him."

"I'll try him again."

Wallander continued to his room. He closed the door and called Ebba. "No calls for the next half hour," he said. "Anything from Svedberg, by the way?"

"Should there be?"

"I was just wondering."

Wallander put his legs up on the desk. He was tired and his mouth was dry. On an impulse, he grabbed his coat and left the room.

"I'm going out," he told Ebba. "I'll be back in an hour or two."

It was still warm and calm. Wallander went down to the central library on Surbrunnsvägen. With some effort he found his way to the medical section. Soon he found what he was looking for: a book about diabetes. He sat down at a table, put his glasses on, and started reading. After an hour and a half he thought he had a better idea of what diabetes entailed. He realised he only had himself to blame. The foods he ate, his lack of exercise, and his on-and-off dieting had all contributed to the disease. He put the book back on the shelf. A sense of failure and disgust came over him. He knew there was no way out. He had to do something about his lifestyle.

It was already 4.20 p.m. when he returned to the police station. There was a note on his desk from Martinsson saying that he still hadn't managed to get in touch with Svedberg.

Once more Wallander read through the summary of events regarding the disappearance of the three young people. He scrutinised the three postcards. The feeling that there was something he was overlooking returned. He still couldn't pin it down. What was there he wasn't seeing?

He felt his anxiety increase and could almost see Eva Hillström in front of him. Suddenly the gravity of the situation struck him. It was very simple. She knew her daughter hadn't written that card. How she knew this was irrelevant. She was sure and that was enough. Wallander got up and stopped in front of the window. Something had happened to them. The question now was what.

CHAPTER THREE

That evening Wallander tried to start his new regime. All he had for dinner was some bouillon soup and a salad. He was concentrating so hard on making sure that only the right things found their way onto his plate that he forgot he had signed up for the laundry, and by the time he remembered it was too late.

He tried to convince himself that what had happened could be viewed as something positive. An elevated blood-sugar level was not a death sentence; he had been given a warning. If he wanted to stay healthy, he would have to take some simple precautions. Nothing drastic, but he would have to make significant changes.

When he was done eating, he still felt hungry, and ate another tomato. Then, still sitting at the kitchen table, he tried to make a meal plan for the coming days from his dietary guidelines. He also decided to walk to work from now on. On the weekends he would drive to the beach and take long walks. He remembered that he and Hansson once talked about playing badminton. Perhaps that could still be arranged.

At 9 p.m. he got up from the kitchen table and went out onto the balcony. The wind was blowing softly from the south, but it was still warm. The dog days were here.

Wallander watched some teenagers walking past on the street below. It was hard to concentrate on his meal plans and recommended weight chart. Thoughts of Eva

Hillström and her anxiety kept returning to him. Her outburst had shaken him. The fear she felt at her daughter's disappearance was plain to see, and it was genuine.

Sometimes parents don't know their children, he thought. But sometimes a parent knows her child better than anyone else, and something tells me that this is the case with Eva Hillström and her daughter.

He went back into the flat and left the door to the balcony open. He had the feeling that he was overlooking something that would indicate how they should proceed; something that would lead them to a well-founded, investigative hypothesis, and to determine whether Eva Hillström's concerns were justified.

He went out into the kitchen and made some coffee, wiping the table clean while he waited for the water to boil. The phone rang. It was Linda. She was calling from the restaurant where she worked, which surprised him since he thought it was open only during the day.

"The owner changed the hours," she said in answer to his question, "and I make more money working in the evenings. I have to make a living."

He could hear voices and the rattle of pots and pans in the background. He had no idea what Linda's plans for her future were. For a time she wanted to become a furniture upholsterer, then she changed her mind and started exploring the world of theatre. Then that plan also came to an end.

She seemed to read his thoughts. "I'm not going to be a waitress all my life," she said. "But I'm saving some money right now and next winter I'm going to travel."

"Where to?"

"I don't know yet."

It wasn't the right time to discuss this in detail, so he

mentioned that Gertrud had moved and that her grandfather's house was on the market.

"I wish we had kept it," she said. "I wish I had the money to buy it."

Wallander understood. Linda had been close to her grandfather. There were even times when seeing them together had made him jealous.

"I have to go now," she said. "I just wanted to hear how you were."

"Everything is fine," Wallander replied. "I went to the doctor today. He didn't find anything wrong with me."

"Didn't he even tell you to lose weight?"

"Apart from that, he said that everything was fine."

"That doctor was too nice. Are you still as tired as you were on holiday?"

She sees right through me, Wallander thought helplessly. And why don't I tell her the truth, that I'm becoming a diabetic, that I may already be one? Why am I behaving as if it were something shameful?

"I'm not tired," he said. "That week on Gotland was an exception."

"If you say so," she said. "I've got to go now. If you want to reach me here in the evenings you'll have to call a new number."

He quickly memorised it. Then the conversation was over.

Wallander took his coffee with him into the living room and turned on the TV. He turned the sound down, then jotted down the phone number she had given him on the corner of a newspaper. He wrote sloppily. No one else would have been able to read the number. It was at that moment that he realised what was bothering him. He pushed his coffee cup away and looked at his watch. It was 9.15 p.m.

45

He wondered briefly if he should call Martinsson, and wait until the following day before making up his mind. He went into the kitchen, got out the phone book, and sat down at the kitchen table.

There were four families called Norman in Ystad, but Wallander remembered seeing the address among Martinsson's papers. Lena Norman and her mother lived on Käringgatan, north of the hospital. Her father was called Bertil Norman and had the title "CEO" next to his name. Wallander knew that he owned a company that supplied heating systems for pre-fabricated houses.

He dialled the number and a woman answered. Wallander introduced himself, trying to sound as friendly as possible. He didn't want to worry her. He knew how unnerving it was to be called by the police, especially after hours.

"Am I speaking to Lena Norman's mother?"

"This is Lillemor Norman."

Wallander recognised the name.

"This conversation could really have waited until tomorrow," he said. "But there is something I need to know and unfortunately policemen work all hours of the day and night."

She did not seem particularly concerned. "How can I help you? Or would you like to speak with my husband? I can get him for you. He's just helping Lena's brother with his maths homework."

Her answer surprised him. He hadn't realised that schools still had anything called homework.

"That won't be necessary," he said. "What I want is a sample of Lena's handwriting. Do you have any letters from her?"

"Well, apart from the postcards, we haven't received anything. I thought the police knew that."

"I mean an old letter."

"Why do you need it?"

"It's just routine procedure. We need to compare some handwriting samples, that's all. It's not particularly important."

"Do policemen really bother calling people at night about such unimportant matters?"

Eva Hillström is afraid, Wallander thought. Lillemor Norman, on the other hand, is suspicious.

"Do you think you can help me?"

"I have a number of letters from Lena."

"One is enough. About half a page."

"I'll find one. Will someone be by to pick it up?"

"I'll come myself. Expect me in about 20 minutes."

Wallander went back to the phone book. In Simrishamn he found only one entry for the name "Boge", an accountant. Wallander dialled the number and waited impatiently. He was just about to hang up when someone answered.

"Klas Boge."

The voice that answered sounded young. Wallander assumed it was Martin Boge's brother. He told him who he was.

"Are your parents home?"

"No, I'm alone. They're at a golf dinner."

Wallander wasn't sure he should continue. But the boy seemed reasonably mature.

"Has your brother Martin ever written a letter to you? Anything you might have saved?"

"Not this summer."

"Earlier, perhaps?"

The boy thought for a moment. "I have a letter he wrote to me from the United States last year."

"Was it handwritten?"

47

"Yes."

Wallander calculated how long it would take him to drive to Simrishamn. Perhaps he should wait until the next morning.

"Why do you want one of his letters?"

"I just need a sample of his handwriting."

"Well, I could fax it over to you if you're in a hurry."

The boy was a fast thinker. Wallander gave him the number of one of the faxes at the police station.

"I'd like you to mention this matter to your parents," he said.

"I'm planning to be asleep when they get back."

"Could you tell them about it tomorrow?"

"Martin's letter was addressed to me."

"It would be best if you mentioned it anyway," Wallander said patiently.

"Martin and the others will be back soon," the boy said. "I don't know why that Hillström lady is so worried. She calls us every day."

"But your parents aren't worried?"

"I think they're relieved that Martin's gone. At least Dad is."

Somewhat surprised, Wallander waited to see if the boy would go on, but he didn't.

"Thanks for your help," he said finally.

"It's like a game," the boy said.

"A game?"

"They pretend they're in a different time. They like to dress up, like children do, even though they're grown up."

"I'm not sure that I follow," Wallander said.

"They're playing roles, like you would in the theatre. But it's for real. They might have gone to Europe to find something that doesn't really exist."

"So that was what they normally did? Play? But I'm not sure I would call a Midsummer's Eve celebration a game. It's just the same eating and dancing as at any other party."

"And drinking," the boy said. "But if you put on costumes, that makes it something else, doesn't it?"

"Is that what they did?"

"Yes, but I don't know more. It was secret. Martin never said much about it."

Wallander didn't completely follow what the boy was saying. He looked down at his watch. Lillemor Norman would be expecting him shortly.

"Thanks for your help," he said, bringing the conversation to an end. "And don't forget to tell your parents that I called and what I asked for."

"Maybe," the boy replied.

Three different reactions, Wallander thought. Eva Hillström is afraid. Lillemor Norman is suspicious. Martin Boge's parents are relieved he's gone, and his brother in turn seems to prefer it when their parents are gone. He picked up his coat and left. On the way out, he reserved a new time at the laundry for Friday.

Although it wasn't far to Käringgatan, he took the car. The new exercise regimen would have to wait. He turned onto Käringgatan from Bellevuevägen, and stopped outside a white two-storey house. The front door opened as he was opening the gate, and he recognised Lillemor Norman. In contrast to Eva Hillström, she looked robust. He thought about the photographs in Martinsson's file and realised that Lena Norman and her mother looked alike.

The woman was holding a white envelope.

"I'm sorry to bother you," Wallander said.

"My husband will have a few words with Lena when she

comes back. It's completely irresponsible of them to go away like this without a word."

"They're adults and can do as they please," Wallander said. "But of course it's both irritating and worrying."

He took the letter and promised to return it. Then he drove to the police station and went to the room where the officer on duty was manning the phones. He was taking a call as Wallander stepped into the room, but pointed to one of the fax machines. Klas Boge had faxed his brother's letter as promised. Wallander went to his office and turned on the desk lamp. He laid the two letters and the postcards next to each other, then angled the light and put on his glasses.

He leaned back in his chair. His hunch was correct. Both Martin Boge and Lena Norman had irregular, spiky handwriting. If someone had wanted to forge any one of the three's handwriting, the choice would have been clear: Astrid Hillström. Wallander felt profoundly disturbed by this, but his mind kept working methodically. What did this mean? It was nothing, really. It didn't supply an answer to why someone would want to write postcards in their names, and who would have had access to their handwriting. Nonetheless, he couldn't shake off his concern.

We have to go through this thoroughly, he thought. If something has happened, they've been missing for almost two months.

He got himself a cup of coffee. It was 10.15 p.m. He read through the description of events one more time but found nothing new. Some good friends had celebrated Midsummer's Eve together, then left for a trip. They sent a few postcards. And that was all.

Wallander shuffled the letters together and put them in the folder along with the postcards. There was nothing more he could do tonight. Tomorrow he would talk to Martinsson and the others, go through this Midsummer's Eve case one last time, and then decide if they would proceed with a missing persons investigation.

Wallander turned off the light and left the room. In the corridor he realised that Ann-Britt Höglund's light was on. The door was slightly ajar, and he pushed it open gently. She was staring down at her desk but there were no papers in front of her. Wallander hesitated. She almost never stayed this late at the station. She had children to take care of, and her husband travelled often with his job and was rarely at home. He recalled her emotional behaviour in the canteen. And now here she was staring down at an empty desk. She probably wanted to be left alone. But it was also possible that she wanted to talk to somebody.

She can always ask me to leave, Wallander thought.

He knocked on the door, waited for her answer, and stepped inside.

"I saw your light," he said. "You aren't normally here so late, not unless something has happened."

She looked back at him without answering.

"If you want to be left alone, just say the word."

"No," she replied. "I don't really want to be left alone. Why are you here yourself? Is something going on?"

Wallander sat down in her visitor's chair. He felt like a big, lumbering animal.

"It's the young people who went missing at Midsummer."

"Has anything turned up?"

"Not really. There was just something I wanted to double-check. But I think that we'll need to do a thorough reexamination of the case. Eva Hillström is seriously concerned."

"But what could really have happened to them?"

"That's the question."

"Are we going to declare them missing?"

Wallander threw his arms out. "I don't know. We'll have to decide tomorrow."

The room was dark except for the circle of light projected onto the floor by the desk lamp.

"How long have you been a policeman?" she asked suddenly.

"A long time. Too long, maybe. But I'm a policeman through and through. That's not going to change, at least until I retire."

She looked at him for a long time before asking her next question. "How do you keep going?"

"I don't know."

"Don't you ever run out of steam?"

"Sometimes. Why do you ask?"

"I'm thinking of what I said in the canteen earlier. I told you I'd had a bad summer and that's true. My husband and I are having problems. He's never at home. It can take us a week to get back to normal after his trips, and then he just has to leave again. This summer we started talking about a separation. That's never an easy thing, especially when you have children."

"I know," Wallander said.

"At the same time I've started questioning my work. I read in the paper that some of our colleagues in Malmö were arrested for racketeering. I turn on the television and learn that senior members of the force are involved in the world of organised crime. I see all this and I realise it's happening more and more. Eventually it leads me to wonder what I'm doing. Or, to put it another way, I wonder how I'm going to last another 30 years."

"It's all coming apart at the seams," Wallander agreed.

"It's been going on for a long time. Corruption in the justice system is nothing new and there have always been police officers willing to cross the line. It's worse now, of course, and that's why it's even more important that people like you keep going."

"What about you?"

"That applies to me too."

"But how do you do it?"

Her questions were full of anger. He recognised a part of himself in her. How many times had he sat staring into his own desk, unable to find a reason to continue?

"I try to tell myself that things would be even worse without me," he said. "It's a consolation at times. A small one, but if I can't think of any other I take it."

She shook her head. "What's happening to our country?"

Wallander waited for her to continue, but she didn't. A truck rattled past on the street outside.

"Do you remember that violent attack last spring?" Wallander asked.

"The one in Svarte?"

"Two boys, both 14 years old, attack a third boy who is only 12. There's no provocation, no reason behind it. When he's lying there unconscious they start stomping on his chest. Finally he's not just unconscious, he's dead. I don't think it ever hit me so clearly before. People have always had fights, but they would stop when the other person was down. You can call it what you like. Fair play. Something you take for granted. But that's not the way it is any more, because these boys never learned it. It's as if a whole generation has been abandoned by their parents. Or as if not caring has become the norm. You have to rethink what it means to be a police officer because the parameters have changed. The experience you've acquired after years and years of grinding work doesn't apply any more."

He stopped. They heard voices from the corridor. Some of the officers on night duty were talking about a drunk driver. Then everything went quiet again.

"How have you been these past few years?" he asked her.

"You mean since I was shot?"

He nodded.

"I dream about it," she said. "I dream that I die or that the bullet hits me in the head. I think that's almost worse."

"It's easy to lose your nerve," Wallander said.

She got up. "The day I get seriously scared I'll quit," she said. "But I'm not quite there yet. Thanks for stopping by. I'm used to dealing with my problems on my own, but tonight I needed someone to talk to."

"It takes some strength to admit that."

She put her coat on and smiled her pale smile. Wallander wondered how well she was sleeping, but he didn't ask her.

"Can we talk about the car smugglers tomorrow?" she asked.

"How about in the afternoon? Don't forget we have to talk about these young people in the morning."

She looked at him closely.

"Are you really worried?"

"Eva Hillström is, and I can't disregard that."

They walked out together. She rejected his offer of a ride home.

"I need to walk," she said. "And it's so warm. What an August it's been!"

"We're in the dog days," he said. "Whatever that saying means."

They said goodbye. Wallander drove home. He drank a cup of tea and leafed through the Ystad daily paper, then went to bed. He left the window slightly open since it was so warm, and fell asleep at once.

A violent pain woke him up with a start. His left calf muscle was locked in a spasm. He lowered his leg onto the floor and flexed it. The pain disappeared. He lay down again carefully, afraid that the cramp would return. The alarm clock on the bedside table read 1.30 a.m. He had been dreaming about his father again, in a disjointed way. They walked around the streets of a city that Wallander didn't recognise. They were looking for someone. Who, he never found out.

The curtain in front of the window moved slowly. He thought about Linda's mother, Mona. He had been married to her for a long time. Now she was living a new life with another man who played golf and probably did not have elevated blood-sugar levels.

His thoughts kept wandering. All at once he saw himself walking along Skagen's endless beaches with Baiba. Then she was gone.

Suddenly he was wide awake. He sat up in bed. He didn't know where the thought came from; it simply appeared among the others and fought its way to the front: Svedberg.

The fact that he hadn't called in sick didn't make sense. Not only was he never sick, if something had happened he would have let them know. He should have thought of it before. If Svedberg hadn't been in contact, it could only mean one thing: something was preventing him from communicating with them.

Wallander felt himself getting worried. Of course it was just his imagination. After all, what could have happened to Svedberg? But the feeling of unease was strong. Wallander looked at the clock again, then went out into

55

the kitchen, searched for Svedberg's number, and dialled it. After a few rings the machine picked up. Wallander hung up. Now he was sure that something was wrong. He put on his clothes and went down to the car. The wind had picked up but it was still warm. It took him only a few minutes to drive to the main square. He parked the car and walked towards Lilla Norregatan where Svedberg lived. The lights were on inside his flat. Wallander felt relieved, but only for a few seconds. Then the worry returned even more strongly. Why didn't Svedberg pick up the phone if he was at home? Wallander tried the door to the building. It was locked. He didn't know the security code, but the crack between the front doors was wide enough. Wallander took out a pocketknife and looked around. Then he slipped the thickest blade between the doors and pushed. They opened.

Svedberg lived on the fourth floor. Wallander was out of breath by the time he made it up the stairs. He pressed his ear against the door but heard nothing. Then he opened the letter slot. Nothing. He rang the bell, the sound echoing inside the flat. He rang three times, then pounded on the door. Still nothing.

Wallander tried to gather his thoughts. He felt a strong urge not to be alone. He groped for his mobile phone but realised it was still on the kitchen table at home. He went down the stairs and pushed a small stone between the two front doors. Then he hurried out to one of the telephone booths on the main square, and dialled Martinsson's number.

"I'm sorry to have to wake you up," Wallander said when Martinsson answered, "but I need your help."

"What is it?"

"Did you ever get hold of Svedberg?"

"No."

"Then something must have happened."

Martinsson didn't reply, but Wallander sensed that he was now fully awake.

"I'm waiting for you outside his block of flats on Lilla Norregatan," Wallander said.

"Ten minutes," Martinsson said. "At the most."

Wallander went to his car and unlocked the boot. He had some tools wrapped up in a dirty plastic bag. He took out a crowbar, then returned to Svedberg's building.

After less than ten minutes Martinsson drove up. Wallander saw that he was wearing his pyjama top under his jacket.

"What do you think has happened?"

"I don't know."

They walked upstairs together. Wallander nodded to Martinsson to ring the doorbell. Still no one answered. They looked at each other.

"Maybe he keeps some spare keys in his office."

Wallander shook his head.

"It'll take us too long," he said.

Martinsson took a step back. He knew what would be next. Wallander wedged the crowbar into the door, and forced it open.

CHAPTER FOUR

The night of 8 August 1996 became one of the longest of Kurt Wallander's life. When he staggered out from the flat building on Lilla Norregatan at dawn, he still hadn't managed to rid himself of the feeling that he was caught up in an incomprehensible nightmare.

But everything he had seen during that long night had been real, and this reality was horrifying. He had witnessed the remains of a bloody and brutal drama many times in the course of his career, but never had it touched him as closely as now.

When he forced open the door to Svedberg's flat he still didn't know what lay in store for him. Yet from the moment he wedged the crowbar in the door he had feared the worst, and his fears had been confirmed.

They walked silently through the hall as if they were about to enter enemy territory. Martinsson stayed close behind. Lights were shining further down the hall. For a brief moment they stood there without making a sound. Wallander heard Martinsson's anxious breathing behind him. In the doorway to the living room, he jerked back so violently that he collided with Martinsson, who then bent forward to look at what Wallander had seen.

Wallander would never forget the sound Martinsson made, the way he whimpered like a child in front of the inexplicable thing before him on the floor.

It was Svedberg. One of his legs was hanging over the

broken arm of a chair that had been knocked over. The torso was strangely twisted, as if Svedberg had no spine.

Wallander stood in the doorway, frozen with horror. There was no doubt in his mind about what he was seeing. The man he had worked with for so many years was dead. He no longer existed. He would never again sit in his usual place at the table in one of the conference rooms, scratching his bald spot with the end of a pencil.

Svedberg didn't have a bald spot any more. Half of his head was blown away.

A short distance from the body lay a double-barrelled shotgun. Blood was spattered several metres up the white wall behind the overturned chair. A confused thought went through Wallander's mind: now Svedberg will never be troubled by his phobia for bees again.

"What happened?" Martinsson said in an unsteady voice. Wallander realised that Martinsson was close to tears. He was a long way from such a reaction. He couldn't cry over something he didn't yet fully comprehend. And he really didn't comprehend the scene in front of him. Svedberg couldn't be dead. He was a 40-year-old police officer who would be in his usual chair again tomorrow when they had one of their regular team meetings. Svedberg with his bald spot, his fear of bees, who used the police station's sauna on his own every Friday night. It simply couldn't be Svedberg who lay there. It was someone else who looked just like him.

Wallander glanced instinctively at his watch. It was 2.09 a.m. They stood in the doorway for a few more seconds, then walked back out into the hall. Wallander turned on the light. He saw that Martinsson was shaking. He wondered what he looked like himself.

"Tell them to put all units on red alert."

There was a phone on a table in the hall, but no

answerphone. Martinsson nodded and was about to pick up the receiver when Wallander stopped him.

"Wait," he said. "We need time to think."

But what was there really to think about? Maybe he was hoping for a miracle, that Svedberg would suddenly appear behind them and that nothing they had seen would turn out to be real.

"Do you know Lisa Holgersson's number?" he asked. He knew from experience that Martinsson had a good head for addresses and numbers. There used to be two with this particular gift: Martinsson and Svedberg. Now only one was left.

Martinsson recited the number, stammering. Wallander dialled and Lisa Holgersson picked up on the second ring. Her phone must be right beside her bed, he thought.

"This is Wallander. I'm sorry to wake you up."

She seemed awake at once.

"You should come down here right away," he said. "I'm in Svedberg's flat on Lilla Norregatan. Martinsson is also here. Svedberg is dead."

He heard her groan. "What happened?"

"I don't know. He's been shot."

"That's terrible. Is it murder?"

Wallander thought about the shotgun on the floor.

"I don't know," he said. "Murder or suicide, I don't know which."

"Have you been in touch with Nyberg?"

"I wanted to call you first."

"I'll be right over, I just have to get dressed."

"We'll contact Nyberg in the meantime."

Wallander handed the phone to Martinsson. "Start with Nyberg," he said.

The living room was accessible from two directions. While Martinsson used the phone, Wallander walked out through the kitchen. A kitchen drawer lay on the floor. The door to a cupboard was ajar. Papers and receipts lay strewn all over the room.

Wallander made a mental note of everything he saw. He could hear Martinsson explaining to Nyberg, the head of forensics in Ystad, what had happened. Wallander kept walking. He looked carefully where he was going before putting his feet down. He came to Svedberg's bedroom. All three drawers in a chest of drawers were pulled out. The bed was unmade and the blanket lay on the ground. With a feeling of boundless sorrow he noted that Svedberg had slept in flowery sheets. His bed was a meadow of wildflowers. Wallander kept going, arriving at a little study between the bedroom and living room. There were some bookcases and a desk. Svedberg was a neat person. His desk at the police station was kept meticulously free of clutter. But here his books had been pulled from their shelves, and the contents of the desk lay on the floor. There was paper everywhere.

Wallander entered the living room again, this time from the other side. Now he was closer to the shotgun, with Svedberg's twisted body at the far end. He stood completely still and took in the whole scene, every detail, everything that had been frozen and left behind as a marker of the drama that had taken place. The questions raced through his mind. Had someone heard the shot or shots? The scene suggested that a burglary had taken place. But when did it happen? And what else happened here?

Martinsson appeared in the doorway on the other side of the living room.

"They're on their way," he said.

Wallander slowly retraced his steps. When he was back in the kitchen he heard the bark of a German shepherd and then Martinsson's agitated voice. He hurried out to the hall and bumped into a dog patrol. Some people in bathrobes were huddled in the background. The patrol officer with the dog was called Edmundsson and had recently moved to Ystad.

"We received a call about a possible burglary," he said uncertainly when he saw Wallander. "At the flat of someone called Svedberg."

Wallander realised that Edmundsson had no idea which Svedberg the caller had been talking about.

"Good. There has been an incident here. By the way, it's Officer Svedberg's flat."

Edmundsson went pale. "I didn't know."

"How could you? But you can go back to the station. Back-up is on its way."

Edmundsson looked inquiringly at him. "What's happened?"

"Svedberg is dead," Wallander answered. "That's all we know."

He immediately regretted having said even that much. The neighbours were listening. Someone could take it into their heads to call the press. What Wallander wanted least of all was to have reporters hanging about. A policeman dying in mysterious circumstances was always news.

As Edmundsson disappeared down the stairs, Wallander thought fuzzily that he didn't know what the dog was called.

"Can you take care of the neighbours?" he said to Martinsson. "If nothing else, they must have heard the shots. Maybe we can establish a time of death."

"Was there more than one shot?"

"I don't know, but someone must have heard something."

The front door slammed below them and they heard approaching footsteps. Martinsson started rounding up the sleepy and anxious people and herded them into the flat next door. Lisa Holgersson came rushing up the stairs.

"I want you to prepare yourself," Wallander said.

"Is it that bad?"

"Svedberg was shot in the head with a shotgun at close range."

She made a face, then steeled herself. Wallander followed her into the hall and pointed to the living room. She went up to the doorway then quickly turned away and swayed as if she were about to faint. Wallander took her by the arm and helped her into the kitchen. She sank down on a blue kitchen chair, and looked up at Wallander with wide eyes.

"Who did this?" she asked.

"I don't know."

Wallander took a glass and gave her some water.

"Svedberg was away yesterday," he said. "Without telling anyone."

"That's unusual," said Holgersson.

"Very unusual. I woke up in the middle of the night with a feeling that things weren't quite right, so I drove over."

"So you don't think it happened yesterday?"

"No. Martinsson is talking to the neighbours to see if anyone heard anything unusual, which they probably did. A shotgun is loud. But we'll have to wait for the autopsy report."

Wallander heard his factual statement echo inside his head. He felt nauseated.

"I know he wasn't married," said Holgersson. "Did he have any family?"

Wallander thought back. He knew that Svedberg's mother had died a couple of years earlier. He didn't know anything about his father. The only relative Wallander knew about for sure was one he had met a few years earlier during a murder investigation.

"He has a cousin called Ylva Brink. She's an obstetric nurse. I can't think of anyone else."

They heard Nyberg's voice out in the hall.

"I'll stay here for a few minutes," said Holgersson.

Wallander went out to talk to Nyberg, who was kicking off his shoes.

"What the hell happened here?"

Nyberg was a brilliant forensic specialist, but he was moody and could be hard to work with. He seemed not to have understood that this emergency concerned a colleague. A dead colleague. Maybe Martinsson had forgotten to tell him.

"Do you know where you are?" Wallander asked carefully.

Nyberg shot him an angry look.

"Some flat on Lilla Norregatan," he answered. "But Martinsson was unusually muddled on the phone. What's going on?"

Wallander looked at him steadily. Nyberg noticed his demeanour and became quiet.

"It's Svedberg," Wallander said. "He's dead. It looks like he's been murdered."

"You mean Kalle?" Nyberg said incredulously.

Wallander nodded and felt a lump in his throat. Nyberg was one of the few who called Svedberg by his first name. His name was actually Karl Evert. Nyberg used his nickname, Kalle.

"He's in there," Wallander said. "Shot in the face with a shotgun."

Nyberg grimaced.

"I don't have to tell you what that looks like," Wallander said.

"No," Nyberg said. "You don't have to do that."

Nyberg went in. He turned away like the others when

64

he reached the doorway. Wallander waited briefly, to give Nyberg a moment to comprehend what he saw in front of him. Then he walked over.

"I already have a question for you," he said. "One of the most important. As you see, the gun is at least two metres away from the body. My question is, could it have ended up over there if Svedberg committed suicide?"

Nyberg thought about it, then shook his head. "No," he said. "That's impossible. A shotgun aimed by himself wouldn't be thrown that far."

For a moment Wallander felt strangely relieved. Svedberg didn't kill himself, he thought.

People were beginning to congregate in the hall. The doctor arrived, as did Hansson. A technician was unpacking his bag.

"Please listen, everybody," Wallander said. "The person lying in there is your colleague, Officer Svedberg. He's dead, probably murdered. I want to prepare you for the fact that it's a terrible sight. We knew him and we grieve for him. He was our friend as well as our colleague and that makes our job much harder."

Wallander stopped. He felt he should say more but couldn't think of anything. He lacked the words. He returned to the kitchen while Nyberg and his assistants got to work. Holgersson was still sitting at the table.

"I have to call his cousin," she said. "If she's the closest living relative."

"I can do it," Wallander said. "After all, I already know her."

"Give me an overview of the events. What happened here?"

"I'll need Martinsson for that. I'll get him."

Wallander went out onto the stairs. The door to the next flat was slightly ajar. He knocked and went in. Martinsson was in the living room with four people. One of them was fully dressed, the others were still in their dressing gowns. There were two women and two men. He signalled for Martinsson to come with him.

"Please remain here for now," he told the others.

They went into the kitchen. Martinsson was very pale.

"Let's start from the beginning," Wallander said. "When was the last time anyone saw Svedberg?"

"I don't know if I was the last one," Martinsson said. "But I caught a glimpse of him in the canteen on Wednesday morning at around 11 a.m."

"How did he seem?"

"Since I didn't think about it, I suppose he must have been like he always was."

"You called me that afternoon. We decided to have a meeting on Thursday morning."

"I went into Svedberg's office straight after our conversation, but he wasn't there. At the front desk they told me he'd gone home for the day."

"What time did he leave?"

"I didn't ask."

"What did you do then?"

"I called him at home and left a message about the meeting. Then I called back a couple of times but I didn't get an answer."

Wallander thought hard. "Sometime on Wednesday, Svedberg leaves the police station. Everything seems normal. On Thursday he doesn't show up, which is unusual, regardless of whether he heard your message. Svedberg never stayed away without letting someone know."

"That means it could have happened as early as Wednesday," Lisa Holgersson said.

Wallander nodded. At what point does the normal suddenly become the abnormal? he thought. That's the moment we have to find.

Another thought struck him – Martinsson's remark about his own answerphone not working.

"Wait here a minute," he said and left the kitchen.

He walked into Svedberg's study. His answerphone was on the desk. Wallander went into the living room where Nyberg was kneeling beside the shotgun, and took him back into the study.

"I'd like to listen to the answerphone, but I don't want to destroy any clues."

"We can get the tape to return to the same place," Nyberg said. He was wearing plastic gloves. Wallander nodded and Nyberg pressed the play button. There were three messages from Martinsson. Each time he stated the time of day. There were no other messages.

"I'd also like to hear Svedberg's greeting," Wallander said.

Nyberg pressed another button.

Wallander flinched when he heard Svedberg's voice. Nyberg also seemed upset by it.

I'm not here, but please leave a message. That was all.

Wallander went back into the kitchen. "Your messages are still on the machine," he said. "But we can't tell if anyone listened to them or not."

The room was quiet. Everyone was thinking about what Wallander had said.

"What do the neighbours say?" he asked.

"No one heard anything," Martinsson answered. "It's quite strange. No one heard a shot and almost everyone was at home."

Wallander frowned. "It's not possible that no one heard anything."

"I'll keep talking to them."

Martinsson left. A police officer came into the kitchen. "There's a reporter outside," he said.

Goddamn it, Wallander thought. Someone had already contacted the press. He looked at Holgersson.

"We have to notify his relatives first," she said.

"We can't put it off any longer than midday," Wallander said.

He turned to the waiting police officer. "No comment right now," he said. "But we'll issue a statement later this morning."

"At 11 a.m.," Holgersson said.

The officer disappeared. Nyberg shouted at someone in the living room. Then everything was quiet again. Nyberg had a bad temper but his outbursts were always brief. Wallander went out into the study and picked up a phone book off the floor. He looked up Ylva Brink's number at the kitchen table and looked questioningly at Holgersson.

"You make the call," she said.

Nothing was as difficult as notifying a relative of a sudden death. Whenever possible, Wallander tried to make sure he was accompanied by a police minister. Although he had gone through this many times, he never became accustomed to it. And even if Ylva Brink was only Svedberg's cousin, it would be hard enough. He heard the first ring and noticed himself start to tense up.

Her answerphone came on with a message saying that she was working the night shift at the hospital. Wallander put the receiver back down. He suddenly remembered visiting her at the hospital with Svedberg two years ago. And now Svedberg was dead. He still couldn't comprehend it.

"She's at the hospital," he said. "I'll have to go and see her in person."

"It really can't wait," Lisa Holgersson said. "Svedberg might have had other relatives that we don't know about."

Wallander nodded. She was right.

"Do you want me to come with you?" she asked.

"That's not necessary."

It occurred to Wallander that he would have liked to have Ann-Britt Höglund with him, and then he realised that no one had contacted her.

She should be here working on this with the others, he thought.

Holgersson got up and left the kitchen. Wallander sat down in her chair and dialled Höglund's number. A man's sleepy voice came on the line.

"I need to speak to Ann-Britt. This is Wallander."

"Who?"

"Kurt. From the police."

The man was still sleepy but now he sounded angry as well.

"What the hell is going on?"

"Isn't this Ann-Britt Höglund's number?"

"There's no bitch by that name around here," the man grunted and slammed down the phone. Wallander could almost feel the impact. He had dialled the wrong number. He tried again slowly and Höglund picked up after the second ring, as quickly as Holgersson had.

"It's Kurt."

She didn't sound particularly sleepy. Maybe she had been awake? Maybe her problems were keeping her awake. Now she'll have one more to add to the list, Wallander thought.

"What's happened?"

"Svedberg has been killed, probably murdered."

"That can't be true."

"Unfortunately it is. It happened in his home, the flat on Lilla Norregatan."

"I know where it is."

"Can you come down here?"

"I'm on my way."

Wallander hung up and remained at the kitchen table. One of the technicians looked in, but Wallander waved him away. He needed to think, if only for a minute. There was something strange about all this, he realised. Something that didn't add up. The crime technician came back into the kitchen.

"Nyberg wants to talk to you."

Wallander got up and went out into the living room, where the discomfort and distress of the people at work was palpable. Svedberg hadn't been a colourful personality, but he was well liked. And now he was dead.

The doctor was kneeling by the body. Now and then a flash went off in the room. Nyberg was making notes. He came over to Wallander, who stopped in the doorway.

"Did Svedberg have any weapons?"

"You mean the shotgun?"

"Yes."

"I don't know, but I can't imagine he did."

"It's just strange that the killer would leave his weapon behind."

Wallander nodded. That had been one of his first thoughts.

"Have you noticed anything else strange around here?" he asked.

Nyberg narrowed his eyes. "Isn't everything about a colleague having his head blown off strange?"

"You know what I mean."

But Wallander didn't wait for an answer. He turned and walked away, bumping into Martinsson in the hall.

"How did it go? Have you established a time?"

"No one heard anything, and if I'm right in my calculations there has been someone in the building continuously since Monday. Either on this level or in the flat below."

"And no one heard anything? That's impossible."

"There was a retired high school teacher who seemed a little hard of hearing, but the others were fine."

Wallander didn't understand it. Someone must have heard the shot or shots.

"You'll have to keep working on this," he said. "I have to drop by the hospital. Do you remember Svedberg's cousin, Ylva Brink? The midwife?"

Martinsson nodded.

"She's probably his nearest relative."

"Didn't he have an aunt somewhere in Västergötland?"

"I'll ask Ylva."

Wallander went down the stairs. He needed to get some air. A reporter was waiting outside the front door. Wallander recognised him as a reporter from Ystad's daily paper.

"What's going on? All units called out in the middle of the night to the home of a police officer by the name of Karl Evert Svedberg."

"I can't tell you anything," Wallander said. "We're issuing a statement to the press at 11 a.m."

"You can't say anything or you won't?"

"I really can't."

The reporter, whose name was Wickberg, nodded.

"That means someone's dead, and you can't say anything until the next of kin has been notified. Am I right?"

"If that were the case I could have picked up the phone."

Wickberg smiled in a firm but not unfriendly way.

"That's not how it's done. You get hold of a police minister first, if one's available. So Svedberg's dead?"

Wallander was too tired to get angry.

"Whatever you want to guess or think is your business," he said. "We'll release information at 11 a.m. Before then I won't say another word."

"Where are you going?"

"I need to get some air."

He walked along Lilla Norregatan and continued a few blocks, then looked back. Wickberg was not following him. Wallander turned right onto Sladdergatan, then left onto Stora Norregatan. He was thirsty and had to take a leak. There were no cars around. He walked up to a building and relieved himself. Then he kept going.

Something's wrong, he thought. Something about this whole thing is completely odd. He couldn't think of what it was, but the feeling became stronger. There was a gnawing pain in his stomach. Why had Svedberg been shot? What was it about the terrible image of the man with his head blown off that didn't add up?

Wallander arrived at the hospital, walked around to the emergency entrance, and rang the bell. He took the elevator to the maternity ward, a rush of images of him and Svedberg on their way to talk to Ylva Brink flitting through his mind. But this time there was no Svedberg. It was as if he had never existed.

Suddenly he caught sight of Ylva Brink through the double glass doors. She met his gaze, and he saw that it took her a couple of seconds to remember who he was. She walked over to the doors and let him in. At that moment he saw that she realised something was wrong.

CHAPTER FIVE

They sat down in the office. It was 3 a.m. Wallander told her the facts. Svedberg was dead. He had been killed with a shotgun. Who the killer was, why it had happened and when, remained unanswered. He avoided giving her too much detail of the crime scene.

When he finished, one of the nurses on the night shift came in to ask Ylva Brink a question.

"Can it wait?" Wallander said. "I've just notified her of a death in the family."

The nurse was about to leave when Wallander asked if he could have a glass of water. He was so dry that his tongue was sticking to the roof of his mouth.

"We're all in shock," Wallander said after the nurse left. "It's completely incomprehensible."

Ylva Brink didn't say anything. She was very pale but had not lost her composure. The nurse returned with the glass of water.

"Let me know if I can do anything else," she said.

"We're fine right now," Wallander answered.

He emptied his glass, but it didn't quench his thirst.

"I just can't get it into my head," she said. "I don't understand."

"I can't either," Wallander said. "It'll be a while before that happens, if ever."

He found a pencil in his coat pocket, but as usual he didn't have a notebook handy. There was a wastepaper basket next to the chair. He took out a piece of paper on which someone had doodled stick figures, smoothed it out, and took a magazine from the table to lean on.

"I have to ask you some questions," he said. "Who were his next of kin? I must admit you're the only one I can think of."

"His parents are gone and he had no siblings. Besides me there's only one cousin. I'm a cousin on his father's side and he has a cousin on his mother's side as well. His name is Sture Björklund."

Wallander noted down the name.

"Does he live here in Ystad?"

"He lives on a farm outside of Hedeskoga."

"So he's a farmer?"

"He's a professor at Copenhagen University."

Wallander was surprised. "I can't recall Svedberg ever mentioning him."

"They hardly ever saw each other. If you're asking which relatives Svedberg had any contact with, then the answer is just me."

"He'll still have to be notified," Wallander said. "As you can understand, this will be making a lot of headlines. A police officer who dies a violent death is big news."

She looked at him carefully. "A violent death? What do you mean by that?"

"That he was murdered."

"Well, what else could it have been?"

"That was going to be my next question for you," Wallander said. "Could it have been suicide?"

"Isn't it always a possibility? Under the right circumstances?"

"Yes."

"Can't you tell by looking at the body if he's been murdered or if he's committed suicide?"

"Yes, we'll probably be able to, but certain questions are a matter of routine."

She thought for a while before answering.

"I've considered it myself during a particularly difficult time. God only knows all that I've been through. But it's never occurred to me that Karl would do anything like that."

"Because he had no reason to?"

"He wasn't what I would call an unhappy person."

"When did you last hear from him?"

"He phoned me last Sunday."

"How did he seem?"

"He sounded perfectly normal."

"Why did he call?"

"We talk to each other once a week. If he didn't get in touch, I did, and vice versa. Sometimes he came over and had dinner, other times I went over to his place. As you may remember, my husband isn't home very often. He works on an oil tanker. Our children are grown up."

"Svedberg could cook?"

"Why wouldn't he be able to?"

"I've never imagined him in a kitchen."

"He cooked very well, particularly fish."

Wallander went back a little. "So he called you last Sunday. That was 4 August. And everything seemed fine?"

"Yes."

"What did you talk about?"

"This and that. I remember him telling me how tired he was. He said he was completely overworked."

Wallander looked at her intently. "Did he really say that he was overworked?"

75

"Yes."

"But he had just taken his holiday."

"I remember it very clearly."

Wallander thought hard before asking his next question. "Do you know what he did on his holiday?"

"I don't know if you know this, but he didn't like to leave Ystad. He usually stayed home. He might have taken a short trip to Poland."

"But what did he do at home? Did he stay in the flat?"

"He had various interests."

"Such as?"

She shook her head. "You must know as well as I do. He had two big passions: amateur astronomy and Native American history."

"I knew about the Indians, and how he sometimes went to Falsterbo to do some bird-watching. But the astronomy is new to me."

"He had a very expensive telescope."

Wallander couldn't remember seeing one in the flat.

"Where did he keep it?"

"In his study."

"So that's what he did on his holidays? Looked at stars and read about Indians?"

"I think so. But this summer was a little unusual."

"In what way?"

"We usually see a lot of each other over the summer, more so than during the rest of the year. But this year he had no time. He turned down several invitations to dinner."

"Did he say why?"

She hesitated before answering. "It was as if he didn't have the time."

Wallander sensed that he was nearing a crucial point.

"He didn't say why?"

76

"No."

"That must have puzzled you."

"Not really."

"Did you notice a change in his behaviour? Did something seem to be bothering him?"

"He was just the same as always. The only thing was that he seemed to be pressed for time."

"When did you first notice this?"

She thought about it. "Shortly after Midsummer, right about the time he took his holiday."

The nurse reappeared in the doorway. Ylva Brink got up.

"I'll be right back," she said.

Wallander looked for a washroom. He drank two more glasses of water and relieved himself. When he came back to the office Ylva was waiting for him.

"I think I'll go now," he told her. "Other questions can wait."

"I can call Sture, if you like. We have to make the funeral arrangements."

"Try to call in the next couple of hours," Wallander said. "We'll be issuing a statement to the press at 11 a.m."

"It still feels unreal," she said.

Her eyes had filled with tears. Wallander had trouble keeping his own eyes from welling up. They sat quietly, both fighting back their tears. Wallander tried to concentrate on the clock hanging on the wall, counting the seconds as they ticked by.

"I have one last question," he said after a while. "Svedberg was a bachelor. I never heard mention of a woman in his life."

"I don't think there ever was one," she answered.

"You don't think that something like that could have happened this summer?"

"You mean that he met a woman?"

"Yes."

"And that was why he was overworked?"

Wallander realised it seemed absurd. "These are questions I have to ask," he repeated. "Otherwise we won't get anywhere."

She followed him to the glass doors.

"You have to catch the person who did this," she said and gripped Wallander's arm tightly.

"You have my word," Wallander said. "Svedberg was one of us. We won't stop until we've caught whoever killed him."

They shook hands.

"Do you know if he used to keep large sums of money in the flat?"

She looked at him with disbelief. "Where would he have got large sums of money? He always complained about how little he earned."

"He was right about that."

"Do you know how much a midwife makes?"

"No."

"I'd better not tell you. You could say we wouldn't be comparing who makes more but who makes even less."

When Wallander left the hospital he drew a deep breath. Birds were chirping. It was barely 4 a.m. There was only a faint trace of wind and it was still warm. He started walking slowly back to Lilla Norregatan. One question seemed more important than the others. Why had Svedberg felt overworked when he had just been on holiday? Could it have something to do with his murder?

Wallander stopped in his tracks on the narrow footpath. In his mind he went back to the moment when he had stood in the doorway of the living room and first witnessed

78

the devastation. Martinsson had been right behind him. He had seen a dead man and a shotgun. But almost at once he was struck by the feeling that something wasn't quite right. Could he make out what it was? He tried again without success.

Patience, he thought. I'm tired. It's been a long night and it's not over yet.

He started walking again, wondering when he would have time to sleep and think about his diet. Then he stopped again. A question suddenly came to him.

What if I die as suddenly as Svedberg? Who will miss me? What will people say? That I was a good policeman? But who will miss me as a person? Ann-Britt? Maybe even Martinsson?

A pigeon flew by close to his head. We don't know anything about each other, he thought. What did I really think of Svedberg? Do I actually miss him? Can you miss a person you didn't know?

He started walking again, but he knew these questions would follow him.

Going into Svedberg's flat again was like walking back into a nightmare. Gone was all feeling of summer, sun, and birdsong. Inside, beneath the harsh beams of the spotlights, there was only death.

Lisa Holgersson had returned to the police station. Wallander beckoned Höglund and Martinsson to follow him into the kitchen. He stopped himself at the last moment from asking them if they had seen Svedberg. They sat down around the kitchen table, grey-faced. Wallander wondered what his own face looked like.

"How is it going?" he asked.

"Can it be anything other than a burglary?" Höglund asked.

"It could be a lot of other things," Wallander answered. "Revenge, a lunatic, two lunatics, three lunatics. We don't know, and as long as we don't know we have to work with what we can see."

"And one other thing," Martinsson said slowly.

Wallander nodded, sensing what Martinsson was about to say.

"The fact that Svedberg was a policeman," Martinsson said.

"Have you found any clues?" Wallander asked. "How is Nyberg's work going? What's in the medical report?"

They both rifled through the notes they had made. Höglund finished first.

"Both barrels of the shotgun were fired," she read. "The pathologist and Nyberg are sure that the shots came in quick succession. The shots were fired directly at Svedberg's head at close range."

Her voice shook. She took a deep breath and continued. "It isn't possible to determine whether or not Svedberg was sitting in the chair when the shots were fired, nor what the exact distance was. From the arrangement of the furniture and the size of the room it cannot have been more than four metres, but it could have been much closer."

Martinsson got up and mumbled something, then disappeared into the bathroom. They waited. He returned after a few minutes.

"I should have quit two years ago," he said.

"We're needed now more than ever," Wallander said sharply, but he understood Martinsson only too well.

"Svedberg was fully dressed," Höglund continued. "That means he wasn't forced out of bed, but we still have no time frame."

Wallander looked at Martinsson.

"I've been over this point again and again," he said. "But none of the neighbours heard anything."

"What about noise from the street?" Wallander asked.

"I don't think it would cover the sound of a shotgun going off. Twice."

"So we have no way of pinpointing the time of the crime. We know that Svedberg was dressed, which may allow us to eliminate the very late hours of the night. I've always been under the impression that Svedberg went to bed early."

Martinsson agreed.

"How did the killer enter the flat? Do we know that?"

"The door shows no signs of a forced entry."

"But remember how easy it was for us to get in," Wallander said.

"Why did he leave his weapon behind? Was it panic?"

They had no answers to Martinsson's question. Wallander looked at his colleagues, who were tired and depressed.

"I'll tell you what I think," he said. "For what it's worth. As soon as I came into the flat I had the feeling that something was odd. What it was I don't know. There's been a murder that suggests a burglary. But if it isn't a burglary, then what? Revenge? Or is it possible to imagine that someone came here not to steal anything but rather to find something?"

He got up, picked up a glass from the kitchen counter, and poured himself some more water.

"I've talked to Ylva Brink at the hospital," he said. "Svedberg had almost no family. He had two cousins, one of whom is Ylva. They seem to have been in close contact. She mentioned one thing that I found odd. When she talked with Svedberg last Sunday he complained of being overworked. But he had just returned from holiday. It doesn't make any sense."

Höglund and Martinsson waited for him to continue.

"I don't know if it means anything," Wallander said. "But we need to know why."

"Was it something to do with Svedberg's investigation?" Höglund asked.

"The young people who went missing?" Martinsson said.

"There must have been something else as well," Wallander said, "since that wasn't a formal investigation. Anyway, he went on holiday just a few days after the parents first notified us."

No one could come up with an answer.

"One of you will have to find out what he was working on," Wallander said.

"Do you think he had a secret of some kind?" Martinsson asked carefully.

"Doesn't everybody have one?"

"So is that what we're looking for? Svedberg's secret?"

"We're looking for the person who killed him. That's all."

They decided to meet again at the station at 8 a.m. Martinsson immediately returned to the flat next door to continue his interviews with the neighbours. Höglund lingered. Wallander looked at her tired and ravaged face.

"Were you awake when I called?"

He regretted the question as soon as it came out. He had no business asking whether or not she had been up. But she didn't seem to mind.

"Yes," she said. "I was wide awake."

"You came down here so quickly that I assume your husband must be at home with the children."

"When you called, we were in the middle of an argument. Just a stupid little argument, the kind you have when you don't have the energy for the big ones any more."

They sat quietly. Now and then they heard Nyberg's voice.

"I just don't understand it," she said. "Who would want to hurt Svedberg?"

"Who was closest to him?" Wallander said.

She looked surprised. "I thought it was you."

"No, I didn't know him that well."

"But he looked up to you."

"I have trouble imagining that."

"You didn't see it, but I did. Maybe the others noticed it as well. He always took your side, even when you were wrong."

"That still doesn't answer our question," Wallander said, and asked it again. "Who was closest to him?"

"No one was close to him."

"Well, we have to get close to him now. Now that he's dead."

Nyberg came into the kitchen, a cup of coffee in his hand. Wallander knew that he always had a thermos ready in case he was called out in the middle of the night.

"How's it going?" Wallander asked.

"It looks like a burglary," Nyberg said. "What we don't know is why the killer left his gun."

"We don't have a time of death," Wallander said.

"That's up to the pathologist."

"I still want to hear your opinion."

"I don't like to make guesses."

"I know, but you have a certain experience in these matters. I promise I won't hold you to it."

Nyberg rubbed his hand over his unshaven chin. His eyes were bloodshot.

"Maybe 24 hours," he said. "I doubt it's less than that."

They let his words sink in. That means Wednesday night or early Thursday, Wallander thought. Nyberg yawned and left the kitchen.

"You should go home now," Wallander said to Höglund. "We have to be ready to organise the investigation at 8 a.m."

The clock on the wall read 5.15 a.m. She put on her coat and left. Wallander stayed in the kitchen. A pile of bills lay on the window sill. He leafed through them. We have to start somewhere, he thought. Next he went in to Nyberg and asked for a pair of rubber gloves. He returned to the kitchen and looked slowly around. He went through the cupboards and drawers methodically and noted that Svedberg kept his kitchen as neat as his office at work.

He left the kitchen and went into the study. Where was the telescope? He sat down in the desk chair and looked around. Nyberg came by and said they were ready to take Svedberg's body away. Did he want to see it again? Wallander shook his head. The image of Svedberg with half his head blown off was forever fixed in his mind. It was an image that didn't spare a single gruesome detail.

He let his gaze continue to wander around the room. The answerphone was on the desk, as well as a pencil holder, some old tin soldiers, and a pocket calendar. Wallander picked up the latter and leafed through it month by month. On 11 January, at 9.30 a.m., Svedberg had had a dentist's appointment. 7 March was Ylva Brink's birthday. On 18 April Svedberg had written the name "Adamsson". The name was also jotted down on 5 and 12 May. In June and July there were no notes at all.

Svedberg had taken his holiday. Afterwards he complained that he was completely overworked. Wallander kept

84

turning the pages, more slowly now, but there were no more notes. The last days of Svedberg's life were a complete blank. 18 October was Sture Björklund's birthday, and the name Adamsson appeared again on 14 December. That was all. Wallander put the pocket calendar back in its place, and leaned back in the chair, which was very comfortable. He felt tired and thirsty. He closed his eyes, wondering who Adamsson was.

Then he leaned forward and picked up the business cards that were tucked into a corner of the brown desk pad. There was a card from *Boman's Second Hand Book Shop* in Gothenburg, and the Audi specialist in Malmö. Svedberg had been a loyal customer and had always driven an Audi, the same way that Wallander always traded in his Peugeot for another Peugeot. Wallander put the desk pad back and looked through a packet of letters and postcards. Most of the letters were more than ten years old, and almost all of them were from Svedberg's mother.

He put them back and looked at a couple of the post-cards. To his surprise he found one that he had sent from Skagen. *The beaches here are amazing*, it said. Wallander sat looking at the card for a while.

That had been three years ago. He had taken an extended medical leave, doubting that he would ever return to active duty. He had spent part of that time wandering along Skagen's wintery and abandoned beaches. He didn't remember writing the postcard. His memories from that period in his life were few.

Eventually he had returned to Ystad and started work-ing again. He remembered Svedberg on his first day back at work. Björk had just welcomed Wallander, and the conference room grew quiet. None of them had expected him to return. The person who finally broke the silence was Svedberg. Wallander could still remember exactly what he said.

"Thank God you finally came back, because I really don't think we could've made it another day without you."

Wallander held on to the memory and tried to see Svedberg clearly. He was the quiet type, but someone who could often ease an uncomfortable situation. He was a good policeman, not outstanding in any way, but good. Stubborn and conscientious. He didn't have a lot of imagination and he wasn't a particularly accomplished writer. His reports were often poorly written, and they irritated the prosecutors. But he had been an important part of the team.

Wallander got up and went into Svedberg's bedroom. There was no sign of the telescope. He sat down on the bed and picked up a book off the bedside table. It was called *A History of the Sioux Indians* and was written in English. Svedberg didn't speak very good English, but perhaps he was better at reading it.

Wallander flipped through the book absentmindedly and found himself staring at a remarkable picture of Sitting Bull. Then he got up and went into the bathroom. He opened a mirrored cabinet and found nothing that surprised him. His own bathroom cabinet was exactly the same.

Now only the living room remained. He would have preferred to skip it, but knew he couldn't. He went into the kitchen and drank a glass of water. It was close to 6 a.m. and he was very tired.

Finally he went out into the living room. Nyberg had put on knee-guards and was crawling around the black leather sofa that stood against a wall. The chair was still overturned and no one had moved the shotgun. The only thing that had been moved was Svedberg's body.

Wallander looked around the room and tried to imagine the events that had taken place. What had happened right before the fatal moment, before the gun went off? But he couldn't see anything. The feeling that he was ignoring something important came over him again. He stood completely still and tried to coax the thought to the surface, but he got nothing.

Nyberg came up to him and they looked at each other.

"Do you understand this?" Wallander asked.

"No," Nyberg answered. "It's strangely like a painting."

Wallander looked closely at him. "What do you mean 'a painting'?"

Nyberg blew his nose and carefully refolded his handkerchief.

"Everything is such a mess," he said. "Chairs have been overturned, drawers pulled out, papers and china thrown all over the place. It's almost as if it's too messy."

Wallander knew what he meant, although he had not yet followed this thought to its conclusion.

"You mean it looks arranged."

"Of course it's only a thought at this point. I don't have anything to back it up with."

"What exactly gave you this feeling?"

Nyberg pointed to a little porcelain rooster that lay on the ground.

"It seems plausible to assume that it came from that shelf over there," he said, and pointed it out to Wallander. "Where else could it have come from? But if it fell because someone was pulling out the drawers and going through them, why would it have landed all the way over here?"

Wallander nodded.

"There's probably a completely rational explanation," Nyberg said. "But if so, you'll have to tell me what it is."

Wallander didn't say anything. He stayed in the living room for a few more minutes, then left the flat. When he came out on the street it was already morning. A police car stood parked outside the building, but there were no onlookers. Wallander assumed that the police officers had been instructed not to give out any information.

He stood completely still and drew a couple of deep breaths. It was going to be a beautiful, late summer's day. Only now was he starting to sense the overwhelming nature of his sorrow, which stemmed as much from genuine affection as from the reminder of his own mortality. Death had come close this time. It was not like when his father had died. This frightened him.

It was 6.25 a.m. on Friday, 9 August. Wallander walked slowly to his car. A cement mixer started up in the distance.

Ten minutes later he walked through the doors of the police station.

CHAPTER SIX

They gathered in the conference room shortly after 8 a.m. and held an impromptu memorial service. Lisa Holgersson lit a candle at the place where Svedberg normally sat. All those at the station that morning were gathered in the room, filling it with a palpable sense of shock and sadness. Holgersson said only a few words, fighting to keep her composure. Everyone in the room prayed for her not to break down. It would make the situation unbearable. After she had spoken, they stood for a minute's silence. Uneasy images floated through Wallander's mind. He was already having trouble picturing Svedberg's face. He had experienced the same thing when his father died, and earlier with Rydberg.

Although one can certainly remember the dead, it's as if they never existed, he thought.

The impromptu service came to an end, people started to leave. Apart from the members of the investigative team, Holgersson was the only one to stay behind. They sat down at the table. The flame of the candle flickered when Martinsson closed one of the windows. Wallander looked questioningly at Holgersson, but she shook her head. It was his turn to speak.

"We're all tired," he began. "We're upset and sad and confused. What we've always feared the most has finally occurred. Normally we try to solve crimes, even violent crimes, that do not affect people from our own world. This time it's happened in our midst, but we still have to try to approach it as if it were a regular case."

He paused and looked around. No one spoke.

"Let's go over the facts," Wallander said. "Then we can begin to plot our strategy. We know very little. Svedberg was shot sometime between Wednesday afternoon and Thursday evening. It happened in his flat, which shows no signs of forced entry. We can assume that the shotgun lying on the floor was the murder weapon. The flat looks like it was burgled, which may indicate that Svedberg was confronted by an armed assailant. We don't know if this was the case; it is simply a possibility. We cannot disregard other scenarios. We have to keep our search as broad as possible. We also cannot disregard the fact that Svedberg was a policeman. This may or may not be significant. We have no exact time of death yet, and a perplexing fact is that none of the neighbours heard any shots. We therefore have to wait for the autopsy report."

He poured himself a glass of water and emptied it before continuing.

"This is what we know. The only thing to add is that Svedberg did not turn up for work on Thursday. We all appreciate how unusual this is. He gave no reason for his absence, and the only rational assumption is that there was something preventing him from coming in. We know what that means."

Nyberg interrupted him with a gesture.

"I'm not a pathologist," he said, "but I doubt that Svedberg died as early as Wednesday."

"Then we have to deal with the question of what could have prevented Svedberg from coming to work yesterday," Wallander said. "Why didn't he call in? When was he killed?"

Wallander described his conversation with Ylva Brink. "Apart from telling me about the only other relative that Svedberg was in touch with, she said something that stuck in my mind. She said that in the last few weeks Svedberg complained about feeling overworked. But he had just returned from holiday. It doesn't make any sense, particularly if you know that he didn't tend to take strenuous trips on his holiday."

"Did he ever leave Ystad?" Martinsson asked.

"Not very often. He made a day-trip to Bornholm or occasionally took the ferry to Poland. Ylva Brink confirmed this. But he seems mostly to have spent time on his two hobbies, which were Native American history and amateur astronomy. Ylva Brink told me that he owned an expensive telescope, but we haven't found it yet."

"I thought he went bird-watching," said Hansson, who had been silent until now.

"Sometimes, but apparently not so often," Wallander said. "I think we should assume that Ylva Brink knew him quite well, and according to her it was stars and Indians that mattered."

He looked around. "Why was he overworked? What does that mean? It may not be important at all, but I can't help thinking that it is."

"I looked over what he was working on before our meeting," Höglund said. "Just before he went on holiday, he spoke to all the parents of the young people who are missing."

"Which young people?" Holgersson asked, surprised. Wallander explained and Höglund continued.

"The last two days before he went on holiday, he visited the Norman, Boge, and Hillström families, one after the other. But I can't find any notes from those visits even though I searched thoroughly."

Wallander and Martinsson looked at each other.

"That can't be right," Wallander said. "All three of us had a thorough meeting with those families. We had never talked about pursuing them for further questioning, since there was no indication of a crime."

"Well, it looks like he went and saw them anyway," Höglund said. "He's noted the exact times of his visits in his calendar."

Wallander thought for a moment. "That would mean that Svedberg was pursuing this on his own without telling us about it."

"That's not like him," Martinsson said.

"No," Wallander agreed. "It's as strange as him staying home from work without notifying anyone."

"We can easily verify this information," Höglund said.

"Please do," Wallander said. "And find out what questions Svedberg was asking."

"This whole situation is absurd," Martinsson said. "We've been trying to meet with Svedberg with regard to these young people since Wednesday and now he's gone and here we are still talking about them."

"Have there been any new developments?" Holgersson asked.

"Nothing apart from the fact that one of the mothers has become extremely anxious. Her daughter sent her another postcard."

"Isn't that good news?"

"According to her, the handwriting was faked."

"Who would do that?" Hansson asked. "Who the hell forges postcards? Cheques I understand. But postcards?"

"I think we should keep the two cases separate for

now," Wallander said. "Let's work out how to tackle the investigation of Svedberg's killer or killers."

"Nothing indicates that there was more than one," Nyberg said.

"Can you be sure that there wasn't?"

"No."

Wallander let his palms fall flat onto the table. "We can't be sure about anything right now," he said. "We have to cast a wide net. In a couple of hours we're going to release the news of Svedberg's death, and then we'll really have to move."

"This will take top priority, of course," Holgersson said. "Everything else can wait."

"The press conference," Wallander said. "Let's take care of that right now."

"A police officer has been murdered," Holgersson said. "We'll tell them exactly what happened. Do we have any leads?"

"No." Wallander's answer was firm.

"Then that's what we'll say."

"How detailed should we get?"

"He was shot at close range. We have the murder weapon. Is there any reason to withhold that information?"

"Not really," Wallander said, and he looked around the table. No one had any objections.

Holgersson got up. "I'd like you to be there," she said. "Maybe all of you should be there. After all, a colleague and friend has been killed."

They decided to meet 15 minutes before the press conference.

Holgersson left. The candle went out when the door closed. Höglund lit it again. They went through what they knew one more time and divided up the work at hand.

They were returning to work mode. They were just about to stop when Martinsson raised one more issue.

"We should probably decide now if the young people should be left aside for now or not."

Wallander felt unsure. But he knew it was up to him.

"We'll put it aside for now," he said. "At least for the next few days. Then we'll revisit it, unless of course Svedberg was asking some extraordinary questions."

It was 9.15 a.m. Wallander got a cup of coffee and went into his office. He got out a pad of paper and wrote a single word at the top of the first page: *Svedberg*. Underneath it he drew a cross that he immediately scratched out. He didn't get any further. He had been meaning to write down all the thoughts that had come to him during the night. But he put down the pen and walked to the window. The August morning was sunny and warm. The thought that there was something not quite right about this case returned. Nyberg felt there was something arranged about the murder scene. If so, then why, and by whom?

He looked for Sture Björklund's number in the phone book and dialled it. The phone rang several times.

"Please accept my condolences," Wallander said, when the man answered.

Sture Björklund's voice sounded strained and distant.

"Likewise. You probably knew my cousin better than I did. Ylva called me at 6 a.m. this morning to tell me what had happened."

"Unfortunately this will make headlines in the papers," Wallander said.

"I know. As it happens it's the second murder case in our family."

"Really?"

"Yes, in 1847, or more precisely on 12 April 1847, a man who was Karl Evert's great-great-great-great-uncle was killed with an axe somewhere on the outskirts of Eslöv. The murderer was a soldier by the name of Brun, who had been given a dishonourable discharge from the army for a number of reasons. The murder was simply a matter of money. Our ancestor was a cattle man and fairly wealthy."

"What happened?" Wallander asked, trying to hide his impatience.

"The police, which I guess consisted of a sheriff and his assistant, made heroic efforts and arrested Brun on his way to Denmark a few days later. He was sentenced to death and executed. When Oscar I became king he took on the business of processing death sentences blocked by his predecessor, Charles XV. As many as 14 prisoners were executed as soon as he came to power. Brun was beheaded, somewhere in the vicinity of Malmö."

"What a strange story."

"I did some research into our ancestry a couple of years ago. Of course the case of Brun and the murder in Eslöv was already known."

"If it's all right with you, I'd like to come out to see you as soon as possible."

Sture Björklund immediately put up his guard.

"What about?"

"We're trying to clarify our picture of Karl Evert." It felt unnatural to use his first name.

"I didn't know him very well, though, and I have to go to Copenhagen this afternoon."

"This is urgent and it won't take much time."

The man was quiet at the other end of the line. Wallander waited.

"What time?"

"Around 2 p.m.?"

"I'll call Copenhagen and let them know I won't be in today."

Sture Björklund gave Wallander directions. His house didn't seem hard to find.

After the phone conversation, Wallander spent a half hour writing out a summary of the case. He was still searching for the thought he had had when he first saw Svedberg lying on the floor – the thought that something wasn't quite right, the same idea that had also struck Nyberg. Wallander realised that it could simply be a reaction to the unbearable and incomprehensible experience of seeing a colleague dead. But he still tried to explore what might have caused it.

A little after 10 a.m. he went to get another cup of coffee. A number of people were gathered in the canteen. There was a general atmosphere of shock and dismay. Wallander lingered for a while, talking to some traffic officers. Then he walked back to his office and called Nyberg on his mobile phone.

"Where are you?" Wallander asked.

"Where do you think?" he replied sourly. "I'm still in Svedberg's flat."

"You haven't seen a telescope, by any chance?"

"No."

"Anything else?"

"We have a number of prints on the shotgun. We'll be able to get complete copies of at least two or three of them."

"Then we'll hope he's already in the database. Is that it?"

"Yes."

"I'm on my way to question Svedberg's other cousin,

who lives outside Hedeskoga. After that I'll be back to do a more thorough search of the flat."

"We'll be done by then. I'm also planning to attend the press conference."

Wallander couldn't remember Nyberg ever coming to a meeting that involved the press before. Maybe it was Nyberg's way of expressing how upset he was. Wallander was suddenly moved.

"Have you found any keys?" he asked after a moment.

"There are some car keys and a key to the basement storage area."

"Nothing in the attic?"

"There don't seem to be storage areas in the attic, only in the basement. You'll get the keys from me at the press conference."

Wallander hung up and went to Martinsson's office.

"Where's Svedberg's car?" he asked. "The Audi."

Martinsson didn't know. They asked Hansson, who didn't know either. Höglund wasn't in her office.

Martinsson looked at his watch.

"It's got to be in a car park close to the flat," he said. "I think I have time to check before 11 a.m."

Wallander went back to his office. He saw that people had started to send flowers. Ebba looked like she had been crying, but Wallander didn't say anything to her. He hurried past her as fast as he could.

The press conference started on time. Afterwards Wallander remembered thinking that Lisa Holgersson conducted the proceedings with dignity. He told her that no one could have done a better job. She was wearing her uniform and standing in front of a table with two bouquets of roses. Her speech was clear and to the point. She told the press the known facts, and her voice did not fail her this time. A respected colleague, Karl Evert Svedberg, had been found murdered in his flat. The exact time of death and the motive were not yet known, but there were indications that Svedberg was attacked by an armed burglar. The police did not have any leads. She concluded by describing Svedberg's career and his character. Wallander thought her description of Svedberg was very good, not exaggerated in any way. Wallander answered the few questions that were asked. Nyberg described the murder weapon as a Lambert Baron shotgun.

It was all over in half an hour. Afterwards, Holgersson was interviewed by the *Sydnytt* newspaper, while Wallander spoke to some reporters from the evening papers. It was only when they asked him to pose outside the block of flats on Lilla Norregatan that he let his impatience show.

At midday Holgersson asked the members of the investigative team to a simple lunch at her home. Wallander and Holgersson spoke about some of their memories of Svedberg. Wallander was the only one who had heard Svedberg explain why he had decided to become a police officer.

"He was afraid of the dark," Wallander said. "That's what he said. The fear had been with him since his earliest childhood, and he had never been able to understand it or overcome it. He became a police officer because he thought it would be a way to fight this fear, but it never left him."

A little before 1.30 p.m. they returned to the station. Wallander drove back with Martinsson.

"She handled that very well," Martinsson said.

"Lisa's good at her job," Wallander answered. "But you knew that already, didn't you?"

Martinsson didn't answer.

Wallander suddenly remembered something. "Did you find the Audi?"

"There's a private car park at the back of the building. It was there. I looked it over."

"Did you see a telescope in the boot?"

"There was only a spare tyre and a pair of boots. And a can of insecticide in the glove compartment."

"August is the month for bees," Wallander said glumly.

They went their separate ways when they arrived at the station. Wallander had got a bunch of keys from Nyberg at the lunch, but before he returned to the flat he drove to Hedeskoga. Sture Björklund's directions were very clear, Wallander thought, as he turned into a little farmhouse that lay just outside the town. There was a fountain in front of the house, and the large lawn had plaster statues dotted all over it. Wallander saw to his surprise that they all looked like devils, all with terrifying, gaping jaws. He wondered briefly what he would have expected a professor of sociology to have in his garden, but his thoughts were interrupted by a man wearing boots, a worn leather coat, and a torn straw hat. He was very tall and thin. Through the tear in the hat Wallander could see one similarity between Svedberg and his cousin: they were both bald.

Wallander was thrown for a moment. He hadn't expected Professor Björklund to look like this. His face was sunburnt, and had a couple of days' worth of stubble. Wallander wondered whether professors in Copenhagen really appeared unshaven at their lectures. But then he reminded himself that the semester had not yet started and that Björklund probably had other business across the strait.

"I hope this isn't too much of an inconvenience," Wallander said.

Sture Björklund threw his head back and laughed. Wallander noted a certain amount of derision in his laughter.

"There's a woman I meet in Copenhagen every Friday," Sture Björklund said. "I suppose you would call her a mistress. Do policemen in the Swedish countryside have mistresses?"

"Hardly," Wallander said.

"It's an ingenious solution to the problems of coexistence," Björklund said. "Each time may be the last. There's no co-dependence, no late-night discussions that might get out of hand and lead to things like furniture buying or pretending that one takes the idea of marriage seriously."

This man in the straw hat with the shrill laugh was starting to get on Wallander's nerves.

"Well, murder is something to take seriously," he said.

Sture Björklund nodded and took off the hat, as if he felt compelled to show a sign of something resembling mourning.

"Let's go in," he said.

The house was not like anything Wallander had ever seen before. From the outside it looked like a typical Scanian farmhouse. But the world that Wallander entered was completely unexpected. There were no walls left on the inside of the house – it was simply one big room that stretched all the way to the rafters. Here and there were little tower-like structures with spiral staircases made out of wrought iron and wood. There was almost no furniture and the walls were bare. One of the walls at the end of the house was entirely taken up by a large aquarium. Sture Björklund led him to a huge wooden table flanked by a church pew and a wooden stool.

"I've always thought that chairs should be hard,"

Björklund said. "Uncomfortable chairs force you to finish what you have to do more quickly, whether it's eating, thinking, or talking to a policeman."

Wallander sat down in the pew. It really was very uncomfortable.

"If my notes are correct, you're a professor at Copenhagen University," he said.

"I teach sociology, but I try to keep my course load down to an absolute minimum. My own research is what interests me, and I can do that from home."

"This is probably not relevant, but what is it you do your research on?"

"Man's relationship to monsters."

Wallander wondered if Sture Björklund was joking. He waited for him to continue.

"Monsters in the Middle Ages were not the same as they were in the 18th century. My ideas are not the same as those of future generations will be. It's a complicated and fascinating world: hell, the home of all terror, is constantly changing. Above all, this kind of work gives me a chance to make extra money, a factor which is not insignificant."

"In what way?"

"I work as a consultant for American film companies that make horror movies. Without boasting, I think I can claim to be one of the most sought-after consultants in the world when it comes to commercial terror. There's some Japanese man in Hawaii, but other than that it's just me."

Just as Wallander was starting to wonder if the man sitting across from him on the little stool was insane, he handed him a drawing that had been lying on the table.

"I've interviewed seven-year-olds in Ystad about monsters. I've tried to incorporate their ideas into my own work and have come up with this figure. The Americans love him. He's going to get the starring role in a cartoon series aimed at frightening seven- and eight-year-olds."

Wallander looked at the picture. It was extremely unpleasant. He put it down.

"What do you think, Inspector?"

"You can call me Kurt."

"What do you think?"

"It's unpleasant."

"We live in an unpleasant world."

He laid the straw hat on the table and Wallander smelt a strong odour of sweat.

"I've just decided to cancel my telephone service," he said. "Five years ago I got rid of the TV. Now I'm getting rid of the phone."

"Isn't that a little impractical?"

Björklund looked at him seriously. "I'm going to exercise my right to decide when I want to have contact with the outside world. I'll keep the computer, of course. But the phone is going."

Wallander nodded and took the opportunity to change the subject.

"Your cousin, Karl Evert Svedberg, has been killed. Apart from Ylva Brink, you are the only remaining relative. When was the last time you saw him?"

"About three weeks ago."

"Can you be more precise?"

"Friday, 19 July, at 4.30 p.m."

The answer came so quickly that Wallander was surprised. "How can you remember the time of day so well?"

"We had decided to meet at that time. I was going to Scotland to see some friends, and Kalle was going to house-sit, like he always did. That was really the only time we saw each other, when I was going away and when I came back."

"What was involved in house-sitting?"

"He lived here."

The answer came as a surprise to Wallander, but he had no reason to doubt Björklund.

"This happened regularly?"

"For the last ten years at least. It was a wonderful arrangement."

Wallander thought for a moment. "When did you come back?"

"27 July. Kalle picked me up at the airport and drove me home. We chatted for a bit and then he went back to Ystad."

"Did you have the feeling that he was overworked?"

Björklund threw his head back and laughed his shrill laugh again.

"I take it you meant that as a joke, but isn't it disrespectful to joke about the dead?"

"I meant the question seriously."

Björklund smiled. "I suppose we can all seem a bit overworked if we indulge in passionate relationships with women, can't we?"

Wallander stared at Björklund.

"What do you mean?"

"Kalle met his woman here while I was gone. That was part of the arrangement. They lived here whenever I went to Scotland or anywhere else."

Wallander gasped.

"You seem surprised," Björklund said.

"Was it always the same woman? What was her name?"

"Louise."

"What was her last name?"

"I don't know. I never met her. Kalle was quite secretive about her, or perhaps one should say 'discreet.'"

Wallander was caught completely by surprise. He had never heard of Svedberg having any relationship with a woman, let alone a long-term one.

"What else do you know about her?" he asked.

"Nothing."

"But Kalle must have said something?"

"Never. And I never asked. Our family is not one for idle curiosity."

Wallander had nothing more to ask. What he needed now was time to digest this latest piece of information. He got up, and Björklund raised his eyebrows.

"Was that it?"

"For now. But you'll hear from me again."

Björklund followed him out. It was warm and there was almost no breeze.

"Do you have any idea who might have killed him?" Wallander asked when they reached his car.

"Wasn't there a break-in? Who knows what criminal is lurking just around the corner?"

They shook hands and Wallander got into the car. He had just started the engine when Björklund leaned down to the window.

"There's just one more thing," he said. "Louise changed her hair colour pretty often."

"How do you know?"

"The hairs left in the bathroom. One year it was red, then black, then blond. It was always different."

"But you think it was the same woman?"

"I actually think Kalle was very much in love with her."

Wallander nodded. Then he drove away. It was 3 p.m.

One thing was certain, Wallander thought. Svedberg, our friend and colleague, may have been dead for just a couple of days, but we already know more about him than when he was alive.

At 3.10 p.m., Wallander parked his car in the town square and walked up to Lilla Norregatan. Without knowing why, he quickened his step. Something about this had suddenly become a matter of urgency.

CHAPTER SEVEN

Wallander went down into the basement. The steep stairs gave him the feeling that he was on his way to something far deeper than a normal basement; that he was journeying to the underworld. He arrived at a blue steel door, found the right key among the ones Nyberg had given him, and unlocked it. It was dark inside and the air smelt dank and musty. He took out the torch he had brought with him from the car and let the beam travel over the walls until he found the light switch. It was placed unusually low, as if for very small people. He walked into a narrow corridor with storage areas behind grilles on both sides. It occurred to him that Swedish basement storage lockers were not unlike rough prison cells, except that they didn't contain prisoners, but instead guarded old sofas, skis, and piles of suitcases. Svedberg's storage locker was all the way at the end of the corridor. The wire netting was reinforced with steel bars. A padlock hung around two of the bars. Svedberg must have reinforced this himself, Wallander thought. Is there something in there that he couldn't risk losing?

Wallander put on a pair of rubber gloves, opened the lock carefully, then turned on the light in the storage area and looked around. It was full of the things one would expect, and it took him only about an hour to go through everything there. He found nothing unusual. Finally, he straightened up and looked around again, looking for something that should have been there but wasn't, like the expensive telescope. He left the basement and locked it up.

He came back up into daylight. Since he was thirsty, he walked over to a café on the south side of the main square and drank some mineral water and a cup of coffee. He fought an inner battle over buying a Danish pastry. He knew he shouldn't but did it anyway.

Less than half an hour later he was back at the door of Svedberg's flat. It was deathly silent inside. Wallander held his breath before going in. The usual police tape was plastered across the door. He unpeeled the tape from the lock, got out the key, and let himself in. Immediately he heard the cement mixer from the street. He walked into the living room, cast an involuntary glance at the spot where Svedberg had lain, and walked over to the window. The rumble of the cement mixer seemed magnified among the buildings. Construction materials were being unloaded from a large truck. A thought suddenly came to Wallander. He left the flat and walked down to the street. An older man who had taken his shirt off was spraying water into the mixer. The man nodded at Wallander and seemed to know immediately that he was a police officer.

"It's terrible what happened," he yelled above the sound of the mixer.

"I need to speak to you," Wallander yelled back.

The man called out to a younger worker who was smoking in the shade. He came over and grabbed the hose. They went around the corner, where it was quieter.

"Do you know what has happened?" Wallander asked him.

"Some policeman by the name of Svedberg was shot."

"That's right. What I want you to tell me is how long

you've been working here. It looks like you're just getting started."

"We started on Monday. We're rebuilding the entryway to the building."

"When did you start using the mixer?"

The man thought about it. "It must have been on Tuesday," he said. "At around 11 a.m."

"Has it been on since then?"

"Pretty much continuously from 7 a.m. until 5 p.m. Sometimes even a little longer."

"Has it been in the same spot the whole time?"

"Yes."

"So you've had a clear view of everyone coming and going from the building."

The man suddenly realised the importance of Wallander's question and became very serious.

"Of course you don't know the people who live here," Wallander said. "But you've probably seen a number of people more than once."

"I don't know what that policeman looked like, if that's what you're asking."

Wallander hadn't thought of this.

"I'll get someone to come down and show you a photograph," he said. "What's your name?"

"Nils Linnman, like the man who does those nature programmes."

Wallander was of course familiar with Nils Linnman, the Swedish television personality.

"Have you noticed anything unusual during the time you've been working here?" Wallander asked while he desperately searched for something to write on.

"How do you mean?"

"Someone who may have seemed very nervous, or as if

they were in a hurry. Sometimes you notice things that just don't seem quite right."

Linnman thought it over and Wallander waited. He needed to pee again.

"No," Linnman said finally. "I can't think of anything. But Robban may have seen something."

"Robban?"

"The young guy who took over for me. But I doubt it. I think the only thing on his mind is his motorbike."

"We'd better ask him," Wallander said. "And if you think of anything later, please call me right away."

For once Wallander had a card with him, which Linnman tucked into the front pocket of his baggy overalls.

"I'll get Robban."

The ensuing conversation with Robban was very brief. His full name was Robert Tärnberg and he had heard only vague mention of someone being killed in the building. He had not noticed anything unusual. Wallander suspected he wouldn't even have noticed an elephant walking across the street, so he didn't bother giving him his card. He returned to the flat. At least he now had a satisfactory answer for why no one had heard the shots.

He went out into the kitchen and called the station. Höglund was the only one available. Wallander asked her to come down with a photo of Svedberg to show to the construction workers.

"We already have officers down there going door to door," she said.

"But they seem to have overlooked the workers."

Wallander walked out into the hall, then stopped and tried to rid himself of all extraneous thoughts. Many years ago, when Wallander had just moved to Ystad from Malmö,

Rydberg had given him the following advice: slowly peel away all the extraneous layers. There are tracks and marks left at every crime scene, like shadows of the event itself. That's what you have to find.

Wallander opened the front door and immediately noticed at least one detail that wasn't right. In a basket under the hall mirror there was a stack of newspapers, all copies of the local paper, *Ystad Allehanda*, which Svedberg subscribed to. But there was no copy on the floor under the post slot, although at least one should have been there.

Maybe even two or three by now. Someone had moved them. He walked into the kitchen and saw that the Wednesday and Thursday editions lay on the counter. Friday's edition lay on the kitchen table.

Wallander called Nyberg's mobile phone. He answered right away. Wallander started by telling him about the cement mixer. Nyberg sounded doubtful.

"Sound travels inwards," he said. "People on the street would be unable to hear shots from inside if the cement mixer had been on, but inside the building it would be a different story. Sound travels differently in buildings. I read about it somewhere."

"Maybe we should do some test shots," Wallander said. "With and without the cement mixer on and without telling the neighbours about it beforehand."

Nyberg agreed.

"But what I'm really calling about is the paper," Wallander said. "*Ystad Allehanda*."

"I put it on the kitchen table," Nyberg said. "But some-one else is responsible for the ones lying on the counter."

"We should test them for prints," Wallander said. "We don't know who might have put them there."

Nyberg was silent for a moment. "You're right," he said. "How the hell could I have missed it?"

"I won't touch them," Wallander told him.

"How long are you going to be there?"

"Two or three hours at least."

"I'll come down."

Wallander pulled out one of the kitchen drawers and found a couple of pens and a pad of paper where he remembered seeing them before. He wrote down Nils Linnman's and Robert Tärnberg's names and noted that someone should talk to the newspaper delivery person. Then he returned to the hall. Traces and shadows, Rydberg had told him. He held his breath while he let his gaze travel over the room. The leather coat Svedberg wore both winter and summer hung by the door. Wallander searched the pockets and found his wallet.

Nyberg has been sloppy, he thought.

He returned with it to the kitchen and emptied the contents onto the table. There was 847 kronor, a cash card, a card for petrol, and some personal identification cards. *Detective Inspector Svedberg*, he read. He compared the police ID and the driver's licence. The photo on the driver's licence was the older. Svedberg stared glumly into the lens. It looked like it had been taken in the summertime; the top of Svedberg's head was sunburned.

Louise should have told you to wear a hat, Wallander thought. Louise. Only two people claimed she existed. Svedberg and his cousin, the monster maker. But he had never seen her, only strands of her hair. Wallander made a face. It didn't make sense.

He picked up the phone and called Ylva Brink at the hospital. He was told she would be in that evening. Wallander looked up her home phone number and got her machine.

He went back to the contents of the wallet. The photo on the police ID was recent. Svedberg's face was a little fuller but just as glum. Wallander looked through the rest of the contents and found some stamps. That was all. He got out a plastic bag and dumped everything into it. Then he went out into the hall for the third time. Peel everything away, find the traces, Rydberg had said.

Wallander went into the bathroom and relieved himself. He thought about what Sture Björklund had said about the different coloured hairs. The only thing that Wallander knew about the woman in Svedberg's life was that she dyed her hair. He went out into the living room and stood beside the overturned chair. Then he changed his mind. You're proceeding too quickly, Rydberg would have told him. Traces of a crime need to be coaxed out, not rushed.

He returned to the kitchen and called Ylva Brink again. This time she answered.

"I hope I'm not disturbing you," he said. "I know you work all night."

"I can't sleep anyway," she said.

"A lot of questions have come up and I need to ask you some of them right away."

Wallander told her about his talk with Sture Björklund and Björklund's claim that Svedberg had a woman called Louise.

"He never told me any of this," she said when Wallander had finished.

He sensed that the information disturbed her.

"Who never told you? Kalle or Sture?"

"Neither one."

"Let's start with Sture. What kind of relationship do you two have? Are you surprised that he never told you about this?"

"I just can't believe it."

"But why would he lie?"

"I don't know."

Wallander realised that the conversation needed to be continued in person. He looked at the time. It was 5.40 p.m. He needed another hour in the flat.

"It's probably best if we meet," he suggested. "I'm free after 7 p.m. tonight."

"How about at the station? That's close to the hospital, and I could come by on my way to work."

Wallander hung up and returned to the living room. He approached the broken and overturned chair, looked around the room, trying to imagine the actions that had taken place. Svedberg had been shot straight on. Nyberg had mentioned the possibility that the buckshot had entered slightly from below, suggesting that the killer held the shotgun at hip or chest level. The bloodstain on the wall confirmed this upward trajectory. Svedberg must have then fallen to the left, most probably taking the chair down with him, at which point one of its arms broke. But had he been about to sit down, or get up?

Wallander realised the importance of this at once. If Svedberg had been sitting in the chair he must have known his killer. If a burglar had surprised him, he would hardly have sat down or remained sitting.

Wallander went over to the spot where the shotgun had been found. He turned around and looked at the room from his new vantage point. This may not have been the point from which the shot was fired, but it would have been close. He kept still and tried to coax the shadows from their hiding places. The feeling that something about the case was very strange grew stronger. Had Svedberg come in from the hall and surprised a burglar? If this was the case, he would have been in the way. This would also have been true if Svedberg had entered from the bedroom. It was reasonable to assume that a burglar would not have had the shotgun at the ready. Svedberg would no doubt have tried to attack him. He may have been afraid of the dark, but he was certainly not afraid to take action when necessary.

The cement mixer was suddenly turned off. Wallander listened. The sound of traffic was not very loud.

There is another alternative, he thought. The person who entered the flat was someone Svedberg knew. He knew him so well that it would not have worried him to see the shotgun. Then something happened, Svedberg was killed, and the unknown assailant turned the flat inside out looking for something.

Perhaps he simply tried to make it look like a burglary. Wallander thought about the telescope again. It was missing, but who could say if anything else was gone? Maybe Ylva Brink would know the answer.

Wallander went up to the window and looked down at the street. Nils Linnman was locking up a work shed. Robert Tärnberg must already have gone. He had heard the roar of a motorbike being started up a couple of minutes ago.

The doorbell rang. Wallander jumped. He opened the door, and Ann-Britt Höglund came in.

"The construction workers have gone home," Wallander said. "You're too late."

"I showed them Svedberg's picture," she said. "No one saw him, or at least they don't remember it."

They sat down in the kitchen and Wallander told her about his meeting with Sture Björklund. She listened attentively.

"If he's right then that changes our picture of Svedberg quite dramatically," she said when Wallander had finished.

"Why did he keep her a secret for so long?" Wallander asked.

"Maybe she was married."

"An illicit affair? Do you think they met only at Björklund's house? That doesn't seem feasible. They only had access to it a couple of times a year. She can't have come to this flat without anyone ever seeing her."

"Whatever the case, we have to find her," Höglund answered.

"There's something else I've been thinking about," Wallander said slowly. "If he kept her a secret, what else might he have hidden from us?"

He could see she was following his train of thought.

"You don't think it's a burglary."

"I doubt it. A telescope is missing, and Ylva Brink may be able to tell us if anything else is gone, but it doesn't add up. There's no coherence to the scene of the crime."

"We've checked his bank accounts," Höglund said. "At least the ones we've managed to find. There's nothing of note, no outlandish deposits or debts. He has a loan of 25,000 kronor for his car. The bank said that Svedberg always managed his affairs conscientiously."

"One shouldn't speak ill of the dead," Wallander said, "but to tell the truth I thought he was downright miserly."

"How do you mean?"

"We'd always share the tab when we went out, but I'd always leave the tip."

Höglund slowly shook her head. "It's funny how differently we can see people. I never thought of him like that."

Wallander told her about the cement mixer. He had just finished when they both heard a key turning in the lock. They were both struck by the same fleeting sense of dread until they heard Nyberg clearing his throat.

"Those damn newspapers," he said. "I don't know how I could have overlooked them."

He put them into a plastic bag and sealed it.

"When can we find out about prints?" Wallander asked.

"Monday at the earliest."

"What about the autopsy report?"

"Hansson's in charge," Höglund said. "But it should be done pretty quickly."

Wallander asked Nyberg to sit down, then recounted the story of Louise one more time.

"That sounds completely implausible," Nyberg said. "Was there a more confirmed bachelor than Svedberg? What about his lone sauna stints on Friday evenings?"

"It's even more implausible that a professor at Copenhagen University is lying to us," Wallander said. "We have to assume he's telling the truth."

"What if Svedberg simply invented her? If I understood you correctly, no one actually saw her."

Wallander thought about this. Could Louise be a figment of Svedberg's imagination?

"What about the hairs in Björklund's bathtub? They're clearly not an invention."

"Why would anyone invent a story like that about himself?" Nyberg asked.

"Because he's lonely," Höglund answered. "People can go to great lengths to invent the companionship missing from their lives."

"Have you found any hairs in the bathroom?" Wallander asked.

"No," Nyberg answered. "But I'll go and have another look."

Wallander got up. "Come with me for a minute," he said.

They went into the living room and Wallander walked them through the various thoughts that had come to him.

"I'm trying to come up with a provisional starting point for this case," he said. "If this is a burglary, there are many issues that need clearing up. How did the killer enter? Why was he carrying a shotgun? At what point did Svedberg appear? What besides the telescope has been stolen? And why was Svedberg shot? There's no sign of a struggle. There's a mess in almost every room, but I doubt they chased each other around the flat. I can't get the various pieces to fit together, and so I ask myself, what happens if we push the burglary hypothesis aside for a moment? What do we see then? Is it a matter of revenge? Insanity? Since there's a woman in the picture, we can entertain the idea of jealousy. But would a woman shoot Svedberg in the face? I doubt it. What other possibilities are there?"

No one spoke. This silence confirmed Wallander's impression that there was no obvious logic to this case, no simple way to categorise it as a burglary, crime of passion, or something else. There was no apparent reason for Svedberg's murder.

"Can I leave now?" Nyberg said finally. "I still have some reports to finish tonight."

"We're going to have another meeting tomorrow morning."

"What time?"

"We'll aim for 9 a.m."

Nyberg left the other two in the living room.

"I've tried to see an unfolding drama," Wallander said. "What do you see?"

He knew that Höglund could be sharp-sighted, and there was nothing wrong with her analytical skills.

"What if we start with the state of the flat?"

"Yes, what then?"

"There are three possible explanations for the mess. A nervous or hurried burglar, a person looking for something, which of course could also apply to a burglar although he wouldn't know what he was looking for. The third possibility is a person bent on destruction for its own sake. Vandalism."

Wallander followed her train of thought closely.

"There's a fourth possibility," he said. "A person who acts out of uncontrollable rage."

They looked at each other, and each knew what the other was thinking. Occasionally Svedberg would become so angry that he lost all self-control. His rage seemed to come out of the blue. Once he had almost destroyed his office.

"Svedberg could have done this himself," Wallander said. "It's not totally out of the realm of possibility. We know it's happened before. It leads us to a very important question."

"Why?"

"Exactly. Why?"

"I was there when Svedberg trashed his office, but I never understood why he did it," Höglund said.

"It was when Björk was chief of police. He accused Svedberg of stealing confiscated material."

"What kind of material?"

"Some valuable Lithuanian icons, among other things," Wallander answered. "It was loot from a big racketeering case."

"So Svedberg was accused of stealing?"

"No – incompetence and sloppy police work. But, of course, the suspicion was implicit."

"What came of it?"

"Svedberg felt humiliated and smashed everything in his office."

"Did the icons ever turn up?" she asked.

"No, but no one was ever able to prove anything. The racketeers were prosecuted successfully anyway."

"But Svedberg felt humiliated?"

"Yes."

"Unfortunately it doesn't help us. Svedberg trashes his own flat, but then what?"

"We don't know," Wallander said.

They left the living room.

"Did you ever hear of Svedberg receiving threats?" Wallander asked her when they had reached the hall.

"No."

"Has anyone else received any?"

"You know how it is – strange letters and calls are par for the course," she said. "But naturally there would be a record of it."

"Why don't you go through everything that's come in lately," Wallander said. "I'd also like you to talk to whoever delivers the newspapers."

Höglund wrote his requests in her notebook. Wallander opened the front door.

"At least it wasn't Svedberg's gun," she said. "He had no registered weapons."

"That's good to know."

She started walking down the stairs and Wallander returned to the kitchen. He drank a glass of water and thought that he should eat something soon. He was tired. He sat down with his head against the wall and fell asleep.

He was surrounded by snowy mountains that sparkled in the strong sun. His skis looked like the ones he had seen down in Svedberg's basement. He was going faster and faster and he was heading straight down towards a thick layer of fog. Suddenly a ravine opened up in front of him.

He woke up with a start. He looked at the kitchen clock and saw that he had been asleep for eleven minutes.

He sat still and listened to the silence. Then the phone rang. It was Martinsson.

"I thought that's where you were."

"Has anything happened?"

"Eva Hillström has been to see me again."

"What did she want?"

"She said she was going to go to the papers if we don't do something."

Wallander thought for a moment before answering. "I think I may have been misguided this morning," he said. "I'd been meaning to talk about it tomorrow morning anyway."

"What about?"

"Naturally our first priority is Svedberg. But we can't shelve the case of the missing young people. Somehow we have to find the time to do both."

"How are we going to do that?"

"I don't know. But it's not the first time we've had so much work to do."

"I promised Mrs Hillström I would call her after speaking with you."

"Good. Try to calm her down. We're going to move on it."

"Are you coming by?"

"I'm on my way. I'm going to see Ylva Brink."

"Do you think we'll solve Svedberg's murder?"

Wallander sensed Martinsson's concern.

"Yes," he said. "Of course we will. But I have a feeling it'll be complicated."

He hung up. Some pigeons flew by the window and a thought suddenly came to Wallander.

Höglund had said that the murder weapon was not registered in Svedberg's name. The reasonable conclusion to make was that Svedberg had no weapons. But reality was rarely reasonable. Weren't there countless unregistered guns floating around Swedish society? It was a constant source of concern for the police. Couldn't a police officer in fact also possibly be in possession of an unregistered weapon? What would that mean? What if the murder weapon did belong to Svedberg? Wallander felt his sense of urgency return. He got up quickly and left the flat.

CHAPTER EIGHT

István Kecskeméti had come to Sweden exactly 40 years earlier, part of that stream of Hungarian immigrants who were forced to leave their country after the failed revolution. He had been 14 years old when he came to Sweden with his parents and his three younger siblings. His father was an engineer who at the end of the 1920s had visited the Separator factories outside of Stockholm. That's where he was hoping to find work. But they never got further than Trelleborg. On the way down the steep stairs of the ferry terminal, he suffered a stroke. His second encounter with Swedish soil was when his body smacked into the wet asphalt. He was buried in the graveyard in Trelleborg, the family stayed in Skåne, and now István was 54 years old. He had long been the owner and manager of one of the many pizzerias dotting the length of Ystad's Hamngatan.

Wallander had heard István's story a long time ago. Wallander ate there from time to time, and if there weren't many customers around, István would happily sit down and talk. It was 6.30 p.m. when Wallander walked in, with half an hour to spare before meeting Ylva Brink. There were no other customers, just as Wallander had expected. From the kitchen came the sound of a radio and of someone banging a meat cleaver. István was just finishing a phone call by the bar, and waved to Wallander as he sat down at a table in the corner. He came over with a serious expression.

"Is it true what I've heard? That a policeman is dead?"

"Unfortunately yes," Wallander answered. "Karl Evert Svedberg. Did you meet him?"

"I don't think he ever came in," István said. "Do you want a beer? It's on the house." Wallander shook his head.

"I'd like to have something that's quick," he said. "And appropriate for someone with high blood-sugar levels."

István looked at him with concern.

"Have you become diabetic?"

"No. But my sugar level is too high."

"Then you are a diabetic."

"Well, perhaps temporarily. I'm in a bit of a hurry right now."

"How about a small steak, sautéed in a little oil, and a green salad?"

"That sounds good."

István left and Wallander wondered why he reacted as if diabetes was something to be ashamed of. Maybe it wasn't so strange. He hated the fact that he was overweight. He wanted to pretend the problem wasn't there.

As usual he ate much too fast. He drank a cup of coffee while István was tending to a group of Polish tourists. Wallander was happy to avoid having to answer questions about Svedberg's murder. He paid his bill and left.

He got to the police station just after 7 p.m. Ylva Brink had not yet arrived. He went straight to Martinsson's office. Hansson was also there.

"How is it going?" he asked.

"There are almost no leads from the public, which is a little unusual."

"Anything from Lund?"

"Not yet," Hansson said. "We'll have to wait until Monday."

"We need to establish the time of death," Wallander said. "As soon as we get that, we'll have a starting point."

"I've checked the files," Martinsson said. "Neither the murder nor the burglary matches any previous case."

"We don't know it was a burglary," Wallander said.

"What else could it have been?"

"I don't know. I have to go and see Ylva Brink now. I'll see you two tomorrow at 9 a.m."

He went to his office and found a note on his desk from Lisa Holgersson, who wanted to speak to him as soon as possible. Wallander tried to call her but she had left. Wallander decided to call her at home later that evening.

A few minutes later Ylva Brink arrived. Wallander asked her if she wanted some coffee but she said no. He decided to use a tape recorder for this interview. Normally he found it distracting, as if a third party were eavesdropping on the person he was interviewing, but he wanted to have access to this conversation word for word. He asked Ylva Brink if she had any objections, but she didn't.

"It's not like it's an interrogation," he said. "It's just that I want to remember what we talk about. This machine is better at that than I am."

He pushed the record button and the tape started turning. It was 7.19 p.m.

"Friday, 9 August, 1996," Wallander stated. "Interview with Ylva Brink in connection with Inspector Karl Evert Svedberg's death by manslaughter or homicide."

"Well, what other possibilities are there?" she asked.

"Police language is full of these redundant expressions," Wallander said. He too had thought that it sounded stilted.

"It's been a few hours," he began. "You've had some time to think. You've probably been asking yourself why it happened. A murder often seems senseless to everyone except the murderer."

"I still can't quite believe it's true. I talked to my husband several hours ago – it's possible to place satellite calls to the boat. He thought I was crazy. But when I heard the words come out of my mouth, the reality hit me."

"I would have liked to be able to wait before pressing you to talk about it. But we can't wait. We have to catch the killer as soon as possible. He has a head start and it's getting bigger all the time."

She seemed to be steeling herself for his first real question.

"This woman Louise," Wallander said. "Apparently Karl Evert had been meeting her for years. Did you ever see her?"

"No."

"Did you ever hear him talk about her?"

"No."

"What was your first reaction when I told you about her?"

"I didn't think it was true."

"What do you think now?"

"That it's true, but still completely incomprehensible."

"You and Karl Evert must have talked at some point about why he had never married. What did he say?"

"That he was a confirmed bachelor and happy that way."

"Was there anything unusual about the way he said this?"

"How do you mean?"

"Did he seem nervous? Could you tell if he was lying?"

"He was completely convincing."

Wallander detected a note of hesitation in her voice.

"I have the feeling you might just have thought of something."

She didn't answer immediately. The tape recorder was whirring in the background.

"Occasionally I wondered if he was different . . ."

"You mean, if he was gay?"

"Yes."

"Why did that occur to you?"

"Isn't it a natural reaction?"

Wallander recalled that he himself had sometimes been conscious of this possibility.

"Yes, of course it is."

"It came up in conversation once. He was invited over for Christmas dinner, quite a few years ago. We were discussing whether or not a person that we both knew was homosexual. I remember very clearly how vehemently disgusted he was."

"By the friend's supposed homosexuality?"

"By homosexuality in general. It was very unpleasant. I had always considered him a tolerant person."

"What happened after that?"

"Nothing. We never spoke of it again."

Wallander thought for a moment. "How do you think we could go about finding this Louise?"

"I have no idea."

"Since he never left Ystad, she must live here or in the near vicinity."

"I suppose so."

She looked at her watch.

"When do you have to be at work?" Wallander asked.

"In half an hour. I don't like to be late."

"Just like Karl Evert. He was always very punctual."

"Yes, he was. What's that saying? Someone you could set your watch by."

"What kind of a person was he, really?"

"You've already asked me that."

"Well, I'm asking you again."

"He was nice."

"How do you mean?"

"Nice. A nice person. I don't know how else to put it. He was a nice person who could sometimes fly into a rage, although that didn't happen very often. He was a little shy. Dutiful. Some people probably thought him boring. He might have seemed a bit aloof and slow, but he was intelligent."

Wallander thought her description of Svedberg was accurate and close to something he might have said if their roles had been reversed.

"Who was his best friend?"

Her answer shocked him.

"I thought you were."

"Me?"

"He always said so. 'Kurt Wallander is the best friend I have.' "

Wallander was dumbstruck. For him Svedberg had always been a colleague. They never saw each other outside of work. He hadn't become a friend in the way that Rydberg had been, and that Höglund was slowly becoming.

"That comes as quite a surprise," he said finally. "I didn't think of him in that way."

"But he may have considered you his best friend, regardless of what you thought."

"Of course."

Wallander suddenly realised how lonely Svedberg must have been. His definition of friendship had been grounded on the lowest common denominator, an absence of animosity. He stared into the tape recorder, then forced himself to continue.

"Did he have any other friends or people he spent a lot of time with?"

"He was in contact with a society for the study of Native American culture. I think it was called 'Indian Science'. But their activities were mainly conducted by correspondence."

"Anything else?"

"Sometimes he mentioned a retired bank director who lives in town. They shared an interest in astronomy."

"What was his name?"

She thought for a moment. "Sundelius. Bror Sundelius. I never met him myself."

Wallander made a note of the name.

"Anyone else you can think of ?"

"Just me and my husband."

Wallander changed the subject.

"Do you recall anything unusual during his last weeks? Was he anxious, or did he seem distracted?"

"He didn't say anything except that he felt overworked."

"But he didn't say why?"

"No."

Wallander realised he had forgotten to ask her something. "Did it surprise you that he said he was overworked?"

"No, not at all."

"So he usually mentioned how he was feeling?"

"I should have thought of this before," she said. "There's one more thing I would add to my description of him – that he was a hypochondriac. The smallest little ache would worry him enormously. And he was terrified of germs."

Wallander could see him, the way he was always running to the bathroom to wash his hands. He always avoided people with colds. She looked at the clock again. Time was running out.

"Did he own any weapons?"

"Not that I know of."

"Is there anything else you would like to tell me, anything that seems important?"

"I'm going to miss him. Maybe he wasn't such an extra-ordinary person, but he was the most honourable person I knew. I'm going to miss him."

Wallander turned off the tape recorder and followed her out. For a moment she seemed helpless.

"What am I going to do about the funeral?" she asked. "Sture thinks the dead should be scattered to the wind without priests and rites. But I don't know what his own thoughts were."

"He didn't leave a will?"

"Not that I know of. I'm sure he would have told me."

"Did he have a safe-deposit box at the bank?"

"No."

"Would you have known about it?"

"Yes."

"The police will attend the funeral, of course," Wallander said. "I'll ask Lisa Holgersson to be in touch."

Ylva Brink went out through the front glass doors. Wallander returned to his office. Yet another name had cropped up: Bror Sundelius. As Wallander looked him up in the phone book, he thought about the conversation with Ylva Brink. What had she really told him that he hadn't already known? That Louise was a well-kept secret. A well-guarded secret, Wallander thought.

He made some notes to himself. Why would you keep a woman secret for so long? Ylva Brink had told him about Svedberg's strong aversion to homosexuality, and about his hypochondria. She had also said he met with a retired bank director from time to time to study the night sky. Wallander laid down his pen and leaned back in his chair.

For the most part, his picture of Svedberg remained the same. The only revelation was this woman, Louise. And nothing seemed to point to an explanation of his death. He felt that he suddenly saw the whole drama clearly in front of him. Svedberg had failed to show up for work because he was already dead. He had caught a burglar by surprise who shot him on the spot, then fled with the telescope in his arms. The crime was unpremeditated, banal and horrifying. There was no other possible explanation.

It was 8.10 p.m. Wallander called Lisa Holgersson at home. She wanted to talk about the funeral and he told her to contact Ylva Brink. Then he told her what they had learned over the course of the afternoon. He also told her that he was starting to lean towards the violent-and-heavily-drugged-burglar theory.

"The national chief of police has called me," she said. "He wanted to express his condolences and his concern."

"In that order?"

"Yes, thank God."

Wallander told her he had arranged a meeting the next morning at 9 a.m., and promised to keep her abreast of any developments. After he'd hung up, Wallander dialled the number for Sundelius, but there was no answer or even an answerphone.

Once he put the phone down again he felt somewhat at a loss. Where should he go from here? He felt a growing impatience, but knew he had to wait for the autopsy report and the forensic evidence to come in.

He started to replay the conversation with Ylva Brink and thought about the last thing she had said, that Svedberg was honourable. There was a knock at the door and Martinsson entered.

"There's a bunch of impatient reporters at the door," he said. Wallander made a face.

"We don't have anything new to tell them."

"I think they'll make do with something old, just as long as they get something."

"Can't you send them away for now? Promise them a press conference as soon as we feel we have something to report."

"Have you forgotten the orders that came from on high instructing us to get along smoothly with the press?" Martinsson said, his voice heavy with irony.

Wallander hadn't forgotten. The national chief of police had recently issued directives to improve relations between the various police districts and local media. Reporters were now to be welcomed and treated with kid gloves.

Wallander got up heavily. "I'll talk to them," he said.

It took him 20 minutes to convince the reporters that he had no new information to give them. He almost lost his temper towards the end, when they continued to regard his claim with suspicion. But he managed to control himself and the reporters finally left. He got a cup of coffee from the canteen and went back to his office. He called Sundelius once more without success.

The phone rang. More reporters, Wallander thought despondently. But it was Sten Widén.

"Where are you?" Widén asked. "I realise you have a lot going on and you have my condolences, but I've been waiting here for a while now."

Wallander swore under his breath. He had completely forgotten his promise to visit Sten Widén at his horse ranch near the castle ruins at Stjärnsund. They had been friends since childhood and shared a passion for opera. As adults, they had started to grow apart. Wallander became a police officer and Sten Widén took over the ranch from his father, where he raised racehorses. A couple of years ago they had started seeing each other again, and they had made plans for this evening. It had totally slipped his mind.

"I should have called you," Wallander said. "I completely forgot."

"They announced it over the radio. Was your colleague murdered or was it manslaughter?"

"We don't know, it's too early to tell. But the last 24 hours have been horrific."

"We can get together some other time."

Wallander made up his mind. "Give me half an hour."

"Don't feel pressured."

"I don't; I need to get away for a while."

Wallander left the station, went to the flat and picked up his mobile phone, then took the E65 out of town. He saw the castle ruins and slowed down to turn into Widén's ranch. Apart from the neighing of a horse, all was quiet.

Widén came out to greet him. Wallander was used to seeing him in dirty work clothes, but now he was wearing a white shirt and his hair was combed back. As they shook hands Wallander smelt alcohol on his breath. He knew that Widén drank too much, but he had never said anything to him. Somehow it never came up.

"What a beautiful evening," Widén said. "Summer finally arrived in August. Or is it the other way around? August finally arrived with summer. Who really arrives with whom?"

Wallander felt a twinge of jealousy. This was what he had dreamed of, living out in the countryside with a dog and maybe even Baiba. But nothing had come of it.

"How's business?" he asked.

"Not so good. The eighties were the golden decade. Everyone seemed to have plenty of money then. Now they don't. People spend most of their time praying they won't lose their jobs."

"Isn't it just the wealthy who buy racehorses? I didn't think they had to worry about unemployment."

"They're still around," Widén agreed. "But there don't seem to be as many of them as before."

They walked down towards the stables. A girl wearing riding gear appeared around the corner with a horse.

"That's Sofia. She's the only one left. I had to get rid of everyone else," Widén said.

Wallander remembered hearing something a couple of years ago about Widén sleeping with one of the girls working on the ranch. What had her name been? Jenny?

Widén exchanged some words with the girl and Wallander caught the name of the horse, Black Triangle. The outlandish names still surprised him.

They went into the stables.

"This is Dreamgirl Express," Widén said, showing him another horse. "Right now she supports me almost all by herself. Owners complain about the upkeep being expensive, and my accountant keeps calling earlier and earlier in the morning. I really don't know how much longer I can get by."

Wallander stroked the horse's muzzle carefully.

"You've always managed before," he said.

Widén shook his head.

"Right now it doesn't look good," he said. "But I can probably get a good price for the place and then I'll take off."

"Where will you go?"

"I'm just going to pack my bags, get a good night's sleep, and decide in the morning."

133

They left the stables and walked up to the main house. Wallander remembered it being a huge mess, but surprisingly everything was very neatly arranged this time.

"A couple of months ago I realised that cleaning could be therapeutic," Widén said in answer to Wallander's obvious surprise.

"That doesn't work for me. God knows I've tried."

Widén gestured for him to sit at the table, where he had set out glasses and a couple of bottles. Wallander hesitated, then nodded and sat down. His doctor wouldn't like it but right now he didn't have the energy to abstain.

"Do you remember that time we went to Germany to hear Wagner?" Widén said, much later in the evening. "It's 25 years ago now. I found some photos the other day. Do you want to see them?"

"Sure."

"I treat them like valuables," Widén said. "I've put them in my secret compartment."

Wallander watched as Widén removed part of the wooden panelling next to the window and took out a metal box that had been jammed into the space underneath. The pictures were in the box. Widén held them out to Wallander, who took them, marvelling at what he saw.

One of the pictures was taken at a roadside rest area outside Lübeck. Wallander had a bottle of beer in his hand and was bellowing at the photographer.

"We had a great time," Widén said. "Maybe more fun than we've ever had since."

Wallander poured some more whisky into his glass. Widén was right. They had never had as much fun after that.

Close to 1 a.m., they called a company in Skurup and

ordered a taxi. Widén agreed to drive his car in the next day. Wallander already had a headache and felt sick to his stomach. He was very, very tired.

"We should go back to Germany sometime," Widén said as they were waiting for the cab.

"No, we shouldn't go back," Wallander said. "We should take a new trip. Not that I have any property I can sell."

The car came and Wallander got into the back seat, leaned back, and fell asleep immediately.

Just as they passed the turn-off to Rydsgård something pulled him up to the surface again. At first he didn't know what it was. Something had flickered through his mind in the dream he'd been having. But then he remembered what it was: Widén had removed a piece of the wood panelling.

Wallander's mind became crystal clear at once. Svedberg had kept the woman in his life a secret for years. But when Wallander had searched his desk he hadn't found anything except some old letters from his parents. Svedberg must have a secret compartment, Wallander thought. Just like Sten Widén.

He leaned forward to the driver and changed the destination from Mariagatan to the town square. A little after 1.30 a.m. he got out of the cab. He still had the keys to Svedberg's flat in his pocket. He remembered seeing some aspirin in Svedberg's medicine cabinet. He unlocked the front door of the flat, held his breath, and listened. Then he poured himself a glass of water and took the aspirin.

Some drunken teenagers walked by on the street below, and then the silence returned. He put the glass down and started looking for Svedberg's secret compartment. By 2.45 a.m. he had found it. A corner of the plastic flooring under the chest of drawers in the bedroom could be peeled away from the concrete base. Wallander repositioned the bedside lamp so that light fell on the exposed area. There was a brown envelope stuffed in the space under the mat. It wasn't sealed. He took it out into the kitchen and opened it.

Like Widén, Svedberg treated his photographs as valuables. There were two pictures inside the envelope. One was a studio portrait of a woman's face. The other photograph was a snapshot of a group of young people who sat in the shadow of a tree and raised their wineglasses towards an unknown photographer.

The scene was idyllic. There was only one thing that struck Wallander as odd. The young people were dressed in elaborate, old-fashioned costumes, as if the party had taken place in a bygone era.

Wallander put on his glasses. His stomach started to ache. He recalled having seen a magnifying glass in one of Svedberg's drawers, and he got it out and studied the photograph more closely. There was something familiar about these young people, especially the girl who sat on the extreme right. Then he suddenly knew who it was. He had seen another picture of her recently, one in which she was not dressed up. The girl on the far right was Astrid Hillström.

Wallander slowly lowered the photograph. Somewhere a clock struck 3 a.m.

CHAPTER NINE

By 6 a.m. on Saturday, 10 August, Wallander couldn't stand it any longer. He had spent most of the remaining night pacing back and forth in his flat, too anxious to sleep. The two pictures he had found at Svedberg's place lay on the kitchen table. They had been burning a hole in his pocket ever since he'd made his way home through the deserted town. It wasn't until he took off his coat that he realised it must have been raining slightly outside.

The photographs in Svedberg's secret compartment were a crucial find. What convinced him of this he couldn't say, but the free-floating anxiety he had felt since the beginning of this case had now escalated into full-blown fear. A case that hadn't even been a case, three young people who were travelling around Europe somewhere, now appeared in the middle of one of the most serious murder investigations the Ystad police had ever undertaken – the killing of one of their own. During the hours after Wallander's discovery, his thoughts were muddled and contradictory. But he knew that this was a crucial breakthrough.

What was it the photographs told him? The picture of Louise was in black-and-white, the snapshot in colour. There was no date printed on the back of either. Did that mean they weren't developed in commercial laboratories? Or were there local businesses that didn't use automatic dating systems? The sizes of the photographs were standard. He tried to decide if the pictures were taken by an amateur or not, since he knew that pictures developed in private darkrooms often did not dry to a uniform finish. But he lacked the expertise to answer his questions.

Next he asked himself what feelings the two photographs evoked. What did they say about the photographer? He was not yet willing to assume that they were taken by the same person. Had Svedberg taken the picture of Louise? Her gaze was impenetrable. The picture of the young people was also hard to pin down. He did not see a conscious sense of composition. The dominating principle appeared to be the inclusion of everyone in the frame. Someone had picked up a camera, told everyone to look over, and pushed the button. Maybe there was a whole series of pictures from this festive occasion. But where were they?

The sheer implausibility of the connection worried him. They already knew that Svedberg had started investigating the disappearance of the young people only a few days before he had gone on holiday.

Why would he have done that? And why would he have done it in secret? Where did the photograph of the young revellers come from? Where was it taken? And then this picture of the woman. It couldn't be anyone but Louise. Wallander studied it for a long time as he sat at the kitchen table. The woman was in her 40s, perhaps a couple of years younger than Svedberg. If they had met 10 years earlier, she might have been 30 and he 35. That seemed pretty reasonable. The woman had straight, dark hair in a style Wallander knew was called a page boy cut. Because it was a black-and-white photograph, he couldn't tell what colour her eyes were. She had a thin nose and face, and her lips were pressed together in the hint of a smile. It was a Mona Lisa smile, but the woman had no glimmer of a smile in her eyes. Wallander thought the picture had been retouched, or else she was heavily made up. There was something veiled about the photograph, something he couldn't place. The woman's face was evasive. It had been captured by the camera but was still not there somehow.

These photographs have been kept in a vacuum, Wallander thought. They lack fingerprints, like two unread books.

He managed to hold out until 6 a.m. and then he called Martinsson, who was an early riser. He answered almost at once.

"I hope I didn't wake you."

"If you call me at 10 p.m. you'd be in danger of doing that. But not at 6 a.m. I was about to go out and work in the garden."

Wallander came right to the point. He told him about the photographs. Martinsson listened without asking any questions.

"I want to meet with everyone as soon as possible," Wallander said when he finished. "Not at 9 a.m. At 7 a.m."

"Have you talked to anyone else?"

"No, you're the first."

"Who do you want?"

"Everyone, including Nyberg."

"Then you'll have to call him yourself – he's so moody in the mornings. I can't deal with angry people until after I've had my morning coffee."

Martinsson volunteered to call Hansson and Höglund, leaving the others to Wallander. He started with Nyberg, who was as sleepy and ill-tempered as expected.

"We're meeting at 7 a.m., not 9 a.m.," Wallander said.

"Has anything happened, or are you just doing this for the hell of it?"

139

"If you ever find you've been called to an investigative meeting just for the hell of it, you should contact your union representative."

He regretted that last comment to Nyberg. He went out to the kitchen and put on some water for a cup of coffee. Then he called Lisa Holgersson, who promised to be there. Wallander took the coffee with him out onto the balcony, where the thermometer indicated that it would be another warm day. There was the sudden clatter from something being pushed through the post slot in the front door.

It was his car keys. And after a night like that, he thought. Sten is amazing. He was weighed down with fatigue. With self-disgust, he suddenly imagined little white icebergs of sugar floating around in his veins.

He left the flat just after 6.30 a.m., and bumped into the person who delivered the newspapers, an older man named Stefansson who had bicycle clips around his trouser legs.

"Sorry I'm late today," he apologised. "There was something wrong with the presses this morning."

"Do you deliver papers at Lilla Norregatan as well?" Wallander asked.

Stefansson understood him at once. "You mean to the policeman who was killed?"

"Yes."

"A lady by the name of Selma works there. She's the oldest delivery person around. I think she started in 1947. What's that, nearly 50 years?"

"What's her last name?"

"Nylander."

Stefansson handed Wallander the paper.

"There's something about you in there," he said.

"Put it in my slot," Wallander said. "I won't have time to read it."

Wallander knew he could make it on time if he walked, but he took the car anyway. The start of his new life would have to be pushed back another day.

He ran into Höglund in the car park. "The person who delivers papers to Svedberg's building is called Selma Nylander," he told her. "Have you talked to her?"

"No, it turns out she doesn't have a phone."

Wallander thought about Sture Björklund's decision to throw out his telephone. Was it becoming a general trend? They went into the conference room. Wallander made himself a cup of coffee, and stood out in the corridor for a while trying to think how to organise the meeting. He was normally very well prepared, but this time couldn't think of anything except putting the photographs on the table and seeing what people had to say.

He closed the door behind him and sat in his usual spot. Svedberg's chair was still empty. Wallander took the pictures out of his coat pocket and told them briefly how he had found them. He omitted the fact that the thought had come to him while he lay in a drunken stupor in the back of a taxi. Since being stopped for driving under the influence by some of his colleagues six years ago, he never mentioned drinking alcohol.

The photographs lay in front of him. Hansson set up the projector.

"I'd like to point out that the girl to the far right in this picture is Astrid Hillström, one of the young people who has been missing since Midsummer."

He put both pictures into the projector. There was silence around the table. Wallander took the opportunity to study the pictures more closely himself as he waited, but couldn't pick out any additional details. He had used the magnifying glass carefully during those early hours.

Martinsson finally broke the silence. "You have to hand it to Svedberg," he said. "She's beautiful. Does anyone recognise her? Ystad isn't a big city."

No one had seen her before, nor any of the young people. It was, however, clear to everyone in the room that the girl to the far right was Astrid Hillström. The picture of her on file resembled this one closely, except for the clothes.

"Is it a masquerade?" Chief Holgersson asked. "What period is it meant to be?"

"The 17th century," Hansson said confidently.

Wallander looked at him with surprise. "How do you know that?"

"Maybe it's more like the 18th century," he said, changing his mind.

"I think it's the 16th century," Höglund said. "King Gustav I Vasa's time. They dressed in the same billowing sleeves and leggings."

"Are you sure?" Wallander asked.

"Of course I'm not sure. I'm just telling you what I think."

"Let's steer clear of educated guesses for a moment. The most important thing here is not how they're dressed up. It will eventually be important to figure out why they were dressed up, but even that can wait."

He looked around at everyone before continuing. "We have a picture of a woman in her 40s and a picture of a group of young people dressed up in some kind of costume. One of these young people is Astrid Hillström, who has been missing since Midsummer, although she's most probably travelling around Europe with two of her friends. This is what we know. I found these pictures hidden in the flat of our colleague Svedberg, who has been murdered. The way we need to begin our investigation is by determining what happened on Midsummer's Eve. That's where we start."

It took them three hours to go through the available material. Most of the time was spent formulating new questions and deciding who would do what. After two hours they took a short break and everyone except Chief Holgersson had coffee. Then they kept going. The team was starting to come together. At 10.15 a.m. Wallander felt they couldn't get any further.

Holgersson had been quiet for a long time, as she often was during their investigative work. Wallander knew she had great respect for their abilities. But now she raised her hand slightly.

"What do you really think has happened to them?" she asked. "If there's been any kind of an accident you would think it would have been discovered by now."

"I don't know," Wallander said. "The very supposition that something has happened to them leads us to conclude that their signatures on the postcards were forged. Why?"

"To cover up a crime," Nyberg suggested.

The room became quiet. Wallander looked at Nyberg and nodded slowly.

"And not just any crime," he said. "People who go missing either stay that way or turn up. There's only one possible explanation for these postcards having been forged, and that is that someone is trying to hide the fact that these three people – Boge, Norman and Hillström – are dead."

"That tells us another thing," Höglund said. "The person who sent these postcards knows what happened to them."

"Not just that," Wallander said. "It's the person who killed them, a person who can forge their signatures and handwriting, and who knows where they live."

It was as if Wallander needed time to get to his final conclusion. "If our supposition is correct," he said, "then we have to assume that these three were the victims of a calculating and well-organised murderer."

His words were followed by a long silence. Wallander already knew what he wanted to say next but wondered if anyone would jump in. Outside in the hall someone laughed loudly. Nyberg blew his nose. Hansson was staring off into space and Martinsson drummed his fingers on the table. Höglund and Holgersson were looking at Wallander.

My two allies, he thought.

"We are forced into the realm of speculation at this point," he said. "One line of reasoning will be particularly unpleasant and unimaginable, but we cannot overlook the part that Svedberg may have played in these events. We know he kept a photograph of Astrid Hillström and her friends hidden in his flat. We know that he conducted his investigations into their disappearance in secret. We don't know what drove him to do these things, but the three of them are still missing and he has been killed. It may have been a burglary of some kind, it may have been the case that someone was looking for something, perhaps for this very picture. But we cannot definitively rule out the possibility that Svedberg himself may have been involved in some way."

Hansson dropped his pen on the table. "You can't mean that!" he said, visibly upset. "One of our colleagues is brutally murdered, we're trying to find his killer, and you're suggesting that he was involved in an even greater crime."

"We have to consider it as a possibility," Wallander said.

"You're right," Nyberg interrupted. "However unappealing

it is. Since the Belgian case I've had the feeling that anything is possible."

Nyberg was right. The macabre string of child murders in Belgium had been linked in unsavoury ways to both the police and politicians. These links were still tenuous, but no one doubted that many dramatic revelations were to come.

Wallander nodded for Nyberg to continue.

"What I'm wondering is how Louise fits into the picture."

"We don't know," Wallander said. "We have to try to proceed in as open-minded a fashion as possible and try to answer all our questions, including who this woman is."

A certain gloom fell over the group as they divided up the tasks and accepted that they would now be working around the clock. Holgersson would see about bringing in extra personnel. They finished a little after 10.30 a.m. Wallander signalled to Höglund to remain behind. When they were alone, he gestured for her to close the door.

"Tell me what your thinking is on this," he said when she had sat down.

"Naturally some thoughts are so repulsive that you try to block them out."

"Of course. Svedberg was our friend. Now we have reason to speculate that he may have been a criminal."

"Do you really think so?"

"No, but I have to consider even what seems impossible, if that makes any sense."

"Then what do you think happened?"

"That's what I want you to tell me."

"Well, a connection has now been established between Svedberg and those three young people."

"No, that's not true. A connection has been established between Svedberg and Astrid Hillström."

She nodded.

"What else do you see?" he asked.

"That Svedberg was someone other than we thought."

Wallander pounced on this. "And how did we think he was?"

She thought a moment before answering. "That he was open, trustworthy."

"But in reality he turned out to be secretive and untrustworthy, is that what you mean?"

"Not exactly, but something like that."

"One of his secrets involved a woman, who may have been called Louise. We know what she looks like."

Wallander got up, turned on the projector, and slipped the picture back into the machine.

"I have the strange feeling that there's something wrong with this face. But I can't think what it is."

Höglund hesitated, but Wallander sensed that his statement didn't surprise her.

"There's something odd about her hair," she said finally. "Although I can't put my finger on it."

"We have to find her," Wallander said. "And we will."

He put the second photograph in the projector and looked at Höglund. Again she answered hesitantly.

"I'm quite convinced that they're wearing clothes from the 16th century. I have a book at home about fashion through the ages. But I could be wrong."

"What else do you see?"

"Young people who seem happy. Excited and drunk."

Wallander suddenly thought of the pictures that Sten Widén showed him from their trip to Germany, especially the drunken one of himself with the beer bottle in his hand. There was a similarity in the expressions on their faces.

"What else do you see?"

"The boy, the second from the left, is yelling something to the photographer."

"They're sitting on a blanket with food spread out, and they're dressed up. What does that mean?"

"A masquerade of some sort. A party."

"Let's assume it's a summer event of some kind," Wallander said.

"The whole picture gives the impression of warm weather. It could very well be a Midsummer's Eve party, but it can't have been taken this summer, since Norman isn't in the picture."

"And Astrid Hillström seems a little younger."

Wallander agreed. "I thought that too. The picture could be a couple of years old."

"There's nothing threatening in the photograph," she said. "At that age, they're as happy as they can be. Life seems endless, the sorrows few."

"I have such a strange feeling about this," Wallander said. "I've never been at the beginning of an investigation like this one. Svedberg is the centre, of course, but the compass needle keeps swinging back and forth. We can't see where we should go."

They left the room. Höglund took the envelope with the two photographs to give to Nyberg so he could check them for fingerprints. First she would make some copies of both. Wallander went to the lavatory and then drank almost a litre of water in the canteen.

Everyone set to work on their assigned tasks. Wallander's job was to talk to Eva Hillström and Sture Björklund again. He sat down in his office and reached for the phone. He was going to start with Hillström, but he decided against phoning her first. Höglund knocked on his door and handed him some photocopies of the pictures. The picture of the young people had been enlarged so that their faces appeared as clearly as possible.

It was around midday when Wallander left the station. He heard someone say that it was about 23°C. He took off his jacket before getting into the car.

Eva Hillström lived on Körlingsväg, which was just outside Ystad's eastern border. He parked the car outside the gate and looked at the house. It was a large, turn-of-the-century villa, with a beautifully maintained garden. He walked up to the front door and rang the bell. Eva Hillström opened the door and jumped when she saw who it was.

"Nothing's happened," Wallander said quickly, anxious to stop her from imagining the worst. "I just have some more questions."

She let him into a big hall that smelled strongly of disinfectant. She was barefoot and wearing a tracksuit. Her eyes darted anxiously around the room.

"I hope I'm not intruding," Wallander said.

She mumbled something unintelligible and he followed her into a spacious living room. The art and furniture gave the impression of being valuable. There was certainly nothing wrong with the Hillströms' finances. He sat down obediently on the sofa that she indicated to him.

"Can I get you anything?" she asked.

Wallander shook his head. He was thirsty but didn't want to ask for a glass of water. She was sitting on the very edge of her seat, and Wallander had the strange impression that she was a runner at the start of a race, waiting for the gun to go off. He took out his photocopies, and handed her the picture of Louise. She looked at it briefly and then up at him.

"Who is this?"

"You don't recognise her?"

"Does she have anything to do with Astrid?"

Her attitude was hostile and Wallander forced himself to sound very firm.

"It is sometimes necessary for us to ask routine questions," he said. "I just showed you a picture, and my question is, do you know who it is?"

"Who is she?"

"Just answer the question."

"I've never seen her before."

"Then we don't have to say anything more about it."

She was about to ask him something else when Wallander gave her the other picture. She looked at it quickly, then got up out of her chair and left the room, as if the starting gun had just gone off. She came back after about a minute and handed Wallander a photograph.

"Photocopies are never as good as the original," she said in response to his puzzled face.

Wallander looked down at the photo. It was the same as the photocopy, the same picture he had found in Svedberg's flat. He felt a step closer to something important.

"Tell me about this photograph," he said. "When was it taken? Who are the other people in it?"

"I don't know exactly where it is," she said. "Somewhere around Österlen, I think. Maybe at Brösarp's hill. Astrid gave it to me."

"When was it taken?"

"Last summer, in July. It was Magnus's birthday."

"Magnus?"

She pointed to the boy who was shouting at the unknown photographer. Wallander pulled out the notebook he had for once remembered to bring.

"What's his full name?"

"Magnus Holmgren. He lives in Trelleborg."

"Who are the rest?"

Wallander took down their names and where they lived. Suddenly he remembered something else.

"Who took the picture?" he asked.

"Astrid's camera had a self-timing mechanism."

"So she took it?"

"I just told you the camera had a self-timer!"

Wallander moved on.

"This is a birthday party for Magnus, but why are they dressed up?"

"That was something they did. I can't see anything strange about it."

"I don't either, I just have to ask these questions."

She lit a cigarette. Wallander felt she was on the verge of breaking down again.

"So Astrid has a lot of friends," he said.

"Not that many," Eva Hillström said. "But good ones."

She took up the photo again and pointed to the other girl.

"Isa wasn't with them this year at Midsummer," she said. "Unfortunately she fell ill."

It took a moment for her words to sink in. Then Wallander understood.

"You mean that this other girl was supposed to have been with them?"

"She fell ill."

"And so it was just the three of them? And they went ahead with the party and then took off together for a trip to Europe?"

"Yes."

Wallander looked down at his notes.

"What's her full name?"

"Isa Edengren. Her father is a businessman. They live in Skårby."

"What has she said about the trip?"

"That nothing had been decided in advance. But she's sure they've gone. They always took their passports with them on these occasions."

"Have they sent her any postcards?"

"No."

"Doesn't she think that's strange?"

"Yes."

Eva Hillström put out her cigarette.

"Something's happened," she said. "I don't know what it is, but Isa's wrong. They haven't left. They're still here."

Wallander saw that there were tears in her eyes.

"Why won't anyone listen to me?" she asked. "Only one person listened, but now he's gone too."

Wallander held his breath.

"Only one person has listened to you," he said. "Is that correct?"

"Yes."

"Do you mean the police officer who visited you at the end of June?"

She looked at him with surprise. "He came many times," she said. "Not just then. During July he came every week, and a couple of times this week as well."

"Do you mean Officer Svedberg?"

"Why did he have to die?" she said. "He was the only one who listened, the only one who was as worried as I was."

Wallander was silent. Suddenly he had nothing to say.

CHAPTER TEN

The breeze was so gentle that sometimes he didn't feel it at all. He counted how often he actually felt the wind on his face, just to make the time go a little faster. He was going to add this to his list of pleasures in life, the joys of the happy person. He had remained hidden behind a large tree for several hours. The fact that he was so early gave him a feeling of satisfaction.

It was still a warm evening. When he had woken that morning, he had known that the time had come to go public. He couldn't wait any longer. He had slept for exactly eight hours, like he normally did. Somewhere in his sub-conscious the decision had been made. He was going to recreate the events that had occurred 50 days ago.

He got up around 5 a.m., again like always, making no exception to his routine although this was his day off. After drinking a cup of the tea that he ordered directly from Shanghai, he rolled away the red carpet in the living room and did his morning exercises. After 20 minutes he measured his heart rate, wrote it down in a notebook, and took a shower. At 6.15 a.m. he sat down to work. This morning he was making his way through a large report from the department of labour that examined possible solutions to the problem of unemployment. He marked some passages with a pen, occasionally also commenting on them, but nothing really struck him as new.

He put down his pen and thought about the anonymous

people who had put this meaningless report together. They are in no danger of becoming unemployed, he thought. They are never to be granted the joy of being able to see straight through daily existence to what actually mattered, the things that gave life meaning.

He read until 10 a.m., and then dressed and went shopping. He made lunch and rested for a while until around 2 p.m. He had soundproofed his bedroom. It was very expensive but worth every penny. No sounds from the street ever intruded. The windows were gone. A soundless air conditioning unit provided him with air. On one side of the room he had a large picture of the world, on which he could follow the progression of sunlight around the globe. This room was the centre of his world. Here he could think clearly about what had happened and what was going to happen. He never had to think about who he was or if he was right. Right about there being no justice in the world.

They had been at a conference in the Jämtland mountains. The director of the engineering firm he worked for had suddenly appeared in his doorway and ordered him to go. Someone had fallen sick. Naturally he agreed, although he had already made plans for that weekend. He said yes because he wanted to please his boss. The conference was on something to do with new digital technology. It was spearheaded by an older man who had invented the mechanical cash registers that were manufactured in Åtvidaberg. He talked about the new era, and everyone stared down at their notebooks. On one of the last evenings, they had all decided to go to the sauna. He didn't really like being naked in front of other men, so he waited for them in the bar. He didn't know exactly how to act. Afterwards they joined him and sat drinking for a long time. Someone started telling a story about good ways to fire employees. All of the men except for him were in important positions at their companies. They told one story after another and finally looked at him. But he had never fired anyone. It never even occurred to him that he would one day be fired. He had studied hard, could do his job, had paid off his student loans, and had learned how to agree with people. Afterwards, after the catastrophe was a fact, he suddenly remembered one of the stories. A small, unpleasantly plump man from a factory in Torshälla told them about how he had once summoned an old worker and said, "I don't know how we could have managed without you here all these years." "It was great," the fat man said, laughing. "The old guy was so proud and happy that he wasn't on guard. Then it was easy. I just said, 'But we'll just have to try, starting tomorrow.'" So the old man was fired. He often thought about that story. If it had been possible he would have gone to Torshälla and killed the person who had fired the old man like that, and had the gall to show off about it afterwards.

He left his flat around 3 p.m. He drove eastwards until he reached a car park in Nybrostrand, where he waited until there were no other people around. Then he quickly switched to another car he had parked there and drove away.

When he arrived at the nature reserve he saw that he was in luck. There were no other cars around, which meant he didn't have to bother with the fake number plates. It was already 4 p.m. and a Saturday, and so he doubted that anyone else would turn up that evening. He had spent three Saturdays watching the entrance to the nature reserve and had noted the pattern of visitors. Almost no one came in the evening. The few who did always left by 8 p.m. He took his tools out of the boot. He had also packed a few sandwiches and a thermos of tea. He looked around, listened, then disappeared down one of the trails.

When the time was right, he started making his way towards the place. He immediately saw that no one had been there. In the space between the two trees that was the only natural opening into the clearing, he had hung a thin thread. He knelt down to examine it and saw that it was untouched. Then he got out his collapsible shovel and started digging. He went about his task calmly and methodically. The last thing he wanted to do was break out in a sweat, which would increase the risk of his catching a cold. He paused after every eighth shovelful and listened for noises. It took 20 minutes to remove the layer of sod and reach the tarpaulin. Before lifting it aside he smeared some menthol ointment under his nostrils and put on a mask. The three plastic bags were lying undisturbed in the ground. There was no unpleasant odour, which meant they hadn't leaked. He lifted up one of the bags and threw it over his shoulder. His workouts had made him strong. It only took him 10 minutes to carry all three bags to their original location. Then he filled the hole, replaced the layer of sod, and stamped the ground on top until it was flat, pausing from time to time to listen out for sounds.

Next he went to the tree where he had placed the three bags. He unpacked the tablecloth, glasses, and the remains of the rotting food that he had stored in his refrigerator. Then he took the bodies out of the bags. Their wigs were a little yellowed and the bloodstains had taken on a greyish tinge. He put the bodies in their places, breaking and cracking what was necessary so that everything looked like it had when he had taken the picture on Midsummer's Eve. His last touch was to pour a little wine into one of the glasses. He listened. Everything was still.

He folded the bags under his arm, stuffed them into a sack, and left. He had already removed his mask and wiped away the menthol. He didn't see a single person on his way back to the car. He drove to Nybrostrand, changed cars again, and made it back to Ystad before 10 p.m. He didn't drive straight home but continued in the direction of Trelleborg. He pulled over at a spot where he could drive down towards the water without being observed. He put two of the big bags inside the third, weighted them down with pieces of steel pipe that he had procured for this purpose, and threw them into the water. They sank immediately.

He returned home, burned his mask, and threw his shoes into the rubbish. He put the menthol ointment in the bathroom cabinet. Then he took a shower and rubbed his body with disinfectant.

Later, he had some tea. When he looked into the tea container, he realised he would soon have to order more. He wrote it down on the noticeboard he kept in the kitchen. He watched a programme about the homeless on TV. No one said anything he didn't already know.

Around midnight he sat down at the kitchen table with a stack of letters in front of him. It was time for him to start thinking of the future. He opened the first letter carefully and started to read.

Shortly before 1.30 p.m. on Saturday, 10 August, Wallander left the Hillströms' villa on Körlingsväg. He decided to drive straight to Skårby, where Isa Edengren, the girl whom Eva Hillström claimed should have been with the others on Midsummer's Eve, lived. Wallander had asked Hillström why she hadn't told him about this earlier, but inside he felt a growing sense of guilt over the fact that he had taken so long to realise that something might be seriously wrong.

He stopped at a café by the bus station and ordered a sandwich and a cup of coffee. He realised too late that he should have ordered his sandwich without butter. Now he was forced to try and scrape it off with his knife. A man at the next table was watching him, and Wallander guessed that he had recognised him from the papers. Probably this would lead to rumours about how the police frittered their time away scraping butter off sandwiches instead of searching for their colleague's killer. Wallander sighed. He had never been able to get used to the rumour mill.

He finished his coffee, went to the lavatory, and left the café. He chose to follow the smaller road that went through Bjäresjö. Just as he left the main road his mobile phone rang. It was Höglund.

"I just spoke to Lena Norman's parents," she said. "I think I've found out something important."

Wallander held the phone more closely to his ear.

"There was supposed to be a fourth person at that Midsummer party," she said.

"I know. I'm on my way to her house right now."

"Isa Edengren?"

"Yes, Eva Hillström picked her out from Svedberg's picture. It turns out that she had the original. Astrid took it last summer with the self-timer on her camera."

"It feels like Svedberg is always one step ahead of us," she said.

"We'll catch up with him soon," Wallander said. "Anything else?"

157

"Some people have called in with leads, but nothing looks promising."

"Do me a favour and give Ylva Brink a call," Wallander said. "Ask her how big Svedberg's telescope was, and if it was heavy. I can't figure out where it's gone."

"Have we already ruled out the possibility of a burglary?"

"We haven't ruled anything out yet, but if someone made off with a telescope, you would think they would've been seen."

"Do you want me to do it right away, or can it wait? I'm on my way to see one of the boys from the photograph who lives in Trelleborg."

"It can wait. Who's going to talk to the other one?"

"Martinsson and Hansson are going together. I gave them his name. Right now they're in Simrishamn with the Boge family."

Wallander nodded with satisfaction. "I'm glad we're getting hold of everyone today," he said. "I think we'll know a lot more about the case by this evening."

They hung up and Wallander continued to Skårby. He followed the directions Eva Hillström had given him. She had told him that Isa Edengren's father had a big piece of property with several full-time landscapers working on it. A private road lined with big trees led up to a two-storey house. A BMW was parked in front. Wallander got out of his car and rang the bell. No one answered. He banged on the door and rang the bell again. It was 2 p.m. He was sweating. He rang the bell once more, then walked around to the back of the house. The garden was large and old-fashioned, with a variety of well-pruned fruit trees. There was a pool and a set of sun loungers that Wallander thought looked expensive. At the bottom of the garden there was a glassed-in gazebo, surrounded and almost completely hidden by bushes and overhanging branches. Wallander walked towards it. The green door was slightly ajar. He knocked but there was no answer. He pushed the door open. The curtains in the windows were pulled shut and it took a while for his eyes to adjust to the dim light.

He saw that there was a person inside. Someone was sleeping on a divan. He could see black hair sticking up over a blanket, but the person's back was turned towards him. Wallander closed the door and knocked again. Still no answer. Wallander walked in and flicked on the light switch. Light flooded the room. He grabbed the sleeper by the shoulder and gave a couple of shakes. When there was still no reaction Wallander knew that something was wrong. He turned the person over and saw that it was Isa Edengren. He spoke to her, and shook her again. Her breathing was slow and laboured. He shook her hard and sat her up but she didn't show any signs of waking. After fumbling in his pocket for his mobile phone, he remembered he had left it on the car seat after talking to Höglund. He ran back to the car and made an emergency call to the hospital on his way back to the gazebo, giving careful directions to the house.

"I think it's either a suicide attempt or serious illness," he said. "What do I do?"

"Make sure she doesn't stop breathing," he was told. "You're a police officer, you should be familiar with the procedure."

The ambulance arrived after 15 minutes. Wallander had managed to get hold of Höglund, who had not yet left for Trelleborg, and asked her to meet the ambulance when it arrived at the hospital. He was going to stay in Skårby for a while. After the ambulance left, he tried the doors of the main house, but they were locked. Then he heard an approaching car. A man wearing rubber boots and over-alls got out of a little Fiat.

"I saw the ambulance," he said.

Wallander saw the look of worry in his eyes. After telling him who he was, Wallander said that Isa Edengren was ill. That was all he could say for the moment.

"Where are her parents?" he asked.

"Away."

The answer seemed deliberately vague.

"Can you be more specific? We'll have to notify them."

"They may be in Spain," the man said. "But they could also be in France. They own houses in both countries."

Wallander thought about the locked doors.

"Does Isa live here even when they're away?"

The man shook his head.

"What do you mean by that?"

"It's really none of my business," the man said and started backing towards his car.

"You've already made it your business," Wallander said firmly. "What's your name?"

"Erik Lundberg."

"Do you live close by?"

Lundberg pointed to a farm that lay south of where they were.

"Now I want you to answer my question: did Isa live here while her parents were away?"

"No, she wasn't allowed to."

"What do you mean by that?"

"She had to sleep in the gazebo."

"Why wasn't she allowed in the main house?"

"There had been trouble in the past. Some parties where things had either been broken or stolen."

"How do you know this?"

The answer came as a surprise.

"They don't treat her very well," Lundberg said. "Last winter when it was ten degrees below zero, they went away and locked up the house. But there's no heating in the gazebo. She came down to our place completely frozen and told us about it. Not me directly, that is, but my wife."

"Then we'll go back to your place," Wallander said. "I'd like to hear what she told your wife."

He asked Lundberg to go ahead of him. Wallander wanted to check the gazebo before he left. He found no trace of sleeping pills or letter, and nothing else of consequence. He looked around one more time then headed back to the car. His phone rang.

"She's just been admitted," Höglund said.

"What are the doctors saying?"

"Not very much for now."

She promised to call as soon as she heard anything. Wallander relieved himself next to the car before he went down to Lundberg's farm. A wary dog met him on the front porch. Lundberg came out and chased it away, and invited Wallander into a cosy kitchen. Lundberg's wife was making coffee. Her name was Barbro and she spoke in a Gothenburg dialect.

"How is she?"

"My colleague will let me know as soon as she hears anything."

"Did she try to kill herself?"

"It's too soon to know," Wallander said. "But I wasn't able to wake her up."

He sat down at the table and put the phone beside him.

"I take it she's attempted suicide before, since you immediately assumed that was the case," he said.

"It's a suicidal family," Lundberg said with distaste.

Then he stopped talking, as if he regretted his remark.

Barbro Lundberg put the coffee pot on the table. "Isa's brother passed away two years ago," she said. "He was only 19 years old. Isa and Jörgen were only one year apart."

"How did he do it?"

"In the bathtub," Lundberg said. "He wrote a note to his parents telling them to go to hell. Then he plugged a toaster into the wall and dropped it in the water."

Wallander felt sick to his stomach. He had a vague recollection of the incident. It came to him that Svedberg had been the one in charge of the investigation. A newspaper lay on an old sofa under the window. Wallander caught sight of a photo of Svedberg on the front page. He reached out for it and showed them the photograph.

"You may have heard about the policeman who was killed," he said. He got his answer before he even asked the question.

"He was here about a month ago."

"Did he come to see you or the Edengrens?"

"First to see them. Then he came here, just like you did."

"Were her parents gone that time as well?"

"No."

"So he met Isa's parents?"

"We don't know exactly who he spoke to," Lundberg said. "But her parents weren't gone then."

"Why did he come down here? What did he ask you about?"

Barbro Lundberg sat down at the table.

"He asked us about the parties they had when Isa's parents were gone, before they started locking her out," she said.

"That was the only thing that interested him," Lundberg said.

Wallander grew more attentive. He realised that this might give him an insight into the way Svedberg had spent his summer.

"I want both of you to try to remember exactly what he said."

"A month is a long time," she said.

"But you sat here at the kitchen table?"

"Yes."

"And you had coffee?"

Barbro Lundberg smiled. "He liked my bundt cake."

Wallander proceeded carefully. "It must have been right after Midsummer."

The couple exchanged looks. Wallander saw that they were trying to help each other remember.

"It must have been right at the beginning of July. I'm sure of it," she said.

"So he came here at the end of June. First to see the Edengrens and then to see you."

"Isa came with him. But she was sick with some kind of stomach bug."

"Did Isa stay here the whole time?"

"No, she only came down with him to show him the way. Then she left."

"And he asked you about the parties?"

"Yes."

"What exactly did he ask?"

"If we knew the people who used to come. But of course we didn't."

"Why do you say 'of course'?"

"They were just young people who came in cars and then left the same way."

"What else did he ask?"

"If any of these parties were masquerades," Lundberg said.

"Did he use that word?"

"Yes."

His wife shook her head. "No, he didn't. He just asked if the people who attended the parties used to dress up."

"Did they?"

They both looked at Wallander with surprise.

"How on earth would we know?" Lundberg asked. "We weren't there, and we don't go around peeking through the curtains."

"But didn't you see something?"

"The parties were sometimes in the autumn, and it was usually dark. We couldn't see how people were dressed."

Wallander sat quietly and thought for a moment. "Did he ask anything else?"

"No. He sat for a while scratching his forehead with his pen. He was only here for about half an hour. Then he left."

Wallander's mobile phone rang. It was Höglund.

"They're pumping her stomach."

"So it was a suicide attempt?"

"I don't think people can ingest this many sleeping pills by accident."

"Are the doctors saying anything at this stage?"

"The fact that she's unconscious suggests she may already be poisoned."

"Will she make it?"

"I haven't heard anything to the contrary."

"Then why don't you go on to Trelleborg?"

"That's what I was thinking. I'll see you later back at the station."

They hung up, and the couple looked at Wallander with anxious eyes.

"She'll make it," he said. "But I will need to contact her parents."

"We have a couple of phone numbers," Lundberg said, and got up.

"They wanted us to call if anything happened to the house," his wife explained. "They didn't say anything about this kind of situation."

"You mean what to do if anything happened to Isa?"

She nodded. Lundberg gave Wallander a piece of paper with the phone numbers.

"Can we visit her in the hospital?" Barbro Lundberg asked.

"I'm sure you can," Wallander answered. "But I think it would be best if you waited until tomorrow."

Erik Lundberg saw him out.

"Do you have any keys to the house?" Wallander asked.

"They would never entrust them to us," the man said.

Wallander said goodbye, returned to the Edengren house, and walked over to the gazebo. He searched it again thoroughly for about half an hour, unsure as to what exactly he was looking for. He ended up sitting on Isa's bed.

Something's repeating itself, he thought. Svedberg came to talk to the girl who didn't make it to the Midsummer celebration and did not go missing. Svedberg asked about parties, and about young people dressing up in costumes. Now Isa Edengren has tried to kill herself and Svedberg has been murdered.

Wallander got up and left the gazebo. He was worried. He wasn't finding anything reliable to point him in the right direction. There seemed to be clues pointing in many directions, but none of them seemed to lead anywhere. He got into his car and headed back to Ystad.

His next aim was to have another talk with Sture

Björklund. It was almost 4 p.m. when he pulled into Björklund's yard. He knocked on the door and waited, but no one answered. Björklund had probably gone to Copenhagen, or else he was in Hollywood discussing his latest ideas for a monster. Wallander banged hard on the door but didn't wait for anyone to open it. Instead he walked around to the back. The garden was neglected. Some half-rotting pieces of furniture were scattered in the long grass. Wallander peered in through one of the windows of the house, then continued down to a little shed. Wallander felt the door. It was unlocked. He opened it wide and pushed a piece of wood underneath it to keep it in place. It was a mess inside. He was about to leave when his attention was caught by a tarpaulin folded over something in the corner. There seemed to be some kind of equipment under it. He carefully pulled off part of the cover. It was a machine all right; or more precisely, an instrument. Wallander had never seen one like it before, but he still knew immediately what it was. A telescope.

CHAPTER ELEVEN

When Wallander walked back outside he noticed the wind had picked up. He turned his back to it and tried to collect his thoughts. How many people owned telescopes? Not many. The telescope had to be Svedberg's. He couldn't think of any other possible explanation. That brought up other questions: why hadn't Sture Björklund said anything?

Did he have something to hide, or didn't he know that the telescope was on his property? Could Sture Björklund have killed his own cousin? He doubted it.

He returned to his car and made some calls, but neither Martinsson nor Hansson was in his office. He asked the officer on duty to send a car out to Hedeskoga.

"What's happened?" he asked.

"I need some people to keep this place under surveillance," Wallander said. "For now you can simply say that it has to do with Svedberg's case."

"Do we know who shot him?"

"No. This is a routine matter."

Wallander asked for an unmarked car and described the intersection where he would meet it. When Wallander reached the intersection the car was already waiting for him. He explained to the patrol officers where they should wait, and that they should call him as soon as Sture Björklund turned up, then he started back to Ystad. He was very hungry and his mouth was dry. He stopped at a takeaway restaurant on Malmövägen and ordered a hamburger. While he was waiting for his food, he drank some soda water. After eating much too quickly he bought himself a litre of mineral water. He needed time to think, but knew he would inevitably be disturbed if he returned to the station, so he drove out of town and parked outside the Saltsjöbaden hotel. The wind was quite strong now but he walked on until he found a sheltered spot. For some reason there was an old toboggan there and he sat down on it and shut his eyes.

There has to be a point of entry into this mess, he thought. A point of connection that I am overlooking. He went through everything that had happened so far as carefully and clearly as he could, but despite his efforts, the facts remained as muddled and obscure as before.

What would Rydberg have done? When Rydberg had been alive, Wallander had always been able to ask him for advice. They would take a walk on the beach or sit in the station late into the night discussing the facts of a case until they arrived at something important. But Rydberg was gone now. Wallander strained to hear his voice in his head, but there was nothing there.

Sometimes he thought Ann-Britt Höglund was on her way to becoming his new partner. She listened as well as Rydberg and didn't hesitate to change track if she felt it could help them break through a new wall.

In time it may work out, he thought. Ann-Britt is a good police officer. But it takes time.

He got up heavily and started walking back to the car. There's only one thing that really sets this investigation apart, he thought. People dressed up in costume. Svedberg wanted to know about parties where people dressed up in costume. We have a photograph of people at a party dressed up in costume. There are people in costume at every turn.

Wallander knew it would be a long night. As soon as everyone had returned from their assignments, they would hunker down in the conference room. He went into his office, hung up his coat, and called the hospital. After being transferred a couple of times he finally reached a doctor who told him that Isa Edengren was in a stable condition and was expected to make a full recovery. He knew this doctor, having met him at least a couple of times before.

"Tell me something I know you aren't allowed to say," Wallander said. "Was it a cry for help or was she really trying to end it all?"

"I'm told you were the one who found her, is that right?" the doctor said.

"That's right."

"Then let me put it this way," he said. "It was lucky you found her when you did."

Wallander understood. He was about to hang up when another question came to him.

"Has anyone been to see her?"

"She's not allowed visitors yet."

"I understand. But has anyone asked to see her?"

"I'll find out for you."

While Wallander waited, he hunted out the piece of paper with Isa's parents' telephone numbers that Lundberg had given him. The doctor returned.

"No one has been here and no one has called," he said. "Who is going to get in touch with her parents?"

"We'll take care of that."

Wallander hung up and tried dialling the first number without knowing whether he was calling France or Spain. He counted 15 rings, then hung up and tried the other number. This time a woman answered almost immediately.

Wallander introduced himself and she said she was Berit Edengren. Wallander told her what had happened. She listened without interrupting. Wallander thought about her son Jörgen, Isa's brother. He tried to keep his details to a minimum, but it was a suicide attempt and he couldn't cover that up.

She sounded calm when she replied. "I'll tell my husband," she said. "We'll have to talk about whether we should return home immediately."

She loves her daughter, Wallander reminded himself, but he couldn't help feeling angry at her response. "I hope you understand that it could have ended badly."

"Thankfully it didn't."

Wallander gave her the number of the hospital and the name of the doctor. He decided against asking any questions about Svedberg yet. What he did ask was for information about the Midsummer's Eve celebration that Isa was to have attended.

"Isa doesn't tell us very much," she answered. "I didn't know anything about a Midsummer's Eve party."

"Would she have told her father?"

"I doubt it."

"Martin Boge, Lena Norman, and Astrid Hillström," Wallander recited. "Do you recognise these names?"

"They're friends of Isa's," she said.

"But Isa hadn't told you about any special plans for Midsummer?"

"No."

"This is a very important question and I need you to think carefully. Could she have mentioned a place where they were to meet?"

"There's nothing wrong with my memory. I know she didn't say anything to us."

"Do you know if she had any fancy dress costumes at home?"

"Is this really important?"

"Yes. Please answer the question."

"I don't go through her cupboards."

"Is there a spare key to the house?"

"We keep a spare hidden key in a drainpipe on the right wing. Isa doesn't know about it."

"And she won't find out about it in the next couple of days."

Wallander had only one more question for her. "Did Isa say anything about going on a trip after Midsummer?"

"No."

"Would she have told you if she was thinking about it?"

"Only if she had needed the money, which she always did."

Wallander had trouble controlling his temper.

"You'll hear from us again," he said.

He slammed down the phone, realising as he did so that he still didn't know whether they were in France or Spain.

He went out to the canteen and got a cup of coffee. On his way back to his office he remembered that he had one more call to make. He found the phone number and dialled it. This time someone answered.

"Bror Sundelius?"

"Speaking."

Wallander introduced himself and was about to explain why he was calling when Sundelius interrupted him.

"I've been waiting for the police to give me a call. It seems to me you've taken a long time."

He was an elderly man with a direct way of speaking.

"I've already called a couple of times and got no answer. Why did you think we would be in touch?"

Sundelius answered without hesitation. "Karl Evert did not have many close friends. I was one of the few. That's why I assumed that you would contact me."

"What do you think we wanted to talk to you about?"

"You should know that better than I do."

True, Wallander thought. At least he isn't going senile.

"I'd like to meet with you," Wallander said. "Here or at your place, preferably tomorrow morning."

"I used to go to work every day. Now I climb the walls," Sundelius said. "I have an endless amount of time that simply goes to waste. You can come tomorrow any time after 4.30 a.m. I live on Vädergränd. My legs aren't so good. How old are you, Inspector?"

"I'll be 50 soon."

"Then your legs are better than mine. At your age it's important to keep moving. Otherwise you'll develop heart problems or diabetes."

Wallander listened to him with surprise.

"Are you still there, Inspector?"

"Yes," said Wallander. "I'm here. How about 9 a.m.?"

They crowded into the conference room at 7.30 p.m. Lisa Holgersson had arrived early with the chief prosecutor filling in for Per Åkeson, who was in Uganda. Åkeson had taken a leave of absence and was working for the International Refugee Commission. He had been gone almost eight months and sent Wallander letters every now and then, describing his daily life, and the dramatic ways in which the new environment and work were changing him. Wallander missed him, even though they had never been close. He also sometimes felt a stab of envy when he thought about the decision Åkeson had made. Would he ever be anything other than a policeman? He would soon turn 50. The chances of starting something new were shrinking rapidly.

The acting chief prosecutor, Thurnberg, had come down from Örebro. Wallander had not had a lot to do with him up until now, as Thurnberg had only started in Ystad in the middle of May. He was a couple of years younger than Wallander, fit and quick-witted. Wallander had not yet decided what he thought about him. On a previous encounter, he had appeared rather arrogant.

Wallander knocked on the table with his pencil and looked around the room. Svedberg's chair was still empty. He wondered when someone was going to start using it. Wallander began by telling them about his find at Björklund's house, since he was expecting him to be back from Copenhagen later that evening.

"Before this meeting we were talking about something else that strikes us as odd," Martinsson said. "There are no diaries. I've asked the others, but none of the three seem to have kept a diary or a pocket calendar."

"There are no letters either," Hansson said.

"These people seem to have erased all traces of themselves," Höglund said.

"Is that the case with the others, too? The ones who were in Svedberg's photograph?"

"Yes," Martinsson said. "But we should probably probe further."

Martinsson flipped through his notes and was about to add something when there was a knock on the door. An officer came in and nodded in Wallander's direction.

"Björklund has just got home."

Wallander got up. "I'll go out there alone. It won't be an arrest, after all. We'll continue when I get back."

Nyberg got up as well. "I should probably have a look at the telescope right away," he said.

They drove out to Hedeskoga in Nyberg's car. The unmarked police car was still parked at the intersection. Wallander got out and spoke to the officer behind the wheel.

"He arrived about 20 minutes ago in a Mazda."

"Then you can go back," Wallander said.

"You don't want us to stay?"

"It won't be necessary."

Wallander got back in the car and they pulled up outside the house.

"He's home," he said to Nyberg. "No doubt about that."

Music was coming from an open window. It had a Latin beat. Wallander rang the bell and the music was turned down. Björklund opened the door wearing only a pair of shorts.

"I have a couple of questions that couldn't wait," Wallander said.

Björklund seemed to think for a moment, then smiled. "Now I understand," he said.

"What do you understand?"

"Why that car was parked up by the turn-off."

Wallander nodded. "I was looking for you earlier today. My questions can't wait."

Björklund let them in and Wallander introduced Nyberg.

"Once upon a time I also thought about becoming a forensic technician," Björklund said. "The idea of dedicating my life to interpreting evidence was appealing to me."

"It's not as exciting as you'd think," Nyberg replied.

Björklund looked mildly astonished.

"I wasn't talking about adventure," he said. "I was talking about being a person who follows traces."

They stopped in the entrance to the big room. Wallander noted Nyberg's amazement at Björklund's menage.

"I'm going to get right to the point," he said. "You have a small shed to the east of the house. There's an instrument in there hidden under a piece of tarpaulin. I think it's a telescope, and I want to determine whether or not it came from Svedberg's flat."

Björklund balked. "A telescope? In my shed?"

"Yes."

Björklund instinctively took a step back. "Who's been snooping around out here?"

"I told you that I came looking for you earlier today. The door to your shed was open and I went in. I found the telescope."

"Is that legal? Are the police allowed to enter other people's homes at will?"

"If you have an opinion to the contrary, feel free to make a report to the ombudsman."

Björklund looked at him with animosity. "I think I will," he said.

"For God's sake," Nyberg interrupted angrily. "Let's just get this cleared up."

"So you claim to have no knowledge of a telescope on your property."

"That's right."

"Do you realise that doesn't sound very believable?"

"I don't care what it sounds like. As far as I'm concerned, there's no telescope anywhere on my property."

"We'll soon determine whether that's the case," Wallander said. "If you refuse to cooperate I'll leave Nyberg here and get a search warrant from the chief prosecutor. You should have no doubts about that."

Björklund was still hostile. "Am I accused of a crime?"

"For now I simply want an answer to my question."

"I've already given you one."

"So you deny knowledge of the telescope? Could Svedberg have put it there without your knowledge?"

"Why would he have done that?"

"I'm simply asking if it's possible, that's all."

"Of course he could have done it while I was away over the summer. I never check what's in the shed."

Wallander sensed that Björklund was telling the truth, and experienced this as a relief.

"Shall we go and look?"

Björklund nodded and slipped on some clogs. His upper body was still bare.

When they had arrived at the shed and turned on the light, Wallander pulled the others back and turned to Björklund.

"Does anything in here look different?"

"Like what?"

"It's your shed. You should know."

Björklund looked around and shrugged. "It looks like it normally does."

Wallander directed them into the corner and lifted the tarpaulin. Björklund's surprise seemed genuine.

"I have no idea how that got there," he said.

Nyberg crouched down to have a better look, directing a strong torch beam at it.

"I don't think we need to speculate further about who it belongs to," he said, pointing to something.

Wallander looked more closely and saw a small metal plate with Svedberg's name on it. Björklund no longer seemed angry.

"I don't understand," he said. "Why would Karl Evert hide his telescope here?"

"Let's go back inside and leave Nyberg to his work," Wallander said.

As they walked back to the house, Björklund asked if he wanted some coffee. Wallander said no. He seated himself for a second time on the uncomfortable pew.

"Do you have any idea how long it could have been there?"

Björklund now seemed to be trying to give thorough answers.

"I don't have a good memory for rooms," he said. "My memory for objects is even worse. I don't think I could come up with any kind of a time frame for you."

Something seemed to occur to him. Wallander waited.

"Is it possible that someone else put it there?" Björklund asked.

"If so, it would probably have been someone who knew you two were related."

Wallander saw that something was troubling Björklund.

"What are you thinking about?"

"I don't know if this means anything," he said doubtfully. "But I had the feeling once that someone had been here."

"How did you get this feeling?"

"I don't know. It was just a feeling."

"Something must have set it off."

"That's what I'm trying to remember."

Wallander kept waiting. Björklund seemed lost in thought.

"It was a couple of weeks ago," he said. "I had been in Copenhagen and returned in the afternoon. It had been raining. As I walked across the yard something made me stop. At first I didn't know what it was, but then I saw that someone had moved one of the sculptures."

"One of the monsters?"

"They're copies of the medieval gargoyles from the cathedral in Rouen."

"I thought you had a poor memory for objects."

"That doesn't apply to my sculptures. Not when someone has changed their position. I was certain that someone had been in the yard while I was gone."

"And it wasn't Svedberg."

"No. He never came out here unless we had arranged it."

"You can't be sure of that, though."

"No, but I feel sure. I knew him, and he knew me."

Wallander nodded, encouraging him to continue.

"A stranger had been here."

"You didn't have anyone looking after the place when you were gone on short trips?"

"No one comes here except the postman."

Björklund sounded convinced and Wallander had no reason to doubt him.

"A stranger, then," he repeated. "And you think this person is the one who might have put the telescope in your shed?"

"I know it sounds unreasonable."

"Can you tell me the exact date when this happened?"

Björklund went and got a little pocket calendar and leafed through to a particular day.

"I was away on 14 and 15 July."

Wallander made a note of it. Nyberg came in, his mobile phone in hand.

"I've called for some equipment," he said. "I'd like to finish working on the telescope tonight. Why don't you take my car back and I'll have a squad car pick me up when I'm finished?"

Nyberg disappeared again. Wallander got up, and Björklund followed him to the door.

"You must have had time to think about what's happened," Wallander said to him.

"I don't understand why anyone would want to kill my cousin. I can't imagine a more meaningless act."

"No," Wallander agreed. "But these are the questions we have to answer: who would have wanted to kill him, and why?"

They parted in the yard. The gargoyles looked somewhat plaintive in the weak light from the house. Wallander returned to Ystad in Nyberg's car. Nothing had been resolved.

The meeting back at the station lasted almost until midnight. Everyone was tired, but Wallander didn't want to let them go.

"There's really just one thing we can do," he said. "We have to declare Boge, Norman and Hillström officially missing. We need to get them back home as soon as possible."

Everyone in the room agreed with him. Holgersson and Martinsson would see that it was done the next morning.

"It seems that all of these young people have been up to something," he said. "But we haven't been able to get them to tell us what it is. You've all said that you feel there's something they're not saying, that they have a secret. Is that right?"

"Yes," said Höglund. "There's something they're not letting us in on."

"But they don't seem particularly concerned, either," Martinsson said. "They're convinced that Boge, Norman and Hillström are travelling."

"I hope they're right," Hansson said. "I'm starting to feel worried."

"So am I," Wallander said. He threw his pen down. "What the hell was Svedberg up to? That's what we have to figure out. And who in God's name is Louise?"

"We've checked all of our photographic records," Martinsson said.

"That's not enough," Wallander said. "We'll have to publish the picture in the papers. We have a murder to solve. Not that she's a suspect. At least not yet."

"Women don't tend to shoot their victims in the face with a shotgun," Höglund said.

No one had anything further to say. They agreed to continue the following day. Wallander would start by visiting Sundelius. He walked out of the station with Martinsson.

"We have to get them home," he said again. "We'll talk to Isa Edengren, and we'll bring in the ones that you've already visited once. We'll get them to tell us what they know."

They walked to their cars. Wallander was extremely tired. The last thing he thought about before falling asleep was that Nyberg was still out in Björklund's shed.

A steady rain fell over Ystad at dawn. Then the clouds blew away. Sunday was going to be a warm and sunny day.

CHAPTER TWELVE

Rosmarie Leman and her husband Mats often drove out to parks and nature reserves to take their Sunday walk, depending on the weather and season. This morning, Sunday, 11 August, they had talked about driving up to Fyledalen but settled on the Hagestad nature reserve instead. The deciding factor was that they hadn't been there for a long time, not since the middle of June.

They were early risers and left Ystad a little after 7 a.m. As usual they were planning to be gone the whole day. They put two rucksacks in the boot. These contained everything they might possibly need, even raincoats. Although it looked like it was going to be a fine day, you could never be sure. They lived a well-organised life. She was a teacher, he an engineer. They never left anything to chance.

They parked at the reserve shortly before 8 a.m., had a cup of coffee, then put on their rucksacks and started walking. At 8.15 a.m. they looked around for a nice place to have breakfast. They heard some dogs barking at a distance but had not yet seen any other people. It was warm and there was no breeze. When they found a good spot they spread out a blanket and sat down to eat. On Sundays they discussed the things they didn't have time for during the week. Today it was buying a new car. The one they had was getting old, but could they really afford a new one? After talking for a while, they decided they would wait another month or so. When they had finished eating, Rosmarie Leman stretched out on the blanket and fell asleep. Mats Leman intended to do the same, but first he had to relieve himself. He took some toilet paper with him and walked to the other side of the path and headed down the slope towards an area surrounded by thick bushes. Before squatting down, he looked around carefully but saw no one.

This is the best part of Sunday, he thought when he had finished. To lie down next to Rosmarie and doze for half an hour. As he had this thought, he noticed something in the bushes. He didn't know what it was, but there was some colour that contrasted with the green foliage. Normally he was not particularly curious, but he couldn't help walking closer and parting the branches for a better look. What he saw he would never forget as long as he lived.

Rosmarie was woken by his screams. At first she didn't know what it was, then she realised to her horror that it was her husband's voice calling for help. She had just managed to stand up when he came running towards her. She couldn't know what had happened or what he had seen, but his face was completely ashen. He made it to her side by the blanket and tried to tell her something.

Then he fainted.

The police station in Ystad took the call at 9.05 a.m. The caller was so hysterical that he was difficult to understand. Finally, however, the policeman taking the call pieced together that the caller's name was Mats Leman and he claimed to have found some dead bodies in Hagestad's nature reserve. Although his account was disjointed, the policeman on duty realised that it was serious. He took down the caller's mobile-phone number and told him to stay where he was. Then he went into Martinsson's office, since he had seen him come in just a few minutes before. The policeman stood in the doorway and told him about the call. There was one detail in particular that made Martinsson's stomach knot up.

"Did he say three?" he asked. "Three dead bodies?"

"That's what he said."

Martinsson got up. "I'll check it out right now," he said. "Have you seen Wallander?"

"No."

Martinsson remembered that Wallander was going to see someone this morning, someone named Sundberg – or was it Sundström? He called Wallander's mobile.

Wallander had walked to Vädergränd from his flat on Mariagatan, stopped in front of a beautiful house that he had admired many times, and rang the bell. Sundelius opened the door, dressed in a neatly pressed suit. They had just sat down in the living room when the phone rang. Wallander saw Sundelius's disapproving look as he pulled it out of his pocket with a quick apology.

He listened to what Martinsson had to say. He asked the same question as Martinsson.

"Did he say three? Three people?"

"It hasn't been confirmed, but that's what he thought he saw."

Wallander felt as though a weight was starting to press against his head.

"You realise what this might mean," he said.

"Yes," Martinsson answered. "We have to hope he was hallucinating."

"Did he give that impression?"

"Not according to the officer who took the call."

Wallander looked at a clock hanging on Sundelius's wall. It was 9.09 a.m.

"Come by and pick me up. I'm at number seven, Vädergränd," he said.

"Should we have full back up?"

"No, let's check it ourselves first."

Martinsson was on his way. Wallander got to his feet. "Unfortunately our conversation will have to wait," he said.

Sundelius said he understood. "I take it there's been an accident of some kind?"

"Yes," Wallander said. "A traffic accident. Unfortunately, there's no way of knowing when something like this will come up. I'll be in touch about visiting you again."

Sundelius walked him to the door. Martinsson pulled up and Wallander jumped in. He reached out and placed the flashing police light on the roof. When they arrived at the nature reserve, a woman ran out to meet them. Wallander could see a man sitting on a rock with his head in his hands. Wallander got out of the car. The woman was distraught and kept pointing and shouting something. Wallander took her by the shoulders and told her to calm down. The man remained where he was. When Wallander and Martinsson walked over to him he looked up. Wallander crouched down beside him.

"What happened?" he asked.

The man pointed into the nature reserve. "They're in there," he mumbled. "They're dead. They've been dead for a long time."

Wallander looked at Martinsson. Then he turned back to the man.

"You said that there were three of them."

"I think so."

One question remained, perhaps the worst one. "Could you tell how old they were?"

The man shook his head. "I don't know."

"I know it must have been a terrible sight," Wallander said. "But you have to lead us to the spot."

"I'm never going back there," he said. "Never."

"I know where it is."

It was the woman. She came up behind her husband and put her arm around him.

"But you never saw them yourself?"

"Our rucksacks and blanket are still up there. I know where it is."

Wallander got up. "Let's go," he said.

She led them into the reserve. The air was very still, and Wallander thought he could hear the faint sound of the sea. He wondered if the sound was simply the jumble of anxious thoughts inside his own head. They walked quickly and Wallander had trouble keeping up with the other two. Sweat ran down his chest. He needed to pee. A rabbit dashed across their path. Wallander couldn't imagine what they were about to find, but he knew that it would not be like anything he had seen before. Dead people are no more alike than the living, he thought. Nothing is ever repeated or the same, just like this anxiety. He recognised the knot in his stomach. It was still as if he were experiencing it for the first time.

The woman slowed down. They were getting closer. When they arrived at the blanket, she turned around and pointed down a slope on the other side of the path. Her hand shook. Until this moment Martinsson had been in front, but now Wallander took the lead. Rosmarie Leman waited by the rucksacks.

Wallander looked down the hillside. There was nothing but bushes below them. He started down the slope with Martinsson close behind. They arrived where the bushes started, and looked around.

"Do you think she might be wrong about the spot?" Martinsson asked. His voice was low, as though he were afraid someone would overhear them.

Wallander didn't answer. Something else had caught his attention. At first he didn't know what it was and then it struck him. A bad smell. He looked at Martinsson, who hadn't caught a whiff of it yet. Wallander started pushing his way through the bushes. He didn't see anything, just some trees up ahead. The smell disappeared, then returned more strongly.

"What's that?" Martinsson asked.

As soon as he had said it he realised what the answer was. Wallander proceeded slowly with Martinsson close behind. Then he stopped suddenly and saw Martinsson flinch. There was something behind the bushes to the left. The smell became stronger.

Martinsson and Wallander looked at each other, and each put a hand over his nose and mouth. A feeling of nausea washed over Wallander. He tried to take some deep breaths through his mouth while he kept his nose shut.

"Wait here," he told Martinsson. His voice quavered.

He forced himself forward and parted the branches. Three young people lay entwined on a blue linen cloth. They had been shot in the head. And they were in an advanced state of decomposition. Wallander shut his eyes and sat down.

After a moment he got up and returned to the place where he had left Martinsson, and pushed him along in front of him as if someone were following them. He stopped only when they were up on the path again.

"I've never seen anything so fucking horrible," Wallander stammered.

"Is it – "

"It has to be."

They stood there in silence. Wallander would later remember that a bird sang in a nearby tree. Everything was like a strange nightmare, and yet at the same time an excruciating reality. Wallander used all his inner resources to force himself to start thinking like a policeman again, to start practising his profession. He got out his phone and called the station. After about a minute he got Höglund on the line.

"It's me, Kurt."

"Shouldn't you be visiting that retired bank manager this morning?"

"We've found them. All three of them. They're dead."

He heard her catch her breath. "You mean Boge and the others?"

"Yes."

"They're dead?"

"Shot."

"Oh my God."

"Listen to me. Here's what we have to do. This is a red alert. I want everybody out here. We're at Hagestad nature reserve. I'll put Martinsson at the turn-off to guide people down here. We need Lisa immediately. And we'll need extra help to keep the area cordoned off from the public."

"Who's going to call the parents?"

Wallander felt a degree of anguish and panic he had never experienced before. Of course the parents had to be notified; they had to identify their children's bodies. But he just couldn't do it.

"They've been dead for a long time," he said. "Do you understand? They may have been dead as long as a month."

She understood.

"I'll have to talk to Lisa about it," he said. "But we can't let the parents see this."

There was nothing else to say. Wallander was left staring down at the phone after they had hung up.

"You'd better get down to the turn-off," he told Martinsson.

Martinsson inclined his head in Rosmarie Leman's direction. "What do we do with her?"

"Get the important facts. Time, address, etcetera. Then send them home. Tell them not to talk to anyone about it until they hear otherwise."

"Are we allowed to do that?"

Wallander stared at Martinsson. "Right now we're allowed to do whatever the hell we want."

Martinsson and Leman left, and Wallander was alone. The bird kept singing. A couple of metres away, hidden behind thick bushes, three young people lay dead. How alone can a person possibly feel, he wondered. He sat down on a rock by the path. The bird flew away.

We didn't get them home, he thought. They never left for Europe. They were here the whole time and they were dead. Maybe even since Midsummer. Eva Hillström was right all along. Someone else wrote those postcards. They were here the whole time, in the same spot where they celebrated their Midsummer feast.

He thought about Isa Edengren. Did she realise what had happened? Was that why she had tried to commit suicide? Did she realise the others were dead, just as she would have been if she'd been with them that night?

There were already things that didn't make sense. Why had no one discovered the bodies for a whole month? Even if the spot was out of the way, someone would have come across it, or smelled them. Wallander didn't understand it, but he also couldn't quite bear to keep thinking about it. Who could possibly have wanted to kill three young people dressed up in costume and celebrating Midsummer together? It was an act of insanity. And somewhere in the network of connections to this act there was another dead body. Svedberg. How had he been involved in all this?

Wallander felt an increasing sense of helplessness. Although he had only gazed at the scene for a few seconds, he had not been able to mistake the bullet holes in their foreheads. The murderer knew what he was aiming at. And Svedberg had been the best shot in the force.

A breeze tossed the trees from time to time. In between the small gusts, all was calm. Svedberg was the best shot. Wallander forced himself to think this through. Could Svedberg possibly have been the one? What was there that spoke against this possibility? For that matter, were there any clear alternatives to choose from?

He got up and started walking to and fro along the path. He wished he could have called Rydberg on the phone. But Rydberg was dead, as dead as these three young people. As he moved along the path he had a sudden impulse to run away from it all. He didn't think he could handle the pressure any more. Someone else would have to take over: Martinsson or Hansson. He was burnt out. And he had developed diabetes. He was on a downward spiral.

Finally he heard people approaching. There were sounds of cars in the distance and branches breaking somewhere down the path. Then they were there, gathering around him. He would have to take charge and tell them what to do. He had known many of them for as long as 15 years. Lisa Holgersson was pale. Wallander wondered what he looked like himself.

"They're down there," he said and pointed to the bushes. "They've been shot. Although they haven't been identified yet, I'm sure they're the three missing young people, the ones we assumed, or hoped, were travelling through Europe. Now we know that isn't the case."

He paused before continuing. "I want to prepare you for the fact that the bodies may have been lying here since Midsummer. You all know what that means. There is every reason to put on a mask."

He looked at Holgersson. Did she want to see them? She nodded. Wallander led the way. The only sounds were rustling leaves and small branches breaking underfoot. When the smell of the bodies came wafting over them, someone groaned. Holgersson grabbed Wallander's arm. Wallander knew it was easier to deal with a macabre scene like this in a group rather than alone. Only one of the younger police officers had to turn away and vomit.

"We can't let their parents see this," Holgersson said with a shaky voice. "It's horrible."

Wallander turned to the doctor who had accompanied them. He was also very pale.

"The investigation has to be as quick as possible," Wallander said. "We need to take the bodies back and get them fixed up as soon as possible before the parents have to identify them."

The doctor shook his head. "I'm not touching this," he said simply. "I'm calling Lund."

He went off to the side and made a call on Martinsson's phone.

"We need to be clear about one thing," Wallander said to Holgersson. "We already have a dead police officer on our hands. Now we have three more murder victims. That means four murders to solve, and it's going to be huge when it gets out. There will be enormous pressure on us to catch the killer. We also have to be prepared for rumours of a connection between the two events. You understand where that may lead."

"The suspicion that Svedberg was the killer?"

"Yes."

"Do you think he did it?"

Her question came so quickly that he was taken by surprise. "I don't know," Wallander said slowly. "There are no indications that Svedberg had a motive. Somewhere there's a connection, yes. But we don't know what it is."

"How much should we say at this point?"

"I don't actually think it matters. We've never been able to protect ourselves from idle speculation."

Höglund was listening to their conversation. He noticed that she was shaking.

"There's one more thing to keep in mind," she said. "Eva Hillström is going to accuse us of not moving on this soon enough."

"She may be right about that," Wallander said. "It may be something we'll have to acknowledge. I'll bear responsibility for it."

"Why you?" Holgersson asked.

"Someone has to," Wallander said simply. "It doesn't matter who it is."

Nyberg gave them all rubber gloves, and they started working. There were specific routines to be followed, tasks that had to be done in a certain order. Wallander walked over to Nyberg, who was instructing someone with a camera.

"I want everything on video," Wallander said. "Both close-up and from far away."

"Will do."

"Try to get someone whose hand won't shake."

"It's always easier to look at death through the lens," Nyberg said. "But we'll use a tripod just in case."

Wallander gathered his team together: Martinsson, Hansson and Höglund. He started looking around for Svedberg but stopped himself.

"They're dressed up," Hansson said. "And they're wearing wigs."

"It's the 18th century," Höglund said. "This time I'm sure."

"So it happened on Midsummer's Eve," Martinsson said. "That's two months ago."

"We don't know that," Wallander broke in. "We don't even know that this is where the crime took place."

He knew how ridiculous it sounded, but it was strange that no one had discovered them for so long. Wallander started walking around the blue linen cloth. He tried to see what had happened. He slowly let his mind pull back from everything else.

They were here to have a party. There were supposed to be four of them but one had fallen ill. They carried food, drink and a tape recorder with them in two big baskets.

Wallander interrupted himself and went over to Hansson, who was talking on the phone. Wallander waited until he was done.

"The cars," he said. "Where are the cars that we assumed were somewhere in Europe? They must have got here somehow."

Hansson promised to look into it. Wallander resumed his slow circling of the tablecloth where the dead lay. They set their things out, they ate and drank. Wallander crouched down. There was an empty bottle of wine in one of the baskets, two more in the grass. Three empty bottles altogether.

When death came for you, you had already emptied three

bottles. That means you were drunk. Wallander got up thoughtfully. Nyberg came up behind him.

"I'd like to know if any wine ran out into the grass or if we can determine if they drank it all."

Nyberg pointed to a stain on the blue cloth.

"Some of it spilled right there. It's not blood, if that's what you're thinking."

Wallander kept going. You ate and drank and became intoxicated. You had a tape recorder, you were listening to music. Someone entered this scene and killed you when you were resting on the blue cloth with your arms around each other. One of you, Astrid Hillström, may in fact have been asleep. It was probably already morning, maybe early dawn.

Wallander paused.

His eyes fell on a wineglass near one of the baskets. He knelt down to examine it and waved a photographer over to get a close-up. The glass was leaning against the basket but there was a little pebble supporting it underneath. Wallander looked around. He lifted the edge of the cloth carefully but didn't see any stones or rocks anywhere. He tried to think what it meant. When Nyberg walked by he stopped him.

"There's a pebble propping up that wineglass. If you see any others like it please let me know."

Nyberg made a note of it. Wallander continued his rounds. Then he pulled back a bit and surveyed the scene from more of a distance.

You spread your feast out at the foot of a tree. You chose a private place where no one would see you. Wallander pushed his way through the bushes and stood on the other side of the tree.

He must have come from somewhere. There are no signs

193

of panic. You were resting on the cloth, and one of you was already asleep. But the other two were perhaps still awake.

Wallander went back and studied the corpses for a long time. Something wasn't right. Then he realised what it was. The picture in front of him wasn't real. It had been arranged.

CHAPTER THIRTEEN

As dusk approached on Sunday, 11 August, and police spotlights gave an unearthly glow to the scene, Wallander did
something unexpected. He left. The only person he spoke
to was Höglund. He needed to borrow her car since his
own was still parked at Mariagatan. He told her to get in
touch with him on his mobile phone if he was needed. He
didn't tell her where he was going. She returned to the
crime scene, where there were no longer any bodies. They
had been carried out around 4 p.m. Once the bodies had
been removed, Wallander felt consumed by fatigue and
nausea. He forced himself to put in a couple more hours;
then he felt the need to leave the scene. When he asked
Höglund for her car keys, he knew where he was going.
He wasn't simply going away. However tired and depressed
he got, he rarely functioned without a clear plan. He drove
off almost in a hurry. There was something he wanted to
see, a mirror he wanted to hold up in front of himself.

Wallander pulled up outside Svedberg's building on
Lilla Norregatan. The cement mixer was still there, and
Svedberg's keys were in his pocket. The air inside the flat
was stale. He went into the kitchen and opened the window.
Then he drank a glass of water and reminded himself that
he had an appointment with Dr Göransson the next morning. He knew he was going to miss it. He hadn't managed
to improve his habits at all since receiving the diagnosis.
He still ate as poorly, and had taken no exercise. At this

point even his own health would have to be put on hold.

The streetlamps cast a faint light into the living room. Wallander stood completely still in the twilight. He had left the crime scene because he needed some perspective on what had happened. But there was also a thought that had occurred to him earlier and that he wanted time to consider. They had all talked about the connections between the crimes and the hideous possibility that Svedberg was involved. But suddenly it occurred to Wallander that they were ignoring the most likely scenario. Svedberg had been conducting his own investigation without telling anyone what he was doing. It looked like he spent most of his holiday investigating the disappearance of these three young people. Of course, this could mean that he had something to hide. But it could also be that he had stumbled upon the truth. He might have had grounds to doubt that Boge, Norman and Hillström were travelling around Europe. He might have believed that something was wrong, and he might have crossed someone's path, only to end up murdered himself. Wallander knew that this did not explain why Svedberg hadn't told his colleagues what he was doing, but he may have had a good reason.

The events of the day slowly passed through his mind. Only an hour or so after they had discovered the bodies, Wallander had come to the conclusion that there was something wrong with the scene. He discovered what it was when the pathologist told him he was certain that the time of death was not as long ago as 50 days. This suggested two possibilities: either the shots were fired later than Midsummer, or else the bodies had been stored somewhere in the meantime, where they would have been better preserved. They couldn't conclude that the place where the bodies were found was necessarily the same place as the location of the crime.

For Wallander and the team, it didn't seem possible that someone had killed the three people where they were found, moved them to an unknown location for storage, then returned them to their original place. Hansson had suggested that they really did go on their European holiday, but that they returned earlier than anticipated. Wallander acknowledged this as a possibility, however unlikely. But he didn't write anything off yet. He made his observations, listened to anyone who had anything to say, and felt he was being forced deeper and deeper into an endless fog.

The warm August day had seemed never-ending. They took refuge in the structure of police routines and made their thorough examination of the scene. Wallander watched his colleagues, downcast and horrified, do what was expected of them. He watched them and wondered if every one of them was wishing that he or she had become anything but a police officer. People left as soon as they got the chance. Some camping chairs and tables were placed along the path where they could drink cups of coffee that got colder each time the thermoses were opened. Wallander didn't see anyone eat anything all day.

It was Nyberg's tenacity that was the most impressive of all. He rummaged around the half-rotten, stinking food remains with sullen determination. He directed the photographer and the policeman doing the videotaping, sealed countless objects in plastic bags, and made detailed maps of the crime scene. Wallander sensed the hatred Nyberg felt for the person who had caused the mess he was now forced to root around in. He knew that no one else was capable of Nyberg's thoroughness. At one point Wallander had realised that Martinsson was exhausted. He took him aside and ordered him to go home, or at the very least to go down to the forensic technicians' van and sleep for a while. But Martinsson simply shook his head and continued his work on the area closest to the cloth. Some dog patrols from Ystad arrived. Edmundsson was there with his dog, Kall. The dogs had picked up a couple of different scents. One of them had found human excrement behind one of the bushes. In other places there were beer cans and pieces of paper. Everything was duly noted on Nyberg's maps. In one particular spot, under a tree a little distance away, Kall indicated a find but after a careful search they were still unable to locate any human object. Wallander returned to the spot behind this tree several times that day. He discovered that it was one of the most sheltered locations from which to observe the place where the Midsummer celebrations had taken place. He felt a cold grip around his stomach. Had the murderer stood in this very place? What had he seen?

Shortly after midday, Nyberg told Wallander to take a look at the tape recorder that lay on its side by the cloth. They found a number of unmarked cassette tapes in one of the baskets. Everyone stopped talking when Wallander turned on the tape recorder. A dusky male voice they all recognised came on: the singer Fred Åkerström interpreting a ballad from the collection *Fredman's Epistles*. Wallander looked at Höglund. She had been right. This was a celebration set in the 18th century, the age of that eternally popular poet Bellman.

Wallander got up and went into Svedberg's study. First he looked around for a minute, then he sat down at the desk. He let images from the investigation come to him. There were the three postcards that Eva Hillström had doubted from the very beginning. Wallander hadn't believed her; no one had. It had been inconceivable that someone would send fake postcards. But now they had found her daughter dead, they knew that the postcards had been sent by someone else. Someone had travelled all over Europe, to Hamburg, Paris and Vienna for this. Why? Even if the three young people were not killed on Midsummer's Eve, there was no doubt that they were killed before the last postcard came from Vienna. But what was the reason for this false trail?

Wallander stared blankly out into the dimly lit room.

I'm afraid, he thought. I've never believed in pure evil. There are no evil people, no one with brutality in their genes. There are evil circumstances and environments, not evil per se. But here I sense the actions of a truly darkened mind.

Wallander reached for Svedberg's pocket calendar and went through it again. There was the recurring name, "Adamsson". Could this be the surname of the woman in the photograph whom Sture Björklund told them was called Louise? Louise Adamsson. He went back to the kitchen and looked in the phone book. There was no Louise Adamsson listed. She could be married, of course, and have a different surname. He made a mental note to ask Martinsson to find out what Svedberg had done on the days marked "Adamsson" in his calendar.

He turned out the light and went to the living room. Here someone had walked across the floor with a shotgun in his hand. It had been aimed and fired at Svedberg's head, then thrown to the floor and left behind. Wallander tried to think whether this marked the beginning or end of a series of events. Or was it part of something even larger? He almost didn't have the energy to follow this last thought to its conclusion. Was there really someone out there who was going to continue the senseless killing? He didn't know. Nothing gave him the mental foothold he was looking for. He walked over to the place where the shotgun had been found and tried to see where Svedberg must have been sitting. The cement mixer would have been rumbling on the street. Two shots, Svedberg thrown to the ground – probably dead before he even hit the floor. Wallander didn't hear any argument or raised voices, only the dry shots from the gun. He changed his position and walked over to the chair that lay on the ground.

You let in a person you know, someone you are not afraid of. Or else someone enters who has his own key. Perhaps someone picks the lock. There are no marks on the door; he didn't use a crowbar. We'll assume it's a he. He has a shotgun, or else you keep an unregistered shotgun in the flat. A shotgun that is loaded, and that the person you have let in knows about. There are so many questions, but in the end it comes down to a who and a why. Only one who. And one lone why.

He went back to the kitchen and called the hospital. Luckily, the doctor he had spoken to before was in.

"Isa Edengren is doing well. She'll be released tomorrow or the day after."

"Has she said anything?"

"Not really. But I think she's happy you found her."

"Does she know it was me?"

"Shouldn't we have told her that?"

"What was her reaction?"

"I don't think I understand your question."

"How did she react when she was told that a policeman had come looking for her?"

"I don't know."

"I need to talk to her as soon as possible."

"Tomorrow will be fine."

"I'd rather talk to her tonight. I need to talk to you, too."

"It sounds rather urgent."

"It is."

"I'm actually on my way out. It would be more convenient to talk tomorrow."

"I wish it were that unimportant," Wallander said. "But I have to ask you to stay. I'll be there in ten minutes."

"Has something happened?"

"Yes. Something I don't think you could possibly imagine."

Wallander drank a glass of water and left the flat. It was still warm outside, with only a faint breeze.

When he arrived at the ward where Isa Edengren was being kept, the doctor was waiting for him. They went into an empty office and Wallander closed the door. On the way over he had decided to level with the doctor completely. He told him what they had found out in the nature reserve, that three young people had been murdered, and that Isa Edengren was meant to have been with them. The only detail he left out was the fact that they had been dressed up. The doctor listened in disbelief.

"I thought about going into pathology," he said afterwards. "But hearing this I'm glad I decided against it."

"You're right. It was a terrible sight."

The doctor got up. "I take it you want to see her now."

"Just one more thing. Naturally I'd like you not to mention this to anyone."

"Doctors have to take an oath."

"So do police officers. But information seems to have a way of getting out anyway."

They stopped outside Isa's door.

"I'll just make sure she's awake."

Wallander waited. He didn't like hospitals. He wanted to leave as soon as possible. He remembered what Dr Göransson said about checking his blood-sugar levels. It was apparently a very simple test. The doctor came back out.

"She's awake."

"One more thing," Wallander said. "This will sound strange, but can you check my blood-sugar level?"

The doctor looked at him with astonishment.

"Why?"

"I have an appointment with one of your colleagues tomorrow morning that I won't be able to attend. But I was going to have it checked."

"Are you diabetic?"

"No. My blood-sugar level is too high."

"Then you're diabetic."

"I just want to know if you can measure it or not. I don't have my insurance card with me but maybe you could make an exception in my case."

A nurse walked by and the doctor stopped her.

"Could you check this man's blood-sugar level? He's going to speak with Edengren afterwards."

"Of course."

The nurse's name tag said "Brundin". Wallander thanked the doctor for his help and followed the nurse. She pricked his finger and squeezed a drop of blood onto a strip of tape in a machine that looked like a Walkman.

"It's very high – 15.5," she said.

"It's way too high," Wallander said. "That's all I wanted to know."

She looked closely at him, but in a friendly way.

"You're a little on the heavy side," she said.

Wallander nodded. He felt suddenly ashamed of himself, like a naughty child.

He went back to Isa Edengren's room. He had expected her to be lying in bed, but she was curled up in an armchair with a blanket drawn tightly around her. The only light in the room came from the bedside lamp. As he came closer he saw something like fear in her eyes. He put out his hand and introduced himself, then sat down on a stool next to her.

She doesn't know what's happened, he thought. That three of her closest friends are dead. Or does she suspect it already? Has she been waiting for this discovery? Is that why she couldn't take it any longer?

He pulled his stool around so he was facing her. Her eyes never left him. When he had first walked into the room she had reminded him of Linda. Linda had also tried to commit suicide, at the age of 15. Wallander later realised it was part of the series of events that had led Mona to leave him. He had never really understood it, even though he and Linda talked about it years later. There was something there that he would never quite grasp. He wondered if he would be able to understand why this girl had tried to take her life.

"I'm the one who found you," he said. "I know you know that already. But you don't know why I came out to Skårby. You don't know why I walked around the back of the locked house and kept looking for you until I found you in the gazebo where you were sleeping."

He paused so she could speak, but she remained silent, watching him.

"You were supposed to have celebrated Midsummer with your friends Martin, Lena and Astrid," he continued. "But you fell ill. You had some kind of stomach bug and stayed at home. Isn't that right?"

No reaction. Wallander was suddenly unsure of how to proceed. How could he tell her what had happened? On the other hand it would be in all the papers tomorrow. She would suffer a great shock in either case.

I wish Ann-Britt were here, he thought. She would be better at this than I am.

"Astrid's mother received some postcards," he said. "They were signed by all three, or just by Astrid, and sent from Hamburg, Paris and Vienna. Had the four of you talked about going away after Midsummer?"

She finally began to answer his questions, but her voice was so low that Wallander had trouble hearing her.

"No, we hadn't decided anything," she whispered.

Wallander felt a lump in his throat. Her voice sounded as if it might break at any moment. He thought about what she was going to hear, that a simple virus had saved her life. Wallander wanted to call the doctor he had spoken to before and ask him what he should do. How would he tell her? He put it off for now.

"Tell me about the Midsummer party," he said.

"Why should I?"

He wondered how such a fragile voice could sound so determined. But she wasn't hostile. Her answers would depend on his questions.

"Because I'd like to know. Because Astrid's mother is worried."

"It was just a party."

"But you were going to dress up like 18th-century courtiers."

She couldn't know how he knew. He was taking a risk in asking the question, but she might be impossible to talk to after she found out what had happened to her friends.

"We did that sometimes."

"Why?"

"It made things different."

"To leave your own age and enter another?"

"Yes."

"Was it always the 18th century?"

There was an undertone of disdain in her answer. "We never repeated ourselves."

"Why not?"

She didn't reply, and Wallander immediately knew he had hit an important point. He tried to approach it from another direction.

"Is it possible to know how people dressed in the 12th century?"

"Yes, but we never entered that age."

"How did you choose an era?"

She didn't answer that either, and Wallander was starting to discern a pattern in the questions she wouldn't answer.

"Tell me what happened that Midsummer's Eve."

"I was sick."

"It must have come on suddenly."

"Diarrhoea usually does."

"What happened?"

"Martin came to get me and I told him I couldn't come."

"How did he react?"

"Like he was supposed to."

"How?"

"By asking me if it was true. Like he was supposed to."

Wallander didn't understand her answer. "What do you mean?"

"You're supposed to tell the truth. If you don't, they kick you out."

Wallander thought for a moment. "You took your

friendship seriously, then. No one was allowed to lie. One untruth meant expulsion?"

She looked genuinely puzzled. "What would friendship be otherwise?"

He nodded. "Of course friendship is always based on mutual trust."

"What else is there?"

"I don't know," Wallander said. "Love, perhaps."

She pulled the blanket up under her chin.

"How did you feel when you realised that they had left to travel around Europe without you?"

She looked at him for a long time before answering. "I've already answered that question."

It took Wallander a moment before he made the connection. "Are you referring to the police officer who visited you earlier this summer?"

"Who else would I be referring to?"

"Do you remember when he came to see you?"

"On 1 or 2 July."

"What else did he ask you?"

She leaned in towards Wallander so suddenly that he pulled back involuntarily.

"I know he's dead. He was called Svedberg. Have you come here to tell me about him?"

"Not exactly, but I'd like to hear more about your conversation with him."

"There's nothing more to tell."

Wallander frowned. "What do you mean? He must have asked you something else."

"He didn't. I have it on tape."

"You recorded your conversation with Svedberg?"

"In secret, yes. I do that a lot."

"And that's what you did when Svedberg came to see you?"

"Yes."

"Where is that tape now?"

"In the gazebo, where you found me. There's a blue angel on the outside of the tape."

"A blue angel?"

"I make the wrappers myself."

Wallander nodded. "Do you mind if I have someone get the tape for me?"

"Why would I mind?"

Wallander called the station and instructed the policeman on duty to send a squad car to the house to get the tape. He also told them to get the Walkman he had seen on the bedside table.

"A blue angel?" the policeman asked.

"Yes, a blue angel on the wrapper. Tell them to hurry."

It took them exactly 29 minutes. While he was waiting, Isa spent more than 15 minutes in the bathroom. When she came back Wallander realised she had washed her hair. It occurred to him that perhaps he should have worried that she was making a second attempt on her life.

An officer came into the room and gave him the tape recorder and tape. Isa nodded in recognition. She took the Walkman and fast-forwarded to the place she was looking for.

"Here," she said and handed the headphones to Wallander.

Svedberg's voice came at him full-strength. He flinched as if he had been struck. He heard Svedberg clear his throat and ask a question. Her answer disappeared in the surrounding noise. He rewound the tape and listened again. He had heard correctly.

Svedberg had asked a similar question. But Isa was wrong – it wasn't the same question. Wallander had asked, "How did you feel when you realised that they had left to travel around Europe without you?"

The way Svedberg phrased his question dramatically altered its meaning: "Do you really think they have gone on a trip to Europe?"

Wallander listened to it a third time. Isa's reply couldn't be heard. He took off the headphones.

Svedberg knew, he thought. By 1 or 2 July, Svedberg had known they weren't travelling around Europe.

CHAPTER FOURTEEN

They continued their conversation, although Wallander was finding it hard to concentrate. By 9 p.m. he didn't think he could hold off telling her the truth any longer. He excused himself by saying he was going to get a cup of coffee. In the hall he called Martinsson, who said that most of the officers were starting to return to Ystad. Soon only the forensic technicians and the security guards would be left. Nyberg and his team would work through the night. Wallander told him where he was and asked to speak to Höglund. She came to the phone, and he told her that he needed her help.

"Isa Edengren has to be notified of the deaths. I don't know how she's going to react."

"Well, at least she's already in the hospital. What do you think could happen to her?"

Her answer seemed unusually cold to Wallander until he realised that she was distancing herself from the situation. Nothing could be worse than the way she had spent this long August day.

"I'd still appreciate it if you could come over," he said. "That way at least I don't have to do this alone. She has just tried to commit suicide."

After they hung up, he looked for the nurse who had checked his blood-sugar levels and got the name and home number of the doctor he had spoken to. He also asked her what her impression of Isa Edengren was.

"Many people who try to commit suicide are very strong," she said. "There are always exceptions to the rule, but it's my impression that Isa Edengren is one such person."

He asked where he could get some coffee and she directed him to a vending machine in the foyer. Wallander called the doctor at home. A child's voice answered the phone, then he got a woman, and finally the doctor.

"I haven't been thinking clearly," Wallander said. "We have to tell her what happened right away, or she'll hear it herself tomorrow morning. Then we may not be able to intervene. I don't know how she's going to react."

The doctor said he would come in. Wallander set off in search of the vending machine, but when he found it he realised that he had no change in his pockets. An elderly man pushing a walking frame came by. When Wallander carefully asked him if he had any change, the old man simply shook his head.

"I'm going to die soon," he said. "In about three weeks or so. What do I need money for?"

He kept going, seemingly in high spirits. Wallander was left with a note in his outstretched hand. When he did find some change, he pushed the wrong button and ended up with cream in his coffee, which he almost never had.

When he returned to the ward, Höglund had arrived. She was pale and had dark circles under her eyes. They hadn't found any significant leads, she told him, and he could hear how tired she was.

We're all tired, he thought. Exhausted, before we've even begun to penetrate this nightmare we're in.

He told her about his conversation with Isa Edengren, and she listened with surprise when he mentioned the recording of Svedberg's voice. He told her his conclusion:

that Svedberg knew, or at least strongly suspected, that the three missing people hadn't set off on a trip.

"How on earth could he have known that," she asked, "unless he was extremely close to what happened?"

"The situation seems clearer to me now," Wallander said. "He is somehow very close to the events, but he doesn't know everything. If he did he would have no reason to be asking these questions."

"That would suggest that Svedberg wasn't the one who killed them," she said. "Not that any of us really thought so."

"It passed through my mind," Wallander said. "I'll admit it. Now the picture has changed. I'm prepared to go a step further and say that Svedberg knew only a couple of days after Midsummer that something was wrong. But what was it that he feared?"

"That they were dead?"

"Not necessarily. He's in the same situation we were in before we found them. But where does his fear or suspicion come from?"

"He knows something we don't?"

"Something makes him suspicious. Perhaps it is only a vague feeling, we'll never know. But he doesn't share these suspicions. He keeps them to himself, conducts a thorough investigation during his holiday."

"So we have to ask ourselves what he knew."

"That's what we're looking for, nothing else."

"But that won't explain why he was shot."

"Nor does it explain why he didn't tell us what he was doing."

She frowned. "Why do you keep something hidden?"

"Because there's information you don't want to get out. Or you don't want to be discovered," he answered. "We may find a link."

"I've thought the same thing. There may very well be a link between Svedberg and the young people. Someone else."

"Louise?"

"Maybe."

They heard a door slam at the end of the corridor and the doctor came walking towards them. It was time. Isa Edengren was still sitting in the chair when Wallander went back in.

"There's one last thing I have to talk to you about," he said, sitting down next to her. "I'm afraid it will be difficult for you to hear. That's why I'd like your doctor to be here while I tell you. And one of my colleagues, Ann-Britt Höglund."

He saw that she was getting scared. But there was no way out now. The others joined them, and Wallander told her the facts. Her three friends had been found, but they were dead. Someone had killed them.

"We wanted to tell you now," he finished. "So you don't read about it in the papers tomorrow."

She didn't react.

"I know this is hard for you," he said. "But I have to ask you if you have any idea who might have done this."

"No."

Her voice was weak but clear.

"Did anyone else know about your plans that night?"

"No outsider is ever told."

It occurred to Wallander that she sounded like she was reciting a rule. Perhaps she was.

"No one knew except you?"

"No one."

"You weren't there since you got sick. But you knew where they were going to be?"

"In the nature reserve."

"And you knew they were going to dress up?"

"Yes."

"Why was it so secret?"

She didn't answer. I've trespassed onto secret territory again, Wallander thought. She refuses to answer when I go too far. But he knew she was right. No one had known about their plans. He had no further questions.

"We're leaving," he said. "Please be in touch if you think of anything else. The people around here know how to get hold of me. I also want you to know that I spoke to your mother."

She jerked her head back. "Why? What has she got to do with this?"

Her voice was suddenly shrill, making Wallander feel uncomfortable.

"I had to tell her," he said. "When I found you, you were unconscious. It's my duty to notify the next of kin."

She seemed about to say more, but then she stopped herself, and started to cry. The doctor indicated that it was time for Wallander and Höglund to leave. When they were out in the corridor again and the door shut behind them, Wallander noticed that he was dripping with sweat.

"Every time it gets worse," he said. "Soon I won't be able to get through this any more."

They arrived back at the station around 10.30 p.m. Wallander was surprised to see that there were no reporters outside. He'd thought the news about the murders would already have been leaked. Wallander hung up his coat and went to the canteen. Tired police officers sat silently over their cups of coffee and the remains of takeaway pizzas. It occurred to Wallander that he ought to say something to cheer them up. But how did you lighten the mood after the killing of three innocent people on a summer picnic? Somewhere in the background was also the murder of one of their own.

Wallander said nothing, but he nodded to them and tried to show that he was there for them. Hansson looked at him with weary eyes.

"When are we meeting?" he asked.

Wallander glanced at his watch. "Now. Is Martinsson here?"

"He's on his way."

"Lisa?"

"In her office. I think things were hard for her in Lund. All the parents, couple after couple, stepped up to identify their child. Although I think Eva Hillström came by herself."

Wallander went straight to Lisa Holgersson's office. The door was slightly ajar, and he could see her behind the desk. Her eyes seemed wet. He knocked and looked in. She gestured for him to come in.

"Do you regret going to Lund?"

"There's nothing to regret. But it was as terrible as you said it would be. There are no words to offer someone at a time like this. Parents are called down on a summer's day to identify their dead child. The people who had fixed up the bodies had done a great job, but they couldn't completely hide the fact that they had been dead for a long time."

"Hansson said Eva Hillström came by herself."

"She was the most restrained, perhaps because she had feared the worst all along."

"She's going to accuse us of not moving fast enough on this. Perhaps with some justification."

"Is that really your opinion?"

"No, but I don't know how much my opinion matters. If we had had more personnel, if it hadn't been in the middle of everyone's holiday time . . . things might have been different. But there are always excuses. And now a mother is forced to confront her worst fear."

"I'd like to discuss the possibility of getting some re-inforcements down here as soon as possible."

Wallander was too tired to argue, but he didn't agree with her. There was always the hope that greater numbers meant greater efficiency. But in his experience this was almost never the case. It was often a small, well-run inves-tigative team that produced the best results.

"What do you think?"

Wallander shrugged. "I think you know my opinion on this. But I'm not going to object if you want reinforce-ments."

"I'd like to talk to the others about it tonight."

"They're exhausted," he said. "You won't get any rational answers. Why don't you wait until tomorrow?"

It was 10.45 p.m. Wallander got up and went to the conference room. Svedberg's chair was still empty. Nyberg came in straight from the crime scene and Wallander saw him shake his head. No new finds.

Wallander started by telling them about his visit to the hospital. He had brought the tape recorder and cassette with him. There was an eerie silence in the room when he played the recording of Svedberg's voice. After Wallander told them about his conclusions, he noticed that the exhaustion of the group seemed to lift a little. Svedberg had known something. Was that why he had been killed?

They slowly went over all the facts of the case again. The meeting stretched long into the night, and the team slowly overcame their tiredness and low spirits. They took a short break just after midnight. When they returned, Martinsson sat down in Svedberg's chair by mistake. He changed his seat when he realised what he had done. Wallander got up to go to the men's room and drink some water. His mouth was dry and his head ached, but he knew he had to push on. During the break he went to his office to call the hospital. After waiting for a long time he finally talked to the nurse who had checked his blood-sugar level.

"She's sleeping," she said. "She wanted a sleeping pill. Naturally we couldn't give her one, but she fell asleep anyway."

"Has anyone called her? Her mother?"

"Only a man who said he was her neighbour."

"Lundberg?"

"Yes, that was his name."

"The full impact of what has happened will probably only hit her tomorrow," Wallander said.

"What is it that's happened?"

Wallander couldn't think of any reason not to tell her. There was a stunned silence.

"I can't believe it," she said.

"I don't know," he said honestly. "I don't understand it any better than you."

He returned to the conference room. It was time for him to summarise the events as they knew them.

"I don't know why this happened," he started. "I see no possible motive and therefore no possible suspect. But I am aware of a chain of events, as you all are. This chain is not completely without gaps, but I'll tell you what I see. Correct me if I leave anything out."

He reached for some sparkling mineral water and filled

his glass. "Some time during the afternoon on 21 June, three young people drove out to Hagestad nature reserve. They probably arrived in two cars, both of which remain missing. According to Isa Edengren, who was supposed to have been with them but fell ill, they had chosen the place for their party in advance. They were going to make it a masquerade, which they had done before. We should try to understand this game as well as we can. I think there were very strong ties between these young people, something more than simple friendship.

"Their era this time was the 18th century, the age of Bellman. They wore costumes and wigs and played songs from *Fredman's Epistles*. We don't know if they were being observed at this point. The spot they had chosen was hidden from view. The killer appeared from somewhere and shot them. They were each shot in the forehead. We don't yet know what kind of weapon was used. Everything points to the killer carrying out the deed deliberately and without hesitation. We find them 51 days later. That's the most likely scenario, but until we know exactly how long they have been dead we cannot rule out that they may not have been killed at the Midsummer feast. It may have happened at a later date. We simply don't know. But we do know that the killer must have been privy to certain information. It's not really believable that this triple homicide was a chance occurrence. We can't rule out the possibility of a lunatic, since we can't rule anything out, but the signs point to a carefully planned and executed killing. The motive for this crime I cannot even begin to speculate about. Who would want to kill young people in the midst of the happiest time of their lives? I don't think I've ever been involved in a case like this before."

He looked around. He wasn't quite done with his

summary of the events, but he wanted to see if there were any questions. No one spoke.

"There is more to this story," he said. "We don't know if it is a beginning, an end, or a parallel event, but Svedberg was also murdered, and we found a photograph of these young people in his flat. We know that he was investigating their disappearance and that he started to do so as soon as he heard from Eva Hillström and the other parents. There is a connection here. We don't know what it is but we have to find it. That's where we have to begin."

He put his pencil down and leaned back in his chair. His back ached. He looked over at Nyberg.

"I should perhaps add that both Nyberg and I feel there is something artificial and arranged about the scene of the crime."

"I just can't understand how they could have lain there for 51 days without anyone finding them," Hansson said despondently. "A lot of people visit the reserve during the summer."

"I don't either," Wallander said. "There are three possibilities. We could be completely wrong about the time of death. Maybe it wasn't Midsummer's Eve; maybe it was later than that. Or else the scene of the crime and the place we found the bodies aren't the same. The third possibility is that these two places are one and the same, but someone moved the bodies and returned them at a later date."

"Who would do that?" Höglund asked. "And why?"

"That's what I think happened," Nyberg said.

Everyone looked at him. It was unusual for Nyberg to speak with such conviction so early on in an investigation.

"At first I just kept seeing the same thing Kurt did," he began. "That there was something fake about the whole scene, like a photographer had arranged it for the camera. Then I found some things that made me rethink."

Wallander waited with excitement, but it was as if Nyberg lost his train of thought.

"Go on," he said.

Nyberg shook his head. "It doesn't make any sense," he said. "Why would anyone move the bodies just to return them at a later date?"

"There might be a lot of reasons," Wallander said. "To delay a discovery or to give himself time to escape."

"Or to send a number of postcards," Martinsson said.

Wallander nodded. "We'll take this step by step. We don't know if our thinking is right or wrong."

"Well, it was the glasses that made me think again," Nyberg said slowly. "There was wine left in two of them. A little less in one, a little more in the other. It should have evaporated a long time ago, but what really surprised me was what wasn't there. There were no insects in the glasses, which there should have been. We know what happens if you let even an empty glass that has had wine in it sit out overnight. In the morning it's full of insects. But there was nothing in these glasses."

"What do you make of that?"

"That the glasses had been sitting out for only a couple of hours when Leman found the bodies."

"How many hours?"

"I can't tell you exactly."

"What about the remains of the food?" Martinsson objected. "The chicken was rotten, the salad mouldy, and the bread stale. Food doesn't go bad that quickly."

Nyberg looked at him. "But isn't that exactly what we're discussing now? That the scene that Mats and Rosmarie Leman discovered had been pre-arranged. Someone puts out a couple of glasses and splashes wine in the bottom.

The food has been decomposing elsewhere, and is distributed on the plates."

Nyberg sounded as certain as he had when he'd begun to speak. "We'll be able to prove it, if it is the case," he said. "We'll be able to determine exactly how long the wine we found in the glasses had been exposed to air. But I already know what I think. I think the Lemans would not have found anything at all if they had gone for their walk on Saturday morning."

The room was silent. Nyberg had followed his train of thought much further than Wallander had realised. It hadn't occurred to Wallander that the bodies might only have been lying out for about a day. The killer must have been close by. What Nyberg said also affected Svedberg's relationship to the crime. He could have killed them and hidden the bodies, but he could not have brought them out again.

"I can tell you feel sure of this," Wallander said. "What's the likelihood that you could be mistaken?"

"None. I may be wrong in the exact hours and times I've been suggesting. But it must have happened in the way I have described."

"Is the place we found them also the scene of the crime?"

"We're not finished yet," Nyberg said. "But it does seem as if blood has seeped through into the ground."

"So you think they were shot there and then moved?"

"Exactly."

"So where were they taken?"

They all sensed the importance of this question. They were charting the movements of the killer. Although they couldn't see him clearly, they were zeroing in on his actions. That was a crucial step.

"I think we should assume that this is the work of a man acting alone," Wallander said. "But there may have been more than one person involved. This seems more probable if it turns out that the bodies were moved and later replaced."

"Perhaps we're using the wrong words," Höglund said. "Perhaps instead of moved we should be saying concealed."

Wallander was thinking the same thing. "The spot is not deep inside the reserve," he said. "It's possible to drive a car up there, but it is not allowed and it would attract attention. The alternative is easy. The bodies could have been concealed somewhere in the area, perhaps quite close to the scene of the crime."

"The dogs didn't pick up any tracks," Hansson said. "Not that that means anything."

Wallander had made up his mind. "We can't wait for all the results to come in. I want to search the area again at dawn for somewhere the bodies may have been concealed. If we're right, it'll be nearby."

It was just after 1 a.m. Wallander knew everyone needed a few hours' sleep before the morning.

He was the last to leave the room. The night air was warm, with no hint of wind. He pulled the air deep into his lungs, walked behind the back of a police car, and relieved himself. He would miss his appointment with Dr Göransson in the morning. His blood-sugar level was way too high at 15.5, but how could he think about his health at a time like this?

He started to walk home through the deserted town. Something was bothering him, a fear he knew he shared with the others although no one had said so. They were close to tracking the killer's movements, but they had no idea what he was thinking or what motivated him. They had no idea if he was planning to strike again.

CHAPTER FIFTEEN

Wallander didn't make it into bed that night. As soon as he stopped outside his door on Mariagatan and fumbled for his keys, anxiety overtook him. He put the keys back in his pocket, walked over to his car and jumped in. Somewhere out there a killer was hiding in the shadows and he would remain there until they caught him. They had to find him. He simply couldn't be allowed to get away, to become one of the people who would haunt Wallander in his dreams.

As he drove through the calm night, he thought about a case in the early 1980s, shortly after he had moved to Ystad with Mona and Linda. Rydberg had called him late one night with the news that a young girl had been found dead in a field outside of Borrie. She had been bludgeoned to death. They drove out there together that November evening. Hard flecks of snow were drifting through the air.

The girl had taken the bus from Ystad after going to the cinema, got off at her normal stop, and followed her usual shortcut through the fields to the farm where she lived. When she hadn't arrived at the time she said she would be home, her father went down to the road to look for her, and found her.

The investigation went on for years and filled thousands of pages of reports, but they never found the killer, nor any possible motive. The only clue was a piece of a wooden clothes-peg found close to the dead girl's body which bore traces of blood. Apart from that there was nothing. Rydberg would often come to Wallander's office to talk about it. During his last days, when he was dying of cancer, he mentioned her again. Wallander understood that he didn't want him to forget about the dead girl in the field. Once he was gone, only Wallander would be left to solve the case. He seldom thought about her now, but occasionally she appeared in his dreams. The image was always the same. Wallander was leaning over her, with Rydberg somewhere in the background. She looked back at him but was unable to speak.

Wallander took the turn-off for the nature reserve. I don't want three young people haunting my dreams, he thought. Nor do I want Svedberg there. We have to find the one who did this.

He parked his car and saw to his surprise that the officer on duty was Edmundsson.

"Where's your dog?" Wallander asked.

"At home," Edmundsson said. "I don't see why he should have to sleep in the car."

Wallander nodded. "How is everything out here?"

"Only Nyberg is here, as well as those of us on duty."

"Nyberg?"

"He arrived a little while ago."

He's also haunted by anxiety, Wallander thought. It shouldn't surprise me.

"It's too hot to be August."

"Autumn will come, just you wait," Wallander said. "It'll come when you least expect it."

He turned on his torch and walked into the reserve.

The man had been hiding in the shadows for a long time. In order to enter the nature reserve without being seen, he had approached it from the sea. He followed the beach, climbed the dunes, and disappeared into the woods. To avoid running into the policemen or their dogs, he took a circuitous route towards the trail that led into the main hiking area. From there he could always make his way onto the road if the dogs picked up his scent. But he wasn't worried. They wouldn't expect him to be there.

Under the cover of darkness he saw police officers come and go along the path. Two of the officers were women. Shortly after 10 p.m. many of them left the reserve, and he sat down to drink the tea he had brought with him in a thermos. The order he sent to Shanghai had already been filled. He would pick it up early the next day. When he finished his tea, he packed the thermos away and made his way to the place where he had killed them. There were no more dogs in the area, so he felt safe. From a distance he could see big spotlights that were set up around the scene, casting an unearthly glow. It was like a theatre production, but one that was closed to the ordinary public. He was tempted to sneak close enough so he could hear what the policemen were saying and watch their faces. But he controlled himself, as he always did. Without self-control you couldn't be sure that you would get away and be safe.

The shadows danced in the spotlights. The police looked like giants, although he knew it was just an illusion. They fumbled around like blind animals in the world he had created. For a moment he allowed himself to enjoy a feeling of satisfaction. But only for a moment. He knew pride was dangerous and could make you vulnerable.

He returned to his lookout beside the main trail. He was thinking of leaving when someone walked by. The beam of a torch flickered over the ground. A face was visible for an instant and the man recognised him from the papers. His name was Nyberg and he was a forensic specialist. He smiled to himself. Nyberg might be able to identify the individual pieces, but he would never see the whole pattern.

He had finished putting his rucksack on and was about to cross the path when he heard another person approaching. Again a torch flickered between the trees and he jumped back into the shadows. The officer was large and moved heavily. The man felt a sudden impulse to make his presence known, to dash out like an animal of the night, before being swallowed up again by the darkness.

Suddenly the officer stopped. He let the torch shine on the bushes to the side of the trail. In a moment that lengthened into sheer terror the man thought that he had been caught. He was frozen and couldn't get away. Finally the light disappeared as the officer walked away. But then he stopped a second time, turned off the light, and waited in the dark. After a while he turned the torch back on and continued.

The man lay still for a long time, his heart pounding. What had caused the policeman to stop? He couldn't have heard anything, or seen him. For once his inner clock failed him. He had no idea how long he lay there before getting up, crossing the path, and making his way back down to the sea. It could have been an hour, maybe more. When he reached the beach it was starting to get light.

Wallander saw the lights from a distance. From time to time he heard Nyberg's tired and irritated voice. One officer was up on the path, smoking. He stopped again and listened. He didn't know where the feeling had come from, the sense that the killer was out there somewhere in the dark. Had he heard something? He stopped and felt a rush of fear. Then he realised that it must be his imagination. He stopped one more time, turned off the light, and listened. But there was only the sound of the sea.

He greeted the officer, who made an attempt to put out

his cigarette. Wallander stopped him. He was a young policeman by the name of Bernt Svensson.

"How's it going?" he asked.

"I think I saw a fox," Svensson said.

"A fox?"

"I thought I saw a shadow back there. It was bigger than a cat."

"There are no foxes in Skåne. They all died from the plague."

"I still think it was a fox."

Wallander nodded. "Then we'll say it was a fox. Just a fox."

He continued on down and into the ring of light. Nyberg was examining the place under the tree where the three bodies had lain. Even the blue cloth was gone now.

"What are you doing here?" he asked when he saw Wallander. "You should sleep. You have to have the energy to keep going."

"I know. But sometimes you can't sleep."

"Everyone should sleep," Nyberg said. His voice was cracking with fatigue. Wallander sensed how distraught he was.

"Everyone should sleep," he repeated. "And things like this shouldn't happen."

"I've been in the force for 40 years," Nyberg said. "I'm going to retire in another two."

"What will you do then?"

"Go crazy with boredom maybe," he said. "But you can bet I won't be standing around forests looking at the half-rotten corpses of some young people."

Wallander remembered what Sundelius had said. I used to go to work every day. Now I climb the walls.

"You'll find something," Wallander said encouragingly.

Nyberg muttered something unintelligible. Wallander tried to shake the tiredness out of his body.

"I came out to start planning the morning's activities," he said.

"You mean digging around for a possible hiding place?"

"If we're right about this, we should be able to deduce where he hid the bodies."

"He, or they. He may not have been alone," Nyberg answered.

"I think he was. It just doesn't make sense for two people to organise this kind of massacre. We're assuming the killer is a man, but I think that's a safe assumption. Women don't shoot people in the head. Especially young people."

"What about last year?"

Nyberg was referring to a case in which the killer of several people turned out to be a woman. But that did not change Wallander's mind.

"Not this time," he said. "So who are we looking for? An escaped lunatic?"

"Maybe. I'm not sure."

"But this gives us a starting point."

"Exactly. If he's alone, he has three bodies to hide. What does he do?"

"He won't move them very far, for practical reasons. He has to carry them, unless he brought a wheelbarrow, which would have drawn attention. I think he's a cautious person."

"So he buries them near here?"

"If he buried them at all," Wallander said. "Did you have the impression that the bodies had been exposed to animals or birds?"

"No. But I'm not a pathologist."

"Still, that confirms our idea that the bodies were in the ground. But animals can dig. That means the bodies have been protected somehow, by a box or plastic sheeting."

"I'm not an expert on these things," Nyberg said, "but

I do know that bodies in sealed containers decompose at a different rate to bodies exposed directly to the earth."

They were closing in on something that could be significant.

"Where does that lead us?" Wallander said.

Nyberg gestured with one arm.

"He wouldn't have gone uphill," he said and pointed back to the path. "Nor would he have crossed a path unless he had to."

They turned their backs to the hillside and looked past the lights, where insects danced in front of the hot lenses.

"To the left of us the ground slopes away steeply, then goes up again almost as sharply. I don't think he'd try there," Nyberg said.

"Straight ahead?"

"It's level, surrounded by thick brush."

"To the right?"

"Also brush, but not as thick. The ground is probably waterlogged from time to time."

"So probably somewhere straight ahead or to the right," Wallander said.

"To the right, I think," Nyberg said. "I forgot to mention something. If you go straight you hit another path."

"So we'll try to the right, once it gets light," Wallander said. "In a spot that looks like it might have been disturbed."

"I hope we're right," Nyberg said.

Wallander was so tired he could no longer speak. He decided to go back to his car and sleep for a few hours. Nyberg followed him up to the main path.

"I had a feeling there was someone sneaking around in the dark when I came up here," Wallander said. "And Svensson said he thought he saw a fox."

"Normal people have nightmares in their sleep," Nyberg

answered. "We have our nightmares when we're awake."

"I'm worried he's going to strike again," Wallander said. "Aren't you?"

Nyberg was silent for a moment before answering. "I'm always worried. But I also have the feeling that what happened here won't be repeated."

"I hope you're right," Wallander said. "I'll be back in a couple of hours."

He returned to the car park, without experiencing the feeling that someone was out there in the darkness. He curled up in the back seat of his car and fell asleep immediately.

It was broad daylight and someone was knocking on the window. He saw Höglund's face and hauled himself out of the car. His whole body ached.

"What time is it?"

"It's 7 a.m."

"Damn it, I've slept in. They have to start looking for a place to dig."

"They've already started," she said. "That's why I came to find you. Hansson's on his way."

They hurried up along the path. "I hate this," Wallander grumbled. "Sleeping in the back of a car, getting up unwashed and looking like hell. I'm too old for this. How am I supposed to think without even having a cup of coffee?"

"I think we can fix that," she said. "If the station hasn't supplied us with anything, you can have some of mine. I'll even give you a sandwich."

Wallander picked up his pace, but she still seemed to walk more quickly than he did. It annoyed him. They passed the place where he had felt as if someone was hiding in the bushes. He stopped and looked around, realising that it was the perfect lookout. Höglund looked at him expectantly, but Wallander didn't feel like explaining.

"Do me a favour," he said. "Get Edmundsson and his dog to search this place. Have them go 20 metres into the woods on either side."

"Why?"

"Because I want them to. That's all the explanation I can give right now."

"What do you want the dog to look for?"

"I don't know. Something that shouldn't be there."

She asked no further questions, and he already regretted not telling her more. It was too late now. They kept walking and she handed him a copy of the newspaper. It had a picture of "Louise" printed on the front page. He read the headline without stopping.

"Who's in charge of this?" he asked.

"Martinsson is organising and checking the leads as they come in."

"It's important that it's done right."

"Martinsson is very careful."

"Not always."

He heard how irritated and disapproving he sounded and knew there was no reason to take his tiredness out on her. But there was no one else around.

When all this is over I'll have to speak to her, he thought helplessly.

At that moment a jogger came towards them. Wallander reacted without a second thought by placing himself in the man's way.

"Haven't they sealed off the area? No one should be here except the police!"

The jogger was in his 30s and was wearing headphones. As he tried to run past, Wallander reached out to stop him. The jogger, thinking he was being attacked, hit back.

He caught Wallander on the side of his jaw. Wallander was taken by surprise and collapsed. When he got his bearings, Höglund had the man pinned to the ground with his arm twisted behind his back. The headphones had fallen onto the path, and Wallander heard to his surprise that the jogger had been listening to opera. Some officers came running down to help them and handcuffed the jogger. Wallander got up gingerly and felt his jaw. It hurt, and he had bitten the inside of his mouth, but his teeth were unharmed. He looked over at the jogger.

"The reserve has been sealed off," he said. "Did that fact escape you?"

"Sealed off?"

The man's surprise seemed genuine.

"Get his name," Wallander ordered. "Make sure the barriers are up. Then take him out and let him go."

"I'm going to report this," the jogger said angrily.

Wallander turned away and felt the inside of his mouth with a finger. Then he slowly turned back around to face him.

"What's your name?"

"Hagroth."

"What else?"

"Nils."

"And what is it you're going to report?"

"Excessive force. Here I am jogging peacefully and then I'm attacked without warning."

"You're wrong," Wallander said. "The person who was assaulted was me, not you. I'm a police officer and I was trying to stop you because you were inside a restricted area."

The jogger began to protest but Wallander lifted his hand. "You can get a year's jail time for assault of a police officer. It's a very serious offence. You're obliged to follow police orders and you were trespassing in a restricted area. You could get three years. Don't think you'll get away with a fine and a slap on the wrist. Do you have a previous criminal record?"

"Of course not."

"Then we'll say three years. But if you forget about this and stay away from here I'll think about letting it drop."

The jogger tried to protest again but once more Wallander's hand went up.

"You have ten seconds to make up your mind."

The jogger nodded.

"Take off the handcuffs," Wallander ordered. "See that you get him out of here and get his address."

Wallander continued walking up the path. His jaw hurt, but he was no longer tired.

"He wouldn't get three years," Höglund said.

"He doesn't know that," Wallander said. "And I don't think he's likely to go to any length to find out if it's true."

"I thought this was exactly the kind of thing the head of the national police wants us to avoid," she said. "Shaking the people's trust in the police."

"It'll be shaken more if we don't find whoever killed Boge, Norman and Hillström. Plus one of our colleagues."

When they finally arrived at the crime scene, Wallander poured coffee into a Styrofoam cup and went looking for Nyberg, who was supervising preparations for the dig. Nyberg's hair was standing on end, his eyes were bloodshot, and he was in a foul mood.

"I don't know why I'm the one who's suddenly in charge of this," he said. "Where the hell is everybody? Why is your face all bloody?"

Wallander felt his cheek with one hand. The corner of his mouth was bleeding.

"I got into a fight with a jogger," he said. "Hansson's on his way."

"A fight with a jogger?"

"It's a long story."

Wallander filled Höglund in on their conversation about where the bodies might be buried, and put her in charge of the search. He made some rapid calculations. With Höglund and Hansson at the crime scene, there was no reason for him to stay. If Martinsson was taking care of things back at the station, that meant Wallander could turn his attention to other tasks.

He dialled Martinsson's number. "I'm coming in," he told him. "Having Hansson and Ann-Britt here is enough."

"Any results?"

"It's too early for that. Have we heard anything from Lund?"

"I can try to call now."

"Good. Tell them it's urgent. What we really need is to establish a time of death. It would also be good to know who was killed first, if possible."

"Why is that important?"

"I don't know if it's important. But it's possible the killer was actually only after one of the three."

Martinsson promised to call Lund straight away.

Wallander put his phone back in his pocket. "I'm going back to Ystad," he told the others. "Let me know if you find anything."

He started walking back to the car and bumped into Edmundsson and his dog along the way. Höglund must already have made the call. Edmundsson had been equally swift.

"Did you fly him in?" Wallander asked, pointing at the dog.

"A colleague drove him in. What was it you wanted us to do?"

Wallander showed him the place and explained what he wanted. "If you find anything, you should let Nyberg know. When you're done, join the search up at the crime scene. They're looking for a place to start digging right now."

Edmundsson went pale. "Are there more bodies?" he asked.

His words jolted Wallander. He hadn't even considered this possibility, but he realised it was improbable.

"No," he said, "we don't expect to find more bodies, just a spot where they might have been buried for a while."

"Why would they have been buried?"

Wallander didn't answer. Edmundsson is right, he thought. Why would the killer hide the bodies? We've raised the question and tried to answer it, but it may turn out to be more important than we thought. He got into his car. His jaw still ached. He was about to start the engine when his phone rang. It was Martinsson.

He's got information from Lund, Wallander thought and felt a rising excitement.

"What did they say?"

"Who?"

"You haven't talked to Lund?"

"No, I haven't had time. I've just had a call."

Wallander could tell that Martinsson was worried, which was uncharacteristic.

Don't let it be someone else, he thought. Not more dead bodies. Not now.

"The hospital called," Martinsson said. "Isa Edengren has disappeared."

It was 8.03 a.m. on Monday, 12 August.

CHAPTER SIXTEEN

Wallander drove straight to the hospital, much too fast. Martinsson was waiting for him when he arrived. He left the car in a no-parking zone.

"What happened?"

Martinsson was carrying a notebook. "No one really knows," he said. "She must have left around dawn, but no one saw her leave."

"Did she call anyone? Did anyone come and pick her up?"

"It's hard to get a straight answer. There are so many patients in her ward, and almost no staff on night duty. But she must have left before 6 a.m. Someone came in at 4 a.m. and saw her sleeping."

"Which of course she wasn't," Wallander said. "She was waiting for the right moment to take off."

"Why?"

"I don't know."

"Do you think she'll try to kill herself again?"

"Possibly. But let's think this through. We tell her what happened to her friends and the next day she makes her escape. What does that mean?"

"That she's scared."

"Exactly. But what is she scared of?"

There was only one place Wallander could think of to start looking for her, and that was the house outside Skårby. He wanted Martinsson with him, if only so he wouldn't have to be alone. When they arrived in Skårby, they stopped first at Lundberg's house. The man was out in the yard inspecting his tractor. He looked surprised when two cars pulled into his driveway. Wallander introduced Martinsson.

"You called the hospital last night and were told that Isa was OK, all things considered. Sometime early this morning, between 4 a.m. and 6 a.m., she disappeared. Escaped. What time do you get up?"

"Early. My wife and I are up by 4.30 a.m."

"And Isa hasn't turned up?"

"No."

"Did you hear any cars go by early this morning?"

The answer was very firm. "Åke Nilsson, who lives up the road, went by at about 5 a.m. He works at the slaughterhouse three days a week. But apart from him there was no one."

Lundberg's wife appeared at the door. She had heard the last part of the conversation.

"Isa hasn't been here," she said. "And there haven't been any cars, either."

"Is there anywhere else she might have gone?" Martinsson asked.

"Not that we know of."

"If she contacts you, you'll have to let us know," Wallander said. "It's very important for us to find out where she is. Is that clear?"

"She never calls," the woman said.

Wallander was already on his way back to his car. They drove to the Edengrens' house. He put his hand into the drainpipe and pulled out the spare keys. Then he showed Martinsson the gazebo in the back of the house. Everything seemed as it had when he was last there. They returned to the main house and unlocked the door. The house looked even bigger from the inside. No expense had been spared on the interior decorating but the impression was chilly, like a museum. There were few traces of the inhabitants. They walked through the rooms on the first floor, then went upstairs to the bedrooms. A large model aeroplane was suspended from the ceiling of one of the bedrooms. There was a computer on a desk, and someone had thrown a sweater over it. It was probably Jörgen's room, the brother who had committed suicide. Wallander went into the bathroom and saw a plug by the mirror. Reluctantly he pointed it out to Martinsson. It was probably here that Isa's brother had died.

"I bet that doesn't happen every day," Martinsson said. "Who kills himself with a toaster?"

Wallander was already on his way out of the bathroom. Next door was another bedroom. When he entered he knew it was Isa's.

"We have to search this room," he said.

"What are we looking for?"

"I don't know. But Isa was supposed to have been out there with them in the nature reserve. She tried to commit suicide, and now she's run away. We both think she's scared."

Wallander sat down at her desk while Martinsson started going through the dresser and the large cupboard that took up a whole side of the room. The drawers in the desk were unlocked, which surprised him. But after going through them he realised there was no need for privacy. The drawers were almost completely empty. He frowned. Had someone emptied them? He picked up a green writing pad. Underneath it was a poorly executed watercolour. "*I.E. '95*" was written in the corner. The watercolour depicted a coastal landscape of sea and cliffs. He put the pad back.

In a bookshelf next to the bed were several rows of books. He recognised some that Linda had read. He felt along the back of the shelves and found two that had fallen behind the others or were concealed. Both of them were in English. One had the title *Journey to the Unknown* by someone called Timothy Neil. The other was called *How to Cast Yourself in the Play of Life* by Rebecka Stanford. The book covers looked similar, with geometric signs, numbers, and letters that seemed to be suspended in a universe of some kind. Wallander took the books with him back to the desk. They were well-thumbed. He put on his glasses and read the blurb on the back cover of the first book. Timothy Neil discussed the importance of following the spiritual map as revealed by people's dreams. Wallander made a face and put the book down. Rebecka Stanford in turn discussed what she referred to as "chronological dissolution". Something caught his attention. There seemed to be a discussion of how groups of people could control time and move back and forth through the ages. She seemed to be arguing that this technique was useful for "self-actualisation in a time of increased meaninglessness and confusion".

"Have you ever heard of an author by the name of Rebecka Stanford?" Wallander asked Martinsson, who was standing on a chair looking through the contents of the highest shelf in the cupboard. He got down and came over to look at the book, then shook his head.

"It must be a young person's book. You'd better ask Linda," he said.

Wallander nodded. Martinsson was right; he should ask Linda, who read a lot. During their holiday on Gotland he had been surprised by all the books she had brought with her. He hadn't recognised the name of even a single author.

Martinsson returned to the cupboard, and Wallander turned to the shelf beside the bed. There were some photo albums there, which he brought back to the desk. Inside were pictures of Isa and her brother. The colours had started to fade. In one, the two of them were standing on either side of a snowman. They both held themselves stiffly, looking unhappy. After this photograph were several pages of Isa by herself. School photographs, images of Isa and her friends in Copenhagen. Then some more of her with Jörgen. Here he was older, perhaps 15, and sombre. Whether his attitude was affected or genuine, Wallander couldn't tell. The approaching suicide could be read in the pictures, Wallander thought, but did he know it himself? Isa was smiling in these pictures, while Jörgen looked miserable. Next were shots of a coastal landscape. Wallander was reminded of the watercolour painting. On one of the pictures he read "Bärnsö, 1989." Wallander kept leafing through the pages. There were no photographs of the parents, just Jörgen and Isa, her friends, and landscape shots of the same coastline and small islands.

"Where is Bärnsö?" Wallander asked.

"Isn't it one of the islands that gets mentioned in the marine weather report?"

Wallander wasn't sure. He looked for a long time at a picture of Isa standing on a rock just below the waves. It almost looked like she was walking on water. Who had taken it? Martinsson suddenly whistled with surprise.

"You'd better take a look at this," he said.

Wallander got up quickly. Martinsson held a wig in his hand that looked like the ones Boge, Norman and Hillström had been wearing. There was a slip of paper attached to a strand of hair. Wallander carefully removed it. *Holmsted's Costume Rental*, he read. *Copenhagen*. There was an address and phone number. He turned the slip over and saw that the wig had been rented on 19 June, to be returned on the 28th.

"Should we give them a call right now?" Martinsson asked.

"Or visit them in person," Wallander said, thinking. "No, let's start by calling."

"You'd better do it," Martinsson said. "Danes never understand my Swedish."

"You're the one who doesn't understand them," Wallander said gently. "Since you never listen properly."

"I'll find out where Bärnsö is. Why did you want to know that?"

"I'm trying to figure that out myself," Wallander answered and dialled the number. A woman answered. He introduced himself and explained what he wanted to know. "The wig was rented by Isa Edengren, from Skårby, Sweden," he said.

"I'll check. Just a moment," she said.

Wallander waited. He could hear Martinsson asking someone for the number of the coast guard. The woman came back to the phone.

"There's no record of any rentals to Isa Edengren," she said. "Not on that day nor the days before."

"I'll give you another name to try," Wallander said.

"I'm the only person working here right now and I have some customers. Can it wait?"

"No. If you can't help me, I'll have to contact the Danish police."

She made no further protests and he gave her the other names – Martin Boge, Lena Norman and Astrid Hillström. Then he waited again. Martinsson sounded irritated. He didn't seem to be getting anywhere. The woman returned.

"Yes, that's right," she said. "Lena Norman came in and rented four wigs and some costumes on 19 June. It was all due back on 28 June but she hasn't shown up. We were just about to send off a reminder."

"Do you remember serving her? Was she alone?"

"My colleague was here that day. His name is Mr Sørensen."

"Can I talk to him?"

"He's on holiday until the end of August."

"Where is he?"

"He's on his way to the Antarctic."

"Where?"

"He's on his way to the South Pole. He's visiting some old Norwegian whale fishing stations along the way. Mr Sørensen's father was a whale fisherman. I think he was even the one who operated the harpoon."

"So there's no one at the shop who can identify Lena Norman, or tell me if she came in alone to rent the wigs?"

"No, I'm sorry. Of course, we would like to have them back. Otherwise we'll have to charge a replacement fee."

"It'll be a little while. They're involved in a case we're working on."

"Has anything happened?"

"You could say that, but I'll explain later. Please tell Mr Sørensen to contact the Ystad police as soon as he returns."

"I'll tell him. Wallander, was it?"

"Kurt Wallander."

Wallander hung up. So Lena Norman had been in Copenhagen. But had she gone there alone?

Martinsson came back into the room. "Bärnsö Island is off the coast of Östergötland," he said. "Or more precisely, it's part of the Gryt archipelago. There's also a Bärnsö way up north, but that's more of a reef."

Wallander told him about his conversation with the fancy dress shop in Copenhagen.

"We should talk to Lena Norman's parents," Martinsson said.

"I would have liked to wait a few days," Wallander said, "but I don't think that will be possible."

They both sat quietly for a moment, considering what lay ahead of them. At that moment they heard the front door open. They were both struck by the thought that it might be Isa Edengren. When they went to the top of the stairs, however, they saw Lundberg standing in the hall. When he caught sight of them he kicked off his boots and walked upstairs.

"Has Isa been in touch with you?" Wallander asked.

"No, it's something else. I don't mean to take up your time, but there was something you said when we were talking in the yard, about me calling the hospital to ask how Isa was."

"It was perfectly natural for you to want to know how she was doing."

Lundberg looked at Wallander with concern. "But that's just it. I didn't call, and neither did my wife. We didn't call to see how she was, although we should have."

Wallander and Martinsson exchanged glances.

"You didn't call?"

"No. Neither one of us."

"Is there another Lundberg who might have called?"

"Who would that be?"

Wallander looked thoughtfully at the man in front of him. There was no reason to doubt he was telling the truth. So someone else had called the hospital. Someone who knew that Isa was in close contact with the Lundbergs. Someone who also knew that she was there. But what had that person wanted to know? That Isa was getting better, or if she had died?

"I just don't understand. Who would pretend to be me?" Lundberg asked.

"You're the one who can best answer that question," Wallander said. "Who knew that Isa used to come to you when she had problems with her parents?"

"Everyone in the village knew," Lundberg said. "But I can't think of anyone who would have called and used my name."

"Someone could have seen the ambulance," Martinsson said. "Did no one call to ask what had happened?"

"Karin Persson called," Lundberg said. "She lives in the hollow down by the main road. She's very curious and keeps tabs on everyone. But I can't imagine she can make herself sound like a man on the phone."

"Was there no one else?"

"Åke Nilsson dropped by on his way back from work. He brought some pork chops. We told him what had happened, but he didn't even know Isa so he wouldn't have called."

"Anyone else?"

"The postman came by with some unexpected news. We won 300 kronor in the Lottery. He wanted to know if the Edengrens were home. We told him that Isa was in the hospital, but what reason would he have to call?"

"There was no one else?"

"No."

"You did the right thing in telling us about this," Wallander said firmly, ending the conversation. Lundberg went back down the stairs, pulled his boots back on and left.

"When I was out at the nature reserve last night,"

Wallander said, "I had the feeling that I was being watched by someone in the darkness. I thought I'd imagined it, but now I'm starting to wonder. This morning I even asked Edmundsson to examine the spot with his dog. Is someone keeping an eye on us?"

"I know what Svedberg would have said."

Wallander looked at Martinsson with surprise. "What would he have said?"

"It was something he said when we were working on the smuggling case, during the spring of 1988, if you remember. That we should stop from time to time and look back over our shoulders. Like the Indians."

"What would we see?"

"Someone who shouldn't be there."

"That would mean we should station men out here to keep watch over the house, in case someone decides to search Isa's room. Is that what you mean?"

"Something like that."

"There's no 'something' about it. You either think that's what we should do, or you don't."

"I'm just telling you what I think Svedberg would have said."

Wallander realised how tired he felt. His irritation lay just below the surface. He knew he should apologise to Martinsson, just as he should have explained himself to Höglund at the nature reserve. But he didn't.

They went back to Isa's room. The wig was lying on the desk next to Wallander's phone. He knelt down and looked under the bed, but found nothing. When he stood up he felt dizzy. He grabbed Martinsson's arm to steady himself.

"Don't you feel well?"

Wallander shook his head. "It's been years since I could

stay up this many nights in a row without really feeling it. It'll happen to you, too."

"We should ask Lisa for extra staff."

"She's already talked to me about it." Wallander said. "I told her we'd get back to her. Is there anything else we need to look at here?"

"I don't think so. There's nothing unusual in the cupboard."

"How about anything that seems to be missing? Anything that should be in a young woman's cupboard that isn't there?"

"Nothing that I can think of."

"Then let's get going."

It was close to 9.30 a.m. when they returned to their cars.

"I'll call Isa's parents myself," Wallander said. "The rest of you will have to take on Boge, Norman and Hillström's parents. I don't want to be responsible for what might happen if we don't get hold of Isa. They may know something, and so might the others in the photo that we found at Svedberg's flat."

"Do you think something's happened?"

"I don't know."

They drove away. Wallander thought back to the conversation with Lundberg. Who had made that call? He had a gnawing feeling that Lundberg had said something else that was important, but he couldn't think what it was. I'm tired, he thought. I don't listen to what people say and then I have the feeling that I missed something important.

When they arrived back at the station, they went off in separate directions. Ebba stopped him as he walked past the reception desk.

"Mona called you," she said.

Wallander came to a complete stop. "What did she want?"

"She didn't tell me."

Ebba gave him her phone number in Malmö. Wallander already knew it by heart, but Ebba was very thoughtful. She also handed him a number of other phone messages.

"Most of them are from reporters," she said consolingly. "You don't have to get back to them."

Wallander got some coffee and went into his office. He had just taken off his jacket and sat down when the phone rang. It was Hansson.

"There's nothing new to report," he said. "Just so you know."

"I want either you or Ann-Britt to come back to the station," Wallander said. "Martinsson and I can't quite keep up with everything that has to be done. For example, who's in charge of searching for the cars?"

"I am. I'm working on it. Has anything happened?"

"Isa Edengren escaped from the hospital this morning. It worries me."

"Which one of us would you rather have?"

Wallander would have preferred Höglund. She was a better police officer than Hansson. But he didn't say so.

"It doesn't matter. Just one of you."

He hung up and dialled Mona's number in Malmö. Every time she called, which wasn't often, he feared that something had happened to Linda. She answered on the second ring. Wallander always felt a twinge of sorrow when he heard her voice. Was it his imagination or was the feeling getting weaker? He wasn't sure.

"I hope I'm not bothering you," she said. "How are you?"

"I'm the one who called you," he said. "I'm fine."

"You sound tired."

"I am tired. You've probably seen in the papers that one of my colleagues is dead. Svedberg. Do you remember him?"

"Barely."

"What did you want?"

"I wanted to tell you that I'm going to get married again."

Wallander was quiet. For a moment he nearly hung up, but he stayed as he was, speechless.

"Are you there?"

"Yes," he said. "I'm still here."

"I'm telling you that I'm getting remarried."

"Who to?"

"Clas-Henrik. Who else would it be?"

"Should you really be marrying a golfer?"

"That's not a very nice thing to say."

"Then I should apologise. Does Linda know?"

"I wanted to tell you first."

"I don't know what to say. Perhaps I should congratulate you."

"That would be nice. We don't have to continue this conversation. I just wanted you to know."

"Why the hell would I want to know? What the hell do I care about you and your fucking golfer?"

Wallander was enraged. He didn't know exactly where it came from. Perhaps it was the tiredness, or the last remnant of pain at realising that now Mona was leaving him for good. The first time he had felt such pain was when she told him she wanted to leave him. And now, when she told him she was getting married again, he discovered that it was still there.

He slammed down the phone so hard that it broke. Martinsson was walking into his office as it happened, and he jumped when the receiver fell apart. Wallander pulled the phone out of the jack and threw the whole mess in the rubbish. Martinsson watched this, obviously afraid to incur Wallander's wrath. He raised his hands up in front of his chest and turned to leave.

"What did you want?"

"It can wait."

"My anger is a private matter," Wallander said. "Tell me what you want."

"I'm going to see Norman's family. I thought I'd start with them. Lillemor Norman may know where Isa has gone."

Wallander nodded. "Either Hansson or Ann-Britt will be in soon. Tell them to take care of the other families."

Martinsson nodded, then remained in the doorway. "You'll need a new phone," he said. "I'll see to it."

Wallander didn't answer. He waved for Martinsson to leave. He didn't know how long he sat there doing nothing. Once more he'd been forced to face the fact that Mona was still the woman he was closest to in his life. It was only when someone showed up at his door with a new phone that he got up and left. Without knowing why, he ended up wandering down the hall and coming to a halt outside Svedberg's office. The door was open slightly and he looked in. The sun coming in through the window revealed a thin layer of dust on the desk. Wallander closed the door and sat down in Svedberg's chair.

Höglund had already gone through all his papers. She was very thorough. It would be a waste of time to go over them again. Then he remembered that, like all of them, Svedberg had a locker in the basement. Höglund had probably checked it, but she had never mentioned having done so. Wallander went out to the reception area and asked Ebba for the keys.

"His spare keys are right here," she said with obvious distaste.

Wallander took them and was about to leave when she stopped him.

"When is the funeral going to be?"

"I don't know."

"It's not going to be easy."

"At least we don't have to face a widow and crying children," said Wallander. "But you're right. It's not going to be easy."

He went down the stairs and found Svedberg's locker. He didn't know what he was looking for; there was probably nothing to find. There were some towels, soap and a shampoo bottle, for Svedberg's Friday night saunas. There was also a pair of old trainers. Wallander felt with his hand along the top shelf. There was a thin plastic folder containing some papers. He took it out, put on his glasses, and looked through it. Inside was a reminder from Svedberg's mechanic to bring his car in for a tune. There were some handwritten notes that looked like shopping lists. But there were also some ticket stubs for the bus and the train. On 19 July Svedberg, or somebody, had taken the morning train to Norrköping. He had returned to Ystad on 22 July. He could tell from the way that the ticket was stamped that it had been used. The stubs from the bus were very blurry. He held them up to the light but couldn't read them. With the help of a magnifying glass he could just decipher the price and the words "Östgöta Public Transit". He called Ylva Brink, who was at home for once, but she had no idea what Svedberg would be doing in Östergötland. He had no family there as far as she knew.

"Maybe this Louise person lives there," she said. "Have you found out who she is yet?"

"Not yet, but you may be right."

Wallander got another cup of coffee. His mind kept returning to his conversation with Mona. He still couldn't comprehend how she could marry that skinny little golfer who supported himself by importing sardines. He returned to his office and kept staring at the ticket stubs. Suddenly he froze, the cup halfway to his mouth.

He should have thought of it at once. What was that island in Isa Edengren's photo album called? Bärnsö? Hadn't Martinsson said that Bärnsö was off the coast of Östergötland? He put the coffee cup down so roughly that some of the liquid spilled, and tried out his new phone by calling Martinsson.

"Where are you?"

"I'm having coffee with Lillemor Norman. Her husband will be home soon."

Wallander could hear from Martinsson's voice that the visit was difficult.

"I want you to ask her something," he said. "Now, while I'm still on the line. I want to know if she's heard of an island called Bärnsö, and if she knows of any connection between the island and Isa Edengren."

"Just that?"

"Just that. Do it now."

While Wallander was waiting, Höglund appeared in the doorway. Perhaps Hansson had sensed that Wallander would rather have her with him. She pointed to his coffee cup and disappeared. Martinsson came back on the phone.

"Well, that was unexpected," he said. "She says that the Edengrens not only have houses in Spain and France, but also one on Bärnsö Island."

"Good," Wallander said. "Finally things are starting to make some sense."

"Wait, there's more. Apparently the others have been there with her many times. Lena Norman, Boge and Hillström."

"I know someone else who's been out there," Wallander said.

"Who?"

"Svedberg. Between 19 and 22 July."

"What the hell? How do you know that?"

"I'll tell you when you get here. Now go back to what you were doing."

Wallander hung up, carefully this time. Höglund came in again. She sensed at once that something was up.

CHAPTER SEVENTEEN

Wallander was right. It had not occurred to Höglund to go down into the basement and look through Svedberg's things. He couldn't help feeling a sense of satisfaction that she had missed this. He thought of her as good at her job. But the fact that she had forgotten about the storage locker meant she wasn't infallible.

They quickly compared notes. Isa Edengren was gone. Wallander wanted the search for her to be their top priority. Höglund encouraged him to spell out what he thought might have happened to Isa. He couldn't get past the facts. Isa was supposed to have been at that party. She had tried to commit suicide. And now she had run away.

"There's a possibility we haven't considered," Höglund said. "Although it's unpleasant and rather improbable."

Wallander sensed what she was thinking. "You mean the possibility that Isa killed her friends? I've considered that, but she was genuinely ill on Midsummer's Eve."

"If that's when it really happened," Höglund said. "We still don't know that for sure."

Wallander knew she was right. "In that case we have even more reason to try to find her as soon as possible. We also shouldn't forget that someone called for her at the hospital posing as Lundberg."

She left his office to visit the Hillström and Boge families, as well as the young people from the photograph they'd found in Svedberg's flat. She promised that she'd ask about Bärnsö Island. Nyberg called just after she had gone. Wallander immediately thought they must have located the place where the bodies had been buried.

"Not yet," Nyberg said. "This process can take a long time. I'm calling because we've received some information on the gun that was found in Svedberg's flat."

Wallander reached for a notebook.

"The national register is a blessing," Nyberg continued. "The gun that was used to kill Svedberg was stolen two years ago in Ludvika."

"Ludvika?"

"The report was filed on the 19 February 1994 to the Ludvika police. It was handled by an officer called Wester. The man who reported the gun stolen was Hans-Åke Hammarlund. He was an avid hunter who kept all his weapons securely locked up in accordance with the law. On 18 February, he went into Falun on business. That night someone broke into his house. His wife, who was sleeping in an upstairs bedroom, didn't hear anything. When Hammarlund returned from Falun the next day, he discovered that a number of his guns were missing and filed the report the same day. The shotgun was a Lambert Baron, a Spanish make. The numbers match perfectly. None of the missing guns ever turned up, nor were they ever able to identify any suspects."

"So other weapons were stolen as well?"

"The intruder left behind a very valuable shotgun designed for shooting elk, but took two revolvers, or rather one pistol and one revolver. It's not clear from the report how the intruder entered the property, but I take it you understand what this may mean?"

"That one of the other weapons might have been the

one used in the nature reserve? Yes, we'll have to get that question answered as soon as possible."

"Ludvika is in the Dalarna region," Nyberg said. "That's quite far away from here, but weapons have a way of turning up where you least expect them."

"You don't think Svedberg stole the gun that was used to kill him?"

"When it comes to stolen weapons, the connections are rarely so straightforward," Nyberg replied. "Weapons are stolen, sold, used and resold. I think there may have been a very long chain of owners before this shotgun ended up in Svedberg's flat."

"It's still important," Wallander said. "I feel as though I'm trying to navigate through thick fog."

Nyberg promised to make the identification of the stolen guns a priority. Wallander was leaning over his notebook, trying to make an outline of recent events, when the phone rang again. This time it was Dr Göransson.

"You didn't come to your appointment this morning," he said sternly.

"I'm sorry," Wallander said. "I don't have much of an excuse."

"I know you're very busy. The papers are full of this terrible crime. I worked at a hospital in Dallas for a few years, and I think the headlines in the Ystad papers are getting frighteningly like those in Texas."

"We're working around the clock," Wallander said. "It's just the way it is."

"I still think you'll have to give your health a little of your time," Göransson said. "A mismanaged case of diabetes is no laughing matter."

Wallander told him about the blood test he had had in the hospital.

"That just emphasises what I'm saying. We have to do a complete check-up on you to see how well your liver, kidneys and pancreas are functioning. I really don't think it can wait any longer."

Wallander knew he'd have to go in. They decided that he would return the following morning at 8 a.m. He promised to come in on an empty stomach and to bring a urine sample.

Wallander hung up and pushed the notebook away. He saw clearly how badly he had been abusing his body these last few years. It had started when Mona told him she wanted a divorce, almost seven years ago. He was still tempted to blame her for it, but he knew deep down that it was his own doing.

He stared at the notebook for a moment longer, then started looking for the Edengrens. He checked the coun try codes in the phone book and saw that Isa Edengren's mother had been in Spain when he had talked to her last. He dialled the number again and waited. He was about to hang up when a man answered.

Wallander introduced himself. "I heard that you had called. I'm Isa's father."

He sounded as though he regretted this last fact, which enraged Wallander.

"I expect you're in the middle of making your arrangements to come home and take care of Isa," he said.

"Actually, no. It doesn't sound as if there's any immediate danger."

"How do you know that?"

"I spoke to the hospital."

"Did you say that your name was Lundberg when you made this call?"

"Why would I have done that?"

"It was just a question."

"Do you really have nothing better to do with your time than ask idiotic questions?"

"Oh, I do," Wallander said and stopped trying to conceal his anger. "For example, I may very well contact the Spanish police to enlist their aid in getting you on the next flight home."

It wasn't true, of course, but Wallander had had enough of the Edengrens' indifference towards their daughter in spite of their son's suicide. He wondered how people could have such a total absence of affection for their children.

"I find your tone insulting."

"Three of Isa's friends have been murdered," Wallander said. "Isa was supposed to have been with them when it happened. I'm talking about murder here, and you're going to cooperate with me or I'm going to go to the Spanish authorities. Am I making myself clear?"

The man seemed to hesitate. "What is it that's happened?"

"As far as I know, they sell Swedish papers in Spain. Can you read?"

"What the hell do you mean by that?"

"Exactly what I just said. You have a summer house on Bärnsö Island. Does Isa have the keys to it, or do you lock her out of that house, too?"

"She has the keys."

"Is there a phone on the island?"

"We use our mobile phones."

"Does Isa have one?"

"Doesn't everybody?"

"What's her number?"

"I don't know. I'm really not sure whether she has one."

"So which is it? Does she have a phone or not?"

"She has never asked me for money to buy one, and she couldn't afford one. She doesn't work, she doesn't do anything to try to get a grip on her life."

"Do you think it's possible that Isa has gone to Bärnsö? Does she often go there?"

"I thought she was still in the hospital."

"She's run away."

"Why?"

"We don't know. Is it possible that she would have gone to Bärnsö?"

"It's possible."

"How do you get there?"

"You take a boat from Fyrudden."

"Does she have access to a boat?"

"The one we have is currently being serviced in Stockholm."

"Are there any neighbours on the island I could get in touch with?"

"No, we're the only house on the island."

Wallander had been taking notes as they talked. For the moment he couldn't think of anything else to ask.

"You'll have to stay close to the phone so I can get hold of you," he said. "Is there any other place you can think of where Isa may have gone?"

"No."

"If you think of anything, you know where to reach me."

Wallander gave him the phone numbers to the station and his mobile phone, then hung up. His hands were damp with sweat. It was already past lunchtime, and Wallander ached from hunger and a headache. He ordered a pizza that arrived after 30 minutes, and ate it at his desk. Nyberg hadn't called back, and he wondered briefly if he should drive out to the nature reserve, but then decided against it. He wouldn't be able to speed anything up. Nyberg knew what he was doing. He wiped his mouth, threw out the pizza box, and went out to the men's room to wash his hands. Then he left the station, crossed the road, and started walking up towards the water tower. There he sat down in the shade and concentrated on a thought that kept returning to him.

His worst fear, that Svedberg was the one who killed the three young people, had started to fade. Svedberg was on the side of the pursuers in this case, still a little ahead of Wallander. It would be a while until they caught him up.

Svedberg could not be the murderer because he had been killed, too. Wallander's worst fear was starting to leave him, only to be replaced by another. Someone was observing their investigation, someone who kept himself very well informed. Wallander knew that he was right about this, even though he couldn't yet see how it all hung together.

The person who had killed Svedberg and killed the three young people had some means of access to the information he required. The Midsummer's Eve party was planned in complete secrecy and yet someone else knew about it, someone who realised that Svedberg was closing in on him.

Svedberg must simply have got too close, Wallander thought, without realising that he had wandered into forbidden territory. That was why he was murdered. There is no other reasonable explanation.

He could make sense of events up to this point, but beyond it the questions piled up one on top of the other. Why was the telescope at Björklund's house? Why had someone sent postcards from all over Europe?

I have to find Isa, he thought. I have to get her to tell

me what she doesn't even know she knows. And I have to follow in Svedberg's footsteps. What had he discovered that we still haven't seen? Or did he have access to some information from the very beginning that we don't have?

Wallander thought briefly about Louise, the woman in Svedberg's life, whom he had kept secret. There was still something about her picture that disturbed him, although he couldn't put his finger on it. The feeling was strong enough that he knew he mustn't give up on it, that he must bide his time. It occurred to him that there was a similarity between the young people in the reserve and Svedberg. They had all had secrets. Was this also significant?

Wallander got up and walked back to the police station. His body still ached from the hours he had spent sleeping curled up on the back seat of his car. His biggest anxiety still lay at the back of his mind – the fear that the killer would strike again.

When he got to the station he realised what he had to do. He had to drive up to Bärnsö and see if Isa Edengren was there. He had to choose between all the important tasks that lay before him. The most important was to find her.

Time was running out. He returned to his office and managed to get in touch with Martinsson, who had finally left the Norman family's home.

"Has anything happened?" Martinsson asked.

"Not nearly enough. Why haven't we heard anything from the pathologist? We're helpless until we have a time of death. Why aren't we getting any good leads? Where are the missing cars? We have to talk. Get here as soon as you can."

While they were waiting for Höglund, Wallander and

259

Martinsson called the young people in Svedberg's photograph. It turned out that they had all visited Isa on Bärnsö at one time or another. Martinsson spoke to the pathologist in Lund and was told that no results were available yet, either for the Svedberg case or the three young people. Wallander worked through a list of the leads that had come in from the general public. Nothing looked significant. The strangest thing was that no one had called to say they recognised the woman they were calling Louise. It was the first thing Wallander brought up with his colleagues in one of the smaller conference rooms. He put the photograph of her on the projector again.

"Someone must recognise her," he said. "Or at least think they do. But no one has called in."

"The picture has only been out there a few hours," Martinsson said.

Wallander dismissed this explanation. "It's one thing to ask people to recall an event," he said. "That can take time. But this is a face."

"Perhaps she's foreign?" Höglund suggested. "Even if she only lives in Denmark. Who bothers to read the Skåne papers over there? The photo won't be published in the national papers until tomorrow."

"You might be right," Wallander said, thinking of Sture Björklund, who commuted between Hedeskoga and Copenhagen. "We'll get in touch with the Danish police."

They looked at the picture of Louise for a long time.

"I can't escape the feeling that there's something unusual about her," Wallander said. "I just don't know what it is."

No one could say what it was. Wallander turned off the projector.

"I'm going up to Östergötland tomorrow," he said. "It's

possible that Isa might have gone there. We have to find her and we have to get her to talk."

"What exactly do you think she can tell us? She wasn't there when it happened."

Wallander knew that Martinsson's objection was reasonable. He wasn't sure that he could give him a good answer. There were so many gaps, so many thoughts that were closer to vague assumption than firm opinion.

"She is a witness, in a way," he said. "We're convinced that this is not a crime of opportunity. Svedberg's murder may still turn out to be just that, although I doubt it, but the deaths of these young people were well planned. The crucial thing here is that they made their own arrangements in secret, but someone else seems to have had access to that information – what they were thinking, where they were going to meet, perhaps even the exact time. Someone was spying on them. Someone managed to find out what they were up to. If it turns out that the bodies were buried fairly close to the place where they were killed, then we'll know this for sure. Holes don't dig themselves. Isa was part of these elaborate preparations. But she fell ill at the moment when everything was to begin. If she had been able to go, she would have. Her illness saved her life. And she is the one who can help us find out what happened that night. Somewhere along the way, without their realising it, she and the others crossed paths with the person who decided to take their lives."

"Is that what you think Svedberg believed?" Martinsson asked.

"Yes. But he knew something else as well. Or at least suspected it. We don't know how this suspicion arose in the first place, or why he conducted his whole investigation in secret. But it must have been important. He dedicated his entire holiday to it. He insisted on taking all of his holiday time. He had never done that before."

"Something's still missing," Höglund said. "And that's a motive. Revenge, hatred, jealousy. It doesn't add up. Who would've wanted to murder three young people? Or four, for that matter. Who could've hated them? Who had reason to be jealous? There's a brutality to this crime that goes beyond anything I've ever seen. It's worse than the case involving the poor boy who dressed up as an Indian."

"He may have chosen this party deliberately," Wallander said. "Although it's almost too terrible to imagine, he could have chosen his moment precisely because their joy was at its peak. Think how alone people can feel over Midsummer."

"In that case we're dealing with a madman," Martinsson said, visibly upset.

"A methodical and deliberate madman, yes," Wallander said. "But the important thing is to try to find the invisible common denominator in these crimes. The murderer got his information from some source. He must have had access to their lives. That's the key we're after. We have to look thoroughly into their lives. We'll find this point of intersection. We may already have come across it and not seen it."

"So you think Isa Edengren should be our focus," Höglund said. "In a way you think she's leading this investigation, and we're carefully following in her footsteps."

"Something like that. We can't overlook the fact that she tried to kill herself. We have to find out why. We also don't know how the killer feels about the fact that she survived."

"You're thinking about the person who called the hospital and pretended to be Lundberg," Martinsson said.

Wallander nodded. "I want one of you to talk to whoever took that call. Find out what the caller sounded like. Was he old or young? What dialect did he speak? Anything could turn out to be important."

Martinsson promised to take on this task. For the next hour they went over what else had to be covered. At one point Holgersson came in to talk about the arrangements for Svedberg's funeral.

"Does anyone know what kind of music he liked?" she asked.

"Strangely enough, Ylva Brink says she has no idea."

Wallander realised to his surprise that he had no idea either. Holgersson left again, after he had given her an update on the investigation.

"I wish we could know what exactly happened and why when we attend his funeral," Martinsson said.

"I doubt we will," Wallander said. "But that's what we'd all like."

It was 5 p.m. They were about to leave when the phone rang. It was Ebba.

"Please, no reporters," Wallander said.

"It's Nyberg. It sounds important."

Wallander felt a twinge of excitement. There was a hiss of static, then Nyberg's voice came on.

"I think we were right."

"Have you found the spot?"

"That's what we think. We're taking pictures now, and we're trying to see if we can get a footprint."

"Were we right about the location?"

"This is about 80 metres from where they were found. It's a very well selected spot. It's surrounded by thick shrub-bery and no one would choose to walk through it."

"When are you going to start digging?"

"I was going to see if you wanted to come and take a look at it first."

"I'm on my way."

Wallander hung up. "They think they've found the place where the bodies were buried," he said.

They quickly decided that Wallander would go out there alone. The others had a number of tasks to take care of as soon as possible.

When he got to the nature reserve, he drove his car past the roadblocks all the way up to the crime scene. A forensic technician was waiting for him, and escorted him to a spot where Nyberg had cordoned off an area of about 30 square metres. Wallander saw at once that the spot was well chosen, just as he had said. He crouched down beside Nyberg, who started to point things out to him.

"The ground over here has been dug up," he said. "Clumps of grass have been taken out and replanted. If you look over there under the leaves you'll see dirt that's been swept aside. If you dig a hole and fill it with something else, there'll be earth left over."

Wallander brushed his hand along the ground. "It's been carefully done."

Nyberg nodded. "It's very precise," he said. "He didn't take any shortcuts. We would never have noticed this place without having set out to look for it."

Wallander got up. "Let's dig it up," he said. "We've got no time to lose."

The work went slowly. Nyberg directed the others. It was beginning to get dark by the time the first layer of earth had been removed. Spotlights were set up around the site. The earth underneath the sod was porous and came out easily. As they removed it, a rectangular hole became visible. By this time it was after 9 p.m. Holgersson had come out with Höglund and they watched in silence. By the time Nyberg was satisfied, Wallander knew what he was looking at. The rectangular hole in front of him was a grave.

They gathered in a semicircle around the edge.

"It's big enough," Nyberg said.

"Yes," Wallander said. "It's big enough. Even for four bodies."

He shivered. For the first time they were following closely in the killer's tracks. They had been right. Nyberg kneeled next to the hole.

"There's nothing here," he said. "It's possible that the bodies were sealed in airtight body bags. If there was also a tarpaulin tucked in around them under the sod, I doubt that even Edmundsson's dog would pick up anything. But of course we'll go over it, down to the last tiny speck of dirt."

Wallander walked back up to the main path with Holgersson and Höglund.

"What is this killer doing?" Holgersson asked, distaste and fear in her voice.

"I don't know," Wallander said. "But at least we have a survivor."

"Isa Edengren?"

Wallander didn't answer. He didn't need to. They all knew what he meant. The grave had been intended for her as well.

CHAPTER EIGHTEEN

At 5 a.m. on Tuesday, 13 August, Wallander left Ystad, deciding to drive along the coast, through Kalmar. He was already at Sölvesborg when he realised he had forgotten his promise to visit Dr Göransson at the clinic that morning. He pulled over by the side of the road and called Martinsson. It was just past 7 a.m. Wallander told him about the doctor's appointment and asked Martinsson to call and give an excuse.

"Tell him an urgent matter called me out of town," Wallander said.

"Are you sick?" Martinsson asked.

"It's a routine check-up," Wallander told him. "That's all."

Afterwards, when he had pulled back out onto the road, it occurred to him that Martinsson must have wondered why he didn't call Dr Göransson himself. Wallander asked himself the same question. Why couldn't he tell people that he had in all likelihood developed diabetes? He was having trouble making sense of his own actions.

He was thirsty, and his body ached. When he passed a roadside café he stopped and had breakfast. On the way out he bought two bottles of mineral water. He made it to Kalmar by 9 a.m. The phone rang. It was Höglund, who was going to help him with directions once he reached Östergötland.

"I talked to a colleague in Valdemarsvik," she said. "I

thought it would be best to make it sound like a personal favour."

"Good idea," Wallander said. "Police officers don't tend to like it when you trespass on their territory."

"Especially not you," she said with a laugh. She was right. He didn't like having police officers from other districts in Ystad.

"How do I get out to the island?" he asked.

"That depends on where you are right now. Are you far away?"

"I've just passed Kalmar. Västervik is 100 kilometres away, and then it's about another hundred after that."

"Then it'll be tight."

"What do you mean?"

"My contact in Valdemarsvik suggested that you take the post boat, but it leaves Fyrudden between 11 a.m. and 11.30."

"Is there no other way?"

"Oh, I'm sure there is. But you'll have to organise that once you get to the dock."

"I may be able to do that. Can't someone call the post office and tell them I'm on my way? Where does the post get sorted? In Norrköping?"

"I'm looking at a map right now," she said. "I think it would have to be in Gryt, if there's even a post office there."

"Where's that?"

"Between Valdemarsvik and Fyrudden harbour. Don't you even have a map with you?"

"Unfortunately I left it on my desk."

"Let me call you back," she said. "But I really think the best thing would be for you to go out with the post boat. If my colleague is right, it's the easiest way for people to get out to the islands. Those that don't have their own

267

boats, of course, or anyone who's willing to come and get them."

Wallander understood what she meant.

"Good thinking," he said. "You mean that Isa Edengren may have taken the post boat herself?"

"It was just an idea."

Wallander thought for a moment. "But do you really think she made it up there by 11 a.m. if she left the hospital at 6 a.m.?"

"She may have," Höglund replied. "If she had a car, and Isa Edengren does have her licence. And we mustn't forget that she could have left the hospital as early as 4 a.m."

She promised to call him back. Wallander increased his speed. The traffic was getting heavier and there were a number of cars with trailers on the road. They reminded him that it was still summer, and holiday time. For a moment he considered turning on his police light, but decided against it. Instead he continued to increase his speed.

Höglund called him back after 20 minutes.

"I was right," she said. "The post gets sorted in Gryt. I even talked to the captain of the post boat. He sounded very nice."

"What was his name?"

"I didn't catch it. But he'll wait for you until midday. Otherwise he can come and get you later in the afternoon but I think that will cost you more."

"I was planning to write this trip off to expenses," Wallander said. "But I'll get there before midday."

"There's a car park next to the wharf," she said. "And the post boat is just across from it."

"Do you have his phone number?"

Wallander pulled over to the side of the road and wrote

268

down the number. As he sat there he was passed by a lorry he had finally managed to overtake a little earlier.

It was 11.40 a.m. when Wallander drove down the hill towards Fyrudden harbour. He found a car park and then walked out onto the pier. There was a soft wind. The harbour was full of boats. A man in his 50s was loading the last of his boxes into a large motorboat. Wallander hesitated, having imagined that the post boat would look different. He had even expected a flag bearing the post office logo. The man, who had just set down a crate of soda water, looked at Wallander.

"Are you the one going out to Bärnsö?"

"That's me."

The man stepped onto the dock and reached out his hand. "Lennart Westin."

"I'm sorry I'm a little late."

"Oh, there's no hurry."

"I don't know if the woman who called told you but I have to get back somehow, either later this afternoon or tonight."

"You aren't spending the night?"

The situation was starting to get confusing. Wallander didn't even know if Höglund had told him that he was a policeman.

"I should tell you I'm a detective with the Ystad homicide unit," Wallander said and got out his identification. "I'm working on a particularly difficult and unpleasant case at the moment."

This postman called Westin was a fast thinker.

"Is it that case involving the young people that I read about in the paper? Wasn't there a police officer killed, too?"

Wallander nodded.

"I thought I recognised them from the picture in the paper," Westin said. "At least one of them. I had the feeling I had given them a ride a year or so ago."

"With Isa?"

"Yes, that's right. They were with her. I think it was late autumn a couple of years ago. There was a storm coming in from the southwest. I wasn't sure we could pull up to the Bärnsö landing. It's a particularly exposed spot when the wind is blowing from that direction. But we made it. One of their bags fell in the water, and we managed to fish it out. That's why I remember. But you should never be too sure of your memory."

"I think you're probably right," Wallander said. "Have you seen Isa recently? Today or the day before?"

"No."

"Does she normally catch a ride out with you?"

"When her parents are out here, they collect her. Otherwise she gets a ride with me."

"So she's not here now?"

"If she is, she went out with someone else."

"Who would that have been?"

Westin shrugged. "There are always people around out here who would be willing to give her a ride. Isa knows whom to call. But I think she would have asked me first."

Westin glanced at his watch. Wallander hurried back to his car to get the little bag he had packed. Then he got on the boat. Westin pointed to the map beside the steering wheel.

"I could take you directly to Bärnsö but that would be out of my way," he said. "Are you in a hurry? If we go to Bärnsö on my regular route we'll be there in an hour. I have three other stops first."

"That's fine."

"When do you want me to pick you up?"

Wallander thought for a moment. Isa was most likely not on the island. He had drawn the wrong conclusion, which was a disappointment. But now that he was here he might as well search the house. He would probably need a couple of hours.

"You don't need to make up your mind right now," Westin said and gave him his card. "You can reach me over the phone. I can either come by this afternoon or this evening. I live on an island that's not too far away."

He pointed it out on the map.

"I'll call you," Wallander said and put the card away.

Westin started both the engines and set off.

"How long have you been delivering the post?" Wallander asked. He had to shout to make himself heard above the engine noise.

"Too long," Westin shouted back. "More than 25 years now."

"What do you do in the winter?"

"Hydrocopter."

Wallander felt his exhaustion lifting. The speed, the experience of being out on the water, gave him a surprising sense of well-being. When had he last felt like this? Perhaps during those days with Linda on Gotland. He knew it must be hard work delivering the post in the archipelago. But right now all suggestion of storms and autumn darkness seemed far away. Westin looked over at him, as if he knew what he was thinking.

"Maybe that would be something for me," he said. "Being a policeman."

Normally Wallander rushed to defend his profession. But here with Westin, as they sped across the smooth surface of the water, the familiar topic coaxed a different response from him.

"Sometimes I have my doubts," he shouted. "But when you reach 50 you're kind of on your own. Most doors are closed."

"I turned 50 this spring," Westin said. "Everyone I know out here threw a big party."

"How many people out here do you know?"

"Everyone. It was a big party."

Westin turned the wheel and slowed the boat down. Right next to a big cliff there was a red boathouse and a pier built out over a row of old stone structures.

"Båtmansö Island," Westin said. "When I was a child there were nine families living out here – more than 30 people. Now there are people out here over the summer, but come winter there's only one. His name is Zetterquist and he's 93 years old, but he still makes it through the winter. He's been widowed three times. He's the kind of old man you don't meet any more. I think the national board of health must have outlawed them."

His last remark took Wallander by surprise and made him laugh.

"Was he a fisherman?"

"He's been a jack-of-all-trades. He worked on a tugboat once upon a time."

"You know everybody. And they all know you?"

"That's the way it goes. If this old chap didn't show up to meet my boat, I'd go up and see if he was sick, or if he'd had a fall. If you're a country postman, either at sea or on land, you end up knowing everybody's business. What they're doing, where they're going, when they're due back. Whether or not you actually want to."

Westin had brought the boat softly alongside the

landing, and now he unloaded a couple of boxes. Quite a few people had gathered on the pier. Westin took the packet of post and walked up to a small red house.

Wallander stretched his legs on the pier, looking at a pile of old-fashioned stone sinkers. The air was cooler. Westin came back after a couple of minutes and they left. Their route took them through the varied landscape of the archipelago. After two more post stops, they approached Bärnsö. They came out on an open stretch of sea called Vikfjärden. Bärnsö lay strangely isolated, as if it had been thrown out of the community of islands.

"You must know the whole Edengren family," Wallander said, when Westin had pulled back the throttle and they were gliding towards the little dock.

"I suppose you could say that," Westin said. "Although I haven't had much contact with the parents. Honestly speaking, I think they're rather snobbish. But Isa and Jörgen have caught a ride with me many times."

"You know that Jörgen is dead," Wallander said carefully.

"I heard he was in a car accident," Westin said. "His father told me. I had to collect him once when there was something wrong with their boat."

"It's tragic when children die," Wallander said.

"I had always thought Isa was the one who would have an accident."

"Why is that?"

"She lives her life to the extreme. At least, if you believe what she says."

"She talks to you? Maybe as a postman you become something of a confidant."

"Hell, no," Westin said. "My son is Isa's age. They were together for a while a couple of summers ago. But it ended, like these things often do at that age."

The boat hit the edge of the pier. Wallander took his bag and got off.

"I'll give you a call this afternoon."

"I eat at 6 p.m.," Westin answered. "Before or after is fine."

Wallander watched the boat disappear around the point. He thought about how Westin had described Jörgen's death. His parents had changed the story. A toaster in the bath had become a car accident.

Wallander walked onto the green, lush island. Next to the dock was a boathouse and a small guest house. It reminded him of the gazebo in Skårby where he had found Isa. An old wooden rowing boat lay turned over on some trestles. Wallander caught a faint whiff of tar. Several large oak trees grew on the hillside leading up to the main house. It was a red two-storey house, old but in good condition. Wallander walked up to it, looking around and listening. There was a sailing boat in the distance, and the dying sound of an outboard motor. Wallander was sweating. He put the bag down, took his coat off and threw it over the railing of the front steps. The curtains were drawn in the windows. He went up the steps and knocked on the door. He waited. Then he banged on it with his fist. No one answered. He felt the handle. It was locked. For a moment he hesitated, then he walked around the back, feeling as though he was repeating his visit to Skårby. There was a garden with fruit trees behind the house – apples, plums and a lone cherry tree. Garden furniture was piled up under a plastic sheet.

A path led away from the house towards the thick woods. Wallander started walking down the path, and came to an old well and an earth cellar. The numbers 1897 were carved into the rock above the door, and the key was in the lock.

Wallander opened the door. It was dark and cool inside, and there was a smell of potatoes. When his eyes became accustomed to the dark he saw that it was empty. He closed the door and continued along the path, catching glimpses of the sea on his left. From the position of the sun he knew he was walking northwards. After about a kilometre he came to a junction where a smaller path led off to the left. He kept walking straight ahead, and after a couple of hundred metres came to the end. Ahead of him were smooth boulders and cliffs. Beyond them, just the open sea. It was the tip of the island. A seagull squawked above him, rising and falling on the wind. He climbed out onto the rocks, sat down, and wiped the sweat from his forehead, wishing that he'd brought some water with him. Gone were all thoughts of Svedberg and the dead young people.

He got up after a while and walked back. At the junction he took the smaller path, which led to a small, natural harbour. Some rusty iron rings were bolted into the rock face. The water was like a mirror, reflecting the tall trees. He turned and walked back to the main house. He checked his phone, went behind one of the oak trees, and took a piss. Then he got out a bottle of water and sat down on the main steps. His mouth was completely dry. As he put the bottle down something caught his attention. He stared at his bag that lay at the foot of the stairs. He was sure he had put it on the higher step. He got off the stairs and went over his actions in his mind.

First I put the bag down, then I removed my jacket and hung it on the railing, he thought. Then I moved the bag to the second step.

It had been moved. He looked around at everything with a new attentiveness. The trees, the bushes, the main house. The curtains were still drawn. He thought of the landing and the guest house, the guest house that reminded him of the gazebo in Skårby. He walked down the hill to the boathouse. The door was latched. He opened it and looked in. It was empty, but he could tell from the size of the berth and the ropes that it housed a big boat. Fishing nets were hanging on the walls. He went out again and locked the door. Part of the guest house was built out over the water with a ladder hanging over the end for swimming. He stood and stared at it for a moment. Then he walked up and felt the door. It was locked. He knocked lightly.

"Isa," he said. "I know you're in there."

He waited.

When she opened the door he didn't recognise her at first. She had tied her hair up in a knot. She was dressed in black, in some kind of overalls. Wallander thought her expression was full of animosity, but perhaps it was fear.

"How did you know I was here?" Her voice was hoarse.

"I didn't. Not until you told me."

"I haven't said anything. And I know you didn't see me."

"Policemen have the bad habit of noticing little things. Like someone lifting a bag, for instance. And not putting it back in the right place."

She stared back at him as if she couldn't understand what he had said. He saw that she was barefoot.

"I'm hungry," she said.

"So am I."

"There's food in the main house," she said and started walking. "Why did you come here?"

"We had to find you."

"Why?"

"Since you know what happened, I don't have to tell you."

276

She walked on in silence. Wallander looked at her. Her face was pale and drawn.

"How did you get out here?" he asked.

"I called Lage, who lives on Wettersö Island."

"Why didn't you get a ride with Westin?"

"I thought you might try to find out if I was here."

"And you didn't want to be found?"

She didn't answer this either. She unlocked the door and let them in, then walked around opening the curtains. She tugged at them in a careless way, as if she actually wanted to break everything around her. Wallander followed her into the kitchen. She opened the back door and connected a bottle of liquid gas to the stove. Wallander had already noticed that there was no electricity in the house. She turned around and looked at him.

"Cooking is one of the few things I can do."

She pointed out the refrigerator and a large freezer that were also hooked up to gas tanks. "They're full of food," she said disdainfully. "That's the way my parents want it. They pay someone to come out here and change the gas. They want food to be here in case they decide to come out for a couple of days. Which they never do."

She sounded like she was spitting. "My mother's an idiot," she said. "She's completely ignorant. She can't help it, I guess. My father, on the other hand, is not an idiot. But he's ruthless."

"I'd like to hear more."

"Not now. When we eat."

It was clear that she wanted him to leave the kitchen, so Wallander went out to the front of the house and called Ystad. He got hold of Höglund.

"I was right," he said. "She's here, just like we thought."

"Like you thought," she corrected him. "To tell the truth, I don't think any of us were so sure."

"Well, everyone's right some of the time. I think we'll be back in Ystad some time tonight."

"Have you talked to her?"

"Not yet."

She told him some calls had come in from people who thought they recognised the picture of Louise. They were still in the process of checking them. She promised to get back to him when they were finished.

Wallander went back into the house. He kept returning to the same thought. He had to get her to tell him what she didn't even know she knew.

She set the table in the large glassed-in veranda that had been added on to the side of the house. She asked him what he wanted to drink and he opted for water. She drank wine. He worried that she would get drunk and become impossible to talk to, but she had only one glass. They ate in silence. Afterwards, she put on some coffee. She shook her head when Wallander started clearing the table. A sofa and some chairs stood in a corner of the veranda. A lone sailing boat drifted by with limp sails.

"It's very beautiful here," he said. "This is a part of Sweden I haven't seen before."

"They bought the house 30 years ago," she replied. "They claim I was conceived out here, which may be true since I was born in February. They bought the house from an old couple who'd lived here their whole lives. I don't know how my father heard about it but one day he came to see them with a suitcase full of 100-kronor notes. It looks very impressive, but it doesn't necessarily mean it's a large sum of money. Neither of them had ever seen so much money in their lives. It took a couple of months to convince them, but they finally accepted the offer. I don't know what the exact amount was but I'm sure he paid nothing close to what it was worth."

"Do you mean that he swindled them?"

"I mean that my father has always been a scoundrel."

"If he simply made a good deal perhaps he should be called an ambitious businessman."

"My father has been involved in deals all over the world. He smuggled diamonds and ivory in Africa. No one really knows what he does now, but lately a lot of Russians have come out to visit him in Skårby. You can't tell me they're up to anything legal."

"As far as I know he's never been in trouble with us," Wallander said.

"Yes, he's good," she said. "And persistent. You can accuse him of a lot of things but he's not lazy. Ruthless people don't tend to rest on their laurels."

Wallander set his coffee cup down. "Let's talk about you instead," he said. "That's why I'm here, and it's been a long trip. We'll be heading back soon."

"What makes you think I'll be coming with you?"

Wallander looked at her for a long time before answering. "Three of your closest friends have been murdered," he said. "You were supposed to have been there when it happened. Both of us know what conclusion to draw from that."

She curled up in her chair and Wallander saw that she was frightened.

"Since we don't know why it happened, we have to take every precaution," he said.

The importance of what he was saying finally seemed to sink in. "Am I in danger?"

"We can't rule that out. We have no motive, therefore we have to consider all possibilities."

"But why would anyone want to kill me?"

"Why would anyone want to kill your friends? Martin, Lena, Astrid?"

She shook her head. "I don't understand it," she said.

Wallander moved his chair closer to hers. "Nonetheless you're the one who's going to help us," he said. "We're going to catch whoever did this. And to get him, we have to know why he did it. You got away. You're the one who's going to tell us."

"But when it's completely incomprehensible?"

"You have to think back," Wallander said. "Who could have targeted you as a group? What united you? Why? There is an answer. It has to be there."

He quickly changed tack, knowing that she was starting to listen to him. He didn't want to lose this opportunity.

"You have to answer my questions," he said. "And you have to tell the truth. I'll know if you're lying. And I don't want that."

"Why would I lie?"

"When I found you, you had just tried to commit suicide," he said. "Why? Did you already know what had happened to your friends?"

She looked at him with surprise. "How could I have known that? I had the same questions as everybody else."

Wallander knew she was telling the truth. "Why did you want to kill yourself?"

"I didn't want to live any more. Is there ever any other reason? My parents have ruined my life, just like they ruined Jörgen's. I just didn't want to live any more."

Wallander waited. Maybe she would keep talking. But she didn't say anything else.

For the next three hours he led her step by step through the events of the summer. He didn't leave anything untouched, however minor. He went through everything, sometimes more than once. There were no limits to how far back he could go. When had she first met Lena Norman? Which year, which month, what day? How had they met, how did they become friends? When she said she couldn't remember, or if she became unsure of herself, he slowed down and started again. An unclear memory could be overcome with patience. The whole time he was trying to get her to think about whether there had been anyone else there.

"A shadow in the corner," he said. "Was there a shadow in the corner? Anything you're forgetting?"

He asked about everything that might have seemed unexpected. As time went on she started to understand his methods, and then it was easier. Shortly after 5 p.m. they decided to stay the night and leave Bärnsö the following day. Wallander called Westin, who promised to come and get them when Wallander called. He didn't ask about Isa, but Wallander was sure he had known she was out there all along. They took a walk on the island, talking the whole time. Now and again Isa interrupted herself to point out places where she had played as a child. They walked out to the northernmost point. To his surprise she pointed to a shelf in the rock where she claimed to have lost her virginity one summer, but she didn't say with whom.

When they returned to the house it was starting to get dark. She walked around turning on the kerosene lamps, while Wallander called Ystad and talked to Martinsson. Nothing much had happened. No one had identified Louise. Wallander told him he was staying the night, and that he would return with the girl the next day.

Isa and Wallander continued their conversation all evening, pausing only to have tea and sandwiches.

Wallander walked out in the dark and relieved himself against a tree. The wind moaned in the treetops. Everything was quiet. He was beginning to understand their games – the way they dressed up, had parties, and travelled to different ages. When the conversation approached the party that had turned out to be their last, Wallander proceeded with painstaking care. Who could possibly have known about their plans? No one? He simply couldn't accept her answer. Someone must have known.

It was 1.30 a.m. when they stopped for the night. Wallander was so tired that he felt nauseated. She still hadn't come up with anything, but they were going to keep going in the long car trip to Ystad. He wasn't going to give up.

She showed him to a bedroom on the second floor. She was sleeping downstairs. She said good night and gave him a kerosene lamp. He made his bed and opened the window. It was very dark outside. He lay down in the bed and blew out the lamp. He heard her cleaning up in the kitchen, then the sound of the front door being locked. Then nothing.

Wallander fell asleep immediately.

No one noticed the boat that crossed Vikfjärden late that evening with its lights turned off. And no one heard it as it glided into the natural harbour on the west side of Bärnsö Island.

CHAPTER NINETEEN

Linda screamed.

She was somewhere close by. Her scream forced its way into his dreams. When he opened his eyes he had no idea where he was, but the faint scent from the kerosene lamp made him realise that it couldn't have been Linda who had screamed. His heart was pounding. It was quiet outside, just the whisper of the wind in the trees. He listened. Had it been a dream? He sat up and fumbled for the matches that he had placed beside the lamp on the table, lit it, and got dressed. He was putting his shoes on when he heard the sound. Something banging against the side of the house. Maybe the sound of a washing line hitting a drainpipe. But it was coming from downstairs. He got up, still with one shoe in his hand, and went over to the door. He opened it carefully and the sound came more clearly. The kitchen. The kitchen door must be open and banging in the wind. His fear came back with a vengeance. He hadn't been dreaming. The scream had been real.

Instead of putting his shoe on, he kicked off the other one, and walked downstairs with the lamp in his hand. He stopped halfway down and listened. The lamplight flickered over the walls. His hands were shaking. He realised that he had nothing to defend himself with. He tried to gather his thoughts. Nothing could happen out here. They were alone on the island. Maybe a bird had cried outside his window. And there was another possibility – that he wasn't the only one who had nightmares.

He went all the way downstairs and stopped outside her door, listened, then knocked. No answer. It's too quiet, he thought. He felt the handle. It was locked. Now he didn't hesitate. He banged the door and rattled the handle. Nothing. He went out to the kitchen. The back door was open and he closed it. He looked in the kitchen drawers and found a screwdriver, and used it to open her door. The bed was empty, the window open without being fastened. He tried to think what might have happened. He remembered seeing a big torch in the kitchen. He got it, and took a hammer as well. He opened the back door, and shone the light out into the darkness.

Once he was outside he realised that he was barefoot. A bird flew away from somewhere nearby. The sound of the wind was stronger. He called Isa's name, but there was no answer. He shone the light below her window. There were footprints on the ground, but they were so faint that he couldn't see where they led. He shone the light out into the darkness and called out again. Still no answer. His heart was pounding. He went back to the kitchen door and examined the lock. It had been forced, just as he'd thought. His fear grew stronger. He turned around and lifted his hammer, but there was no one there. He returned to the house. His phone was on the table next to his bed. He tried to imagine what had happened.

Someone breaks in through the kitchen door. Isa wakes because someone is trying to get into her room. Then she jumps out the window.

He couldn't think of any other explanation. He looked at his watch. It was 2.45 a.m. He dialled Martinsson's home number. He answered on the second ring. Wallander knew he had a phone by his bed.

"It's Kurt. I'm sorry to wake you."

"What's wrong?" Martinsson was still half-asleep.

"Get up," Wallander said. "Splash some cold water on your face. I'll call back in three minutes."

Martinsson started to protest, but Wallander hung up and looked at his watch. In exactly three minutes he called back, worrying about the battery to his phone running out.

"Listen carefully," he said. "I can't talk for long, my battery is going to run out. Do you have a pen and paper?"

Martinsson was wide awake now.

"I'm writing this down as we speak."

"Something's happened out here. I don't know what. Isa Edengren screamed, and I woke up. Now she's gone. The back door to the house has been forced. There's someone else on the island besides us. Whoever it is, he's come for her. I'm afraid she's in danger."

"What do you want me to do?"

"For now, just get the phone number of the coast guard in Fyrudden. Be prepared for my next call."

"What are you going to do?"

"Find her."

"If the killer's out there it'll be dangerous. You need help."

"And where would that come from? Norköpping? How long would that take?"

"You can't search an entire island by yourself."

"It's not that big. I'm going to hang up now, I want to conserve the battery."

Wallander put his shoes on and slipped the phone into his pocket, tucked the hammer into his belt, and left the house. He walked down to the landing and shone the torch. No boat. The boathouse and guest house were empty. He was calling her name. He ran back up to the main house, and started down the path. The bushes and trees looked white in the strong light. There was no one in the earth cellar.

He continued, calling her constantly. When he came to the junction in the path, he hesitated. Which way should he go? He looked at the ground, but couldn't see any prints. He headed for the northern tip of the island. He was out of breath when he reached the end. The wind coming in off the open sea was icy. He let the beam from the torch play over the rocks. Two eyes gleamed in the light. It was a little animal, a mink perhaps, that scuttled away between the rocks. He walked to the very end of the rocks, shining his light in the crevices. Nothing. He turned around to start back.

Something made him stop. He listened. The waves hit the shore in a rhythmic motion, but there was another sound. At first he didn't know what it was. Then he realised that it was an engine. The sound came from the west.

The harbour, he thought, and started running. I should have taken the other path.

He stopped only when he was about to reach the shore. He stepped out and flashed his light over the water. There was nothing there, and the sound had disappeared. A boat has just left, he thought. His fear increased. What had happened to her? He walked back along the path, trying to decide how to continue his search. Did the coast guard have dogs? Even though the island was small, he wouldn't be finished until morning. He tried to think out how she would have reacted. She had fled her bedroom in panic. The person trying to break in had blocked her way up to his room. She jumped out the window and

286

took off into the darkness. He doubted that she'd had a torch.

Wallander reached the junction again. Suddenly he knew. As they were walking around the island, she had mentioned a favourite hiding place she and Jörgen had when they were little. He thought back to where they had been standing when she had pointed to the rock face that was the highest point on the island. It had been closer to the house, and he remembered two juniper trees. He left the path. Fallen trees and thick shrubbery slowed his progress. There were large boulders strewn about, and he shone his light on them as he walked by. As he was nearing the beginning of the rock face, he caught sight of a deep crevice behind some ferns. He walked up to the rock wall, parted the ferns, and shone his torch inside.

She was there, curled up against the side of the rock, wearing only a nightgown. Her arms were wrapped around her legs and her head was leaning against one shoulder. It looked like she was sleeping, but he knew at once that she was dead. She had been shot in the head.

Wallander sank down on the ground. The blood rushed to his head. He felt like he was dying, and he didn't really mind. He had failed. He hadn't managed to keep her safe. Even the hiding place where she had played as a child hadn't protected her. He hadn't heard a shot. The gun must have had a silencer.

He got up and leaned against a tree. The phone slid out of his grasp. He leaned down, picked it up, and started staggering back towards the house as he called Martinsson.

"I'm too late," he said.

"Too late for what?"

"She's dead. Shot, just like the others."

Martinsson didn't seem to understand. Wallander had to repeat himself.

"My God," Martinsson said. "Who killed her?"

"A man in a boat," Wallander said. "Call the police in Norrköping. They'll have to do this. And talk to the coast guard."

Martinsson promised to do what he said.

"You might as well wake up the others," he said. "Lisa Holgersson, everyone. Once I get some help out here I'll call you again."

The conversation was over. Wallander sat on a chair in the kitchen, with the beam resting on a tapestry with the words "home sweet home". After a while he forced himself to get up, go into her room, and pull the blanket from her bed. Then he went out into the dark. Once he got back to the crevice he wrapped the blanket around her.

He sat down by the ferns that covered the opening. It was 3.20 a.m.

The wind picked up in the early, pale dawn. Wallander heard the coast guard arriving and went to the landing. The policemen approached him with suspicion. Wallander could understand their reaction. What was a police officer from Skåne doing out here on one of their islands? If he had been on holiday, it would have been different. He led them to the crevice, and turned away as they lifted the blanket. One of the officers demanded to see Wallander's police ID. Wallander lost his temper. He tore his wallet from his pocket and threw his ID card on the ground. Then he walked away. His fury left him almost immediately, replaced by a paralysing fatigue. He sat down on the front steps to the house with a bottle of water.

Harry Lundström came and found him. He'd seen

Wallander lose his temper and had thought how tactless it had been to ask him for his police badge at that moment. It was clear, after all, that he was a fellow police officer. The call had come from the Ystad police, with very specific information. A detective by the name of Kurt Wallander was on Bärnsö Island. He had found a dead girl, and he needed assistance.

Harry Lundström was 57 years old. He had been born in Norrköping and was considered the best detective in the city by everyone but himself. When Wallander flew into a rage, Lundström had understood his reaction. He didn't know what events lay behind the murder, but he knew that it had to do with the dead police officer and the three young people. Beyond that it was very unclear. But Harry Lundström had a huge capacity for empathy. He could imagine what it might have felt like to find a girl dressed only in her nightgown, curled in a crevice, with a bullet hole in her head.

Lundström sat down next to Wallander on the steps.

"That was a thoughtless thing of them to do," he said. "Asking for your ID like that."

He stretched out his hand and introduced himself. Wallander immediately felt that he could trust him.

"Should I speak to you?"

Lundström nodded.

"Then let's go inside," Wallander said.

They sat in the living room. After he'd called Martinsson on Lundström's phone, and arranged for Isa's parents to be notified of her death, he took more than an hour to explain who the dead girl was, and the circumstances surrounding her murder. Lundström listened without taking notes. Now and again they were interrupted by officers with questions. Lundström provided simple and clear instructions. When Wallander had finished talking, Lundström asked about a few details. Wallander thought that they were exactly the questions he would have asked himself.

It was already 7 a.m. and through the windows they could see the coast guard's boat scraping against the dock.

"I'd better get back up there," Lundström said. "You can stay here, of course. You've seen more than enough."

The wind was very strong now, and Wallander shivered.

"It's an autumn wind," Lundström said. "The weather has started to turn."

"I've never been in this archipelago before," Wallander said. "It's very beautiful."

"I played handball when I was young," Lundström said. "I had a picture of the Ystad team on my bedroom wall, but I've almost never been to your parts."

As they walked along the path, they could hear dogs barking in the distance.

"I thought it would be best to comb the island," Lundström said, "in case the killer is still here somewhere."

"He arrived by boat," Wallander said. "He anchored on the west side."

"If we had more time, we'd arrange to put some of the nearby harbours under surveillance," Lundström said. "But it's too late now."

"Maybe someone saw something," Wallander said.

"We're on to it," Lundström said. "I've considered the possibility. Someone may have seen a boat anchoring here late last night."

Wallander remained at a distance while Lundström walked up to the crevice and had a brief discussion with his colleagues. He felt sick to his stomach. What he wanted most of all was to get off the island as soon as possible.

His feeling of being somehow responsible for the crime was very strong. They should have left the island last night. He should have realised the danger of staying. The murderer seemed always to be in a position of knowing what they were doing. It had also been a mistake to let her sleep downstairs. He was aware that blaming himself was unreasonable, but he couldn't help it.

Lundström reappeared, and at the same time an officer with a dog came from the opposite direction. Lundström stopped him.

"Find anything?"

"There's no one on the island," the officer said. "She traced him to a bay on the west side, but the scent ended there."

Lundström looked at Wallander. "You were right," he said. "He came and left by boat."

They walked down to the main house again. Wallander thought about what Lundström had just said.

"The boat is important," he said. "Where did he get hold of it?"

"I was just thinking the same thing," Lundström said. "If we assume that the killer is not from around here, which I think we have to, then we have to find out where he got the boat from."

"He stole it," Wallander said.

Lundström stopped. "But how did he find his way here in the middle of the night?"

"He may have been out here before, and there are maps."

"Do you really think he's been out here before?"

"We can't rule that out."

Lundström started walking again.

"A stolen or borrowed boat," he said. "It must have happened near here. Either in Fyrudden, Snäckvarp or

291

Gryt. If he didn't steal it from a private dock, that is."

"He can't have had a lot of time," Wallander said. "Isa ran away from the hospital yesterday morning."

"Criminals in a hurry are always the easiest to trace," Lundström said.

They reached the landing and Lundström talked to a police officer who was adjusting one of the ropes. They took shelter from the wind by the boathouse.

"There's no reason to keep you here," Lundström said. "I assume that you want to go home."

Wallander felt a need to describe his feelings. "It shouldn't have happened," he said "I feel responsible. We should have left here yesterday. And now she's dead."

"I would have done the same thing that you did," Lundström said. "This was where she ran to. This was where you could start to get her talking. You couldn't have known what was going to happen."

Wallander shook his head. "I should have realised how much danger she was in."

They walked up to the house, and Lundström said he would do his best to ensure cooperation between the Norrköping and Ystad police.

"I'm sure there'll be the odd complaint about our not being informed that you were up here, but I'll see that they keep quiet."

Wallander got his bag and they returned to the landing. The coast guard would drop him back on the mainland. Lundström remained on the landing and saw them off. Wallander lifted his hand in a gesture of gratitude.

He threw his bag in the car and went to pay his parking ticket. As he was walking back he saw Westin on his way into the harbour. Wallander walked out to meet him, noting Westin's sombre expression as he stepped ashore.

"I take it you've heard the news," Wallander said.

"Isa is dead."

"It happened last night. I woke up when she screamed, but I was too late."

Westin looked at him grimly. "So it wouldn't have happened if you hadn't come out here last night?"

There it is, Wallander thought. The accusation. The one I can't defend myself against.

He took out his wallet. "How much do I owe you for yesterday's trip?"

"Nothing," Westin said.

Westin began to walk away. Wallander remembered that he had one more question to ask him.

"There's one more thing," he said.

Westin turned.

"Sometime between 19 and 22 July, you took someone to Bärnsö."

"In July I had a lot of passengers every day."

"This was another detective," Wallander said. "His name was Karl Evert Svedberg. He spoke with an even stronger Skåne accent than I do. Do you remember him?"

"Was he wearing his uniform?"

"I doubt it."

"Can you describe him?"

"He was almost completely bald, about as tall as me, solid but not overweight."

Westin thought it over.

"Between 19 and 22 July?"

"He would probably have crossed in the afternoon or early evening on the 19th. I don't know when he came back, but it would have been the 22nd at the latest."

"I'll check my records," Westin said. "But I don't remember off hand."

Wallander followed him out to the boat. Westin got out a notebook that lay under his chart, and came out of the wheelhouse.

"There's nothing here," he said. "But I do have a vague recollection of him. There were a lot of people on board, though. I might be confusing him with someone else."

"Do you have access to a fax machine?" Wallander asked. "We can send you a picture of him."

"I can get faxes at the post office."

Another possibility occurred to Wallander.

"You might already have seen a picture of him," he said. "Maybe on TV. He's the police officer who was murdered in Ystad a couple of days ago."

Westin frowned. "I heard about that," he said. "But I can't remember seeing a picture."

"You'll get one over the fax," Wallander said. "Give me the number."

Westin wrote it down for him in his notebook and tore out the page.

"Do you know if Isa was out here between 19 and 22 July?"

"No, but she was here a lot this summer."

"So it's a possibility?"

"Yes."

Wallander left Fyrudden. He stopped at a petrol station in Valdermarsvik, then took the coast road. There wasn't a cloud in the sky. He rolled down the window. When he reached Västervik he realised that he didn't have the energy to continue. He had to eat something, and sleep. He found a roadside café and ordered an omelette, some mineral water and a cup of coffee. The woman who took his order smiled at him.

"At your age you shouldn't stay up all night," she said.

Wallander looked at her with surprise. "Is it so obvious?"

She bent down and got her bag from behind the counter, then fished out a make-up mirror and handed it over to him. She was right. He was pale and had dark circles under his eyes. His hair was a mess.

"You're right," he said. "I'll have my omelette, then I'll catch up on a bit of sleep in my car."

He went outside and sat down in the shade. She brought the food out on a tray.

"There's a small room off the kitchen with a bed in it," she said. "You could use it for a while if you'd like."

She walked away without waiting for an answer. Wallander watched her departing figure with surprise. After he'd finished eating he walked over to the door of the kitchen. It was open.

"Is the offer still open?" he asked.

"I don't go back on my word."

She showed him the room and the bed, which was a simple folding cot with a blanket.

"It's better than the back seat of your car," she said. "Of course, policemen are used to sleeping anywhere."

"How do you know I'm a policeman?"

"I saw your police ID in your wallet when you paid. I was married to a policeman, so I recognised it."

"My name is Kurt. Kurt Wallander."

"I'm Erika. Sleep well."

Wallander lay down on the bed. His whole body ached and his head felt completely empty. He knew he should call the station and let them know that he was on his way, but he couldn't be bothered. He closed his eyes and fell asleep.

When he woke he had no idea where he was. He looked down at his watch. It was 7 p.m. He sat up with a jerk. He had slept for more than five hours. Cursing, he got the phone and called the station. Martinsson didn't answer, and so he tried Hansson.

"Where the hell have you been? We've been trying to reach you all day. Why wasn't your phone on?"

"There must have been something wrong with it. Has anything happened?"

"Nothing more than us wondering where you were."

"I'll be there as soon as I can. By 11 p.m. at the latest."

Wallander hung up. Erika appeared in the doorway.

"I think you needed that," she said.

"An hour would have been plenty. I should have asked you to wake me."

"There's coffee, but no hot food. I've closed for the day."

"You've been waiting for me?"

"There are always things that need doing around here."

They went out into the empty restaurant, and she brought him a cup of coffee and some sandwiches, and sat down across from him.

"I just heard on the radio about the girl who was killed in the archipelago, and the police officer who found her," she said. "I take it that was you."

"Yes, but I'd rather not talk about it. So, you were married to a policeman once?"

"When I lived in Kalmar. I moved here after the divorce, when I had the money to buy this place."

She told him about the first few years, when the restaurant didn't make enough money. But it was doing better now. Wallander listened, but all the while he was looking at her. He wanted to reach out and touch her, to hold on to something normal and real. He sat with her for half an hour, then paid and walked to his car. She followed him out.

"I don't really know how to thank you," he said.

"Why do people always need to thank each other?" she said. "Drive carefully."

Wallander reached the station at 11 p.m. and met with everyone in the large conference room. Nyberg and Holgersson were there. During the drive back, he had thought through everything that had happened, beginning on the night that he had woken thinking that something was wrong with Svedberg. He still felt guilty about Isa, but now he also felt anger at her death. His rage caused him to speed up without noticing it, and at one point he found himself doing more than 150 kilometres per hour.

His rage stemmed not only from her senseless murder, but also from his feeling of failure at their inability to see which way to turn. And now Isa Edengren had been shot out on Bärnsö Island, practically before his eyes.

Wallander told everyone about the events on the island. After answering their questions and listening to a report on developments in Ystad, he summed up the situation in a few sentences. It was well past midnight.

"Tomorrow we have to start from the beginning," he said. "We have to start from the beginning and work from there. We'll find the killer sooner or later. We have to. But I think that the best thing to do now is to go home and get some sleep. It's been hard up till now, and I think that it's just going to get harder."

Wallander finished. Martinsson looked as though he was about to speak, but then changed his mind. Wallander was the first to leave. He closed his office door, making it clear that he didn't want to be disturbed. He sat down and thought about what he hadn't brought up at the meeting, what they would have to discuss the following day.

Isa Edengren was dead. Did that mean that the killer had completed his task, or was he now preparing for something else?

No one knew the answer.

Part Two

CHAPTER TWENTY

On the morning of Thursday, 15 August, Wallander finally went back to Dr Göransson's office. He didn't have an appointment but was seen immediately. He hadn't slept well and was extremely tired, but he left the car at home. He knew that each new day would carry with it fresh excuses for not exercising. This day was just as inconvenient as any other, so he might as well start getting used to it.

The weather was still beautiful and calm. As he walked through the town he tried to recall when they had last had an August this warm. But his mind kept turning back to the investigation, and not just during his waking hours. It haunted him in his sleep as well.

Last night he had dreamed of Bärnsö. He kept hearing her scream. When he woke up he was halfway out of bed, drenched in sweat, his heart pounding. It had taken him a long time to fall back to sleep.

He sat at the kitchen table for a while after he woke. It was still dark outside. He couldn't think of a time when he'd felt as helpless as he did at that moment. It wasn't just the fatigue caused by the little icebergs of sugar floating around in his blood. It also came from a feeling of having been overtaken by age. Was he really too old? He wasn't even 50.

He wondered if he was simply starting to crumble under the weight of all the responsibility and was now on a downward trajectory to a point where only fear remained.

He was very close to making a new decision: to give up. To ask Holgersson to put someone else in charge.

The question was who to appoint in his place. Martinsson and Hansson both came to mind, but Wallander knew neither one of them was up to it. They would have to bring someone in from outside, which was not ideal. That would be like labelling themselves inadequate.

He didn't come to any conclusion. When he decided to go to the doctor it was in the hope that he'd hear the words that would free him, give him the chance to be forced to take leave on medical grounds.

But it turned out that Dr Göransson had no such plans for him. After telling Wallander that his blood sugar was still too high, that he was leaking sugar into his urine and had worryingly high blood pressure, he simply gave him a prescription for some medication and ordered him to make a radical change in his diet.

"We have to attack your symptoms from all sides," he said. "They're connected and have to be treated as such. But it's not going to be possible unless you take charge of your health."

He gave him the phone number of a dietician. Wallander left the office with the prescription in hand. It was a little after 8 a.m. and he knew he should go directly to the station, but he didn't feel ready. He went up to the café by the main square and had a cup of coffee, but this time he passed on the pastry.

What do I do now, he thought. I'm in charge of solving one of the most brutal serial killings in Sweden in years. Every police officer's eye is on me, since one of the victims was in the force. The press are hounding me. I'll probably be criticised by the victims' parents. Everyone expects me to find the killer in a few days and to have collected the kind of evidence against him that would make even the most hardened prosecutor weep. The only problem is that in reality I have nothing. Soon I'll gather my colleagues together and we'll start again. We aren't even close to anything like a breakthrough. What we're in is a vacuum.

He finished his coffee. A man was reading the paper at the next table. Wallander saw the big black headlines, and left the café in a hurry. Since he had time to spare, he decided to squeeze in an errand before returning to the station. He went to Vädergränd and rang the doorbell at Bror Sundelius's house. There was a chance that Sundelius didn't welcome surprise visits, but Wallander knew it would not be because he wasn't up yet.

The door opened. Even though it was only 8.30 a.m., Sundelius was dressed in a suit. The knot of his tie was an exercise in perfection. He opened the door wide without hesitation, invited Wallander in, and disappeared into the kitchen for coffee.

"I always keep the water hot," he said, "in case I have unexpected visitors. The last time that happened was about a year ago, of course, but you never know."

Wallander sat down on the sofa and pulled the cup towards him. Sundelius sat down across from him.

"Last time we spoke we were interrupted," Wallander said.

"The reason for that has become exceedingly clear," Sundelius replied dryly. "What kind of people do we let into this country anyway?"

His comment puzzled Wallander.

"There's no evidence that this was the work of an immigrant," he said. "Why would you think that?"

"It seems obvious to me," Sundelius said. "No Swede could have done anything like this."

He knew the best thing to do was to steer the conversation to safer ground. Sundelius did not seem like the kind of man who was easily swayed in his convictions. But Wallander couldn't keep himself from articulating his objections.

"Nothing points to a killer of foreign extraction. That much we know. Let's talk about Karl Evert instead. You knew him quite well?"

"He was always 'Kalle' to me."

"How long had you known each other?"

"Which day did he die?"

Wallander was puzzled again. "We haven't established that yet. Why?"

"If you had, I would have been able to give you an exact answer. Let me provisionally say that we knew each other 19 years, seven months, and around 15 days when he passed away so tragically. I have kept careful records my whole life. The only data I won't be able to record is the exact time of my own death, unless I commit suicide, which I have no plans to do. But my lawyer has instructions to burn all my notebooks when I die. They are of value only to me, not anyone else."

Wallander was starting to sense that Sundelius was one of these old people who did not get enough chances to talk to others. Wallander thought briefly of his father – one of the few people he had known who had been an exception to this rule.

"You were both interested in astronomy, is that correct?"

"That is correct."

"You don't have a Scanian accent. You moved here at some point?"

"I moved here from Vadstena on 12 May 1959. My furniture arrived on the 14th. I thought I would stay a few years, but it has been much longer than that."

Wallander cast his gaze hastily around the room. He didn't see any pictures of family. Sundelius wasn't wearing a ring.

"Are you married?"

"No."

"Divorced?"

"I'm a bachelor."

"Like Svedberg."

"Yes."

He might as well come right to the point. He still had a copy of the picture of Louise in his breast pocket. He took it out and laid it on the table.

"Have you ever seen this woman before?"

Sundelius put on some glasses after polishing the lenses with his handkerchief, and studied it carefully.

"Isn't that the same picture that was published in the paper the other day?"

"That's right."

"Members of the public were asked to call the police if they had any information regarding who she was."

Wallander nodded. Sundelius laid the photograph back on the table.

"So I should already have contacted you if I had known anything about her."

"Do you?"

"No. And I have a gift for faces. It's a necessity for a banker."

Wallander couldn't help himself. Why would bank directors need to have a gift for faces? He asked the question and got another long answer.

305

"There was a time when I was young when it was the only kind of credit information there was," Sundelius said. "That was before our society started recording its citizens' every move. We speak of before and after the birth of Christ, but it would be more accurate to speak of before and after the invention of personal identification numbers. When I was young, you had to make your decision on the spot. Was the person standing before you honest? Did he mean what he said? Did he have integrity, or was he a liar? I remember an old clerk in Vadstena who never gathered any credit reports on his clients, and this even after the regulations were tightened and it was easier to collect such information. However large the loan in question, he would simply study the person's face. And he was never wrong, not once over the course of his whole career. He rejected the scoundrels, and helped the honest and hardworking. Of course, he could never foresee a person's luck."

Wallander nodded and continued. "This woman has been connected with Kalle," he said. "According to reliable information, they saw each other for about ten years. Or, to be more precise, they had a relationship for ten years. Kalle remained a bachelor, but he was apparently involved with this woman for a very long time."

Sundelius froze with the coffee cup halfway to his mouth. When Wallander finished speaking, he slowly lowered it onto the saucer.

"That was not very reliable information," he said. "You're wrong."

"In what way?"

"In all ways. Kalle didn't have a girlfriend."

"We know these meetings took place in secret."

"They didn't take place at all."

Sundelius was sure of himself. But Wallander also

sensed something else in the tone of his voice. At first he couldn't tell what it was. Then he realised that Sundelius was upset. He maintained his self-control, but an edge had crept into his voice.

"Let me make it clear that none of his colleagues nor anyone else knew about this woman," Wallander said. "Only one person knew about her. So we're all very surprised."

"Who knew about her?"

"I'd rather not tell you for now."

Sundelius looked at Wallander. There was something resolute and yet vacant in his gaze. But Wallander was sure: the indignation and irritation were there. It was not his imagination.

"Let us leave this unknown woman for a while," Wallander said. "How did you meet?"

Sundelius's manner was altered. Now his answers came reluctantly and without his previous fluency. He had been led into an area where he hadn't been expecting to go.

"We met in the home of mutual friends in Malmö."

"Is that what it says in your notebook?"

"I really don't know why the police would be interested in what my calendar does or does not say."

Now he's completely dismissive, Wallander thought. A photograph of an unknown woman changes everything. He continued carefully.

"But it was at that time that you started maintaining a friendship?"

Sundelius seemed to have realised that his new attitude was noticeable. He resumed his calm and friendly manner, but Wallander still felt his attention was elsewhere.

"We would study the night sky together. That was all."

"Where did you go?"

"Out into the countryside, where it's dark. Especially in

307

the autumn. We would go to Fyledalen, among other places."

Wallander thought for a moment. "You were surprised when I first contacted you," he said. "You said you were surprised that I hadn't been in touch earlier, since Kalle didn't have many close friends. Did you count yourself among them?"

"I remember what I said."

"But now you describe a relationship based on a mutual interest in the night sky. Was that all it was?"

"Neither he nor I was the intrusive type."

"But it hardly qualifies you as a close friend, does it? Nor as the kind of friend we as his colleagues would have heard about."

"It was what it was."

No, Wallander thought. It wasn't. But I still don't know what it was.

"When was the last time you saw each other?"

"In the middle of July. The 16th, to be precise."

"You went to look at the stars?"

"We went out to Österlen. It was a very clear night, although summer is not the best time."

"How was he?"

Sundelius looked at him blankly. "I don't understand the question."

"Was he his normal self? Did he say anything unexpected?"

"He was exactly as he always was. You don't talk much when you look at stars. At least we never did."

"And after that?"

"We didn't see each other again."

"Had you decided when you would see each other again?"

"He said he was going away for a few days and that he had a lot to do. We said we would be in touch in August, when he was due to take his holidays."

Wallander held his breath. Three days later Svedberg had gone to Bärnsö. What Sundelius had just said seemed to indicate that Svedberg had already decided to go. He'd said he had a lot to do, and that he was due to take his holiday in August, although he was actually in the middle of his holiday already.

Svedberg was lying, Wallander thought. Even to Sundelius, who was his friend, he had lied about the way he was spending his holiday. He didn't tell people at work either. For the first time Wallander felt that he was very close to a revelation. But he still didn't see what it could be.

Wallander thanked him for the coffee. Sundelius followed him to the door.

"I'm sure we'll be seeing each other again," Wallander said as he took his leave. Sundelius had completely regained his composure.

"I'd be grateful if you would let me know when the funeral is going to be."

Wallander promised him he would be notified. He walked along Vädergränd and sat down on a bench outside Café Bäckahästen. As he watched the ducks swimming in the pond, he went over his conversation with Sundelius. There were two moments of particular significance: one when Wallander had showed him the photograph, the other when he had realised that Svedberg was lying. He stayed with the photograph for a moment. It wasn't just the picture that had upset him; it was also the fact that Wallander had spoken of a ten-year love affair.

Perhaps it's that easy, he thought. Maybe there wasn't

one love affair but two. Could Sundelius and Svedberg have had a relationship? Was there something to the rumour that Svedberg was gay? Wallander grabbed a handful of gravel and let it fall through his fingers. He still had doubts. The photograph was of a woman, and Sture Björklund was very sure of the fact that a woman called Louise had long been a part of Svedberg's life. That raised another important question. Why did Sture Björklund know about this woman when no one else did?

Wallander wiped off his hands and got up. He remembered the prescription, and stopped at a pharmacy to have it filled. When he took out the prescription slip, he noticed that his phone was turned off. He continued on to the station at a more rapid clip. His conversation with Sundelius had propelled him deeper into the investigation.

When Wallander walked through the station doors, Ebba told him that everyone was looking for him. He told her to tell people that they were meeting in half an hour. On his way to his office he bumped into Hansson.

"I was just coming to find you. Some results have come in from Lund."

"Can the pathologist give us a time of death?"

"It seems like it."

"Then let's have a look."

Wallander followed Hansson to his office. When they walked past Svedberg's office, he noticed to his surprise that the nameplate was already gone. His surprise turned into dismay, then anger.

"Who removed Svedberg's nameplate?"

"I don't know."

"Couldn't the bastards at least have waited until after the funeral?"

"The funeral is on Tuesday," Hansson said. "Lisa said that the minister of justice will be attending."

Wallander knew her from her TV appearances to be a very determined and self-confident woman. Right now her name escaped him. Hansson hastily brushed some racing forms off his desk and got out the pathologist's report. Wallander leaned against the wall while Hansson was rifling through the report.

"Here we are," he said finally.

"Let's start with Svedberg."

"He was hit with two shots from the front. Death was instantaneous."

"But when?" Wallander said impatiently. "Skip the rest unless it's important. I want a time."

"When you and Martinsson found him he couldn't have been dead more than 24 hours, and not less than ten."

"Are they sure? Or will they change their minds?"

"They seem sure. And just as sure that Svedberg was sober when he died."

"Were there speculations to the contrary?"

"I'm just stating what the report says. His last meal, taken a couple of hours before he died, was of yogurt."

"That suggests he died in the morning."

Hansson nodded. Everyone knew that Svedberg ate yogurt for breakfast. When he was forced to work a night shift he always put a container of yogurt in the fridge in the canteen.

"There it is," Wallander said.

"There's a lot more," Hansson continued. "Do you want the details?"

"I'll go over those myself later," Wallander said. "What does it say about the three young people?"

"That it's difficult to ascertain their time of death."

"We knew that already. But what's their conclusion?"

"Their tentative conclusion is that there needs to be further research done, but they don't rule out the possibility that the victims could have been killed as early as 21 June, Midsummer's Eve, with one stipulation."

"That the bodies weren't left out in the open air."

"Exactly. Of course, they're not sure."

"But I am. Now we can finally draw up a time frame. We'll start with that at the meeting."

"I haven't located the cars yet," Hansson said. "The killer must have disposed of them too somehow."

"Maybe he buried them as well," Wallander said. "Whatever he did with them, they have to be found as soon as possible."

He walked back to his office, got out his medication, and read the label. It was called Amaryl, and the instructions said to take it with food. Wallander wondered when he would have a chance to eat next. He got up with a heavy sigh and walked to the canteen, where he found some old biscuits on a plate. He managed to get them down and took his pills when he was finished.

He returned to his office, gathered up his papers, and went to the conference room. Just as Martinsson was about to close the door, Lisa Holgersson turned up with Thurnberg, the chief prosecutor, in tow. Wallander realised when he saw him that he hadn't really kept him informed of the investigation's progress. As might be expected, Thurnberg had a disapproving look on his face. He sat as far from Wallander as he could get.

Holgersson told them that Svedberg's funeral was to be held on Tuesday, 20 August, at 2 p.m.

She looked at Wallander. "I'll give a speech," she said. "So will the minister of justice and the national chief of police. But I wonder if one of you shouldn't also say a few words. I'm thinking especially of you, Kurt, since you've been here the longest."

Wallander held up his hands. "I can't give a speech," he said. "Standing in church next to Svedberg's coffin, I won't be able to get a single word out."

"You made a great speech when Björk retired," Martinsson said. "One of us should say something, and it ought to be you."

Wallander knew he couldn't do it. Funerals terrified him.

"It's not that I don't want to do it," he said pleadingly. "I'll even write the speech. I'm just not going to be able to deliver it."

"I'll do it if you write it." Höglund said. "I don't think anyone should be forced to speak at a funeral unless they want to. It can be so overwhelming. I can give the speech, unless anyone objects."

Wallander was sure that neither Hansson nor Martinsson actually thought this was the best solution. But neither one of them said so, and it was agreed that Höglund would speak.

Wallander quickly turned the discussion to the case. Thurnberg sat motionless at his end of the table, an inscrutable expression on his face. His presence made Wallander nervous. There was something disdainful, even hostile, in his manner.

They went through the latest developments. Wallander gave them an abbreviated version of his conversation with Sundelius, completely leaving out Sundelius's reaction to hearing of Svedberg's ten-year relationship with an unknown woman.

Leads kept being phoned in to the station, but there were no credible reports about the woman's identity yet. Everyone agreed that this was unusual. They decided to send the picture to the Danish papers, as well as to Interpol.

After a couple of hours, they reached the matter of the pathologist's report and Wallander suggested they take a short break. Thurnberg got up immediately and left the room. He hadn't said a single word. Lisa Holgersson lingered after the others had left.

"He doesn't seem very happy," Wallander said, referring to Thurnberg.

"No, I don't think he is," she answered. "I think you should talk to him. He thinks this is taking too long."

"We're working as hard as we can."

"But do we need reinforcements?"

"We'll discuss this issue, of course, but I can tell you right now that I for one am not going to oppose it."

His answer seemed to relieve her. He went out and got a cup of coffee. Then they all filed back into the room. Thurnberg returned to the same seat, his face as blank as before. They began to go through the autopsy report. Wallander sketched the possible time frame on the board.

"Svedberg was killed not more than 24 hours before we found him. Everything indicates that he was killed in the morning. As far as the young people go, it turns out that our hypothesis works better than we had imagined. It doesn't supply us with a motive or a killer, but it does tell us something significant."

He sat down before he continued. "These young people made the arrangement for their celebration in secret. They chose a place where they were sure they would be left alone. But someone knew about their plans. Someone kept himself incredibly well informed, and had the time to make meticulous preparations. We still have no motive for what happened in the nature reserve, but we have a killer who didn't give up until he had traced the only remaining survivor of this night and killed her too. Isa Edengren.

He knew she fled to Bärnsö, and he found her out there among all those islands. This gives us a place to start. We're looking for a person who knew about the plans for the Midsummer celebration. Someone close to the source."

No one spoke for a long time.

"Where do we find this person who had access to so much information?" Wallander said. "That's where we have to start. If we do, then sooner or later we'll find out where Svedberg fits into the picture."

"We already have," Hansson said. "We know he started his investigation only a few days after Midsummer."

"I think we can say more than that," Wallander said. "I think Svedberg had a definite suspicion who killed, or was about to kill, the young people in the reserve."

"Why did the killer wait so long to kill Isa Edengren?" Martinsson asked. "He took more than a month to do it."

"We don't know why," Wallander agreed. "She wasn't particularly hard to find."

"And one more thing," Martinsson added. "Why did he dig up the bodies? Did he want them to be discovered?"

"There's no other explanation," Wallander said. "But it raises another set of questions about what motivates this killer. And in what way he and Svedberg had anything to do with each other."

Wallander sat back and looked at everyone gathered around the table.

Svedberg knew what had happened to the young people when they didn't return after Midsummer, he thought. Svedberg knew who the killer was, or at least had a very strong suspicion. That's why he was killed. There just isn't any other explanation. Which brings us to the most important question of all. Why didn't he want to tell us who the killer was?

CHAPTER TWENTY-ONE

Shortly after 2 p.m., Wallander asked Martinsson a question regarding a call that had come in from a man who had a news-stand in Sölvesborg. This man had stopped at Hagestad's nature reserve on the afternoon of Midsummer's Eve on his way to a party in Falsterbo. He had realised he was going to be too early, and had stopped to take a break. He thought he remembered two cars parked at the entrance. But Wallander never heard what additional details the man remembered. When he finished asking Martinsson his question, he fainted.

One moment he was waving his pencil in Martinsson's direction. The next he fell back in his chair, his chin to his chest. For a split second no one knew what had happened. Then Holgersson and Höglund reacted almost simultaneously, before the others. Hansson later confessed that he had thought Wallander had had a stroke and died. What the rest of them thought, or feared, he never heard. They dragged him out of the chair and laid him out on the floor, loosened his collar, and took his pulse. Someone grabbed a phone and called an ambulance. But Wallander came to before it arrived. As they helped him to his feet, he was already thinking that his blood-sugar level must have dropped. He drank some water and took some lumps of sugar from a tray on the table. He was starting to feel his normal self again.

Everyone around him looked worried. They thought he

should go down to the hospital for an examination or at the very least go home and rest. But Wallander didn't want to do either. He excused the episode as due to lack of sleep and then returned to the matter at hand with such determined energy the others had to back down.

The only one who didn't show signs of either worry or fear was Thurnberg. He hardly had any reaction at all. He stood up when Wallander was laid on the ground, but he didn't leave his place. No one really noticed a significant shift in expression either.

When they took a break Wallander went to his office and called Dr Göransson, and told him about the fainting episode. Dr Göransson did not seem surprised.

"Your blood-sugar level will continue to fluctuate," he said. "It'll take us a while to get it stabilised. We may have to reduce your medication if it keeps happening, but until then keep an apple handy in case you get dizzy."

After that day Wallander walked around with lumps of sugar in his pocket, as if he were expecting to see a horse. He didn't tell anyone about his diabetes. It was still his secret.

The meeting dragged on until 5 p.m., but by then they had managed to go through every aspect of the investigation thoroughly. There was a new infusion of energy in the room. They decided to call for reinforcements from Malmö, although Wallander knew that it was the people gathered around the table who would remain the core members of the investigative team.

Thurnberg remained behind after everyone had filed out of the room, and Wallander realised he must want to have a word with him. As he made his way to the other side of the table, he thought regretfully of Per Åkeson, who was somewhere under an African sun.

"I've been expecting a debriefing for quite a while," Thurnberg said. His voice was high-pitched and always sounded on the verge of cracking.

"We should have done this earlier, of course," Wallander said in a friendly tone. "But the direction of the investigation has shifted dramatically over the last couple of days."

Thurnberg ignored Wallander's last comment. "In the future I expect to be continuously apprised of the situation without having to ask. The justice department is naturally very interested when a police officer is killed."

Wallander felt no need to answer. He waited for him to continue.

"The investigation up to this point can hardly be called successful or even as thorough as one would hope," Thurnberg said, gesturing to a long list of points he had written on a pad of paper in front of him. Wallander felt as if he was back at school being told he had failed a test.

"If the criticisms are warranted we'll take the steps necessary to remedy the situation," he said.

He tried hard to sound calm and friendly, but he knew he would be unable to conceal his anger much longer. Who did this visiting prosecutor from Örebro think he was? How old was he? He couldn't be more than 33.

"I'll see to it that you have my list of complaints about the handling of the case on your desk tomorrow morning," Thurnberg said. "I'll be expecting a written response from you."

Wallander stared back at him quizzically. "Do you really mean you want us to waste time writing letters to each other while a killer who's committed five brutal murders is still running around out there?"

"What I mean is that the investigation so far has not been satisfactory."

Wallander hit the table with his fist and got up so violently that the chair fell to the ground. "There are no perfect investigations!" he roared. "But no one is going to accuse me or my colleagues of not having done everything that we can."

Thurnberg's expression finally changed. His face drained of all colour.

"Go ahead and send me your little note," Wallander said. "If you are right, we'll do as you say. But don't expect me to write you any letters in reply."

Wallander left the room and slammed the door shut behind him.

Höglund was on her way into her office and turned around when she heard the noise.

"What was that all about?" she asked.

"It's Thurnberg," Wallander said. "The bastard's whining about the investigation."

"Why?"

"He doesn't think we're thorough enough. How could we possibly have done more?"

"He probably just wants to show you who's boss."

"In that case he's picked the wrong man."

Wallander went into her office and sat down heavily in her visitor's chair.

"What happened in there?" she asked. "When you fainted."

"I haven't been sleeping well," he said, dodging her question. "But I feel fine now."

He got the same feeling he had when he was in Gotland with Linda. She didn't believe him either. Martinsson poked his head round the door.

"Am I interrupting anything?"

"No, it's good that you're here," Wallander said. "We should talk. Where's Hansson?"

"He's working on the cars."

"He should be here too," Wallander said. "But you'll have to fill him in later."

He gestured to Martinsson to close the door, then told them about his conversation with Sundelius, and his feeling that Svedberg might have been gay after all.

"Not that it matters one way or the other," he added. "Police officers are allowed to have whatever sexual orientation they like. The reason I'm not going public with this is that I don't want to start unnecessary rumours. Since Svedberg didn't talk about his sexuality while he was alive, I don't see the need for public speculation now that he's dead."

"It complicates this matter with Louise," Martinsson said.

"He may have been a man of many interests. But what is it that Sundelius knows? I had a strong feeling that he wasn't telling me everything. That means we have to dig deeper into both their lives. Are there other secrets? We have to do the same thing with these young people. Somewhere there's a point of intersection. A person who is a shadow to us right now, but who is there just the same."

"I have a vague recollection that someone lodged a complaint against Svedberg with the justice department's ombudsman a number of years ago," Martinsson said. "I forget what it was about."

"We should look into it, like everything else," Wallander said. "I thought we could divide these things up. I'll take Svedberg and Sundelius. I also have to talk to Björklund again, since he's the only one who knows anything about Louise."

"It's incomprehensible that no one's seen her," said Höglund.

"It's not just incomprehensible," Wallander said. "It's an impossibility. We just have to find out why."

"Haven't we gone a little easy on Björklund?" Martinsson asked. "After all, we found Svedberg's telescope at his house."

"He's innocent until proven guilty," Wallander said. "It's a hackneyed phrase, but there's some truth to it."

He got up. "Remember to tell Hansson about this," he said and left the room.

It was 5.30 p.m. and he hadn't eaten anything all day except the dry old biscuits in the canteen. The thought of going home and cooking a meal was too overwhelming. Instead he went down to the Chinese restaurant on the main square. He drank a beer while he was waiting. Then another. When the food came he ate too fast, as usual. He was about to order dessert when he stopped himself, and headed home. It was another warm evening and he opened the door to the balcony. He tried to call Linda three times, then gave up. Her phone was constantly busy. He was too tired to think. The TV was on, with the sound down. He lay down on the sofa and stared up at the ceiling. Shortly before 9 p.m. the phone rang. It was Lisa Holgersson.

"I think we have a problem," she said. "Thurnberg spoke to me after your argument."

Wallander grimaced, sensing what she was about to say. "Thurnberg was probably upset because I shouted at him. I made a lot of noise, thumped my fist on the table, that sort of thing."

"It's worse than that," she said. "He says you're not fit to be in charge of the investigation."

That came as a surprise. Wallander hadn't thought Thurnberg would go so far. He should have felt angry, but instead he was frightened. It was one thing to question your own abilities, but had it never occurred to him that someone else might do so.

"What were his reasons?"

"Mostly things to do with the running of the investigation. He's particularly concerned about the fact that he's been kept so poorly informed."

Wallander protested. What more could they have done?

"I'm just telling you what he said. He also thinks it was a serious lapse of judgment not to contact the police in Norrköping before you went up to Östergötland. He questions the validity of the trip itself, in fact."

"But what about the fact that I found Isa?"

"He thinks the police in Norrköping could have done that, while you were down here leading the team, and he seems to imply that she might have lived if this had been the case."

"That's absurd," Wallander said flatly. "I hope that's what you told him."

"There's one last thing," she said. "Your health."

"I'm not sick."

"Look, you fainted right in front of everyone. In the middle of a meeting."

"That could happen to anyone who is overworked."

"I'm telling you what he said."

"But what did you say to him?"

"That I would speak to you. And consider it."

Suddenly Wallander felt unsure of her opinion. Could he still assume she was on his side? His suspicion flared up in an instant, and it was strong.

"So now you've talked to me," he said. "What do you think?"

"What do you think?"

"That Thurnberg is an annoying little man who doesn't

322

like me or any of the others. Which is mutual, by the way. I think he looks on his time here simply as a springboard to greater things."

"That's hardly an objective statement."

"But true. I believe I did the right thing in going up to Bärnsö Island. The investigation here continued just the same. There was no reason to notify the police in Norrköping because no crime had been committed, nor was there any reason to assume one would occur. On the contrary, there was every reason in the world to keep things quiet. Isa Edengren could easily have become even more frightened."

"Thurnberg understands all that," she said. "And I agree with you that he can seem very arrogant. What seems to worry him most is your health."

"I don't think he's worried about anyone but himself. The day I'm no longer up to leading the investigation I promise you'll be the first to know."

"I suppose Thurnberg will have to accept that as his answer for now. But it might be best if you kept him better informed from now on."

"It's going to be hard for me to trust him in the future," Wallander said. "I can stand a lot of things, but I hate it when people go behind my back."

"He hasn't gone behind your back. Telling me about his concerns was the right thing to do."

"No one can force me to like him."

"That's not what this is about. But I think he's going to react to any signs of weakness from now on."

"What the hell do you mean by that?"

The sudden flare of anger came from nowhere, and Wallander didn't manage to control it.

"You don't have to get upset. I'm just telling you what's happened."

"We have five murders to solve," Wallander said. "And a killer who's cold-blooded and well-organised. There are no apparent motives and we don't know if he's going to strike again. One of the victims was a close colleague. You have to assume people are going to get a little upset. This investigation isn't exactly a tea party."

She laughed. "I haven't heard that expression used before in this context."

"Just so you understand where I'm coming from," Wallander said. "That's all."

"I wanted to let you know about this as soon as possible."

"I know, I'm grateful that you did."

When the conversation was over, Wallander went back to the sofa. His suspicions still hadn't left him, and he was already plotting how he would get even with Thurnberg. Perhaps it was out of self-defence, perhaps self-pity. The thought of being relieved of his responsibilities frightened him. Being in charge of an investigation like this meant being under an almost unbearable strain, but the thought of humiliation was worse.

Wallander felt a great desire to talk to someone, anyone who could give him the kind of moral support he needed. It was 9.15 p.m. Who could he call? Martinsson or Höglund? Most of all he wanted to talk to Rydberg, but he lay in his grave and couldn't speak. He thought of Nyberg. They never really talked about private matters, but Wallander knew Nyberg would understand. His irascible and outspoken nature was an advantage in this situation. Above all, Wallander knew Nyberg respected his abilities. He doubted that Nyberg would be able to stand working under anyone else.

Wallander dialled Nyberg's home number. As usual he

answered the phone in an irritable voice. Wallander often said to Martinsson that he'd never heard Nyberg sound friendly on the phone.

"We need to talk," Wallander said.

"What's happened?"

"Nothing to do with the case. But I need to see you."

"Can't it wait?"

"No."

"I can be at the station in 15 minutes."

"Let's meet somewhere else. I thought we could go out and have a beer."

"We're going to a bar? What's this all about?"

"Do you have any suggestions where we could go?"

"I never go out," Nyberg said dismissively. "At least not in Ystad."

"There's a new restaurant and bar by the main square," Wallander said. "By the antiques shop. I'll see you there."

"Do I have to wear a suit and tie?"

"I can't imagine you would," Wallander answered.

Nyberg promised to be there in half an hour. Wallander changed his shirt, then left the flat on foot. There weren't many people in the restaurant. When he asked, they told him it closed at 11 p.m. He realised he was quite hungry, flipped through the menu, and was shocked by the prices. Who could afford to eat out any more? But he wanted to treat Nyberg to something to eat.

Nyberg arrived in exactly half an hour. He was dressed in a suit and tie, and had even slicked his normally wayward hair down with water. The suit was a little old and looked too big. Nyberg sat down across from Wallander.

"I had no idea there was a restaurant here," he said.

"It opened fairly recently," Wallander answered. "Five or so years ago. Let me treat you to something."

"I'm not hungry," Nyberg said.

"Then have a starter," Wallander said

"I'll leave it up to you," Nyberg said and pushed his menu away.

They had a couple of beers while they waited for the food to arrive. Wallander told him about his conversation with Holgersson. He recounted it in detail, but he also added the things he had thought and not said.

"It doesn't sound like the kind of thing you should pay much attention to," Nyberg said when Wallander had finished. "But I understand why it upset you. Internal disputes are the last thing we need right now."

Wallander pretended to take Thurnberg's side for a moment. "Do you think maybe he's right? Should someone else take charge?"

"Who would that be?"

"Martinsson?"

Nyberg stared back at him in disbelief. "You're joking."

"What about Hansson?"

"Maybe in ten years. But this is the worst case we've ever had. That's not a good time to suddenly weaken the leadership of the investigation."

The food appeared on the table and Wallander kept talking about Thurnberg. But Nyberg gave only one-word answers and offered no further comments. At last Wallander realised he was going too far. Nyberg was right. There was nothing more to say. If necessary, Nyberg would back him up. A couple of years earlier Wallander had taken up the matter of his unreasonable workload with Holgersson, soon after she had replaced Björk as chief of police. Nyberg's situation improved after that. They had never talked about it, but Wallander was sure Nyberg knew the part he had played in the matter.

Nyberg was right. They shouldn't waste any more of their energy on Thurnberg, but save it for more pressing matters. They ordered more beers and were told it was the last round. Wallander asked Nyberg if he wanted coffee, but he declined.

"I have more than 20 cups a day," he said. "To keep my energy up. Actually, maybe just to keep going."

"Police work wouldn't be possible without coffee," Wallander said.

"No work would be possible without coffee."

They pondered the importance of coffee in silence. Some people at a nearby table got up and left.

"I don't think I've ever been involved in anything quite as strange as these murders," Nyberg said suddenly.

"Neither have I. It's senseless brutality. I can't imagine a motive."

"It could simply be for the love of killing," Nyberg said. "A killer with a lust for blood who carefully plans and arranges his crimes."

"You may be right," Wallander said. "But how did Svedberg get onto him so fast? That's what I can't understand."

"There's only one rational explanation, which is that Svedberg knew whoever it was. Or had a definite suspicion. Then the question of why he didn't want to tell anyone about this becomes crucial, perhaps the most important question of all."

"Could it be that it was someone we know?"

"Not necessarily. There's another possibility. Not that Svedberg knew who it was, or that he had definite suspicions, but that he feared it was someone he knew."

Wallander saw the logic of Nyberg's statement. To suspect someone and to fear something were not necessarily the same thing.

"That would explain the need for secrecy," Nyberg continued. "He's afraid the killer is someone he knows, but he's not sure. He wants to be convinced before he tells us about it, and he wants to be able to bury the whole thing in silence if his fears turn out to be mistaken."

Wallander watched Nyberg attentively. He was seeing a connection that had not been apparent to him earlier.

"Let's assume that Svedberg hears about the disappearance of the young people," he said. "Let's assume that he is driven by fear that is grounded in a reasonable suspicion. Let's even assume that he knows he's right and that he knows who is responsible for their disappearance. He doesn't even have to know they're dead."

"It isn't very likely that he knew," Nyberg said. "Since he would then have felt compelled to come clean. I can't imagine that Svedberg would have been able to carry a burden like that."

Wallander nodded. Nyberg was right.

"So he doesn't know they're dead," he said. "But he has strong fears and enough conviction to confront this particular person. Then what?"

"He's killed."

"The scene of the crime is hastily rearranged, so that our first thought was that there had been a burglary. And something's missing: the telescope. Which is then hidden in Sture Björklund's shed."

"The door," Nyberg said. "I'm convinced that the killer was let into Svedberg's flat. Or maybe even had his own set of keys."

"It must be someone he knows, someone who's been there before."

"Someone who knows he has a cousin. The killer tries

to push the blame onto him, by planting the telescope at Björklund's place."

The waitress came over with the bill, but Wallander was reluctant to end their conversation.

"What's the common denominator? We really have only two people in the picture: Bror Sundelius and an unknown woman by the name of Louise."

Nyberg shook his head. "A woman didn't commit these murders," he said. "Although we said the same thing a couple of years ago and were proved wrong."

"It can hardly have been Bror Sundelius either," Wallander said. "His legs are bad. There's nothing wrong with his mind, but his health isn't the best."

"Then it's someone we still don't know about," Nyberg said. "Svedberg must have had other people he was close to."

"I'm going to go back a little," Wallander said. "Tomorrow I'm going to start searching Svedberg's life."

"That's probably the right way to do it," Nyberg agreed. "I'll check on the results of our forensic tests, especially the fingerprinting. Hopefully that'll tell us more."

"The weapons," Wallander said. "They're important."

"Wester in Ludvika is very pleasant," Nyberg said. "I'm getting full cooperation."

Wallander pulled the bill towards him. Nyberg wanted to split it with him.

"We could try to put it on the expense account," Wallander said.

"You'll never get this through," Nyberg said.

Wallander felt around for his wallet. It wasn't there. Suddenly he saw it in his mind's eye, lying on the kitchen table.

"I still want to treat you, but it seems I've left my wallet at home."

Nyberg took out his wallet and counted out 200 kronor. But the bill was almost twice that.

"There's a cashpoint around the corner," Wallander said.

"I don't use cards like that," Nyberg said firmly.

The waitress, who had turned the lights on and off several times, approached them. They were the only people left. Nyberg showed her his ID, which she regarded sceptically.

"We don't let guests have tabs here," she said.

"We're police officers," Wallander said angrily. "I just happen to have left my wallet at home."

"We don't give credit," she said. "If you can't pay I'll have to report you."

"Report us to who?"

"The police."

Wallander almost lost his temper, but Nyberg restrained him. "This could get interesting."

"Are you paying or not?" the waitress asked.

"I think you should call the police," Wallander said pleasantly.

The waitress walked off and made the call, making sure to lock the front door first.

"They're on their way," she said. "You'll have to stay until then."

They waited five minutes, then a police car pulled up outside and two officers got out. One of them was Edmundsson. He stared at Wallander and Nyberg.

"We seem to have a little problem," Wallander said. "I've left my wallet at home and Nyberg doesn't have enough cash to cover the bill. This lady doesn't give credit, nor was she impressed by Nyberg's ID."

Edmundsson took this in, then burst into laughter. "What's the bill?" he asked.

"It's 400 kronor."

He took out his wallet and paid.

"It's not my fault," the waitress said. "My boss says we should never give credit."

"Who owns this place?" Nyberg asked.

"His name's Fredriksson. Alf Fredriksson."

"Is he a big man?" Nyberg asked. "Does he live in Svarte?" The waitress nodded.

"Then I know him," Nyberg said. "Nice man. Say hello to him from Nyberg and Wallander."

The squad car was already gone when they walked out onto the street.

"This is the strangest August I've ever known," Nyberg said. "It's already the 15th and it's still warm."

They parted ways when they got to Hamngatan.

"We just don't know if he's going to strike again," Wallander said. "That's the worst thing."

"That's why we have to get him," Nyberg said. "As fast as we can."

Wallander walked home slowly. He was inspired by his talk with Nyberg but felt no real peace of mind. He didn't want to admit it, but Thurnberg's reaction and his conversation with Holgersson had depressed him. Was he being unfair to Thurnberg? Was he right? Should someone else be in charge of this investigation?

When Wallander got home he put on a pot of coffee and sat down at the kitchen table. The thermometer outside the window read 19°C. Wallander got out a pad of paper and a pencil, then looked for his glasses, and found a pair under the sofa.

Coffee cup in hand, he found himself walking around the kitchen table a couple of times as if to coax himself into the right frame of mind for the task ahead. He had never written a speech in memory of a murdered colleague

331

before. Now he regretted having agreed to do it. How did you describe the feeling of finding your colleague with his face blown off in his flat only one week earlier?

Finally he sat down and got started. He could still remember when he first met Svedberg, 20 years earlier, when Svedberg had already begun to bald. He was halfway through when he tore everything up and started again. It was after 1 a.m. when he'd finished. This time it was good enough.

He walked out onto the balcony. The town was quiet, and it was still quite warm. He recalled his conversation with Nyberg and let his mind wander. Suddenly the image of Isa Edengren was there, curled up in the cave that had protected her as a child but no longer could. Wallander went back in, leaving the door to the balcony open. There was a thought that wouldn't go away. That the man out there in the darkness was preparing to strike again.

CHAPTER TWENTY-TWO

It had been a long day. There were many packages, certified letters, and international money orders. He wasn't done with the bookkeeping until it was almost 2 p.m.

His old self would have been irritated by the fact that the work took longer than expected. Now it didn't affect him any more. The enormous change he'd undergone had made him impervious to time. He realised there was no such thing as past or future. There was no time that could be lost or won. The only thing that counted was action.

He put away his postbag and cashbox, then showered and changed his clothes. He hadn't eaten since early that morning, before he'd driven to the depot to start sorting his post. But he wasn't hungry. This was a feeling that he remembered from his childhood. When something exciting lay in store for him, he lost his appetite. He went into the soundproofed room and turned on all the lights. He'd made the bed before leaving that morning, and now he spread the letters out over the dark-blue bedspread. He sat cross-legged in the middle of the bed. He had read these letters before. That was the first step, to pick out letters that caught his eye. He opened them carefully, without doing any damage to the envelope. He copied them and then he read them. He didn't know exactly how many letters he had opened, copied and read this past year. It must have been close to 200. Most of them were nothing special. They were vacuous, boring. It wasn't until he had opened the letter from Lena Norman to Martin Boge . . .

He interrupted the thought. That was over and done with. He didn't need to think about them any more. The last phase had been so difficult and tiring. First there was the trip to Östergötland, then he had hunted around for a suitable boat in the darkness, one that was big enough to take him to the little island at the far edge of the archipelago.

It had been a bothersome undertaking, and he hadn't liked having to put in the extra effort. It meant overcoming his own resistance, something he tried to avoid. He looked at the letters spread around him on the bed. Choosing a couple that were planning to get married had not occurred to him until sometime in May. The idea came to him by chance, like so much else in life. During his years as an engineer, chance had not been allowed in his orderly existence. Now everything had changed. The interplay of luck and coincidence meant a person's life was a steady stream of unexpected opportunities. He could pick and choose what he wanted.

The little raised flag on the letter box told him nothing. But when he knocked on the door and entered the kitchen, he found more than a hundred invitations lying on the table. The bride-to-be let him in. He could no longer remember her name, but he remembered her joy, and it enraged him. He took her letters and posted them, and if he hadn't been so embroiled in complicated plans for participating in the upcoming Midsummer celebration he would perhaps have become involved in her wedding.

New opportunities kept presenting themselves. All six envelopes in front of him were wedding invitations. He had read their letters, got to know each couple. He knew where they lived, what they looked like, and where they were to be married. The invitations in front of him were merely printed cards, there to remind him of the different couples.

Now he faced his most important task, deciding which of the couples was the happiest. He went through the envelopes one by one, reminding himself of other letters that they had written, to each other or their friends. He savoured the moment, suffused with contentment. He was in charge. In this soundproofed room he could not be touched by the things that had made him suffer in his earlier life – the feeling of being an outsider and being misunderstood. In here he could bear to think about the great catastrophe, when he was shut out and declared superfluous.

Nothing was hard any more. Or almost nothing. He still couldn't bear to think about how he had subjected himself to humiliation for more than two years. He had answered ads in the paper, sent in his CV, gone to countless interviews.

That was before he cut himself off from his former existence and left everything behind. Becoming another.

He knew he was one of the lucky ones. Today he would never have got a job as a substitute postman. There were blocks to most professions. People were laid off. He noticed this as he went along his post route. People sat in their houses waiting for letters. More and more of them ended up on the outside and had not yet learned how to break free.

He finally picked the couple getting married on Saturday, 17 August, at their home just outside Köpingebro. They had invited a lot of people. He couldn't even remember how many invitations they had given him. But both of

335

them had been standing there when he came in through the door, and their happiness seemed limitless. He could have killed them on the spot. But as usual he controlled himself. He congratulated them, and no one could have guessed what he was really thinking.

It was the most important art a person could learn: self-control.

On Friday morning, Wallander began the task of mapping out Svedberg's life in earnest. He arrived at the station shortly after 7 a.m. and went about his task with some reluctance. He didn't know exactly what he was looking for, but somewhere in Svedberg's life there had to be a point leading to the reason for his murder. It was like trying to find a trace of life in a person who had already died.

What interested him most this morning was a man called Jan Söderblom, who Ylva Brink said knew Svedberg when he was young, during his days of compulsory military service and police training. The connection was severed when Söderblom married and moved away, she thought to Malmö or Landskrona. What interested Wallander was that Söderblom had become a police officer just like Svedberg. He was about to call the station in Malmö when Nyberg appeared at the door. Wallander could tell from his expression that something was up.

"Things are happening," Nyberg said and waved some faxes at him. "We can start with the murder weapons, if you like. Turns out the revolver stolen in Ludvika along with the shotgun could have been the same as the one in the nature reserve."

"Could have been?"

"In my language that means it's the one."

336

"Good," Wallander said. "We needed that."

"Then there are the fingerprints," Nyberg continued. "We found a good right thumbprint on the shotgun. We found another good thumbprint on a wineglass out in the reserve."

"Same thumb?"

"Yes."

"Previous record?"

"Not in our files. But we're going to send that thumbprint all around the world if we have to."

"So it is the same man," Wallander said slowly. "At least we know that much."

"There were no fingerprints on the telescope, however, other than Svedberg's own."

"Does that mean he hid it at Björklund's place himself?"

"Not necessarily. The person could have been wearing gloves."

"We have this thumbprint on the shotgun," Wallander said. "But what about in Svedberg's flat in general? We have to know who created that chaos, if it was Svedberg or someone else. Or both."

"We'll have to wait on that, but they're working on it."

Wallander got up and leaned against the wall. He felt that there was more to this.

"We found none of Svedberg's prints on the shotgun," Nyberg said. "That may or may not mean anything."

"We've come a long way," Wallander said. "We have a single killer."

"Maybe we should notify the chief prosecutor," Nyberg said, smiling. "That might cheer him up."

"Or not. We're not living up to our bad reputation. But we'll make sure he gets his report."

Nyberg left the room and Wallander grabbed the phone,

called Malmö and asked to speak to Officer Jan Söderblom. Sure enough there was a detective by that name who worked mainly on theft cases, but he was on holiday on a Greek island until the following Wednesday. Wallander left a message that he wanted to speak to him as soon as possible. He also made a note of Söderblom's home phone number. He had just hung up when Höglund knocked on the half-open door. She held his speech about Svedberg in her hands.

"I've read it," she said. "And I think it's honest and moving. I suppose those two things always go together. No one's touched simply by empty talk of eternity and light conquering the darkness."

"It's not too long?" Wallander asked anxiously.

"I read it aloud to myself and it took less than five minutes. I don't usually speak at funerals, but I think it's just the right length."

She was about to slip out again when Wallander told her Nyberg's news.

"That's a huge step forward," she said when he had finished. "If we could only find the person or people who stole the guns."

"It'll be hard, but of course we'll try. I was wondering if it wouldn't be worth it to put pictures of the guns in the papers. Both the revolver and the shotgun."

"There's a press conference at 11 a.m.," she said. "Lisa has been overrun by the press lately. Maybe we should tell them about the weapons. What do we really have to lose by telling them there's a connection between the two cases? It'll be murder on a scale this country hasn't seen for a long time."

"You're right," Wallander said. "I'll be there."

She lingered in the doorway. "Then there's the elusive

Louise," she said. "Whom no one seems to have seen. There have been a lot of calls but nothing reliable."

"That's strange," Wallander said. "But someone somewhere knows her. We talked about trying Denmark."

"Why not all of Europe?"

"Yes," he agreed. "Why not? But let's start with Denmark and let's do it now, as soon as possible."

"I'm on my way to Lund to go through Lena Norman's flat," she said. "But I'll ask Hansson to do it."

"Not Hansson," Wallander said. "He's still working on finding the cars. There has to be someone else who can do it."

"We're going to need those reinforcements," Höglund said. "Lisa says some people are arriving from Malmö this afternoon."

"We need Svedberg," Wallander said. "That's what it is. We just aren't used to not having him around."

They were silent for a while after this; then she left. Wallander opened the window. It was still warm, and there was only a gentle breeze. The phone rang. It was Ebba. She sounded tired, and Wallander thought how much she had seemed to age during the last few years. Before, she had always helped them keep their spirits up. Now she was often down herself, and sometimes she forgot to pass along their messages. She was due to retire next summer, but no one could bring themselves to think about it.

"There's a call here from an officer called Larsson. He says he's from the police in Valdemarsvik," she told him. "Can you take it? Everyone else is busy."

Larsson spoke with an Östgöta dialect.

"Harry Lundström from Norrköping told us to inform you about anything stolen around Gryt on the day that girl was shot out on Bärnsö Island."

339

"That's right."

"We may have something that will interest you, stolen from Snäckvarp. The owner can't say exactly when, because he wasn't there when it happened. But it was found in an inlet just south of Snäckvarp. It's a six-metre fibreglass boat with a raised steering platform."

Wallander felt his usual insecurity in discussing boats.

"Is it big enough to take out to Bärnsö?"

"If the wind wasn't too strong it could take you all the way out to Gotland."

Wallander thought for a moment. "Any fingerprints?" he asked.

"We've checked," Larsson said. "There was oil on the steering wheel so we found a couple of good prints there. They're already on their way over to you, via Norrköping. Harry is the one in charge of the whole thing."

"Was there a road near where the boat was found?" Wallander asked.

"The boat was hidden in a mass of reeds. But you can walk to Snäckvarp in about ten minutes and there's a dirt road from there."

"This is important," Wallander said.

"How are things going? Are you closing in on the killer?"

"Yes, but these things take time."

"I never met the girl, but I had a run-in with Edengren a couple of years ago."

"Oh, what happened?"

"Illegal fishing. He was putting nets and eel traps in other people's water."

"Isn't it free fishing out there?"

"It varies. Not that he bothered to find out. If I may speak plainly, I thought he was a royal pain in the arse. But of course I feel sorry for him now, with the girl and all."

"Was that it? Illegal fishing?"

"As far as I know."

Wallander thanked him for the call. Then he tried to reach Harry Lundström in Norrköping, and was directed to his mobile phone. Lundström was in a car somewhere out in Vikboland. Wallander told him they had a positive ID on the murder weapon from the reserve, and that they would soon know about the gun used on Bärnsö Island. Lundström in turn told him they weren't sure of any prints found on the island, but he assumed the stolen boat in Snäckvarp was the one the killer had used.

"People out here on the islands are getting worried," he said. "You have to get this man."

"Yes," Wallander said. "Yes, we do. And we will."

He went and got a cup of coffee when he was done with the conversation. It was already 9.30 a.m. Something occurred to him, and he went back to his office and looked up the number for the Lundberg family in Skårby. The wife answered. Wallander realised he hadn't spoken to them since Isa was murdered, and so he began by offering her his condolences.

"Erik is still in bed," she said. "He doesn't have the energy to get up. He says we should sell the house and move away. Who could do something like this to a child?"

Isa was like a daughter to her, Wallander thought. I should have thought of it earlier.

He couldn't really answer her question, but he sensed that she held him responsible for Isa's death.

"I called to see if her parents have come home," he said.

"They came back last night."

"That was all I wanted to know," he said. He expressed his regrets once again and then hung up.

He planned to drive out to Skårby immediately after the

press conference. He wanted to go right away, but there wasn't time. He picked up the phone and called Thurnberg. Without mentioning what he had heard the previous night, he gave him a short update on the latest findings from the forensic investigation. Wallander concluded by stressing that the findings meant they could now concentrate on searching for a single killer. Thurnberg said he looked forward to seeing the written report, and Wallander promised to send him a copy.

"There will be a press conference at 11 a.m.," Wallander said. "I think we should reveal these latest findings to the press and have pictures of the guns published."

"Do we have any pictures of them available now?"

"We'll get them tomorrow at the latest."

Thurnberg made no objections, and said he would participate in the press conference. They kept the conversation brief, but Wallander noticed by the end that he had broken into a sweat.

They held the press conference in the largest room available. Wallander couldn't remember another case ever getting so much attention. As usual he got terribly nervous when he walked up to the podium. To his surprise, Thurnberg began. That had never happened in all the years he had worked there. Per Åkeson always let Wallander or the chief of police take on that task. Thurnberg spoke as if he was accustomed to speaking to the press. It's a new era, Wallander thought. He wasn't sure that he didn't feel a tiny bit envious. He listened carefully to what Thurnberg said, and couldn't deny that he expressed himself well.

Next it was his turn to speak. He had made some notes on a piece of paper to remind himself of what to say, but now, naturally, couldn't find it. He told them they had traced the murder weapons to Ludvika, with a possible link to a robbery in Orsa. He also told them that they were still waiting for a positive ID on the weapon used on Bärnsö Island in the Östergötland archipelago. As he spoke he thought of Westin, the postman who had taken him out to the island. Why he thought of him at that moment he couldn't say. He also talked about the findings regarding the stolen boat. When he finished, there were many questions. Thurnberg handled most of them, with Wallander jumping in from time to time. Martinsson was listening to the proceedings from the very back of the room.

Finally a woman from one of the evening papers indicated that she wanted to ask a question. Wallander had never seen her before.

"Would it be accurate to say that the police have no leads at this time?" she said, turning directly to Wallander.

"We have many leads," Wallander said. "We're just not close to making an arrest."

"It seems to me that the police investigation hasn't yielded any results. It seems more than likely that this killer will strike again. After all, I think it's clear to all of us that we're dealing with a madman."

"We don't know that," Wallander answered. "That's why we're keeping our approach as comprehensive as we can."

"That sounds like a strategy," the reporter said. "But it could also give the impression that you don't know where to turn, that you're helpless."

Wallander glanced at Thurnberg, who encouraged him to continue with an almost invisible nod of his head.

"The police are never helpless," Wallander said. "If we were, we wouldn't be police officers."

"Don't you agree that you're looking for a madman?"

"No."

"What else could this person be?"

"We don't know yet."

"Do you think you'll catch whoever did this?"

"Yes, without a doubt."

"Will he strike again?"

"We don't know."

There was a brief pause. Wallander got up, which the others took as a signal that the conference was over. Wallander thought Thurnberg had probably intended to end it in a more formal manner, but Wallander left the room before Thurnberg had a chance to talk to him. TV news teams were waiting to interview him in the reception area. Wallander told them to speak with Thurnberg. Later Ebba told him that Thurnberg was more than happy to oblige.

Wallander went into his office to get his coat. He tried to think what it was that made him think of Westin during the press conference. He knew it was significant. He sat down at his desk and tried to coax the thought to the surface, but it wouldn't come. He gave up. As he was putting his coat on, Hansson called.

"I found the cars," he said. "Norman's and Boge's: a 1991 Toyota and a Volvo that's one year older. They were in a car park down by Sandhammaren. I've already called Nyberg. He's on his way there."

"So am I."

At the edge of town, Wallander pulled over at a take-away bar and ate a hotdog. It had become habit now to buy one-litre bottles of mineral water. He had forgotten to take the medication that Dr Göransson had prescribed for him, and he didn't have it with him.

He drove back to Mariagatan in a bad temper. There was a heap of post on the floor in the hall, and he noticed a post-card from Linda, who was visiting friends in Hudiksvall, and a letter from his sister Kristina. Wallander took the post with him into the kitchen. His sister had put the name and address of a hotel on the back of the envelope. It was in Kemi, which Wallander knew was in northern Finland. He wondered what she was doing there, but he let the post wait, and took his medicine instead. Before he left the kitchen, he glanced at the post lying on the table and again his thoughts returned to Westin. Now he was able to catch hold of the thought.

There was something Westin had said during their trip out to Bärnsö Island, something that Wallander's subconscious had been turning over and was trying to send to the surface. He tried to reconstruct their conversation in the noisy wheelhouse without success. But Westin had said something important. He decided to call him after he had looked at the two cars.

Nyberg was already there when Wallander got out of his car. The Toyota and Volvo were parked next to each other. Police tape was plastered all around the area and the cars were being photographed. The doors and boots were wide open. Wallander walked up to Nyberg, who was getting a bag out of his car.

"Thanks again for meeting me last night," he said.

"An old friend came down to see me from Stockholm in 1973," Nyberg replied. "We went out to a bar one evening. I don't think I've been out since then."

Wallander remembered that he hadn't paid Edmundsson back.

"Well, anyway, I had a nice time," he said.

"There's already a rumour going around that we were caught trying to get out of paying the bill," Nyberg said.

"Just as long as Thurnberg doesn't get wind of it. He might take it the wrong way."

Wallander walked over to Hansson, who was making some notes.

"Any doubt they're the right ones?"

"The Toyota is Lena Norman's, the Volvo belongs to Martin Boge."

"How long have they been here?"

"We don't know. In July the car park is full of cars coming and going. It's only in August that it starts to slow down and that people start noticing which cars haven't been moved."

"Is there any other way to find out if they've been here since Midsummer?"

"You'll have to talk to Nyberg about that."

Wallander went back to Nyberg, who was staring at the Toyota.

"Fingerprints are the most important," Wallander said. "The cars must have been driven here from the reserve."

"Someone who leaves his prints on a boat might well leave us a greeting on a steering wheel."

"That's what I'm hoping."

"That probably also means our killer is fairly sure his prints don't appear in any records, either here or abroad."

"I was thinking the same thing," Wallander said. "We'll just have to hope you're wrong."

Wallander didn't need to stay any longer. As he passed the turn-off to his father's house, he couldn't resist having a look. There was a For Sale sign by the driveway. He didn't stop. Seeing the sign gave him a funny feeling. He had just made it back to Ystad when the mobile phone rang. It was Höglund.

"I'm in Lund," she said. "In Lena Norman's flat. I think you should come here."

"What is it?"

"You'll see when you get here. I think it's important."

Wallander wrote down the address and was on his way.

CHAPTER TWENTY-THREE

The block of flats was on the outskirts of Lund. It was four storeys high, one of five buildings comprising a large housing estate. Once, many years ago when Wallander had come down to Lund with Linda, she had pointed them out to him and told him they were student flats. If she had chosen to study in Lund, she would have lived in a place like this. Wallander shivered, imagining Linda out in the reserve.

He didn't have to guess which building it was, as a police car was parked outside one of them. Wallander put his phone in his pocket and got out. A woman was stretched out in the sun on one of the lawns. Wallander wished he could lie down beside her and sleep for a while. His tiredness came and went in heavy waves. An officer stood inside the doorway, yawning. Wallander waved his identification in front of him and the officer pointed up the stairs absentmindedly.

"All the way up. No elevator."

Then he yawned again and Wallander felt a sudden urge to whip him into shape. Wallander was the superior officer, and one from another district at that. They were trying to catch a man who had killed five people so far. He didn't need to be greeted by an officer who yawned and could hardly bring himself to speak.

But he said nothing. He walked up the stairs. Apart from the loud, raucous music coming from one flat, the building seemed abandoned. It was still August and the autumn term had not yet begun. The door to Lena Norman's flat was slightly ajar but Wallander rang the bell anyway.

Höglund came to the door herself. He tried to read her expression without success.

"I didn't mean to sound so dramatic over the phone," she said quickly. "But I think you'll understand why I wanted you to see this."

He followed her into the flat, which hadn't been aired out for a while. The air had that characteristic but indescribable dry quality he had so often encountered in concrete buildings. He had read somewhere that the FBI had developed a method for determining how long a house had been locked up. He didn't know whether Nyberg had the technique at his disposal.

At the thought of Nyberg he made another mental note to repay Edmundsson. The flat had two rooms and a kitchen. They reached the combined living room and study. The sun was shining in through the window and dust drifted slowly in the still air. There were a number of photographs tacked up on one wall. Wallander put on his glasses and peered at them. He recognised her at once. Lena Norman was dressed up in a scene that looked like it was supposed to be from the 17th century. Martin Boge was also in the picture, which was taken with what appeared to be a castle in the background. The next picture was also of a party. Lena Norman was in that one too, and now Astrid Hillström was there. They were indoors somewhere, half-naked. Wallander guessed they were staging a bordello scene. Neither Norman nor Hillström was particularly convincing. Wallander straightened up and cast a glance over the entire wall.

"They play different roles at their parties," he said.

"It goes further than that," she said and went over to a desk that stood at right angles to one of the windows. It was covered with binders and plastic folders.

"I've gone through this material," she said. "Not completely, of course, but what I've seen so far worries me." Wallander lifted his hand to interrupt her.

"Wait a second. I need to drink a glass of water, and use the bathroom."

"My father has diabetes," she said.

Wallander froze on his way to the door. "What do you mean by that?"

"If I didn't know any better I'd think you had it too, the way you drink water these days. And need to go to the loo constantly."

For a moment Wallander thought he was going to break his silence and tell her the truth: that she was right. But instead he just muttered something inaudible and left the room. When he came out of the kitchen, the toilet was still flushing.

"The flushing mechanism is broken," he said. "I guess that's not our problem."

She was looking at him as if she was expecting him to talk.

"Why are you worried?" he asked.

"I'll tell you what I've found so far," she said. "But I'm convinced there's more, and that it'll become apparent when we've gone through everything."

Wallander sat down on a chair by the desk. She remained standing.

"They dress up," she started. "They have parties, and move between our own time and that of past ages. From time to time they even go into the future, but not very often. Probably because it's harder – no one knows how people will dress in a thousand years, or even 50. We know all this, of course. We've talked to the friends who weren't with them at Midsummer. You even had a chance to talk to Isa Edengren. We know they rented their costumes in Copenhagen. But there's a deeper level to this."

She picked up a folder covered in geometric figures. "They appear to have belonged to a sect," she said. "It has its roots in the United States, in Minneapolis. It strikes me as an updated version of the Jim Jones cult or the Branch Davidians. Their rules are horrifying, something akin to the threatening letters people who have broken chain mail or pyramid schemes hand over to us. Anyone who divulges their secrets will suffer violent retribution – always death, of course. They pay dues to the head office that in turn sends out lists of suggestions for their parties and explains how to maintain their secrecy. But there is also a spiritual dimension to their activities. They think that people who practise moving through time like this will be able to choose the age of their rebirth at the moment of their death. It was highly unpleasant reading. I think Lena Norman was the head of the Swedish chapter."

Wallander was listening with rapt attention. Höglund had called him down here with good reason.

"Does the organisation have a name?"

"I don't know what it would be in Swedish. In English they call themselves the Divine Movers."

Wallander flipped through the folder she had given him. There were geometric figures everywhere, but also pictures of old gods and the mutilated bodies of tortured people. He put the material down with disgust.

"Do you think what happened in the nature reserve was

a result of vengeance? That they had divulged the secret and had to be killed?"

"In this day and age I hardly think that can be ruled out."

Wallander knew she was right. Only a short time ago a number of members of a sect in Switzerland and France had committed mass suicide. In May, Martinsson had taken part in a conference in Stockholm devoted to the role of the police in stemming this increased activity. It was getting harder, since modern sects no longer circled around a single crazed individual. Now they were well-organised corporations that had their own lawyers and accountants. Members took out loans to pay fees they couldn't really afford. It wasn't even clear these days if the emotional blackmail that took place could be classified as criminal activity. Martinsson had told Wallander after he returned from the conference that new laws would have to be enacted if they were to have any hope in prosecuting these soul-sucking vampires who were profiting from the increased sense of helplessness in society.

"This is an important discovery," he said to Höglund. "We're going to need help with this. The national police have a special division devoted to working on new sects. We'll also need help from the United States on the Divine Movers. Above all, we have to get the other young people involved in this to talk, get them to divulge their carefully guarded secrets."

"They take their vows and then eat horse liver. Raw," she said, leafing through the folder.

"Who officiates at these ceremonies?"

"It must be Lena Norman."

Wallander shook his head, baffled. "And she's dead now. Do you think she would have broken her vows? Was there someone waiting to replace her?"

"I don't know. Maybe we'll find a name among these papers when we've had a chance to go through them properly."

Wallander stood up and looked out the window. The woman was still down on the lawn. He thought of the woman he had met at the roadside restaurant outside Västervik. He searched for her name for a while before it came to him: Erika. He had a sudden longing to see her again.

"We probably shouldn't get too distracted by all this," he said in an absentminded way. "We shouldn't rule out our other theories."

"Which are?"

He didn't need to spell it out for her. The only possible theory was a deranged killer acting alone. The theory you always worked with when you had no leads.

"I have difficulty seeing Svedberg getting tangled up in all this," he said. "Even though he's surprised us."

"Maybe he wasn't directly involved," Höglund said. "He may simply have known someone who was."

He thought again of Westin, the seafaring postman. Wallander was still desperately trying to catch hold of something he had said during that boat trip. But it remained out of reach.

"There's really only one thing we need to know," Wallander said, "as in all complicated cases. One thing, that would set everything else in motion."

"The identity of Svedberg's killer?"

He nodded. "Exactly. Then we would have an answer to everything, except perhaps the question of the motive. But we could piece that together as well."

Wallander returned to the chair and sat down. "Did you have time to talk to the Danes about Louise?"

"The photograph will be published tomorrow."

Wallander got up again. "We have to go through this flat thoroughly," he said. "From top to bottom. But I think I'll be of more use in Ystad. If we have time, we'll contact Interpol today and get the Americans involved. Martinsson will love taking charge of that."

"I think he dreams about being a federal agent in the United States," Höglund agreed. "Not just a policeman in Ystad."

"We all have our dreams," Wallander said, in an awkward and completely unnecessary attempt to come to Martinsson's defence. He gathered the papers from the desk while Höglund looked around the kitchen for some plastic bags to put them in. They talked for a while in the small hall before he left.

"I keep having this feeling that I'm overlooking something," Wallander said. "I think it has something to do with Westin."

"Westin?"

"He was the one who took me out to Bärnsö Island. He's the postman in the archipelago. He said something when we were standing in the wheelhouse. I just can't remember what it was."

"Why don't you call him? The two of you might be able to reconstruct the conversation. Maybe simply hearing his voice will bring whatever it was back to you."

"You may be right," Wallander said doubtfully. "I'll call."

Then he remembered another voice. "What happened with Lundberg? I mean the person who wasn't him, but who pretended to be. The one who called the hospital and asked about Isa."

"I passed that on to Martinsson. We exchanged a couple of tasks; I can't remember now what they were. I took on

353

something he hadn't had time to do. He promised to talk to the nurse."

Wallander sensed a note of criticism in her voice. They all had so much to do. The tasks were piling up.

Wallander drove back to Ystad, thinking over the latest events. How did the revelations in Lena Norman's flat alter the picture? Were these parties much more sinister than he had thought? He recalled the time a few years earlier, when Linda had undergone what might be described as a religious crisis. It was right after the divorce. Linda was as lost as he was, and one night he had heard a soft mumbling from inside her bedroom that he thought must be prayer. When he found books in her room about Scientology, he'd become seriously concerned. He tried to reason with her without much success. Finally Mona sorted things out. He didn't know exactly what happened, but one day the soft mumbles behind her door stopped and she went back to her old interests.

He shivered at the thought of sects. Were the answers to this case lying somewhere in these plastic bags? He accelerated. He was in a hurry.

The first thing he did back at the station was to find Edmundsson and pay him the money he owed. Then he went to the conference room where Martinsson was briefing the three police officers from Malmö who were joining the investigation. Wallander had met one of them before, a detective in his 60s by the name of Rytter. He didn't recognise either of the other two, who were younger. Wallander said hello, but didn't stay. He asked Martinsson to try to catch him sometime later that evening. Then he went to his office and started going through the papers from Lena Norman's flat. He was about half finished when Martinsson appeared. It was a little after 11 p.m. Martinsson was pale and bleary-eyed. Wallander wondered how he looked himself.

"How's it going?" he asked.

"They're good," Martinsson said. "Especially the old guy, Rytter."

"They're going to make a real difference," Wallander said enthusiastically. "It will give us the break we need."

Martinsson pulled off his tie and unbuttoned his collar.

"I have a project for you," Wallander said. He told him in some detail about the materials that had turned up in Lena Norman's flat. Martinsson became more and more interested. The thought that he would be contacting colleagues in the U.S. was clearly invigorating.

"The most important thing is to get a clear picture of these people," Wallander said.

Martinsson looked at his watch. "I guess this isn't the best time of day to get in touch with the U.S., but I'll give it a shot."

Wallander got up and gathered the papers together, and they went to copy the material that Wallander hadn't had time to look through.

"Apart from drugs, sects are the thing I'm most afraid of for my children," Martinsson said. "I'm afraid of them getting pulled into some religious nightmare they won't be able to get out of, where I won't be able to reach them."

"There was a time when I had those exact worries about Linda," Wallander said. He didn't say anything more, and Martinsson didn't ask any questions.

The copier suddenly stopped working. Martinsson reloaded it with a new sheaf of blank paper. Wallander left Martinsson and returned to his office. A report on the charges once filed against Svedberg was lying on his desk. He read through it quickly to get a sense of what had happened. It was dated 19 September 1985. A man named Stig Stridh, the complainant, was assaulted by his brother, an alcoholic, who had come to ask him for money. He knocked out two of Stridh's teeth, stole a camera, and demolished a large part of his living room. Two police officers, one by the name of Andersson, showed up at the flat and took down details of the incident. Stridh was called down to the police station on 26 August for a meeting with Inspector Karl Evert Svedberg. Svedberg explained to him that there would not be an investigation into the case since there was no evidence. Stridh argued vehemently that a camera was missing and a large part of his living room was damaged, and that the two officers had seen his cuts and bruises. According to Stridh, at this point Svedberg's manner became threatening and he ordered him to drop the charges. Stridh left and later wrote a letter to Björk, in which he complained about the treatment he had received.

Two days later Svedberg showed up at Stridh's door and repeated his threats. After some deliberation with friends, Stridh had decided to file charges against Svedberg with the department of justice. Wallander read the report with a growing sense of disbelief. Svedberg's response to the report was brief and denied all charges. Svedberg's behaviour in the case simply couldn't be explained. But this was exactly the kind of thing they had to get to the bottom of.

It was past midnight when Wallander had finished reading the report. He hadn't managed to fit in the visit to Isa Edengren's parents. He couldn't find a Stig Stridh in the phone book. Both matters would have to wait until the morning. Now he had to get some sleep. He took his coat and left the station. There was a faint breeze outside, but it was still warm. He found his car keys and unlocked the door.

Suddenly he jerked around. He couldn't say what had frightened him. He listened hard and stared into the shadows at the edge of the car park. There was no one there, he told himself. He got into his car. I'm always afraid that he's out there, close by, he thought. Whoever he is, he keeps himself well informed, and I'm afraid he will kill again.

CHAPTER TWENTY-FOUR

On Saturday, 17 August, Wallander woke to the sound of rain drumming against the bedroom window. The alarm clock read 6.30 a.m. Wallander listened to the sound of the rain. Soft morning light was streaming in through a gap in the curtains. He tried to recall when it had last rained. It had to have been before the night when he and Martinsson found Svedberg's body, and that was eight days ago. It's an unfathomable length of time, he thought. Neither long, nor short. He went out to the bathroom and had a pee, then drank some water at the kitchen counter and returned to bed. The fear from the night before was still with him, just as mysterious, just as strong.

He was showered and dressed by 7.15 a.m. For breakfast he had a cup of coffee and a tomato. The rain had stopped and the thermometer read 15°C. The clouds were already starting to clear. He decided to make his calls from the flat rather than the station. First he would call Westin, then the operator to try and get Stig Stridh's phone number. He had already found the piece of paper with Westin's numbers on it. He was counting on Westin having Saturdays off, but he probably wasn't the type to stay in bed, either. Wallander took his coffee with him into the living room and dialled the first of the three numbers on the scrap of paper. A woman answered after the third ring. Wallander introduced himself and apologised for calling so early.

"I'll get him," she said. "He's chopping wood."

Wallander thought he could hear the sound of wood splitting in the background. Then the sound stopped and he heard children's voices. Westin finally came to the phone, and they exchanged greetings.

"You're chopping wood," Wallander said.

"The cold weather always comes sooner than you think," Westin said. "How are things going? I've been trying to follow the case in the papers and on the news. Have you caught him yet?"

"Not yet. It takes time. But we'll get him."

Westin was silent on the other end. He probably saw right through Wallander's optimism, which was as hollow as it was necessary. Pessimistic policemen rarely solved complicated crimes.

"Do you remember any of our conversation when we were heading out to Bärnsö?" Wallander asked.

"Which part?" Westin answered. "We talked all the way there, if I recall. Between stops."

"One of our conversations was a little longer – I think it was the very first part of the trip."

Suddenly Wallander remembered. Westin had slowed the boat down and they were coasting in towards the first or perhaps the second island. It had a name that reminded him of Bärnsö.

"It was one of the first stops," Wallander said. "What were the names of those islands?"

"You must be thinking of Harö or Båtmansö Island."

"Båtmansö. That was it. An old man lived there."

"Zetterquist."

It was starting to come back to him now. "We were on our way in towards the dock," he said. "You were telling me about Zetterquist, who spends the winters out there all alone. Do you remember what you said?"

Westin laughed, but in a jovial way. "I'm sure I could have said any number of things."

"I know this seems strange, but it's actually quite important," Wallander said.

Westin seemed to sense that Wallander was serious. "I think you asked me what it was like to deliver the post," he said.

"Then I'll ask you that same question. What's it like being a postman in the islands?"

"It gives you a sense of freedom, but it's also hard work. And no one knows how long I'll keep my job. I wouldn't put it past them to cut my route entirely and stop servicing the archipelago. Zetterquist once told me he might even have to put in an advance order to have his body collected, just to make sure he wasn't left lying out there indefinitely when his time came."

"You didn't say that. I would have remembered it. I'll ask you again. What's it like to be a postman in the islands?"

Westin hesitated this time. "I don't recall saying much else."

But Wallander knew there had been something else. Something mundane, about what delivering post to people who lived out there was like.

"We were on our way in towards the landing," Wallander said. "That much I remember. The boat had slowed down a lot and you were telling me about Zetterquist."

"Maybe I said something about how you end up looking out for people. If they don't come down to meet you, you go up and make sure they're all right."

Almost, Wallander thought. We're almost there now. But you said something more, Lennart Westin. I know you did.

"I can't think of anything else. I really can't," Westin said.

"We're not giving up just yet. Try again."

But Westin couldn't come up with anything else and Wallander wasn't able to coax it out of him.

"Keep at it," Wallander said. "Call me if it comes back to you."

"I'm not normally the curious type, but why is this so important?"

"I don't know," Wallander said simply. "But when I do, I'll tell you, I promise."

Wallander felt despondent after the call. Not only had he been unable to get Westin to remember what he'd said, it was probably irrelevant anyway. His thoughts of giving up, and letting Holgersson put someone else in charge returned more strongly. But then he thought of Thurnberg and felt an even stronger urge to prove him wrong. He called the operator and asked for a number for Stig Stridh. It was unlisted but not private. He dialled the number and counted nine rings before someone answered. The voice was old and drawling.

"Stridh."

"This is Inspector Kurt Wallander from the Ystad police."

Stridh sounded like he was spitting when he replied. "It wasn't me who shot Svedberg, but maybe I should have."

His attitude angered Wallander. Stridh should show more respect, even if Svedberg had acted inappropriately towards him in the past. He had trouble holding back his irritation.

"You filed charges against Svedberg ten years ago. They were dismissed."

"I still can't understand how they could do that," Stridh said. "Svedberg should have lost his job."

"I'm not calling to discuss the decision," Wallander said curtly. "I want to talk to you about what happened."

"What's there to talk about? My brother was drunk."

"What's his name?"

"Nisse."

"Does he live in Ystad?"

"He died in 1991. Cirrhosis of the liver, what a surprise."

Wallander was momentarily at a loss. He had assumed the call to Stig Stridh was the first step towards eventually meeting the brother who played the leading role in the whole strange episode.

"You have my condolences," Wallander said.

"The hell I do. But whatever. I'm not particularly sorry. I get left in peace now and I have the place to myself. At least more often."

"What do you mean by that?"

"Nisse has a widow, or whatever one should call her."

"Is she his widow?"

"That's what she says, but he never married her."

"Do they have children?"

"She did, but not with him. That was just as well. One of hers is doing time."

"What for?"

"Robbed a bank."

"What's his name?"

"It's a she. Stella."

"Your brother's stepdaughter robbed a bank?"

"Is that so strange?"

"It's unusual for a woman to commit that kind of crime. Where did it take place?"

"In Sundsvall. She fired a number of shots at the ceiling."

A vague recollection of this event was coming back to Wallander. He looked for something to write with. Wallander turned back to the matter at hand. Stridh's answers came slowly and with great unwillingness. It took what seemed like an eternity, but Wallander finally had a clearer picture of the events. Stig Stridh had been married, had two grown sons who now lived in Malmö and Laholm. His brother, Nils, called Nisse, who was three years younger, became an alcoholic early on. He began a career in the military but was discharged on account of his heavy drinking. At first Stig tried to be patient with his brother, but the relationship deteriorated, not least because he always came asking for money. Tensions had reached breaking point eleven years earlier. This was the point Wallander wanted to reach.

"We don't have to go through the events in detail," he said. "I just want to know one thing: why do you think Svedberg acted the way he did?"

"He said we had no evidence, but that was bullshit."

"We know that. We don't have to go into it. What I want to know is why you think he acted like this."

"Because he was an idiot."

Wallander was prepared for the answers to anger him, and he knew that Stig had good reasons for his hostility. Svedberg's behaviour had been incomprehensible.

"Svedberg was no idiot," Wallander said. "There must be another explanation. Had you ever met him before?"

"When would that have been?"

"Just answer my questions," Wallander said shortly.

"I'd never met him before."

"Have you had any run-ins with the law yourself?"

"No."

That answer came a little too fast, Wallander thought. It isn't true.

"Stick to the truth, Stridh. If you tell me lies I'll have you hauled straight down to the station in the blink of an eye."

It worked. "Well, I did a little car-dealing in the 1960s,"

he said. "There was some trouble once about a car that was supposed to be stolen, but that's all."

Wallander decided to take him at his word.

"How about your brother?"

"He probably did all kinds of things, but he never did any time for anything except his drinking."

Again, Wallander felt that Stridh was telling the truth. The man didn't know of a connection between his brother and Svedberg. It's hopeless, he thought. I'm banging my head against the wall. Wallander ended the conversation, having decided to talk to Rut Lundin, the "widow".

He left the flat and walked to the station.

Shortly after 11 a.m., as he went to get another cup of coffee, he realised that most of his colleagues were around, including the officers from Malmö, and took the opportunity to call a meeting in the conference room. He started by going through his own attempts to shed light on the events surrounding the complaint filed against Svedberg eleven years ago. Martinsson told him that Hugo Andersson, the policeman who'd answered Stridh's call that night, now worked as a janitor at a school in Värnamo. The officer who'd been his partner was a policeman by the name of Holmström, who now worked in Malmö.

Martinsson promised to check up on both of them. Wallander told them he was driving out to meet Isa Edengren's parents. After the meeting, Wallander shared a pizza with Hansson. All day he had been trying to keep track of how much water he had drunk and how many times he'd relieved himself, but he had already lost track. He called Rut Lundin. Once she understood why he was calling, she answered most of his questions – but she had nothing useful to add. He asked her specifically about Nisse's drinking buddies, and she said she remembered a few. When he pressed her for names, she said she needed time to think. He told her he would drop by later that afternoon.

At 4 p.m. he called Björk, their former chief of police, who now lived in Malmö. They started by catching up on the latest gossip, and Björk expressed deep sympathy at their having to deal with the case at hand. They talked at length about Svedberg. Björk said he was planning to attend the funeral, which surprised Wallander, although he didn't know why. Björk had nothing to say about the complaint filed against Svedberg. He couldn't remember any more why Svedberg had dismissed the investigation, but since the department of justice hadn't intervened, he was sure the whole thing was above board.

Wallander left the station at 4.30 p.m., on his way to Skårby. First he stopped by Rut Lundin's flat to pick up the list of names she had promised him. When he rang her doorbell she opened the door at once, as if she had been waiting for him in the hall. He could see that she was drunk. She thrust a piece of paper in his hand and said it was all she could remember. Wallander saw she didn't want him to come in, so he thanked her and left.

Back out on the footpath, he stopped under the shade of a tree and read through what she had written. He immediately saw a name he recognised about halfway down the list. Bror Sundelius. Wallander caught his breath. A pattern was finally starting to emerge. Svedberg, Bror Sundelius, Nisse Stridh. He didn't get any further. The phone in his pocket rang.

It was Martinsson, and his voice was shaking.

"He's done it again," he said. "He's done it again."

It was 4.55 p.m. on Saturday, 17 August 1996.

CHAPTER TWENTY-FIVE

He knew he was taking a risk. He hadn't done that before, since taking risks was beneath him and he had devoted his whole life to learning how to escape. But he was attracted by the challenge, and the situation was much too tempting.

He had almost lost control when he came by to pick up their invitations. Their joy was so great that it felt like a physical blow, an act specifically aimed at humiliating him, which of course it was.

Then, when he read the letter, he made up his mind. Between the ceremony at the church and the reception, they were going to stop off at a nearby beach to have their wedding portraits taken. The photographer was very clear in his directions and had even drawn a little map for them. The couple agreed. They would meet him there at 4 p.m., weather permitting.

He went there to scout it out. The photographer's directions were so clear that he had no problem in locating the exact spot. The beach was big, with a camping ground at one end. At first, he wasn't sure that he'd be able to carry out his plans, but then he saw that they would be quite sheltered in their spot among the sand dunes. There would be others on the beach, but they would keep their distance while the photographs were being taken. The challenge was figuring out which direction to approach them from. Disappearing afterwards would be relatively easy, since it was only about 200 metres to the car. If anything went wrong and he was chased, he had his gun. Someone might notice what kind of car he was driving, but he would have three different cars standing by so he could switch them.

He didn't solve the question of his approach on the first visit. But on the second visit, he saw what he had overlooked on the first. He saw the dramatic solution that would enable him to transform the comedy into tragedy.

Suddenly everything was planned and he was running out of time. Cars had to be stolen and parked in their various locations. A small revolver wrapped in plastic had to be buried in the sand. He also put a towel in with it.

The only thing he couldn't count on was the weather, but August had been beautiful this year.

They were married in the church where she had been confirmed nine years earlier. The minister who had officiated then had died, but she had a relative who was a minister and he agreed to step in. Everything went according to plan. The church was bursting with family and friends, and once the photo session was over they would have a big reception. The photographer was at the church with them taking pictures. He had already planned out the pictures he wanted to take at the beach. He had used the spot before and it worked well. He had never been as lucky with the weather as today.

They arrived at the beach just before 4 p.m. The camping ground was full of people, and a number of children were playing on the beach. A lone swimmer was out in the water. It took the photographer only a few minutes to set up his gear, which included the tripod and the light reflectors. They were completely undisturbed.

Everything was ready. The photographer paused behind

the camera while the bridegroom helped his bride check her make-up in a small mirror. The swimmer was on his way up out of the water. His towel lay on the beach. He sat down on it, with his back to them. The bride thought it looked like he was digging a hole in the sand. They were ready. The photographer told them what he had planned for the first photo. They debated whether they should be serious or smiling, and the photographer suggested trying it both ways. It was 4.09 p.m. They had plenty of time.

They had just taken the first picture when the man on the beach below them got up and started walking. The photographer was getting ready to take the next picture but at that moment the bride saw that the man had changed his course and was heading towards them. She held up her hand to stop the photographer from taking the picture, thinking it best to wait until he had passed. He was almost upon them now, carrying his towel like a shield in front of his body. The photographer smiled at him and turned back to the couple. The man smiled in return, unwrapped the towel from his gun, and shot the photographer in the neck. He quickly advanced a couple of steps and shot the bride and groom in turn. All that was heard were some dry crackles. He looked all around. No one had noticed anything.

He continued on over the sand dunes and waited until he was out of sight of the camping ground. Then he started running. He reached the car safely, unlocked it, and jumped in. The whole thing had taken less than two minutes.

He realised that he was cold. It was another risk he had taken, as he could have caught cold. But the temptation had simply been too great. It was wonderful to emerge from the water like that, like the invincible person he really was.

At the edge of Ystad he stopped the car and pulled on the tracksuit he had laid out on the back seat. Then he settled in to wait.

It took a little longer than he expected. Was it one of the children playing on the beach, or someone at the camping ground taking a walk? He would read about it in the papers soon enough.

Finally he heard the noise of the sirens. It was just before 5 p.m. The vehicles drove past him at high speed, among them an ambulance. He felt like waving at them, but controlled himself. He drove home. He had again achieved what he had set out to do. And escaped again, with dignity.

Wallander was picked up outside Rut Lundin's building. The officers assigned to get him didn't know anything other than that they were to take him to Nybrostrand. From the information on the police radio, he gathered that several people were dead. He hadn't managed to get anything more out of Martinsson. Wallander leaned back in his seat. Martinsson's words still echoed in his head. "He's done it again."

He opened the door before the car had even come to a halt. A woman stood there crying, her hands in front of her face. She was wearing shorts and a T-shirt with a slogan supporting Sweden joining NATO.

"What happened?" Wallander asked.

People from the camping ground were rushing around, waving and gesturing. They were running all over the sand dunes. Wallander made it out there before the rest. He stopped dead. The nightmare was repeating itself. At first he couldn't take in what he was seeing, and then he understood that three bodies lay before him. There was a camera on a tripod.

"They had just been married," he heard Höglund say, somewhere nearby. Wallander walked closer and crouched down. All three of them had been shot. The shots had struck the bride and groom in the forehead. The bride's white veil was stained with blood. He touched her arm very carefully. It was still warm. He stood up again and hoped he wouldn't get dizzy. Hansson arrived, as well as Nyberg. He walked over to them.

"It's him again. This happened minutes ago. Are there any tracks? Has anyone seen anything? Who found them?"

Everyone around him seemed dumbstruck, as if they had been looking to him to supply them with the answers.

"Don't just stand there – move!" he shouted. "It just happened! This time we've got to get him!"

Their paralysis lifted, and after a couple of minutes Wallander was able to get a clearer idea of what had happened. The couple had come here to have their wedding pictures taken. They had gone into the sand dunes. A child playing on the beach had left his friends because he needed to pee. He had discovered the dead bodies and run screaming to the camping ground. No one had heard shots, and no one had noticed anything unusual. Several witnesses confirmed that the photographer and the couple had arrived alone.

"Some of the children saw a man swimming in the water," Hansson said. "According to their accounts, he came up out of the sea, sat down in the sand, and then disappeared."

"What do you mean, 'disappeared'?" Wallander was having trouble concealing his impatience.

"A woman who was hanging up her laundry when the couple arrived said the same thing," Höglund said. "She thought she saw a swimmer, but when she looked again he was gone."

Wallander shook his head. "What does that mean? That he drowned? Buried himself in the sand?"

Hansson pointed to the stretch of beach that lay directly below the crime scene.

"The place he sat down was right there," he said. "At least according to one child who seems believable. He had his eyes open."

They walked down on the beach. Hansson ran over to a dark-haired boy and his father. Wallander made them all walk in a wide circle to avoid ruining the tracks in the sand and making it harder for the dog to pick up a scent. They could see the marks of someone sitting in the sand, the remains of a little hole and a piece of plastic sheeting.

Wallander shouted for Edmundsson and Nyberg to join him.

"This plastic reminds me of something," he said, and Nyberg nodded. "Maybe it matches the plastic sheeting we found in the nature reserve."

Wallander turned to Edmundsson. "Let her smell this and see what she finds."

They walked off to the side and watched the dog, who immediately took off into the sand dunes. Then she veered to the left. Wallander and Martinsson followed at a distance. The dog was still excited. They arrived at a small road, and there the scent ended. Edmundsson shook his head.

"A car," Martinsson said.

"Someone may have seen it," Wallander said. "Get every police officer out here to work on this: we're looking for a man in a bathing suit. He left about an hour ago in a car that was parked here."

Wallander ran back to the crime scene. One of the forensic technicians was making a mould of a footprint in the sand. Edmundsson's dog was searching the area.

Hansson was just ending a conversation with a woman from the camping ground. Wallander waved him over.

"More people saw him," Hansson said.

"The swimmer?"

"He was down in the water when the couple arrived. Then he walked up onto the beach. Someone said it looked as though he started to build a sand castle, then got up and disappeared."

"No one's seen anyone else in the area?"

"One man, who is clearly under the influence, claimed two masked men were riding down the beach on bicycles, but I think we can safely disregard this."

"Then we'll stick with the swimmer for now," Wallander said. "Do we know who the victims are?"

"The photographer had this invitation in his pocket," Höglund said and handed it over to Wallander. He was overcome by such a wave of despair that he wanted to scream.

"Malin Skander and Torbjörn Werner," he read out loud. "They were married at 2 p.m. this afternoon."

Hansson had tears in his eyes. Höglund was staring at the ground.

"They were man and wife for two whole hours," he said. "They came down here to have their pictures taken. Who was the photographer?"

"We found his name on the inside of the camera bag," Hansson said. "His name was Rolf Haag and he had a studio in Malmö."

"We have to notify the next of kin," Wallander said. "The press will be all over this place before we know it."

"Shouldn't we put up roadblocks?" Martinsson asked. He had just joined them.

"Why? We have no idea what the car looked like. Even though we know when this happened, it's already too late."

"I just want to nail the bastard," Martinsson said.

"We all do," Wallander said. "So let's go through everything we know at this point. The one lead we have is a lone swimmer. We have to assume he's our man. We know two things about him: he's well informed and plans his crimes meticulously."

"You think he was out there swimming in the ocean while he waited for them?" Hansson asked hesitantly.

Wallander tried to imagine the chain of events. "He knew the newly-weds were having their wedding pictures taken here," he said. "On the invitation it said the reception was starting at 5 p.m. He knew the photo session would be around 4 p.m. He waited out in the water, having parked his car nearby in a spot where he could get down to the beach without walking through the camping ground."

"He had his gun with him the whole time he was out in the water?" Hansson was clearly sceptical, but Wallander was starting to see how it hung together.

"Remember that this is a well-informed and meticulous killer," he said. "He's waiting for his victims out in the water. That means he's only wearing a bathing suit, and with his hair wet his whole appearance is altered. No one pays any attention to a swimmer. Everyone saw him and knew he was there, but no one could describe him."

He looked around and they nodded in agreement. None of the witnesses had managed to describe him yet.

"The newly-weds arrive with their photographer," Wallander said. "That's his cue to come up out of the water and sit down on the beach."

"He has a towel," Höglund added. "A striped one. Several people recalled that detail."

"That's good," Wallander said. "The more detail the

better. He sits down on his striped towel, and what does he do?"

"He starts to dig in the sand," Hansson said.

The pieces were starting to fit together. The killer followed his own rules, and often varied them, but Wallander was starting to see a pattern.

"He's not building a sand castle," he said. "He's uncovering a gun that he's buried in the sand under a piece of plastic sheeting."

Now they followed his train of thought. Wallander continued slowly. "He planted the gun there at some earlier point," he said. "He just has to wait for the right moment, when no one happens to be walking by. He gets up, probably shielding the gun from view with his towel. He fires the gun three times. The victims die immediately. He must have had a silencer on the gun. He continues past the sand dunes, gets to the road where his car is parked, and escapes. The whole thing doesn't take longer than a minute. But we don't know where he went."

Nyberg walked over and joined them.

"We don't know anything about this killer, other than what he's done," Wallander said. "But we're going to find similarities between these crimes, and new details will emerge."

"I know something about him," Nyberg interjected. "He uses snuff. There's some down there in the hole in the sand. He must have tried to kick some sand over it, but the dog found it. We're sending it to the laboratory. You can find out quite a lot about a person from his saliva."

Wallander saw Holgersson approaching from a distance, with Thurnberg a couple of steps behind. The sense of failure washed over him again. Even though he had acted in good faith, he had failed. They hadn't found the man who had killed their colleague, three young people in a nature reserve, a girl curled up in a cave on an island in the Östergötland archipelago, and now some newly-weds and their photographer. There was only one thing he could do, and that was ask Holgersson to put someone else in charge. Maybe Thurnberg had already asked the national police to step in.

Wallander didn't have the energy to go over the events with them. Instead, he walked to Nyberg, who was turning his attention to the tripod.

"He was able to take one picture before it happened," Nyberg said. "We'll get it developed as soon as possible."

"They were married for two hours," Wallander said.

"It seems like this madman hates happy people, sees it as his life's calling to turn joy into misery."

Wallander listened absently to Nyberg's last comment, but he didn't reply. He still didn't have the energy to comprehend the enormity of what had happened. He had been convinced that the killer would strike again, but he was hoping he would be proved wrong.

A good policeman always hopes for the best outcome, Rydberg had often said. And what else? That fighting crime is simply a question of endurance; about which side can outlast the other.

Holgersson and Thurnberg appeared at his side. Wallander had been so lost in thought that he jumped.

"The road should have been blocked off," Thurnberg said, by way of greeting.

Wallander looked back at him stonily. At that moment he decided two things. He wasn't going to relinquish leadership in this case willingly, and he was going to start speaking his mind, the latter effective immediately.

"Wrong," he answered. "The roads shouldn't have been

blocked off at all. You can of course order us to do so, but it won't receive my endorsement."

This wasn't the answer Thurnberg was expecting, and he looked taken aback.

He was too puffed up, Wallander thought with satisfaction. He was so puffed up by his own sense of importance that he burst. Wallander turned his back on Thurnberg. Holgersson looked paler than he'd ever seen her before. He could see his own fear in her eyes.

"It's the same man?"

"I'm sure of it."

"But a couple of newly-weds?"

It was the first thought that had come to him as well.

"You could say that wedding clothes are a kind of costume."

"Is that what he's after?"

"I don't know."

"What else could it be?"

Wallander didn't answer. The only possibility he could see was a madman. A madman who wasn't a madman, but who had killed eight people, including a police officer.

"I've never been involved in anything so horrible in my whole life," she said. After a moment she added, "I heard they were married nearby."

"In Köpingebro," Wallander told her. "The reception is about to begin."

She looked at him and he knew what she was thinking.

"I'm going to ask Martinsson to contact the photographer's family," he said. "He can contact the Malmö police for help. You and I will drive out to Köpingebro."

Thurnberg stood a short distance away, talking to someone on his mobile phone. Wallander wondered who it was.

He gathered everyone around him and asked Hansson to take charge until he returned.

"Answer all of Thurnberg's questions," Wallander said. "But if he tries to tell you what to do, let me know."

"Why on earth would a chief prosecutor try to tell the police how to do their work?"

Now there's a good question, Wallander thought. But he left without answering and joined Holgersson, who was waiting silently in her car.

At 10 p.m. on Saturday, 17 August, it began to rain. Wallander was already back at the crime scene. Notifying the next of kin, entering that room of joy with his brutal news, was even worse than he had imagined. Holgersson was strangely passive during the visit, perhaps because her encounters with the parents of the young people in the reserve the week before had drained her of any remaining energy. Maybe we have a set quota for these kinds of experiences, Wallander thought. I must have met mine by now.

It was a relief to get back to Nybrostrand. Holgersson had already returned to Ystad by then. Wallander had been in touch with Hansson by phone several times, but there was nothing new to report. Hansson told him that Rolf Haag was unmarried and childless. Martinsson had delivered the news to his aged father, who was in a nursing home. A nurse assured Martinsson that the old man had long since forgotten he even had a son.

Nyberg had just been given a freshly developed copy of the one photograph Rolf Haag had taken. The bride and groom smiled into the camera. Wallander looked at it intently for a moment. He suddenly remembered something Nyberg had said to him earlier.

"What was it you said?" he asked. "When we were standing here before. You had just discovered that he had managed to take a picture."

"I said something?"

"It was some kind of comment."

Nyberg thought hard. "I think I said that the killer didn't like happy people."

"What did you mean by that?"

"Svedberg is the exception, of course. But with the young people in the nature reserve, I think their celebration could be characterised as joyous."

Wallander sensed he was on to something. He looked at the wedding picture again, then gave it back to Nyberg and was about to say a few words to Höglund when Martinsson pulled him aside.

"I thought you should know that someone has filed charges against you."

Wallander stared back at him.

"Against me? Why?"

"For assault."

Martinsson scratched his head apologetically. "Do you remember that jogger in the nature reserve? Nils Hagroth?"

"He was trespassing."

"Well, he filed the charges anyway. Thurnberg's got wind of it and seems to take it seriously."

Wallander was speechless.

"I just wanted to tell you," Martinsson said. "That's all."

It was raining harder now. Martinsson left.

A police spotlight illuminated the place where, a few hours earlier, a couple of newly-weds had been murdered. It was 10.30 p.m.

CHAPTER TWENTY-SIX

It stopped raining shortly after midnight. Wallander walked down to the sea to think. It was what he most needed to do at this point. A fresh smell was rising up from the ground after the rain. There were no more wafts of rotting seaweed. The hot weather had lasted for two weeks. Now that the rain had passed, it was warming up again and there was still no wind. The waves against the shore were almost imperceptible.

Wallander pissed into the water. In his mind's eye he could see the little white grains of sugar congealing in his veins. He was constantly dry-mouthed, had trouble keeping his eyes focused on an object, and feared that his blood-sugar levels were increasing.

As he walked along the dark beach, his thoughts returned to the latest events. He was convinced that the lone swimmer, the man with the striped towel, was the one they were looking for. There was no other plausible suspect. He was the one who had been in the nature reserve, probably hidden behind the tree that Wallander had pinpointed. Later he had been in Svedberg's flat. And now he had emerged from the ocean. His weapon was concealed in the sand, his car parked on a nearby road.

The swimmer had been to this place more than once. He must have gone to the same spot and dug a hole in the sand. It could even have been in the middle of the night. Wallander felt he was getting closer to unlocking the secret now, but he wasn't quite there yet. The answer is quite simple, he thought. It's like looking for the pair of glasses on your nose.

He began walking slowly back. The spotlights shone in the distance. Now he tried following in Svedberg's footsteps. Who was the person he had let into his flat? Who was Louise? Who had sent those postcards from all over Europe? What was it you knew, Svedberg? Why didn't you want to tell me, even though Ylva Brink says I was your closest friend?

He stopped. The question he'd posed suddenly seemed more important than before. If Svedberg hadn't wanted to tell anyone what he was up to, it could only have been because he was hoping he was wrong. There was simply no other reason for it. But Svedberg had been right, and that was why he was killed.

Wallander had almost reached the police barricades. There was still a little group of people gathered around the perimeter, trying to see something of the sombre tragedy that had taken place. When Wallander came over the sand dunes, Nyberg had just finished making some notes.

"We have some footprints," Nyberg said. "I mean that quite literally, since the killer was barefoot."

"Have you pieced together what happened?"

Nyberg put the notebook away. "The photographer was hit first," he said. "There's no doubt about that. The bullet entered his neck at an angle, so he may have had his back partially turned. If the first shot had been aimed at the couple, he would have turned around and been shot from the front."

"And next?"

"It's hard to say. I think the groom was probably the

next to go. A man is more of a threat, physically. Then the girl last."

"Anything else?"

"Nothing you don't already know. This killer is in total control of his weapon."

"His hand doesn't shake?"

"Hardly."

"You see a calm and determined killer?"

Nyberg looked grimly at Wallander. "I see a cold-blooded and heartless madman."

When Wallander returned to the police station, the phones were going mad. One of the officers on duty gestured for him to come over. Wallander waited while he finished a phone call about a drunk driver sighted in Svarte. The officer promised to send out a squad car as soon as possible, but Wallander knew no squad car would be making it to Svarte for another 24 hours.

"A police officer from Copenhagen called you. The name was something like Kjær or Kræmp."

"What was it about?"

"The photograph of that woman."

Wallander took the piece of paper with the name and number on it and sat down at his desk to make the call without even removing his coat. The call had come in just before midnight. Kjær or Kræmp might still be there. The call was answered and Wallander said who he was looking for.

"Kjær."

Wallander was expecting a man's voice, but Kjær was a woman.

"This is Kurt Wallander from Ystad. I'm returning your call."

"We have some information for you about the picture

of that woman. We've had two calls from people who claim to have seen her."

Wallander banged the table with his fist.

"At last."

"I've spoken with one of the callers myself. He seemed very reliable. His name is Anton Bakke. He's a manager at a company that makes office furniture."

"Does he know her personally?"

"No, but he was absolutely convinced he had seen her here in Copenhagen at a bar, close to the Central Station. He's seen her there several times."

"It's extremely important that we speak to this woman."

"Has she committed a crime?"

"We don't know that yet, but she is wanted in connection with a growing murder investigation. That's why we sent you her photograph."

"I heard about what happened over there. Those young people in the park. And the police officer."

Wallander told her about the latest events.

"And you think this woman had something to do with it?"

"Not necessarily, but I would like to ask her some questions."

"Bakke says there have been periods when he went to this bar as often as several times a week. He saw her there about half the time."

"Was she usually alone?"

"He wasn't sure, but he thought she sometimes came with someone else."

"Did you ask him when he saw her last?"

"When he was there last, sometime in the middle of June."

"What about the other caller?"

"It was a taxi driver who claimed he gave her a ride in Copenhagen a couple of weeks ago."

"A taxi driver sees a lot of people. How can he be sure?"

"He remembered her because she spoke Swedish."

"Where did he pick her up?"

"She waved him down on the street one night, or rather, early one morning. It was around 4.30 a.m., and she said she was catching the first ferry back to Malmö."

Wallander knew he had to make a decision. "We can't ask you to arrest her," he said. "But we do need you to bring her in. We must talk to her."

"We should be able to do that. We can invent a reason."

"Just tell me when she next shows up at that bar. What was its name?"

"The Amigo."

"What kind of a place is it?"

"It's pretty nice, actually, even though it's down on Istedgade."

Wallander knew that the street was in downtown Copenhagen.

"I appreciate your help on this."

"We'll let you know when she turns up."

Wallander wrote down Kjær's full name and her phone numbers. Her first name was Lone. Then he hung up.

It was 1.30 a.m. He rose slowly to his feet and went to the men's room, then drank some water in the canteen. Some dried-up sandwiches lay on a plate, and he picked one of them up. He heard Martinsson's voice out in the hall, speaking to one of the Malmö officers. They came into the canteen a few minutes later.

"How's it going?" he asked, between bites of the sandwich.

"No one's seen anyone other than that one swimmer."

"Do we have a description of him yet?"

"We're trying to piece together everything we've received so far."

"The Danish police called. They may have found Louise."

"Really?"

"Seems like it."

Wallander poured himself a cup of coffee. Martinsson was waiting for him to continue.

"Have they arrested her?"

"They have no grounds to do so. But reports have come in from both a taxi driver and a man who saw her in a bar. They recognised her from the photograph in the paper."

"So her name really is Louise?"

"We don't know that yet."

Wallander yawned. Martinsson did the same. One of the Malmö officers tried to rub the tiredness from his eyes.

"I'd like to see everyone in the conference room," Wallander said.

"Give us 15 minutes," Martinsson said. "I think Hansson's on his way over now, and I'll call Ann-Britt at home."

Wallander took his coffee with him to his office. He looked up and studied the map of Skåne hanging on his wall. First he located Hagestad, then Nybrostrand. Ystad lay nestled in between. The area was small, but this fact didn't lead anywhere in itself. Wallander finally picked up his notebook and walked over to the conference room. He was met by tired, despondent faces. Their clothes were wrinkled, their bodies heavy.

Our killer's probably sleeping peacefully as we speak, Wallander thought, while we're fumbling around in his footsteps.

They went through the various points that were currently

under investigation and reported the latest findings. The biggest breakthrough was the fact that no one had seen anyone other than the lone swimmer. That strengthened the case against him.

Wallander looked through his notes. "Unfortunately our description of him is strange and rather contradictory," he said gloomily. "The witnesses can't seem to agree whether he has very short hair or is bald. Those who think he has hair can't agree on the colour. Everyone, however, seems to concur that he doesn't have a round face. It seems to be long, or 'horsey', as two independent witnesses have said. Furthermore, everyone seems to agree that he wasn't very tanned. He was of average height – though in reality that could mean anything between a dwarf and a giant. He was of average build and there was nothing remarkable about the way he moved. No one has been able to say what colour his eyes were. The area of greatest confusion is in regard to his age. We have reports that range from 20 to 60. More people have his age between 35 and 45, but no one seems to have any grounds for these statements."

Wallander pushed the notebook away. "In other words, we really have no description at all," he said.

The silence lay heavy in the room. Wallander realised he had to try to lighten the mood.

"We have to remember that it's impressive how much information we've been able to gather in such a short time," he said. "We'll be able to do even more tomorrow. And it's an enormous step to be able to focus on one suspect. I wouldn't hesitate for a moment to call this a breakthrough."

At 2.40 a.m. he called the meeting to an end. Martinsson was the only one who stayed on. He wanted to fill Wallander in on the information he had received regarding the Divine

Movers. He started going through the reports that had come in from the United States and Interpol, but Wallander interrupted him impatiently.

"Has there ever been an incidence of violent crime?" he said. "Have members of this sect ever been the targets of attack?"

"Not from what I can see so far. But I've been told that more files are on their way, both from Washington and Brussels. I'll read through them tonight."

"You should go home and sleep," Wallander said sternly.

"I thought this was important."

"It is, but we can't do everything at once. We have to concentrate on Nybrostrand right now. That's where we got the closest to this madman."

"So, you've changed your mind?"

"What do you mean?"

"Well, now you're talking about a 'madman'."

"A murderer is always crazy. But he can also be cunning and cowardly. He can be like you and me."

Martinsson nodded tiredly and didn't manage to stifle his yawn.

"I'm going home," he said. "Remind me why I ever became a policeman."

Wallander didn't answer. He went into his office to get his coat and remained standing in the middle of the room. What should he do now? He was too tired to think, but he was also too tired to sleep. He sat down in his chair and looked at the picture of Louise that was lying on his desk. He was struck again by the feeling that there was something strange about her face, but he still couldn't put his finger on it. In an absentminded way he picked up the photo and slipped it into his coat pocket. He closed his eyes to let them rest from the light, and fell asleep almost immediately.

He woke with a start without knowing where he was. It was just before 4 a.m. He had slept for almost an hour. His body ached, and he sat for a long time without a single thought in his head. Then he went to the men's room and splashed cold water on his face. Although he was still plagued by indecision, he knew he needed to sleep, if only for a few hours. He needed to bathe and change his clothes. Without having made a firm decision, he left the station and headed home.

But once he was in his car, he turned in the direction of Nybrostrand. There would be nobody there at 4 a.m., only the officers assigned to guard the area. Being alone at the crime scene could make it easier to see new details. It didn't take him long to get there. As he expected, there were no longer any onlookers crowded around the police barricades. One squad car, with someone sleeping behind the wheel, was parked down on the beach. Another officer was outside it, smoking a cigarette. Wallander walked over and said hello. He saw that it was the same man who had been assigned to the nature reserve that night.

"Everything looks pretty quiet," he said.

"Actually the last of the gawkers didn't leave until just a little while ago. I always wonder what they expect to see."

"They probably get a thrill from being in the presence of the unthinkable," Wallander said. "Knowing that they themselves are safe."

He crossed the police line to the crime scene. A lone spotlight was illuminating the well-trodden grass. Wallander walked over to where the photographer had stood, then slowly turned around and walked down the dune to where the hole was.

The guy with the striped towel knew everything, Wallander thought. He wasn't just well informed, he knew everything down to the last detail. It was as if he had been there when they made their plans.

Was that a possibility? If the killer was Rolf Haag's assistant, that would explain his knowledge of this photo session. But how would such an assistant know about the party in the nature reserve? And Bärnsö Island? And what about Svedberg?

Wallander dropped the thought for now, although he meant to take it up again. He walked back up the side of the dune, thinking about the motive for killing young people dressed up in costume. Svedberg was the exception, but this was easy enough to interpret. Svedberg had never been a target; he had simply come too close to the truth.

It occurred to him that Rolf Haag could be dismissed: he had simply been in the way. That left six victims. Six young people in different kinds of costume, six very happy people. He thought about Nyberg's words: seems like this madman hates happy people. So far it made some sort of sense, but it wasn't enough.

He walked up to the road where the getaway car must had been parked. Again, the killer had planned things down to the last detail. There were no houses nearby, no potential witnesses. He returned to the crime scene, where the officer on duty was still smoking.

"I'm still thinking about the gawkers," he said, throwing the butt on the ground and grinding it into the sand, where many others were already strewn about. "I guess we would be there too if we hadn't joined the force."

"Probably," Wallander said.

"You see so many strange people. Some of them pretend not to be interested, but they hang around for hours. One of the last people to leave this evening was a woman. She was already here when I arrived."

Wallander was only half-listening, but decided he may as well stay and chat while he was waiting for dawn.

"At first I thought it was someone I knew," the policeman said. "But it wasn't. I just thought I had seen her somewhere before."

It took a while for his words to sink in. Finally Wallander looked over at the policeman.

"What was that last thing you said?"

"I thought the woman hanging around here was someone I had seen before. But it wasn't."

"You thought you had seen her somewhere before?"

"I thought maybe she was someone I was related to."

"Well, which was it? Someone you thought you knew, or someone you thought you had seen before?"

"I don't know. There was something familiar about her, that's all."

It was a long shot, perhaps just grasping at straws, but Wallander hauled out the photograph of Louise that he had tucked into his coat pocket. It was still dark, but the policeman took out his torch.

"Yeah, that's her. How did you know?"

Wallander held his breath. "Are you sure?"

"Absolutely. I knew I had seen her somewhere before."

Wallander swore under his breath. A more attentive officer might have identified her on the spot and alerted the others. But he knew that was unfair. There were so many people coming and going. At least this policeman had noticed her.

"Show me where she was standing."

The policeman shone a torch over to a spot close to the beach.

"How long was she here?"

"Several hours."

389

"Was she alone?"

The policeman thought for a moment. "Yes." His tone was definite.

"And she was one of the last to leave?"

"Yes."

"Which direction did she go?"

"Towards the camping ground."

"Do you think she was staying there?"

"I didn't see exactly where she was headed, but she didn't look like a camper."

"Well, what do campers look like, in your opinion? And how was she dressed?"

"She was dressed in a blue suit of some kind, and in my experience campers tend to wear casual clothing."

"If she turns up again, let me know immediately," Wallander said. "Tell the others. Do you have this picture in the car?"

"I'll wake up my partner. He'll know."

"Don't bother."

Wallander gave him the photograph he had been holding. Then he left. It was almost 5 a.m., and he was already feeling less tired. His sense of excitement was mounting. The woman called Louise was not their lone swimmer. But she might just know who he was.

CHAPTER TWENTY-SEVEN

He woke up when the phone rang, sat up in bed with a jerk, then staggered out into the kitchen. It was Lennart Westin.

"Were you sleeping?" Westin asked apologetically.

"Not at all," Wallander answered. "But I was in the shower. Can I call you back in a couple of minutes?"

"No problem. I'm at home."

There was a pen on the table, but no piece of paper in sight, not even the newspaper. Wallander wrote the number down on the table. Then he hung up and put his head in his hands. He had a pounding headache and he was more tired now than before he had gone to bed. He rinsed his face with cold water, looked around for some aspirin, and put water on for coffee. But there was no more coffee. That was the last straw. Almost 15 minutes went by before he called Lennart Westin back. The kitchen clock read 8.09 a.m. Westin answered.

"I think you must have been asleep after all," he said. "But you did say to call if I thought of anything that might be important."

"We work around the clock," Wallander said. "It's hard to get enough sleep. But I'm glad you called."

"It's two things, really. One is about that policeman who came by earlier, the one who was shot. When I woke up this morning, I remembered something he had said as we were going out to the islands."

Wallander stopped him and went to the living room to get a notebook.

"He asked me if I had ferried any women to Bärnsö Island recently."

"And had you?"

"Yes, as a matter of fact."

"Who?"

"A woman called Linnea Vederfeldt, who lives in Gusum."

"Why was she going out to Bärnsö?"

"Isa's mother had ordered new curtains for the house. She and Vederfeldt knew each other from childhood. She was going out there to measure everything."

"Did you tell Svedberg this?"

"I didn't think it was any of his business, so I avoided going into details."

"How did he react?"

"Well, that's just it. He insisted that I tell him more about her. Finally I told him she was a childhood friend of Isa's mother and then he completely lost interest."

"Did he ask anything else?"

"Not that I can think of. But he became agitated when he realised that I had taken a woman out to Bärnsö. I remember it so clearly now that I don't know how I ever forgot it."

"What do you mean by agitated?"

"I'm not so good at describing these things, I guess. But I would say 'afraid' even."

Wallander nodded. Svedberg had been afraid it was Louise.

"What about the other thing? You said there were two."

"I must have slept really well. This morning I also thought of what it was I said to you as we were approaching that first landing. I said that you end up knowing everything about people, whether or not you want to. Do you remember that?"

"Yes."

"That's all. I hope it helps."

"Yes, it does. I'm glad you called."

"You should come out here sometime in the autumn," Westin added. "When it's quiet."

"Do I take that to mean you're inviting me?" Wallander asked.

"Take it any way you like," Westin laughed. "But you can normally take me at my word."

After they had finished the conversation, Wallander walked slowly into the living room. He remembered the conversation now, about delivering post in the islands. Suddenly he caught hold of the thought he had been trying to grasp for so long. They were looking for a killer who planned everything about his terrible crimes down to the last detail. This approach depended on his being able to get access to very specific information about his victims' lives without their knowing. Like being able to read other people's post. Wallander stood frozen in the middle of the living room. Who would have unlimited access to other people's letters? Lennart Westin had suggested a possibility: a postman. Someone who opened letters on the way, read them, sealed them again, and made sure they got to the intended address. No one would ever know they had been opened.

Something told Wallander it couldn't be this simple. This wasn't the way things worked. It was too far-fetched. Nonetheless, it answered one of the most difficult questions in the investigation: how the killer managed to gather all his information.

All trace of sleepiness was gone now. He realised he had

hit on a possible explanation. There were weaknesses, of course, not least the consideration that the victims did not live along a single postal route. But perhaps it wasn't actually a postman. Could it be someone who sorted the post before it was carried out?

He quickly showered, put his clothes on, and left. It was 9.15 a.m. when he walked through the main doors of the police station. He felt the need to discuss his latest ideas with someone, and he knew exactly who that person was. He found her in her office.

"I hope I don't look like you do," said Höglund as he walked through her door, "if you'll excuse me for being so blunt. Did you sleep at all last night?"

"A couple of hours."

"My husband's leaving for Dubai in four days. Do you think we'll have closed the door on this hell by then?"

"No."

"Then I don't know what I'm going to do," she said and let her arms fall by her sides.

"You'll just work when you can, it's as simple as that."

"It's not simple at all," she replied. "But men rarely understand that."

Wallander didn't want to be pulled into a conversation about the problems of finding childcare, so he quickly changed the topic to the latest events. He told her about the policeman who had seen Louise out at Nybrostrand. He also told her about his conversation with Lone Kjær.

"So Louise exists. I was beginning to think she was a ghost."

"We still don't know if that really is her name, but she exists. I'm sure of it. And she's very interested in our investigation."

"Is she our killer?"

"I suppose we can't rule her out completely, but she could also be someone who has found herself in Svedberg's situation."

"Following in someone else's tracks?"

"Yes, something like that. I want everyone alerted to the fact that she may return to the crime scene."

Wallander now turned the conversation to Westin's phone call. Höglund listened attentively, but he could tell that she was sceptical.

"It's worth looking into," she said when he finished. "But I see a number of potential problems with your idea. For one, do people even write letters any more?"

"It's not perfect, but I see it more as an answer to part of the problem. An idea that may complete the picture, rather than give us the entire solution."

"We've come across a couple of postmen in the course of this investigation already, haven't we?"

"There have been two," Wallander said. "Westin, and the postman that Isa's neighbour, Erik Lundberg, mentioned had come by the day that Isa was taken to the hospital."

"Maybe we should find out if his voice matches the one that made the phone call to the hospital."

It took a moment for Wallander to follow her. "You mean the person who said he was Lundberg?"

"Yes. The postman knew she was in the hospital since Lundberg told him. He also knew that Lundberg knew."

Wallander's head was starting to spin. Was there something to all this? His fatigue was returning and he wasn't sure he could trust his own ability to reason any more.

"Then there's this matter with Svedberg," he said. He told her about the charges that had been filed. "I don't understand why he wouldn't investigate the alleged attack by Nils Stridh on his brother. He even resorted to threatening Stig Stridh, to protect Nils Stridh at all costs. Why? He was lucky the whole thing was dropped by the authorities. He could have been severely reprimanded."

"It doesn't sound like Svedberg at all."

"That's what makes me suspicious. He must have felt pressured to act in that way."

"By Nils Stridh?"

"Who else could it have been?"

They thought for a moment. "It sounds like blackmail to me," she said finally. "But what could Stridh have known about Svedberg?"

"That remains to be seen. But I think Bror Sundelius knows more than he's telling."

"We should put a little pressure on him."

"We will," Wallander answered. "As soon as we have some time to spare."

They had a meeting at 10 a.m. Martinsson, Hansson and the three officers from Malmö were there. Nyberg was still at the crime scene and Holgersson had barricaded herself in her office. She was dealing with the press. Thurnberg was keeping his distance, although Wallander caught sight of him in the hall. The meeting took a light-hearted turn when someone started passing around the complaint that had been filed by the jogger, Nils Hagroth, about Wallander's assault on him at the nature reserve. Wallander was the only one who failed to find it funny, not because he was bothered by the report itself, but because he didn't want his team to become distracted.

They had a lot to do. Wallander and Höglund would drive out to Köpingebro to talk with Malin Skander's parents, while Martinsson and Hansson would handle

Torbjörn Werner's relatives. Wallander nodded off the moment he got into Höglund's car, and she let him sleep.

He woke up when she stopped the car, at a farm just outside Köpingebro. Although it was a beautiful day, an unnatural quiet reigned in the house and garden. All the doors and windows were shut. As they walked up to the main house, a man wearing a dark suit came walking towards them. He was well into middle age, tall and strongly built. His eyes were red. He introduced himself as Lars Skander, father of the bride.

"You'll have to talk to me," he said. "My wife isn't up to it."

"We offer you our condolences," Wallander said. "We're also sorry we couldn't leave you in peace, but it's imperative that we get answers to a few questions."

"Of course, if it can't wait." Lars Skander didn't try to hide either his bitterness or his sorrow. "You have to get this maniac."

The look he gave them was pleading. "How can someone do this? How can someone murder two people about to have their wedding pictures taken?"

Wallander was afraid that the man was going to break down, but Höglund took charge of the situation.

"We're only going to ask you a few essential questions," she said. "Only as much as we need in order to catch whoever did it."

"Can we sit outside?" Lars Skander asked. "It's so oppressive inside."

They walked in silence to the garden at the back of the house. A table and four chairs stood under an old cherry tree.

"Can you think who might have done this?" Wallander asked after they had gone through the most straightforward details about the murdered couple. "Did they have any enemies?"

Lars Skander stared back at him, uncomprehending. "Why would Malin and Torbjörn have had enemies? They were friends with everyone. You couldn't find more peace-loving people."

"It's an important question. I need you to think very carefully before answering."

"I have thought about it. I can't think of a single person."

Wallander moved on. Information, he thought. What we need to know is how the killer got the information he needed.

"When did they choose the day for their wedding?"

"I can't recall exactly. Sometime in May, I think. First week of June at the latest."

"When did they decide upon Nybrostrand as the place where their wedding pictures would be taken?"

"That I don't know. Torbjörn and Malin planned everything carefully in advance, and Torbjörn and Rolf Haag went way back, so I'm sure the plans for the photography were made early."

"Two months ago, then?"

"Something like that."

"Who knew that the wedding pictures were going to be taken on the beach?"

The answer came as a surprise. "Almost no one."

"Why not?"

"They wanted to be left alone during that time, between the church and the reception. Only they and Rolf knew where they were going. They said it would be like a secret honeymoon for a couple of hours."

Wallander and Höglund exchanged glances.

"This is extremely important," Wallander said. "I have to make sure I've understood you correctly. Apart from

Malin and Torbjörn, only the photographer knew where the pictures were going to be taken?"

"That's right."

"And the location was chosen sometime at the end of May or beginning of June."

"Originally, they were going to have the pictures taken up by the Ale stones," Lars Skander said. "But then they changed their minds. It's become commonplace for couples to have their pictures taken up there, apparently."

Wallander frowned. "So you did know where they were going to have the pictures taken."

"I knew about the Ale stones plan. But then they changed their minds, like I said."

Wallander drew his breath in sharply. "When was it that they changed their minds?"

"Just a couple of weeks ago."

"And the new location was kept a secret?"

"Yes."

Wallander studied Lars Skander without speaking. Then he turned to Höglund. He knew they were thinking the same thing. The location had been changed only a few weeks ago, and the couple had been sure it was their secret. But someone had still managed to trespass into their private plans.

"Call Martinsson," Wallander said to Höglund. "Get him to confirm this with the Werner family."

She got up and walked away to make the call.

We haven't been this close before, Wallander thought. He tried to go through all the possibilities in his head. He still didn't know for sure if Rolf Haag had an assistant or not, and it was still possible that a close friend had known about the plans, despite what Lars Skander had told them.

At that moment, a window on the top floor of the house was flung open. A woman leaned out, screaming.

CHAPTER TWENTY-EIGHT

Wallander would retain the image of the screaming woman in his head for a long time. It had been one of the most beautiful days of an unusually warm summer, the garden was green and lush, and Höglund was leaning against the pear tree talking on her mobile phone while he sat across from Lars Skander in a white wooden chair. Both he and Höglund immediately thought it was too late, that the woman who had flung open the window was about to hurl herself down onto the flagstones. They would never get to her in time.

There was a moment of complete calm, as if everything was frozen. Then Höglund dropped her phone and ran towards the window, while Wallander yelled something – he hardly knew what. Lars Skander got to his feet very slowly. The woman in the window continued to scream. She was the mother of the dead bride, and her pain cut that warm August day like a diamond cuts glass. They agreed afterwards that it was her scream that shook them the most.

Höglund disappeared into the house, while Wallander remained under the window with outstretched arms. Lars Skander stood at his side like a ghost, staring up at the distraught woman in the window. Then Höglund appeared out of nowhere behind her and pulled her into the room. Everything went quiet.

When Wallander and Lars Skander entered the bedroom, Höglund was sitting on the floor with her arms around the woman. Wallander went back downstairs and called an ambulance. They returned to the garden at the back of the house once the ambulance had come and gone. Höglund picked up the phone that lay in the grass.

"Martinsson had just answered when it happened. He must have wondered what was going on," she said.

He sat back down in one of the chairs. "Call him," he said.

She sat down across from him. A bee buzzed back and forth between them. Svedberg had a phobia of bees. Now he was dead. That's why they were there, in the Skanders' garden. Many others were also dead. Too many.

"I'm afraid he's going to strike again," Wallander said. "Every second I think I'll get a call telling me he's done it again. I'm going crazy looking for signs that the nightmare will soon be over, that we won't have to kneel over any more bodies of people who have been shot, but I can't find them."

"All of us have that fear," she replied.

That was all that needed to be said. Höglund called Martinsson who, as expected, demanded to know what had happened. Wallander moved his chair over into the shade and took hold of his thoughts.

If the decision to move the photo session to Nybrostrand was made only a couple of weeks ago, who would have had access to that information? Why hadn't anyone confirmed whether or not Rolf Haag had an assistant?

Höglund finished her conversation and also moved her chair into the shade.

"He'll call me back," she said. "Apparently the Werners are both very old. Martinsson can't tell whether they're in shock or just senile."

"What about the question of Rolf Haag's assistant?"

Wallander asked brusquely. "The Malmö police were going to take care of that for us. Do you remember Birch? We worked with him on a case last year."

"How could I forget?"

Birch was a police officer of the old school. It had been a pleasure to meet him.

"He moved to Malmö," she said. "I think he was put in charge of this."

"Then he's already done the work," Wallander said firmly.

He took up his phone and dialled the Malmö police station. He was in luck: Birch was in his office. After exchanging greetings, Birch got straight to the point.

"I called Ystad with my report," he said. "It hasn't reached you?"

"Not yet."

"Then I'll tell you the main points of interest. Rolf Haag's studio is located close to the Nobel plaza, and his main occupation was studio photography, though he also published some travel books."

"I'm going to interrupt you here," Wallander said. "What I really need to know is whether or not he had an assistant."

"Yes, he did."

"What's his name?" Wallander gestured for Höglund to give him a pen.

"Her name is Maria Hjortberg."

"Have you talked to her?"

"I couldn't. She's at her parents' house outside Hudiksvall for the weekend. It's a small place in the woods and they have no phone. She's coming back to Malmö this evening and I'm planning to meet her at the airport. But I very much doubt she's the person who shot her boss and this young couple."

This wasn't the answer that Wallander was looking for, and it irritated him, which he thought was probably a sign that he was a bad policeman.

"What I need to know is whether someone else knew where the wedding pictures were going to be taken."

"I searched the studio last night," Birch said. "It took half the night. I found a letter from Torbjörn Werner to Haag dated 28 July. In it he confirmed the time and place for the photo session."

"Where was it posted?"

"Ystad appears at the top of the page."

"There's no envelope? No postmark?"

"There's a big bag of paper in Haag's office, so it could be in there. Otherwise, I'm afraid it might already have been thrown away. It was written several weeks ago, after all."

"I need that envelope."

"Why is it so important? Can't we assume it was posted in Ystad, since that's where it was written?"

"I need to know if the envelope was opened by someone before it reached Haag. I want our forensics team to have a look at it, if only to rule out this possibility."

Birch didn't need further explanation. He promised to go down to the studio at once.

"That's some theory you've got," he said.

"It's all I have right now," Wallander answered.

Birch promised to call if he found anything.

It was already midday. Wallander went home, fried some eggs for lunch, then lay down to rest for half an hour. At 1.10 p.m. he was back at the police station.

Going through the notes in his office, he decided that the theory about someone having opened the letters needed to be explored before they dismissed it. He went out to the front desk and talked to the girl who filled in for Ebba on the weekends. He asked her if she knew where the post in Ystad was sorted. She didn't.

"Maybe you could find that out for me," Wallander said.

"But it's Sunday," she said.

"A regular working day, as far as I'm concerned."

"But surely not for the post office."

Wallander was starting to get angry, but he controlled himself.

"Post is collected even on Sundays," he said. "At least once. That means that someone is working down at the post office today."

She promised to try to find the answer to his question. Wallander hurried back to his office, feeling that he had disturbed her. Just as he closed his door, it struck him that he was wrong about one thing. He had told Höglund that two postmen already figured in this investigation. But there were actually three. What was it Sture Björklund had said that day? He had the feeling that someone had been at his house when he wasn't there. His neighbours knew how much he valued his privacy. The only person who came by regularly was the postman.

Could it have been the postman who put Svedberg's telescope in Björklund's shed? It wasn't just a wholly unreasonable idea, it was crazy. He was grasping at straws. He growled angrily to himself and started leafing through the various reports that lay on his desk. Before he'd got very far, Martinsson appeared in the doorway.

"How did it go?" Wallander asked.

"Ann-Britt told me about the woman who tried to jump out the window. We didn't have quite as bad a time of it, but it's so tragic. Torbjörn had just taken over the farm. The old couple were getting ready to hand over all the responsibility to the next generation. One son died in a car crash a few years ago. And now they have no one."

"The killer doesn't consider things like that," Wallander said.

Martinsson walked over and stood by the window. Wallander could see how shaken he was. Once upon a time, he had been an eager young recruit with all the best intentions – and at a time when becoming a police officer was no longer seen as something noble. Young people seemed to despise the profession, in fact. But Martinsson held fast to his ideals and genuinely wanted to be a good policeman. It was only during the last few years that Wallander had noticed his faith starting to slip. Now Wallander doubted that Martinsson would make it to retirement.

"He's going to do it again," Martinsson said.

"We don't know that for sure."

"Why wouldn't he? He kills for the sake of killing – there's no other motive."

"We don't know that. We just haven't found his motive yet."

"You're wrong."

Martinsson's last words were delivered with such force that Wallander took them as an accusation.

"In what way am I wrong?"

"Until a few years ago, I would have agreed with you: there's an explanation for all violence. But that just isn't the case any more. Sweden's undergone a fundamental change. A whole generation of young people is losing its way. They don't know what's right or wrong. And I don't know what is the point of being a policeman any more."

"That's a question only you can answer."

"I'm trying."

Martinsson sat down. "You know what Sweden has

become?" he asked. "A lawless nation. Who would have thought that could ever happen?"

"We're not quite there yet," Wallander said. "Even though I agree with you that it's where things seem to be heading. This is why it's so important for us not to give up."

"That's what I used to say to myself. But I'm not sure I think it's possible for us to make a difference any more."

"There isn't one police officer in this country who hasn't asked himself these same questions," Wallander said. "But that doesn't change the fact that we have to keep working, we have to resist the direction our society has taken. We have to stop this madman, and we're very close to him right now. We're going to get him."

"My son is convinced that he wants to be a policeman too," Martinsson said after a while. "He asks me what it's like. I never know what to say."

"Send him to me," Wallander said. "I'll have a talk with him."

"He's eleven."

"That's a good age."

"All right, I'll send him."

Wallander took advantage of the shift in their conversation to return to the matter at hand.

"How much did the Werners know about the photo session?"

"Nothing more than the time."

Wallander let his hands fall onto the table.

"Then we have a breakthrough. Tell everyone I want a meeting at 3 p.m. this afternoon."

Martinsson nodded and got ready to leave. He turned when he reached the door.

"Do you mean what you said about talking to my son?"

"I'll do it the moment all this is over," Wallander said.

"I'll answer all his questions and even let him try on my policeman's cap."

"You have one of those?" Martinsson asked with surprise.

"Somewhere. I just have to find it."

Wallander went to the meeting that afternoon with the feeling that he was going to end up having another confrontation with Thurnberg. Apart from the unfortunate incident in Nybrostrand, there had been no further contact. Wallander was still unsure what would come of the charges the jogger had filed against him. Although Thurnberg hadn't said anything about it, Wallander felt that there was an ongoing war between them.

After the meeting, he realised he was wrong. Thurnberg surprised him by offering support when the others faltered or started to disagree. Whenever he made a comment, it was short and to the point. Perhaps Wallander had been too quick to judge him. Was Thurnberg's arrogance just a bluff, perhaps a sign of insecurity?

Wallander paused for a moment as they were getting ready to leave, wondering if he should say something to Thurnberg. But he couldn't think of anything.

It was now 4.30 p.m. In two hours, Haag's assistant would be arriving at the airport. Wallander tried to call Birch, but there was no answer. He decided to do something he had never done before. He had an old alarm clock in his desk drawer, and he got it out and set it. He locked the door of his office, stretched out on the floor, and pushed an old briefcase under his head for a pillow. Someone knocked on the door right before he fell asleep, but he didn't answer. If he was going to have the energy to keep working, he would need an hour of sleep.

* * *

A rapid succession of disjointed images passed before him. A glimpse of his father, the smell of turpentine, the holiday in Rome. Suddenly Martinsson was there, standing at the foot of the Spanish Steps. He looked like a small child. Wallander called out to him, but Martinsson couldn't hear him. Then the dream was gone.

It took some effort to get to his feet. His joints cracked as he walked to the men's room. He hated this crippling fatigue. It was getting harder and harder to bear as he got older. He splashed cold water on his face and took a long leak. He avoided looking at his face in the mirror. He reached Sturup Airport at 6.45 p.m. When he entered the arrivals area, he spotted Birch's imposing figure almost immediately. He was leaning against the wall, his arms crossed. When he saw Wallander, his sombre face broke into a wide smile.

"You're here as well?"

"I thought you wouldn't mind the company."

"Let's go and grab a cup of coffee. Her plane's not due in for a while."

As they stood in line at the cafeteria, Birch told him he hadn't found the envelope Wallander was hoping for. "But I did talk to one of our forensic technicians," Birch said, as he helped himself to a piece of cake and a Danish pastry, "and he told me I'd never be able to tell if a letter had been opened and resealed. There have been new advances in this area, it seems. No more steam, like in the old days."

"I need that envelope," Wallander said. He forced himself not to follow Birch's example and kept to a cup of coffee. They walked over to the gate. Birch wiped crumbs from his mouth.

"I'm not sure I understand the relevance of the envelope. Of course, I'm also wondering why you decided to come out here. Maria Hjortberg must be important."

Wallander began to tell him about the latest developments as passengers started to stream in from the plane. Birch surprised Wallander by pulling a piece of paper from his coat pocket with Maria Hjortberg's name on it. He walked out into the middle of the gate area and held it up, while Wallander watched from the side.

Maria Hjortberg was a very beautiful woman, with intense dark eyes and long dark hair. She had a rucksack slung over one shoulder. She probably still didn't know that Rolf Haag was dead, but Birch was already telling her. She shook her head in disbelief. Birch took her rucksack, then led her over to Wallander and introduced him.

"Is anyone coming to pick you up?" Birch asked.

"I was going to take the bus."

"Then we'll give you a ride. Unfortunately we have some questions to ask you and they can't wait. But we can do this either at the police station or the studio."

"Is it really true?" she asked in a dazed voice. "Is Rolf really dead?"

"Yes. I'm sorry," Birch said. He asked her if she had more luggage, but she didn't. "How long have you worked as his assistant?"

"Not very long. Since April."

Her answer came as a relief to Wallander. Her grief wouldn't be too intense – unless, of course, she had been in a relationship with him. She told Birch that she preferred to speak to them at the studio.

"You take her in your car," Wallander said to Birch. "I have some phone calls to make."

∗ ∗ ∗

Two hours later it became clear that Maria Hjortberg didn't have any crucial information to give them. She hadn't even known about Rolf Haag's photo session at Nybrostrand. He had told her that he would be attending a wedding on Saturday, but she had thought it was a personal invitation, not a job. She had never heard of Malin Skander or Torbjörn Werner. They had a calendar in the office where they noted their appointments, but there was nothing down for Saturday, August 17. When Birch showed her the letter he had found, she merely shook her head.

"He opened all the post," she said. "I helped him with the photo sessions, that was all."

"Who else could have seen this letter?" Wallander asked. "Who else has access to this studio? A cleaner?"

"We do our own cleaning. And clients didn't go into the office."

"So it was just you and Rolf?"

"Yes, although I was hardly ever here."

"Have there been any burglaries?"

"No."

"I looked for the envelope that this letter came in," Birch said. "I couldn't find it anywhere."

"It must have been thrown away," she said. "Rolf likes to keep things tidy. The rubbish is collected every Monday."

Wallander looked at Birch. There was no reason for her to lie. He didn't think they could get any further.

"How close was your relationship?" he asked.

She understood what he was getting at, but didn't seem to mind. "It was nothing personal," she said. "We worked well together and I learned a lot from him. I'm hoping to set up my own studio one day."

It was over. Birch said he would drive her home while

Wallander drove back to Ystad. They parted outside on the street.

"I still don't understand it," she said. "I spent the last two days in an isolated house in an equally isolated forest, and I come back to this."

She began to cry and Birch put an arm around her protectively.

"I'll take her home now," he said. "Will you give me a call later?"

"I'll call you from Ystad," Wallander said. "Where are you going to be?"

"I'm going to search his flat later tonight."

Wallander made sure that he had Birch's mobile number, then crossed the street to his car. It was 10.30 p.m.

Before he had a chance to start the car, the phone buzzed in his pocket and he answered.

"Is this Kurt Wallander?"

"Yes."

"Lone Kjær here. I just wanted to tell you that the woman we're calling Louise is at the Amigo right now. What do you want us to do?"

Wallander made a quick decision. "I'm already in Malmö. I'll be right over. If she leaves, have someone follow her."

"There's a boat leaving at 11 p.m., I think. That brings you to Copenhagen at around 11.45 p.m. I'll meet you on this side."

"Just don't lose her," Wallander said. "I need this one."

"We'll watch over her well, I promise."

Wallander hung up and stared unseeing into the darkness, his excitement growing.

CHAPTER TWENTY-NINE

Wallander picked her out as soon as he got off the boat. She was wearing a leather coat, she had short blond hair, and she was younger than he imagined, and smaller. But there was no doubt that she was in the force. Why, he couldn't have said, but he could always pick out the police officer in a group of strangers.

He stopped in front of her and they exchanged greetings.

"Louise is still at the bar," she said.

"If that really is her name," Wallander said.

"Why is she so important to your investigation?"

Wallander had been thinking about this on the way over. He couldn't connect her to the crimes in any way. All he wanted to do was talk to her. He had so many questions.

"I think she may have interesting information for us. Of course, a bar is hardly the best place for this kind of a conversation."

"You can always use my office."

A police car was waiting for them, and they drove away in silence. Wallander thought about the last time he had been in Copenhagen. It was when he'd attended a performance of *Tosca* at Det Kongelige theatre. He'd gone to a bar after the performance and was dead drunk by the time he caught the last boat for Malmö.

Lone Kjær was speaking to someone on the car radio.

"She's still there," she said, pointing out the window. "It's across the street. Do you want me to wait for you?"

"Why don't you come in?"

The broken neon sign simply read "igo". Wallander was about to meet the woman he'd been wondering about since he'd found her photograph in Svedberg's secret compartment under the floorboards.

They opened the door, pushed aside the heavy red curtain, and entered the bar. It was warm and smoky inside, the lighting was tinged red, and it was full of people. A man walked towards them on his way out.

"All the way at the end of the bar," he said to Lone Kjær.

Wallander nodded to him, then left Kjær by the door and started making his way through the crowd.

He caught sight of her. She was sitting at the far end of the bar. Her hair looked just as it had in the photograph. Wallander stood frozen, watching her. She looked like she was alone, although there were people on either side of her. She was drinking a glass of wine. When she turned her head in his direction, he slipped behind a tall man who was drinking a beer. When Wallander looked again she was staring down at her glass of wine. Wallander turned, nodded to Kjær, and made his way over to Louise.

He was in luck. Just as he reached her, the man on her left stood up and left. Wallander sank down on the bar stool, and she glanced at him quickly.

"I think your name is Louise," Wallander said. "My name is Kurt Wallander, and I'm a police officer from Ystad. I need to speak to you."

She tensed up for a moment, then relaxed and smiled.

"All right, but I'd like to visit the ladies' room first, if you don't mind. I was just about to get up when you sat down."

She got up and walked towards the back of the room, where there were signs to the men's and women's lavatories.

The bartender caught Wallander's eye, but he shook his head to indicate he wouldn't be ordering anything. She doesn't speak with a Scanian dialect, he thought. But she is Swedish.

Kjær came closer. Wallander gave her a sign that everything was proceeding smoothly. The clock hanging on the wall advertised a brand of whisky that Wallander had never heard of. Four minutes went by. Wallander looked over at the area leading to the lavatories. A man walked by, then another. He tried to concentrate on his questions, wondering which he should ask first.

Seven minutes had gone by now, and he realised something was wrong. He got up and walked towards the lavatories. Kjær appeared at his side.

"Go into the ladies' room and look around."

"Why? She hasn't come out again. I would have seen her if she had tried to leave."

"Something's wrong," Wallander said. "I want you to check for me."

Kjær went into the women's lavatory and Wallander waited. She was back again almost immediately.

"She's not in there."

"Damn it," Wallander said. "Is there a window in there?"

Without waiting for an answer he jerked the door open and went in. Two women were adjusting their make-up in front of the mirror. Wallander hardly noticed them. Louise was gone. He ran out again.

"She must still be here somewhere," Kjær said in disbelief. "I would have seen her."

"But she isn't," Wallander said.

He made his way to the front door through a throng of people that seemed to be getting thicker all the time. The bouncer looked like a wrestler.

"Ask him," Wallander said. "We're looking for a woman with medium-length dark hair. Did anyone like that leave recently? It would have been ten minutes ago at the most."

Kjær asked the bouncer but he shook his head, and said something that Wallander didn't catch.

"He's sure," she yelled over the noise in the room.

Wallander turned and started pushing his way through the crowd again. He was looking for her, but part of him knew she was already gone.

Finally he gave up, and made his way over to the bartender. He couldn't see the glass of wine Louise had been drinking.

"Where's the glass that was here?" he asked.

"I've already washed it."

Wallander waved to Kjær and she came over. He pointed to the top of the bar.

"I don't know how likely we are to get anything, but let's try for some fingerprints."

"It'll be a first for me," she said. "I've never had to cordon off a section of a bar before. But I'll make sure it's done."

Wallander left and walked out into the street. He was drenched with sweat and shaking with anger. How could he have been so stupid? That smile, her willingness to speak with him, just a trip to the ladies' room first. Why hadn't he seen through it?

Kjær came out after ten minutes. "I really don't know how she did it," she said. "I know I would have seen her if she had tried to leave."

But the pieces were starting to fit together. Slowly Wallander understood what must have happened. There was only one answer. It was so unexpected that he needed time to grasp its full implication.

"Can we go to your office?" he asked. "I need time to think."

When they got there, Kjær brought him a cup of coffee and repeated her question.

"I just don't understand how she got away without being seen."

"That's because she never left," Wallander said. "Louise is still in there somewhere."

She looked at him with surprise. "Still there? Then why did we come here?"

Wallander shook his head dully. He was frustrated at his lack of awareness. He had sensed that there was something strange about her hair the first time he'd seen her picture in Svedberg's flat.

I should have seen it back then, he thought. That it was a wig.

She repeated her last question.

"In a way, Louise is still in the bar," he answered, "because Louise is just an act, put on by someone else. A man. That wrestler who was guarding the door said three men left the bar during the last ten minutes. One of them was Louise, with her wig in her pocket and all her make-up wiped off."

She didn't believe him, and he was too tired to go into more detail. The important thing was that he knew it. Still, he owed her an explanation. She had helped him. Although it was past midnight, he continued to explain.

"When she went into the lavatory, she took off her make-up and the wig, and then she walked out again," Wallander said. "She probably altered something about the way her clothing looked as well. Neither of us noticed anything, because we were waiting for a woman to come out. Who would have noticed a man?"

"The Amigo doesn't have a reputation as a transvestite bar."

"He may simply have gone there to play the role of a woman," Wallander said thoughtfully. "Not to be among his own kind."

"What does this mean for your investigation?"

"I don't know. It probably means a great deal, but I haven't thought it through yet."

She looked down at her watch.

"The last boat to Malmö has already left. The earliest leaves at 4.45 a.m. in the morning."

"I'll stay in a hotel," Wallander said.

She shook her head. "You can sleep on the sofa at my place," she said. "My husband comes home around this time. He's a waiter. We have sandwiches and a beer together before we go to bed."

They left the police station.

Wallander slept uneasily. At one point he got up and walked over to the window. He stared down at the empty street and wondered why all city streets resembled each other at night. He kept waiting for someone to appear, but all was quiet. He felt his anxiety grow stronger. The victims so far had been dressed up in costume. Just like Louise. When Wallander had told her who he was, she left.

It was him, he thought. There's no other explanation. I had the killer by my side without knowing it. But I didn't manage to see through his disguise, and he disappeared. Now he knows we're closing in, but he also knows we haven't guessed his real identity.

Wallander went back to the sofa and dozed until it was time to take the ferry back to Malmö.

417

He called Birch when he got to the other side, hoping he was an early riser. Birch answered and said he was just drinking his morning coffee.

"What happened to you last night? I thought we were going to be in touch."

Wallander explained what had happened.

"Were you really that close?"

"I let myself be fooled. I should have stood guard by the lavatories."

"It's easy to say so in hindsight," Birch said. "You're back in Malmö now, aren't you? You must be tired."

"The worst thing is that I can't get the car started. I left my lights on."

"I'll come over. I have jump leads," Birch said. "Where are you?"

Wallander gave him directions.

It took Birch less than 20 minutes to get there, during which time Wallander napped in his car.

Birch looked closely at Wallander. "You should really try to sleep for a few hours," he said. "It won't help matters if you collapse."

While they put the jump leads on, Birch told him he had searched Haag's flat but hadn't found anything significant.

"We'll do another search of the studio and his flat," Birch said. "And we'll stay in touch."

"I'll tell you how things go at our end," Wallander said.

He left Malmö. It was 6.25 a.m. At the turn-off for Jägersro, he pulled over to the side of the road and called Martinsson.

"I've been trying to reach you," Martinsson said. "We were supposed to have a meeting last night, but no one could contact you."

"I was in Denmark," Wallander said. "Tell everyone I want a meeting at 8 a.m."

"Has anything happened?"

"Yes, but I'll tell you about it later."

Wallander continued on towards Ystad. The weather was still beautiful. There were no clouds in the sky and no wind. He was feeling less tired, and his mind was starting to work again. He went through the meeting with Louise over and over, trying to home in on the face behind the wig and make-up. Sometimes he almost had it.

He reached Ystad at 7.40 a.m. Ebba was at the front desk. She sneezed.

"Caught a cold?" he asked. "In the middle of summer?"

"Even an old bag like me can have allergies," she replied good-naturedly. Then she looked sternly at him.

"You haven't had a wink of sleep, have you?"

"I was in Copenhagen. That's not conducive to a good night's sleep."

She didn't seem to see the humour in this. "If you don't start taking your health seriously, you'll pay for it," she said. "Mark my words."

He didn't answer. He was sometimes annoyed by her ability to see right through him. She was right, of course. He thought about the clumps of sugar in his bloodstream.

He got himself a cup of coffee and went into his office. Soon his colleagues would be waiting for him in the conference room. He would have to tell them what had happened the night before, how the killer had been there, gone to the lavatory, and disappeared.

A woman went up in smoke by taking on the form of a man. There was no Louise any more. All they had was an unknown man who simply removed his wig and disappeared without a trace. A man who had already killed eight people, and who might be preparing to strike again.

He thought about Isa Edengren, curled up in the cave behind the ferns, and shivered.

What do I tell them, Wallander thought. How do I find the right path through this unknown territory? We're pressed for time and can't afford to think through every possibility, every possible lead. How can I know which is the right way?

Wallander left his own questions unanswered and went to the men's room. He stared at his image in the mirror. He was swollen and pale, with watery bags under his eyes. For the first time in his life, the sight of his face made him nauseated.

I have to catch this killer, he thought. If only so I can go on medical leave and start taking control of my health.

It was now just after 8 a.m. Wallander left the men's room.

Everyone was already in the conference room when he entered. He felt like the tardy schoolboy, or perhaps the flustered teacher. There was Thurnberg, fingering his perfectly knotted tie. Holgersson smiled her quick, nervous smile. The others greeted him to the best of their exhausted capability: simply by being there.

Wallander sat down and told them exactly where things stood. How he had been inches away from the killer, and how he had let him slip away under his very nose. He told the story calmly, starting with Maria Hjortberg and ending with Louise's smile and her apparent willingness to talk to him, saying she just had to visit the lavatory first.

"He must have removed the wig while he was in there," he said. "It was the same one as in the picture, by the way. He must have wiped off his make-up as well. He's careful by nature, and he must have foreseen the risk of being recognised. He probably had some make-up remover with him. I didn't notice him slip out because I was waiting for a woman."

"What about his clothes?" Höglund said.

"Some kind of trouser suit," Wallander said. "And low-heeled shoes. I suppose it might have been obvious that he was a man if one knew to look carefully. But you couldn't see while he sat at the bar."

Höglund's was the only question.

"I have no doubts that he's the one," Wallander said after a pause. "Why else would he leave like that?"

"Did you consider the fact that he might have been on your boat this morning?" Hansson asked.

"I did think of it," Wallander said. "But by then it was too late."

They should blame me for this, he thought. For this and for many other aspects of the investigation. I should have known it was a wig from the moment I first saw the photograph. If we had known we were looking for a man from the beginning it would all have been different. The search for him would have taken precedence over everything else. But I didn't see it. I didn't understand what I was looking at.

Wallander poured himself a glass of mineral water. "We have to assume he could strike again at any moment, so we have no time to lose. We have to re-examine the facts of this investigation to see if we can find any trace of this man."

"The photograph," Martinsson said. "We can manipulate it on the computer and make it look more like a man."

"That's at the top of our list right now," Wallander said. "We'll have that done as soon as we leave this meeting. A face can be significantly altered with make-up and a wig, but it can't be completely changed."

There was a new surge of energy in the room. Wallander didn't want to keep them any longer, but Holgersson sensed he was about to bring the meeting to a close, and raised her hand.

"I want to remind you that Svedberg's funeral is tomorrow at 2 p.m. With the best interests of this investigation in mind, I'm cancelling the reception afterwards."

No one had any comments. Everyone seemed eager to leave.

Wallander went to his office to get his coat. There was something he wanted to follow up on even though it would most likely lead nowhere. He was just about to leave when Thurnberg appeared.

"Do we really have the resources to manipulate that photograph here?" he asked.

"Martinsson knows the most about that sort of thing," Wallander said. "If he has any doubts about his ability to do the job properly, he'll turn it over to the technicians, don't worry."

Thurnberg nodded. "I just wanted to make sure." But he clearly had something else to say. "I don't think you should blame yourself for letting him slip away in the bar. You couldn't have been expected to see through his disguise."

It seemed as if he really meant it. Was this his way of making amends? Wallander decided to accept him at face value.

"I appreciate your opinion," he said. "This investigation has been far from clear-cut."

"I'll get in touch if I think of anything that might be helpful," Thurnberg said.

Wallander left the station. He hesitated for a moment in the car park before deciding to walk. All he had to do was walk downtown, and he had to keep moving or else sleep would overtake him.

It took him ten minutes to reach the red building that was the central postal depot. Post was being unloaded from yellow postal vans. Wallander had never been down here before. He looked around for an entrance and found one. It was locked. He pressed a small buzzer and was let in.

The man who greeted him was the manager, a young man hardly more than 30 years old. His name was Kjell Albinsson, and he made a good impression. Albinsson escorted him to his office, where a fan placed on top of a filing cabinet was going at high speed. Wallander got out a pen and paper, wondering how he should go about phrasing his questions, such as "Do your postal workers ever open other people's post?" It was an impossible question to ask, an insult to the profession. Wallander thought of Westin, who would no doubt have been deeply offended. He decided instead to start from the beginning.

It was 10.43 a.m. on Monday, 19 August.

CHAPTER THIRTY

A map hung on the wall in Albinsson's room. Wallander started there, asking him about the rural postal routes. Albinsson wanted to know why the police were so interested in this information, and Wallander came close to telling him. Then he realised how preposterous it would sound if he said that the police suspected one of his staff of being a mass murderer, so he kept his explanations as vague as possible, making sure that Albinsson knew not to expect further clarification.

Albinsson described the various routes to him with great enthusiasm. Wallander took occasional notes.

"How many postmen work here?" Wallander asked after Albinsson had finished with the map and sat down at his desk.

"Eight."

"Do you have their names written down anywhere? Photographs would be helpful too."

"The Post Office is a proactive business these days," Albinsson said. "We have an information brochure that I think is just what you're looking for."

As Albinsson left the room, Wallander thought to himself that he had just had a stroke of luck. From the photographs of the postal workers he would immediately be able to determine if the man in Copenhagen worked here or not. Then he would have identified the killer in a single stroke.

Albinsson came back with the brochure, and Wallander looked around for his glasses, to no avail.

"Maybe mine will work," Albinsson suggested. "What's your prescription?"

"I don't know, around ten-point-five, I think."

Albinsson looked at him curiously. "That would mean you were blind," he said. "I take it you mean one-point-five. I'm a two, so go ahead and try them."

Wallander put on the glasses and found that they helped. He unfolded the brochure and looked closely at the pictures of the eight postal workers. There were four men and four women. Wallander studied the men's faces, but none of them bore any likeness to Louise. He hesitated for a moment at the face of a man called Lars-Göran Berg, but quickly realised that it couldn't be him. He looked briefly at the women, and recognised one who regularly delivered post to his father's house in Löderup.

"Can I keep this?" he asked.

"You can have more copies if you like."

"Just one will do."

"Have I answered all your questions?"

"Not quite. There's one more point I need to cover. All of the post is sorted here in this building, right? Do the postmen sort their own post?"

"Yes."

He gave the glasses back to Albinsson. "That's all. I won't keep you from your work any longer."

He stood up. "What is it you're trying to find out?" Albinsson asked.

"Just what I said. This is a routine check."

Albinsson shook his head. "I don't believe that. Why would the chief inspector on a pressing murder case drop by as a matter of routine? You're trying to solve the murder of one of your colleagues, as well as that of those young-sters in the Hagestad nature reserve, and the newly-weds. Your visit here has something to do with all that, doesn't it?"

"That wouldn't change the fact that this is still a routine check," Wallander said.

"I think you're looking for something in particular," Albinsson said.

"I've told you as much as I can."

Albinsson didn't ask any more questions. They parted at the front door, and Wallander walked out into the sunny yard. What a strange August this is, he thought. The heat just won't let up, and there's never even a hint of a breeze.

He walked back to the station, wondering whether to wear his uniform at Svedberg's funeral. He also wondered whether Höglund was regretting having promised to give a speech, let alone one she hadn't written herself.

When he walked into reception, Ebba said that Holgersson wanted to speak to him. Ebba seemed depressed.

"How are things with you these days?" he asked. "We never have time to talk any more."

"Things are as they are," she said.

It was the kind of thing his father used to say when he spoke of getting old.

"As soon as all this is over, we'll talk," he said.

She nodded. Wallander sensed that something was differ-ent about her, but he had no time to ask more. He went to Holgersson's office. Her door was wide open as usual.

"This is a significant breakthrough," she said as soon as he had sat down in the comfortable armchair across from her. "Thurnberg is impressed."

"Impressed by what?"

"You'll have to ask him that. But you're living up to your reputation."

Wallander was surprised. "Are things really so bad?"

"I'd say just the opposite."

Wallander made an impatient gesture with his hand. He didn't want to talk about his own performance, especially since he knew it was seriously flawed.

"The national chief of police will officiate at the funeral tomorrow," she said, "together with the minister of justice. They're landing at Sturup tomorrow morning at 11 a.m. I'll be there to greet them and escort them back here. They have both requested a briefing on the state of our investigation, so I've scheduled that for 11.30 a.m., in the large conference room. It'll be you, me, and Thurnberg."

"Could you handle it on your own, or with Martinsson? He can speak more eloquently than I can."

"You're the one in charge of the investigation," she said. "It'll only take half an hour, then we'll break for lunch. They fly back to Stockholm straight after the funeral."

"I'm dreading this funeral," Wallander said. "It's different when the dead person has been brutally murdered."

"You're thinking about your old friend Rydberg?"

"Yes."

The phone rang and she picked it up, listened for a moment, and then asked the caller to get back to her later.

"Have you chosen the music?" Wallander asked.

"We let the cantor choose it for us. I'm sure it'll be appropriate. What is it usually? Bach and Buxtehude? And then the old standard hymns, of course."

Wallander got up to leave. "I hope you'll make the most of this opportunity," he said. "What with the national chief of police and the minister of justice here."

"What opportunity?"

"To tell them they can't let things go on like this. The cuts in staff and funding are starting to look like a conspiracy to make us unable to do our jobs, not like a matter of fiscal responsibility. The criminal element is taking over. Tell them it will be the end of all of us if they don't do something to stop it. We're not quite there yet, but we will be soon."

Holgersson shook her head in amazement. "I don't think we see eye to eye on this."

"I know you've noticed it too."

"Why don't you tell them yourself?"

"I probably will. But I have a killer to track down in the meantime."

"Not you," she corrected him. "We."

Wallander went to Martinsson's office. Höglund was with him and they were studying a picture on the computer screen: Louise's face. Martinsson had erased her hair.

"I'm using a programme developed by the FBI," Martinsson told him. "We can add details such as hairstyles, beards and moustaches. You can even add pimples."

"I don't think he had any of those," Wallander said. "The only thing I'm interested in is what was under his wig."

"I called a wigmaker in Stockholm about that," Höglund said. "I asked him how much hair you could hide under a wig, but it was hard to get a clear answer from him."

"So he could have bushy hair for all we know," Wallander said.

"The programme can do other things, too," Martinsson said "We can fold out the ears and flatten the nose."

"We don't have to fold out or flatten anything," Wallander said. "The photograph is already so similar to his face."

"What about the eye colour?" Martinsson asked.

Wallander thought for a moment. "Blue," he answered.

"Did you see her teeth?"

"Not her teeth. His teeth."

"Did you see them?"

"Not very closely. But I think they were white and well kept."

"Psychopaths are often fanatics about oral hygiene," Martinsson said.

"We don't know if he's a psychopath," Wallander said.

Martinsson entered the information about eyes and teeth into the computer.

"How old was she?" Höglund asked.

"You mean he," Wallander said.

"But the person you saw was a woman. You only realised later that she had to be a man."

She was right. He had seen a woman, not a man, and that was the image he had to return to in order to judge the person's age.

"It's always hard to tell with women who wear a lot of make-up," he said. "But the photograph we have must be fairly recent. I would say around 40 years old."

"How tall was she?" Martinsson asked.

Wallander tried hard to remember. "I'm not sure," he answered. "But I think she was quite tall, between 170 and 175 centimetres."

Martinsson entered in the numbers. "What about her body?" he said. "Was she wearing falsies?"

Wallander realised he hadn't noticed very much about her at all.

"I don't know," he said.

Höglund looked at him with a hint of a smile. "The latest studies indicate that the first thing a man notices about a woman is her breasts," she said. "He registers whether they are small or large, then usually proceeds to her legs, and finally her behind."

Martinsson chuckled from his place at the computer. Wallander saw the absurdity of the situation. He was supposed to describe a woman who was actually a man, but who should still be regarded as a woman, at least until Martinsson had finished entering the data into the computer.

"She was wearing a jacket," he said. "Maybe I'm an unusual male, but I really didn't notice her breasts. And the bar hid most of her body. I didn't see much of her when she stood up and went to the ladies' room, because she was swallowed up by the crowd. It was a full house."

"We have quite a lot already," Martinsson said reassuringly. "We just have to work out what kind of hairstyle he had under the wig."

"There must be a hundred different styles," Wallander said. "Let's try circulating the face without any hair. Someone may recognise his features."

"According to the FBI, that's almost impossible."

"Let's do it anyway."

Something else occurred to Wallander. "Who questioned the nurse who received the call from the man pretending to be Erik Lundberg?"

"I did," Höglund said.

"What did she remember about his voice?"

"Not very much. He had a Scanian accent."

"Did it sound real?"

She looked at him with surprise. "Actually, no. She said there was something funny about his dialect, although she couldn't put her finger on it."

"So it could have been fake?"

"Yes."

"Was it a low or high voice?"

"Low."

Wallander thought back to his time in the Amigo. Louise had smiled at him, then excused herself, and her voice had been deep, although she had tried to make it sound feminine.

"I think we can assume it was him," Wallander said. "Even though we have no proof."

He told them about his visit to the postal depot. "I've only been able to find one common denominator so far," he said. "Isa Edengren and Sture Björklund had the same postman. The other people in this investigation bring the number of postmen involved to three, in addition to someone who works outside of Ystad altogether. It therefore seems reasonable to ditch this theory, since it's absurd to think there's a conspiracy between postal workers."

He sat back in his chair and looked at the other two. "I see no pattern yet," he said. "We have costumes and secrets, but nothing more."

"What happens if we ignore the costumes?" Höglund said. "What do we have then?"

"Young people," Wallander said. "Happy people, having a party or getting married."

"You don't think Haag is a target?"

"No. He falls outside the parameters."

"What about Isa Edengren?"

"She was supposed to have been there."

"That changes our picture," Höglund said. "A new motive emerges. She's not allowed to escape, but escape what? Is it revenge, or hatred? There also doesn't seem to be any point of connection between the young people and the

431

wedding couple. And then there's Svedberg. What lead was he following?"

"I think I can answer the last question," Wallander said. "At least for now. Svedberg knew this man who dresses as a woman. Something made him suspicious. Over the course of the summer, his investigation confirmed his suspicion. That's why he was killed – he knew too much. But he didn't have time to tell us what he knew."

"But what does it all add up to?" Martinsson said. "Svedberg told his cousin he was involved with a woman called Louise. Now it turns out she's a man. Svedberg must have known that after all these years, so where does that lead us? Was Svedberg a transvestite? Was he homosexual after all?"

"A number of explanations are possible," Wallander said. "I doubt that Svedberg had a passion for dressing up in women's clothing, but he may very well have been homosexual without any of us knowing about it."

"One person in our investigation seems to be growing in importance," Höglund said.

Wallander knew to whom she was referring: Bror Sundelius.

"I agree," he said. "We need to maintain that end of the investigation, not as an alternative but as part of our search for the killer. We need to know more about the people involved in charges filed against Svedberg. He may very well have been the victim of blackmail or had some other reason to keep Stridh quiet."

"If Bror Sundelius has deviant tendencies then it all starts to make sense," Martinsson said.

Wallander bristled at Martinsson's words. "In this day and age, homosexuality can hardly be regarded as 'deviant'," he said. "Maybe in the 1950s, but not now. That people

432

might still want to conceal their sexual preferences is another matter entirely."

Martinsson registered Wallander's disapproval, but said nothing.

"The question is what connected these three men, Sundelius, Stridh, and Svedberg," Wallander said. "A bank director, a petty criminal and a policeman, whose surnames all start with the letter 'S.'"

"I wonder if Louise was in the picture at that point," Höglund said.

Wallander made a face. "We have to call him something else," he said. "Louise disappeared in the lavatory of that bar back in Copenhagen. We'll confuse ourselves if we don't use another name."

"What about Louis?" Martinsson said. "That would make it easy."

They all agreed, and Louise was renamed. Now they were looking for a man called Louis. They decided that Martinsson should spend part of his time keeping an eye on Sundelius. Wallander left the room and went back to his office. He bumped into Edmundsson on his way.

"We didn't find anything in that area of the nature reserve you wanted us to search," he said. It took Wallander a moment to remember what this had been about.

"Nothing?"

"We found a wad of chewing tobacco by a tree," Edmundsson said. "That was it."

Wallander looked closely at him. "I hope you collected that wad of chewing tobacco, or at least alerted Nyberg."

Edmundsson surprised him with his answer. "Actually, I did."

"This could be more important than you realise," he said.

He kept walking towards his office. He was right. The killer had been there that night, hiding where he had the best view of their comings and goings. He had spat out a wad of chewing tobacco, just like on the beach. And later he had turned up outside the police barricades at Nybrostrand, although this time he was disguised as a woman.

He's following us, Wallander thought. He's somewhere close by, both a step ahead and a step behind. Is he trying to find out what we know? Or is he trying to prove to himself that we can't find him?

Something occurred to him and he called Martinsson. "Is there anyone who has shown an unexpected interest in our investigation?"

"You mean like a journalist?"

"Let people know to be on the lookout for someone who takes an interest in the case, something out of the ordinary. I don't think I can give you a more precise description – just someone who seems odd."

Martinsson promised to pass it on. Wallander hung up.

It was midday and he felt nauseated with hunger. He left the station and walked to a restaurant in the middle of town. He got back at 1.30 p.m., took off his coat, and looked through the brochure that he had picked up at the post office.

The first postman was called Olov Andersson. Wallander picked up the receiver and dialled his number, wondering how long he could keep going.

He returned to Ystad shortly after 11 a.m. Since he didn't want to risk running into the policeman who had found him in Copenhagen, he took the ferry from Helsingør. When he arrived at Helsingborg, he took a taxi to Malmö where his car was parked. The unexpected inheritance he'd received from a relative meant he no longer had to worry about money. He watched the car park from a distance before approaching his car. There had never been a moment when he doubted that he would get away with it, just as he hadn't doubted the fact that he would get away the night before at the Amigo. That had been a major triumph. He hadn't expected a policeman to stroll in and sit down beside him, but he hadn't panicked or lost control of himself, only done what he had long ago planned to do in such a situation.

He walked calmly into the women's lavatory, took off his wig and tucked it inside his shirt above his belt, removed his make-up with the cream he always carried with him, and then left, timing his departure so it coincided with a man leaving the men's room. He still had the ability to escape. It had not failed him.

When he was certain that the car park wasn't under surveillance, he got into the car and drove to Ystad. Once he was back at home he'd taken a long shower and crawled into bed in the soundproofed room. There was so much he had to think through. He didn't know how that policeman Wallander had found him. He must inadvertently have left a trace of himself behind. That upset him more than it worried him. The only thing he could think of was that Svedberg had kept a photo of him in his flat after all. A photograph of Louise. He hadn't found it during his search. Nonetheless, this thought calmed him. The policeman was expecting to talk to a woman. Nothing suggested that he had seen through the disguise, although by now he might have put two and two together.

The thought of his narrow escape excited him. It spurred him on, although he now encountered a problem. He hadn't selected any more people to kill. According to his original plans, he was going to wait for a whole year before acting again. He needed to plan his next move carefully so he could outdo himself. He would wait just long enough for people to start to forget about him, and then he would show himself again.

But his recent encounter with the policeman changed everything. Now he couldn't stand the idea of waiting a whole year before striking again. He stayed in bed all afternoon, analysing his situation methodically. There were a number of courses of action to be evaluated. A few times he almost gave up.

At last he thought he had hit upon a solution. It went against the original plan, which was its biggest flaw, but he felt he had no alternative. It was also a great temptation. The more he thought about it, the more it struck him as ingenious. He would create something completely unexpected, a riddle no one would see through.

It would have to be Wallander, the policeman, and soon. Svedberg's funeral was tomorrow. He would need that day for his preparations. He smiled at the thought that Svedberg would actually come to his aid. During the funeral, the policeman's flat would be empty. Svedberg had told him on several occasions that Wallander was divorced and lived alone. He would wait no longer than Wednesday. The idea filled him with exhilaration. He would shoot him first, and then give him a disguise. A very particular disguise.

CHAPTER THIRTY-ONE

Monday had been a wasted day. That was the first thought that went through Wallander's mind when he woke up Tuesday morning. For the first time in a long while he felt fully rested, as he'd left the station at 9 p.m. the night before.

It was 6 a.m. and he lay motionless in his bed. Through the gap in the curtains he saw blue sky. Monday had been a wasted day because it hadn't brought them closer to their goal. He'd spoken to two of the postal workers assigned to rural routes, but neither one had been able to tell him anything of significance. Around 6 p.m., Wallander had conferred with the other members of the investigative team. By then they had covered all six postal workers. But what were they supposed to have asked, and what answers had they been expecting?

Wallander was forced to admit that his hunch had been wrong. And it wasn't just the postmen who had proved a dead end; Lone Kjær had called from Copenhagen to say that they hadn't been able to recover any prints from the bar top at the Amigo. They had even worked on the bar stool. Wallander knew it had been unlikely that they'd get anything, but he'd still been hoping that they would. A print would have identified the killer beyond doubt. Now they had to carry around that vague and disconcerting anxiety that this lead would also turn out to be false; that the man in the dark wig was only a step along the path, not the answer itself.

They'd spent a long time wondering whether or not to publish the digitally enhanced picture of Louis – too long for Wallander's liking. He'd sent for Thurnberg. The members of his team had wildly differing opinions, but Wallander had insisted that it should be published. Someone might recognise the face now that the wig was gone. All they needed was one person. Thurnberg had joined the discussion for the first time, supporting Wallander. In his opinion, the picture should be released to the press as soon as possible.

They decided to wait until Wednesday, the day after the funeral.

"People love these composite sketches," Wallander had said. "It doesn't matter if it really looks like him or not. There's something extraordinary, almost magical about this act of throwing out a half-finished face in the hope that someone will bite."

They had worked non-stop all Monday afternoon. Hansson had searched the various databases of the Swedish Police for information on Bror Sundelius. As expected, there was nothing. In terms of digital records at least, he was clean. They'd decided that Wallander would go back and talk to him on Wednesday, pressing him harder this time. Wallander knew that Sundelius was coming to the funeral, and he'd reminded the others of this fact.

Other things had come up on that Monday afternoon, even though Wallander now saw the day as a waste. Shortly after 4 p.m., a journalist from one of the national papers had called him to say that Eva Hillström had been in contact with them. The parents of the young murder victims were planning to criticise the police investigation. They didn't think the police had done enough, and they felt they had been denied information that they'd had a right to. The reporter had told him that their criticism was strong. In addition, Eva Hillström seemed to regard Wallander as the person responsible, or rather, the one who was not responsible enough. It would be a big article, and it would come out the day after next. The reporter had called to give Wallander a chance to respond to the allegations. Somewhat to his own surprise, Wallander had sharply declined to comment. He'd said he would be in touch when he had read the article and seen for himself what the parents had to say. If he had any reason to disagree with their claims, he would send a rebuttal. End of story.

After speaking to the journalist he'd felt a new knot in his already overtaxed stomach. This one took up residence right next to the fear that the killer was going to strike again. He'd gone over it all again in his mind, asking himself if they could have done more, if they had really done everything in their power up to this point. The reason that they hadn't caught the killer yet was because the investigation was so complicated, not because of laziness, lack of focus, or poor police work. They had so little to go on. The internal blunders made along the way were another matter. The perfect investigation didn't exist; not even Eva Hillström could claim otherwise.

After the 6 p.m. meeting, when they had ruled out the postal workers and studied different images of Louis with exhausted eyes, Wallander told them about his conversation with the newspaper reporter. Thurnberg, immediately concerned, had questioned Wallander's decision not to respond to the allegations.

"There just isn't time to do everything at once," Wallander had said. "We're so overworked right now that even these allegations will have to wait."

"The national chief of police is going to be here tomorrow," Thurnberg had replied, "and the minister of justice. It's particularly unfortunate that this article is going to coincide with their visit."

Wallander had suddenly understood Thurnberg's real concern. "Not even a shadow of these allegations falls on you," he'd said. "It seems that Eva Hillström and the other parents are critical of the work of the police, not the chief prosecutor's office."

Thurnberg had had nothing else to say. Shortly afterwards they'd called it a day. Höglund had followed Wallander out into the hall and told him that Thurnberg had been asking questions about events in the nature reserve on the day the jogger, Nils Hagroth, claimed to have been assaulted by Wallander. On hearing this, Wallander had been hit by another a wave of exhaustion. Didn't they have enough on their plates without Nils Hagroth's absurd charges? That had been the moment when, despite the consistently high level of activity, the entire day had begun to seem like a waste.

Wallander reluctantly got out of bed at 7.30 a.m. He was already dreading this day. His uniform hung on the cupboard door. He had to put it on now, because there wouldn't be enough time between his meeting with the national chief of police and the minister of justice and the funeral itself. He looked at himself in the mirror after he put it on. The trousers strained alarmingly across his belly. He would have to leave the top button undone. He couldn't remember when he had last worn his uniform but it must have been a long time ago.

On the way to the station he stopped at a news-stand and bought a paper. The reporter had not been exaggerating.

It was a big article, with pictures. The parents' allegations were threefold. First, the police had waited too long before acting on the disappearance of their children. Second, they felt the investigation had not been as organised as it could have been. Third, they felt they had been poorly informed of the developments in the case.

The national chief isn't going to be very happy, Wallander thought. It's not going to matter if we tell him that these allegations are unjust. The fact that they've been made will hurt the police.

Wallander approached the station feeling shaken and angry. It was just before 8 a.m. It was going to be a long and depressing day, although the weather was still warm and beautiful.

Holgersson called him from her car at 11.30 a.m. They were on their way from Sturup and would arrive at the station in five minutes. Wallander walked out to reception to greet them. Thurnberg was already there. They exchanged pleasantries, neither of them mentioning the article. The car pulled up outside and everyone got out. The national chief of police and the minister of justice were appropriately dressed for a funeral. Everyone was introduced, and they all proceeded to Holgersson's office for coffee. Before they entered the room, Holgersson pulled Wallander aside.

"They read the article on the plane," she said, "and the national chief is not pleased."

"What about the minister?"

"She seemed more eager to hear your side of the story before giving an opinion."

"Should I say something?"

"No. Only if they bring it up."

They sat down with their coffee and Wallander received

their condolences for Svedberg's death. After that, it was his turn to say something. As usual he had forgotten to bring the piece of paper he'd scribbled some notes on. But it didn't really matter. He knew what he wanted to tell them: that they had a lead. They had identified the killer. Things were picking up, there were new developments.

"This whole matter is very unfortunate," the national chief said when Wallander finished. "A policeman and some innocent youngsters murdered. I hope we can count on you to wrap this up shortly. I'm pleased to hear you have a breakthrough."

It was clear that he was extremely anxious.

"No society will ever be free of lunatics," the minister said. "Mass murders happen in democracies and dictatorships the world over."

"And lunatics don't act according to a predictable pattern," Wallander added. "They can't be easily categorised. They plan their deeds carefully, often appearing from nowhere, with no previous criminal record."

"Community policing," the national chief said. "That's where it has to start."

Wallander didn't quite understand the link between lunatics and community policing but he said nothing. The minister asked Thurnberg some questions, then it was over. As they were about to leave for lunch, the national chief noticed that some papers were missing from his briefcase.

"I have a temporary secretary right now," he said glumly. "I never know where anything is. I hardly have time to learn their names before they leave again."

As they toured the station, the minister of justice fell in beside Wallander.

"I heard someone's filed charges against you. Is there anything to it?"

"I'm not concerned about it," Wallander said. "The man was trespassing at the scene of a murder investigation. There was no assault involved."

"I didn't think so," she said encouragingly.

Once they had returned to the reception area, the national chief asked Wallander the same question.

"The timing is very unfortunate," he said.

"It's always unfortunate," Wallander said. "But I have to give you the same answer that I gave the minister. The allegations of an assault are unfounded."

"Then what was it?"

"A man who was trespassing on the scene of a police investigation."

"It's important for the police to maintain a good relationship with the public and the media."

"Once this case is completed, I'll issue a statement to the papers," Wallander said.

"I'd like to see that before it goes to press," the national chief said.

Wallander promised to oblige. He declined to accompany them to lunch, and stopped by Höglund's office instead. It was empty. He returned to his own office and sat down at his desk. The germ of an idea was dancing somewhere deep in his mind, but he couldn't quite catch it. Was it something the minister had said? The national chief? It was gone.

At 2 p.m., Saint Mary's Cathedral by the main square was full of people. Wallander was one of the pallbearers. The coffin was white and simply adorned with roses. They carried it into the church.

Wallander searched the crowd for a man's face, although he wasn't expecting Louis to be there. He didn't see him.

But Bror Sundelius was there. Wallander greeted him. Sundelius asked him how the investigation was proceeding.

"We've had a breakthrough," Wallander replied. "That's all I can tell you."

"Just be sure you get him," Sundelius said.

Svedberg's murder had obviously shaken him. Wallander wondered if Sundelius knew what Svedberg had known. Did he feel the same fear? He must talk to him again as soon as possible.

Wallander sat in the front row of the cathedral with a sense of dread in his stomach. Dread at the idea of his own annihilation. He wondered if funerals really had to be such an ordeal. The minister of justice spoke about democracy and the right to a secure life, the national chief of police about the tragic nature of this death. Wallander wondered if he was going to weave in a piece about community policing, then decided he was being unfair. There was no reason for him to question the man's sincerity. When the national chief was finished, it was Ann-Britt Höglund's turn. Wallander had never seen her in her uniform before. She read Wallander's words in a loud, clear voice, and to his surprise he didn't cringe when he heard them.

It was towards the end of the service, right before the processional, when Wallander finally seized the thought that had been skirting the edges of his consciousness. The national chief had said something while rifling through his papers, something about temporary employees who came and went and whose names one never learned before they were gone. At first he didn't know why this comment had stayed with him, but then he suddenly saw the connection. Postal workers must have substitutes who filled in for them when they were away.

It was past 5 p.m. when Wallander was able to return home and take off his tight uniform. He called the postal depot, but no one answered. Before trying to reach Albinsson, he showered and changed, found a pair of glasses and looked in the phone book. Kjell Albinsson lived in Rydsgård. He dialled the number and Albinsson's wife answered. Her husband was playing football for the post office team. She didn't know where the game was being played, but she promised she would have him return Wallander's call.

Wallander heated up tomato soup and ate some slices of crisp bread, then lay on his bed, exhausted despite his good night's sleep. The funeral had tired him out. He was woken by the phone at 7.30 p.m. It was Kjell Albinsson.

"How was the game?" Wallander asked.

"Not so good. We were playing a slaughterhouse team. They have some good players. But it was only a pre-season game. The regular season doesn't start for a while."

"It's a great way to stay in shape."

"Or get your bones broken."

Wallander decided to launch straight into his question. "There was one thing I forgot to ask you the other day. I take it you sometimes employ substitute postal workers."

"That's right. Both short-term and long-term."

"Who do you normally use?"

"We prefer to use people with experience, and we've been pretty lucky. With today's unemployment, we have many to choose from. There are two people who do most of our substituting. One is a woman called Lena Stivell. She had a permanent position, but chose to go to part-time and then to occasional work."

"Is the other one also a woman?"

"No, he's a man called Åke Larstam. He used to be an engineer, but he retrained."

"To become a postal worker?"

"It's not as strange as it sounds. The hours are good and you meet a lot of people."

"Is he working at the moment?"

"He subbed for someone about a week ago. I'm not sure what he's up right now."

"Is there anything else you can tell me about him?"

"He's a very private person, but conscientious. I think he's about 44 years old, and he lives here in Ystad – at number 18, Harmonigatan, if I'm not mistaken."

Wallander thought for a moment. "And these substitutes might be placed on any of your routes?"

"It's supposed to work that way. You never know when someone's going to come down with a cold."

"Which route was Larstam working on last time?"

"The district to the west of Ystad."

Wrong again, Wallander thought. Neither the nature reserve nor Nybrostrand lay to the west.

"Thanks, that's all I wanted to know," he said. "I appreciate you taking the time to call me back."

Wallander hung up and decided to return to the station. The investigative team had no plans to meet that evening, but he would use the time to re-examine material in the case files. The phone rang. It was Albinsson again.

"I made a mistake," he said. "I mixed up Lena's and Åke's assignments. Lena took the route to the west of Ystad."

"And was Åke Larstam also working?"

"That's where I was wrong. He last subbed on a route in Nybrostrand."

"When was that?"

446

"In July. The assignment was only for a couple of weeks."

"Do you remember the route he had before that?"

"He had a long-term assignment out towards Rögla. That must have been from March to June."

"Thanks for telling me," Wallander said.

He replaced the receiver. Åke Larstam had recently been delivering post in the area where Torbjörn Werner and Malin Skander lived. Before then, he had been delivering post in an area that included Skårby, where Isa Edengren lived. It was probably mere coincidence, but he couldn't help taking out the phone book and looking for Larstam's entry. There was no one by that name in the book. He called information and was told that Larstam had an unlisted number.

Wallander dressed and went down to the station. To his surprise, Höglund was also there. She was in her office, looking through a thick pile of papers.

"I didn't think anyone else would be here," he said.

She was still dressed in her uniform. Wallander had already complimented her on her speech earlier in the day.

"My babysitter is there tonight," she said. "I have to make the most of it. There's so much paperwork to do."

"Same here. That's why I came down too."

He sat down in her visitor's chair. She saw he wanted to discuss something with her, and she pushed her pile of paper to the side. Wallander told her about the idea he'd had after hearing the national chief mention his temporary secretary. Then he described his conversation with Albinsson.

"From his description, he hardly sounds like a mass murderer," she said.

"Who does? My point is that we finally have someone whose activities we can trace to three of the victims' homes."

"So what are you suggesting we do?"

"I just came here to talk to you about it, nothing more."

"We've talked to the regular postal workers, so we should talk to these substitutes too. Is that what you want?"

"I don't think we need to bother with Lena Stivell."

Höglund looked down at her watch. "We could take a short walk," she said. "Get some fresh air. We could walk by Harmonigatan and ring Larstam's bell. It's not that late."

"Even I hadn't thought that far," he said. "But I like your idea."

It took them ten minutes to walk to Harmonigatan, which lay in the western part of the city. Number 18 was an older, three-storey block of flats. Larstam lived on the top floor. Wallander rang the bell and they waited. He rang it again.

"I suppose he isn't home," she said. Wallander crossed the street and looked up at the flat. Two of the windows were lit. He went back and tried the front door. It was open, so they walked in. There was no elevator. They walked up the wide stairs. Wallander rang the doorbell, and they heard it ring inside. Nothing happened. He rang it three times. Höglund bent down and looked through the post slot.

"There's no sound," she said. "But the light's on."

Wallander rang the bell one last time, then Höglund banged on the door.

"We'll have to try again tomorrow," she said.

Wallander was struck by the feeling that something wasn't quite right. She noticed it immediately.

"What are you thinking?"

"I don't know. That something doesn't add up."

"He's probably not home. The manager at the post office

448

said that he's not working at the moment. He might have gone somewhere for a few days. That's a logical explanation."

"You're probably right," Wallander said doubtfully.

She started down the stairs. "Let's try again tomorrow," she said.

"That is if we don't try to go in tonight anyway."

She looked up at him with genuine surprise. "Are you suggesting that we break in? Is he even a suspect?"

"It's just that we happen to be here now."

She shook her head vigorously. "I can't let you do it. It goes against all the rules."

Wallander shrugged. "You're right. We'll try again tomorrow."

They returned to the station. During the walk they discussed how the workload should be distributed over the next couple of days. They parted in reception, and Wallander returned to his office to deal with some pressing paperwork.

Shortly before 11 p.m. he dialled the number of the Stockholm restaurant where Linda worked. For once he succeeded in getting through, but Linda was very busy. They agreed that she would call him in the morning.

"How is everything?" he asked. "Have you decided where you're going to go?"

"Not yet. I will."

The conversation gave him a burst of energy. He returned to his paperwork. At 11.30 p.m., Höglund came to say she was leaving.

"I'll try to be here before 8 a.m.," she said. "We can start by visiting Larstam again."

"We'll fit it in when we have the time," Wallander said.

Wallander waited for five minutes, then took a set of

skeleton keys out of his desk drawer and left the office. He had already made up his mind while they were deliberating outside Larstam's door. If she didn't want to be party to breaking in, he would do it alone. There was something about Åke Larstam that bothered him.

He walked back to Harmonigatan. It was just before midnight and there was a soft, easterly breeze. Wallander thought he could feel a touch of autumn chill in the air. Maybe the heat wave was nearing its end. He rang the bell from downstairs and noted that the same lights were on. When there was no answer, he pushed open the front door and walked up the stairs.

He had a feeling of being back where it all began; of reliving the night when he and Martinsson had gone up to Svedberg's flat. He shuddered, then listened intently outside the door of the flat. Not a sound. He carefully opened the post slot. No sound, just a soft beam of light. He rang the doorbell and waited, then rang it again. After waiting for five minutes, he got out the skeleton keys, and looked closely at the door. It was fitted with the most elaborate set of locks he had ever seen in his life. Åke Larstam was clearly a person who valued his privacy. There was no way he would be able to open these locks with his skeleton keys. At the same time, the need to get inside seemed more pressing than ever. He hesitated for only a moment before getting out his phone and calling Nyberg.

Nyberg answered in his usual irritated tone. Wallander didn't need to ask if he had been asleep.

"I need your help," he said.

"Don't tell me it's happened again," Nyberg groaned.

"No one's dead," Wallander said. "But I need your help opening a door."

"You don't need a technician for that."

"In this case I do."

Nyberg growled on the other end, but he was fully awake now. Wallander described the locks to him and gave him the address. Nyberg promised to come. Wallander walked quietly down the stairs and waited for him out on the street. He would need to explain to him what was going on, and Nyberg was probably going to protest loudly. With good reason.

Wallander knew he was doing something he shouldn't.

Nyberg arrived within ten minutes. Wallander guessed he was wearing pyjamas under his coat. As he had expected, Nyberg immediately issued a furious protest.

"You can't just break into the homes of innocent people."

"I need you to open the door," Wallander said. "Then you're free to go. I take full responsibility, and I won't tell a soul you've been here."

Nyberg still expressed his reluctance, but when Wallander insisted he walked up the stairs and studied the locks carefully.

"No one will believe you," he said. "There's no way you'd get past this on your own."

Then he got to work. At just before 1 a.m., the door finally opened.

CHAPTER THIRTY-TWO

The first thing he noticed was the smell. After he stepped into the hall, he stood absolutely still to and listened for sounds within the flat. That's when it hit him. Nyberg stayed where he was on the other side of the door. The smell was overpowering.

He realised that it was merely the smell of a place that was never aired. The air had actually gone bad. Wallander gestured for Nyberg to follow him in, which he did unwillingly. Wallander told him to wait there and walked into the rest of the flat on his own. There were three rooms and a little kitchen, all clean and orderly. The neatness contrasted strongly with the bad air.

The door to one of the rooms differed from the others. It looked as if it had been specially made. When Wallander pushed it open he saw that it was extremely thick. It reminded him of a door to a recording studio, like the ones he had seen on the few occasions he'd done radio interviews. Wallander stepped inside. There was something strange about the room. There were no windows and the walls were reinforced. There was a bed and a lamp in the room, nothing else. The bed was made, but there was a faint imprint of a body on the bedspread. It took him a while to put it together: the room looked as it did because it had been soundproofed. His curiosity piqued, Wallander walked through the rest of the flat again, hoping to find a picture of the man who lived there. There were shelves full of porcelain figures, but not a single photograph. Wallander came to a halt in the living room, suddenly overtaken by the sense that he was violating someone's privacy.

He had no business being here. He should leave at once. But something held him back. He returned to the hall where Nyberg was waiting.

"Five more minutes," he said. "That's all."

Nyberg didn't reply. Wallander returned to the flat, conducting a methodical search now. He knew what he was looking for. He went through the three cupboards one by one. In the first two he found only men's clothing. He was about to close the door of the third when he caught sight of something. He reached into one end of the cupboard, where some clothes had been hung behind the others, and pulled out a hanger. It held a red dress. He started going through the drawers with equal concentration, feeling underneath the neatly folded piles of men's clothing. The sense that time was running out, that he had to hurry, spurred him on. Again, he came up lucky. Various articles of women's underclothing were hidden away. He returned to the third cupboard, crept around on hands and knees, and found some women's shoes. He was careful to return things as they had been. Nyberg came out into the living room as he worked.

Wallander could see that he was furious. Or possibly afraid.

"It's been almost 15 minutes," he hissed. "What the hell are we doing here?"

Wallander didn't answer. Now he was looking around for a desk. There was an old secretary's desk in the corner. It was locked. He motioned for Nyberg to work on it, but Nyberg objected.

Wallander interrupted his protests, giving him the shortest possible answer he could think of.

"Louise lives here," he said. "You know, the woman in the picture we found in Svedberg's flat. The woman in Copenhagen. The one who doesn't really exist. She lives here."

"You could have said that a little earlier," Nyberg said.

"I didn't know for sure," Wallander said. "Not until this moment. Could you open that desk for me, without leaving any marks?"

Nyberg unlocked it quickly with his tools. The lid folded down into a writing surface.

It had often seemed to Wallander that police work was characterised by a series of expectations that were inevitably disappointed. What he had been expecting at this particular moment, he was later unable to determine, but it could not have been what actually awaited his gaze.

There was a plastic folder full of newspaper clippings, all related to the murder investigation. There was a copy of Svedberg's obituary, which Wallander hadn't seen until then.

Nyberg was waiting behind him. "You should take a look at this," Wallander said slowly. "It'll explain what we're doing in this flat."

Nyberg took a few steps forward, flinched, then looked at Wallander.

"We could leave," Wallander said, "and put the house under surveillance. Or we could call for reinforcements and start going through the flat right away."

"He's killed eight people," Nyberg said. "That means he's armed and dangerous."

It hadn't occurred to Wallander that they might be in danger. That made up his mind for him: they'd get reinforcements. Nyberg closed the desk. Wallander went into the kitchen, where he had seen some glasses on the counter. He wrapped one of them in paper and put it in his pocket. He was about to leave the kitchen when he noticed that the back door was slightly ajar. He felt a wave of fear so powerful it almost knocked him over. He thought someone was about to push the door open and shoot. But nothing happened. Gingerly he approached the back door and nudged it gently. The back stairs were empty. Nyberg was already on his way out of the flat by the front door. Wallander joined him.

They listened carefully. Nothing. Nyberg softly closed the front door. He examined the threshold with a torch.

"There are a few scratches," he said. "But they're not noticeable unless you're really looking for them."

Wallander thought about the back door that had been slightly ajar. He decided to keep it to himself for now. When they got to the station, Wallander literally ran down the corridor to his office. The first person he called was Martinsson, since he wanted him there as soon as possible.

During the next ten minutes he talked to a number of sleepy people who became surprisingly alert when he told them about his find. Martinsson was the first to arrive, then Höglund and the others in rapid succession.

"I'm lucky," she said. "My mother's visiting."

"I went back to Harmonigatan," Wallander said. "I had the feeling it couldn't wait."

By 2 a.m., everyone was assembled. Wallander looked around the table. He wondered briefly how Thurnberg had found the time to get such a perfect knot in his tie. Then he told them about his discovery.

"What made you go over there in the middle of the night?" Hansson asked.

"I'm usually sceptical of my intuition," Wallander said. "But this time I was right."

He shook off his tiredness. Now he had to shape his investigative team into hunters, stalking their prey in ever-narrowing circles until he was caught.

"We don't know where he is right now," he said. "But the back door was open. Given the nature of the locks on his front door, I think we can assume he heard us working on them and fled. In other words, he knows we're closing in on him."

"That means he's not likely to return," Martinsson said.

"We don't know that for sure. I'd like to put the place under surveillance. One car is fine, as long as there are several others close by."

Wallander brought his palms down heavily on the table.

"This man is extremely dangerous," he said. "I want everyone to be fully armed."

Hansson and one of the reinforcements from Malmö volunteered to take the first watch. Nyberg said he would take them to the flat and see if there had been any change in the lights in the window.

"I want to talk to Kjell Albinsson in Rydsgård," Wallander continued. "A car should be sent out to bring him in."

No one remembered Albinsson. Wallander explained that he was the manager at the postal depot and moved on.

"We need to check if Åke Larstam turns up in any police records," he said. "That's your responsibility, Martinsson. It may be the middle of the night to everyone else, but to us it's a normal working day. Feel free to call anyone you can think of who may have important information. Albinsson will give us some details about Larstam, but it may not be enough. This man dresses up as a woman and

456

takes on other personas. His name may not even be Larstam. We have to look everywhere we can think of for clues. Everywhere."

Wallander now took out the glass he had taken from the flat and placed it on the table.

"If we're lucky, there are prints on this glass," he said. "And if I'm right, they're going to match the ones we found in Svedberg's flat, as well as the ones in the nature reserve."

"What about Sundelius?" Höglund asked. "Shouldn't we wake him up as well? He may know something about Larstam."

Wallander nodded and glanced briefly at Thurnberg, who seemed to have no objections.

"Why don't you do the honours, Ann-Britt? Don't let him off easily this time. He's been hiding something from us, I'm sure of it. Now we have no more time for secrets."

Thurnberg nodded. "That sounds reasonable enough," he said. "But let me just ask this: is there any possibility that we're mistaken?"

"No," Wallander said. "We're not mistaken."

"I just want to make sure, since the only thing we really have on this man is a file of newspaper clippings."

Wallander felt perfectly calm as he answered. "It's him. There's not a single doubt in my mind."

They made the conference room their provisional headquarters. Wallander was still in his chair at the end of the table when they brought in Kjell Albinsson. He was very pale and seemed bewildered at having been woken up in the middle of the night and brought to the police station. Wallander asked someone to bring him a cup of coffee. In the background he saw Höglund go by with an indignant Sundelius.

"I want to explain the whole situation to you," he began.

"We think Åke Larstam is the person who killed a police officer by the name of Svedberg a few weeks ago, the same man who was buried yesterday."

Albinsson went whiter still. "That's just not possible."

"There's more," Wallander said. "We're also convinced he killed three young people in Hagestad's nature reserve, as well as a young woman on an island in the Östergötland archipelago, and finally a couple of newly-weds out in Nybrostrand. What I'm telling you is that this person has killed eight people in a relatively short space of time, making him one of the worst mass murderers that Sweden has ever had."

Albinsson simply shook his head. "There has to be some mistake. It can't be Åke."

"I wouldn't be talking with you now if I wasn't utterly certain. You must take my word for it, and make sure you answer my questions as thoroughly as you can. Do you understand?"

"Yes."

Thurnberg walked in and sat across the table from Albinsson without a word.

"This is chief prosecutor Thurnberg," Wallander said. "The fact that he's here means you're not being charged with anything."

Albinsson didn't seem to understand. "I'm not charged with anything?"

"That's what I said. Now try to concentrate on my questions."

Albinsson nodded. The realisation of where he was and why seemed slowly to be sinking in.

"Åke Larstam lives at number 18, Harmonigatan," Wallander said. "We know he isn't there now, and we suspect he's fled. Do you have any idea where he might have gone?"

"I don't really know him outside work."

"Does he have a summer house? Any close friends?"

"Not that I know of."

"You must know something."

"There's some information about him in the employee records. But all that's kept at the depot."

Wallander swore under his breath. He should have thought of that himself. "Then we'll get it," he said. "Now."

He called in some patrol officers and sent them off with Albinsson. When he returned to his seat, Thurnberg was making notes on a pad.

"How did you enter the flat in the first place?" he said.

"I broke in," Wallander said. "Nyberg was present but the responsibility was wholly mine."

"I hope you're right about Larstam. Otherwise this is going to look very bad."

"I envy you that you should have time to think about such things right now."

"You have to understand my position," Thurnberg said. "Sometimes people make mistakes."

Wallander controlled his temper with some difficulty.

"I don't want another murder on my hands," he said. "That's the bottom line. And Åke Larstam is the man we've been looking for."

"No one wants any more murders," Thurnberg said. "But we also don't want any more police errors."

Wallander was about to ask Thurnberg what he meant by this when Martinsson came in.

"Nyberg called," he said. "The lights in the window haven't changed."

"What about the neighbours?" Wallander asked.

"Where do you want me to start?" Martinsson asked. "With Larstam and the police records? Or with the neighbours?"

"You should do both at the same time. But if we can find anything on Larstam in our files, it would be useful."

Martinsson left and silence filled the room. Somewhere a dog barked and Wallander wondered absently if it was Kall. It was just before 3 a.m. Wallander left to get some coffee. The door to Höglund's office was closed. She was in there with Sundelius. For a moment he wondered if he should go in, but he decided against it.

Wallander returned to the conference room and saw that Thurnberg had left. He glanced at his pad to see what Thurnberg had written. *Dashes, ashes, lashes.* A random series of rhyming words. Wallander shook his head.

Five minutes went by, then Albinsson came in. He was less pale now. He held a yellow folder in his hands.

"These are confidential records," he said. "I should really consult the postmaster before handing them over."

"If you do that I'll get the chief prosecutor back in here," Wallander said, "and have you arrested for obstruction of justice and aiding a criminal."

Albinsson seemed to take this seriously. Wallander stretched out his hand and took the file. The records confirmed what Albinsson had already told him. From the beginning of March to the middle of June Larstam had worked on the Skårby route. In July he had delivered post in Nybrostrand.

There was little personal information. Åke Larstam had been born on 10 November 1952, in Eskilstuna. His full name was Åke Leonard Larstam. He had graduated from high school in 1970, had done his compulsory military training in Skövde the following year, then had enrolled at the prestigious Chalmers School of Engineering in Gothenburg in 1972. He had graduated from Chalmers in 1979 and taken a job in Stockholm with Strand Consulting. He'd worked there until 1985, when he'd given notice and started to retrain for the postal service. That year he had moved first to Höör and then to Ystad. He was unmarried and had no children. The space allotted to "emergency contact" was blank.

"Doesn't this man even have any relatives?"

"Apparently not," Albinsson said.

"But he must have socialised with someone."

"He was very private, as I said."

Wallander put down the file. All of the facts would be verified, but for now Wallander had to concentrate on finding where Larstam was.

"No one is completely without personal relationships," Wallander said. "Who did he talk to? Who did he have coffee with? Did he have any strong opinions? There has to be something more you can say about him."

"We talked about him sometimes," Albinsson said. "He was so hard to get to know. But since he was always so friendly and helpful, everyone left him alone. You can grow fond of people you know nothing about."

Wallander thought about what Albinsson had just said. Then he chose a different tack.

"Some of these jobs were long term, some just a matter of days. Did you ever know him to turn down an assignment?"

"No."

"So he didn't seem to have another job?"

"Not that we knew about. He could get ready at a few hours' notice."

"That means you always managed to get hold of him."

"Yes."

"He was always at home waiting for the phone to ring?"

Albinsson was very serious when he answered. "It seemed like that."

461

"You've described him as conscientious, helpful, careful and responsible. And introverted. Did he ever do anything that surprised you?"

Albinsson thought for a while. "He sang to himself."

"Sang?"

"Yes. He hummed melodies under his breath."

"What kinds of things?"

"Mainly hymns, I think. He would do it as he was sorting the post, or as he was walking out to his car. I don't know how to describe it. He sang in a very low voice, probably because he didn't want it to bother anyone."

"He sang hymns?"

"Or religious songs."

"Was he religious?"

"How would I know that?"

"Just answer the question."

"There's a thing called freedom of religion in this country. Åke Larstam could be a Buddhist for all I know."

"Buddhists don't go around shooting people," Wallander said sharply. "Did he have any other peculiar characteristics?"

"He washed his hands a lot."

"Anything else?"

"The only time I saw him in a bad mood was when people around him were laughing. But that seemed to pass quickly enough."

Wallander stared at Albinsson. "Can you elaborate on what you just said?"

"Not really. It's just what I told you."

"He didn't like people being happy?"

"I wouldn't say that, but he seemed to withdraw more when other people were laughing. I suppose you could call that being happy. It seemed to irritate him."

Wallander had a flashback to the crime scene at Nybrostrand. Nyberg had turned to him and said that the killer didn't seem to like happy people.

"Did he ever show any violent tendencies?"

"Never."

"Any other tendencies?"

"He had no tendencies. You hardly noticed him."

Wallander sensed there was something else that Albinsson was trying to get at. He waited.

"Maybe you could say that his strongest characteristic was the fact that he didn't seem to want to be noticed. He was the kind of person who never turns his back to a door."

"What do you mean by that?"

"That he always wanted to know who was coming and going."

Wallander thought he knew what Albinsson was saying. He looked at his watch. It was 3.41 a.m. He called Höglund.

"Are you still with Sundelius?"

"Yes."

"I'd like to see you out in the hall for a moment."

Wallander got up. "Can I go home now?" Albinsson asked. "I know my wife must be worried."

"Please feel free to call her. But you can't go home just yet."

Wallander went out into the hall and closed the door. Höglund was already waiting for him.

"What did Sundelius say?"

"He claims he doesn't know who Åke Larstam is. He keeps repeating that he and Svedberg never did anything but look at stars, and that once they went to a natural healer together. He's very upset. I don't think he's comfortable talking to a female police officer."

Wallander nodded thoughtfully. "I think we can send

him home for now," he said. "He probably didn't know Larstam. I think what we have is two separate nests of secrets. We have Larstam, who eavesdropped on his victims' most intimate affairs. And we have Svedberg, who kept a part of his life secret from Sundelius."

"And what would that have been?"

"Just think about it."

"You mean there's a love triangle of sorts behind all this?"

"Not behind. In the middle of."

She nodded. "I'll send him home. When are Hansson and the others supposed to be relieved?"

Wallander realised he had already made up his mind.

"They can stay. We're going in. Åke Larstam isn't coming back tonight. He's holed up somewhere – the question is where. If we're going to find the answer, our best place to start is in his flat."

Wallander returned to the conference room while Albinsson was talking on the phone to his wife. Wallander signalled for him to finish his call.

"Have you been able to think of anything else?" he asked. "Where could Åke Larstam have gone?"

"I don't know. But that makes me think of another way to describe him."

"How?"

"That he was always trying to hide."

Wallander nodded. "I'll have someone take you home now," he said. "But give me a call if you think of anything else."

They went back into Åke Larstam's flat at 4.15 a.m. Wallander gathered everyone outside the door to the soundproofed bedroom.

"We're looking for two things," he said. "The first is where he could be hiding. Does he have a secret hiding place? How do we force him to show himself? The second is whether he is planning to kill again. That's the most important point. It would also be useful if anyone found a picture of him."

He took Nyberg aside when he finished. "We need fingerprints," he said. "Thurnberg is nervous. We have to have something that places Larstam at the scene of the crime. This has to take precedence over anything else."

"I'll see what I can do," Nyberg said.

"Don't see what you can do, just do it," Wallander said.

Wallander went into the soundproofed room and sat down on the bed. Hansson appeared in the doorway, but Wallander waved him away.

Why build a soundproofed room? To keep sounds out, or to keep them in? Why, in a town like Ystad? Traffic is never that bad. His thoughts wandered. The bed was uncomfortable to sit on. He got up and looked under the sheets. There was no mattress, just the hard platform of the bedframe. He's a masochist, Wallander thought. Why? He stooped to peer under the bed. There was nothing there, not even a speck of dust. Wallander tried to summon forth the spirit of the man who lived here. Åke Larstam, 44 years of age. Born in Eskilstuna, a graduate of Chalmers. An engineer turned postal worker. You suddenly go out and kill eight people. Apart from Svedberg and the photographer, your victims were all dressed up. The photographer just happened to be in the way, and you killed Svedberg because he was on to you. His worst fears were confirmed. But the others were dressed up, and they were happy. Why did you kill them? Was it in here, in your soundproofed chamber, that you planned everything?

Wallander didn't feel any closer to the killer's thoughts. He walked out into the living room, and looked around at all the porcelain figures. Dogs, roosters, dolls in 19th-century dress, gnomes and trolls. It's like a doll's house, Wallander thought. A doll's house inhabited by a lunatic with bad taste. He wondered why Larstam kept all these kitsch souvenirs.

Höglund came in from the kitchen and interrupted his train of thought. Wallander knew immediately that she had found something.

"I think you'd better take a look at this," she said. Wallander followed her into the kitchen. One of the drawers had been pulled out and placed on the table. At the top of a pile of papers in the drawer was a piece of mathematical paper. Something was written on it in pencil. If that was Larstam's handwriting, he wrote in an unusually spiky style. Wallander put on his glasses and read what it said.

There were only ten words, forming a macabre poem of sorts. *Number 9. Wednesday 21. He giveth and He taketh away.* The meaning was immediately clear to Wallander, as it must have been to Höglund.

"He's already killed eight people," Wallander said. "This is about victim number nine."

"It's the 21st today," she said. "And it's Wednesday."

"We have to find him," Wallander said, "before he gets a chance to do this."

"What about the last part? What does he mean by 'He giveth and He taketh away'?"

"It means Larstam hates happy people. He wants what they have to be taken from them."

Wallander told her what Albinsson had said.

"How do you go about locating happy people?" she asked.

"You go out and look for them."

He felt the knot in his stomach return.

"One thing is strange," she said. "This number nine sounds like a single person. But if you disregard Svedberg, he's always gone for a group of some sort in the past."

"You're right to disregard Svedberg. He's not part of the pattern. It's a good point."

It was 4.20 a.m. Wallander walked over to the window and looked out into the night. It was still dark. Åke Larstam was out there in that darkness. Wallander felt a sudden twinge of panic. We're not going to get him in time, he thought. We're going to be too late. He's already chosen his victim and we have no idea who it is. We're scurrying around like blind mice, not knowing where to turn. We know nothing.

Wallander put on a pair of rubber gloves and starting going through the rest of the papers in the drawer.

CHAPTER THIRTY-THREE

The sea. That would be his place of last resort, if it ever came to that. He imagined himself walking straight out, slowly sinking down to the place where eternal darkness and silence reigned. A place where no one would ever find a single trace of him.

He took one of his cars and drove down to the sea, just west of Ystad. Mossbystrand was deserted this August evening. Few cars went by on the road to Trelleborg. He parked so that none of the lights from oncoming traffic would hit him, and so that he could make a quick getaway if he was being followed.

There was one detail about the latest events that disturbed him. He had been lucky. If his bedroom door had been completely closed, as it usually was, he would never have heard them breaking into the flat that evening. He had woken up with a start, realised what was happening, and slipped out the back door. He had no idea if he had remembered to close it behind him. The only thing that he had grabbed, apart from some clothes, was his gun.

Although he had been shaken, he'd forced himself to drive calmly. He didn't want to risk having an accident.

Now it was 4 a.m. and it would be a while before the sun came up. He thought about everything that had happened and wondered if he had made a mistake. But he couldn't find anything. He was not going to alter his plans.

Everything had gone well. During Svedberg's funeral he

had gone to the policeman's flat on Mariagatan. It was easy enough to pick the lock. He'd looked through the flat and quickly established that the man lived alone. Then he'd made his plans. It was easier than he expected; he found a set of spare keys to the flat in a kitchen drawer. He wouldn't have to pick the lock next time. For fun he lay down on the policeman's bed, but it was much too soft. He felt as though he was drowning.

Afterwards he had gone home, showered, eaten and rested in the soundproofed room. Later he'd done something that he had been planning to do for a long time. He polished all his porcelain figurines. That had taken quite a while. When he was done, he'd eaten his supper and gone to bed. He had been sleeping for several hours when he'd heard the policemen at the door.

He thought about the fact that the police were in his flat right now, pulling out drawers, dirtying the floor, moving his porcelain figurines around. It enraged him, and he could hardly control his desire to rush back and shoot them all. But self-preservation was more important than revenge, and he knew they would find nothing in the flat to help them in their search. He kept no photographs there, no private documents, nothing. They didn't know about the safe-deposit box he kept at the bank under an assumed name. That's where all the important documents were, such as his car registration and his financial information.

They would probably be in his flat for many hours but sooner or later the policeman would return home, exhausted after his sleepless night. And he would be there waiting for him.

He returned to the car. The most important thing was for him to catch up on the sleep he had missed. He could of course sleep in one of his cars, but there was a slight chance that he could be discovered. He also disliked the idea of curling up in the back seat. It was undignified. He wanted to stretch out in a real bed, one where he could remove the mattress to give him the firm support he liked.

He considered checking into a hotel under a false name, but dismissed the possibility when he had a sudden flash of inspiration. There was one place he could go where no one would disturb him. And there was always the back door if someone turned up unexpectedly. He started the engine and turned on the headlights. It was almost time for the sun to rise. He needed to sleep, to rest in preparation for the coming day.

He turned on to the main road and drove back to Ystad.

It was close to 5 a.m. when Wallander started to realise how best to describe the kind of person Åke Larstam was. He was someone who left no trace of himself. They had nearly finished their search of the flat and hadn't managed to find even one object that revealed anything about the person who lived there. There was no post, not even a piece of paper with Åke Larstam's name on it.

"I've never seen anything like it," Wallander said. "Åke Larstam doesn't seem to exist. We can't find a single document that verifies his existence, even though we know he's real."

"Maybe he keeps another flat somewhere," Martinsson said.

"Maybe he has ten other flats," Wallander answered. "He might have all kinds of villas and summer houses, but if so we have nothing here that will lead us to them."

"Perhaps he took everything with him when he fled,"

Hansson said. "He may have known we were closing in on him."

"The state of this flat doesn't suggest that," Wallander said. "I think he lived like this. The man has a professionally soundproofed room. But you may be right. I hope you are; then perhaps we'll find something after all."

The piece of paper lay on the table in front of them.

"Are we misinterpreting it?" Höglund asked.

"It says what it says. Nyberg claims it was written recently. He can tell that from the consistency of the graphite, or something like that."

"Why do you think he wrote it?"

Martinsson was the one who asked the last question, and Wallander knew it was an important one.

"You're right," he said. "It stands out as the only personal item we've found. What does it mean? I'm assuming that he was here when Nyberg and I were at the door. The unlocked back door seems to imply a hasty departure."

"Then this was something he left behind inadvertently?" Martinsson asked.

"That's the most plausible explanation. Or rather the most obvious. But is it the right one?"

"What would the alternative be?"

"That he wanted us to find it."

No one seemed to grasp what Wallander was getting at. He knew it was a flimsy theory.

"What do we know about Åke Larstam? We know he's good at getting the information he needs. He ferrets out other people's secrets. I'm not saying he has access to our investigation, but I think the information he does have is aided by a fair amount of foresight. He must have considered the possibility that we would find him. The fact that I turned up at that bar in Copenhagen, if nothing else, would have forced him to think about this. What does he do? He prepares to flee, but first he prepares a greeting for us. He knows we'll find it, since there's nothing much else here to find."

"But that still doesn't tell us why," Martinsson said.

"He's teasing us. That's not so unusual. Lunatics like this often enjoy taunting the police. He must have exulted over his triumph in Copenhagen. There he was, parading around as Louise just after the Danish papers had run her picture, and he still managed to get away."

"It still strikes me as strange that we would find this piece of paper on the very day he's planning to kill again."

"He couldn't have known when we would get here."

But the words sounded unconvincing even to his ears. Wallander let it drop.

"We have to take his threats seriously," he said. "We have to assume he intends to strike again."

"Do we have any leads whatsoever?" The question came from Thurnberg, who had appeared in the doorway.

"No," Wallander said. "We have nothing. We might as well be honest about that."

No one said anything. Wallander knew he had to counteract the sense of hopelessness that was spreading through the team. It was 5.20 a.m. Wallander suggested that they report back at 8 a.m. That would give everyone an opportunity to rest for an hour or so. They would station a couple of officers outside the block of flats, and they would also start questioning the neighbours about Larstam.

Nyberg waited until everyone except Wallander had left the room.

"He keeps a clean house," he said. "But we have finger-prints."

"Anything else?"

"Not really."

"Any weapons?"

"No, I would have already told you about something like that."

Wallander nodded. Nyberg's face was ashen with exhaustion.

"I think you were right about the killer and happy people."

"Will we find him?"

"Sooner or later. But I dread what may happen today."

"Couldn't we make some kind of announcement?"

"Saying what exactly? That people should avoid laughing today? He's already chosen his victim. It's probably someone who isn't giving a thought to the idea of being followed."

"I guess we might have a better chance of locating his hideout if we keep quiet."

"That's my thought, too. I just don't know how much time we have."

"Shouldn't we also consider the possibility that he may not have an extra flat or summer house to run to? What then? Where would he go?"

Nyberg was right. Wallander hadn't considered this possi-bility. The fatigue had wrung his brain dry. "What do you think?" he asked.

Nyberg shrugged. "We know he has a car. Maybe he's curled up in the back seat. It's still warm enough to sleep outside. That's another possibility. Or he may have a boat. There are a number of options."

"Too many," Wallander said. "We have no time to look for him."

"I understand the hell you're in right now," Nyberg said. "Don't think I don't."

It was rare for Nyberg to express anything remotely close to emotion. Wallander sensed his support, and for once felt somewhat less alone.

Once Wallander was out on the street, he was no longer sure what to do. He knew he needed to go home, shower, and sleep for at least half an hour. But anxiety drove him to keep going. A squad car took him back to the station. He felt queasy and thought about trying to eat something, but instead he drank some more coffee and took his medication. He sat down at his desk and started working through the file again. He saw himself back at Svedberg's flat, with Martinsson close behind. Åke Larstam was the one who had been there and killed Svedberg. Wallander still couldn't see their relationship clearly, but the photo Svedberg had was of Larstam dressed as a woman. Now he knew why the flat had looked the way it did. Larstam's greatest fear was leaving traces of himself. After shooting Svedberg, he had turned the flat upside down looking for that photograph. But Svedberg had had a secret of his own.

The team met promptly at 8 a.m. When Wallander saw the fatigue and anxiety on the faces around him, he worried that he had failed them. Not that he had led them down the wrong path, but that he hadn't led them down the right one. They were still fumbling around in a no-man's-land, not knowing which way to turn. He had one clear thought in his head.

"From now on we work together," he said. "This room will be our headquarters and our meeting place."

The others went to their offices to get the materials they needed. Only Martinsson lingered in the doorway.

"Have you slept at all?" he asked.

Wallander shook his head. "You have to," Martinsson said firmly. "We can't do this if you collapse."

"I can keep going a while longer."

"You've already crossed the line. I slept for an hour. It helped."

"I'll take a walk soon," Wallander said. "I'll go home and change my shirt."

Martinsson looked as if he was going to add something, but Wallander held his hand up to stop him. He didn't have the energy to listen. He didn't know if he was ever going to have the energy to get up from his chair again. They all filed back into the room and closed the door. Thurnberg loosened his tie and actually looked tired. Holgersson sent a message saying that she was in her office dealing with the press.

Everyone looked at Wallander.

"We have to try to understand the way he thinks," he said. "And we have to figure out where can we look for answers. We're not only going to look back through our files on this investigation; some of us will have to examine this man's past. We need to know if he has any living relatives at all, if anyone remembers him from his time at Chalmers, or his old workplace. Where did he retrain to become a postal worker? Our biggest problem is time. We have to assume that the note we found was a message to us about his intentions. Somehow we have to decide what information to look for first."

"We should find out about his parents," Höglund said. "We can only hope his mother is still alive. A mother knows her children; we've learned that lesson."

"Why don't you look into that?" Wallander said.

"One more thing," she said. "I think there's something

475

strange about his career switch from engineer to postal worker. That needs to be explored."

"I recently heard about a bishop who started driving a taxi," Hansson said.

"This is different," she said. "I heard about that bishop, too. He was already 55 – maybe he wanted to try something completely different before he got too old. But Åke Larstam made his switch before he turned 40."

Wallander sensed that this was important. "You mean that something happened?"

"Yes, something significant had to have happened to make him change his life so completely."

"He moved, too," Thurnberg said. "That suggests that Ann-Britt is right."

"I'll look into this myself," Wallander said. "I'll call that engineering firm – what was it called?"

Martinsson flipped through his papers. "Strand Consulting. He left in 1985, which means he was then 33 years old."

"We'll start there," Wallander said. "The rest of you will keep looking through the material we already have. You're trying to find out where he might be, and who his next victim is."

"What about bringing in Kjell Albinsson again?" Thurnberg asked. "He might think of something else, particularly if he participates in our discussion."

"You're right," Wallander said. "We'll bring him back. Someone also has to run Larstam's name through the database."

"His name isn't there," Martinsson said. "I've already checked."

Wallander was surprised that he had found the time to do it, but then he realised that Martinsson must have lied

when he said he had slept for an hour. He had been working as hard as Wallander, but had lied out of consideration. He didn't know if he should be touched or angry. He
decided against both, and pushed on.

"Get me the number of that firm."

He dialled the number that was read out to him and
reached a recording stating that the number had been
changed. He dialled the new number, which was in
Vaxholm, an island very close to Stockholm. This time
someone answered.

"Strand Consulting," a female voice said.

"My name is Kurt Wallander. I'm a detective with the
criminal division in Ystad. I need some information about
a former employee at your company."

"And who might that be?"

"An engineer by the name of Åke Larstam."

"There's no one here by that name."

"I know. That's what I just said. He's a former employee.
Please listen."

"There's no need to take that tone with me. How do I
know you're really from the police, anyway?"

Wallander was about to pull the phone out of the wall
but managed to calm himself.

"Of course you have no way of knowing who I am," he
said. "But all the same, I need information on Åke Larstam.
He left the firm in 1985."

"That was before my time. You'd better speak with Persson."

"Why don't I give you my number? That way he can
double-check that I'm calling from the Ystad police station."

She wrote down the number.

"This is an urgent matter. Is Persson available?"

"He's meeting with a client right now, but I'll have him
call you when he's done."

"That's not soon enough," Wallander said. "He'll have to interrupt his meeting and call me back immediately."

"I'll tell him it's important, but that's all I can do."

"Then tell him this: if he doesn't return my call in three minutes, a police helicopter will be dispatched from Stockholm to bring him in for questioning."

Wallander hung up, aware that everyone was staring at him. He looked over at Thurnberg, who burst out laughing.

"I'm sorry about that," Wallander said. "I had to say something."

Thurnberg nodded. "I didn't hear you say anything."

The phone rang in less than two minutes. The man on the other end said he was Hans Persson. Wallander told him what he needed to know, without saying that Åke Larstam was wanted for murder.

"According to our information, he stopped working for you in 1985," Wallander said.

"That's right. It was in November, if I recall."

"You remember?"

"Vividly."

Wallander pushed the receiver closer to his ear.

"Why was it so memorable? What happened?"

"He was fired. He's the only engineer I've ever let go. I should explain at this point that I founded this company. There's never been a 'Strand' here, I just thought Strand sounded better than Persson."

"So you fired Åke Larstam. Why?"

"It's hard to explain, but he just didn't fit in here."

"Why not?"

"It will sound strange when I explain it."

"I'm a policeman, I'm used to strange things."

"He wasn't independent enough. He always agreed with

478

everything, even when we knew he had a different opinion. It isn't possible to have constructive discussions with people who are only out to please others. You can't get anywhere with them."

"That's how he was?"

"Yes. It just wasn't working out. He never came up with any ideas of his own."

"How were his technical abilities?"

"Excellent. That was never the issue."

"How did he react to his termination?"

"He didn't show any emotion at all, as far as I could tell. I was expecting to keep him on for another half a year at least, but he left immediately. He walked out of my office, got his coat, and just left. He didn't even pick up the severance pay due to him. It was as if he vanished into thin air."

"Did you have any contact with him after that?"

"I tried to, but I never managed to speak with him in person."

"Did you know he went to work for the post office?"

"I heard about it. There was some paperwork that came through from the employment office."

"Did he have any close friends that you were aware of?"

"I knew nothing about his personal life. He wasn't particularly close to anyone at this office. Sometimes he looked after other people's flats when they were gone, but otherwise I think he simply kept to himself."

"Do you know if his parents were still alive, or if he had any siblings?"

"I have no idea. His life outside this office was a complete blank. That's a real problem at a small firm."

"I understand. Thanks for your help."

"You'll understand if my curiosity has been piqued," Persson said. "Can you tell me what this is about?"

479

"You'll hear about it soon enough," Wallander said. "I can't tell you more than that right now."

Wallander hung up abruptly. He was struck by something Persson had said, something about how Larstam looked after other people's flats when they were away on holiday. He hesitated, but decided it should be looked into.

"Has anything been done with Svedberg's flat?" he asked.

"Ylva Brink said at the funeral that she was going to empty it soon, but she hasn't started yet."

Wallander thought about the keys that were still in his desk drawer.

"Hansson," he said. "You and someone else should go down to his flat and look around. See if you can tell if anyone's been there recently. The keys are in my top drawer."

Hansson left with one of the officers from Malmö. It was just before 9 a.m. Höglund was trying to find Larstam's parents. Martinsson went back to double-check the database. Wallander went to the men's room, refusing to look at himself in the mirror. When he returned to the conference room, someone was passing around a plate of sandwiches, but he shook his head. Höglund appeared in the doorway.

"Both of his parents are dead," she said.

"Any siblings?"

"Two older sisters."

"Find them."

She left, and Wallander thought about his own sister, Kristina. How would she describe him if the police came around asking questions?

He heard someone shouting in the corridor. Wallander got up quickly as a policeman appeared in the door.

"Gunfire," he shouted. "Down at the main square."

Wallander knew what it meant. "It must be Svedberg's flat," he shouted back. "Anyone injured?"

"I don't know. But the gunfire has been confirmed."

Four cars with blaring sirens were on their way in less than a minute. Wallander sat in the back seat with his gun held tightly in his hand. Larstam was there, he thought. What had happened to Hansson and the colleague from Malmö? He feared the worst, but pushed the thought away. It was too unbearable.

Wallander was out of the car before it came to a halt. A crowd had gathered at the door to the block of flats on Lilla Norregatan. Wallander dived through the crowd at full speed, bellowing, he was later told, like a charging bull. Then he saw both Hansson and the officer from Malmö. They were unhurt.

"What happened?" Wallander yelled.

Hansson was pale and shaking. The Malmö officer was sitting on the kerb.

"He was there," Hansson said. "I had just unlocked the door and stepped inside. He appeared out of nowhere and fired his gun. Then he was gone. It was pure luck we weren't hit. We turned and ran. It was sheer luck."

Wallander didn't say anything, but he knew luck had nothing to do with it. Larstam was an excellent marksman. He could have taken out both of them if he had wanted to. But he hadn't. Someone else was marked as his victim.

The flat was now empty. The back door was ajar. A greeting, Wallander thought when he saw it. A second door left open. He's showing us how good he is at getting away.

Martinsson emerged from Svedberg's bedroom.

"He's been sleeping in there," he said. "Now at least we know how he thinks. He takes shelter in empty nests."

"We know how he thought," Wallander corrected. "He won't do the same thing twice."

"Are you sure?" Martinsson said. "He's probably trying to figure out how we think. Maybe it makes sense to leave some men here. We don't expect him to return here, so that may be exactly what he does."

"He can't read our thoughts."

"It seems to me," Martinsson said, "that he gets pretty damn close to that. He always manages to stay one step ahead of us and one step behind at the same time."

Wallander didn't reply. He was thinking the same thing.

It was 10.30 a.m. There was only one thing Wallander was sure of and that was that Larstam had not yet killed victim number nine. If he had, Hansson would have been number ten, and their colleague from Malmö number eleven.

Why is he waiting, Wallander thought. Because he has to? Is his victim out of reach, or is there another explanation? Wallander left Svedberg's flat with nothing but more questions. I might as well face it, he thought. I'm back to square one.

CHAPTER THIRTY-FOUR

He felt a sense of regret when it was over. Should he have aimed at their heads after all? He knew that it had to be the police. Who else would have reason to visit Karl Evert's flat, now that he was dead and buried? He also knew that they were trying to track him down. There was no other reasonable explanation.

Once again he had managed to escape, something that was both reassuring and satisfying. Although he hadn't expected them to come looking for him there, he had taken the necessary precautions by unlocking the back door and propping a chair against the front door. It would fall to the ground if someone tried to enter. The gun lay loaded on the bedside table. He slept with his shoes on.

The noise from the street disturbed him. It wasn't like sleeping in his soundproofed room. How many times had he tried to convince Karl Evert to renovate his bedroom? But nothing had come of it, and now it was too late.

The images had been blurry and indistinct, but he'd known he was dreaming of his own childhood. He was standing behind the sofa. He was very young. Two people were fighting, probably his parents. There was the harsh, domineering voice of a man. It swooped over his head like a bird of prey. Then there was a woman's voice, weak and afraid. When he heard it, he thought he was hearing his own voice, though he was still safely hidden behind the sofa.

That was when he was woken by the sounds from the hall. They entered his dreams by force. By the time the chair fell over, he was on his feet, the gun cocked in his hand. It would have meant changing his plans, but he should have shot them. He had left the building, his gun tucked into his coat pocket. The car was parked down at the railway station. He'd heard sirens in the distance. He'd driven out past Sandskogen, towards Österlen. He stopped in Kåseberga and took a walk down to the harbour. He thought about what he should do next. He needed more sleep, but it was getting late and he had no idea when Wallander would return home. He had to be there when he did. He had already decided that it should happen today, and he couldn't risk changing his plans.

When he arrived at the far end of the pier, he made up his mind. He drove back to Ystad and parked at the back of the block of flats on Mariagatan. No one saw him slip in through the front door of the building. He rang the doorbell and listened carefully. No one was home. He unlocked the door, walked in, and sat down on the sofa in the living room. He put his gun down on the coffee table. It was a few minutes after 11 a.m.

Hansson and the Malmö officer were still so shaken that they had to be sent home. This meant that the team shrank by two people, and Wallander detected a new level of tension among members of the group when they gathered after the chaotic events at Lilla Norregatan.

Holgersson took him aside to ask if it was time to send for more reinforcements. Wallander wavered, exhausted and starting to doubt his judgment, but then answered with an emphatic no. They didn't need reinforcements, they just needed to focus.

"Do you really think we can find him?" she asked. "Or are you just hoping there will be another breakthrough?"

"I don't know," he admitted.

They sat back down at the conference table. Martinsson had still not been able to find anything on Larstam in the police registers, so he turned the matter over to a subordinate who would search the files in the basement. Höglund hadn't yet managed to find anything on the two sisters. Now that Hansson was out of the game, Wallander asked her to hold off on that. He needed to have her close by; the sisters would have to wait. They had to concentrate on finding Larstam before he turned to victim number nine.

"We have to ask ourselves what we know," Wallander said, for the umpteenth time.

"He's still in town," Martinsson said. "That must mean he's preparing to strike somewhere close by."

"He's not unaffected by us," Thurnberg said, who rarely commented on the action. "He knows we're on his heels."

"It's also possible he likes it this way," Wallander said.

Kjell Albinsson, who was sitting silently in a corner of the room, now indicated that he wanted to speak. Wallander nodded to him and he got up and approached the table.

"I don't know if this is anything," he said. "But I just remembered that last summer someone at work claimed to have seen Larstam down at the marina. That might mean he owns a boat."

Wallander hit the table with the flat of his hand. "How seriously can we take this?"

"It was one of the other postmen who saw him. He was sure it was him."

"Did he ever actually see Larstam climb onto one of the boats?"

"No, but he said he was carrying a container of petrol."

"Then it can't be a sailing boat," said one of the Malmö officers. But this comment met with a storm of protests.

"Sailing boats often have engines as well," Martinsson said. "We can't rule anything out, even a little sea plane."

Martinsson's last suggestion met with even more protests. Wallander silenced them.

"A boat is a good hiding place," he said. "The question is how much stock we put in this."

He turned to Albinsson again. "Are you sure you're right?"

"Yes."

Wallander looked over at Thurnberg, who nodded.

"Get some plainclothes officers to look around the marina," Wallander said. "Make the whole thing as discreet as possible. If there's even a hint of a suspicion that Larstam is there, they should turn back. We'll have to decide how to proceed at that point."

"There are probably a lot of people down there," Höglund said, "with this weather we've been having."

Martinsson and one of the Malmö officers headed down to the marina. Wallander asked Albinsson to sit at the table.

"If you have any more of these boat stories up your sleeve, I'd love to hear them."

"I've been trying to think of everything I can, but it's just making me realise how little I knew about him," Albinsson said.

Wallander checked his watch. It was 11.30 a.m. We're not going to get him in time, he thought. At any moment the phone will ring with the news of another murder.

486

Höglund started talking about Larstam's motive.

"It must be some kind of revenge," Wallander said.

"For what?" she asked. "Because he was fired from his job? What would the newly-weds have to do with that?"

Wallander got up to get some coffee and Höglund came along.

"You're right. There's another motive here," Wallander said, as they were nursing their mugs of coffee in the canteen. "There may be an element of revenge at the bottom of it, but Larstam kills people who are happy. Nyberg was struck by this thought in Nybrostrand. Albinsson confirmed it. Åke Larstam doesn't like it when people laugh."

"Then he's more disturbed than we realised. You don't kill people just because they're happy. What kind of world is this?"

"Good question," Wallander said. "We ask ourselves what kind of world we live in, but it's too painful to face the truth. Maybe our worst fears have already been realised – maybe the justice system has collapsed. More and more people are feeling overlooked and superfluous, and that feeds the escalation of senseless violence we're seeing. Violence has become part of our daily reality. We complain about the way things are, but sometimes I think things are even worse than we're admitting."

Wallander was about to continue with this line of thought when he was told that Martinsson was on the phone. He spilled coffee on his shirt as he ran back to the conference room.

"We haven't found anything," Martinsson said. "There isn't a boat registered under Larstam's name."

Wallander thought for a moment. "He may have registered his boat under someone else's name," he said.

"These marinas are so small that people generally know each other," Martinsson said. "I doubt he would have felt safe using an assumed name."

But Wallander wasn't prepared to let go of the idea just yet. "Did you check under Svedberg's name?"

"I did, actually. But there wasn't anything."

"I want you to check the register one more time. Try anyone's name who's been associated with this investigation, either centrally or otherwise."

"You're thinking of names like Hillström and Skander?"

"Exactly."

"I see what you're saying, but do you really think it's a reasonable assumption?"

"Nothing is reasonable. Just do it. Call me if you find anything."

Wallander hung up, and looked down at the large coffee stain on his shirt. He was fairly sure he had at least one clean shirt in his cupboard, and it would take him only 20 minutes to go home and change. But he decided to wait until he heard from Martinsson again.

Thurnberg came over. "I'd like to send Albinsson home," he said. "I don't think he has anything to add at this point."

Wallander got up, walked over to Albinsson, and shook his hand. "You've been a great help to us."

"I still don't understand any of this."

"None of us do."

"Nothing should go further than this room," Thurnberg said.

Albinsson promised to keep quiet.

"Does anyone know where Nyberg is?" Wallander asked.

"He's using the phone in Hansson's office."

"That's where I'll be if Martinsson calls."

Wallander went to Hansson's office, where Nyberg sat

with the telephone receiver pressed to his ear. He was writing something on a pad. He looked up when Wallander came in.

"We'll know whether or not it's Larstam's thumb before the end of the day," Nyberg said when he'd hung up.

"It is his thumb," Wallander said. "We just need confirmation."

"What will you do if it isn't his thumb?"

"Resign from this investigation."

Nyberg pondered these words. Wallander sat down in Hansson's chair.

"Do you remember the telescope?" Wallander asked. "Why was it over at Björklund's house? Who put it there?"

"You don't think it was someone other than Larstam, do you?"

"Why did he put it there?"

"Maybe to cause confusion. Perhaps a half-hearted attempt to pin the blame on Svedberg's cousin."

"He must have thought of everything."

"If he hasn't, we'll get him."

"His prints should be on the telescope."

"If he didn't think to wipe it off first."

The phone rang and Wallander grabbed it. It was Martinsson.

"You're right," he said.

Wallander jumped to his feet so fast the chair was knocked over.

"What do you have?"

"A berth registered in Isa Edengren's name. I even saw the contract and it looks like he imitated her signature. I recall what her handwriting looked like. Someone in the office remembers the person who signed it. He says it was a dark-haired woman."

"Louise."

"Exactly. She even told them her brother would often be using the boat."

"He's good," Wallander said.

"It's a small wooden boat," Martinsson said. "Big enough for a couple of sleeping berths below deck. There's another boat on one side but nothing on the other."

"I'm coming down," Wallander said. "Keep your distance, and above all stay vigilant. We have to assume he's being very careful now and he won't approach the marina unless he's sure the coast is clear."

"I guess we haven't kept as low a profile as we should have."

Wallander hung up and told Nyberg what had happened. He returned to the conference room and placed Höglund and Thurnberg in charge of coordinating assistance in the event that he needed it.

"What will you do if you find him?" she asked.

Wallander shook his head. "I'll think about that when I get there."

It was almost 1 p.m. when Wallander arrived at the docks. It was warm, and there was an occasional breeze from the southwest. He took out the binoculars he had remembered to bring and took his first look at the boat.

"It looks empty," Martinsson said.

"Is there anyone on the boat to the left?" Wallander asked.

"No."

Wallander let the binoculars glide over the rest of the boats. There were people on many of them.

"We can't risk any shots being fired," Martinsson said. "But I also don't see how we can evacuate the entire marina."

"We can't wait," Wallander said. "We have to know if he's there or not, and if he is, we have to bring him in."

"Should we start cordoning off the area around the boat?"

"No," Wallander said. "I'm climbing aboard."

Martinsson jumped. "Are you insane?"

"It would take us at least an hour to secure the area. We don't have the luxury of time in this case. I'm going in, and you'll have to back me up from the pier. I'll be as quick as I can. I doubt he's keeping a lookout. If he's there, he's probably sleeping."

"I can't let you do this," Martinsson said. "It's suicide."

"Keep in mind that Larstam didn't kill Hansson or the Malmö officer, and not because he missed. Neither was his ninth victim. This man is very particular about who he kills, and when."

"So he won't shoot you?"

"I think I have a good chance, that's all."

But Martinsson wasn't about to give in. "He has no escape route this time. What's he going to do? Jump into the water?"

"We have to take that chance," Wallander said. "I know that his not having an escape route could change everything."

"It's irresponsible."

Wallander's mind was made up. "All right then, we'll proceed with the necessary caution. Return to the station and see to it that we get the proper reinforcements. I'll stay here and keep an eye on the boat."

Martinsson left. Wallander instructed the Malmö officer to guard the car park. He walked out onto the pier, thinking that he was about to violate the most fundamental rule of police work. He was about to confront a ruthless killer, alone, without a single person to back him up, in an area that wasn't properly secured. Some children were playing on the pier. Wallander made himself sound as stern as possible and ordered them to move their games. His hand squeezed the gun in his pocket. He had already disengaged the safety catch. He studied the boat carefully and realised there was no way to approach it from the pier. If Larstam was on board he would see him. The only chance he had was to approach the boat from behind, but for that he needed a dinghy. He looked around. There was a party going on in the boat next to him, and a little red dinghy lay tied to its side. Wallander didn't hesitate. He climbed aboard and showed the surprised revellers his police identification.

"I need to borrow your dinghy," he said.

A bald man with a glass of wine in his hand stood up. "Has there been an accident?"

"No," Wallander said. "But I have no time to explain it to you. Everyone stays put, no one climbs out onto the dock. Understood?"

No one argued with him. Wallander stepped clumsily into the dinghy and fumbled with the oars, dropping one. As he reached for it, the gun almost slid out of his pocket. He swore and broke out into a sweat. Eventually he got the oars under control and made his way into the harbour. He wondered if the dinghy was going to sink under his weight, but managed to approach the back of Larstam's boat without a mishap. He grabbed it with one hand and felt his heart pounding. He secured his dinghy, careful to avoid setting the other boat in motion. Then he stopped and listened. The only sound he heard was his own heart. Gun in hand, he slowly undid the fastenings of the covering on the back of the boat. Still no sound. Once he had undone a big enough portion of the covering he faced the hardest part. Now he had to flip the covering off and then throw himself to one side to avoid the person who might be waiting inside with a gun aimed at his head. His mind was blank, and the hand holding his gun was trembling and sweaty.

All at once he performed the manoeuvre. The dinghy rolled so hard he thought he was going to end up in the water. But he grasped a railing on the side of the boat and kept his balance. Nothing happened. He peeked inside and saw that the boat was empty. The small doors to the lower cabin were open, and he could see all the way in. No one was there. He climbed aboard, still holding his gun in front of him. It was two steps down to the bunk area. He saw that the bunks were not made up. The mattresses were covered with plastic.

The man with the bald head grabbed the mooring line when Wallander returned the dinghy. "Now maybe you'll tell us what that was all about," he said.

"No," Wallander replied.

He was in a hurry now. The others might already be on their way and he had to stop them. Larstam wasn't in the boat. That could mean they were one step ahead of him for the first time. Wallander paused on the pier and called Martinsson.

"We're on our way," Martinsson said.

"Abort!" yelled Wallander. "I don't want to see a single car! Come down here alone."

"Has anything happened?"

"He's not here."

"How do you know for sure?"

"I just know."

Martinsson was silent. "You went aboard," he said finally.

"We're under pressure," Wallander said. "We'll discuss this some other time."

Martinsson arrived in five minutes and Wallander told him about his hunch that they were one step ahead of Larstam at last. When Martinsson caught sight of the flapping covering at the back of the boat, he shook his head in disapproval.

"We'll have to fix that," Wallander said quickly. "You stand guard in case he's on his way."

Martinsson stayed on the pier while Wallander climbed aboard and into the cabin. He looked around but saw nothing. When he had fastened the covering, he returned to the pier.

"How did you manage it?" Martinsson asked.

"I borrowed a dinghy."

"You're crazy."

"Maybe. But I don't think so."

Wallander walked up to the Malmö officer guarding the car park and told him to keep an eye on the harbour and the marina. He also called the station and posted more officers on the job.

"You should go home and change your shirt," Martinsson said, staring at Wallander.

"I will," he said. "I just want to talk this through with the others."

No one at the station asked him how he had got onto the boat. No one seemed to think to ask him if he had done it alone. Martinsson sat through the meeting as if he had been struck dumb. Wallander realised how upset he was, but he would have to deal with that later.

"We have to keep looking for him," Wallander said. "He used Isa Edengren's name to rent his berth. He doesn't seem to be following a pattern, but somewhere we're going to run across a clue that will blow this whole case wide open. I'm sure of it."

Wallander felt for a moment as if he were preaching to the converted, but he didn't know what else to do.

"Why did Larstam choose Isa Edengren's name?" he said. "Is it a coincidence, or is there something more here?"

"Isa's funeral is the day after tomorrow," Martinsson said.

"Call her parents. Tell them I want them to come down so someone can ask them about the boat."

Wallander got to his feet. "Right now I'm going to excuse myself for 20 minutes so I can run home and change my shirt."

Ebba came into the room with a plate full of sandwiches. "If you give me your keys, I'll go and get it for you," she said. "It's no bother."

Wallander thanked her but declined her offer. He needed to get away, if only for a short while. He was about to leave the room when the phone rang. Höglund answered and immediately gestured for him to stay in the room.

"It's the Ludvika police," she says. "That's where one of Åke Larstam's sisters lives."

Wallander decided to stay. He looked around for Ebba, but she had left. Martinsson took over the call from Ludvika, while Höglund called Isa Edengren's parents. Wallander stared down at his coffee stain. Martinsson hung up.

"Berit Larstam," he said. "She's 47, an unemployed social worker. She lives in Fredriksberg, wherever that is."

"That's where the weapons were stolen," Wallander said. "Maybe Larstam was visiting his sister at the time."

Martinsson waved a small piece of paper at him, then dialled the number.

Wallander felt he was no longer needed for the moment. He looked for Ebba in reception, but couldn't see her, so he returned to the conference room.

"Axel Edengren, the father, has promised to come in," Höglund said. "I think we can expect a pompous arse who doesn't think much of the police."

"What makes you say that?"

"He lectured me at length about how incompetent we were. I almost lost my temper."

"That's what you should have done."

Martinsson ended his conversation. "Åke Larstam visited her about once every three years. They weren't particularly close."

Wallander stared at him with surprise. "Is that all?"

"What do you mean?"

"Didn't you ask her anything else?"

"Of course I did, but she asked if she could return my call later. She was in the middle of something."

Wallander was starting to get irritable, and Martinsson was on the defensive. Tension filled the air. Wallander left and went to reception. Ebba was there.

"I think I will ask you to get it for me after all," he said, handing her the keys. "There should be a clean shirt in the cupboard. If not, you'll have to take the cleanest one you find from the hamper."

"I'll take care of it."

"Can anyone give you a ride?"

"I have my trusty old Volvo," she said. "You haven't forgotten about it, have you?"

Wallander smiled. He watched her as she walked out the front doors. He thought again about how hard these last few years had been on her. He returned to the conference room and apologised to Martinsson for his bad temper. They continued their work.

CHAPTER THIRTY-FIVE

Ebba still wasn't back with his shirt by the time Axel Edengren arrived at the station. Wallander started wondering what was taking so long. Was she having trouble finding a clean shirt? Wallander felt somewhat ill at ease as he walked out to reception to greet Axel Edengren. Not so much because of the large coffee stain on his chest as because of his recollection of the strange way in which the Edengrens had treated their daughter. Wallander wondered what kind of man he was about to meet, and for once the reality matched his expectations. Axel Edengren was a big, powerfully built man, with a spiky crew-cut and intense blue eyes. He was one of the largest men Wallander had ever seen, and there was something unappealing about his bulk. His handshake was dismissive. As Wallander showed him to his office, he felt as though he was being followed by a bull about to skewer him with his horns. Axel Edengren started speaking before they sat down.

"You were the one who found my daughter," he said. "What brought you to Bärnsö in the first place?" He used the polite form of the Swedish "you" in addressing Wallander.

"Please feel free to use the informal 'you' with me," Wallander said.

Edengren's reply was swift and unexpected. "I prefer to use the polite form of address with people I don't know, and whom I plan to meet only once. What were you doing in Bärnsö, Inspector?"

Wallander felt a spark of anger, but he didn't think he had the energy to wield his usual authority.

"I had reason to believe Isa had gone there. And it turned out I was right."

"I've heard about the sequence of events. I can't believe you allowed it to happen."

"I didn't let anything happen. If I had had even the slightest inkling of what was about to happen, I would have done everything in my power to prevent it. I assume that goes for you too, not only in the case of Isa, but with Jörgen."

Edengren flinched at the sound of his son's name. It was as if he had been knocked to his knees while running at top speed. Wallander took the opportunity to turn the conversation around.

"We're pressed for time, so let me simply express my condolences for what happened. I met Isa several times and thought she was a nice young woman."

Edengren was about to say something, but Wallander pressed on. "There's a berth at the marina here in Ystad that has been rented in Isa's name."

Edengren regarded Wallander with suspicion. "That's a lie."

"No, it's quite true."

"Isa doesn't have a boat."

"That's what I thought. Do you have a berth here?"

"No, my boats are in a marina in Östergötland."

Wallander had no reason to doubt him. "We think someone else rented the berth in your daughter's name."

"Who would that be?"

"The person we believe killed your daughter."

Edengren stared at him. "Who is that?"

"His name is Åke Larstam."

There was no reaction. Edengren didn't recognise the name.

"Have you arrested him?"

"Not yet."

"Why not? You believe he killed my daughter, don't you?"

"We haven't managed to locate him. That's why we asked you to come down. We're hoping you can make our task easier."

"Who is he?"

"For security reasons I can't give you all the information right now. Let's just say he's been working as a postman for the past couple of years."

Edengren shook his head. "Is this some kind of joke? The postman killed my daughter?"

"Unfortunately it's no joke."

Edengren was about to ask him something else, but Wallander stopped him. The moment of low energy had passed.

"Did Isa have any contact with the sailing club that you know of? Did any of her friends have boats?"

Edengren's answer came as a surprise. "Not Isa, but Jörgen did. He had a sailing boat. In the summer he kept it in Gryt. He sailed all around Bärnsö. The rest of the year it was kept down here."

"But Isa never used the boat?"

"Only with her brother. They got along well together, at least most of the time."

For the first time Wallander sensed something like sorrow in his voice. There was nothing to read on the surface, but Wallander thought there was probably a volcano of feelings locked up inside his enormous body.

"How long did Jörgen sail for?"

"He started in 1992. He had a little informal sailing club with regular meetings. They had parties and sent letters back and forth in bottles. Jörgen was often the secretary. I had to show him how to write up the minutes."

"Do you still have those records?"

"I remember putting all the minutes in a box after he died. They must still be there."

I need names, Wallander thought.

"Can you think of the names of any of his friends?"

"Some, but not all."

"But the names are probably recorded in the minutes."

"Probably."

"Then I'd like you to go and get them," Wallander said. "It could be important."

Wallander offered to send a police car to Skårby, but Edengren wanted to get them himself. He turned around in the doorway.

"I don't know how I'm going to stand it," he said. "I've lost both my children. What else is there?"

He didn't wait for an answer, and Wallander would not have been able to give him one. He got up and walked to the conference room. Ebba wasn't there, and no one had seen her. Wallander called his home number. The phone rang eight times but no one answered. Ebba must be on her way back.

Edengren returned after 40 minutes, and handed Wallander a big brown envelope.

"That's all I have. I think there are eleven sets of minutes in there. They seem not to have taken it so seriously."

Wallander leafed through the papers. They were type-written and contained a number of mistakes. He found seven names altogether, but recognised none of them. Another dead end, he thought. I'm still looking for a pattern, but Åke Larstam doesn't follow one. He went to the conference room, showed the material to Martinsson and asked him to look over the names. Wallander was about to walk out the door when Martinsson gave a yell. Wallander turned and walked back. Martinsson pointed to the name "Stefan Berg".

"Wasn't one of the postmen called Berg?"

It had slipped Wallander's mind, but he now realised that Martinsson was right.

"I'll call him," Martinsson said.

Wallander returned to Edengren. He paused before walking into the room. Was there anything else he needed to ask? He didn't think so. He pushed open the door. Edengren was standing at the window and turned when he heard Wallander come in. To his surprise, Wallander saw that his eyes were red.

"You're free to go home now," he said. "We have no reason to keep you."

Edengren looked searchingly at him. "Will you get him? The bastard who killed Isa?"

"Yes, we'll get him."

"Why did he do it?"

"We don't know."

Edengren shook his hand and Wallander followed him out to reception. Still no sign of Ebba.

"We'll stay in Sweden until after the funeral," Edengren said. "Then I don't know. Maybe we'll leave Sweden, sell the house in Skårby and in Bärnsö too. The thought of going back there is too unbearable."

Edengren left without waiting for a response. Wallander stood for a long time after he had gone. When he returned to the conference room, Martinsson was getting off the phone.

"We were right," he said. "Stefan Berg is the postman's son. He's enrolled in a college in Kentucky right now."

"Where does that lead us?"

"Nowhere, really. Berg told me everything he could, I think. He said he often talked about himself and his family when he was at work. That means Åke Larstam would have had many opportunities to hear about Stefan and the sailing club."

Wallander sat down. "But where does it really lead us? Is there anything here that can point us in the right direction?"

"It doesn't seem like it."

Wallander suddenly erupted and swept the pile of papers in front of him onto the floor.

"We're not going to find him!" he yelled. "Where the hell is he? Who the hell is the ninth victim!"

The others in the room looked at him to see if he was done. Wallander threw his arms out in apology and left the room. He started walking up and down the hall. He checked to see if Ebba had come back, but she was still gone. She probably had trouble finding a clean shirt and went to buy me a new one, he thought.

It was 3.27 p.m., and there were only eight and a half hours left for Åke Larstam to do what he had promised to do.

Wallander went back to the conference room and waited until he caught Höglund's eye. When she came over to talk to him, he told her to get Martinsson and join him in his office.

"Let's think this through together," Wallander said when they were assembled. "We still have two questions. We need to know where he is, and who he's planning to kill. Even if he's planning his deed for the stroke of midnight, we have less than nine hours to go."

He knew that Martinsson and Höglund must have thought of this as well, but it seemed as if the full implications were only hitting them now.

"Where is he?" Wallander repeated. "What is he thinking? We found him in Svedberg's flat, which suggests he didn't think we would look for him there. But we did. Then there's his boat. But he may already assume it's too dangerous to use it. Then what will he do?"

"If his earlier crimes are anything to judge by," Martinsson said, "he'll choose a victim and a situation that poses little threat to himself. The way in which he's toying with us is different. He knows we're after him. He knows we've seen through his disguise."

"He's asking himself how we think," Höglund said.

Wallander felt that they were all thinking along the same track now. "You're Larstam," he said. "What are you thinking?"

"He's intending to go through with number nine. He's fairly sure we don't know who that is."

"How can he be so sure of that?"

"Because if we knew, we would have surrounded that person with police protection. He's made sure of the fact that this hasn't been done."

"We could also come to a different conclusion," Martinsson said. "He could be concentrating on finding a secure hiding place. He may not be overly concerned about getting to number nine yet."

"That may be what he wants us to think," Höglund said.

"So we have to think differently," Wallander said. "We have to take yet another step into the unknown."

"He must have chosen the most unlikely place for us to look for him."

"In that case he should be here, in the basement of the station," Martinsson said.

Wallander nodded. "Or some symbolic equivalent to the station. What could that be?"

None of them had a suggestion.

"Does he assume we know what he looks like as a man by now?"

"He can't take any chances."

Wallander suddenly thought of something. He turned to Martinsson. "Did you ask his sister for a photograph?"

"I did, but she said the only one she had was of Larstam as a 14-year-old, and that it wasn't a very good one."

"No help there then."

"Where is Åke Larstam at this exact moment?"

No one had an answer, because there was nothing to go on. Just this strenuous speculation. Wallander felt a hint of panic. Time was ticking inexorably by.

"What about the person he's after?" Wallander said. "He's killed six young people so far, as well as an older photographer and a middle-aged policeman. I think we should discount the last two. That leaves us with six young people, killed on two separate occasions in two groups."

"Three," Höglund objected. "He killed Isa Edengren on a separate occasion, alone on an island in the middle of nowhere."

"That tells us that he finishes what he starts," Wallander said. "He follows through, whatever it takes. Is there anything unfinished in his present situation? Or is he embarking on a new project?"

Before anyone could answer this last question, there was

a knock on the door. It was Ebba. She held a shirt on a hanger in her hand.

"I'm sorry it took so long," she said. "I took the opportunity to run some other errands, and then I had a lot of trouble with the lock on your front door."

Wallander frowned. There was nothing wrong with his lock as far as he knew. Ebba must have tried the wrong key. He took the shirt and thanked her for her efforts. Then he excused himself to go and change.

"Even when you're on your way to your own execution, it feels good to be wearing a clean shirt," he said when he came back. He stuffed the stained shirt in his desk drawer. "Where were we?"

"There's no unfinished business that we can think of," Martinsson said. "No one except for Isa was also due to attend the Midsummer celebration. And only two people get married at a time."

"We have to start again," Wallander said. "The worst possible case. We have nothing to go on."

The room became silent. There seemed to be nothing else to say. Of two impossible alternatives, we have to choose the one that seems less impossible, he thought.

"We're never going to figure out where he's hiding," he said finally. "Our only choice is to focus on his potential victim. This is what we have to concentrate on from now on, before he has a chance to do his deed. Are you with me?"

Wallander knew this was still an impossible task.

"Do you think it will do any good?" Höglund asked.

"We can't give up," Wallander replied.

They started again. It was past 4 p.m. Wallander's stomach ached from hunger and anxiety. He was so tired it was starting to feel like his natural state. He sensed the same desperate fatigue in the other two.

"In broad strokes," Wallander prompted, "what do we have? Happy people. Joyful people. What else?"

"Young people," Martinsson said.

"People in costume," Höglund added.

"I don't think he repeats himself," Wallander said. "But we can't be sure of that. The question then is where we can find out about happy, young people in costume who are gathering for some reason today, other than for a wedding or a midnight picnic in a nature reserve."

"Perhaps someone's having a masquerade?" Martinsson suggested.

"The newspaper," Wallander said suddenly. "What's going on in Ystad tonight?"

He had hardly finished the sentence before Martinsson had rushed out of the room.

"Should we return to the conference room?" Höglund asked.

"Not just yet. We'll go back soon enough. But I'd like to have something to bring to the table, even if it's just a red herring."

Martinsson stormed back into the office with the *Ystad Allehanda* in his hand. They laid it on the table and leaned over it. There was a fashion show in Skurup that immediately drew Wallander's attention.

"Models are dressed up," he said. "And we can assume they're generally feeling good about themselves."

"That's not until next Wednesday," Höglund said. "You misread it."

They kept flipping the pages, then all three of them saw it at the same time. That evening there was going to be an event at the Continental Hotel for the "Friends of Ystad" Society. Members were asked to attend in 17th-century dress. Wallander was doubtful from the start. Something told him it wasn't right, but Martinsson and Höglund didn't share his doubts.

"This must have been planned in advance," Martinsson said. "He's had a long time to make his preparations."

"The members of this type of society are rarely very young," Wallander said.

"The ages are often quite mixed," Höglund said. "That's my impression, anyway."

Wallander couldn't shake off his doubts, but they didn't have anything to lose. The dinner was scheduled for 7.30 p.m. They had a couple of hours to go. Just in case, they finished looking through the paper to see if there were any other events to consider, but found nothing.

"It's up to you," Martinsson said. "Do we focus on this or not?"

"It's not my decision," Wallander said. "It's ours. And I agree with you: what do we have to lose?"

They returned to the conference room. Wallander wanted both Thurnberg and Holgersson to be present, so someone was sent to get them. While they were waiting, Martinsson was trying to find out who was responsible for arranging the party that evening.

"Call the hotel," Wallander said. "They'll know who made the reservation."

Although Martinsson was standing right next to him, Wallander heard himself raise his voice. The fatigue and tension were taking their toll.

When Thurnberg and Holgersson entered the room, Wallander made a point of closing the door, underscoring the seriousness of the moment. He described the reasoning that had led them to the conclusion that Åke Larstam was planning to strike at a party at the Continental Hotel later that evening. They could be wrong in their assumptions; it might turn out to be another dead end. But it was all they had. The alternative was simply to wait. He thought Thurnberg would have strong objections and might dismiss the plan out of hand, but to his great surprise Thurnberg approved. He used the same argument they had: what else was there to do?

At these words they were under way. It was 5.15 p.m. and they had two hours to make their preparations. Wallander took Martinsson and went down to the Continental, while Höglund remained in the conference room. They called in reinforcments for the evening and Wallander insisted everyone be equipped with the highest level of protection. Åke Larstam was a dangerous man.

"I don't think I've ever worn a bulletproof vest," Wallander said. "Except during training exercises."

"It'll help, if he's still using his gun," Martinsson said. "The only problem is that he shoots people in the head."

Martinsson was right. Wallander made a call from the car and ordered helmets to go with the vests. They parked outside the main entrance to the hotel.

"The manager of the restaurant is called Orlovsky," Martinsson said.

"I've met him before," Wallander said.

Orlovsky had been notified of their visit and was waiting for them in the lobby. He was a tall, trim man in his 50s. Wallander decided to tell him exactly what was going on. Together they walked into the room where preparations for the evening's festivities were under way.

"We need to be as efficient as possible," Wallander said. "Could someone show Martinsson around while you and I talk?"

Orlovsky beckoned to a waiter who was setting the table. "He's been here for 20 years."

The waiter's name was Emilsson. He looked surprised at the request but obediently accompanied Martinsson out of the room. Wallander told Orlovsky enough to let him know what was going on.

"Wouldn't it be best to cancel the event altogether?" Orlovsky asked when Wallander had finished.

"Perhaps. But we won't do that unless we decide that the security of the guests will be compromised, and we're not quite there yet."

Wallander wanted to know how the guests would be seated and asked to see the seating arrangement. They were expecting 34 people. Wallander paced around the room and tried to imagine Larstam's preparations. He doesn't want to be caught, Wallander thought. He'll have his avenue of escape well prepared. I doubt he's planning to kill all 34 people, but he'll need to get close to the tables.

A thought struck him. "How many waiters will be working tonight?" he asked.

"Six altogether."

"Do you know them all personally?"

"All except one who's been hired for this evening."

"What's his name?"

Orlovsky pointed to a small, pudgy man of around 65 who was setting out the glasses.

"His name is Leijde and he's often called in to help with larger dinners. Would you like to talk to him?"

Wallander shook his head. "What about the kitchen staff? The bartender? Who's working the coat check?"

"They're all permanent employees."

"Do you have any guests staying at the hotel?"

"A couple of German families."

"Will anyone else be here tonight?"

"No, the whole dining area has been reserved for the

party, although we have room for more. That leaves only the receptionist."

"Is it still Hallgren?" Wallander said. "I've met him before."

Orlovsky confirmed that Hallgren still worked there. Martinsson and the waiter Emilsson returned from the kitchen. Emilsson went back to setting the table, while Martinsson sat down to sketch an approximation of the dining area, lavatories, and kitchen with Orlovsky's help. Wallander wondered briefly if the staff should be given protective gear as well, but decided against it. It would tip Larstam off. All of a sudden Wallander had the distinct impression that he was somewhere close by, that he was surveying the comings and goings at the hotel.

Time was running out. Wallander and Martinsson returned to the station, where they were told that reinforcements were on their way. Höglund and Holgersson had moved quickly.

Martinsson's sketch was put onto a transparency. "Here's what we're going to do," Wallander said. "At some point Larstam will try to enter the hotel. Meanwhile we have to surround the entire building, although I want our men to be invisible, hard as I know that is. Otherwise we'll scare him off."

He looked around, but no one had any comments. He continued. "If he somehow manages to break through our outer ring of officers, we'll have a team placed inside the dining room. I suggest Martinsson and Höglund dress up as members of the waiting staff."

"With a bulletproof vest and helmet?" Martinsson said.

"No. If he enters the dining room, we have to get him at once. All exits from the dining room have to be blocked. I'm going to be circulating the entire area, since

I'm the only person who can actually identify him."

Wallander paused. Before the meeting broke up he had one more thing to add.

"We can't overlook the fact that he may be dressed up as a woman. Not Louise, but someone else. We can't even know he's going to turn up for sure."

"What if he doesn't?"

"Then we go home and get a good night's sleep. That's what we need most, after all."

They took up their positions at the hotel a little after 7 p.m. Martinsson and Höglund put on waiters' uniforms, and Wallander positioned himself behind the reception desk. He was in radio contact with eight other officers outside the building, as well as one stationed in the kitchen. He had his gun in his pocket. The guests started arriving. Höglund was right. Many of them were quite young, as young as Isa Edengren. They were dressed up and the atmosphere was joyful. Laughter filled the lobby and dining room. Åke Larstam would have hated this display of happiness.

It was now 8 p.m. Wallander checked continually with the other officers, but no one saw anything suspicious. At 8.23 p.m. there was an alarm from Supgränd, just south of the hotel. A man had stopped on the footpath and was looking up at the hotel windows. Wallander rushed to the spot but the man was gone before he arrived. One of the police officers identified him as the owner of an Ystad shoe shop. Wallander returned to the lobby, where he heard drinking songs coming from the dining room. Someone got up and made a toast.

Still nothing happened. Martinsson showed up at the entrance to the dining room. Wallander felt the constant grip of tension. It showed no sign of letting up. There were more drinking songs, more toasts. At 10.40 p.m., the party was beginning to come to a close. Larstam hadn't showed up. We were wrong, Wallander thought. He didn't show up. Or else he saw our men.

He felt a mixture of disappointment and relief. The ninth person, whoever he was, was still alive. Tomorrow they would go through the evening's guest list one by one and try to identify the intended victim. But Larstam was still on the loose somewhere.

At 11.30 p.m. the streets were deserted once more. The guests had gone home, all the officers were back at the station. Wallander made sure that the marina and the flat on Harmonigatan would be kept under surveillance all night. He returned to the station along with Martinsson and Höglund, but none of them had the energy to discuss what had happened. They decided to meet at 8 a.m. the next morning. Thurnberg and Holgersson agreed. They would have to figure out why Larstam hadn't shown up the next day.

"We've gained some time," Thurnberg said. "If nothing else, this manoeuvre gave us that."

Wallander went back to his office and locked his gun in one of the drawers. Then he drove back to Mariagatan. It was just before midnight when he started up the stairs to his flat.

CHAPTER THIRTY-SIX

Wallander put his key in the lock and turned it. From the back of his mind came Ebba's words about the lock having been stiff. The door was hard to open if it was locked from the other side with the key still in it, which only happened if someone was already there. Linda did this. When he came home and the lock was stiff, it was a reminder that she was staying with him.

His exhaustion was slowing down his thought processes. He unlocked the door, thinking about what Ebba had said, but now the lock was working smoothly. The reason for this dawned on him as he opened the door. He sensed more than saw the figure at the end of the hall. He threw himself to one side and felt a scaring pain as something tore open his right cheek. He then flung himself down the stairs, thinking each moment was about to be his last.

Larstam.

This was not the situation Hansson and the Malmö officer had encountered earlier in the day. Nor was it the situation Ebba had been in, although Larstam must have been there when she entered the flat. I am the ninth victim, Wallander thought. He reached the bottom of the stairs, ripped open the front door, and ran. When he reached the end of the street he stopped and turned. There was no one there. The street was deserted. Blood gushed from the wound on his cheek. His whole head thudded with pain. He reached for the gun in his pocket, then remembered he had locked it in his desk. The whole time, he kept his eyes on the door to his building, waiting for Larstam to come out. He took cover in the shadows of another doorway. The only thing he could do when Larstam showed up was to keep running. Now he finally knew where he was, and this time there was no back door for Larstam to use for his escape.There was only one way out, and that was through the front door.

Wallander fumbled for his mobile phone with his bloody hands. Was it in his car? But then he remembered putting the phone down on his desk at work. He let out a stream of curses under his breath. No gun and no phone. He couldn't call anyone for help. His mind worked frantically to find a solution, but nothing came to him. How long he stood there in the shadows, his coat collar pressed against his bleeding cheek, he didn't know. He kept his eyes on the door the whole time. Every once in a while he cast a glance at the dark windows of his flat. Larstam is up there, he thought. He can see me down here, but he doesn't know I'm unarmed. After a while, when no police cars show up he'll get the picture. That's when he'll make his move.

He looked up at the sky. There was nearly a full moon, although clouds obscured it. What am I doing, he thought, and what is going through Larstam's mind? He looked at his watch. It was 12.07 a.m., on Thursday, 22 August. The fact that it was past midnight wasn't likely to help him now. Larstam had trapped him. Had he guessed Wallander and his colleagues would be distracted by the masquerade party at the hotel?

Wallander tried to work out how Larstam had broken into his flat. Suddenly he saw what must have happened, and it gave him a sense of how Larstam worked. He took advantage of opportunity. The day before, during

Svedberg's funeral, every police officer in town had been at the church. That would have given Larstam plenty of time to work on the lock. Once inside, he had probably found the spare keys.

Wallander's thoughts were racing, his cheek burned, and fear still throbbed in his body. The most important question was why Larstam had chosen him as his victim, but he pushed it aside for the time being.

I have to do something, he thought. Without merely attracting enough attention for someone to call the police. If they do, I won't have a chance to explain to the patrol officers the situation they're heading into. Chaos will result.

He heard footsteps. A man came around the corner and walked straight towards Wallander, who emerged from his shadowy doorway. He was youngish, probably in his 30s. His hands were pushed deep into the pockets of his suede jacket. When he saw Wallander, he pulled them out with a start and took a step back, looking frightened.

"I'm a police officer," Wallander said. "There's been an accident. I need your help."

The man looked at him, uncomprehending.

"Don't you understand what I'm saying? I'm a police officer and I need you to contact the station. Tell them Larstam is in Wallander's flat on Mariagatan. Tell them to be careful. Understood?"

The man shook his head, then said something in a foreign language. It sounded like Polish. Oh, hell, Wallander thought. That's just my luck. He tried his speech in English, but the man said only a few broken words in reply. Wallander, about to lose his patience, moved closer to the man and raised his voice, and the man fled.

Wallander was alone again. Larstam was still up there behind the dark windows, and soon, very soon, he would guess why no one was showing up. Then Wallander's only option would be to run. He tried to gather his thoughts. There had to be something he could do. He lifted his hand as if signalling to someone across the street. He pointed up to his flat and yelled a few words. Then he walked around the corner, out of sight of the dark windows where he presumed Larstam was standing. He can't know there's no one there, Wallander thought. Maybe it'll buy me some time, although there's also a chance he'll just take off.

Then something he hadn't even been hoping for happened. A car turned onto the street. Wallander jumped out in front of it, waving his arms. The driver seemed reluctant to have anything to do with him, especially after he saw Wallander's bloody face. But Wallander thrust his hand in through the half-open window and opened the door. A man in his 50s was driving the car, a much younger woman at his side. Wallander immediately had a bad feeling about them, but pushed these thoughts aside.

"I'm a police officer," he said. "There's been an accident and I need to use your phone." He managed to get his police badge out to show them.

"I don't have a phone."

Doesn't everybody have mobile phones these days? Wallander thought desperately. "What's happened?" the man asked anxiously.

"Never mind that. I need you to drive straight down to the police station. Do you know where that is?"

"No, I'm not from around here," the man said.

"I know where it is," the woman said.

"Just go there and tell them that Larstam is in Wallander's flat. Can you repeat that for me?"

The man nodded. "Larstam is in Wallgren's flat."

"It's Wallander, damn it."

"Larstam is in Wallander's flat."

"Tell them Wallander needs assistance, but that they must approach carefully."

The man repeated his words, then they drove off. Wallander hurried back to the corner of Mariagatan and surveyed the scene. He couldn't have been gone more than a minute, hardly enough time for Larstam to get away. Wallander looked down at his watch. It would take ten minutes at most for the first police car to arrive. How long was Larstam planning to wait?

A quarter of an hour went by with no sign of the police. Wallander finally realised the couple had lied. They had no intention of delivering his message. That put him back where he had started. He was trying to think of another solution when he heard a noise.

It was the sound of a car engine and it came from the back of the building. Without being able to explain why, he immediately knew it was Larstam. How had he escaped without being seen? He must have gone over the roof. There was a window leading to the roof in the stairwell just above his flat. Larstam must have seen it and climbed down to street level from the back of the house.

Wallander made it to the end of the street in time to see a red car flash by. He didn't catch a glimpse of the driver but he knew it was Larstam. Without a second thought, he jumped into his own car and took up the chase. He soon had Larstam's rear lights in view. He knows I'm after him, Wallander thought. But he doesn't know I'm unarmed.

They turned onto Highway 19 in the direction of Kristianstad. Larstam drove very fast. Wallander looked down at his fuel indicator and saw it was approaching the red strip just before "empty". He tried to think where

Larstam could be headed. He was probably simply driv-ing aimlessly. They drove through Stora Herrestad. There was almost no traffic. Wallander had passed only two cars going in the opposite direction.

What do I do if Larstam suddenly stops his car? he thought. What if he gets out holding his gun? He had to be ready to stop if need be. Larstam suddenly increased his speed. They were at a section of the highway where there were a number of tight bends in the road. Wallander started losing sight of Larstam's car, and tried to steel himself for the possibility that Larstam was stopped around the next bend, ready to take aim at him as he appeared. He tried to think of what he should do. He was alone. No one knew where he was; he wasn't going to be able to tell anyone to send him the help he needed.

Then he caught sight of Larstam's car again. It was making the turn into Fyledalen, and Larstam had turned off his headlights. Wallander slammed on the brakes and approached the turn-off carefully. The moon appeared through the clouds from time to time, but otherwise it was pitch black outside. Wallander parked by the side of the road and turned off his own lights. There was no sound. Larstam must have parked his car as well. Wallander headed out into the darkness, tucking his white shirt collar inside his dark blue jacket. He brushed his cheek, which started bleeding again. Wallander clambered down through a ditch and reached a meadow. His foot came down on something that made a sudden crunching noise. He swore silently and crept away from the spot. I'm not the only one listening for sounds, he thought.

He continued carefully towards some bushes, where he paused. If he was right, he was now straight across from the road leading into the nature reserve. When he shifted his foot, he came up against another object. He put down his hand and realised it was a broken-off piece of timber. He picked it up.

I'm turning into a man from the Stone Age, he thought. The Swedish Police Force has started incorporating wooden planks in their armoury. Is this the truth about the way things are going in Sweden? A return to the age-old laws of revenge and retaliation that justify the taking of blood?

Now the moon emerged from behind the clouds. Wallander crouched down, smelling the earth and clay. He saw Larstam's car. It was parked just a little way in from the main highway. There was no movement around it. Wallander scoured the area, but the clouds came back and darkness returned.

Larstam must have left the car, he thought. But what is he planning? He knows that I'm still pursuing him. He probably still thinks I'm armed, but he must also know by now that I've failed to establish contact, and that we're completely alone out here in Fyledalen. Two armed men.

Wallander tried to work out what his options were, while straining to hear any sound. Several times he felt an unpleasant puff of chilly air on the back of his neck that made him think Larstam was right next to him, the gun pointed at his head. The gun that had already been fired once at his forehead. Wallander never heard the gun go off – all he had felt was the pain and something cutting open his cheek. Larstam had used a silencer.

How was his mind working right now? He couldn't have anticipated this chase, and so he couldn't have planned his escape route. Wallander sensed that Larstam was as confused as he was. He couldn't remain in the car, he didn't know whether he was staying close to it or whether he was proceeding deeper into the nature reserve. He can hardly see in this darkness either, Wallander thought. We're in the same boat.

Wallander decided to cross the street and approach the car from the side. The moon was still completely covered, so he ran in a crouched position across the road and plunged into some bushes on the other side. Larstam's car was now only 20 metres away. He listened, but there were no sounds. He held the plank firmly in his hands. That's when he heard it. A twig snapped somewhere in front of him. Wallander pressed closer into the bushes, then heard the sound again, fainter this time. Larstam was moving away from the car in the direction of the valley. Larstam must have been biding his time, just like Wallander. But now he had started moving. If Wallander hadn't crossed the road when he did, he would never have heard the faint sounds.

I finally have the advantage, he thought. I can hear you, but you have no idea I'm close by. There was another crunching noise. Larstam must have brushed up against a tree. The sounds were getting further and further away. Wallander slid out from behind the bushes and started walking along the road. He stayed in a crouch the whole time, and kept close to the undergrowth along the side of the road. After every fifth step he stopped and listened. When he had gone about 50 metres he stopped for 5 minutes or so. An owl hooted nearby. There was no further sound of Larstam moving. Had he stopped as well, or was he somewhere up ahead, out of earshot? Wallander's fear returned. Was he walking into a trap? Had Larstam snapped those branches knowingly, to attract Wallander's attention? His heart thudded loudly in his chest. Larstam and his gun must be somewhere close by.

Wallander glanced up at the sky. A break in the clouds

was approaching. Soon the moon would be out, and he couldn't stay where he was when that happened. If Larstam was springing a trap, he had to be somewhere just up ahead. Wallander crossed to the other side of the road and moved up a small incline. There he positioned himself behind a tree and waited.

The moon came out. Suddenly the landscape was awash in blue. Wallander stared at the road in front of him, but saw nothing. The bushes were thinning ahead, and he was approaching a rolling hillside. At the top of the hill was a single tree.

The moon was swallowed up by the clouds. Wallander thought about the tree at the crime scene in the nature reserve. He was sure Larstam had used it as his hiding place. He's like a cat, Wallander thought. He seeks out lofty and secluded places in order to maintain his sense of control.

He was convinced that Larstam was hidden behind that tree on the hill. There was no reason for him not to keep going until he killed Wallander, both to secure his escape and because he had singled him out as an intended victim. This was Wallander's only opportunity. Larstam's attention would be on the road. That's where he thought Wallander would be coming from.

Wallander knew what he had to do. He had to make a long detour down along the road, across to the left side of the hill and then up to some point right behind the tree from the back. What he would do then he didn't know, nor did he care to think about it just now.

He proceeded in three phases. First he walked back down along the road. Then he crept up the hillside, very slowly so he wouldn't attract any attention. Then he walked up, parallel to the road. He stopped. The clouds blocking the moon became thicker, and he had trouble seeing where he was. It was 2.06 a.m.

The moon didn't shine again until 2.27 a.m. It was enough to show Wallander that he was positioned some distance below the tree. He couldn't tell if there was a person behind it or not. He was too far away, and there was thick brush in the way. But he tried to memorise the terrain between him and the tree.

The moon disappeared. The owl hooted more distantly. Wallander tried to reason with himself. Larstam doesn't think I'll be creeping up on him from behind, he thought. But I can't underestimate him, either. Larstam will be ready for me wherever I come from.

Wallander started making his approach. He went very slowly, like a blind person fumbling in the darkness. Sweat poured from his body and his heart was beating so hard he thought it was loud enough for Larstam to hear. At last he reached an area of thick brush that he knew was 20 or 30 metres away from the tree.

It took almost 20 minutes for the moon to come out again, but when it did he finally saw him. Larstam. He was leaning up against the tree trunk, and seemed completely absorbed in watching the road. Wallander could see both his hands. The gun must be tucked in his pocket. It would take him a few seconds to get it out and turn around. That's all the time Wallander had. He tried to estimate the exact distance to the tree, searching out every possible obstacle in his path. He couldn't see one. He looked up at the sky and saw that the moon was about to go behind a cloud again. If he was to have any hope of reaching Larstam he would have to make his approach at the very moment the moon disappeared. He clenched the plank in his hands.

This is insanity, he thought. I'm doing something I know I shouldn't do. But I have to do it.

The moonlight was fading now. He slowly rose to his feet. Larstam hadn't moved. At the moment the light disappeared, he sprang up. Somewhere deep inside he felt the desire to utter a war cry. It would maybe give him a couple of extra seconds, if it scared Larstam. But no one knew how that man was likely to react. No one.

Wallander leaped forward and dashed at the tree. He was nearly there and Larstam hadn't turned around. There was almost no light. Then his foot hit a rock or root. He lost his balance and pitched forward at Larstam's feet just as he turned around. Wallander grabbed his leg, but Larstam grunted and pulled away. As he tried to get his gun out, Wallander rushed him again. With the first swing of his plank, he hit only the tree behind Larstam. There was a splintering sound. He aimed what remained of the plank at Larstam's chest, then threw a punch. He didn't even know where the sudden surge of strength came from, but with sheer luck he hit Larstam right on the jaw. It gave way with a wet, unpleasant sound and Larstam slumped down. Wallander threw himself on top of him and hit him again and again, before he realised that the man under him was unconscious. Then he reached for Larstam's gun, the one that had killed so many people. For a split second he wanted to place it against Larstam's forehead and pull the trigger. But he restrained himself.

He dragged Larstam down along the road. He was still unconscious, and it was only once they had reached Wallander's car that he started making low moans. Wallander got a length of rope out of the back of the car and tied his arms together behind his back, then tied him securely to the front seat. Wallander got in behind the wheel and looked over at Larstam.

Suddenly it seemed to him that the person in the other seat was Louise.

Wallander arrived at the station at 3.45 a.m. When he got out of the car, it was starting to rain. He let the drops run down his face before he went in to speak to the officer on duty. To his surprise he saw that it was Edmundsson. He was drinking a cup of coffee and eating a sandwich. Edmundsson flinched at the sight of Wallander's face. His clothes were muddy and covered with twigs and leaves.

"What's wrong?"

"No questions," Wallander said firmly. "There's a man tied to the front seat of my car. Get someone to go with you and bring him in. Make sure he's handcuffed."

"Who is it?"

"Åke Larstam."

Edmundsson stood up, his sandwich still in his hand. It looked like ham and cheese. Without thinking twice, Wallander took it out of his hand and started eating it. It made his cheek hurt, but his hunger won out.

"You mean to say the killer is tied up in your car?"

"You heard what I said. Put some handcuffs on him, take him to a room, and lock the door. What's Thurnberg's number?"

Edmundsson quickly brought it up on his computer and then left. Wallander finished the sandwich, chewing slowly. There was no reason to hurry any more. He dialled Thurnberg's number. After a long time a woman answered. Wallander told her who he was, and Thurnberg came on the line.

"It's Wallander. I think you should come down here."

"What for? What time is it?"

"I don't care what time it is, you have to come down here and make the formal arrest of Åke Larstam."

Wallander heard Thurnberg catch his breath. "Can you repeat that?"

"I have Larstam."

"How in God's name did you do that?"

It was the first time Wallander had heard Thurnberg caught completely off guard.

"I found him out in the woods."

Thurnberg seemed finally to have understood that he was in earnest. "I'll be right there."

Edmundsson and another officer walked by with Larstam between them. Wallander met his gaze. Neither of them spoke. Wallander walked to the conference room and laid Larstam's gun on the table.

Thurnberg arrived quickly. He too flinched at the sight of Wallander, who still hadn't been to the men's room to check his appearance, although he had managed to find some painkillers in a desk drawer. He also found his mobile phone, which he threw into the rubbish in a sudden rage.

Wallander told Thurnberg what had happened as succinctly as possible. He pointed to Larstam's gun. As if to mark the solemnity of the moment, Thurnberg fished a tie out of his pocket and put it on.

"So you got him. Not bad."

"Oh, it was bad all right," Wallander said. "But we can go into that another time."

"Maybe we should call the others and let them know," Thurnberg said.

"What for? Why not let them sleep for once?"

Thurnberg dropped the suggestion. He left to go and see Larstam. Wallander got heavily to his feet and walked to the men's room. The cut in his cheek was deep and probably needed stitches, but the thought of dragging himself to the hospital made him weak. It would have to wait. It was now 5.30 a.m. He went to his office and closed the door behind him.

Martinsson was the first to arrive the next morning. He had slept badly and anxiety had forced him to come into the station. Thurnberg was still there and told him the news. Martinsson then called Höglund, Nyberg and Hansson in quick succession. Shortly afterwards Holgersson arrived. It was only when they had all gathered at the station that someone asked where Wallander was. Thurnberg told them he had disappeared. They assumed he had gone to the hospital to have his cheek looked at.

At 8.30 a.m. Martinsson called Wallander at home but there was no answer. That was when Höglund wondered whether he was in his office. They went there together. The door was closed. Martinsson knocked gently. When there was no answer, they pushed open the door. Wallander was stretched out on the floor, the phone book and his jacket tucked under his head for a pillow. He was snoring.

Höglund and Martinsson looked at each other. Then they pulled the door shut and let him rest.

EPILOGUE

On Friday, 25 October, rain fell steadily over Ystad. When Wallander stepped out onto the footpath on Mariagatan shortly after 8 a.m., it was 7°C. Although he was trying to walk to work as often as possible, this time he took the car. He had been on sick leave for two weeks, and Dr Göransson had just ordered him to remain off duty for one more. His blood-sugar levels were much lower, but his blood pressure remained high.

He wasn't driving to the station this morning in order to work. He had an important meeting to attend, one that he had agreed to during those chaotic August days when they were still searching blindly for the man who had carried out the most appalling series of murders they had ever investigated.

Wallander could still recall the particular moment quite clearly. Martinsson had come to his office, and at the end of their conversation he had told him that his 11-year-old son was thinking of becoming a police officer. Martinsson had complained that he didn't know what to say to his son, and Wallander promised to speak to him once the investigation was over. Now the time had finally come. He had even promised to let the boy, David, try on his his policeman's cap, and had spent the entire evening looking for it.

Wallander parked the car and hurried into the building, hunching his shoulders against the rain and wind. Ebba had a cold. She warned him to keep his distance and blew her nose. Wallander thought about the fact that she wouldn't be working there in a little less than a year.

David was due at 8.45 a.m. While he was waiting, Wallander cleaned up his desk. In a few hours he was leaving Ystad. He still wasn't sure if this was the right decision or not, but he looked forward to the prospect of driving his car through the autumn landscape, listening to opera.

David was punctual. Ebba showed him to Wallander's office.

"You have a visitor," she said smiling.

"A VIP by the looks of it," Wallander said.

He looked like his father. There was something introverted about him, something that Wallander noticed in Martinsson as well. Wallander put his policeman's cap on the table.

"What should we start with?" he asked. "Your questions or the cap?"

"The questions."

David took a piece of paper out of his pocket. He was well prepared. "Why did you become a policeman?"

The simple question threw Wallander. He was forced to think for a minute, since he had already decided to take the meeting seriously. He wanted to make his answers honest and thoughtful.

"I think I believed I would make a good policeman."

"Aren't all policemen good?"

This was not a question written on the sheet.

"Most of them, but not all. In the way that not all teachers are good."

"What did your parents say about you becoming a policeman?"

"My mother didn't say anything. She died before I had made up my mind."

"What about your dad?"

"He was against it. He was so much against it, in fact, that we almost stopped talking to each other."

"Why?"

"I don't even really know. That may sound strange, but it's the way it was."

"You must have asked him why."

"I never got a good answer."

"Is he dead?"

"He died not so long ago. So now I can't ask him any more, even if I wanted to."

Wallander's answer seemed to worry David. He hesitated over his next question.

"Have you ever regretted becoming a policeman?"

"Many times. I think everyone does."

"Why?"

"Because you have to see so much suffering. You feel helpless, and you wonder how you're going to hold out until your retirement."

"Don't you ever feel that you're helping people?"

"Sometimes, but not always."

"Do you think I should become a policeman?"

"I think you should take your time to make a decision. I think you have to be 17 or 18 years old before you really know what you want to do."

"I'm going to be either a policeman or a road construction worker."

"Road construction?"

"Helping people get around is also good."

Wallander nodded. This was a thoughtful child.

"I only have one question left," David said. "Are you ever scared?"

"Yes."

"What do you do then?"

"I don't know. I end up sleeping badly. I try to think of other things, if I can."

The boy put the piece of paper back in his pocket and looked at the cap. Wallander pushed it towards him and he tried it on. Wallander gave him a mirror. The cap was so large it fell down over his ears.

Wallander accompanied him out to the reception area. "Feel free to come back and see me again if you have more questions."

He watched the boy walk out into the blustery cold. Then he returned to his office in order to finish cleaning it out, although his desire to leave the station was growing. Höglund appeared in the doorway.

"I thought you were on sick leave."

"I am."

"How was your meeting? Martinsson told me about it."

"David is a smart boy. I tried to answer his questions as honestly as possible, but I think his dad could have done as well."

"Do you have time to talk?"

"A little. I'm about to leave town for a couple of days."

She closed the door and sat down in the chair across from his desk.

"I don't know why I'm telling you this," she said. "I want you to keep it to yourself for the time being."

She's quitting, Wallander thought. She can't take it any more.

"Promise?"

"I promise."

"Sometimes it's such a relief just to tell one other person."

"I'm the same."

"I'm getting a divorce," she said. "We've finally agreed

on it, if you can call it that when there are two young children involved."

Wallander wasn't surprised. She had indicated that they were having serious problems early in the summer.

"I don't know what to say."

"You don't have to say anything. I just wanted you to know."

"I've gone through a divorce myself," he said. "Or was divorced. I know what hell it can be."

"But you've done so well."

"Have I? I would tend to say the opposite."

"In that case you hide it well."

The rain outside was falling harder.

"There was one other thing I wanted to tell you," she said. "Larstam is writing a book."

"A book?"

"About the murders. About what it felt like to do it."

"How do you know that?"

"I saw it in the papers."

Wallander was upset. "Who's paying him?"

"Some publishers. They're keeping the advance a secret, but I think we can safely assume it's quite large. I'm sure a mass murderer's memoirs will be a bestseller."

Wallander shook his head angrily. "It makes me sick."

She got to her feet. "I just wanted you to know."

She turned when she reached the doorway. "Have a nice trip," she said. "Wherever you're going."

She disappeared. Wallander thought about what she had told him, about her divorce and the book. They had caught Larstam before he had managed to kill his ninth victim. Afterwards everyone who came into contact with him was struck by his gentle and reserved manner. They were expecting a monster, but this wasn't someone Sture Björklund would have been able to copy for a horror film. Wallander sometimes thought Larstam seemed like the most normal person he had ever met.

He had spent many days interrogating him. It struck him repeatedly that Åke Larstam wasn't just an enigma to the world around him but also to himself. He seemed to answer Wallander's questions honestly, but his answers shed no light.

"Why did you kill the young people celebrating Midsummer in the nature reserve?" Wallander had asked him. "You opened their letters, you followed their preparations for the party, and you shot them. Why?"

"Is there a better way for life to end?"

"Was that why you killed them? Because you thought you were doing them a favour?"

"I think so."

"Think? You must know why you did it."

"It's possible to plan things and still not be sure why you do them."

"You travelled all around Europe and sent postcards in their names. You hid their cars and buried their bodies. Why?"

"I didn't want them to be found."

"But you buried them in a way that gave you the option of disinterring them again."

"I wanted to have that option, yes."

"Why?"

"I don't know, to make my presence known perhaps. I don't know."

"You took the trouble of following Isa Edengren to Bärnsö and killing her there. Why not let her live?"

"You should finish what you start."

Sometimes Wallander had to leave the room, knowing

he was in fact talking to a monster and not a human being, despite the smiling and gentle exterior. But he always returned, determined to cover all the aspects of the case, from the newly-weds whose joy Larstam had been unable to tolerate, to Svedberg.

Svedberg. They discussed their long and complicated love affair. Bror Sundelius hadn't known that Svedberg was betraying him with another man. Nils Stridh found out and threatened to talk. They talked about Svedberg's growing fears that the man he had loved in secret for ten years was somehow connected with the disappearance of the young people.

Wallander never felt satisfied with the answers he received. There was something absentminded about Larstam's way of speaking. He was always polite, always apologetic when he couldn't recall an event to his satisfaction. But there was a space within him that he never managed to penetrate. Wallander never fully understood the relationship between Larstam and Svedberg.

"What happened that morning?" he asked.

"Which morning?"

"When you shot Svedberg."

"I had to kill him."

"Why?"

"He accused me of being involved with the disappearance of those young people."

"They didn't just disappear, they were killed. How did Svedberg start to suspect your involvement in this?"

"I talked to him about it."

"You told him what you had done?"

"No, but I told him about my dreams."

"Which dreams?"

"That I got people to stop laughing."

"Why didn't you want people to laugh?"

"Happiness always turns into its opposite sooner or later. I wanted to spare him this fate. So I told him about my dreams."

"Your dreams of killing people who were happy?"

"Yes."

"So he started to suspect you?"

"I didn't realise it until a few days before."

"Before what?"

"Before I shot him."

"What happened?"

"He was starting to ask questions. It was almost like he was interrogating me. It made me nervous. I didn't like feeling nervous."

"So then you just went over to his place and shot him?"

"At first I was planning to ask him to stop making me so nervous, but he kept asking his questions. That's when I realised I had to do it. I went out into the hall and got my shotgun. I had brought it with me just in case. I got it out and I shot him."

Wallander didn't say anything for a long time. He tried to imagine what Svedberg's last moments had been like. Did he have time to see what was coming? Or did it all happen too fast?

"That must have been very hard for you," he said finally. "To be forced to kill the person you loved."

Larstam stared back at him without answering, devoid of any expression. Even when Wallander asked the question a second time, there was no answer. He finally brought up the evening when Larstam ambushed him in his flat on Mariagatan.

"Why did you choose me to be your ninth victim?"

"I didn't have anyone else."

"What do you mean?"

"I was going to wait, maybe a year, maybe longer. But then I felt the need to keep going since things had turned out so well."

"But I'm not a happy person. I don't laugh a lot."

"You had a job and a reason to get up every morning. I had seen pictures of you in the papers where you were smiling."

"But I wasn't dressed up. I wasn't even wearing my uniform that day."

Larstam's answer came as a surprise. "I was planning to give you one."

"Give me what?"

"A costume, a disguise. I was planning to put my wig on you and try to make your face look like Louise. I didn't need her any more. She could die. I had decided to make myself into another woman."

Larstam looked him right in the eye and Wallander returned his gaze. He was never sure afterwards what it was he had seen there. But he knew he would never forget it.

There came a time when he had no more questions. Wallander arrived at an understanding of a man who was crazy, who never fitted in anywhere, and who finally exploded in uncontrollable violence. The psychological examination corroborated this picture. Larstam had been constantly threatened and intimidated as a child and had concentrated on mastering the ability to hide and get away. He had lacked the resources to deal with his termination from the engineering firm and had come to believe that all smiling people were evil.

It occurred to Wallander that there was a frightening social dimension to all of this. More and more people were being judged useless and were being flung to the margins

535

of society, where they were destined to look back enviously at the few who still had reasons to be happy. He was reminded of a conversation he and Höglund had once begun but never had the chance to finish. They were debating whether or not the decline of Swedish society was more advanced than people generally admitted. Irrational violence was almost an accepted part of daily life these days. It gave him the feeling that they were already one step behind, and for the very first time in his life Wallander wondered if a complete collapse of the Swedish state was a real possibility. Bosnia had always seemed so far away, he thought. But maybe it was closer than they realised. Thoughts like these kept returning to him during the long sessions with Larstam, who maybe wasn't as much of a riddle as he should have been. Maybe Larstam's breakdown could be tied to the breakdown of society itself. There was nothing more to say. Wallander declared himself finished; Larstam was taken away and that was that.

A few days later, Eva Hillström committed suicide. Höglund was the one who told Wallander. He listened to the news in silence, left the station, bought a bottle of whisky, and drank himself into a stupor. He never spoke about it afterwards, but he always thought of her as Larstam's ninth victim.

He turned into the roadside retaurant outside Västervik around 2 p.m. He knew it was closed in the winter, but he still hoped she would be there. That autumn there had been many times when he wanted to call her, but he never had. He didn't know what he wanted to say to her. He got out of the car. The blustery weather seemed to have followed him from Skåne. Autumn leaves clung damply to the ground. The building looked deserted. He walked around the back to the room where he had slept on his return from Bärnsö. It had been only a few months ago but it already felt unreal.

The sight of the deserted building made him feel uneasy. He returned to his car and continued his journey. In Valdemarsvik he stopped and bought a bottle of whisky, then had a cup of coffee and some sandwiches in a café. He told them not to butter the bread.

It was 5 p.m. and already dark when he started down the winding road along the Valdemarsvik bay towards Gryt and Fyrudden. Lennart Westin had called him out of the blue one afternoon at the beginning of September, after the Larstam case had ended. Wallander had been interviewing a young man who had assaulted his father. It was slow going and Wallander wasn't getting anywhere with him. Finally he gave up and handed the matter over to Hansson.

When he got back to his office, the phone rang. It was Westin. He asked him when Wallander was planning to come to see him. Wallander had forgotten all about the standing invitation and an earlier phone call when he had actually agreed to visit, thinking nothing would ever come of it. They decided on a date in October, Westin had called him a few weeks later to confirm it, and now here he was on his way.

They agreed to meet in Fyrudden at 6 p.m. Westin would pick him up in his boat. Wallander was going to stay until Sunday. Wallander was grateful for the invitation, of course, but it also made him nervous. He almost never socialised with people he didn't know. The autumn had been marred by health concerns. He constantly worried about having a stroke, although Dr Göransson tried to reassure him. His blood-sugar levels had stabilised and he was losing weight and had adopted a healthy diet. But Wallander felt it was already too late. Although he hadn't even turned 50 yet, he felt like he was living on borrowed time.

When he swung down towards Fyrudden harbour it was raining harder than before. He parked the car in the same spot he had used that summer, turned off the engine and heard the waves smack against the pier. Shortly before 6 p.m. he saw the lights from an approaching boat. It was Westin.

Wallander got out of his car, grabbed his bag, and headed over. Westin popped his head out of the wheelhouse. He smiled.

"Welcome!" Westin yelled, trying to make himself heard above the wind. "I'm taking you back right away. Dinner's ready."

He took Wallander's bag while Wallander climbed aboard unsteadily. He was freezing. It was rapidly getting much colder.

"So you finally made it up here," Westin said when Wallander entered the wheelhouse.

At that moment Wallander no longer felt hesitant. He was glad to be there. Westin swung the boat around and Wallander grabbed at the side to keep his balance. When they made their way out of the harbour, he felt the hold of the waves on the boat getting stronger.

"Do you get seasick or nervous in this kind of weather?" Westin asked.

He asked the question in a light-hearted manner but there was real concern in his voice.

"Probably," Wallander said.

Westin increased his speed and they sped out onto open water. Wallander suddenly realised he was enjoying himself. No one knew where he was, no one could reach him. For the first time in a long while, he could relax.

INSIGHT GUIDES

The world's largest collection of illustrated travel guides

PHILIPPINES

Update Editor: Bill Williams
Executive Editor: Scott Rutherford

Editorial Director: Brian Bell

APA PUBLICATIONS

L

Part of the Langenscheidt Publishing Group

ABOUT THIS BOOK

When it was first published in 1980, this book won the PATA (Pacific Area Travel Association) Award of Excellence of Publications and the Singapore National Book Development Council's Gold Medal Award for best-designed book. Since then, the Insight Guide series has grown to a total of more than 190 titles spanning every continent.

This latest, updated edition of *Insight Guide: Philippines* is the ideal guide to one of Asia's most fascinating countries. The Philippines is a country of breathtaking beauty and graceful, warm people. But, too, it is a country with an incredible string of adverse episodes in its history, whether colonial occupation, volcanoes and typhoons, or a greedy dictator. Yet somehow, and it is no small measure of the resilience of its people, the Philippines remains a place of optimism and opportunity.

Such a destination lends itself especially well to the approach taken by the *Insight Guide* series, created in 1970. Each book encourages readers to celebrate the essence of a place rather than try to tailor it to their expectations. The books are edited in the belief that, without insight into a people's character and culture, travel can narrow the mind, not broaden it.

Insight Guide: Philippines is carefully structured: the first section covers the archipelago's history, and then analyzes its culture in a series of magazine-style essays. The main Places section provides a comprehensive rundown on the things worth seeing and doing. Finally, a listings section contains useful addresses, telephone numbers and all those other little details so useful to the traveler.

Veronica M. Garbutt was the original project editor for *Insight Guide: Philippines*. Born in northern England, after graduating from her hometown university of Leeds she flew for a decade as an airline flight attendant, based in Europe, Central America and the Middle East. In 1983, on a short assignment to the Philippines for the Dubai-based *Khaleej Times* newspaper, she fell in love with the country and has remained there since. She has produced features and photos for many international publications.

Garbutt

Extensively updating and rewriting this new edition was writer-photographer **Bill Williams**, based in Osaka, Japan, and a frequent contributor to publications around the world. With thirty years of experience in covering East Asia, Williams has contributed to other Insight publications, including *Insight Guide: Japan* and *Insight Pocket Guide: Macau*.

Working with Williams and contributing to this edition was **Catherine Daynos**, a graduate of Philippine University. For the past eight years, Daynos has served on the staff of the Philippine Department of Tourism (DOT), where she works in the Ancilary Services Division, in the National Capital Region.

Manila-born **Alfred A. Yuson** has at various times been a sportswriter, film and television scriptwriter, documentary filmmaker, film and music reviewer for a Manila daily, book designer and literary editor. He has also published two volumes of poetry, and has written columns for the Manila dailies and edited the art magazine *San Juan* and the poetry journal *Caracoa*.

Yuson

Sylvia L. Mayuga spent 14 years in

four different convent schools in Manila, after which she became a feature writer for practically all Manila magazines. Mayuga surveyed the local, political and cultural landscape as a columnist for the *Philippine Daily Inquirer*. She has published a book of essays, *Spy in My Own Country*.

A traveler and journalist, **Elizabeth V. Reyes,** who researched and wrote on the cultural minorities and Filipino food, was born in the US, raised in Manila and graduated from Syracuse University, New York. She has worked for Manila-based publications, and has contributed travel as well as culture pieces to Asian periodicals.

International contributors to *Insight Guide: Philippines* include **Tony Wheeler,** who researched and wrote the travel section on Luzon's southeast peninsula, Bicol. Wheeler combines travel writing with running Australla-based Lonely Planet Publications.

Wheeler

Scotland-born **Marcus Brooke,** who co-wrote the travel section for Mindanao, has been an agriculturalist, bacteriologist, biochemist and immunologist on the faculty of Harvard University and the Massachusetts Institute of Technology. Leaving academia, he has traveled extensively and has been a prolific writer/photographer/contributor to newspapers and magazines all over the world, as well as many *Insight Guides*.

Brooke

Theon Banos Cross contributed pieces on Philippine history and the arts. Born and educated in Boston, she gained experience as an editor working at Random House in New York City. Since then, Cross has been on writing assignments in Africa and Asia, worked as an advertising copywriter in Athens and Tokyo, and edited several specialty publications on Tokyo and Singapore.

Photographer **Catherine Karnow** contributed dozens of new photographs for this edition. Karnow, based in San Francisco, is a widely-respected photojournalist whose work has appeared in periodicals around the world, numerous books, and Insight Guides covering Asia, North America and Europe.

Patrick N. Lucero, born in Hawaii of a Japanese mother and a Filipino father, has covered the changing fortunes of the Philippines political and economic front since 1985. His work has been published in *Asiaweek, Travel and Leisure* and *Businessweek International*.

The extensive photographic coverage in this book also includes work by **Alain Evrard, Alfred Yuson, Blair Seitz, Dr. Christian Adler, Frederic Lontcho, G.P. Riechelt, Hans Höfer, Ingo Jezierski, Leonard Lueras, Max E. Lawrence, Noli Yamsuan Jr., Pierre Alain-Petit, Roberto Yniguez** and **Veronica Garbutt.**

Karnow

Lucero

CONTENTS

Preceding pages: Manila Bay sunset and fishermen; modern fashion designed by Pitoy Moreno recalls the yesteryears.

TRAVEL TIPS

INTRODUCTION

They lay like lovely gems atop Asia's continental shelf, these 7,107 islands, straddling where two tectonic plates collide to create islands with fluid names like Luzon, Mindoro, Palawan and Sulu.

Only a couple thousand of these islands can be considered inhabited by the 70 million Filipinos, or as they call themselves, *Pinoy*, who represent 111 different linguistic, cultural and racial groups. Their national language is Pilipino, based on Tagalog, a dialect of the Tagalog people of Manila and southern Luzon. Another 70 languages and dialects, all belonging to the Austronesian family of tongues, are also spoken. Pilipino and, interestingly for Asia, English are the national languages.

Geographically, the Philippines is a sprawl of half-drowned mountains, part of a great cordillera extending from Japan south to Indonesia. The nation's archipelago stretches 1,840 kilometers (1,140 mi) north to south, spanning 1,100 kilometers (690 mi) at its widest. The northernmost island, in the Batanes group, is but 240 kilometers (150 mi) from Taiwan; the southernmost island, in the Tawi-Tawi group, is only 50 kilometers (30 mi) east of Malaysia's Sarawak, on Borneo. West 1,000 kilometers (620 mi) is China, inescapable in its 4,000-year-old shadow, and in its increasing sway over the region today.

Slightly larger in land area than the British Isles or New Zealand, the Philippine archipelago is anchored to the north by Luzon and to the south by Mindanao; together, these two largest islands comprise 65 percent of the country's total land area and 60 percent of its population. This archipelago was born from powerful forces – great tectonic pressures pushing islands upwards, mighty volcanoes depositing their ash to enrich plains nurtured by monsoon rains. The first humans to see this land walked here during the ice ages, when seas were hundreds of meters lower. Later, after the ocean once again flooded the land bridges, waves of colonizers came from Borneo in seagoing *barangay* to settle the coastal areas, pushing the earlier arrivals into the mountains. The Spanish came much later and ruled for three centuries, and then the Americans for half a century. For half a century, these people have been independent.

Nearly everything that the Malay people brought has lasted, including language, custom and culture. To this foundation the endowments of the Spanish and Americans have been added. (Three centuries in a convent followed by 50 years in Hollywood, goes the old saying.) Also threaded through both culture and lineage are the textures of India, Arabia, China and Europe.

It was Ruy Lopez de Villalobos who, in 1542, named them *Filipinas,* after the infant who later became King Philip II, of Spain. Today, they are the Republic of the Philippines, although simply the Philippines suits most just fine.

The combination of sea and mountains hindered the archipelago's development as a nation, and thus as a regional influence in Asia. China, Indonesia, India, Vietnam, Cambodia and Laos saw the rise and fall of great dynasties and empires over tens of centuries. The archipelago, on the other hand, saw no great kingdoms flourishing on its islands, no ambitious generals leading conquering armies. Even when, ten centuries ago, Islam gained a foothold in the southern islands, it stayed there and spread no further. (Today, the Philippines is the only predominately Christian nation in Asia.)

When the Spanish stumbled upon the islands in the early 1500s, they found a collection of small sultanates and fiefdoms, no match for conquering worldliness of the Spanish soldiers and friars. Given the over three centuries of Spanish rule, it is not surprising, if one is permitted a generalization, that the Filipino usually seems more Latin than Asian to the visitor.

The Philippines has always been the odd one out in Asia, unsure of its own identity and of unknown cast in the minds of other Asians. Even in matters of food, the Philippines seems out of place. No fiery curries, no spicy satays. The Filipino's cuisine is instead a strangely sedate mixture of an ascetic atoll diet, Chinese imagination, and Spanish conservatism, although there are a few areas where chilies come into their own.

For the past few decades, the Philippines has been the butt of regional jokes, a perceived sad-sack country that can't get its act together and that seems determined to promote its own decay. But those who encouraged such stereotypes are back-pedaling nowadays, as the Filipinos have tossed off the debilitating yoke of the Marcos years, when the country was plundered of its wealth and peppered with monuments to presidential ego. The country is prospering, if not undergoing a renaissance of self-esteem, and it is showing an ability to navigate a forward course. Much of this ability became apparent during the 6-year presidency of Fidel Ramos, who led the country with a mixture of military discipline and corporate elan in the 1990s. A new president, former actor Joseph Estrada, was elected in 1998, and both Filipinos and others are watching carefully to see if the nation's progress was a six-year aberration defined by Ramos, or if the country can keep its self-confidence and carry itself into the next millennium.

Few travelers find the Philippines to be boring. It is, in fact, an intoxicating place, whether one is seeking beach solitude or fiesta fire. What it has most of all is an abundance of warmth and friendship. Filipinos radiate genuine Malay warmth and charm, mixed with a hauntingly delightful Latin temperament, not to mention an American flourish of extremes.

Right, outriggers from Zamboanga, Mindanao.

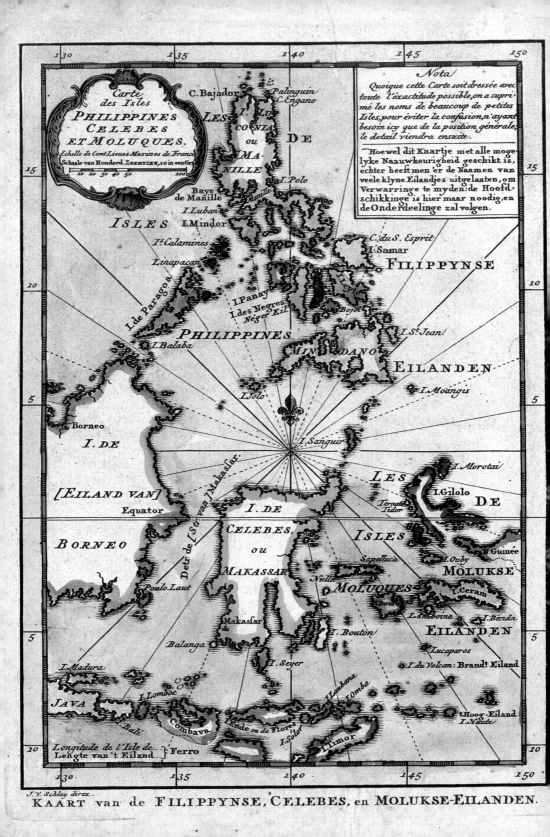

Carte
des Isles
PHILIPPINES
CELEBES
ET MOLUQUES.
Echelle de Cent Lieues Marines de France.
Schaale van Honderd Zeemylen, 20 in een Graad.
0 10 20 30 40 50 100

Nota
Quoique cette Carte soit dressée avec
toute l'exactitude possible, on a supri-
mé les noms de beaucoup de petites
Isles, pour éviter la confusion, n'ayant
besoin icy que de la position générale,
le détail viendra ensuite.

Hoewel dit Kaartje met alle moge-
lyke Naauwkeurigheid geschikt is,
echter heeft men 'er de Naamen van
veele klyne Eilandjes uitgelaaten, om
Verwarringe te myden: de Hoofd-
schikkinge is hier maar noodig, en
de Onderdeelinge zal volgen.

C. Bajador
Palinguin
C. Engano
I. LUCONIA ou MANILLE
LES
DE
C. du S. Esprit
I. Samar
FILIPPYNSE
Baye de Manille
I. Polo
Manille
I. Luban
I. Mindor
ISLES
I.s Calamines
Linapacan
Leyte
I. Panay
I. des Negres
Néger Eil.
Bojol
I. St. Jean
EILANDEN
I. de Paragoa
PHILIPPINES
I. Balaba
MINDANAO
I. Moangis
I. Jolo
Borneo
I. Sanguir
I. DE
I. Morotai
I. Gilolo
[EILAND VAN]
Equator
I. DE
Ternate
Tidor
LES
DE
CELEBES
ou
MAKASSAR
ISLES
BORNEO
Sapelluca
N. Guinée
I. Ouby
MOLUKSE
Detr. de l'Str. van Makassar.
Nulle
MOLUQUES
I. Ceram
Poulo Laut
I. Bouro
L. Amboina
I. Banda
Makassar
I. Bouton
EILANDEN
Balanga
I. Lucaparos
I. Madura
I. Seyer
I. du Volcan: Brandt Eiland
JAVA
I. Lomboc
Lembara
Comba
Hoog-Eiland
I. Haute
Bali
Combava
Ende ou de Flores
I. Solor
I. Timor
Longitude de l'Isle de...
Lengte van 't Eiland...
Ferro

In the beginning, there were only the primordial waters and a low-hanging sky. People had no place in the chaos, where all the elements of life floated in total confusion. With the passing of time, the bottom of the ancient ocean opened to spew up bits of earth. Islands rose precariously, threatened on every side by huge waves. There was need to fix them firmly in the midst of the dancing waters, if people were to have a place to live.

There are echoes of this recurring motif of unstable land in the creation myths still told by the indigenous tribes of the Philippine archipelago. A number of the archipelago's 7,100-plus islands continue to grow, while every year, typhoons threaten low shorelines and monsoon rains tear at the mountain ranges in a powerful memory of a time when the land first emerged from the depths.

Vast, earthshaking movements began it all. The Philippine tectonic plate sat squeezed between the vast Pacific and Asiatic plates. As the Pacific Plate, the world's largest, slid along its ever-moving northwest track, it twisted and buckled the smaller Philippine Plate and ground it into the adjacent Asiatic Plate. At the same time, the much heavier Pacific Plate dived, in what is called subduction, under the Philippine Plate to produce vast amounts of molten material deep in the earth.

When the Philippine Plate buckled, fissures formed and the trapped molten mass to spewed forth in colossal volcanic eruptions in over 200 known volcanoes in the archipelago of the Philippines.

Northern Luzon sits on the western edge of the Philippine Plate, while the rest of the archipelago rests on the eastern edge of the Asiatic Plate. A narrow belt running southeast from Zambales Province to Legazpi in Albay Province roughly follows the boundary between the two plates. This belt contains the most vigorous of the Philippine's two dozen active volcanoes, including Pinatubo, Taal, Banahaw, Iriga and Mayon.

Previous pages: lithographs of mestizo aristocrats and indigenous people; MacArthur monument, Leyte. Left, 17th-century Dutch-French map. Above, wild orchids of the Philippine rain forest.

Unrelenting land building and tearing down is the legacy of the Philippine's geographic position. The earth's crust buckled under tectonic pressure to push up land masses, and volcanoes added their enormous debris. But persistent monsoon rains and ruthless ocean storms ripped at the land as it was pushed up from the depths. Volcanoes spit forth billions of cubic meters of ash and molten lava, and the winds and rains washed it down into vast plains in a process that continues to reshape the Philippine landscape.

By some two million years ago, at the beginning of the Pleistocene epoch, the land was already well formed. But events taking shape in the earth's far polar regions were soon to change its appearance from the archipelago known today. Three successive ice ages lowered sea levels by one hundred meters or more. One large land area reached out into the Pacific Ocean from the Asian continent. Only the South China, Sulu and Celebes basins remained awash as mostly landlocked seas.

Flora and fauna: The so-called Wallace Line defines most Philippine flora and fauna, but not all. Named after the English naturalist, explorer and writer Alfred Russel Wallace (1823–1913), who first noted the zoological-geographical differences between the Asian and Australian continents.

The Wallace Line runs up the Lombok strait between Bali and Lombok islands in the Indonesian archipelago. It then continues north through the Makassar Strait that separates Borneo and Sulawesi, and then turns east into the Pacific and then back north again to encompass the Philippines. All of the animals to the east of the line, including those of the Philippines, owe their biological heritage to species originating in Asia. Those to the west of the line owe their heritage to species originating in Australia.

makes up the country's primary tracts of forests, as it also does in Thailand, Indochina and Indonesia.

In the wilds of Palawan and nearby Calamianes, the same mouse-deer, weasel, mongoose, porcupine, skunk, anteater and otter are found as in Borneo's interior. Species of Palawan shrews, as well as a rare bat found in Mindanao, have kin in Sulawesi.

Fish in the waters of eastern Sumatra and western Borneo are much like those in southwestern Philippines, as are the fish between eastern Mindanao and New Guinea. Many Malaysian and Bornean birds make their home in Palawan. Indeed, the Philippines offers unparalleled nature watching.

However, when sea levels sank during the last Ice Age, a series of land bridges cut through the shallow waters between the Philippines' Palawan and Mindanao and Indonesia's Sulawesi and Borneo. Like the tentacles of a multiform octopus, these land bridges made possible an alliance of flora and fauna, but with adaptations and mutations in succeeding isolation as the land links sank again.

Sixty species of Bornean plants are found in the southern islands of Mindoro, Palawan and Mindanao. Flora identified with Sulawesi and Moluka are widespread in the Philippines, mainly in the form of ferns, orchids, and a great wood, the dipterocarp, which

(Unfortunately, as in Borneo and the Indonesian archipelago, numerous species are threatened by excessive logging and mineral extraction, both of which irreversably damage the ecosystem. The threat extends to the oceans, where coral reefs and their animal species have been damaged to such a degree – and in such a short time – by dynamite and poison fishing that they may be forever lost.)

There is evidence also that an even older land bridge than the two southern ones formerly connected the Philippine north with Taiwan at a time when that island was itself connected to the Asian mainland. The remains of the stegodon, a pygmy elephant, have been dug up both in Taiwan and in the northern Philippines.

Early humans were soon following grazing herds onto the newly exposed grassy plains. Over thousands of years, bands of early hunters pushed farther and farther out onto the continental bulge.

At times, the rising waters isolated them on islands for scores of generations. They necessarily adapted to their changing environment or perished. Some took to the rising sea, while others took to the high mountains. Both developed unique patterns of life in a human mosaic as varied as the earlier plants and animals they followed.

Much of early human history remains

skeletal remains have been carbon-dated to over 20,000 years ago.

The domestication of animals and the beginnings of agriculture marked the neolithic period at the end of a stone age. A neolithic site in Dimolit, Cagayan, has already yielded the earliest pottery in the Philippines, datable to 5,000 years ago. Another neolithic site is at Cal-lo, in the Cagayan Valley, where stone tools and pottery were excavated and have been dated to 4,000 years ago. Even the fabled rices terraces of the Ifugao have been dated as 2,000 to 3,000 years old.

Finds at the Butuan site in Agusan del Norte, on Mindanao, and in caves on Palawan show that inhabitants of the archipelago were

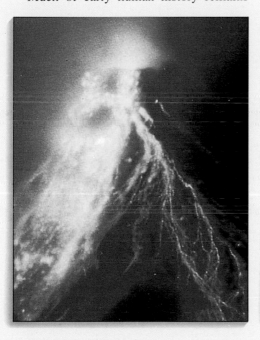 

rooted in speculation, but what is known about early human existence in the Philippine archipelago is remarkably well documented. Archaeologists have dated humans in the Cagayan Valley, on northern Luzon, to over 400 centuries ago. No human skeletons have yet to be found, but scientists agree that the flake and cobble tools unearthed in beds of stegodon, *elephas*, rhinoceros and bublalus fossils are proof of Paleolithic human existence in the area. Out on Palawan, human

Left, primal mists shroud a Mindanao rain forest. Above left, Mt. Mayon erupts, 1968; above right, an early Filipino at the turn of the century.

engaged in far-reaching trade in early times. Ancient boats, gold ornaments, pottery, and evidence of metalworking, unearthed at Butuan, give evidence to long-distance maritime commerce as early as the 10th century. Excavations on Palawan yielded sophisticated burial jars, porcelains and stoneware of the Song dynasty (960-1279), indicating strong trade links with China as early as the 10th or 11th centuries. Historians have uncovered accounts of trade missions to China from the Philippine archipelago as early as the 10th century. Chinese records show that several tributary missions were made to China between the 10th and 15th centuries.

Since the prehistoric ages, the islands were populated by peoples of Malay racial origin. Most of them lived in small, scattered villages at the mouths of rivers. Their houses of bamboo and palm-thatch were set on stilts, and the main sources of their livelihood were rice cultivation and fishing. Other more primitive groups lived in the mountains of the interior, where they practiced hunting, gathering, and slash-and-burn farming.

Until 3,000 years ago, contact with the outside world was minimal, but the following centuries saw increasingly frequent visits by Chinese, Indian, Arab and Indonesian traders, who brought pottery, textiles, iron weapons, tools, jewelry and trinkets to barter for pearls, coral and gold. They also introduced the first truly modern influences.

In the 12th century, the Chinese established a permanent presence ashore. Exercising great commercial power but little political influence, they supplied prestige wares that acquired ceremonial significance in the archipelago – pottery and metal objects, for example – and which have been recovered from ancient graves in recent years.

In the early 14th century, a wave of new traders from the south introduced Islam, sweeping through the Sulu Archipelago and further north. The new faith served to consolidate and invigorate groups that were later, vigorously, to resist Spanish, American and, recently, Philippine national rule.

Treaty of Tordesillas: The archipelago's recorded history began half a world away in a small, dusty town in southwestern Spain. Under the guidance of the Vatican, the Treaty of Tordesillas was inked in 1494, dividing between Spain and Portugal the yet-unexplored world – everything to the east of a line 370 leagues west of the Cape Verde Islands in the Atlantic belonged to Portugal, and everything to the west belonged to Spain. (Little thought, however, was then given as to where the two might meet on the other side of the world.)

The Portuguese set off around Africa's Cape of Good Hope in search of the riches of the Spice Islands, while the Spanish headed in the opposite direction, across the vast Pacific, in search of the same riches.

Magellan: The captain of Spain's search was in fact Portuguese, sailing under a Spanish name and whom later would be best remembered by his English name. Fernao de Magalhaes was a sailor who renounced his Portuguese citizenship, taking up the flag of Castile and the Spanish name Hernando de Magallanes; the English-speaking world later came to know him as Ferdinand Magellan.

In search of the legendary Spice Islands, Magellan took some 109 days to cross the Mar Pacifico, as he dubbed it and what we

call the Pacific Ocean. He also managed to miss every island in the Pacific Ocean, save the tiny atoll of Poka Puka, in the Tuamotu group, and Gua'han, or Guam. In 1521, he made landfall on the island of Homonhon, off the southern tip of Samar in the Visayas. Calling the new lands Lazarus, after the saint's day on which he first sighted them, Magellan sailed on through the Gulf of Leyte and the Surigao Strait to the island of Limasawa. (The Philippines did not get its present name until 1542, when Ruy Lopez de Villalobos named it *Filipinas*, after the infant who would later become King Philip II of Spain.)

While Magellan stands credited as the first European to encounter the Philippines and Villalobos with giving it the name, it was a Malay slave that uttered the first greeting between Spaniard and Filipino. Enrique de Molucca, Magellan's Moluccan slave, on the captain's orders hailed a small boat of eight locals, who understood him; the world had been circled linguistically, and Enrique de Molucca became the first human to circumnavigate the globe, though he has never been credited with the deed.

fended his island from 48 armor-clad Spaniards in April of 1521. During the battle, Magellan was slain. Today, a tall white obelisk stands near the spot where he fell.

The conquistadors: Four subsequent Spanish expeditions failed to establish significant contacts in the Philippines, and it was not until 1565 that Miguel Lopez de Legazpi, sailing from Mexico, gained a foothold in Cebu. Over the next few years the Spanish pushed doggedly northward, finally defeating the Muslim chieftain Sulayman and tak-

Six weeks later, Magellan was dead. From Limasawa, he had sailed up through the Canigao Channel to the island of Cebu, where he Christianized the local rajah and his followers. A minor rajah of Mactan – a flat, muddy island where Cebu's international airport now sits – stood in rebellion to the Rajah of Cebu and his new found foreign guests. Now known to all Filipinos as Lapu Lapu, Rajah Cilapulapu (*ci* means the) de-

Left, Spanish expedition leaders Villalobos, Legazpi and Magellan are fancifully juxtaposed in an old engraving. **Above**, baptism scene from Magellan memorial, Cebu.

ing over his palisaded fortress of Maynilad, at the mouth of the Pasig River and on what is now Manila Bay. Here, in 1571, Legazpi built the walled Spanish city of Intramuros.

Bands of conquistadors, newly arrived from Mexico, fanned out from Intramuros to conquer Luzon and the Visayas. They encountered sustained but unformidable opposition, and soon entrenched themselves as lords of great estates worked by Filipinos. The friars who accompanied the conquistadors rapidly converted and Westernized the population, building churches, schools, roads and bridges, and gradually accumulating vast land holdings for the Catholic Church.

A Spanish governor-general, responsible to the Viceroy of Mexico, presided over Intramuros and the islands through rival civil, ecclesiastical and military establishments. Intramuros, which in the early decades had a population of no more than a thousand Europeans, including soldiers of the garrison, was menaced from the outset by enemies: Japanese *wako*, Dutch fleets, Chinese pirates and disgruntled Filipinos.

The Chinese community was vital to Manila's welfare, as the city surrounding Intramuros became known. A great fleet of Chinese junks converged upon the city each year carrying exquisite porcelains, silks, lacquer and enamel wares, paintings, house-

part collected, a ransom of four million pesos for sparing the city from razing and burning. But his troops nevertheless looted the city; indeed, the English civil governor, Dawson Drake, stripped the Governor's Palace of its lavish fittings and shipped them back to England in packing cases marked "Rice for Drake". The British occupation was short, ending early in 1764.

In the late 18th and early 19th centuries, the Spanish introduced important political, economic and social reforms, allowing some local Filipino participation in government. Also introduced were sugar, tobacco, indigo and hemp as major cash crops; at the same time, the galleon monopoly on foreign com-

hold furnishings, and a wealth of other products from Persia, India, Siam and Indonesia.

The Spanish population eagerly bought this merchandise for re-export to Mexico, via the Manila Galleon, taking payment in Mexican silver carried by the vessel on its return voyage. This 2,000-ton treasure ship sailed annually between Manila and Acapulco, from 1572 until 1815, carrying cargo worth millions, and in which every Spanish resident of Intramuros had equity.

British interlude: Late in 1762, as a minor episode in the Seven Years' War with Spain, Intramuros was seized by England's Gen. William Draper, who demanded, and in large

merce ceased. But the reforms had been late in coming, and there was already an incipient nationalist movement led by the liberal clergy, professionals, and a clique of Filipino students studying in Spain.

Rise of nationalism: A minor uprising in Cavite, in 1872, panicked the Spanish authorities into extreme measures. Three well-known Filipino priests – Jose Burgos, Mariano Gomez and Jacinto Zamora – were garrotted in a public execution in Manila's Luneta after conviction on suspicious evidence of inspiring subversion.

Their deaths fanned the development of nationalist movements in the last two decades of the 19th century. Jose Rizal, Andres Bonifacio and Emilio Aguinaldo emerged as leaders, respectively, of the Propaganda Movement (for Filipino equality with the Spanish), the Katipunan (a secret society advocating armed insurrection), and the first declaration of independence in 1898.

The Katipunan organized a major revolt in 1896. Many revolutionaries were captured and executed, as was Rizal, who, despite being a proponent of nonviolent action, was accused and found guilty of complicity in the revolt on unsubstantiated evidence. He was executed by firing squad in the Bagumbayan Luneta, now Rizal Park in Manila, and is regarded as *the* Philippine national hero.

guerrilla troops had sided with the Americans against the Spanish, but were now angered because the Americans offered not independence but a new style of colonialism. Staging a rebellion in 1900, the islands were not really pacified until early in 1902. The Americans, defining their role as one of trusteeship and tutelage, promoted rapid political, economic and social development. In 1935, the Philippines was made a commonwealth, with the promise of independence in 1945. But World War II intervened.

Japanese occupation: On 10 December 1941, the Japanese landed an expeditionary force in the Philippines, which fought its way down the Bataan Peninsula (despite the

Bonifacio was forcibly exiled by rival revolutionaries. Aguinaldo accepted payment from the Spanish to go into exile, but he returned to be inaugurated as president of the first Philippine republic in 1899.

American occupation: In the meantime, Spain and the United States had gone to war over Cuba. With the end of the Spanish-American War, Spain ceded the Philippines, Puerto Rico and Guam to the United States, and paid an indemnity of US$20 million. Filipino

Left, Ibaloi schoolchildren and American missionary, early 1900s. Above, Gen. MacArthur returns, Leyte, 1945.

heroic resistance of Gen. Douglas MacArthur's American and Filipino troops), stormed the fortress island of Corregidor, occupied Manila, and eventually overran the whole of the archipelago.

On leaving besieged Corregidor, MacArthur pledged, "I shall return". He kept his word, and in autumn of 1944, brought the Americans back to the Philippines with an expeditionary force landing in Leyte, in the Visayas. With the highly effective aid of Fil-American troops, many of whom had campaigned as anti-Japanese guerrillas during the Japanese occupation, the Americans fought their way back into Manila. The liberation of the Philippines cost the Filipinos enormous losses in lives and property, but it was greeted with jubilation.

Problems and opportunities: After the war, American authorities devoted themselves, first, to desperately needed emergency relief, then to the Philippines' long-delayed independence – proclaimed on 4 July 1946 – and finally to the colossal task of rebuilding, rehabilitation and development.

Manuel Roxas served as the first president of the Philippines, followed by Elpidio Quirino, Ramon Magsaysay, Carlos Garcia and Diosdado Macapagai. Ferdinand Marcos was elected president in 1965 and re-elected in 1969. Confronted with student unrest,

1986 to renew his mandate. As expected, amidst unsubtle election fraud, Marcos was proclaimed the winner over Corazon (Cory) Aquino, the widow of assassinated Benigno Aquino. But he could no longer sustain power; his political cronies began jumping ship and, in February, a four-day bloodless revolution climaxed with a standoff between Marcos's tanks and citizens at EDSA, in Manila.

Marcos and Imelda were bundled off in an American plane to Hawaii, where they retired to an expensive villa overlooking Honolulu and whined for the old days. Marcos died there in 1989. (Imelda Marcos would later return to the Philippines and dabble in politics and rhetoric, and self-pity.)

Muslim revolts in Mindanao, and a rural communist insurgency, Marcos imposed martial law from 1972 until 1981, ruling with an iron fist, erecting monuments to himself and accumulating a vast fortune.

Marcos and his infamous wife, Imelda, prospered until the 1983 assassination of Benigno "Ninoy" Aquino, a popular opposition leader. Returning to the Philippines after self-imposed exile in America, Aquino was shot dead, in highly suspicious circumstances, at Manila airport as he stepped off the plane. The assassination invigorated discontent; faced with a restless populace, Marcos called a "snap" election in February

The specter of the Marcos' legacy lingered long after he and Imelda left; the economy and national treasury were pillaged during those years, and even the best management has taken time to heal the country's economy. On the other hand, to the relief of the government, the return of a dead and refrigerated Ferdinand Marcos to Ilocos Norte did not upset the country's increasing stability. In torrential rain, thousands of hometown villagers joined Imelda Marcos (who subsequently, and modestly, re-entered politics) in a funeral ceremony.

The Aquino era: The overthrow of Ferdinand Marcos was completed with an event that would have been inconceivable a few years earlier: the inauguration of Cory Aquino as president. The challenges of her presidency were daunting: an overhaul of the government and military, restoration of public trust, revival of a constipated economy – in short, rebuilding the nation.

But the continuing communist insurgency, infighting within her own coalition, persistent undermining by Marcos supporters, and deeply-embedded corruption worked against her. Her presidency survived seven coups, including one that required American military assistance to suppress. In hindsight, her transitional administration accomplished little, but it was an important symbol and

the American military from Philippine soil. The American involvement had become a national irritant that focused on Subic Bay Naval Base and Clark Air Force Base, both north of Manila. Yet the bases were a significant factor in the country's economy, and the Americans claimed that the area's security depended on them; if so, the Filipinos replied, the United States should pay substantially more for the leases.

The bilateral posturing ended abruptly in 1991 with the dramatic eruption of Mount Pinatubo. Clark was covered by volcanic ash, and the Americans simply packed up and left. A year later, after a new lease on Subic Naval Base was refused, the Ameri-

esteem booster for the Filipino people.

Economic stagnation eventually dampened the national exhilaration that had followed Aquino's election. Symbolic of the stagnation, if not decay, were the daily electrical brownouts in Manila. (A joke of the time: What did Filipinos use for reading before there were candles? Electricity.)

Most symbolic of the Philippines' post-Marcos renaissance was the withdrawal of

Left, Ferdinand Marcos pointing the prosperous way on National Day. **Above**, Cory Aquino after her retirement from the presidency. Her efforts provided the nation an essential transition.

cans hauled up anchor and sailed away. Clark has now been developed into an industrial and economic zone where a new international airport may be built. Subic has also been transformed into a successful duty-free industrial and commercial zone with its own international airport already in operation, and numerous multinational corporations setting up operations there.

Pragmatic revival: In the 1992 presidential election, Fidel Ramos, Aquino's defense minister and a strong ally who backed her during the numerous coup attempts, won a seven-way presidential election with just 24 percent of the vote.

Like Aquino, Ramos (and, no doubt, his successor, as Ramos can serve only one six-year term, although towards the end of his term there were substantial efforts to change the constitution, as there was no viable alternative candidate) faced numerous problems.

While the Philippines' foreign policy problems have typically been less than challenging, the country has been sparring with China over some small, almost nonexistent, islands – including the Spratlys – in the South China Sea. The islands sit astride potentially rich oil fields, thus encouraging China, Taiwan, Malaysia, Vietnam and the Philippines to make claims on them. (China's claim, quite invalid under international law, is that the

waters of the South China Sea and even beyond belong to it because of a brief period of naval power centuries ago.) Several times during the late 1990s, Ramos sent military units to the area to openly signal Manila's claim. Some analysts have suggested that the next significant threat to global peace could start because of these islands.

Besides a population that is increasing too rapidly (at a higher rate than Thailand and Indonesia), the most immediate domestic problem is the Muslim succession movement in Mindanao, which has claimed over 50,000 lives since the 1970s. The majority of the rebels, including their primary leader,

have made peace with Manila and rejoined the political system, with many former guerillas now regulars in the national army, but radical splinter groups are still a threat.

But, in fact, the future has rarely looked better – and more certain – for the Philippines and its people. After his election, Ramos promised to strengthen the economy, enabling the Philippines to share in the boom enjoyed by Pacific rivals such as Malaysia, Korea and Taiwan. He also promised improvements in electrical power supplies, and in other areas of infrastructure, not to mention a general house cleaning of the traditionally corrupt political system. Such boasts are tired promises everywhere and quickly forgotten. But a funny thing happened as Ramos set to work – he kept his promises.

After years of exceeding its annual quota for institutional corruption and feuding, army coups, rebel insurgences, earthquakes, volcanoes and typhoons, the Philippines has been showing steady signs of improvement in its attempts to stabilize and modernize the country's infrastructure. For example, shortly after he was elected president, Ramos immediately got Manila's lights back on – and reliably on – by having private industry build simple, oil-burning power plants, eliminating the half-day brownouts.

The country's economic growth has been excellent, given its past two decades of stagnation. Still, in the late 1990s, the Philippine economy was hit by the economic downturn and exchange-rate shifts that sent the economies of Thailand and other Asian tigers into a tumble. Still, most amazing for any developing country is that Ramos asked the country's creditors if the Philippines could accelerate repayment of its loans.

The year preceding the 1998 election of Joseph Estrada as president – an actor popular for his appreciation of women and drink, and for his portrayals in film of hard-edged characters with a Robin Hood sensitivity for the poor – was peppered with debate about changing the constitution to allow Ramos to run for a second term. A one-term limit had been instituted to prevent another Marcos. The 1998 elections continued the Filipino propensity for political theater, including the political revival and fizzle of Imelda Marcos.

Left, Fidel Ramos tends to important matters. **Right**, the national flag.

Filipinos have a justifiable reputation as one of the most hospitable people in the world, especially in rural areas where traditional attitudes still survive. As in most Asian societies, guests are honored.

In the cities, despite a large number of new hotels and guest houses, a foreign visitor lucky enough to have the name of a local resident is usually fed and shown around, if not offered a place to stay for free. But the foreign visitor should avoid taking advantage of the generous hospitality.

Filipinos are especially concerned with pride and self-esteem; public confrontation, criticism or argumentation can lead to rather uncomfortable situations. Strong and fixed eye contact between males is aggressive. Filipinos often communicate with eyes, lips and hands. Eyebrows raised with a smile are a silent *hello* or *yes* to a question. Polite language and gentle conversation are important, and direct questions should be avoided, or talk about politics, corruption and religion. Families, however, are good topics.

While custom dictates a somewhat late arrival for social engagements, punctuality is expected for business meetings. Unlike elsewhere in Asia, women are on an equal footing in the Philippine business world.

FILIPINO WAYS

Clannishness: This is the rule of survival, both the main strength and source of corruption in Filipino society. Kinship ties of both blood and marriage, often up to three generations removed, are kept well-defined and operative in all levels and facets of life. Clans operate as custodians of common experiences (many old families religiously keep family trees), and the memory of geographical and racial origins. They are act as disciplinary mechanisms, placement agencies and informal social-security systems. When there is a marriage between two clans, it is rarely a matter of choice as much as an alliance.

Preceding pages: farmer and carabao in Iloilo Province; doing business, Philippine Stock Exchange. **Left**, boy with smile and guitar, Visayas. **Above**, mother and child.

Within the sometimes tyrannical embrace of the clan, members of all ages find their place in an orderly world, where children are cared for by aunts, uncles, cousins and grandparents, and the elderly are given care and reverence through to their last days.

If foreign guests find themselves in the middle of clan hospitality, it is considered good form to give special acknowledgement to family elders. It does not hurt to use the honorifics of *lolo* and *lola* for the grandfather and grandmother, and other elder members

of the clan. Greet them by putting their right hand to your forehead in a time-honored Filipino gesture of respect, which goes a long way in establishing relations.

One notable first question to a foreign guest is, Where do you come from? The name of a country does not say much, but the name of a hometown does, even if the Filipino does not have the vaguest notion of where that might be. There is something psychologically comforting for the Filipino to know that visitors, too, wandering so far from home, have a family.

Relationships: Local sociologists have coined the phrase "smooth interpersonal relationships", or SIR for short, to indicate the key premise of human contact among Filipinos: the edges of face-to-face communication must be kept smooth at all times by courtesy and gentle speech, no matter that the content of conversation must sometimes be unpleasant.

Direct confrontations are generally avoided. When forced to deliver negative messages, Filipinos are fond of emissaries and subtle indirection relying for its effective communication of the sensitivity of the other party. Many Westerners accustomed to direct statements and blunt approach find this hypocritical and cowardly. In the Filipino context, however, smooth interpersonal

Another practice falling under the general heading of smooth interpersonal relationships is the custom of offering one's house and goods to anyone within the immediate vicinity. Guests arriving at or around meal time are always asked to stay and share food, so people are usually careful not to come at inconvenient times unless they are sure of their welcome. Even the merest strangers sitting together on a park bench will offer each other the contents of their lunch boxes. Friends and acquaintances sharing a ride on public transportation invariably struggle to pay the other's fare.

Hiya, literally translated as shame but better defined as a delicacy of sensitivity to the

relationship has its value by giving everyone room to maneuver and for amending foolish or hasty statements.

Part of the ritual of SIR are polite forms of address when conversing with strangers, especially older people and people of high social rank. The basic forms are the words *po* and *ho* to end sentences. Use *opo* and *oho* to say yes, and *hindi po* and *hindi ho* to say no. Even in face-to-face conversation, one refers to a new acquaintance, an older person or a dignitary in the third person-plural *sila.* The intention is to maintain a respectful distance, beginning on the verbal level, from which to slowly establish a pleasant relationship.

feeling of others, prevents individuals from taking each other for granted. Related to hiya is *pakiramdaman,* or feeling each other out. Beyond words, Filipinos often intuit or divine what the other means to communicate.

A second strand in the fabric of social relationships is *utang na loob,* or debt of gratitude. Favors long past are never forgotten and always returned in an invisible bond of reciprocity. Of course, utang na loob (both individual and collective) has also been responsible for sluggish bureaucracies resistant to impersonal but rational management procedures, but that is the price of transition from a traditional system to a more modern one. To this day, it is a coarse individual who forgets utang na loob.

A third concept is *pakikisama*, for which there is no exact English equivalent, but which can be defined as "getting along" or submitting to group will. As with all cultural traits, this one has negative applications, such as when teenagers fall in with bad company, adults find themselves in a circle habitually living beyond their means, or government officials fall into webs of compromise. Positively applied, though, pakikisama has tremendous power to mobilize individual energies for common goals.

Bahala na: Perhaps the crowning glory of local sociology is this Filipino expression

The image of today's Filipina emerged from a checkered history. Walking the world today as nurse and beauty queen, scholar and chambermaid, career girl, torch singer and roving ambassador, her origins can well be traced – far into the misty beginnings of her native land – to a long line of priestesses.

It is no longer well remembered, but the majority of the Philippines' early tribes relied on the woman to perform their most sacred rites. *Catalonan* to the Tagalog, *baliana* to the Bicolano, *managanito* to the Pangasinense, *babaylan* to the Bisaya – the priestess healed with herbs, exorcised the

that one anthropologist has traced to a linguistic root of *Bahala na,* or leave it to God. This is a typical Filipino reaction to crises and insoluble problems. Development experts have often decried Bahala na as passive and fatalist, the sole factor in the delayed maturity of the Filipino. Some other students of the Filipino character, however, praise its deeply philosophical origins. As proof, they point to how Bahala na at its best has successfully supported Filipino morale through the trials of destiny.

Left, a tight-knit family in Iloilo Province. **Above**, Manila socialite and hairdresser, Forbes Park.

devil-possessed and, receiving the spirits in trance, guided her tribe through crucial junctures of communal life.

At times, the catalonan or babaylan was male. If so, he had to perform his functions in the robes of a priestess, with simulated feminine voice and gestures, almost as if the gods would not speak to a male without the thinly-veiled ruse.

There is no cause for wonder, then, that women furiously fought the European's arrival. Feeling the cornerstone of tribal life threatened, priestesses of Cagayan, Pangasinan and the Visayas let out one long wail of incantation against the conqueror. As

Catholic missionaries cursed them for being agents of the devil, the priestesses moved their tribes to poison the cowled strangers, burn their altars, and all else failing, flee to thick forest and higher ground.

The Filipina who stayed behind to be Christianized proved to be the colonist's delight. She traded and parlayed with the white man, often helping him pacify warlike neighboring tribes. Here began the special relationship between friar and Filipina.

Once daughter and consort to proud and free men, she became an adopted waif to be melted in the Castellan mold. The friar who was father figure to whole villages fancied her a naive child, tenderheartedly teaching

with all her thoughts on chastity became a tempting morsel. Over and over again, and much to her trauma, the Filipina was seduced by her good father in sacristy and confessional, and in dim quarters of stone convents during the stillness of siesta hour. There are no statistics, but today's third generation after the Spanish counts many grandparents who are mestizo *anak pare*, or friar bastards.

These indiscretions caused a subtle fissure in tribal life. Friar children, though illegitimate, enjoyed a slightly higher status as Castellan progeny. In the care of mothers worshipping at altars full of fair-haired saints with blue and green eyes, the anak pare aroused new visions of beauty. To be white

her his alphabet. He gave her only enough to keep her serving and worshipful, withholding higher education from her eager grasp until as late as the 19th century.

Christian fervor: The enthusiasm with which she once worshipped nature and ancestral spirits was rechanneled to Christian piety. She said endless rosaries, put flowers prettily on the altar, sang songs to the Virgin as she walked – a holy fertility queen – in spring processions. A cheerful presence around the church, she embroidered vestments, cooked and cleaned for her friar-father.

Bound now and "saved" from former joyous abandon to life, the solemn young thing

became the object of many a silent prayer for the next generation. To find a rich, handsome Spaniard to marry became the goal for which many daughters were whipped when they played too long in the sun. The bias against a suntan lasts to this day.

The effect on the Filipino male was devastating. Battered by forced labor and exorbitant taxes, he found his status even more galling when wife or daughter was raped by a powerful Spaniard. There was no recourse, except perhaps in drink, and many a young Filipina grew up only to be torn between her own longing for a better life and her father's wounded and festering pride.

46

The revolution against Spanish rule was a chance to gamble for freedom. In death's embrace, both *indio* and *india* sought to overthrow their common tyrant. He plodded and fought; she hid his arms, carried his secret documents, nursed his wounds, aided his escape. Brave widows, foremost among them Gabriela Silang of the Ilocos, took to the battlefield in place of slain husbands, charging at fortresses at the head of troops.

But the moment was not to last. As the Americans took over soon after, they walked on ground laid smooth by predecessors who had staked strong foundation in the Filipino male's psyche. White was still somehow better; not wiser, but stronger.

of colonial thinking. Under two kinds of white rule, the relationship between the sexes in the Philippines has lived through severe imbalances, giving it both comedy and tragedy. The Spaniard molded the Filipina to an Old World charm. The American touched her ambitions to the quick, kindling a fire that still smolders today. Now one encounters the Filipina in a great variety of professions, jockeying for public office, running modern corporations, even governing the country as president. She does it all without losing whit or grace.

In recent decades, new blandishments – Miss Universe and Miss International titles – have done their bit in turning the Filipina

With the same earnestness that she had memorized the catechism, the Filipina now knelt to worship at the altar of formal education. The more egalitarian cast of the American mind prodded her now into giddy new experiences – voting for the first time, shedding the *saya* (long skirt) for tennis shorts, bobbing her long tresses, driving a car, speaking her mind.

It was a relatively easy thing to declare political independence. It has been a totally different effort in coping with the loose ends

head, as they toast her subtle combination of dusky Malay and fair Spanish, with a touch of Chinoise. The Filipina now graces fashion shows and political stages with equal aplomb, an observation borne out by Corazon Aquino, who rose from being an ordinary housewife to becoming Asia's first female leader.

Yet, all the while, the laws of her country continue to remind the Filipina of her former status as a friar ward. She still cannot draw up or sign contracts without her husband's consent, her adultery is more stiffly punished than his, and a separated wife is not given the same tax exemption as her spouse. These inequities rankle, but the Filipina – now

Left, young Filipina, and Cory Aquino. Above, beauty pageants are ubiquitous in the Philipines.

advocating divorce, family planning and even abortion, along with other particulars of women's freedom – is told she shares equality with her man.

RELIGION

The story is told that when Magellan landed in the thriving coastal kingdom of Cebu, it was not his sonorous promise of friendship with a white king, nor the gleam of Spanish cannons nor the symbol of the cross that won the day for the Great Navigator. Rather, it was a local queen's first intriguing look at a statue of the Christ child. The idol was alien as could be, but before those lambent Castil-

next three centuries of conversion, the friars were to perfect that initial encounter with indigenous psychology.

Kinship was the glue of early Filipino society, and in no time at all, the souls of departed ancestors, the spirits of nature and not a few mythical monsters were replaced (and in many cases, incorporated with) by an extended Christian family consisting of both the human and divine. God, of course, played the stern father, various saints were kindly aunts and uncles, the Virgin Mary the merciful mother and her child the powerful darling of the family.

After the hardier business of conquest subjugated the heads of families into paying

ian eyes, and the crown, scepter and tiny hand grasping all of the known world, the queen of a child-loving kingdom could hardly resist conversion to the new faith.

At the mass baptism that ensued, the queen (who was given the Christian name of Juana, while her husband, Rajah Humabon, was renamed Carlos) received the icon as a gift from Antonio de Pigafetta, historian of the expedition. Henceforth, promised the queen, the little one, Santo Niño of the Spanish, would replace the *anito* (idols) of her people.

The promise was not kept for very long; the records show a rapid return to animism after the conquistadors left, but through the

tribute, pacification was pursued through the women and children. After generations of inculcation, women were convinced that true femininity lay in devotion, chastity and obedience, while children were to perfect their trust in the Father. In lieu, of course, of visible divinities, the friars and governors would do as objects of these virtues.

Depending on the temperamental and cultural quirks of the settlement, emphasis varied between either Mother, the Virgin Mary, or the Child, Jesus. In the shrines and churches of Luzon, where women's equality with men had long ago extended into roles of power as priestesses, Mary became the standard-bearer of Catholicism. In the Visayas of Queen Juana, where children to this day are indulged in extended childhood, the Santo Niño was king. The difference can be seen today in the oldest churches of the country, particularly in the Tagalog provinces, Cagayan, Ilocos, Cebu and Panay Islands.

Propaganda was part and parcel of the missionary kit. Friars made sure that every important event in the lives of their flock was properly attributed to divine intervention. Thus Mary and her son (along with the various patron saints of particular places) became agents for fire prevention, earthquake-proofing (especially of churches), counter spells to outside invasions by the

All over the Philippines, at least 50 major icons of Mary and the Holy Child are surrounded with wondrous stories of miracles. Several of them, in fact, have been recognized by the Catholic Church as authentic miracle workers.

Practically all large Christian towns and cities have their own special image of the Virgin and Child: polished ivory by the classic skills of medieval European carvers; stained ebony fashioned by Mexican artisans; intricately carved in soft wood by Chinese sculptors (many displaying the almond eyes belonging to their own immortals); or carved by the indigenous hands of local Filipino craftsmen.

Dutch, British, Muslim, Portuguese and Chinese, as well as deities of rain, fertility and the entire range of human needs.

Miraculous icons: In the mysterious mechanics of prayer and mass worship, it would seem that many of these wishes, pleas and heart-cries were indeed granted. Tradition continues to claim that in such a place and at such a time, crops were saved from destruction by locust and drought, floods were diverted, and brigands turned away by the heavenly protectors.

Left, ritual cult practice on Mt. Banahaw, south of Manila. **Above,** collection of niño dolls.

Ubiquitous shrines: In the same tradition, there is hardly a Catholic home without its own Virgin and Child enshrined, usually near the master bedroom. Less in the city and more in the country, the Virgin is ever present in garden shrines – grottoes simulating her recorded apparition in Fatima, Lourdes and Carmel. The usual spot is on a mound, hillock or full-fledged mountain side that is carved out with hundreds of tortuous steps to the shrine.

Just a generation ago, it was a standard practice to affix a *Maria* or a *Jesus Maria* to a Filipino child's given name. The practice is dying out for the most part.

Ethnic groups weave a dazzling strain of color into the Philippine cultural fabric. Over 80 different ethnic groups have been identified, and for the most part, they live scattered in relative isolation about the islands. However, many inhabit accessible villages, where visitors can catch glimpses of their customs and lifestyles.

Of the Philippine population, now approaching 70 million, some 10 percent are classified as cultural or ethnic minorities. Most of these people live outside the cultural mainstream of lowland Filipino Christians. They comprise the most diverse and exotic

Mangyan. Considered by their neighbors the Tagalog and Visayan, with whom they associate and trade in the lowland towns, to be half-savages with a low level of culture, the Mangyan are a simple, submissive people who are frequently prey to exploitation.

Tagbanua: Mindoro's neighboring island, Palawan, harbors the Tagbanua tribe. Known as the "people of the country," they have in recent years yielded their shores to intrusive outsiders, yet have managed to retain their own animist culture.

The Tagbanua wear scanty dress, maintain a religion intimately joined with nature, and carve bamboo tubes with an old alphabet of Hindu origin.

population of the nation, with the vast majority of these minorities, some 60 percent, made up of various Muslim groups living on the southern islands of Mindanao and the Sulu Archipelago. The remaining peoples – mostly animists – inhabit the mountain provinces of northern and central Luzon, and the highland plains, rain forests and the isolated seashores of Mindanao and Palawan.

The numerous ethnic groups of the Philippine archipelago include the following tribes:

Mangyan: The hut-dwelling, sweet-potato-eating tribes of Mindoro island – Iraya, Tagaydan, Tatagnon, Buid, Alangan and Hanunoo – are collectively known as

Negrito: The Aeta, Ati, Ita and Eta are collectively known as Negrito. Numbering some 40,000, these short, dark-skin and kinky-haired people are now faced with cultural extinction. The Aetas live in the mountain jungles of Negros, Samar, and Leyte; in the rolling hills of Nueva Ecija on Luzon; and along the untamed shorelines of northern Luzon. The dark-skinned Ati group of Panay are probably the best known of the Negritos. They are credited with welcoming history's first Malay *datus* from Borneo in the 14th century, and also being the represented center of attraction in the annual festival of Ati-Atihan in Aklan Province.

Mountain people: There are five major ethnic groups spread across the Cordillera highlands of northern Luzon: Benguet, Bontoc, Ifugao, Kalinga and Apayao. Other indigenous groups of northern Luzon include the Kalinga and Tingguian.

These people are the unconquered people of the north who have evolved robust indigenous cultures and traditions in highland seclusion, far removed from lowland colonial history. These mountain tribes live sedentary lives based upon a highly-developed agricultural economy. They worship tribal ancestors or spirits of nature, and turn a suspicious faces upon the "intruders" from the lowlands.

tribe, raised within a community system of wards. The *ato* is the meeting place of the village elders and the sleeping place of the adolescent boys. The *ulog* is the dormitory for girls and unmarried women.

Ifugao: The Ifugao of the eastern and central Cordillera are the master architects of the most famous rice terraces in the world, the Ifugao rice terraces, first constructed between 2,000 and 3,000 years ago and covering over 260 square kilometers (100 sq. mi) of steep mountain sides in Ifugao Province. If placed end-to-end, they would reach halfway around the world. No doubt visitors today are happier to find them conveniently in one place, however.

Benguet and Bontoc: The Benguet tribes of the western and southern Cordillera speak Ibaloy and Kankanay. They grow rice, coffee, vegetables and raise livestock on their terraced hillsides. They also mine precious metals like gold and copper in the upland region of Lepanto.

The Bontoc of northwest Cordillera blend American missionary teaching with their ancestral religion. They are probably the best-known people of the mountains. Culturally, the Bontoc are a highly individualistic

Left, Maranao dance troop from Marawi, Mindanao. **Above,** Ifugao elders, northern Luzon.

Muslims: Considered as a whole, the Muslims of the south – also called Moros – constitute the largest cultural minority of the Philippines. Some claim Mindanao and the Sulu Archipelago farther to the south as their own holy land. The Muslims, fiercely independent and combative, are classified into five major groups: Tausug, Maranao, Maguindanao, Samal and Badjao.

The Tausug were the first tribe in the archipelago to be converted to Islam. They are, historically, the ruling people of the ancient Sultanate of Jolo, and regard themselves superior to other Philippine Muslims. As a cultural group, the "people of the current," as they are known, lead a combative, "very muscular" life, where violence is often an expression of the social process. The Tausug are traders, fishermen and artisans of fine Muslim textiles and metal works.

The Maranao are the graceful "people of the lake", living on the northern edge of Lake Lanao, at 700 meters (2,300 ft) above sea level. In cool and aloof isolation, Mindanao's last group to be converted to Islam uphold their complex but vigorous sultanates.

The Maguindanao are the "people of the flood plain," inhabiting an unappealing area of Cotabato Province, where land is periodically flooded by overflowing rivers. The largest group of Muslims, the Maguindanao

are a hardy clan, surviving on agriculture and fishing, and weaving fine mats and baskets.

The Samal are the poorest and least independent of the major Muslim groups. They serve as the "loyal commoners" in the hierarchy of Muslim minorities here. Their lives are literally over the sea, where villages stand on stilts above the coastal waters.

The Badjao are the "sea-gypsies," the true wanderers of the Sulu seas. They are born on the water, live upon their tiny craft for a lifetimes – turning tawny and blonde in the sun and salt – and set foot on the land only to die. The Badjao are a superficially Islam tribe numbering some 20,000.

Another unique cultural group of Sulu, living on Basilan Island south of Zamboanga, are the Yakan. They are a gentle people of partial Polynesian origin, with mixed Muslim and animist beliefs. They are the most superb textile weavers of the southern archipelago. On backstrap looms they turn fine cottons and silks into remarkable geometric works of art.

The non-Muslim ethnic tribes of the Mindanao highlands are the least studied of the Philippine cultural minorities, and among the most highly costumed and colorful. There are over ten tribes living in relative isolation in the Mindanao interior.

The Tiruray are of Malay stock. They are a horse-riding hill people occupying the mountains of southwest Mindanao. The T'boli tribe of Lake Sebu in Cotabato have a wealth of crafts, elaborate ethnic costumes, and vivacious dances and music. They are also admired for their handsome brasswork, which finds its way into figure statuary, heavy belts, chains, and noisy anklets worn by much-beaded and embroidery-bedecked tribal women. The heavily ornamented Bagobo live along the desolate eastern coast of the Gulf of Davao. In imitating the metal arts of the Moros (Muslim warriors), the tribe has produced an ornate tradition in weaponry, and inlaid, bell-bejangled metal boxes. The Bagobo also weave abaca cloths of ruddy earth tones, and weave baskets.

The Subanon of western Lanao originated one of the country's highest traditions of pottery. The 50,000-strong Bukidnon of east Lanao are a tribe of fiercely independent highland dwellers.

Tasaday: The cave-dwelling Tasaday of southern Mindanao have been the focus of furious anthropological debate since their discovery in 1971. They were portrayed as a stone-age tribe of some 25 people living in harmony with nature and with one another, and with no prior contact to the outside world. However, some anthropologists consider the Tasaday a hoax. They argue that the tribe's habitat cannot support their hunter-gatherer existence; the Tasaday language is closely related to the nearby Manobo tribe; and that no trash heaps, showing long-term occupation, have been found near their caves.

<u>Above</u>, **Bukidnon woman in tribal headdress.**
<u>Right</u>, **Bontoc man with woven baskets.**

The present shape of the Filipino fiesta comes from the wisdom of old Spanish friars, who were disturbed by early symptoms of forced – and seemingly incomplete – conversion to Catholicism by Filipinos. When natural calamities and tribal enemies threatened the life of Christian settlements, the friars took the opportunity to lead everyone to the church in quest of a "miracle". The guardian spirits of traditional harvest feasts were gradually replaced by Christian saints, and as summer heat rose in the blood – prompting ancient chants of fertility – friars would scurry through their memories of Spain for songs, dances and colors to woo a musical people in the worship of the Virgin Mary.

January: Kalibo's Ati-Atihan festival, held during the third week of January, is the Philippines' most famous fiesta.

Ati-Atihan means "making like Atis", and refers to the black Negrito aborigines, the original inhabitants of Panay. In 1212, 10 Bornean lords escaping religious tyranny in the south fled northwards with their followers. Upon their arrival in Panay, they sought rights to this island and struck an accord with the local king. Later, the peace pact was reinforced by a lavish harvest feast prepared by the Bornean immigrants for their Ati neighbors. Ever eager to please, the Borneans enlivened up the welcome with gongs and cymbals, smeared soot on their faces and started dancing in the streets in merry imitation of their Ati guests. The Christ-child figure of Santo Niño was introduced in later years, when the Borneans successfully fought off marauding Muslim attackers.

Today, as column upon column of sooted Atis-garbed warring locals beat out drums and cymbals and march in syncopated rhythm, wild dancing breaks out everywhere. The unceasing and deafening Ati-Atihan beat overloads the senses, but everyone ends up joining in the madcap fun.

February: The giant ring road encircling Metro Manila, Epifanio de los Santos Avenue, or EDSA, was the focus for the Febru-

ary 1986 revolution that toppled former dictator Ferdinand Marcos, without violence or bloodshed. It was perhaps the Filipinos' finest hour in modern times. There was tension, of course, when the banners of revolt were first unfurled over Camp Crame. Nevertheless, despite their fears, hundreds of thousands of Filipinos converged on this road of resistance to form a protective human wall. There, confronted with tanks and troops, they brought their personal weapons of prayers, smiles, rosary beads and flowers to

bear on the forces of discredited authority.

Since then, Filipinos have celebrated EDSA People's Power anniversary with moving masses, stage shows, dancing, displays, singing and fireworks. Center stage of the celebration is the portion of EDSA between Camp Crame and Aguinaldo and the EDSA memorial on Ortigas Avenue. A month-long Silayan Arts Festival is held during February at the Cultural Center of the Philippines, on Roxas Boulevard in Manila, with exhibitions of paintings, prints, murals, banners and photos, along with plays, films, lectures, and books. Dances (from ballet to folk) and music concerts range the gamut.

Preceding pages: *gigantes* and young escorts, Angono. **Left,** papier-mâché *gigantes*, or giants. **Above,** fire-breathing during Ati-Atihan.

March: When Easter arrives, Holy Week becomes a colorful celebration throughout the islands. The heart-shaped island of Marinduque especially becomes the stage for a unique spectacle: the Moriones festival and the re-enactment of the ancient Biblical legend of Longinus and his miracle.

The drama unfolds as the villages of Boac, Gasan and Mogpog are converted into immense stages. All-male participants don wooden masks carved from coral wood, and resembling Roman soldiers wearing perpetual scowls. During Ash Wednesday they roam the streets to terrorize – not for real, naturally – the locals. It's all good fun, of course. On Good Friday, a stand-in for Jesus

April: Who has not heard of the jeepney, that four-wheeled Filipino oddity without which no travel in the Philippines would be complete? So baroque and yet so Filipino, jeepneys have for years served as the country's most important mode of transport. They were originally a solution to the problem of what to do with army jeeps abandoned by American soldiers at the end of World War II. Today, no Filipino street scene is complete without the speed, flash and dazzling humor of the King of the Road.

In the late 1960s, a Manila-based oil company, in a flash of public relations genius, launched a search for a so-called Jeepney King. Amid the typical hoopla of a native

is crucified with Longinus' assistance. By Easter Sunday, the Moriones and thousands of spectators crowd into an enormous open-air arena alongside the Boac River. With great theater, Christ's resurrection is then dramatically re-enacted.

The wrath of the Roman legionnaires is immediately aroused. Longinus is pursued by the soldiers and brought to trial. He is thrown before Pontius Pilate, judged, and then ceremoniously beheaded. With his mask held high by a Roman soldier, Longinus' headless body is carried on a bamboo stretcher to the church, bringing to an end the festival of Moriones.

fiesta, jeepney drivers from all over the archipelago compete in contests designed to test their judgement and reflexes on the road and steadiness at the wheel. A showy parade of jeepneys, typical of the Filipino's innate spirit of fun and macho competition, draws the festivities to a splashy and noisy close.

May: The first of May is an important day throughout the Philippines, with May a merry month of flowers, dainty maidens in pretty gowns and the Queen of the Philippine festivals, the Santacruzan, or Queen of Heaven.

Sampaguitas, *ilang-ilang* and hibiscus surround the month-long tribute to the Queen of Heaven, or the Virgin Mary, which begins with a riot of flowers and ends with a glittering parade of crowns and costumes on the last Sunday of May. Indeed, the celebration that was traditionally a religious affair has evolved into a paramount social event.

The Santacruzan is a Spanish legacy that commemorates the search for the True Cross of Christ. According to legend, Constantine the Great was converted to the Christian faith through the vision of a flaming cross in heaven, which is said to have led him to victory in the battle.

As a gesture of thanksgiving, the Roman leader ordered that Christians should from then on be tolerated, and thus Christianity was further spread. Constantine's mother,

procession that closes the Santacruzan is heady with romance, for it is the coming out of females who have reached adulthood. The last celebration before the monsoon rains of June, the Santacruzan is a puberty rite sublimated into a religious ceremony, leading young girls into adulthood and many young boys to their circumcision.

June: At the centerpiece of any Filipino fiesta table, the *lechon*, or whole roast pig, is king. So revered is the aroma of this succulent dish that the folks of Balayan and Batangas have highlighted the feast of their patron saint, St John, with a tribute to golden-red crispy lechon. On the eve of the fiesta, an anniversary ball is held at the town plaza,

Queen Helena, the first Christian empress and who was canonized after her death, led a pilgrimage in search of the Cross, and claimed to have found it in Jerusalem, in 324.

Throughout the archipelago, every town and barrio stages its own Santacruzan. The fiesta is managed by a *hermana* or *hermano mayor* (big sister or brother) or a *capitana* (lady-in-charge), who recruits pretty girls to be the *sagalas* (maidens) of the night. The

Left, masks used in Marinduque's *Moriones* festival during Holy Week. **Above**, the May harvest festival of Lucban, Quezon; colored rice wafers called *kiping* adorn house facades.

where the lechon queen is crowned. Next morning, after mass at the Immaculate Conception Church, an array of at least 50 lechons is gathered to await the festivities. The dressing of the roast pig reflects the theme of the participating civic and social organizations. Medical associations, for instance, present their pig wearing a doctor's uniform, complete with a stethoscope and mask.

The crisp-skinned array of roasts soon becomes the object of mischief. Pranksters hurl water or beer over the roast pigs, drenching the bearers, the lechons, and eventually onlookers. A wet free-for-all ensues and the only objects left unscathed are the few lechons clad in raincoats. A few daredevils invariably attempt to snatch patches of the lechon's prized crispy skin. Rising to the challenge, some participants cover their lechons with barbed-wire enclosures to prevent thieving hands from grabbing free samples.

After the parade, the lechons are taken to their respective home or club headquarters, where the noontime feasting and drinking begin in earnest. But, true to the festive spirit of sharing, some groups surrender their prized roast to the crowds of merrymakers. Whichever way it ends, the *Parada ng Lechon* remains one of the most riotous fiestas held in the Philippines.

July: A colorful procession highlights the festival of Santa Ana Kahimonan Abayan, held on 27 July in the northern Mindanao city of Butuan. In earlier times, human-eating crocodiles infested the Agusan River, biting, so to speak, into the town people's life. Faced with a common enemy, the townspeople implored their patron saint Santa Ana to give them bountiful harvests and safe passage over the river. Santa Ana heard their prayers and destroyed the creatures.

Today, the river-people honor their patron saint by staging a waterborne high mass. Hundreds of boats strung with multicolored bunting and festooned with decorations are linked side by side to form a long platform spanning the river, with the statue of Santa Ana taking center stage. She is borne high on the shoulders of devotees and positioned in the middle of the floating platform. The ensuing mass is celebrated by several priests, sacristans and a choir. After the mass, the choir's chants and the beating of drums fire the celebration into a frenzy.

The Santa Ana Kahimonan Abayan festival also provides an avenue of interaction among the various northern Mindanao ethnic tribes, and is when the Terurai, Manobo, Mandaya and Bukidnon people converge each year at Santa Ana, on Butuan, to sell their wares and perform dances.

August: Four-meter-high (14 ft) papier-maché *gigantes*, or giants, strut through the Quezon town of Lucban representing Juan Cruz, a farmer, his wife and their two children. During the month of August, a full-blown fiesta is dedicated to these symbolic, fun-loving gigantes.

Bamboo framework is garbed in the year's creation, which is paid for by Lucban's more affluent residents. The basic frame is encased in papier-maché through the cooperative hands of the townspeople, who gather every day until the creation takes shape.

Manning the gigantes on bamboo frames over the shoulders, especially while balancing on stilts, requires great discipline and involves considerable discomfort. The men inside the figures have earlier vowed to perform the service in thanksgiving for an answered prayer. With much skill after months of practice, they can march, dance, curtsy and bow before the spectators, and even peer inside second-floor windows of houses along the way. Heightening the fun is the *toro*, an enormous papier-maché bull painted bright

red and rigged with firecrackers. Throughout the parade, the bull scampers around the town plaza, scattering spectators as fireworks inside are shot off.

September: The tiny statue of Our Lady of Peñafrancia, patroness of the Bicol region in southern Luzon, is one of the most revered Marian images in the Philippines. Come September, thousands of devotees travel by any means to catch a glimpse of her at the festival in Naga.

The religious observance begins on the second Friday of September, nine days before the actual feast day. From her shrine, the statue of Our Lady of Peñafrancia is carried on the shoulders of male devotees to the Metropolitan Cathedral. A nine-day *novena* is then held before the statue is returned to her shrine down the Bicol River.

The ritual transfer is known as the *translucion*, and during the one-mile trek, devotees vie for the honor of carrying the statue on their shoulders. Thousands of eager arms stretch up from a sea of bodies desperate to touch the image, while shouts of *Viva la Virgen* fill the air.

As the statue reaches the river, it is placed carefully aboard an elaborate pagoda and rowed down river by an all-male crew, escorted by a flotilla of outrigger canoes, bamboo rafts, and brightly-decorated motorboats.

for "mask" and "many faces". The Masskara festival was first conceived in 1980 to add color and gaiety to the city's celebration of its Charter Day anniversary, on 19 October. The symbol of the festival – a smiling mask – was adopted by the organizers to dramatize the Negrenses happy spirit, despite periodic economic downturns in the sugar industry.

Throughout the week, people from all over the Visayas, the grouping of islands in the central part of the Philippines, flock to the town plaza. They join Bacoleños in the non-stop round of festivities, trying their luck and testing their skills in mask-making contests, greased-pig catching games, pole climbing, sack races, disco king and queen competi-

As dusk approaches, candles light the way, giving the river procession the magnificent impression of a sea of brilliant jewels in an ocean of darkness.

October: Come hell or high water, crisis or no crisis, for seven music- and laughter-filled nights in October, Bacolod, the capital city of the Philippines' sugar-producing province of Bacoleños, becomes one big party.

Masskara is coined from two words: *mass*, meaning crowd or many, and the Spanish word *cara*, or face; thus the double meaning

Left, festive fiesta clown. **Above**, a Sinulog dancer in the spirit of festive celebration.

tions, coconut-milk drinking, and banana- and bread-eating competitions.

The more energetic and athletic sports aficionados compete in basketball, walkathons, cycling and motocross. Throughout the week, too, rehearsals are held to make sure that all runs smoothly at the culmination of the festival the Sunday Masskara parade.

Masks are the order of the day at the Masskara parade, as brightly-costumed men and women dance and prance in the streets. Their beaming faces are be-dimpled, grinning and laughing in molded clay or papier-maché. Every group is represented: civic associations, commercial establishments, schools, even private and government organizations. They march out in enthusiastic throngs wearing their painted masks and elaborate costumes, all vying for prizes in the judging that will be held in the afternoon.

November: Built in the 16th century, Manila's Intramuros district is a stellar example of a medieval fortress town. The heart of this Spanish-style city is Plaza Real, with its gardens, statues and fountains, around which are grouped a cathedral, the governor-general's palace and government buildings.

Today, in the quiet shady gardens and elegant colonial houses, visitors can almost imagine the carriages passing nearby with their *señoritas* and *caballeros*.

In November is a festival of regal revelry, when the walled city relives its colonial golden age. There are exhibitions of historical artifacts, cultural presentations at sprawling Fort Santiago, and parades of Manila's women clad in the traditional Maria Clara costume of the Spanish era.

The Casa Manila choral competition, called *Centar Villancios*, is held for visitors to enjoy the Spanish and Tagalog Christmas carols popular during the 18th century. The underlying theme of these varied activities is the dated traditions observed during the Spanish colonial period. It is a trip back into colonial times, and a re-enactment of that elegant age. Manileños love it. Serving as the culminating activity of the Intramuros Festival is the procession of the Feast of Our Lady of the Immaculate Conception, who is also the patroness of Intramuros. This is a parade of some 75 statues of the Blessed Virgin Mary brought from all over the country, and many of them are believed to be miraculous. Glittering with gold and festooned with sampaguita, ilang-ilang and *dama de noche* flowers, the image-bearing *carrozas* (floats) are paraded at sunset from the old San Agustin Church to the Quirino Grandstand, beside the bay in Rizal Park. It is a not-to-be-missed experience, and a grand build-up to the Christmas festive season.

December: The scene is the town plaza of San Fernando, in the northern Philippine province of Pampanga. Three days before Christmas, at sunset, lanterns glow like phantasmagorical stars along the streets, illuminating the dark of the night. Through the streets, townspeople dance to the beat of a lively brass band, the air cool and filled with the sound of Christmas carols. Children playing the traditional festive *pabitin* game scramble up a trellis to grasp at candies. An unforgettable welcome to the Christmas lantern festival, Filipino-style.

The lanterns, or *parols* as they are known, are specimens of pyrotechnic splendor, representing the synergistic endeavor of every town barrio. The finest exhibits are entered in a grand competition on Christmas Eve. There is friendly rivalry over who will be awarded the coveted Star of Bethlehem title, as almost everyone will have spent much time and effort on their particular exhibit.

On 22 December, the lanterns go on parade accompanied by music, feasting and dancing. Life for the housewives of San Fernando is turned upside down as visitors flock to the houses to sample traditional Noche Buena – Christmas Eve – specialties of chicken *relleno*, rice a la Valenciana, lechon, *menudo, bibingka*, and more.

Most everyone – save the local grinch – in the town smiles and shouts the greeting *Maligayang Pasko* – Happy Christmas!

Left, delicate constructions of bamboo strips, silver tinfoil and colored *papel de Hapon* (Japanese paper) make up the *parol* or Christmas lantern of San Fernando. **Right**, painted 'warriors' for the Pintados fiesta, Leyte.

Manong Paul Bastawang lives in a little shack on a low hillock among the pines of Baguio, north of Manila. His handkerchief-sized yard is thick with old gasoline cans, rubber tires and giant fern stumps recycled into pots of plants.

Indoors, he disappears into a tiny bedroom and emerges with several bottles of dried seeds, bark and leaves, all neatly labeled in his Igorot dialect. Laying them on a wooden table, he proceeds to explain their uses for curing cancer, malaria, snakebites, rheumatism, asthma and several other ills. The portrait is classic – the original apothecary.

It is cold in the house and Manong Paul offers herbal tea to prevent stomach cramps – bitter stuff, to be taken only with brown sugar. Sipping, the visitor notes two flying saucers, glowing like a pair of eyes, on an adjacent wall. One is a crude watercolor; the other, a magazine clipping.

"Have you seen them, Manong Paul?"

"Yes," he answers quietly. "They like to hover directly over churches." There is, in fact, an unusual concentration of various churches in Baguio.

"Why do you suppose they do?" The questions are beginning to sound like those of the ingenuous Carlos Castañeda.

"They could be recharging their batteries," he answers in his best Don Juan manner. "The watercolor is what I saw the other night. You see the lights surrounding it? It's like the light I see around plants that yield medicine.

"I pray everyday. When the right time has come, my Voice tells me to go to the forest. I am guided by white flowers that are friends of medicinal plants. I just follow their trail and I am led right to the useful plants. They are very beautiful, glowing in different colors like the halos of the saints."

Second coming: Four o'clock on a Sunday afternoon at the prayer and meeting hall of the *Watawat ng Lahi* (Flag of the Race), an organization whose central belief is that Jose Rizal was a reincarnation of Christ and, as

such, will come again. The main headquarters of the faith is perched on top of a hill that folk-memory calls *burol na ginto*, hill of gold, near Calamba, Laguna, Rizal's birthplace south of Manila.

This afternoon, members are gathered for the monthly meeting with the oldest and most respected Watawat associates – 16 dead Filipinos now known as national heroes. Through a trance medium, some of them will speak this afternoon in the *Banal na Tinig*, the holy voice of prophecy.

Everyone falls silent while resonant tones echo in the hall. The day, says the Voice, is not long in coming when the new age shall be known in the Philippines by the building of a golden church and a golden palace, and the waving of a golden flag.

The subok: Good Friday in the lush hills of lakeside Tanay town in Rizal Province. High noon creeps overhead. A gathering of men, hollow-eyed from fasting and overnight meditation, shuffle their feet around the courtyard of an old church. Creaking and groaning, a flower-decked *carroza* emerges from the dim interiors, carrying the Santo Sepulcro, a wooden statue of the Dead Christ. There is

Left, a mystic healer in meditation. **Above**, a wine-and-chicken sacrifice by an Ifugao tribesman to appease the spirits of nature.

a rush toward it, then an ensuing scramble to insert strange objects in the folds of the robes, under the feet, in the holy hands.

The image – now loaded with handkerchiefs, bronze medals, pieces of paper inscribed with Latin phrases and images of Christ and the Virgin, pebbles, tektites, bones, prayer books, crucifixes, catfish eyes - is encircled by a chain of linked hands. The procession moves on. Soon after, with a merciless sun beating a still afternoon into an oppressive silence, the same gathering of men appears at a nearby seafood restaurant. They share a meal, laugh, kid around. Then, as if by signal, they fall quiet again. There is a silent reaching for *anting-antings*, the ob-

The gathering of men knits a collective brow in silent approval. One of them moves to touch the anting-anting in his open hand. He claims that it feels as hot as a kettle at boiling point. Held between thumb and index finger, the bronze medal spins with a life of its own.

The others step forward now. Lethal weapons are passed around – horse-hair whips, revolvers, more bolos.

Throughout the rest of Good Friday afternoon and Holy Saturday, each one will test the efficacy of his own talisman – asking to be shot at, whipped, stabbed. Some get hurt. Others leave the subok unscathed, exuding an even deeper solemnity than that with which they came.

jects that had taken a ride with the Santo Sepulcro to become talismans against death and physical harm. It is time to test their efficacy in the ritual of the *subok*, the trial.

Aman, in his forties, walks forward. He appears to be a fisherman, judging from the calluses on his thumb and index finger. He sharpens a long bolo in deliberate motions. Satisfied that it is sharp enough, he then sits at a table, stretches his left arm with a fist tightly clasping his anting-anting. He raises a right arm with the bolo, brings it down suddenly, coolly hacking away at the stretched left arm. No cuts, no blood appear. Again, he strikes. Not the smallest scratch.

Magbabarang: On the island of Siquijor, off the island of Negros, lives the *magbabarang*. He collects certain bees, beetles, and centipedes (collectively called *barang*) chosen because they all have one extra leg. The magbabarang keeps them inside a bamboo tube worn smooth by constant handling.

On Fridays, the magbabarang performs a ritual from which his name derives. He takes a list of names and addresses, writes them on separate pieces of paper, and puts them in the bamboo tube. In a while, he opens the tube. If the papers have been torn to shreds, the insects are willing to attack the owners of the names. The ritual of vengeance begins.

The magbabarang proceeds to tie a white string on the extra legs of his assistants. He then lets them loose, with instructions to lodge themselves inside the victim's body, bite his internal organs, and wreak havoc in his whole system until he dies. Then they go back to their master. If their strings are red with blood, the hex was successful. If clean, the intended victim was innocent and was able to resist the magic. The magbabarang has to let things be.

Bolobolo: A woman arrives at the home of a *bolobolo* complaining of severe chest pains. The bolobolo diagnoses her, then produces a small bamboo tube from his pocket. An assistant hands him a glass half-filled with

The ritual had taken three minutes. In three hours, the bolobolo says, the woman can move about normally. She offers to pay. The bolobolo refuses. That, says he, would be the loss of his God-given powers.

Truth in between?: What to make of it all? Could these mostly unlettered Filipinos really be tuned to power sources that people through the ages have classified as divine? Could they, on the other hand, be (as the strictly rational mind irritably snaps) just a lot of see-through frauds or facile practitioners of hypnosis and sleight of hand, unscrupulously trafficking in ignorance for personal gain? Is there, as the scales balance delicately, some truth in between?

water, into which he carefully drops a moonstone. The bolobolo swallows some of the water, gargles and spits it all out the window. He opens his mouth wide to show that it is empty. After praying in a low mumble, he dips one end of the bamboo tube into the glass, takes the other end of the reed into his mouth and begins to blow.

The water begins to darken to the color of mud. Soon, worms are wriggling in the glass. You are cured, the bolobolo tells the woman.

Left, an apothecary's display of ointment and herbal medicine outside Quiapo Church. **Above**, a cave-dwelling faith healer in Marinduque.

Most of what is known in the West today, both good and bad, about the gray areas of the occult in the Philippines stems from the discovery of Pangasinan psychic surgery in the late 1940s by some Americans. The details of the encounter are now unclear. What is known is that a few diseased individuals were given "miracle cures", unexplainable even by educated Filipinos who, though dimly aware of strange healing practices in the barrios of their childhood, had been schooled long enough in the rational, or Western, way of thought to dismiss them as superstition.

The first major healer encountered by the Americans was a man called Eleuterio Terte, who began as a magnetic healer. His method was a simple laying on of hands, similar to the practice of any number of spiritual healers in Brazil, Hawaii, England, and the southern United States. As reported, however, shortly after World War II, Terte suddenly noticed bodies opening spontaneously under his hands.

This is where the story of psychic healing in the Philippines began. By the time Harold Sherman, an American psychic researcher, came to document the so-called psychic surgery in the mid 1960s, Terte had already trained 14 of the 30 surgeons now known the world over as Filipino faith healers. A controversial bunch, they are both praised and damned by a miracle-hungry century.

Psychic surgery, of course, has been the most impressive example of spirit healing to the Western eye. Diagnosis is done in meditation. Bodies appear to open up without even a single knife stroke, but by short, cavalier slashes of the finger a full half meter away from the diseased part. (Sometimes a finger of an eyewitness held in the healer's hand is used). Then the operation is performed. A few gropes, pulls, twists, and out comes a supposed organ, or an eyeball, followed by quick dabs of alcohol-soaked cotton on blood-drenched areas and a closing of the body cut.

When the parts removed are not thrown into a gory pail of other organic material, they are deposited in bottles of alcohol, which then become the much-prized booty of visiting scientists and the scientifically inclined.

More often than not, requests for these bottles have been refused. Those who have acquired them testify to one of three results. First, laboratory examinations testify that the contents were genuine, diseased human organs or tissues. Or, second, they turned out to be animals parts and fluids. Or third, that the contents vanish from the bottles – whether through evaporation, theft, or what some claim is "dematerialization" into their original "etheric" state.

To make the whole phenomenon even more baffling, sometimes what appears to emerge out of a patient's body are not even pig or chicken parts (substituted in sleight-of-hand by some healers), but totally foreign material – the likes of which have included dried wax, twine, rusty razor blades, coconut husks and old coins.

Little in scientific experience can even begin to explain this sort of impudence, and as the mind stutters in disbelief, it lets in a suggestion from a totally other sphere. The healers churning up these objects from human bodies matter-of-factly call them witchcraft. Parallels to the experiences in South America – where African spiritual rituals and Latin spiritualism combine in a manner similar to the Filipino – have been drawn, making the explanation plausible.

But faith cannot evade aggressive empiricism. Several Filipino healers have been collared by Japanese, German, Swiss, and American scientists and brought to their laboratories. They have been interviewed, nailed down on details of life histories, and asked to enter their healing frame of mind at the precise moment when all the EEG, EMG (electromyograph), pulse rate, blood pressure, and adrenalin-level measuring devices were turned on. In the case of Antonio Agpaoa, possibly the most controversial Pinoy healer of all, the machines in the Tokyo laboratory of Dr. Hiroshi Motoyama, simply, irrespressibly, all broke down. Dr. Motoyama soberly says in his book *Psychic Surgery in the Philippines* that the first and most important condition for being able to heal is "to meet a god", followed by fasting, prayer and initiation to the "mission" and finally, constant contact with the god.

Kahuna ancestry?: A recent theory of somewhat dubious merit purports that Filipino faith healers are descendants of the *kahuna*, the ancient healers in old Tahiti and Hawaii. Their shamans – making the connection between a higher self of consciousness, a middle self of rationality, and a lower self of age-old instinctive power – are said to have had the ability to dematerialize tissues and bones and to rematerialize them in perfect order. The kahunas vanished with the coming of Christianity to Polynesia. Prayers became magic spells. A new pantheon of white saints became guardian spirits.

This synthesis is perhaps the source of today's explosion of so-called psychic power and other similar phenomena, a spouting fountain of charisma feeding the life of even the humblest Filipino.

Right, San Fabian's Apo Ruping, Supreme Pontiff of Crusaders of the Divine Church of Church, at his center-seminary for magnetic healing.

Drawing origins from various cultures but displaying regional characteristics, Filipino food was prepared by Malay settlers, spiced by Chinese traders, stewed in 300 years of Spanish rule, and hamburgered by American influence in the Philippine way of life. The multiracial features of the Filipino – a Chinese-Malayan face, a Spanish name and an American nickname – thusly inform Philippine cuisine, producing dishes of oriental and occidental extraction.

– Monina A. Mercado

Nowhere else is the Philippines' long history of outside influences more evident than in its food, which is remarkably varied. Philippine cuisine, an intriguing blend of Malay, Spanish, and Chinese influences, is noted for the use of fruits, local spices and seafood.

Food, to the Filipino, is an integral part of local art and culture, and of communal existence, and the result is a tribute to the Pinoy's ingenuity in concocting culinary treats from Asian and Western ingredients.

When ordering, it's best to watch the Filipinos. Note, for example, that even before the food arrives, sauce dishes are brought in and people automatically reach for the vinegar bottle with hot chili, or perhaps for the soy sauce, which they mix with *kalamansi*, or small lemons. Most grilled items are good with crushed garlic, vinegar and chili.

It's a good idea to start a meal with *sinigang*, a clear broth slightly soured with small nature fruit and prepared with *bangus* (milkfish) or shrimp.

In the surrounding Asian lands burning with hot chilly curries and spicy satays, Philippine cuisine is often labeled bland. Perhaps this is so, considering the surplus of cooks who have stirred the national broth. But to put it more tastefully, Filipino food is a blend of many cultures – and seeking to avoid conflict, it is a cuisine fit for the more sedate and sensitive taste buds.

Preceding pages: a roasting suckling pig, or lechon. Left, a resort's seafood spread. Right, *lumpia shanghai* **is the Pinoy version of Chinese spring rolls.**

Rice is the natural staple and substance of the Philippine diet, served up in fluffy, steamy mounds on the humblest tin plate or the fanciest porcelain dish. Rice appears before every person at every meal – at breakfast, when the previous night's meal is lightly turned in a morning smother of garlic, and for *merienda*, which is the midday snack time, when rice is turned into rice cakes. Rice is the Filipino's food for bulk, nourishment, and as the backdrop for all the fresh and varied flavors found in simple cooking.

Simple cooking means fish, big or small, from the wide marine catch along the archipelago's long coastline. Filipinos like their fish – and crabs and shrimps and shellfish – as fresh and unfettered as can be. The tasting of seaside freshness is complemented but undrowned by sauces and spices. Seafood is appreciated at its best, in fact, uncooked – in a vinaigrette or *kilawin* matrix, or roasted over coals – *ihaw* or *inihaw* – sometimes stuffed with onions and blanketed with a banana leaf, or aswim in sinigang.

The coconut is another sturdy foundation of the island menu that lends itself to all the parts and intimations of a Filipino meal:

from the luscious soup, *binakol*, cooked in a bamboo tube, to the most stupefying local liquor, *lambanog*. Cooking meats and vegetables with coconut milk makes for hearty *guinatan*, dishes straight from the Malay side of the Filipino cuisine. In the southern Tagalog region and among the underside provinces of Bicol, Filipinos light up their guinatan dishes with fiery chilies – a practice uncharacteristic of their fellow chefs working in other regions.

Coconut generally graces the Philippine table on gentler levels: in delicate salads made from hearts of palm, *ubod*; in fresh *buko*, the young nut's sweet water; in the thick dessert jam called *macapuno*; in the

National fare: There are probably just a handful of "national" dishes on the archipelago's common menu – fiesta fare, known and celebrated across the country's isles and including *adobo, dinuguan, pancit, lumpia,* and *lechon*. Hefty brown adobo, today often classified as the Filipino national dish, is said to be a vagrant descendant of the Spanish *adobado*, a more elaborate preparation doused in garlic and oil. The original dish, however, is whole loin of pork cured for weeks in vinegar, olive oil and spices. Adobo of the Filipino palate is generally a dark, saucy stew of chicken and pork, flavored liberally with light vinegar and soy sauce, garlic and liver bits.

popular merienda stew simply called guinatan; and as the grated flesh called *niog*, that carries off or accompanies many a Filipino sweet and cookie.

Filipino vegetables point to the northern provinces – or rather, the hardy Ilocanos themselves point to vegetables. The wildest and plainest of local leaves and greens have been turned into interesting meals by the ingenious cooks of the harsh northern territory. *Pinakbet* and *dinengdeng* are two vegetable concoctions full of *kangkong* (a leafy green), eggplant and squash, spiced up with *bagoong*, the all-Filipino specialty sauce made from fish fermented in brine.

Other local stews, weighed down with heavy Hispanic notions of meat-and-vegetable meals, are *pochero, kari-kari* and *paella*. The classic pochero consists of beef and pork chunks flavored with spicy Bilbao sausages and escorted by the whole local vegetable garden. Kari-kari is ox tail and tripe, plus the retinue of greenery, all coated in a thick peanut broth, or else served with *bagoong*, an anchovy-based sauce. Paella is good old Andalusian paella, with the accent placed on basic chicken, pork and shrimps atop tomato-colored rice.

Oily fish are also made into adobo, as are beef and chicken. In some regions a variation of adobo is based on coconut milk sauce. This is known as *adobo sa gata*. In a country as diverse as the Philippines, even the national dish has variations. Manila adobo, for example, is a dark, saucy dish, thickened with flour and enriched with soy sauce. A dry adobo is when the pork is fried crisp, and yet another type of adobo comes with a sauce of baby shrimp.

Lechon: All grand celebrations in the Philippines – family reunions, *despedida* parties, anniversaries, homecomings, graduations – must have lechon, or whole roast pig. It is perhaps the definitive social or festive icon.

Served full-form, with crisp brown skin and generally with a bright red apple stuffed

in the mouth, this is the centerpiece of any fiesta or family celebration – the juicy treat of the lechon, basted on a turning spit for hours before the celebration. The usual way is to have a fairly large-sized pig carved by everyone. Lavish party-givers can serve a whole suckling pig per table of six.

Many a befuddled foreigner, as guest of honor, has found herself led to the whole roast pig and invited to take the first serving.

Left, street vendors in Manila's Intramuros, like everywhere, offer economical meals. **Above**, sidewalk vendor sells popular snacks: pancit noodles, sandwiches and peanuts.

Filipino tradition requires the guest to approach the pig armed with not even a knife, fork or other weapon. The first pinch must be taken with the fingers. The secret to a graceful performance is to know the most vulnerable spot of the animal.

There are two such spots: one around the ears and the other near the tail. As the guest pulls off a ear of the roast, the skin comes off, morsel by morsel. The rest of the party then take turns at helping themselves to the crisp skin. With the roast completely removed of its skin, the carver slices the juicy flesh.

Dessert: The provinces of Pampanga and Bulacan are known for their exquisite concoctions from the ubiquitous rice flour, sugar and coconut. Filipino snacks come in pinwheels, puffs and diamond cuts of *puto bumbong, malagkit, bibingka,* and *puto cuchinta.* Alongside the native cakes remains one Spanish handover – *leche flan*, the popular sweet egg custard.

Puddings are generally made with coconut rice or coconut milk. Among the most famous is *bibingka*, which consists of ground rice, sugar and coconut milk, baked in a clay oven and topped with fresh, salted duck eggs. *Guinatan* is a cocoa pudding, served with lashings of coconut cream. Ice creams are made in several fruit flavors, including tropical flavors such as *nangka* (jackfruit), *ube* and mango, as well as the more usual vanilla, chocolate and strawberry.

The Philippines is a fruitful land, a year-round paradise laden with seasonal temptations: mangoes, papayas, bananas of a dozen varieties, chicos, guavas, rambutans, durians, watermelon, jackfruit, duhat, lanzones. And what doesn't come along in the fresh might come colorfully stacked under shaved ice – in that scrumptious Filipino institution called *halo-halo*, literally mix-mix, distilling the essence of Filipino food in its joyous slush-and-synthesis.

Establishments: Filipino cuisine has recently come into its own in the public culinary scene, particularly in two charming fashions: first in the *turo-turo* eatery – or the modern version of the fast-food center – where one "point-points" to preferences in a wide and ready-to-eat smorgasbord.

Then, there is the *kamayan* restaurant just upcoming, where diners go strictly local, quite simply, and very cheap... Eating with the hands off a banana leaf.

Just as the Filipino may have a Spanish name, a distinctly Asian face and an American vocabulary, so Filipino art reflects the cultural accumulation of the country's people over the centuries.

Dance: A young woman moves slowly and confidently with a regal air, her head held high. She carries two large gilded fans. The opulence of her much-adorned and exquisite dress indicates that she is wealthy and privileged. She approaches attendants carrying bamboo poles and begins to dance between

Traditional dance written and choreographed by Filipinos can also be seen in Manila, performed by lithe and talented dancer-interpreters. The most popular companies are Ballet Philippines, Ramon Obusan Dance Company and Seasonal Ballet Company. The best-known classical ballerina is Lisa Macuja, who made her name with the Kirov Ballet in Russia.

Music: Over the past decades, the local music scene has become quite sophisticated, with a local Filipino twist. European and

the moving poles with grace and tranquility. The poles, crossed together on the floor, beat faster and louder, clacking furiously between her nimble feet as she moves with serene grace and ease, never changing expression.

This dance is the Muslim *singkil*. It is a showpiece number often performed by professional folk dancers, and one such group, called the Bayanihan (literally, working together), has become an internationally-known troupe that aims to preserve and popularize traditional Filipino dance forms. Polished and theatrical, the Bayanihan functions as a dancing promotional group for the Philippines around the world.

American pop tunes are translated into Pilipino (Tagalog) or often sung in *Taglish* (a mixture of Tagalog and English). As in many of Asia's developing countries, local pop stars are society's most popular role models.

One of the music culture's most popular queens was Nora Aunor, who started as a warbler peddling soft drinks to stopover passengers at the whistle-stop train station of Iriga, Albay, in Bicol. However, from the moment the little 14-year-old hit Manila on *Tawag ng Tanghalan*, the country's most popular amateur contest, she was on her way to becoming the 1960s' biggest success story, with a TV show and movie production company of her own. (In this music-loving country, future minstrels of Asia present their efforts at stardom on television programs such as *Eat Bulaga* and *Sang Linggo Napo Sila*. Amateur competitions abound.)

Other big names on the local music scene have included Ryan Cayabyab, a composer, music arranger and director, pianist, and vocalist. Bobby Enriquez – The Wildman – is the undisputed king of Filipino jazz.

Folk music is best sampled at Malate's Hobbit House on A. Mabini Street, where

monic Orchestra, the Choral Ensemble, the Philippine Madrigal Singers.

Ethnic music, a stark contrast to Western musical heritage, is the music of indigenous and Islamic religions. Instruments include Muslim gongs (*ku-lintang*); *git-git*, or fiddles using human hair for strings that are played by Mangyans and Negritos; and *kubing*, or the Jew's harp.

Theater: There's much to say, or rather to see, as far as theater goes in the Philippines. Truly another Western tradition, the stage

popular Freddie Aguilar, one of the few internationally-known Filipino singers, has regularly performed over the years. In the early 1980s, his *Bayan Ko* (My Country) was the anthem of the anti-Marcos movement in the 1980s.

More traditional music proliferates as well. Modern composers produce work that includes marches, suites, chamber music, chorales and sonatas. Best-known performers of classical music are the Philippine Philhar-

Left, concerts for the public are popular in Manila's Rizal Park. **Above**, noted artist Arturo Luz at his Makati home.

play was eagerly assimilated by Filipinos, first in Spanish-influenced passion plays. These plays inevitably became street theater under the broader term of fiesta. Indeed, the fiesta is the ultimate street theater, complete with drama, religious passion and revelous audience participation.

Filipino theater is generally coupled with dance and music. While an ethnic, spoken drama may stand wanting, a rich layer of performing arts in dance and music still exists. Within the traditional fiesta, the comedy or *moromoro* is often performed. This folksy story always told of the historical conflict between Christians and nonbeliev-

ce. In cosmopolitan ... musical comedy form ...om the Italian opera, ... revival.

...ners, Filipinos hold the ...ry college or university ...nd Western drama flourished ...ry playwrights write in Filipino ... duce fiery comedies and dramas. Undoubtedly, the biggest Filipino name to date in theater is the actress and singer Lea Salonga, who became an international star for her captivating performance as Kim in the musical *Miss Saigon*.

Cinema: Filipinos saw their first moving pictures in Manila in 1904. For the most part, they were European films with Spanish subtitles. The first Filipino-made film, in 1919, was about a virtuous country girl, and it set the tone of the art for the next 30 years. Filipino cinema was not particularly distinguished by anything but a love of sentimentality and overacting.

In the past two decades, films have digressed to flesh-and-blood epics, and the usual action genre, but more recently, Filipino cinema has come into its own.

For the politically aware, film director Lino Brocka is possibly the Philippines' most interesting cinema personality. His first non-commercial film, *Tinimbang Ka Ngunit Kulang* (You Were Weighed and Found Wanting), a story of a small town's outcasts seen through a young man's eyes, drew rave reviews and shook the local movie industry. Since then he has made several films with a political message, including *Bayan Ko* (My Country), an anti-Marcos film, and more recently, *Fight for Us*, a story of a former priest and political detainee whose post-EDSA revolution optimism fades as he witnesses the escalating violence of vigilante groups. A new arrival on the cinema scene, also with a sociopolitical message, is Briccio Santos, whose film *Damortis* criticizes the Catholic Church.

Literature: Before the arrival of the Spanish, the indigenous people had a distinct oral tradition that included creation myths, native legends and folk tales. Proto-historic peoples even used a syllabic writing system.

The first printed book in the archipelago, *Doctrina Christiana*, appeared in the 16th century, in Spanish. For almost 300 years in the archipelago, the printed word was mostly Spanish, and typically related to religious themes, except for a few works in the indigenous Tagalog language.

Contemporary Filipino literature is written in Pilipino and English, the former becoming increasingly popular as the search for national identity becomes more distinct. National hero Jose Rizal set the standard for prose and poetry with his pre-revolutionary *Noli Me Tangere* and *El Filibusterismo*.

After 1930, there was little Filipino writing in Spanish because of the widespread use of English, and also the increasing use of Tagalog as a medium of literary expression. During the period of American rule, the short story became an increasingly popular form among writers.

In his seventies, Nick Joaquin became the lion of literary gatherings in Manila. An essayist, poet, playwright, short story-writer and novelist, he has spanned the worlds of both *belle lettres* and journalism in the country over the past several decades.

On Joaquin's literary heels stands writer F. Sionil Jose, who not only owns the Solidaridad Bookshop, in Manila on Padre Faura Street, but who also has written short stories and novels, and an epic series of novels about the people of the land, both in Manila and in the countryside. Jose Garcia Villa, named a National Artist and often called the country's greatest, if most eccentric poet, calls himself "Doveglion" – a contraction of dove, eagle and lion.

Painting and sculpture: As early as 1821, a Filipino Academy of Painting was established. Throughout the 19th century, painting in the Philippines was heavily influenced by Spanish trends. Juan Luna and Felix Resureccion Hidalgo reached international fame when they won prizes at the Madrid Exposition of 1884. Luna painted epics and scenes of social significance, while Hidalgo was best known for his neo-Impressionist scenics. Contemporary Filipino artists have transcended the governmental schools of social realism to produce a body of provocative expression. Some of the more prominent artists are Arturo Luz, Vicente Manansala, Jose Joya Jr. and Carlos Francisco.

Roberto Feleo is a name to watch. In his work, executed in wood and glass cut into human and plant shapes, runs the theme of the indigenous confronted with aggressive Western technology.

78 Paquito starred in this film & went to the Cannes Film Festival to show it.

JEEPNEYS

They catch the eye long before a traveler makes the conscious decision to engage in the local lifestyle – public transport the likes of which you've never seen before, and certainly nothing as decorously gaudy.

The jeepney is in a class by itself, by right of dementia say some. Take one army surplus jeep, strip it down to the essentials, lengthen it considerably, deck it out with developmental accessories, embellish with lights as one would a Christmas tree, daub the sides with splashes of macho mythology, add a tassel here, a chrome fender there, plant a nickel stallion on the hood, surround that with non-functional antennas, festoon those with plastic steamers, paste a portrait of the Virgin Mary on the dashboard, hang a *sampaguita* flower garland on the rearview mirror. The formula, like most simple ones, lacks a convenient conclusion.

But this is exactly what Filipinos have done, and one assumes they've never stopped being amused by their creations. Possibly swept away by the great crest of emotion following their liberation from the Japanese in 1945, they whooped it up by converting the jeeps left by the American forces into their own image.

Nowadays manufactured from scratch in special factories, the jeepney is a piece of mobile art, or environmental art, if you please. Curiously enough, it has become a serviceable mass transport system, although they are a significant factor in Manila's traffic mess with their anarchistic stopping without logic or system.

The backseat passengers get in through the open rear end, styled into appropriate curves with a glistening series of handrails, lateral supports and hooks for the kind of carry-alls one would take to market. When a backseat passenger calls for a stop, the driver swivels around to reach out for the fare with his right hand, sometimes keeping his left on the wheel. The fare is relayed to him if it comes from way in back, and everyone on that lightened row then slides closer to the rear. Thus they get nearer the escape hatch, while ensuring a difficult passage through the gamut of knees for any incoming passenger.

Choicest seat: It isn't a futile exercise to read passengers' personalities by their choice of space in an empty jeepney. Most prefer to sit by the open rear so that they may slouch in comfort against the corner padding or gaze out at the miserable traffic in their wake. Those unfamiliar with their destination prefer to stay close to the driver. They crouch low and look warily ahead through the windshield – a futile exercise since the glass is often covered by a variety of aphorisms and campy stickers. Shrill, nervy types

also stay here so that they can admonish the driver for excessively wild maneuvers. Then there are the usual middle-roaders who prefer the warmth and safety of being trapped between fellow passengers, especially if they're of the opposite sex. (At least men think this way.)

The choicest seat is up front, by the open side entrance. This is the true shotgun position; from here, one revels in the occasional hair-raising ride while keeping the option of leaping out in desperation at a moment's notice.

This prime space – handmaiden to the wind – is fought for. The stakes are high, for the loser is likely to languish in the worst seat, which is beside the driver. The gear stick stabs into his thigh, the fare whizzes by the ear, the dried sampaguita garland sways across the face. He will glare at the Virgin Mary and pray that the bully

beside him gets off soon, so that he can try to bluff the next pretender that comes along by saying he's getting out shortly. If the Virgin fails to hear him through the stereo blare of Dire Straits, he has no choice but to scan the cute graffiti before him: *A woman without a lover is like a jeepney without a driver*, or *Don't do unto others what you can do for today*.

The driver, front row left, enjoys a special privilege. Protecting his open side is the spare tire, a curve of rubber over which he drapes his left arm in order to look in control.

Driving in Manila is an immense responsibility and the driver knows it. Daily he makes a pact with daring-do, crossing himself with one hand and trusting the other to steer a country's souped-up psyche.

Political stability and major economic reforms under the administration of President Fidel Ramos have triggered a remarkable economic turnaround for the Philippines. Anchored by Ramos's idea of "Philippines 2000", which aims to transform the country into a newly industrialized one by the turn of the century, the economy has posted steady growth since 1992.

Although considerably below the norm amongst Asia's so-called tiger economies, the economic growth of the Philippines in the past few years has given credence to Ramos's description of the Philippines as a "tiger cub in training".

After posting an unimpressive average growth rate of two percent in 1992 and 1993 - primarily due to the debilitating effects of recurring power outages – the gross national product rose by over 5 percent in 1994 and 1995, and is expected to reach 7 percent in 1996 and 8 percent in 1997.

Decades-old protectionism and state intervention have finally given way to economic liberalization and industry deregulation during the past three years. Foreign-owned companies are now welcome in most areas of the economy, including such key sectors as telecommunications, banking and insurance. Liberal terms under the government's build-operate-and-transfer scheme have attracted foreign investors to infrastructure development, which was a major factor behind the resolution of Manila's earlier electrical brownouts. The telephone industry, which used to be a private monopoly, was opened to new players. With the privatization of major state-owned companies now almost complete, plans for the next wave of privatization include the sale of public utilities and some basic social services. Among the reforms that are expected to be in place by 1997 include the full deregulation of the petroleum industry and a major overhaul of the tax system.

The Philippines's economy has traditional strengths and advantages – strategic location in the heart of the world's fastest-growing

Preceding pages: Philippine Stock Exchange. Left, Makati mall. Right, Jaime Zobel de Ayala.

region; abundant natural resources; a working democracy; a high standard of urban living; and a highly Westernized business environment. Added to this, the Philippines has the advantage of a large pool of educated, English-speaking managers and workers.

Although much of the economic activity remains concentrated in Metro Manila, the present recovery has spawned a number of dynamic growth centers elsewhere in the archipelago. North of the capital is the success story of the Subic Bay Freeport Zone, a

former American naval base that has been successfully transformed into a commercial and industrial center. The zone offers generous investment incentives, such as a 5 percent final tax on gross income, a no-visa rule for foreign visitors, and exemption from all national and local taxes. With a new international airport, Subic has been chosen by Federal Express as its operations hub in the Asian region.

Modern industrial estates have sprouted several kilometers south of Metro Manila. These provinces are being developed into an agro-industrial corridor designed to lure away factories from the overcrowded capital. While the Philippine's constitution prohibits foreigners from owning land, a new law now allows land leases of up to 75 years. Numerous electronic and machine companies from Japan and North America have productively invested in the region.

In addition to Cebu, in the central part of the country and which has traditionally been the primary commercial center outside of Manila, major cities in the southern island of Mindanao are in an economic boom. Despite separatist problems in the island's rural areas, investments have poured into Mindanao's major cities.

Back in Manila, a property boom is underway. While property prices remain

growth in 1993 – becoming the best performer in Asia and the third-best in the world. While foreign interest has somewhat tapered off, a decline prompted by the Mexican debacle in 1994 and a bull run in the American stock market in 1995, long-term market prospects are definitely bullish.

From raw material exports consisting of agricultural and mineral products, the country has begun to diversify into higher-value manufactured goods. While agriculture employs more than 40 percent of the population and contributes 20 percent of the GNP, the top-dollar earners now include electronics, garments and textiles, metal products and processed foods. Major export markets in-

among the lowest in Asia, in both rent and capital values, prices have strongly appreciated in prime areas. Two new central business districts – one adjacent to the financial district of Makati and another in south Metro Manila – are on the drawing boards. Anticipating rising incomes and stable interest rates, real estate developers have started to shift their attention to mass-housing projects.

That the Philippines has finally regained the confidence of the international business community is best shown by the spectacular growth of the local stock market. Emerging from that of a basket case, the local exchange surprised everyone by posting a 150 percent

clude the United States, Japan, Singapore, Holland and Great Britain. However, in the past two years, trade with other Asian nations has increased significantly, particularly with Malaysia, Thailand, Indonesia and South Korea.

Unfortunately, much of the good news has been confined to bustling industrial estates and busy financial centers. Agriculture continues to be the economy's weak spot. In stark contract to the dynamism of industry, the rural sector is one of stagnation. Except with the corporate farms that are devoted to pineapples and bananas for export, modern farming methods have yet to take root. Moreover, the government's agrarian reform program has yet to make headway in the breaking up of concentrated land ownership. With the majority of farmers working as landless tenants, it's not surprising that two-thirds of poor families are found in rural areas.

The relatively high level of poverty has led some investors to underestimate the potential of the domestic market. In fact, however, there are intangibles that make for a more viable market than what the numbers suggest. One finds that urban Filipino consumers are young, highly literate, and with a Westernized lifestyle and aspirations. Doubts on the potential of such a market are easily belied by the overwhelming success of new

shopping malls, the growth of retail chains, and the proliferation of fast-food outlets.

Visitors who have been to overcrowded shopping malls in Metro Manila and Cebu invariably wonder where people's purchasing power comes from, given official statistics on poverty and unemployment. The answer to these questions lies in the fact that such numbers miss two important facets of the Philippines's economy: the informal economy and the number of Filipinos working overseas. Unlike in more developed

Left, the Philippines Stock Exchange is one of the world's most active. **Above**, Makati at night.

economies, a lot of business activity in the Philippines remains outside the scope of government monitoring – small businesses, direct-selling activities by people with other regular jobs, and personal services. Various estimates on the size of the informal sector range from a low of 25 percent to a high of 40 percent of the gross national product. With easily over a million Filipinos living or working abroad, dollar remittances have been a significant economic boost to the country's economy. From just a little over US$1 billion in 1990, dollar remittances are now US$5 billion annually, a trend that is expected to be sustained in the coming years.

Over the long term, the size of the domestic market should become an almost irrelevant issue. In the next five years, per-capita income is projected to double to almost US$2,000, a development that should translate into substantially higher discretionary spending. More importantly, the coming years will see the seven ASEAN member nations move closer to their goal of establishing a free-trade area in the region. Under the ASEAN preferential tariff scheme, member countries will progressively reduce tariff rates for member-produced products until a free-trade area is realized. A company operating in the Philippines will thus have access to a huge potential market.

As President Ramos approaches the end of his term in 1998, the business community has started to focus its attention to the question of succession. With the country's history of political instability and policy inconsistency, their primary concern is whether or not the policies on economic liberalization laid down by Ramos will be sustained.

At this point, the emerging consensus among analysts gives a favorable answer. Ten years after the overthrow of Ferdinand Marcos, the country's democratic institutions are now firmly in place. The successful holding of the 1992 elections, and the midterm elections in 1995, underscore the vibrancy of a maturing democracy, and this should serve as an assurance for a smooth transition in 1998. Looking at the list of possible presidential contenders, practically all are expected to continue the same set of free-market policies. Moreover, the nation's commitments under various trade agreements will ensure further opening of the economy. There is no choice, really.

Unexpectedly for the outsider, basketball is the national passion of the Philippines. Indeed, inch for inch, Filipinos are among the best basketball players in the world, and the sport is marked by a year-round spate of amateur competitions, school championships, provincial meets, professional tournaments and international contests.

At one time or another, nearly every Filipino male tries his hand at the game, reveling in showy creativity, then dribbling the ball and scrambling to shoot a basket. Simplicity

of equipment lies at the root of basketball fever, and every town plaza sports a basketball court alongside the church and town hall. From an early age, boys go through their paces using a makeshift basket.

Like his professional counterpart, the backstreet Filipino basketball player loves theater. He does not just pass the ball, he leaps to lofty heights before executing a behind-the-back feed that, for want of accuracy, ensures a torrid scramble. If he lays emphasis on a feint, it's a sterling performance. The longer he holds the ball, the more chance of stealing the limelight. Not always effective basketball to be sure, but a feast for the spirit.

Jai alai: Brought to the Philippines over a century ago from the Basque area of Spain, *jai alai* is believed to have been invented by Mayan Indians and imported into Spain by returning colonists. Even in distant Manila, many of the *pelotaris* (players) are still Basques. They are all fairly young men in their early 20s or 30s and incredibly fit because of playing the strenuous game several nights a week.

Vying with basketball and cockfighting as the most popular national sport, jai alai is a version of the Spanish handball (*pelota*) played between pairs of players. The basic idea is that the server, armed with a *cesta* (wicker basket) laced tightly to the right hand, must hurl the hard-rubber ball against the granite wall and it must land back in what is called fair territory. The opponent must in one motion catch and hurl the ball once more. Points are scored when a player fails to return a service – either by missing the ball entirely or by mistakenly throwing it into the wrong zone.

What makes the game so thrilling is the shattering speed at which the ball is thrown and returned. The ball becomes almost a deadly missile, traveling at speeds of up to 240 kilometers an hour (150 mph) and why the players now wear helmets. The match is a remarkable and exciting spectacle. Players wear traditional colored shirts and leap around the court with astonishing agility, sometimes clambering up the wire netting separating *fronton* (court) from the spectators in order to return a difficult ball.

The granite blocks of the former Manila fronton on Taft Avenue were imported from Shanghai, where the stadium had been dismantled by the Chinese government as being part of the decadent past. Its inauguration in 1940 by President Manuel Quezon was billed as the most elaborate sporting and social event in the history of Manila.

Today, the games begin every afternoon. There are 14 games each session with a 20-minute break between each game. There is no admission fee to the fronton gallery, so it is jammed every night with both serious aficionados and tourists on a four-hour fronton-and-dinner tour. Spectators are noisy, partisan and totally involved, as betting is both legal and frantic.

Also, because it is a spectator sport, jai alai rouses strong feelings, and cries of *Mata! Mata!* (Kill! Kill!) are shouted constantly at the players as they charge to and fro trying to outwit their rivals with mighty throws and cunning placements. On the wall of the court is a stern warning in Spanish, *El fallo del juez es inapelado*, or the referee's judgment is final, but the crowd hoots, boos, hisses, stamps feet and curses if they disagree with a close decision. Manila's off-course jai alai betting is big business, and it has been estimated that more than half a million bets are placed daily, involving 20 per cent of the capital's population.

Cockfighting: Banned in most countries, the sport of kings in the Philippines is cockfighting, but it is not for the squeamish. No self-respecting town in the Philippines, however, will do without a cock pit (*sabungan*), and every Sunday or public holiday the galleries around the central pits are packed with raucous and excited crowds seated in tiers reaching to the roof.

The pre-fight shouting is directed at the bookmakers (*kristo*), who are minor attractions in themselves because of their uncanny ability to absorb all the bets and odds without writing anything down to the shouted bets, with fingers raised high in a juggling mime of the odds and bets. Thousands of pesos change hands at each fight – and there are many fights per day.

Combat proper begins after the arbiter has unsheathed the razor-sharp spur attached to both cocks' right legs and allowed each combatant a sharp peck at the other's neck. Thus teased and aroused into a fighting mood, the cocks are let loose from opposite ends of the arena, and the dance of death begins. With hackles up, the duelists fix each other in a chilly stare and in the next instance lunge at each other, their talons taut with intent to destroy. In mid-air, the combatants do a swift combination of pecking, clawing and stabbing with their miniature scimitars. The loser

Left, *jai alai* is a game of shattering speed. **Right**, a fighting cock, yet intact.

scurries to one end of the arena, where it crumples into a heap. The game is over, and the betters are ready for the next match.

Martial arts: Most visitors to the Philippines have heard of or seen demonstrations of karate, kung-fu or other forms of Asian martial arts, but few people anywhere have heard of, and fewer have seen, *arnis de mano*, Filipino stick fighting. The sport is so old that it was first banned by the conquering Spanish. The origin of arnis was the defense of the traveler from robbers. The art is played

with a one-meter-long hardwood stick, or *tungkod*. Opponents armed with two tungkods swing and parry at each other. Out of the movements of arnis evolved *eskrina*, a martial art that substituted the wooden sticks of arnis for bladed weapons.

The decline of these practices came as a result as their ineffectiveness against Spanish guns and cannons. Having no more validity for battle, arnis and eskrina became demonstration sports. More complicated movements characteristic of arnis were later added in an approximation of dance and mere spectacle. Arnis is played regularly by aficionados in Manila as well as around the islands.

Demonstrations are occasionally held at Manila's Nayong Pilipino.

Chess: No room for subtle transition here, leaping wildly – in the spirit of place – from the raucous arena of stickfighting to the clinical quietude of a chess hall. All eyes are on a good-looking man studying the pieces before him with calculated aplomb. He is Eugene Torre, Philippine champion and Asia's first world-class grandmaster. Since 1973, Torre represented Asia in high-rating tournaments, in the process winning over some of the world's chess superstars. For the legion of chess fanatics in the country, Torre's ascendancy can only confirm the remarkable national affinity for the game.

serious book study and single-mindedness to emerge national champion at age 18.

It is safe to say, however, that somewhere out there, astride a *carabao* perhaps, some 10-year-old has already set his sights on Torre's crown. If he is disciplined enough to attract the necessary backing, he will certainly make it. It's as good an assumption as saying that in these romance-happy isles, chess has found a more-then-willing mate.

Horseracing: The race track of the Philippine capital is on Felix Huertas Street, in the district of Santa Cruz. It is known to the locals as San Lazaro. In the cool of the early morning, the horses come prancing across the sands from the nearby stables. The jock-

Since the postwar period, Filipino chess players have proven to be some of Asia's best representatives. But not until Torre (whose name appropriately means "rook") became grandmaster did there seem enough justification for the thousands of chess aficionados battling in clubs, corner stores, barber shops and under mango trees. The traditional approach has been similar to that in basketball; tactical genius is given a premium in favor of safe solid strategy. The idea has been to attack, and to create romantic situations of cut-and-thrust in the manner of Mikhail Tahl's precarious but inventive games. Beneath this overlay, Torre inserted

eys are sitting high-kneed but relaxed and loose in the lightweight English saddles.

Horseracing in the Philippines has come quite a long way from the 1860s, when fashionable races organized by the Manila Jockey Club were held only twice a year at the Hippodrome. At that time, fans arrived in flamboyant carriages, the women in flowing skirts with parasols and the men with buttoned coats and Ascot ties. After the races, the gentlemen and their ladies would repair to a ball held at the same site.

Today, jockeys in colorful silks mount thoroughbred horses bred from imported stock. There are electronic totalizers, computers and photo-finish cameras, and air-conditioned booths with push-buttons that summon club personnel to place bets on the horses, plus cocktail lounges and bars. Racing in Manila is undeniably big business.

At the start of the day's races, fans gather in the compound fronting the grandstand beside the paddock. The small but spunky Philippine ponies come into the paddock, breathing gently, some skittish, kicking and throwing their heads in the air, ears laid back, eyes rolling and tugging at the reins held by trainers who talk soothingly, reassuring and calming the animals.

It is like a race track scene that one might find anywhere in the world. And yet, apart

The track on Felix Huertas Street is a near-perfect oval – its immensity telescoped by the tricky light of the early morning. It is six furlongs (1,300 meters) around the track, which is made of sea sand over a soft rock and charcoal base. Encircling the outer track are dozens of stables, on top of which perch stable lads all eagerly monitoring the progress of their charges.

As the horses come down from the stables, their hooves kick up the fine dust-like sand – it hangs around them, softening the shining beauty of their coats as if one is looking at them through gossamer. Then the jockeys are weighed complete with whips and saddles. Everything is ready for the start.

from the similarities, it is unique. A Philippine race track is different from anything that horseracing enthusiasts will have seen in Europe or America. There is no green of the turf (the track is of sand), no ridiculous hats, elaborate dresses, checkered suits or the paraphernalia that has grown alongside a sport elsewhere. Horseracing in the Philippines is a sport still in its purest form, something to see and enjoy for anyone who loves to see superb animals in motion.

Left, *arnis* **or Filipino stick fighting, and street chess, Mabini Street.** Above, **horseracing, San Lazaro, and Manila polo.**

There is some fine, honest racing around San Lazaro, the horses running smoothly and with a dull thunder on the packed sand track. You can see the muscles smoothly moving beneath the soft shine of their coats, moving magnificently, stretching out, heads forward, and tails high. As the race draws to a close, the excited crowd breaks into a loud cheer, and lucky, even more excited, bettors rush off to collect their winnings.

While the Gran Copa Cup is the main event of the racing year, other highlights at San Lazaro are the Founders Cup, the Presidential Cup and the National Grand Derby. Acknowledged as the Philippine version of the English Derby race held at Epsom Downs, the National Grand Derby has become one of the most colorful spectacle of local racing.

Polo: There is no denying that polo remains elitist even in Manila. Golf and other once-upmarket sports may have passed on to more everyday usage. But with polo, you need money, and lots of it. Good polo ponies can cost upwards to $50,000 plus maintenance, training and veterinary care of the horse, not forgetting saddles, mallets, balls, riding habits, transportation, tips – six ponies are needed to play a full match.

Polo is played by two opposing teams of four players equipped with long-handled mallets. Points are scored when a wooden

ball is hit through the opponent's goal, not unlike "hockey on horseback". Each match consists of six periods known as chukkers (from the Indian word *chukka*, for one full turn of a wheel), lasting seven minutes each. Play is continuous except for short intervals after each chukka, when players change horses. In Manila, only about 12 players are fully mounted. In polo jargon, it means having six horses at disposal, one per chukka.

The Manila polo season opens at the end of the rainy season and continues until the rains start again. At regular meetings, major tournaments are scheduled on traditional dates and open slots are sponsored by individual groups. Esteemed old tourneys like the Cameron Forbes Cup and the Past President's Cup are held on 24 January and 7 February, respectively.

It was not surprising that Manila Polo Club, founded in 1909 by Governor Forbes, drew its membership from the capital's *creme de la creme*. The history of the club mirrors American presence in the archipelago until Pearl Harbor. World War II changed the club's character and composition from largely American (top echelon civil government and military officers, and later corporate chiefs) through a cosmopolitan grouping to predominant Filipino gentry.

In pre-war Manila, the polo club, headed by the American governor-general, then the American high commissioner and, later, the American ambassador, was the bastion of the American community. The dressiest parties focused on American holidays such as the Fourth of July, Washington's Birthday, Halloween and Thanksgiving. (So engrossed were the club's members with concerns like ensuring an adequate supply of imported fodder for the ponies and keeping the swimming pool water crystal-clear that they almost failed to notice external events.)

During World War II, the club was demolished by the Japanese and its members were scattered by the winds of war. A temporary club, opened in Parañaque in 1946 with a wider membership, at last included Filipinos. The once-segregated club was now considered incompatible with postwar nationalistic sentiments.

In 1950, the club relocated to Forbes Park, Manila's version of Beverly Hills, in Makati. Then, much of Forbes Park was still countryside. Riders spent many carefree hours exploring natural bridle paths as far as the lakeshore towns of Laguna de Bay. Today, the club stands on the gentlest swell of ground: a long slung building at the end of a driveway flanked by flame trees off McKinley Road. On the polo ground, the maintenance men are busily working while at the old bull rings, instructors teach the rudiments of riding. So vast and rolling are the club's premises that it's hard to believe all this lies in the heart of uptown Makati, Manila's business district and home to the Philippines' corporate world.

Left, golfer at Calatagan. **Right**, free-spirited baseball, introduced by the Americans.

Philippine Archipelago

100 km / 62 miles

South China Sea

Philippine Sea

Luzon Sea

LUZON

BABUYAN I.
CALAYAN I.
DALUPIRI I.
BABUYAN ISLANDS
FUGA I.
CAMIGUIN I.

Abulug
Laoag
Tuguegarao
Ilagan
Banaue
Santiago
San Fernando
Bayombong
Baguio
Dagupan
San Carlos
San Jose
Tarlac
Cabanatuan
Aneles
Olongapo
MANILA
POLLILO ISLANDS
Mariveles
Calamba
Nasugbu
Daet
Batangas
Lucena
S. Pedro
Lopez
Naga
Pili
CATANDUANES
Calapan
Boac
Virac
Mamburao
Naujan
MARINDUQUE IS.
Mt. Mayon
Pinamelayan
Legazpi
Sorsogon

MINDORO

San Jose

BUSUANGA ISLAND

Coron

CULION ISLAND

CUYO ISLANDS

El Nido
Taytay

DUMARAN I.

Kalibo
Roxas

Catarman
Laoong

SAMAR

Calbayog
Catbalogan
Borongan

MASBATE

Daanbantayan
Tacloban

PANAY

Passi
Sagay
San Jose
Iloilo City
Bacolod

CEBU

Ormoc
LEYTE
Baybay

Danao

PALAWAN

Bahell
Puerto Princesa

Palawan Passage

Quezon
Narra

Brooke's Point

BALABAC ISLAND

P. BANGGI
P. MALAWALI
P. JAMBONGAN

Kabankalan

NEGROS

Carcar
Talibon
Argao

Cebu City

BOHOL

Maasin
Surigao

Sta. Catalina
Damaguete

Bohol Sea

Butuan
Tandag
Gingoog
Bayugan
Prosperidad

PHILIPPINES

Laut Sulu

Dapitan
Dipolog

Cagayan de Oro

Sindangan

Oroquieta
Ozamiz

Iligan
Marawi

Malay Balay

Bislig

Pagadian

MINDANAO

Parang

Tagum

Sandakan

MALAYSIA

BORNEO

PILAS GROUP

Zamboanga City

Isabela
Lamitan

BASILAN I.

Moro Gulf

Cotabato City
Pikit

Davao City

Sta. Cruz
Digos

Mati

PANGUTARAN GROUP

Jolo

TAPIANTANA GROUP

Tacurong
Koronadal

Malita

SAMALERS GROUP

JOLO GROUP

General Santos

TAPUL GROUP

Glan

TAWITAWI ISLAND

SIBUTU ISLAND

Celebes Sea

100

PLACES

It's a mood that begins with a flight attendant's smile the moment one boards a Manila-bound flight – a prelude of friendly encounters to come. Call it warmth, call it friendliness, or wrap it up in other clichés, but there is no disguising the sincerity of the much-repeated *mabuhay,* or welcome.

Manila, the in-your-face capital of the archipelago's 7,000-plus islands, is the usual starting point for most journeys in the Philippines. The traveler leaving Europe or North America for the first time finds the city immensely intimidating in its chaos and frantic energy. Worry not, for aside from the predictable scam artists and the like, it is a city with merit for the traveler. It is an old city, with a history that lingers in its architecture: Malacañang Palace, the old walls and inner city of Intramuros, the statues and boulevards.

Beyond Manila, within a day or travel of travel, are active volcanoes like Taal, beach resorts like Cavite, mountainside cult groups on Banahaw, and rain-forest river rapids at Pagsanjan.

Manila is on the southern end of Luzon, the largest island and on the northern end of the archipelago. Northward out of Manila leads into the lofty highlands of Baguio and beyond, or along the western coast of Ilocos. This is the land of cascading rice terraces, so immense that no point on ground can take them in at one time.

South of Luzon are the Outlying Islands and the Visayas, a gathering of variously-shaped islands that can keep travelers engaged for years. Central to the Visayas is the island, and city, of Cebu. This is not only the gateway to resorts and coral reefs, it is an entrepreneurial city, noted within and outside the Philippines as the nation's place to do efficient business. (Too, it's noted for guitars.)

The Palawan archipelago, on the southwestern fringes of the Visayas, is made up of some 1,700 islands, most of them large enough for a single village, if that. Palawan is best known for its exotic wildlife, including such rare species as great sea turtles, peacock pheasants, purple herons, wild parrots and scaly anteaters. Too, it has a couple of resorts in stunning locations that leave one with the memory of being at the end of the explored earth.

Less than two hours by air from Manila is the deep south of the archipelago, where there are sunny shores and cool mountains on Mindanao, and a gathering of cultures that is unique from the northern islands, including the various Muslim groups and the Badjao sea gypsies, who live their lives literally on the water. Even further south, for the most part out of bounds to the rambling traveler, are the Sulu islands, known for fiercely-independent people, smuggling and pirates.

Preceding pages: on the road; Makati disco; rural road; Mindanao village.

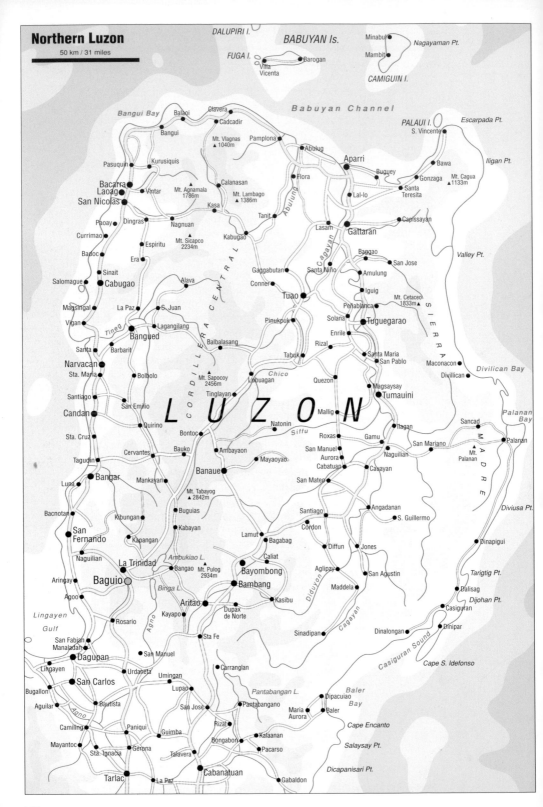

Northern Luzon

50 km / 31 miles

DALUPIRI I.

BABUYAN Is.

Minabul
Nagayaman Pt.

FUGA I.

Mambit

Villa
Vicenta
Barogan

CAMIGUIN I.

Babuyan Channel

PALAUI I.
Escarpada Pt.
S. Vincente
Iligan Pt.

Bangui Bay
Balaoi
Claveria

Cadcadir
Bangui

Pasuquin
Kurusiquis

Mt. Vlagnas
▲ 1040m

Pamplona
Abulug

Aparri
Buguey
Bawa
Gonzaga
Mt. Cagua
▲ 1133m

Santa
Teresita

Bacarra
Laoag
San Nicolas

Vintar

Mt. Agnamala
1786m

Calanasan
Flora

Lal-lo

Mt. Lambago
1386m

Capissayan

Paoay
Dingras

Nagnuan
Kasa

Tanit

Lasam
Gattaran

Currimao
Espiritu

Mt. Sicapco
2234m
Kabugao

Baggao
San Jose

Badoc
Era

Gaggabutan
Santa Niño
Amulung

Salomague
Sinait
Cabugao

Alava

Conner

Iguig

Valley Pt.

Magsingal
La Paz
S. Juan

Pinukpuk
Tuao
Peñablanca
Mt. Cetaceo
1833m

Vigan
Lagangilang
Solana
Tuguegarao

Santa
Bangued
Balbalasang

Enrile

Narvacan
Barbarit

Tabuk
Rizal

Santa Maria
San Pablo
Maconacon
Divilican Bay

Sta. Maria
Bolbolo

Mt. Sapocoy
2456m

Chico

Quezon
Divilican

Santiago
Candon

San Emilio

Tinglayan

Lubuagan

Magsaysay
Tumauini

Palanan
Bay

Sta. Cruz

Cervantes

Bontoc

Siffu
Mallig
Ilagan
Sancad

Tagudin
Bauko

Roxas
Gamu
San Mariano
Palanan

Bangar
Mankayan

Ambayaon
Mayaoyao

San Manuel
Aurora

Naguilian
Mt.
Palanan

Luna

Banaue

San Mateo
Cabatuan
Cauayan

Diviusa Pt.

Bacnotan

Buguias

Angadanan

Kibungan
Kabayan

Santiago
S. Guillermo

San
Fernando
Kapangan

Lamut
Cordon

Dinapigui

Naguilian
La Trinidad

Bagabag
Diffun
Jones

Aringay
Baguio

Ambukiao L.
Bangao
Mt. Pulog
2934m

Bayombong
Aglipay
San Agustin

Tarigtig Pt.

Agoo

Binga L.

Bambang
Maddela

Dalisag

Aritao

Kasibu
Dijohan Pt.

*Lingayen
Gulf*
Rosario

Kayapo
Dupax
de Norte

Casiguran
Dinipar

San Fabian
Manaladan
San Manuel

Sta Fe

Sinadipan
Dinalongan

Casiguran Sound
Cape S. Idefonso

Dagupan
Lingayen

Urdaneta
Umingan

Carranglan

Pantabangan L.
*Baler
Bay*

San Carlos
Bugallon

Bautista

Lupao

San Jose
Pantabangano

Maria
Aurora
Dipacuiao
Baler

Aguilar

Camiling

Paniqui
Guimba
Rizal
Kalaanan

Cape Encanto
Salaysay Pt.

Mayantoc
Sta. Ignacia
Gerona

Bongabon
Pacarso

Talavera

Tarlac
La Paz
Cabanatuan
Gabaldon

Dicapanisari Pt.

CORDILLERA CENTRAL

L U Z O N

SIERRA MADRE

Tineg

Cagayan

Abulug

Agno

Diduyon

Cagayan

102

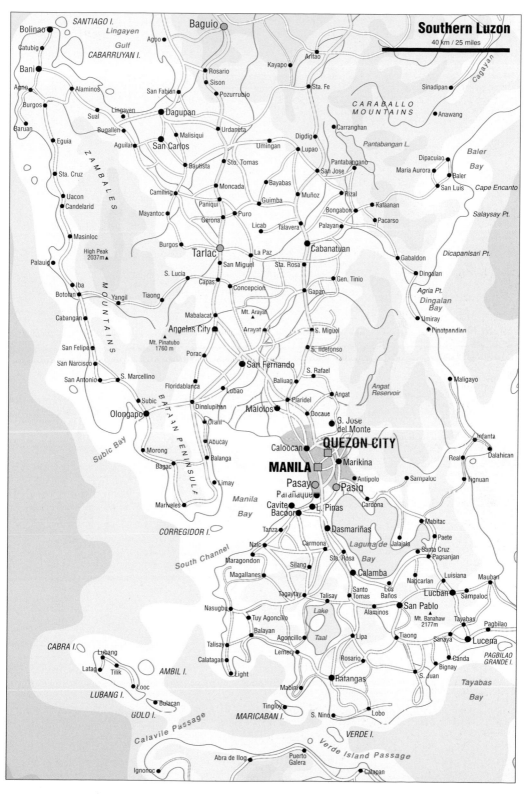

Southern Luzon

40 km / 25 miles

SANTIAGO I.
Bolinao
Catubig
Bani
Agno
Burgos
Baruan
Eguia
Sta. Cruz
Uacon
Candelario
Masinloc
Palauig
Iba
Botolan
Cabangan
San Felipe
San Narciso
San Antonio
Olongapo
Subic Bay
CORREGIDOR I.
Mariveles
Bagac
Morong
Balanga
Limay
Abucay
Orani
Dinalupihan
Subic
S. Marcellino
Floridablanca
Lubao

Lingayen
Gulf
CABARRUYAN I.
Alaminos
Lingayen
Sual
Bugallen
Aguilar
Dagupan
San Carlos
Bautista
Camiling
Mayantoc
Burgos
Tarlac
S. Lucia
Capas
Tiaong
Mabalacat
Angeles City
Mt. Pinatubo
1760 m
Porac
San Fernando

Agoo
San Fabian
Pozurrubio
Malisiqui
Urdaneta
Sto. Tomas
Moncada
Paniqui
Puro
Gerona
Licab
La Paz
San Miguel
Concepcion
Mt. Arayat
Arayat
Baliuag

Baguio
Rosario
Sison
Digdig
Umingan
Lupao
Bayabas
Guimba
Muñoz
Rizal
Bongabon
Talavera
Palayan
Cabanatuan
Sta. Rosa
Gen. Tinio
Gapan
S. Miguel
S. Ildefonso
S. Rafael

Kayapo
Aritao
Sta. Fe
Carranghan
Pantabangan L.
San Jose
Kalaanan
Pacarso
Gabaldon

CARABALLO
MOUNTAINS
Sinadipan
Anawang
Dipacuiao
Maria Aurora
San Luis
Baler
Baler
Bay
Cape Encanto
Salaysay Pt.
Dingalan
Dicapanisari Pt.
Agria Pt.
Dingalan
Bay
Umiray
Pinotpandian

ZAMBALES

MOUNTAINS

High Peak
2037m

Cagayan

BATAAN PENINSULA

Maligayo

Malolos
Docaoe
Plaridel
Angat
Angat
Reservoir
G. Jose
del Monte
Caloocan
QUEZON CITY
MANILA
Marikina
Pasay
Parañaque
Pasig
Antipolo
Sampaloc
Real
Infanta
Dalahican
Tignuan

Manila
Bay
Cavite
Bacoor
Tanza
Naic
Maragondon
Magallanes
Tagaytay
Nasugbu

South Channel

Cardona
L. Piñas
Dasmariñas
Carmona
Silang
Sta. Rosa
Santo
Tomas
Los
Baños
Talisay
Alaminos
Mabitac
Paete
Jalajala
Santa Cruz
Pagsanjan
Calamba
Nagcarlan
Luisiana
San Pablo
Mt. Banahaw
2177m
Mauban
Sampaloc
Lucban
Tayabas
Pagbilao

Laguna de
Bay

CABRA I.
Lubang
Latag
Tilik
AMBIL I.
Looc
LUBANG I.
Bulacan
GOLO I.
MARICABAN I.

Lake
Taal

Tuy Agoncillo
Balayan
Talisay
Calatagan
Light

Agoncillo
Lemery
Mabini
Tingloy
S. Niño

Batangas
Lipa
Rosario
Lobo

Tiaong
Bignay
S. Juan
Sariaya
Canda
Lucena
PAGBILAO
GRANDE I.
PAGBILAO
GRANDE I.
Tayabas
Bay

Calavite Passage
Ignonoc
Abra de Ilog
Puerto
Galera
Verde Island Passage
VERDE I.
Calapan

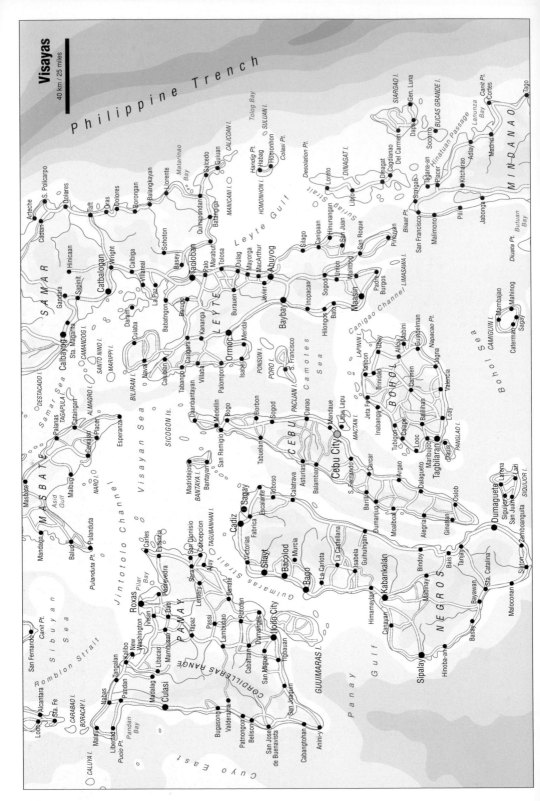

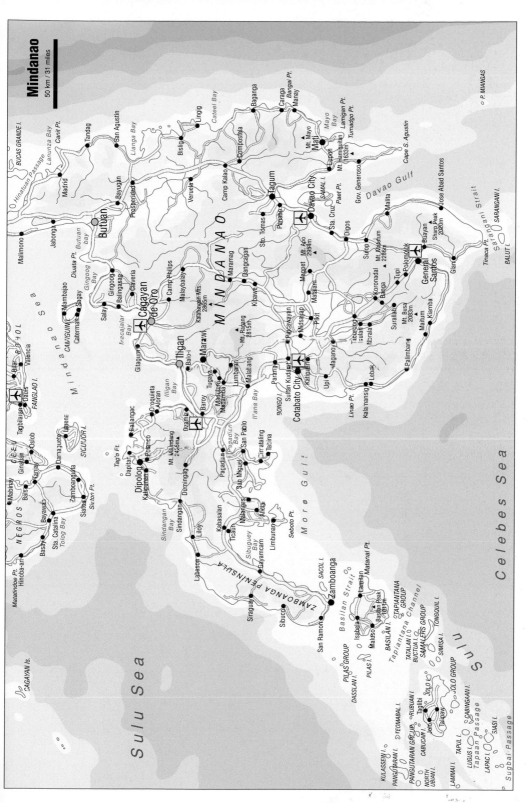

Mindanao

50 km / 31 miles

BUCAS GRANDE I.

Hinatuan Passage

Lanuza Bay

Canit Pt.

Tandag

San Agustin

Madrid

Jabonga

Malimono

Lianga Bay

Bislig

Lingig

Cateel Bay

Baganga

Carga

Bangai Pt.

Manay

Mayo

Bay

Mt. Mayo

P. MIANGAS

Compostela

Bayugan

Prosperidad

BUTUAN

Duata Pt. Butuan

bay

Gingoog Bay

Mambajao

Sagay

Gingoog

Balingasag

Salay

Gaveria

Camp Philips

Malaybalay

Maramag

Dangcagan

Camp Kalao

Verueja

Sto. Tomas

Mati

Lupon

Mt. Hamiguitan

1633m

Tumadgo Pt.

Lamigan Pt.

Cape S. Agustin

TAGUM

DAVAO CITY

SAMAL I.

Paet Pt.

Gov. Generoso

Panabo

Davao Gulf

Jose Abad Santos

Tinaca Pt.

Sarangani Strait

SARANGANI I.

BALUT I.

CAMIGUIN

Catermam

Mt. Apo

2954m

Sta. Cruz

Malita

Digos

Sulop

Sarangani Bay

Sharp Peak

2070m

Glan

CAGAYAN DE ORO

Kalatungan Mts.

2865m

M I N D A N A O

Mt. Ragang

2815m

Kihave

Kabacan

Pikit

Pigcawayan

Midsayap

Megget

Matalam

Koronadal

Banga

Tupi

Polomolok

GENERAL SANTOS

Surallah

Tboli

Mt. Busa

2083m

Maitum

Kiamba

Kalamansig

Lebak

Palimbang

Mt. Matutum

2286m

Malaybalay

Lambayong

Kabuntalan

Cotabato City

Upi

Linao Pt.

Kalamansig

Tacurong

Isulan

Iligan

Marawi

Balo-i

Tugaya

Baroy

Maranding

Matungao

Kapatagan

Malabang

Parang

Sultan Kudarat

Kalinuan

Baganian

Lumbatan

Malalang

Iligan Bay

Illana Bay

BONGO I.

Gitagum

OZAMIZ

Aloran

Clarin

Oroquieta

Fangangan

Tago Ft.

Dapitan

Dipolog

Katipunan

Dinaigan

Mt. Malindang

2435m

Pagadian

San Miguel

San Pablo

Aurelio

Tatina

Pagadian Bay

ZAMBOANGA PENINSULA

Labason

Liloy

Kabasalan

Ticaun

Malangas

Ailela

Limbunan

Siraguan

Sibuco

San Ramonh

Zamboanga

Basilan Strait

Isabela

Maluso

Basilan Peak

1107m

BASILAN I.

Matanal Pt.

SACOL I.

Matanal Pt.

TAPIANTANA GROUP

TATALAN I.

BUCTUA I.

TONGQUIL I.

SAMALERS GROUP

SIMISA I.

Tapiantana Channel

PILAS GROUP

PILAS I.

DASSALAN I.

KULASSEIN I.

PANGUTARAN I.

PANGUTARAN GROUP

TEOMABAL I.

RUBUAN I.

CABUCAN I.

NORTH UBIAN I.

Tapul

Jolo

JOLO GROUP

CABINGAAN I.

Tapaan Passage

LAMMAI I.

TAPUL I.

LUGUS I.

LAPAC I.

SIASI I.

Subgai Passage

Sulu Sea

Celebes Sea

Mindanao Sea

B O H O L

PANGLAO I.

Tagbilaran

Dauis

Oslob

Gualan

SICUJOR I.

Larena

Siaton Pt.

Zamboanguita

Siaton

Sta. Catalina

Tolog Bay

Basay

Bayawan

NEGROS

Matatindoe Pt.

Hinoba-an

CAGAYAN Is.

Sulu Sea

More Gulf

Seboto Pt.

Sindangan Bay

Sibuguey Bay

Payamcam

Illana Bay

Sulu Sea

105

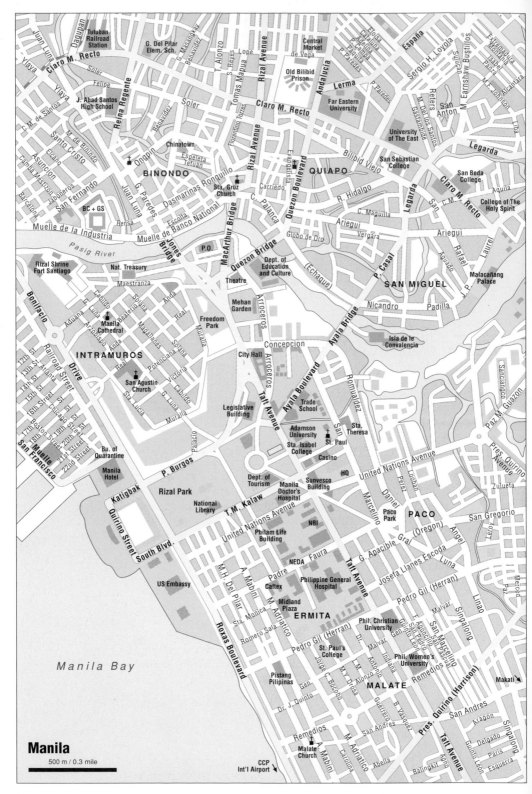

Manila

500 m / 0.3 mile

MANILA

No doubt about it: Manila is one crazy place. It's chaotic and filled with bizarre vignettes. It's sprawling and sprawling even more. It's the city of cliché contrasts and contradictions. And in the end, it's truly an intriguing place.

Fortunately, it has a waterfront that limits its rambunctiousness. Manila Bay, once the harbor of Spanish galleons and Chinese corsairs, defines the western limits of the city. Roxas Boulevard runs directly along it, a promenade that yields some fine sunsets. Along the boulevard, from south to north, are the Cultural Center of the Philippines (CCP) and convention center; a number of hotels; the old bourgeois neighborhood of Ermita, once famous for its night-life; Rizal Park, where the Philippine hero Jose Rizal was executed and which is Manila's central park; the American Embassy with its long queues of visa applicants; and then the classic Manila Hotel.

Just beyond, the old Spanish colonial city of Intramuros awaits at the northern end of Roxas Boulevard, on the south side of the Pasig River flowing into Manila Bay. Intramuros is old history, a walled enclave surrounded, incongruously, by a golf course. Inside are the elegant San Augustin Church, Manila Cathedral, a few – though not enough – renovated colonial homes, and, at the northern tip on the banks of the Pasig, Fort Santiago and a shrine and museum to Rizal.

Like many urban rivers, the Pasig defines districts and neighborhoods. On the northern side of the Pasig, fussy but vigorous places like Binondo, Quiapo and San Miguel embrace the old Chinatown, an intense concentration of universities, and the former presidential residence, Malacañang Palace, on the river's banks.

Returning to Roxas Boulevard and the Manila Bay seawall that lures locals and travelers alike, south of the CCP is Epifanio de los Santos Avenue, or EDSA, where the People's Power revolt against Marcos was anchored. East along EDSA two kilometers is the district of Makati, long the nation's banking and business center and thus peppered with modern high-rises – but increasingly where hip nightlife and expensive shopping is to be found. Some of Manila's swankiest hotels are here, along with most of the foreign embassies and much of the elite money. Just to the southeast is Forbes Park, for lack of a better analogy the Beverly Hills of Manila. Beyond is the elitist Fort Bonifacio golf club, and the egalitarian US Memorial Cemetery, with its thousands of World War II dead.

A number of places outside of Metro Manila pull travelers: Bataan Peninsula and Corregidor, sites of the Death March and MacArthur's last holdout against the Japanese; the rapids of Pagsanjan, primal and wet; the lake-side villages ringing Laguna de Bay; the often-crowded beach resorts of Cavite; and the volcano of Taal, simmering in its own lake.

Preceding pages: wedding at San Augustin Church, Intramuros.

MANILA'S PAST

Deep in the heart of Chinatown, a pedestrian steps into a *panciteria,* or restaurant, picks up a menu, and weighs the choices: Po Guisantes, Almondigas de Pescado Frito Crisp, Shanghai Rice can Kabuti. As classic as it is pidgin, this engaging mixture of Spanish, Chinese, Tagalog, and English is, for the hungry Manileño, only too familiar, a reflection of the confused talk of the city.

Eye, ear and tongue are assaulted by a myriad influences in Manila. It is said that a chop-suey consciousness prevails over the place – the favored terms of endearing definition being milange, baroque, eclectic, hodgepodge, collage, ragout, and potpourri.

El Insigne y Siempre Leal Ciudad. The Spanish called Manila the Noble and Ever Loyal City. With hindsight, the honorific might now be said to mean ever loyal only to the Malay tradition of wide embrace, a communal warmth and quality of acceptance.

Manila had always been openly minded, acknowledging each historic layer as another mantle with which it could embrace and join all previous ones. To look back in time requires stripping away these garments, and the task is not easy. Throwbacks to different eras have, over the years, melded with contemporary images, held together in a gentle flux.

Pasig River: Manila falls easy prey to floods, since most of the city's streets are lower than sea level. The **Pasig River**, which bisects the city, aggravates the condition when it swells at high tide. Cutting a 16-kilometer (10-mi) serpentine course from Laguna de Bay to the seas, the Pasig has served as historical foundation to Manila since the days of the areas earliest settlements. The prevailing etymological theory for the name of *Manila* has it that the *nilad* plant, which grew along the river's banks, lent the place its original name, Maynilad.

On both sides of the river's mouth, the first trading communities formed as early as the fifth century. Through the 12th and 13th centuries, the river trade center flourished with the yearly arrival of merchants – from Arabia, Siam, Borneo, Java, Sumatra, Malacca, India, China and Japan – who found the crescent-shaped bay here an excellent harbor. Cargoes of silk and brocade, porcelain ware, musk, colored glass beads, black damask, iron incense burners, lead and tin and other foreign exotica were bartered for beeswax and honey, pearls, tortoise shells, betel nuts, jute, and gold. The middlemen of Maynilad easily procured these commodities of the archipelago from the less-sophisticated people of the interior, by way of the river.

By the middle of the 16th century, Muslims of royal lineage with ancestry extending back to Borneo had entrenched themselves here, making Maynilad a palisaded city-state of about 2,000 people. A young warrior, Sulayman, ruled the city with his two uncles, Lakandula and Matanda.

The Spanish conquistador Miguel Lopez de Legazpi arrived in 1571. After two epic battles, he took over the ashes of Sulayman's bamboo fortress, which, according to legend, the recalcitrant chieftain razed to the ground upon sensing his impending defeat.

Legazpi founded Spanish Manila the same year, constructing a medieval and fortified town that was to become Spain's most durable monument in the Far East. The city fortress, defended by moats and turreted walls that were 6.5 meters (21 ft) thick and with well-positioned batteries, was called **Intramuros**, literally "within the walls".

For two centuries, the Spanish succeeded in keeping other foreign powers at bay, and Manila passed through a period of enforced insularism. Within the walled city, only the members of the Castilian upper class – friars, soldiers and government administrators – were privileged enough to live. Trade and commerce were conducted outside the walls in the rapidly expanding suburbs across the river, and where the burgeoning Chinese populace was confined – under close scrutiny.

Left, overview of Intramuros, Manila.

In 1762, the English took control of Intramuros for two years, driving the Spanish northward. The walled city was eventually recaptured by starving out the English, and the British interlude, at least from the Spanish view, was kept mercifully short. For another 100 years, the Spanish defended the city against the repeated assaults of the English, Dutch, and Portuguese.

Life in Manila had assumed an air of idyllic uniting of Old World charm with Pacific ease. The Malays accommodated the ways of the conquistadors to the point of gratuitousness, while their attitude of relaxed acquiescence in turn positively rubbed off on the Europeans. In fact, not a few observers had remarked that Spanish rule in Manila and the rest of the islands was characterized by a mellowness and facility in sharp contrast to most other colonizing powers of the period.

Outside the walls: Five gates connected the Walled City to the outlying boroughs, where the *indio*, as the Spanish called the locals, lived along with mestizos, Chinese, Indians, Armenians, Japanese and other foreigners, not to mention large numbers of Spanish commoners. Trade and commerce flourished to such an extent in these suburbs that they soon outstripped the city proper both in area and population.

The Chinese, whose number and industry provoked suspicion from the ruling class, were originally quartered in a district called the Parian, and to where the Filipinos brought their legumes, fruits, vegetables and cotton weavings, and where the Spanish vied for odd purchases, from lead shoe-buckles to silver-plated altars.

Located north of Intramuros, the Parian was eventually eclipsed in importance by Binondo, the Christian Chinese commercial district across the Bridge of Spain, which spanned the Pasig River. Here were housed shops of all sizes and categories, including cigar factories where thousands of women found employment, and warehouses full of opium eventually destined for smuggling into China.

Spanish map of Intramuros.

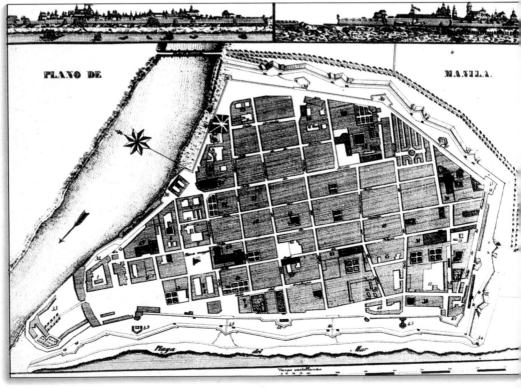

Next to Binondo was the district of Tondo, where blacksmiths, carriage makers, carpenters, masons, printers, booksellers, shoemakers, tailors, and cleaners of noses and ears established themselves. Other boroughs expanded to form well-integrated communities on both sides of the river, among them Santa Cruz, Quiapo and San Miguel in the north, and the residential districts of Dilao, Ermita and Malati in the south.

Towards the close of the 18th century, the Spanish finally realized that neither the annual galleon trade between Manila and Acapulco nor the royal subsistence received from Mexico proved enough of a boost for local economic activity. Not even direct trade between Spain and the Philippines in later years ever became economically viable.

As a result, foreign ships were soon allowed to help handle the increasing volume of Asian trade, and foreign companies were permitted to establish themselves in Manila. Rice, sugar and hemp were exported in great quantities, but what was probably more important, liberal ideas and attitudes of the English and American traders, among others, hastened the cultural uplifting of the city onto a truly cosmopolitan plane.

Musical bands and large numbers of locals welcomed the arrival of each foreign ship, and a festive atmosphere often pervaded Manila.

The liberalization of trade in the 19th century brought an influx of modern political ideas in its wake, and it was just a matter of time before the Castilian sword and cross fell in this Noble and Ever Loyal City.

Enter America: After two years of waging guerrilla battle against the Spanish, the Filipino *revolucionarios* found themselves beaten with the capture of their capital city by the Americans, who were at war with Spain. Four more years of struggle against the Americans followed, until the Americans forced the last *insurrecto,* or rebel, to capitulate.

From 1902 until 1946, when the Philippines was officially granted independence, the people of Manila and the rest of the islands lived under another period

Old Manila postcard of a downtown street.

M-15   Escolta, Main Street of Manila, Philippin

of colonial if somewhat benevolent rule. The Americans, in fact, left the legacy of a valuable educational system, a democratic form of government, salient lessons in technology, and Western mores and manners, which so enchanted the Filipinos that for decades they took pride in being called "the brown Americans" or "little brown brothers", oblivious to contemptuous snickering from their Asian neighbors.

It was a happy, carefree period for most of the city's residents, intoxicated as they were with the "brand-new" and "genuine" feel brought from America. It was a period of sharkskin suits, grand cabarets and big band music, spats or tango shoes marking time to the Charleston and the boogie-woogie, Coca-Cola billboards, and Superman and Batman comics. There were endless discussions on "buy-and-sell" and "import-export", as typified by what came to be known, after Manila's main commercial street at the time, as the Escolta Walking Corporation, a loosely formed gathering – or perhaps breed –

of disenfranchised yet talk-happy and dream-cocky young men, who whiled away their days in the fashionable coffee shops expounding on one flamboyant scheme after another.

The Manileño, suddenly privy to the great big spirit of free enterprise and the bright promise of independence, was in no hurry to do away with his innate Malay sense of timelessness, nor the subtle devices of rhetoric and hyperbole inherited from the Castilian.

The old made way for the new, but only to a certain extent. Jose Rizal was officially decreed by the Americans as the national hero. Team sports such as basketball and baseball were introduced to a people for whom physical play, as fostered by the Spanish, was apparently confined to individual competition. The Bridge of Spain was renamed Jones Bridge. Similarly, a number of streets lost their Spanish heritage in favor of American associations. The city proved itself capable, as time and again it had in the past, of maintaining differing traditions side by side.

American troops embark at the Pasig River at the turn of the century.

114

Wartime Manila: In December of 1941, Japanese bombers emerged from the horizon and Manileños had a brief foretaste of still another outside foreign power. Convinced by the Filipinos that the city and its beloved monuments had to be spared at all costs, the Americans quickly gave up Manila, paving the way for a Japanese occupation that lasted a little over three years. Typical of the ironies of history and true to the nature of assimilation exhibited by the city, the University of Santo Tomas, the oldest such institution established by the Spanish Dominicans for the indios, was turned by the Japanese into one huge concentration camp for the Americans.

Some families evacuated the city, reacquainting themselves with long-forsaken homesteads in the country. Their young men allied themselves with the Americans against the Japanese, and did so with outstanding valor and nobility in the losing battles fought in Bataan and Corregidor. The Americans saw fit to repay the gesture by granting independence barely a year after they recaptured the islands.

Gen. Douglas MacArthur, whose father had fought against the Filipino insurrectos a generation earlier, made good his retreat promise to return in 1944. And, as they had in 1898, American troops once again entered Manila to liberate the city from another power. But this time the Japanese resistance encountered was not quite like the token one offered by the Spanish earlier. The Americans had to fight their way from south of the city, block by block. When the Japanese retreated, they destroyed bridges and razed buildings to the ground. It was more like Rajah Sulayman's spiteful gesture when he abandoned his kingdom to the Spanish.

As a result, Manila became the second-most devastated city in World War II, second only to Warsaw. Still and all, the city people rejoiced, hailing the American liberators as near-gods who rode proudly into the city on awesome tanks. Kids lined the streets shouting "Victory Joe!" and waving V-signs at the returning heroes, who in turn tossed them chewing gum and chocolates. City-wise men took the occasion to cajole their women into sewing fake Japanese flags, which they either sold or exchanged for food-rations with the souvenir-hungry troops.

Except for a few fortunate monuments and public buildings, Manila had been practically leveled to the ground during the war. Once again, American and Filipino worked together to salvage what they could from the ruins, and then to start a structure anew.

On the morning of 4 July 1946, thousands of Manileños and hundreds of representatives from the provinces assembled at the Luneta, now called Rizal Park and near the Manila Hotel. On the same field where, 50 years earlier, Rizal had been executed, the American flag was lowered in favor of the Philippine flag. The Philippines was now an independent republic. To a people who now gazed upwards at the symbol flapping alone against the bay's soft breeze and the familiar blue sky, the image could not help but resolve itself as the culmination of one dream and the fresh start

Former president Diosdado Macapagal and his wife.

of another. Filipinos have always had an intense sense of pride and belonging.

Political passage: For 26 years, Manila remained the seat of a Philippine government that tried its best to carry on the American political tradition, priding itself on being the "showcase" of democracy in Asia.

In 1972, however, in the wake of bombings and student unrest, martial law was declared, and some residents were quick to lament the passing of Manila's free-swinging if often anarchic spirit. But apart from the effects of a midnight-to-dawn curfew that cut short the city's fabled night life, it seemed presumptuous to conceive of a Manila without its usual reckless abandon.

Little has changed over the years, in fact if not in spirit. The cut-and-thrust precocity of horn-happy motorists creating unnerving tangles of traffic during rush hours, cat-quick commuters grasping at handrails of a speeding bus, jeepney drivers weaving in and out of the mess of convoluted streets with their loud music, jaywalkers and cigarette

sellers darting across busy avenues, beggars begging, street urchins urging and taunting, vendors taking over sidewalks with their bulky carts and cases which miraculously become portable when, at a whim's notice, some police officers decide to make a raid. Manila's familiar rites of passage remained the same, and it was difficult to imagine that they would not go on unchanged.

Metro Manila: A presidential decree laid out in 1976 linked 10 existing suburban cities and seven municipalities with the Manila of old to form what is now called Metro Manila, or, rarely, the National Capital Region.

A former governor of the city, Imelda Marcos, availed herself of what was then the latest technocracy of the time to map out the city's growth, building extravagant monuments to so-called progress and national (if not that of the Marcos family) image, including the Philippine Cultural Center, the Philippine Heart Center for Asia, and Manila International Airport, now called Ninoy Aquino International Airport.

Today, Metro Manila, with an estimated population of 11 million, has become a much-too-large heart of a country whose many other parts are sorely lacking in progress and development. As the one massive nerve center, its heaving pulse has always been an indication of whatever strengths or weaknesses characterize the Philippines and its people as a whole.

But the post-People's Power images presented by the Manileño still offer a stunning array. He could be the stock market yuppie who shucks off his business suit at the end of the day and cozies up with the latest Bruce Springsteen record, or the tout in polo *barong* (short-sleeved shirt) lobbying his lore on exactly which bureaucratic palms to grease and by how much. She is the *colegiala* or convent school girl who coyly conceals her modern outlook behind a demure facade, or a media mercenary on the prowl for special projects. He is the hawker who'd rather keep on trucking for a few pesos each day in the hub of glitter than go back to his province and tend his small farm in pastoral quiet.

Left, Manila Bay. **Right,** Manila shopping center.

MANILA

Of course, Manila is not the Philippines, though countless tourists leave Manila with what they think is an image of the Philippines: happily-Westernized Asians on the move and in the know, flashing their best hospitality smiles. It is a shallow impression, and false, too.

But one typically starts in Manila. Old Manila. New Manila. Metro Manila. National Capital Region. Where to begin? Old Manila is likely.

Intramuros: For its small space and relatively out-of-the-way location, **Fort Santiago** has become a popular promenade for lovers and artists, and is easily reached by taxi from nearly anywhere in Metro Manila. Within the inner gate of Fort Santiago is a stately building housing the memorabilia of Dr. Jose Rizal, a Philippine national hero. On another end of the quadrangle is Rizal's cell, where he wrote his last legacy of poetry to the Filipino people.

From Fort Santiago, cross over to **Manila Cathedral**, an imposing Romanesque structure constructed of adobe. A plaque on its facade tells of a phoenix-like cycle that holds true for most other old churches of the country: a relentless history beginning in 1571 of construction and reconstruction after the repetitive ravages of fire, typhoon, earthquakes, and war. Several statues by Italian artists grace the facade, the saints to whom Manileños owe special devotion: St Andrew the Apostle, on whose November feast day in 1574 the Spanish repulsed Chinese invaders; St Anthony the Abbot, founder of Oriental monasticism; St Francis Xavier, the apostle of the Indies; St Rose of Lima, patroness of the Philippines; and St James the Greater, or Santiago Matamoros, patron saint of Spain and the Philippines, and whose name became the conquistadors' battle cry in their perennial wars with the Muslims.

Fronting the cathedral is **Plaza Roma**, named such in 1961 when the city of Rome renamed one of its squares Piazzale Manila, on the occasion of the elevation to the cardinalate of the first Filipino, then Archbishop of Manila, Rufino J. Santos. This square, where colonial solders once drilled, was originally called Plaza de Armas. Later the Spanish rechristened it Plaza Mayor when it became the government center in Intramuros. It was also briefly been known as Plaza McKinley during the American occupation at the end of World War II.

From a bird's-eye view, Intramuros was laid out as a pentagon, but its uneven sides more approximate a triangle. The western wall facing the sea (before reclamation began at the turn of the century) is now flanked by Bonifacio Drive, leading southward to Roxas Boulevard (where further reclamation continues to encroach on Manila Bay).

Intramuros' perimeter measures nearly 4.5 kilometers (3 mi). Following Legazpi's blueprint for the capital, succeeding Spanish governors constructed 18 churches, chapels, convents, schools, a hospital, a printing press, a university (in as early as 1611), palaces for the

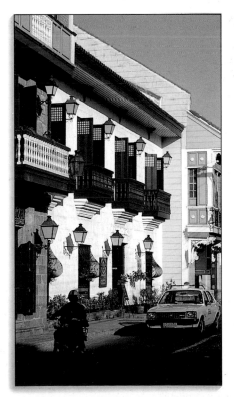

governor-general and the archbishop, soldiers' barracks, and houses for the assorted elite.

Today, much of Intramuros is a jumble of broken buildings – reminders World War II or just plain neglect. Many of them have been taken over by trucking companies and other enterprises that tack on sheets of plywood and tin to old shells to make them weather-tight. However, some of the old city has been restored, with particular focus on the Ayuntamiento (City Hall), Intendencia buildings and San Ignacio Church.

Part of the continuing restoration plan is to replicate eight houses illustrating different styles and periods through which local architecture has evolved. Three are already open to the public, including splendid **Casa Manila**. This grand 19th-century-style home now houses craft and curio shops, an art gallery and one of Manila's best restaurants, Ilustrado.

Outside the stone walls of Intramuros, the Philippine Tourism Authority maintains and operates **Club Intramuros**, a well-kept 18-hole golf course open to the public.

From Plaza Roma, walk down General Luna Street, past the western side of the cathedral, for four blocks to the intersection of General Luna Street and Calle Real. Here, incongruous Chinese *fu* dogs carved of granite guard the entrance to the courtyard of the single structure of Intramuros that was spared by the American bombing of 1945 – **San Agustin Church**. The church facade is notable for its combination of styles – Doric lower columns and Corinthian upper columns – and the evident absence of one of its original twin towers, the left one falling victim to the earthquakes of 1863 and 1889. The remarkable main door is carved out of a Philippine hardwood called *molave*, and is divided into four panels depicting Augustinian symbols and the figures of St Augustine and his mother, St Monica.

Adjoining the church is the monastery-museum containing a treasure trove of Philippine artifacts, religious art, and an extensive collection of Chinese, Span-

ish and Mexican pottery. The cloister gallery exhibits several fine large paintings depicting scenes in the life of St Augustine and portraits of notable Augustinian friars, among them the prodigious Fr. Manuel Blanco, who produced the classic *Flora de Filipinas*. (Guided walking tours are available.)

Pasig River: From San Agustin Church, there are several options. Turn right at Calle Real and prowl the remains of Intramuros until reaching Muralla Street. Here, follow the walls or pass through one of the restored gates leading back to the Pasig River, or to a plaza, **Liwasang Bonifacio**. On this busy square is a statue of the revolutionary leader Andres Bonifacio, with the **Central Post Office** just to the north.

Between these two landmarks is a system of overpasses and underpasses handling, at all hours, a great bulk of Manila's traffic. The left lane leads to Jones Bridge, the center lane to MacArthur Bridge, and the right one to Quezon Bridge. These three bridges are the major passageways across the river,

leading to the half of Manila known as "north of the Pasig". Just next to the post office, beneath MacArthur Bridge, board the Metro Ferry and chug along the Pasig River to **Guadalupe**, near Makati, glimpsing river life, dusty old buildings and Malacanang Palace.

Left at Calle Real ends up at Bonifacio Drive. This leads north to the Delpan Bridge, which also crosses the Pasig into the districts of San Nicolas and Tondo. Southwards, Bonifacio Drive leads to Roxas Boulevard. It's an enjoyable walk along these parts, with the walls of Intramuros rising to the left, its ancient moats now converted into lawns and the Club Intramuros golf course.

Rizal Park: Formerly known as **Luneta** (or little moon, for its crescent shape), **Rizal Park** is a large rectangular field broken up into three sections, with an elevated strolling ground bounded by Roxas Boulevard and ending at the sea wall facing Manila Bay. On this section is the **Quirino Grandstand**, where local officials led by the president gather to preside over Independence Day pa-

Manila contrasts.

rades and other such national occasions. In the early morning hours, a number of Chinese do *tai chi* exercises here, with the more conventional calisthenics enthusiasts and joggers filling up the rest of the vast space.

At the central portion of Rizal Park is **Rizal Monument**, a memorial to the national hero and the object of much wreath-laying by visiting dignitaries. Under 24-hour guard, the regular drill maneuvers of the sentries are an attraction in themselves. (This spot also has the distinction of being Kilometer Zero, or the point of reference for all road distances throughout the largest and main island of Luzon.)

Behind the monument is a series of plaques on which are inscribed Rizal's poem *Mi Ultimo Adios* (My Last Farewell) in the original Spanish and in various translations. A marble slab marks the spot where Rizal met his martyr's death by firing squad, while an obelisk stands on the site of the earlier executions of the Filipino priests Gomez, Burgos, and Zamora.

This central section of the park, where the Rizal Monument is located, is bordered by Roxas Boulevard to the west, T.M. Kalaw Street to the south, M. Orosa Street to the east, and Padre Burgos Street to the north. Close to the Burgos side are the Japanese and Chinese gardens, and an orchidarium, all of which charge token fees for entrance. On this side, too, is the City Planetarium, where an interesting audiovisual show is conducted twice a day for a nominal charge. If you cross Burgos at this point, you come the clubhouse of Club Intramuros golf course. Here one can also enter Intramuros through General Luna Street.

Along the Kalaw Street side of Rizal Park's sits the **National Library**. Close to the park's center is the Rizal Park Cafeteria, run by the speaking- and hearing-impaired. With waitresses communicating via hand signals or with pen and paper, this cafeteria serves decent snacks at reasonable prices. It is a cooling spot to rest over coffee or tea and people-watch. Alternatively, try the **Fountain in Rizal Park.**

Harbor View Restaurant for a beer and pulutan (cocktail snacks Filipino-style) while watching the blossoming sunset over Manila Bay.

The park's eastern section, across Orosa Street, is dominated by the **Department of Tourism (DOT) Building**, on the right side coming from the Rizal Monument. Travelers may call upon the tourism staffers for guides, maps, information and other assistance. Fronting the building is a somewhat lurid globe fountain, bounded by an all-night skating rink, where stylists do their thing in the evening hours.

Further on is another concession to the demands of kitsch: a topographic map of the archipelago set in a lagoon, on both sides of which are viewing platforms that really are not much help in minimizing the obvious distortion of one's view of the miniature islands. Beyond is a children's playground featuring gigantic prehistoric beasts cast in utilitarian cement.

The eastern side of the park is bounded by Taft Avenue, one of the major arteries cutting through Manila south of the river. Both Burgos and Kalaw streets end at Taft Avenue. Follow Burgos leads past the **Old Congress Building**, which once housed the Philippine Senate and still houses the **National Museum**. Northward is Manila City Hall, and beyond, Liwasang Bonifacio, from where the three bridges give the option for further exploring north of the Pasig.

Directly across Taft from the children's playground is an abandoned building that once housed the Jai Alai Fronton, the first such establishment in Asia and one of the few outside Spain.

From this point on Taft Avenue, one can reach practically any section of the southern part of the city by public transport. Jeepneys and buses starting from across the river follow this road leading to all points south, including Pasay City and the municipality of Parañaque. The financial district of Makati is also reached by following Taft Avenue and making a left turn at Buendia Avenue.

This south-of-the-river section of the city is quite easy to learn. On the westernmost side is Roxas Boulevard, running from Rizal Park to Parañaque, near the international airport.

Ermita: From Taft, turn right at any of the perpendicular streets beginning with United Nations Avenue, where the Holiday Inn Manila Pavilion Hotel stands. This will lead to **Ermita**. (The other side of Taft doesn't offer that much, except **Paco Park**, a circular promenade area originally a Spanish cemetery in the 1820s.)

Ermita is an unusual district in many respects, its tourist-belt reputation built on the strength of its proximity to Rizal Park, the seawall along Manila Bay, and a number of government buildings, such as the Department of Justice on Padre Faura Street. Consequently, many hotels and lodging houses have opened in the area, in turn attracting a conglomeration of eateries, nightspots, boutiques, antique shops, handicraft and curio stalls, and travel agency offices.

When the Spanish arrived, Ermita was a seaside village called Laygo, whose residents were found venerating a small female icon carved out of dark

Backstage at a drag-queen show.

wood and set atop a clump of pandanus by the seashore. Although stupefied at the statue's pre-Christian look and intrigued by its origin, Legazpi's men quickly turned the image to their advantage, telling the villagers that the image's name was Nuestra Señora de Guia (Our Lady of Guidance), and that it had been brought by the angels. They installed it in a wooden chapel not far from the spot where it was found. This church, which has undergone eight reconstructions, still stands at the original site on M.H. del Pilar Street, opposite Plaza Ferguson.

Legend has it that around 1591, a Mexican secular and hermit made the small seaside village his retreat. Four years later, an Augustinian priest founded the hermitage dedicated to Nuestra Señora de Guia, and the name *Ermita* (hermitage) has stuck ever since. By the 19th century, the district had become an aristocratic suburb, together with the adjacent district of **Malate** further south. To this day, Ermita and Malate people still carry a faint whiff of snob appeal, although recent years have seen the twin districts burgeoning into commercialism, so that they are often likened to aging aristocrats' daughters now forced to make a living.

Until a few years ago, this assessment was not altogether unjustified, certainly not to the visitor walking the bar strip along del Pilar Street, where the evening hours brought out ladies from the clubs to lure men into them, or elsewhere, for sexual recreation.

Indeed, Ermita was once a hot-spot for foreign men, second in Asia only to Bangkok. After years of benign tolerance by his predecessors, the mayor of Manila closed Ermita's bars and strip shows in the early 1990s. Now with the bars remaining padlocked and the music and the girls long gone, the strip is relatively quiet at night. But for the visitor seeking the less erotically challenging, Ermita still offers diverse and safe nightspots featuring Filipino folk singers and rock and jazz groups. Here, still, another facet of the Ermita spirit may be glimpsed – the bohemian life-

Trendy Mabini diner antics.

style of its younger residents made up of artists, writers, musicians and dancers. Ermita has also given generic birth to a group called the Mabini painters, named after the street where their tiny gallery shops elbow out one another for the indiscriminate eye hooked on cheap cultural souvenirs. Hundreds of studios, landscapes, portraits, and some specimens of a curious genre, oil on velvet, are churned out daily by these so-called artists, not a few of whom sometimes show genuine talent despite their damning prodigiousness. Close to these painters' shops is Cortada Street, which has evolved into a tiny quarter for crafts and brassware from the Muslim Philippines in the south.

An informal and popular hang-out is **Hobbit House**, on Mabini, near the corner of Remedios. Midgets wait on tables and young singers take turns on stage. If you tire of the music or the novelty of the waiters, try a game of billiards upstairs. A number of other good restaurants are also in the area. Down Mabini and del Pilar is an assortment of antique shops, where pottery, religious icons, ethnic ware, old bottles and assorted junk command prices from the *rara avis* sublime to the *gratis* ridiculous. Two of the better shops are Likha and Vizcarra, on Mabini, while Tesoro's, beside the Tower Hotel on Mabini, offers a large collection of curios and Filipino handicrafts. Further south on Mabini lies **Pistang Pilipino**, a huge open-air shopping promenade of arts and artifacts from around the archipelago. At its center is a *nipa* restaurant, where one may sample digital dining – using one's ten fingers.

On the sidewalks, close to the lobbies of the big hotels, are hawkers, almost all of them men and parading their assortment of souvenir items. When a tourist coach comes to a stop, they swing into action in pick-up Japanese as they thrust forward their stuffed tortoises, *carabao* horns, shell figurines, dried flower garlands and *puka* necklaces.

Roxas Boulevard: Paralleling Manila Bay is Roxas Boulevard and its seawall. The **Roxas Boulevard seawall** begins,

Roxas Boulevard and Manila Bay sunset.

not without some hint of appropriateness, where the sprawling grounds of the **American Embassy** – hard to miss with the long lines of visa seekers outside – end. On the Malate side there's a break in the line of buildings facing the bay, and the **Malate Church** and plaza. The church is dedicated to Nuestra Señora de los Remedios (Our Lady of Remedies), whose image, brought over from Spain in 1624, is still venerated on the main altar. In front of the church, modern bronze statues of Our Lady of Remedies and the young Rajah Sulayman make an odd couple as they confront the sunset.

Along President Quirino Avenue, the **Manila Yacht Club** and **Philippine Navy Headquarters**, both standing on reclaimed land, intrude on the sea view. On the landward side is a government complex that includes the Ospital ng Maynila (Manila Hospital), **Metropolitan Museum of Manila**, and the Central Bank of the Philippines. Behind the hospital is the **Manila Zoo**.

Past the Navy Headquarters and on the seaward side of Roxas Boulevard is the immense **Cultural Center of the Philippines**, the centerpiece of what has become known as the **Cultural Center Complex** (CCC). The main building houses two theaters and two art galleries, and a museum and library. The rest of the Cultural Center Complex, which is constructed on reclaimed land, includes the Folk Arts Theater, Design Center of the Philippines, Philippine Center for Industrial and Trade Exhibits (Philcite), Philippine International Convention Center (PICC), the World Trade Center, and the most architecturally interesting structure in the complex, the Government Services Insurance System (GSIS) building, which also houses the Philippine Senate and the GSIS Museum, an interesting art museum. Also here, at the end of the reclaimed land on the bay's waterfront, is the **Westin Philippine Plaza**. During the Christmas season, Philcite transforms into Star City, a carnival-cum-shopper's delight, where people come from all around for fun and shopping.

Transvestite television talent show.

128

Lying just a stone's throw away from the Westin is a former Marcos guest house, the **Coconut Palace**, which although it can now be rented for private functions, it is not open to the general public. Built entirely from indigenous materials, the palace was originally designed to house performing artists and film stars. Today's lucky visitors will have a fascinating time ogling at guest rooms such as the Visayas Room, which showcases thousands of shells; the Mountain Province Room, executed in the bold red and black colors of the highland people; and the Ilocos Room, with its priceless mother-of-pearl furniture. The dining room and gardens are the venue of many fancy parties.

Presently, the palm-fringed Roxas Boulevard continues to hold sway over the bay's crescent, leading to the heart of the city from the international airport, a short distance from the boulevard's southern end. Double-decker buses provide a leisurely sightseeing ride from one end of the boulevard to the other, starting at Rizal Park. Hotels, restaurants, and nightclubs dominate this bayfront area.

Towards the airport: Manila ends immediately past the CCP, just before Senator Gil Puyat Avenue, still called by its old name of Buendia. Some of the bars that were driven out of Ermita have found a new home here, just across the boundary in **Pasay City**. A left turn under the Buendia flyover leads straight to Manila's business center, Makati. Down from the flyover is the **Cuneta Astrodome**, an inappropriately named box structure where professional basketball games are held every Tuesday, Thursday and Sunday. Close to the end of the boulevard is Redemptorist Road forking left to **Baclaran**, an area on the Pasay-Parañaque boundary famous for its *lechon* (roast suckling pig) stalls fringing the **Redemptorist Church**. Wednesdays are bedlam days in this area, with the popular weekly *novenas* to the Virgin Mary drawing crowds as much for the candle offering and devotional singing as for the lechon and the bounty of the dry-goods market at the

Dinner at the Coconut Palace, and a jeepney.

back of the church. Not far from the church is a **Light Rail Transit** station, an elevated spot and ride for a bird's-eye view of Manila. The line runs northwards to the terminus at Monumento, in Caloocan City, and takes approximately 30 minutes.

NAIA Avenue at boulevard's end heads straight to **Ninoy Aquino International Airport**, as well as the domestic flight terminal. Down NAIA Avenue, turn right at the narrow Quirino Avenue and past Parañaque towards the historical attractions of Cavite Province. From NAIA Avenue, it is barely an hour's drive to Tagaytay Ridge, the traditional viewing point overlooking Taal Lake and its Volcano Island. A little way past Parañaque is the Las Piñas Church and its historic bamboo organ.

Close to the airport is another favorite tourist haunt, **Nayong Pilipino** (**Philippine Village**), next to the Philippine Village Hotel. The country's regions are represented in miniature amidst this landscaped village, which has been designed to allow short-term visitors a glimpse into the archipelago's attractions and diverse cultures. Jeepneys provide ferrying services within the grounds, and cultural performances are sometimes scheduled in the evenings.

Makati: From NAIA Avenue, take a short bus or taxi ride to **Makati** via **Epifanio de los Santos Avenue** (**EDSA**), Makati's main east-west street and site of the February 1986 People's Power revolution. **Makati**'s main north-south street, Ayala Avenue, has been dubbed the Philippine Wall Street, as it is the financial hub of the Philippines. Much of what Makati is today – tall and elegant buildings, smart residential "villages" for the up-market crowd, modern shopping complexes, first-class restaurants and international hotels like the Peninsula, Mandarin Oriental, and Shangri-La – can be traced to the development foresight of Zobel de Ayalas, an old family descended from the Spanish and who refused to rest on the laurels of vain aristocracy. Finding themselves holding on to a tract of swampland long considered worthless, the Ayalas saw **Makati.**

the value of its proximity to crowded Manila. They bided their time until the 1950s, when they gradually started the development that transformed swamp into swank. The Ayalas continue to take the lead in urban development, building even more large hotels, fancy restaurants, and state-of-the-art shopping complexes in the business district. Nowhere is the new affluence from the country's economic turnaround more evident than in **Ayala Center**'s Greenbelt and Quad shopping malls. Rows of glittering boutiques have sprung up in this area during the last two years to tempt shoppers with fashion's most well-known names.

At the junction of Paseo de Roxas and Ayala Avenue is a bronze **statue of Benigno Aquino, Jr.**, who was assassinated in August 1983. It stands on the site of the regular Friday rallies that showered yellow confetti and increasing opposition to the administration of former president Ferdinand Marcos.

On Makati Avenue is the **Ayala Museum**. The museum has an outstanding archive and a permanent exhibit of dioramas portraying significant episodes in Philippine history, along with detailed replicas of ships that have plied Philippine waters.

From Ayala Avenue's end at the EDSA, cross the highway to **Forbes Park**, which was built by the Ayalas, of course. The original Makati "village", it continues to enjoy the highest status among all the affluent neighborhoods in this area. Forbes Park's McKinley Road leads to the Manila Polo Club and to **Fort Bonifacio**, a military camp once housing the headquarters of the Philippine Army. Recently sold by the government to a private developer, the 214-hectare (535-acre) camp will one day become the country's newest business and financial district.

Nearby is the **Manila American Memorial Cemetery**, where the remains of 17,000 Allied dead rest below rows of white crosses. The **Libingan ng Mga Bayani (Graveyard of Heroes)** is close by with its eternal flame burning by the Tomb of the Unknown Soldier.

Returning to EDSA via Forbes Park,

Guard and mansion, Forbes Park.

turn right and follow the highway's curve towards north of the Pasig. Makati ends at **Guadalupe Bridge**, beyond which are the areas of Mandaluyong and Pasig. The **Ortigas Center**, which straddles these two extensions of Manila, has become a worthy rival to Makati as the country's premier business district. Three large malls in the area, including the Megamall, reputedly the country's biggest shopping center, and two deluxe hotels, the EDSA Shangri-La and the Galleria Suites, have become an alternative to the congested Ayala Center.

Turning right before Guadalupe Bridge, follow the winding road beside the river to the town of **Pateros**, center of the *balut* duck egg industry. The sandy soil of the area provides the indigenous Pateros duck with an abundance of snails for forage, and these then produce the balut. A unique Filipino treat, baluts are neither duck nor egg but somewhere in-between. Unlike a newly-laid egg, with yolk and white, the balut is really an embryonic duck in a shell, boiled for a few minutes. Balut vendors

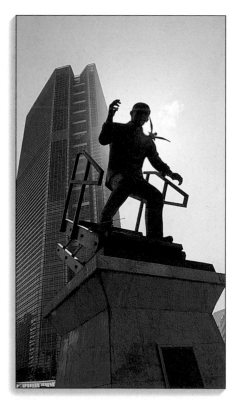

sell their wares at night in the busy Manila cafe areas. Filipinos often wager on the number of baluts that can be eaten at one sitting, but a balut-eating melee frequently turns into a beer drinking contest, and no one remembers to count.

Past Forbes Park and left at EDSA winds in the direction of Pasay City and Parañaque. The South Super Highway, now called J.P. Rizal Superhighway, traverses EDSA before reaching Pasay, and here a right turn will lead back to Malate and the crowded residential districts of Santa Ana, Paco, and Pandacan. A left turn at the Super Highway leads out of Metro Manila and into the lakeshore towns of Laguna Province.

North of the Pasig: The half of Manila north of the **Pasig River** does not carry as many obvious attractions for the traveler as the southern side, except perhaps for the areas close to the river and a few landmarks scattered around the residential districts further north.

Across from Intramuros lie the districts of Binondo and Tondo, once villages that were contemporary with Sulayman's Maynilad. These are now heavily-congested areas characterized by small business shops and cramped residential quarters. Chinatown, which occupies most of Binondo, may be reached by crossing over Jones Bridge from Liwasang Bonifacio. At the foot of the bridge is a small street, Escolta, formerly a major commercial street of Manila. A number of banks have retained their central locations on this short street, together with an assortment of restaurants, department stores, haberdasheries, shoe stores, record shops, and a couple of first-run cinemas, among the city's oldest.

Chinatown: Thanks to its predominantly Chinese community and proximity to the river, **Binondo** became the city's richest mercantile borough at the height of the Manila–Acapulco galleon run. (Manila still has one of the world's largest overseas Chinese population, estimated at over one million.) Evidence of past grandeur may be intimated from the old colonial houses that are now threatened by the continuing encroachment of modern concrete build-

Ninoy Aquino statue, Makati.

ings. The sad, decaying look of these houses fails to obscure certain features once marking an era's resplendence – arched wooden windows, fancy wrought-iron grillwork on balconies, massive wooden doors, brick walls, and tiled roofs where tufts of grass now grow as organic counterpoint to the century's own signature, the TV aerial.

Manila's Chinatown is a maze of such eclectic arrangements. The traditional Chinese apothecary selling dried seahorses and ginseng tea huddles close to a modern bank outfitted with automatic doors and shotgun-carrying guards (of which there are many throughout the city). Chinese restaurants, a favorite destination whenever Manileños go slumming, stand across from a row of Western sports shops, above which are tiny cubicles euphemistically labeled as massage clinics. Acupuncture clinics and kung-fu schools operate on the upper floors of jewelry establishments. And down the choked grid of narrow streets still bearing Iberian names, the *calesas* and *carretelas,* deposed kings of Philippine roads, clip-clop their way a horse-length past romantic oblivion.

Binondo is bounded on the north by Recto Avenue, formerly Azacarraga, beyond which is **Tondo**, a district once the spawning ground of revolutionaries during Spanish times. Now it has a dread reputation as a tough, densely-populated slum area. Its proximity to the harbor's piers has no doubt contributed to its present character, as well as its high population density.

Divisoria: Towards the western end of Recto Avenue, separating Tondo from the district of San Nicolas, is Divisoria, Manila's wild bargain basement. Sprawling over several blocks on the fringes of both districts, Divisoria is a mad emporium where shoppers of all economic levels go to fortify their sense of serendipity. Textiles from the lowly sack cloth to the rare cut of lace, along with fruits and imported handicrafts and hardware, are peddled in a thousand stalls, above where the drunken ghost of *caveat emptor* seems to hang in a thoroughly blissful state of abandon. If preferring a mall, Divisoria has two: the Divisoria Shopping Mall and the Tutuban Center.

East along Recto Avenue is the **Tutuban Railroad Station**, hub of rail travel to points east as well as within the city. Names change, of course, or are compelled to under the guise of new patronage. And so Tutuban now carries the official name of **Philippine National Railway Station**, or PNR for short. From this central station, one can take a train ride (though it's not generally recommended) that will snake past the dingier back sections of the city, including the districts of Tondo and Sta. Cruz in the northern section; Sampaloc and Pandacan in the east; south through Sta. Ana and Makati to the terminal point at Carmona in Laguna province.

Recto Avenue is an important thoroughfare and one of the city's busiest, crossing through five districts that are the city's most populous. Its west end lies at the foot of Roxas Bridge, in the San Nicolas district, so that it is possible to go to Divisoria and Tutuban by going down Bonifacio Drive from Ermita and

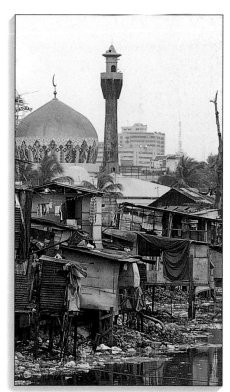

Manila backwater.

crossing over Roxas Bridge. Recto Avenue, after it has passed through Tondo and Binondo, is then intersected by Rizal Avenue, or, as the local folk are wont to call it, Avenida Rizal, or simply, Avenida. This is another important road that services the Sta. Cruz district from its southern end, from the foot of MacArthur Bridge all the way northward to Caloocan City.

This southern end is marked by a heavy concentration of cinemas, department and hardware stores, magazine stands, and a host of sidewalk vendors retailing everything from cheap clothing apparel, toys, sunglasses, watches, and padlocks to playing cards and Playboy magazines. This juncture of Recto Avenue and Avenida Rizal competes with the Quiapo Church area for the distinction of bearing the highest pedestrian traffic in Manila.

Quiapo: Past Avenida Rizal, Recto Avenue is marked by a stretch of small shops selling new and second-hand schoolbooks for the university belt, an area that begins right after Recto Avenue's juncture with Quezon Boulevard. Turning left at Quezon Boulevard leads to **Central Market**, really more of a textile emporium, and eventually to España, which leads to the vast residential and governmental area of Quezon City. Turning right at Quezon Boulevard from Recto Avenue will end up at **Quiapo Church**, at the foot of Quezon Bridge. The area beside the church is the terminal point for most public road transport plying north–south routes of the metropolis. An insane quarter, it has long been considered the heart (some say the armpit) of downtown Manila.

Outside the church patio are Quiapo's fabled herb sellers. Ills of all persuasions from menstrual cramps to a lackluster love life find an answer in these women's organic cornucopia of leaves, stems, twigs, seeds and various oils culled from local plants. To meet the possible contingency of a sudden rise in national health standards, they double as sellers of amulets, candles, religious calendars, local almanacs and hopeful lottery tickets.

Quiapo's Black Nazarene procession.

134

The church interior itself reeks of the appropriate ambience for the Filipino's peculiarly viscous form of devotion. It is dark, dank and heavily-peopled at all hours. Down the length of the aisle, old women walk on their knees in fervent prayer. Men wipe their handkerchiefs on the icons and touch these to their lips. A second dab goes to the brows of their little kids. And a third is a final accord with spiritual power, the token of which is then folded with solemn contentment and placed back into the pocket close to the heaving breast.

Quiapo Church is the devotional arena for the First Friday of the month novenas. It is also the shrine and home of the Black Nazarene, a life-sized Christ kneeling on a platform and bearing a huge cross on his shoulder. On the ninth of January, the image is borne forth in a frenzied all-male procession leading a massed throng of barefoot devotees down the back streets of the district.

In front of Quiapo Church is **Plaza Miranda**, where the public pulse is taken come political kite-flying time.

Bounding this plaza are several streets catering to the common person's needs. Carriedo Street is the shoe-store lane. On Evangelista and Hidalgo are flower vendors, camera shops, crypt sculptors. Down Villalobos leading to the Quinta Market are tinsmiths and clothiers. Before the market, right under the span of Quezon Bridge where jeepneys heading northwards make their U-turns, there are makeshift stalls for cheap handicrafts. These popular stalls are called, simply, **Ilalim ng Tulay** (Under the Bridge).

Carriedo leads to Avenida Rizal, as do the parallel streets of Paterno, Ronquillo, and Gonzalo Puyat. The last, still more popularly known as Raon, is Manila's short but strident version of Tin Pan Alley, where overstocked record shops engage in fierce battles of decibels till late in the evening, adding to the usual street pandemonium.

Down Quezon Boulevard towards Recto Avenue is another conglomeration of textile shops, army surplus stores, pawnshops, bicycle stores, restaurants,

Malacañang Palace.

hole-in-the-wall palmists and astrologers, martial arts schools, dental clinics, notary public offices and movie houses.

At the juncture of Quezon Boulevard and Recto Avenue, turn right into the latter to enter the university belt, where several colleges and universities disgorge tens of thousands of students to add to downtown Manila's transport problems. The University of the East, for instance, lays claim to having the largest enrollment in Asia, with its more than 60,000 students. Close to where Recto Avenue becomes Mendiola Street is the **San Sebastian Church**, reputedly the only prefabricated steel church in the world. Every single piece of its structure was fabricated in Belgium and shipped here for assembly in the closing years of the 19th century.

Malacañang Palace: Mendiola Street threads past several private colleges to **Malacañang Palace**, formerly the office-residence of Philippine presidents. It is now open to the public as a museum, housing memorabilia of all Philippine past presidents. Originally a country estate owned by a Spanish nobleman, Malacañang became the summer residence of Spanish governor-generals in the middle 1800s. Nineteen Spanish executives took turns ruling the country from Malacañang before it was turned over to the first of what would become 14 American governor-generals. Since Independence Day in 1946, nine Filipino chief executives have set up shop in the Presidential Palace, the last being Ferdinand Marcos. Corazon Aquino broke with tradition by choosing to operate from the adjacent Guest House.

Backtracking up Mendiola and Recto Avenues, turn right at Nicanor Reyes Street and shortly find yourself on España Street, where the campus of the **University of Santo Tomas** is located. The oldest university in Asia, it is a point of honor among Filipino historians that this university antedates Harvard by a good 25 years, having been founded by the Dominicans in 1611.

Quezon City: España Street leads straight to the boundary between Manila proper and **Quezon City**, once the country's official capital before its integration into Metro Manila. At best, however, Quezon City only served nominally as the capital; Manila retained the important government institutions.

Where España ends, Quezon City's **Welcome Rotunda** marks the beginning of the former capital's two major thoroughfares. Forking right is Rodriguez Avenue, formerly, and still to most people in the city, known as España Extension. This leads to **Cubao**, Quezon City's commercial center, a popular place among most Manileños but derided by some city aesthetes as a crude, traffic-infested jungle of shops and supermarkets that, unlike Makati, doesn't quite make the grade. Cubao's landmark is the Araneta Coliseum, which was billed as the world's largest domed coliseum way back in the 1960s.

Quezon City's other major street, Quezon Boulevard Extension, leads straight from the Welcome Rotunda to the higher ground of Diliman, site of the sprawling main campus of the University of the Philippines. Just before Diliman is the old Capital Site.

Left, clock tower, University of Sto. Tomas. **Right**, simple transport.

CAVITE AND BATANGAS

Bound together by the low-slung Dos Picos Mountains south of Cavite and north of Batangas, not to mention by history and circumstances, the provinces of Cavite and Batangas lie directly south of Manila.

Both provinces share in a powerful common memory: the Philippine Revolution of 1896. Cavite and Batangas have yielded a high ratio of revolutionary heroes – lawyers, men of battle, poets, merchants – devoted to the overthrow of 333 years of Spanish rule and establishing an independent republic.

Las Piñas: On the way to Taal or on way back to Manila, be sure to visit the **Sarao Jeepney Factory** (closed Sundays), in **Las Piñas**, to see jeepneys being hand-molded and painted by artists, with designs that make each one distinctive. Another stop in Las Piñas is the **San Jose Church**, which sports the only bamboo organ in the world, built in 1821 and refurbished in 1975. Its 954 pipes – 832 bamboo and 122 metal – still reverberate in regular services on Sundays, and during the week-long Bamboo Organ Festival in February.

In many ways, Cavite is a sociological gem. Tattered at its northern boundary towns of **Zapote** and **Bacoor** by factories and refineries, neon lights and beer drinkers, this part of Cavite hums with the rhythm of rock music floating out of crazily painted bars. Southward, a tradition in fine seafood has been layered over by beach resorts.

The beaches at Noveleta, Rosario and Tanza (the last two are old shipbuilding towns) have been trodden by generations of weekenders from Manila. Too, the towns' proximity to industry has made the waters less and less inviting.

Cavite takes its name from the hook shape of its old population center – *kawit*, Tagalog for hook. At the tip of this hook is the city of **Cavite** (*cavite* is the Hispanized form of *kawit*), until recently the provincial capital. Around here, the Spanish outfitted galleons for the Manila–Acapulco run, as well as

small boats to fend off the constantly marauding Moros. It was here that an attack by a Dutch squadron in 1647 damaged a stone fort, whose ruins still stand at **Porta Vaga**.

In the 1870s, a mutiny among Filipino workers around the docks provided the Spanish government with the perfect excuse to punish the leaders of an increasingly powerful movement. The ensuing martyrdom of *indio* priests ignited the sparks of revolution. When the revolution finally happened, the newly arrived Americans aborted the new republic when they took over the Philippines after defeating Spain in the Spanish-American War, in 1898. Cavite found itself once more the site of a colonial naval station, and until the late 1960s, Sangley Point remained an important U.S. naval installation.

Kawit is the birthplace of Emilio Aguinaldo, general of the province's revolutionary forces and eventually president of the first but short-lived Philippine Republic. Long after the revolution in Manila had collapsed from disor-

ganization, Aguinaldo and his men were planning and implementing strategy in Kawit, building a solid southern front which was to hold out against the Spanish for two years. By June 1898, revolutionaries hoisted the Philippine flag from Aguinaldo's balcony, to a battle hymn soon to become the national anthem.

At the center of these rites, the **Aguinaldo Shrine**, a whitewashed home of late colonial vintage, displays the mementos of the period. Among the murals and symbols on display, the photo gallery stands out, portraying the young indios revolutionaries.

Continuing along the southwestern coast and the southern hills of the province, the coastal town of **Maragondon** puts not only history but the untouched natural attractions of Cavite into high relief. Approached from the plains, the hills and the low mountains ahead form a grand rim that sets off the sunset with a poet's touch. In those elevations is this old Jesuit town with its gem of a church, undoubtedly one of the loveliest in an archipelago of churches. It at first ap-

pears deceptively plain until one approaches the intricately-carved door of natural wood and enters the rococo splendor of the interior. Trumpeting angels on the altar and friezes on the pulpit conjure up images of the rattling swords and whizzing bullets of a revolution that overflowed into this church. Andres Bonifacio, that problematic head of the Katipunan, was also imprisoned here by the Caviteños for trying to divide and rule the struggle in their province. Later, he was bludgeoned to death in one of Maragondon's hills and buried on Mt Buntis.

North of Maragondon, another bit of history regarding the Jesuits lingers. In 1663, the Spaniards decided to withdraw their forces from the Moluccan islands of Ternate, Tidore, and Siao. The Spanish Jesuits in those Indonesian posts took their converts to the Philippines and built the settlement north of Maragondon that would, like their old home, be called Ternate.

Intriguing is a visit to Imelda Marcos' favorite country retreat in **Ternate**. The **Bamboo House** sits on a 4-hectare (10-acre) estate amid bougainvillea and hibiscus, and boasts a well-appointed four-bedroom main house as well as cottages. It is built in the indigenous style, or at least what the locals would like if they had a few million pesos to spare, and lies in the grounds of the exclusive Puerto Azul Beach Resort.

Batangas Province: There are three entry points into Batangas: through the Batulao Mountain Range in the north (on the Cavite border); through the agricultural town of Santo Tomas (on the Laguna border); and, perhaps the most thrilling, down a steep road separating Tagaytay from the town of Talisay.

To Batangas Province can be traced some of the oldest ancestors of Tagalog culture. Archaeologists have traced human habitation here to 250,000 years ago, around the southwestern coastline of Balayan Bay.

Tradition fills in the events of a few thousand years later with the story of the Bornean chieftains who fled the tyrant Makatunaw, sometime in the 13th century. They came northward to the Phil-

Selling the local coconut liquor.

ippines, landed on Panay in the Visayas, then continued north in search of a better area to settle. When they reached Balayan Bay, they followed the Pansipit River to the shores of Lake Taal.

With their families and slaves, they settled the fertile land, building an orderly community skilled in rice cultivation and weaving. Literate and possessing a codified law, the Borneans eventually exerted leadership over a wide area embracing what are now Batangas, Oriental and Occidental Mindoro, Quezon, Laguna Provinces, and part of Bicol.

Bombon was the old name of this far-flung area. Archaeological evidence in grave sites in Calatagan and Lemery shows that Bombon conducted a lively trade with Arab, Chinese, and Indian merchants over the centuries.

Batangas was a major discovery for the *conquistadores* Juan de Salcedo and Martin Goiti, in 1570. Settlements abounded along the Pansipit River, a journey that gave Salcedo an arrow in the foot, let fly by a mistrustful local chieftain. That, however, seems to have been the extent of local protest to the *conquista*. As Jose Rizal points out in his annotations to the Spanish historian Morga: "The people, accustomed to the yoke, did not defend their chiefs from the invader... The nobles, accustomed to tyrannize by force, had to accept foreign tyranny when it showed itself stronger than their own."

Delighted by the rivers and "excellent meadows" of the place, the Spanish soon began the settlement pattern they enforced wherever they had gained a foothold in the country. Instead of money, the penurious Spanish Crown granted tracts of land called *encomiendas* to individuals and religious orders most useful to their colonization effort. Inhabitants were classified into the *tributos* or tribute-paying heads of families, and the *almas* or souls, baptized individuals.

A century and a half after Batangas became a province, the indios began to take up arms against the Spanish authorities, one grievance being that their land had been expropriated by Augustinians and Jesuits, who now

Catches of the day.

owned and administered the large cattle ranches found all over Bombon. There were also other problems. The orderly settlements of Batangas attracted Moro plunders all through the 17th century. Their main purpose was the taking of slaves for their new kingdoms in the Mindanao wilderness. The ruins of stone coastal lookouts and defenses can be found in Lemery, Bauan, and Batangas.

In 1732, the Spanish government transferred the capital from coastal Balayan to inland Taal. At the same time, they chose to rename the territory after the new capital. This was the beginning of the "civilization" of Batangas, a process that accompanied a period of rapid economic growth, especially after the coffee bean was introduced from Mexico in 1841. Coffee thrived in the rich volcanic soil to seed of the growth of the Taaleño middle class, who by the 19th century would be dining on golden plates and sending their sons to schools in Madrid and Paris. With this economic impetus, the Taaleños started trading with enthusiasm, transporting produce from island to island. Soon an ornate church that would be the toast of the region would rise in Taal's center.

Touring **Batangas Province** can be divided into two parts – around Lake Taal and along the irregular coastline west, south and southeast. The jagged coast of Batangas has one of the most interesting collections of bays, coves, and peninsulas in the archipelago. In the northwest, the towns of **Nasugbu** and **Lian** lead to beach strips with the usual collection of simple bamboo cottages that can be rented for the night, as well as clusters of up-market beach houses.

The **Calatagan Peninsula** in the southwest has an old Spanish town set in what used to be a large *hacienda* and forest preserve owned by the old and very wealthy Zobel-Ayala family. Calatagan not only has a relatively unspoilt strip of white-sand beach, but also boasts a decent resort called Punta Baluarte, which is hewn out of a rocky cliff, and was named by its mestizo Spanish Ayala proprietors after the finest of the Costa Blanca.

Prawn farming.

Lake Taal: Two hours' drive south from Manila is the **Taal Volcano**. As one of the most active volcanoes in the world, it smolders and occasionally rumbles, and always presents a dramatic sight. The best place to view it is from the heights of **Tagaytay Ridge**, where the major roads intersect. From here, the volcanic islands are clearly visible within the massive crater lake.

Since its first known eruption in 1572, Taal has erupted 32 times. The last eruption took place in 1977, with the center of eruption shifting from the main crater to places on the island. In the mid 1990s, Taal threatened to erupt again, but failed to make good on its threat.

A pleasant spot for lunch is Gourmet's, on Aguinaldo Highway and just north of **Tagaytay**. It's an old plantation house refurbished as a restaurant. If picnicking, try Picnic Grove, just east of Tagaytay. This Philippine Tourism Authority-run park offers good picnic facilities, a fine view of the volcano and horseback riding. West of Tagaytay sits the Taal Vista Lodge and Casino. While the lodge offers minimal facilities and dank, bunker-like rooms, it does have a good view of the volcano. (A new hotel is planned to open at Taal Vista in 1999, as is a new Westin resort, Splendido Taal, nearby. Until then, the best place to stay overnight in the Taal area is the Tagaytay Highlands, a golf resort on the backside of Tagaytay Ridge, a short drive from Tagaytay. The resort lies below the unfinished and now-ruined Marcos country mansion known as The Palace in the Sky, not worth the visit.

The ionic and corinthian columns of **Taal Church** are now nicely covered in moss, but the original grandeur still strikes visitors. From the belfry of the old church, a favorite tourist perch, unfolds a panoramic sweep of this former belle of Batangas: the fields of sugar cane, the blue meandering of the Pansipit River and the present century's own television antennas sprouting like a newly-laid bamboo grove over the roof tops of the 100-year-old houses.

Drying in the sun, on the scrollwork around the public market, are frames of

Fishing on Lake Taal, and embroidering on pineapple fiber.

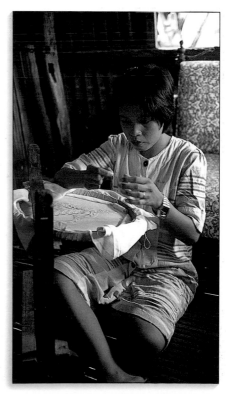

bleached *piña* – woven from near-transparent pineapple fibers – used in embroidery. A tradition of the provinces, this detailed needlework is what gives the *barong tagalog* its distinction. Another Taal original is the flip-open knife of the same name, sold along the road.

Perhaps it was needlework that gave Marcela Agoncillo of Taal a whole page of Philippine history – she sewed the first Filipino flag for the young generals of the revolution. A marker on the Agoncillo House also praises her for pawning her jewels to finance her husband's revolutionary activities.

The town of **Mabini**, eastward off Balayan Bay, is popular with scuba divers. Farther east, off Batangas Bay in the municipality of **Lobo**, isolated white sand beaches can be found. Maricaban and Verde Islands, lying to the southwest and southeast of Lobo, are even more remote and pristine.

To the west of Taal, **Lipa** is interesting for its collection of old ancestral homes, varied flower gardens, and coffee plantations. In the center of town sits

Casa de Segunda, a typical Bahay na Bato that has been lovingly restored to its original glory by the Luz family. History records that the house was named after Segunda Katigbak, the first love of Jose Rizal, whom eventually married Manual Luz.

Los Baños: Be sure to visit **Los Baños**, just over an hour from Manila on the South Super Highway and the home of the **International Rice Research Institute** (IRRI). In 1960, the Rockefeller and Ford foundations joined forces to fund "Erie", as it is called. In a few short years, IRRI developed what's been called a miracle rice. The test fields at IRRI are the most intensely planted rice fields in the world, and visitors can stroll around the fields, which are marked, and see rice from every corner of the world. The Riceworld Museum (weekdays from 8:00 am to 5:00 pm), in the IRRI's main complex, is one of the only museums in the world dedicated to rice, offering an excellent introduction to the history, culture and science of rice cultivation.

On the southern slope of the extinct volcano of **Mt Makiling**, beyond Los Baños, lies **Hidden Valley Springs**, in **Alaminos**. This mountain hideaway is an extremely pleasant private resort, where several springs – hot, cold and soda – have been channeled into specially-constructed bathing pools. A series of paths lead through the jungle of fruit trees, giant ferns and wild orchids to the gurgling pools and a natural waterfall. Hike to a waterfall for a swim in the waters, said to be therapeutic.

From Los Baños, the next town is **Calamba**, the birthplace of Jose Rizal. The old Rizal house on the main street is now a national shrine, landscaped with all the fruit trees of the Philippine lowlands interspersed with varieties transplanted from other Asian orchards.

It is a treat to wander in this garden, fragrant with giant *mabolo*, *santol* and mango, and then to go indoors to the wealthy appointments of a home typical of Laguna gentry. Rice harvested from private fields was stored in huge grain baskets, coffee was ground in the kitchen, and reading was done by the soft light of kerosene lamps.

Left, Jose Rizal's house. **Right**, coffee established the Batangas aristocracy.

RIZAL AND LAGUNA

Long before the Spanish first laid eyes on **Laguna de Bay**, the largest lake in what was to become the Philippines, the heart-shaped body of water already cradled a thriving community. The lake waters spread out over 90,000 hectares (220,000 acres), with the Sierra Madre range looming in the east and the twin peaks of Makiling and Banahaw in the south. Farmers grew rice on the surrounding fertile plain, fishermen harvested from the abundant waters, and traders transported their goods to lakeside towns on slim gliding *bancas*. Regularly, large *cascos*, or barges, roofed over with woven bamboo mats – Malay versions of interisland cargo ships – traveled to the northwest shores and down the Pasig River. This 16-kilometer-long (10 mi) waterway, connecting the lake to Manila Bay, flowed heavy with loads of rice, fish, ducks, and vegetables for sale to the Taga-Ilog in Maynilad, now Manila.

The Spanish named the lake Laguna de Bay (Lake of Bay), establishing a trading settlement on the southern shore that was regularly visited by Chinese traders. Simply called Bay, it served as the first capital of the province of Laguna.

Rizal Province. In 1901, two years after Spain ceded the Philippines to America, Rizal was created out of 19 towns belonging to the old Spanish province of Manila (excluding the city proper) and 14 towns of the former political and military district of Morong, northwest of the lake, which once were part of old Laguna.

Postwar Filipino historians contend that the Americans named the province after Jose Rizal in a canny public relations move. Well aware that most of the towns incorporated into the new province were among the first to rise in rebellion against Spain in the 1890s, the Americans sought to soothe inflamed local sentiment in their aborted revolution with a bow to the cause's martyr.

Three routes lead from Manila to the Rizal countryside. The northern road runs from Caloocan to Marikina. The middle route runs from Epifanio de los Santos Avenue (EDSA) to Pasig. The southern road passes through the salt-producing town of Parañaque. Getting through these municipalities provides an appropriate metaphor on the outmoded infrastructure struggling to cope with the traffic of a growing population.

Twenty kilometers (12 mi) from Manila the road between Marikina and Pasig forks. To the east lies **Cainta** and **Taytay**, the first towns to be subjugated by the Spanish, and in recent times the first to succumb to creeping industrialization. In Cainta, however, lingers a stray bit of trivia. Many of the inhabitants are said to be descendants of British soldiers that invaded the lakeshore in 1762. Traditionally, they are called *sepoy*, for their bronze-colored skin.

Five kilometers (3 mi) beyond Taytay lies hilly **Antipolo**, celebrated in song and legend as the home of the icon of Our Lady of Peace and Good Voyage, widely touted for miraculous powers. This dark icon carved by a Mexican

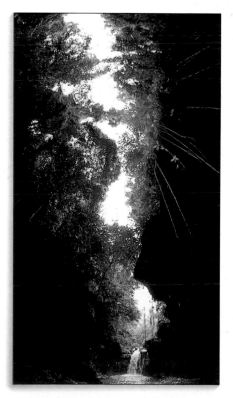

craftsman first gained stature by safely crossing a turbulent Pacific Ocean in 1626. She was first enshrined by Franciscans in an acacia-shaded barrio on the plains; the Jesuits later transferred her to the present hillside shrine in 1632. Ever since, Antipolo has been the site of many pilgrimages, as, traditionally, no trips abroad should be taken without a visit to Nuestra Señora. Antipolo stands in a bedlam of carnival crowds and peddlers of candles, medallions and rosary. T-shirts with silkscreen prints of baroque images are even sold in the plaza.

From Cainta, the road leads southeast to **Angono**, one of the Philippines' better art centers and but a 30-minute drive from Manila. The Balaw Balaw Restaurant and Lake Island Resort here are both worth a stop. Balaw Balaw offers an eclectic collection of local art works and local culinary treats, like assorted lizard and monkey dishes. The Lake Island Resort pushes out on a peninsula into Laguna de Bay, with views of the fishing community.

Angono's best sights, though, are its local artists. The Nemiranda Arthouse, in Dona Justa, is the home and studio of Nemi R. Miranda, Jr. (a.k.a. Nemiranda). Born in Angono in 1949, and graduated from the University of Santo Tomas, Nemiranda stands as one of the Philippines' best contemporary artists working today. A stop at his studio is a rare treat, especially if he is there working on one of his massive folklore or environmental works.

The **Blanco Family Museum** is also in Angono, with hundreds of works by the family's seven working artists. Jose Blanco, nicknamed Pitok, started it all in the mid-1960s. Now Pitok, his wife Loreto and all seven of their children contribute to the Philippine art world.

Past Angono, along the lakeshore, sits the prosperous fishing town of **Cardona**, the balconies of its houses hanging over the lapping waters of the lake. It is a main center of the milkfish industry that spreads over 3,900 hectares (9,600 acres) of the lake.

Just beyond Cardona lies the old Span-

Banca on Laguna de Bay.

ish center of **Morong**. The dome and belfry of its church rise over a sea of green fields. The church, the main attraction of Morong, has an exquisitely carved facade of Filipino baroque. When the baroque movement swept Europe in the 17th century, echoes were heard in the Spanish colonies. In the Philippines, the excitement moved the clergy to refurbish older, plainer structures. Two centuries after construction, the Morong church was redesigned by a wealthy citizen of the town of Paete. It is one of the finest examples of tropical baroque in the Philippines.

Further along the lakeshore lies **Tanay** and its lovely waterfalls. On the outskirts of town, a 14-meter (46-ft) cascade spills into an opaline pool. Called Daranak, a series of small falls gurgle among giant tree roots and writhing stone pathways called Butlag, an idyllic setting for many Filipino movies.

From Tanay, through Pililla and on into Laguna Province runs a 20-kilometer (13 mi) stretch of winding mountain road. Laguna de Bay gleams blue below, while a mist hangs over the dark outlines of the peaks Makiling and Banahaw on the opposite shore.

Laguna Province: What was lost in the relationship between Rizal and Manila can still be found in the green nooks and crannies of Laguna. The 400-year-old marriage between *conquista* and the insular Malay settlements are still tangible here in polite forms of address, sweets on the table, ornate balusters, and colorful flower boxes adorning nearly every window.

The presence of the volcanoes **Makiling** and **Banahaw** dominates life in Laguna. On the periphery of these two extinct volcanoes, sulfur springs gush forth with a force as strong as the mountain myths and legends that haunt the imagination of the foothill people.

Mt Makiling, they say, is where the goddess Maria, the beautiful guardian of the forests, resides. Mt Banahaw, her male counterpart, is where the stouthearted must go to gain strength and wisdom. Up on Banahaw's slopes live several occult sects practicing home-

Mt. Banahaw cult ritual.

grown versions of the cabala and ancient Egyptian mythology. Where they come from, and how they got there, no one seems to know. In the towns around the foot of Mt. Banahaw also live amulet makers, faith healers, and soothsayers, all of whom claim to draw strength from the towering mystic mountain.

At the northeastern boundary, the road dips and moves closer to the lakeshore. The first Laguna towns are Mabitac and Siniloan, in the foothills of the Sierra Madre. **Mabitac** has a magnificent 17th-century church on a hilltop, built high enough to protect it from flood waters pouring down the mountain sides.

Next on the route, Pangil, Pakil and Paete are nothing if not set pieces of colonial Spanish style and scale. Approached from the highway, their narrow streets and tiny houses with carved balusters and scroll-worked eaves take on an elfin quality. Here you might see residents in straw hats, swinging their canes on a sunset *paseo*, and conversing in Spanish with the mellifluous accent of Laguna.

The three exemplary churches of these towns are as tiny as they are exquisite, the most outstanding being the one in **Paete**. A long woodcarving tradition is evident on its facade, executed with exuberant license. On it, St James, the town's patron saint, rides off to battle the Moors, surrounded by a cornucopia of palms and blossoms characterizing Filipino baroque.

While Paete is known for wood carving, **Pakil** to the north is noted for its delicate and fanciful carvings. The delicate toothpicks topped by fanned peacock's tails, butterflies or spiralling trees found in Manila's hotels come from Pakil. A local joke: the carvings of Pakil are the recycled woodcraft of Paete.

South of Paete, an ascending road on the left leads to the Lake Caliraya Country Club. The lake was dug out during the American period to provide water for a hydroelectric plant. The country club is a popular weekend retreat for water-skiing Manileños.

Pagsanjan: Pagsanjan (pron. *pag-san-han*) awaits along the Magdapio River,

Lighting candles, Mt. Banahaw.

156

often called the Pagsanjan River and offering classic whitewater experiences. At the **Pagsanjan Rapids**, visitors change into swimsuits or shorts and travel upriver in open boats, or *banca*. Often the boatman has to get out to push or lift the banca over shallows and other obstructions, but the return journey is thrilling as the boats negotiate the rapids, often getting drenched.

Before coming to the waterfalls that are the focus of the trip, the banca slides between the sides of a picturesque gorge, sheer and glistening with small water falls, and vibrant moss and lichen. The walls rise nearly 100 meter (300 ft), the air still and softly humming with forest sounds. Finally, the waterfalls are reached. At the second falls, passengers from the banca transfer onto rafts guided by long ropes from the shore into the mouth of a cave behind the falls. There is nothing compared to the sensation of going under this ice-cold water right into the walls of a cavern. (Weekdays are best to avoid the crowds.)

The next destination toward the lake is the provincial capital, **Santa Cruz**. Like Pagsanjan, this old town is laid out in grander colonial style than the smaller settlements by the lake. The burgeoning provincial capital was transferred to Pagsanjan in 1688, and in 1858 it was moved once more to the up-and-coming Santa Cruz. This town not only makes excellent white cheese, it has also cornered the market in antique Chinese pottery dug up in surrounding coconut plantations and in the area of old Morong.

Not surprisingly, most of the pottery was found in graves, attesting to the value attached by the old Malays to the ceramics acquired through trade with the Chinese. Collecting fever, fanned by traveling Manila collectors, has spawned several roadside stands advertising antiques for sale. For those interested in the more scholarly value of these items, however, there is a small museum in **Pila**, south of Santa Cruz, where they are properly showcased.

A small but recommended side-tour from Santa Cruz leads into the southern underbelly of the province, where the

Three faces with three smiles.

traveler can drift in another century, moving through a world that continues to be serene and self-contained.

To get there, travel southeast through Pagsanjan's backdoor, away from the patently packaged tour groups, toward Cavinti and Pinagsangahan. The vegetation thickens approaching **Luisiana**, as groves of giant pandanus trees growing in the swampy soil line the road. The entry into the town winds through a cemetery and past long lines of giant pandanus leaves laid out along the sides of the road. After drying, they are made into bags and mats.

Out of Luisiana, the road runs southwest to **Majayjay**, the oldest settlement in the area. There is a Brigadoon quality to Majayjay, laid out on a series of small hills with roads twisting and curving to reveal one colonial treasure after another. Mt Banahaw sits beyond. White-haired grandmothers sit contemplating travelers from the ground floors of squat stone houses, while children at the plaza stop to stare. As elsewhere in the Philippines, everything converges on the church at the center of town, but there is added drama to Majayjay's elevated structure, twice built and thrice restored, with its walls three layers thick. This church is the repository of both the written and oral memory of Majayjay's much troubled history, marked by ongoing tension between Franciscan missionaries and the locals they had forced to labor on its construction and repair for years on end. Rather than be counted among the population of Majayjay subject to compulsory labor, many people built their huts in fields just outside the town boundaries, only to have them burned by friars hard put to find labor to support their infrastructure. The hatred engendered by these acts eventually led to the division of Majayjay into three towns and, ultimately, into indigenous participation in the revolution of 1896.

Liliw, next on the route, has a remarkable church located right at the end of a road that seems to head straight for Mt Banahaw in the background. This town is known for its high-quality, handmade footwear. Along the bank of the rushing **Fiesta meal.**

river, women congregate to make laundry day a social occasion.

West of Liliw lies **Nagcarlan**, another gem of history and the last of the southern Laguna towns on this little side trip. A church and an underground cemetery here can be considered undeclared national treasures. The same Franciscan, Fray Juan de Plasencia, who built the foundations of several Rizal, Laguna and Quezon towns, laid the groundwork for Nagcarlan.

What gives the church and cemetery their fascinating and intoxicating flavor, however, were the renovations done by Father Vicente Velloc, who restored the former and constructed the latter in the mid 1900s. Baroque, Moorish and Javanese styles add a mystifying touch to these two structures. Glazed blue ceramic tiles decorate parts of the church and a wall of the cemetery's underground crypt.

On the landing leading to the underground tombs – now sealed off – are faded epigraphs in Spanish, too blurred to translate. These lead to the legend of

Statue of Jose Rizal, one of dozens in the archipelago.

Father Velloc's crypt. It is said that he had an underground passage built leading to an underground chapel, where he said solitary masses, and on all the way to Mt Banahaw. In 1896, the crypt was the clandestine meeting place of Katipuneros, the secret society whose activities flamed into revolution.

The excursion into Laguna's heartland finished, take the southwestward route into **San Pablo**, a commercial center where charm dissipates into the mundane concerns of trade. Commercial routes north from Bicol and Quezon in the south to Manila converge in this city. A transient air pervades, relieved somewhat by a charming plaza and a promenade area beside the largest of the city's seven lakes.

January is the time to dine well here, because an abundance of fish teems near the lake shores, driven there by the rising sulfuric content of the waters in what are, scientists say, the craters of extinct volcanoes. From San Pablo, there is a choice between going west to Santo Tomas or northwest to Los Baños.

QUEZON

At dawn on a gentle day, light falls on the first artifact of aristocracy: the province's boundary marker, a triumphal arch with two art-deco angels trumpeting entry into Quezon, and with humorous pomposity. Welcome, then, to another genteel stretch of Philippine road, memorable for summer's firebushes and September's yellow lanzones fruit.

Named after native son and former Commonwealth President Manuel L. Quezon and his First Lady, long and narrow **Quezon** and the province of Aurora to the north stretch a third of the length of Luzon's eastern shoreline.

The longest, and by some tallies, the largest province on Luzon, this snakelike pair share boundaries with mountainous Nueva Vizcaya and Isabela to the north, and the mine-rich Camarines provinces of the Bicol region to the south. The grand basalt sweep of the Sierra Madre range, beginning at the

northeastern most tip of the archipelago and running the entire length of Aurora and Quezon, buffers typhoons that wreak yearly havoc on a ruggedly beautiful coastline lying full-face to the Philippine Sea.

Geography is destiny in Quezon. People live concentrated along the western – and sheltered – side of the mountains, in inland valleys that isolate them from each other. Moreover, Quezon has always been isolated between north and south. The small, relatively flat area to the south has an ample road network, while the mountainous four-fifths of the province to the north remains practically inaccessible by land. Much of its forested terrain is home to nomadic people and wildlife, and loggers. East of the Sierra Madres, a relatively flat coastline – in many places falling sharply from 30-meter-high (100-ft) cliffs – encourages a scattering of isolated villages that live off marine-rich coastal waters.

Exploring Quezon: The better-known southern portion of Quezon is in many ways a continuation of Laguna Province, but more deeply marked by the pace of the coconut industry, to which the province owes a large percentage of its agricultural revenue. The deeply Hispanized lordly classes of yesteryear – horseriding gentry resting secure on the income and farm labor of their coconut plantations – has left tangible relics of their lifestyle all through the area, beginning in the town of **Tiaong** on Quezon's southwestern boundary and wending its way eastward.

Barely one kilometer past the arch and art-deco angels lies **Villa Escudero**, an old-time coconut plantation of 800 hectares (2,000 acres). Reputed to be one of the best-managed in the country, this plantation is a self-contained community of some 300 interrelated families, many of them third-generation.

Sariaya, 12 kilometers (8 mi) farther east, is a prosperous trading town and the old home grounds of farm aristocracy. Antique houses loom over narrow streets, the highest of them overlooking the dome of Sariaya's church, a hush of stained-glass windows bathing an unusually bloody crucified Christ. Old in **Young Filipina.**

the ways of leisure, Sariaya also has a reputation as the home of a distinguished cottage industry marketing Quezon's heirloom pastry and fruit candy recipes.

Tayabas, six kilometers (4 mi) northeast of Sariaya, was once the capital of Quezon before Lucena to the south was chosen as the more promising commercial center, by virtue of its coastal location. There was good fortune in the choice, as this hilly town has been left to its own devices, its small houses standing in familial repose.

From Tayabas, it is six kilometers (4 mi) northward to **Lucban**, a provincial border town where isolation has ripened an exotic fruit to fullness. It could have been only yesterday that the Spanish came and left from here. The church bells still ring out at four in the morning, shaking a sleepy old town from dreams of moss and mountain pools. **Mt Banahaw** looms like a forbidding parent chilling the climate of this tropical Gothic outpost.

Come mid-May, Lucban, like Sariaya, springs alive to the festival of *pahiyas*, literally the "enjewelment", when all doors and windows are loaded with summer's papayas and citruses, squashes, cucumbers and corn in a festoonery among rainbow-colored sheets of *kiping* – delicate leaf impressions made of pounded, melted and dyed rice starch. Giant *carabaos* and scarecrows of papier-machi dance past the courtyard of Lucban's 400-year-old church, bowing to its moss-covered stone angel transformed into images of a childhood.

The Franciscans must be blessed for having invented this magical ritual celebrating the feast of San Isidro Labrador, the Catholic saint declared patron of the farmer and the worker. For even today, the spectacle of color and childlike revelry set to the music of an outdoor mass does not fail to touch a chord in Filipino and foreign heart alike.

Coastal ramble: The long and varied coast of Quezon Province plunges into rich and relatively unexploited fishing waters. Lamon Bay off the mid-eastern shores, Tayabas Bay south of Lucena, and Ragay Gulf, which separates the

A May festival in Lucban.

southeastern extremity of the province from the western shores of Camarines Sur in the Bicol region, all draw commercial trawlers and anglers, and recently deep-sea divers as well. These waters, in turn, lap the shores of some of the finest beaches in the country, rimming both mainland and offshore islands. On the scenic south road from Tiaong to Lucena, for instance, is the route to the coastal town of **Padre Burgos**, a jumping-off point to the paired islands of Pagbilao Grande and Pagbilao Chico, on Tayabas Bay.

Connected by a sandy isthmus, this pair of islands is actually a million-year-old coral reef, riddled with hundreds of coves and caves. To listen to sentimental islanders talking, one would think that all this geographical evolution had happened only to accommodate the well-loved legend of Bulaklak and Hangin.

The god Hangin (lit. wind), already betrothed to a goddess, once wandered the earth. One day, his eye lit on Bulaklak (lit. flower), a mortal woman of haunting beauty. They fell in love, but tugged and pulled by divine edict and mortal law, they were left no other choice but suicide. Divine compassion would not look the other way. Afterwards, the lovers' bodies were turned into two islands, forever linked by a bridge of sand – **Pagbilao Grande**, the larger of the two islands, and **Pagbilao Chico**, the lesser. *Barangay* say that on this bridge of sand each May, Bulaklak and Hangin cause a child to drown, joining them as offspring in the other world.

The legend makes good company as you walk through wildly overgrown patches of tropical forest and crescent-shaped coves of staggering variety, many of them lined with giant yucca plants. It could well be Hangin himself whistling on **Estamper Point**, a cave lookout high on the peak of Pagbilao Chico. From this peak, the local people say, hundreds of Japanese sailors whose ships had been sunk by American submarines once hurled themselves to death to avoid capture. It is probably true, given the history of similar episodes elsewhere.

Communal spirit of bayanihan sharing the load.

There are other beach strips to be discovered along the coastlines of Quezon and Aurora, but a particular stretch of coast in the southern portion of Aurora holds out singular attraction: the surfing waters of **Baler Bay**.

The old Franciscan town of Baler is today a medium-sized trading center, with a large migrant Ilocano population. Known as the homeland of Manuel L. Quezon, the first president of the Commonwealth and once known as "the poor boy from Baler", it still retains the distinct flavor of a Spanish settlement.

To its market come the basket-weaving Ilocano farmers and fishermen, as well as the nomadic Atis Negritos. To add to the melting pot, Baler has a small airport and a port for the logging boats plying the eastern shoreline of Luzon. Come March and continuing on through June, an assortment of modern nomads brave the 13-hour bus ride via the dusty flatlands of Nueva Ecija and narrow Sierra Madre roads, through rain forest lined with 10-meter-high (30-ft) ferns. Breathless with tales of darting civet cats and exotic birds, the adventurous hike off and travel to **Cemento**, a fishing village on Cape Encanto. The charms of the seacoast are well complemented by the charms of wildlife thriving all over Quezon.

North of Pagbilao Grande, accessible via the south road proceeding from the town of **Pagbilao**, lies **Quezon National Park**, a short detour from the main highway.

Here, birds twitter among large trees and writhing ancient vines and roots. Doves and orioles, woodpeckers and red-crested royal *kalaw* birds light on this place in droves, and wild monkeys snatch sandwiches off picnic tables. The peak of this elevated jungle – an hour's walk though moist vegetation – affords a good view of Pagbilao, set against the blue of Tayabas Bay.

In this archipelago of diverse flora and fauna, most travelers forget to experience some of the pristine and wild areas. Do so here, and for the enterprising traveler, more beaches and white sandy coves await discovery.

Smiles amidst the rice fields.

BATAAN AND CORREGIDOR

That famed sunset over Manila Bay does not always sink into a watery horizon. Rather, depending on the season, it may fall behind faint mountains.

These vague, dull-blue contours outline the elongated peninsula of Bataan, an infamous byword from World War II. At the peninsula's southern tip, guarding the mouth to Manila Bay, is Corregidor, hallowed ground for veterans. Wreath-laying is a year-round affair at **Mt. Samat**, site of a fierce battle in 1942 before the Filipino-American forces eventually surrendered to the Japanese. Near the summit is a memorial shrine, Dambana ng Kagitingan (Shrine of Valor).

Corregidor: A small rocky island laying some 40 kilometers (25 mi) west of Manila at the entrance to Manila Bay, **Corregidor** – The Rock, as it has long been known – remains a lonely place peppered with echoing tunnels, ruined buildings, huge, rusting mortars and deep memories – an island memorial for the Filipinos and Americans who sought to defend Manila and the Philippines from the advancing Japanese.

Two monuments have been erected on the island. One is a domed white-marble memorial, with an altar built in honor of those who were killed in 1942 during the Japanese invasion. The second is a modern steel sculpture that shoots upwards, representing the flame of freedom.

Corregidor is only a one-hour trip from downtown Manila, via comfortable jetboat from the CCP Complex on Roxas Boulevard. Once on the island, a bus takes visitors on a guided two-hour tour, visiting MacArthur's headquarters in **Malinta Tunnel**, the mile-long barracks, gun batteries, military structures, a ruined hospital and a small museum displaying numerous photographs of Corregidor prior to World War II.

Around the island, tangles of cogon grass and wildflower bushes half con- **Guns on Corregidor.**

ceal rusting artillery and abandoned barracks, shafts of light piercing through the punctured walls of their still-standing shells. At the harbor where the boat from Manila lands, colorful tropical fish play about the rotting pylons of an old pier, and cartridge shells catch the eye among the many polished pumice stones on the island's beaches.

At present, much of the war memorabilia has been subjected to an ongoing restoration program, including the establishing of tourist facilities. For example, a 31-room hotel, the Corregidor Inn, was built a few years ago atop a breezy hill, and a 17-cottage beach resort now sits on the narrow beach.

Bataan: On the peninsula of Bataan, zero-point kilometer markers are found in the towns of **Mariveles** and **Bagac**, World War II starting points of the dreadful Death March, which took a heavier toll on Bataan among the Allied prisoners of the Japanese than the actual fighting itself. Over 75,000 Filipino and American prisoners were forced to hike under miserable conditions 100 kilometers (60 mi) up the peninsula to Japanese concentration camps in Pampanga. A tenth of them perished along the way, a route now marked along Bataan's east coast.

Mariveles: Once a quiet fishing port on the peninsula's southern tip, Mariveles has slowly become industrialized since the opening of the Bataan Export Processing Zone. Cottage products, sports equipment, garment factories, assembly plants and shipyards have helped boost the economy of this depressed region.

To get to Mariveles, follow the North Expressway, which is part of the **Pan-Philippine Friendship Highway** (sometimes called the National Highway, and once called MacArthur Highway) north from Manila to **San Fernando**, in Pampanga Province. In San Fernando turn off onto Highway 7, which leads to Olongapo, Zambales. Soon, the massive destruction of the **Mt. Pinatubo** eruption, in 1990, is apparent in the bleak, volcanic ash-covered landscape. At the Layac junction

before Dinalupihan, turn left onto the road to Balanga and Mariveles.

Several beach resorts are located between Orani and Mariveles, but the ones along Bataan's west coast, facing the South China Sea, are probably by far the better of the lot. Tour buses departing from Manila are available and frequent, and regular bus service to Mariveles from Metro Manila is provided by Victory Line, with offices on the Rizal Avenue Extension in Manila.

North of Bataan lies **Zambales Province**, noted for its rugged mountain range and picturesque coastline. Zambales is unfrequented by foreign visitors due to its often poor roads, although it is possible to drive up through **Olongapo City**, and then all the way up the coast to Pangasinan Province.

Together with Bataan, Zambales was among the first provinces in Luzon to be brought under Spanish rule, when Juan de Salcedo plundered the region's western coastal areas in 1572. He encountered fierce and proud mountain people, the Zambal, who gave him such trouble

that he mounted a punitive expeditions to eradicate them.

Today, the southern part of Zambales has been resettled by outsiders, mostly by Tagalogs. Ilocanos have taken over much of the central region, and the indigenous Zambals have been pushed north, to near Pangasinan, where in the mountain areas are government reservations for Aeta Negritos.

Subic Bay: The country's major freeport sits on Subic Bay, next to Olongapo, Zambales. The former U.S. naval base at **Subic Bay** boasts a world-class infrastructure and facilities, and has become one of the country's most successful duty-free industrial and commercial centers. Although it still retains the look and feel of a military base – and it once was an immense one – hotels and other accommodation are available within the zone, including the Subic Bay International Hotel, in what was once the base's bachelor enlisted quarters, and the Subic Bay Resort and Casino, in the old bachelor officer quarters.

Inside Subic Bay, guests can play a round of golf on the former base's 18-hole golf course, or take advantage of the multitude of water sports offered. Nature enthusiasts can enjoy jungle treks in the virgin Pamulaklakin jungle, with indigenous Aeta guides. Wildlife such as iguanas, pythons, monkeys and wild boar can often be seen during rambles throughout the area.

This stretch of unspoiled jungle was once the jungle survival training center for American naval forces deploying to Vietnam during the long war there. Many of the original Aetas instructors now serve as tourist guides.

In addition to the three smallish beaches found in the Subic area, a 30-minute boat ride takes travelers to the exclusive, 47 hectare (118-acre) Grande Island Resort. The resort offers various water sport activities and has great dive opportunities on the coral reefs off the coast. There are three duty-free stores in the freeport, but the selection and quality is far below what seasoned travelers expect to find in duty-free stores. Food items for the local populace are the main fair in Subic's duty-free outlets.

Left, wave play. **Right**, a guide on Corregidor with American and Filipino flags.

Immediately north from the alluvial fill surrounding Manila Bay are the central plains of Luzon, where Tagalog culture once blossomed, and where nagging gadflys – and later serious opposition – to the Spanish colonial powers prospered. Provinces just north of Manila were pivotal in the revolution against the Spanish, although the revolution's martyr, Jose Rizal came from south of Manila.

The Americans who replaced the Spanish established two large military bases north of Manila — an air base near Angeles, and a naval base at Olongopo — that both gave the area some prosperity but which, increasingly, tainted Filipino-American relations. But it was an explosive Mt. Pinatubo, not tedious negotiations, that finally persuaded the Americans to leave in the early 1990s. The Philippines is now pinning significant hope that these two former bases, converted into industrial zones and international airport, will be kingpins in a revived Philippine economy.

Pangasinan caps the central plains, and is where lush harvests of rice, sugar cane and tobacco make the region one of the nation's most productive agricultural areas.Pangasinan's history is richly endowed, including an unsuccessful attempt by an ancient Chinese emperor to make it part of his empire; the Chinese invaders had to dig an escape tunnel back to the sea. A few Chinese remained behind, leaving a Chinese texture that remains today.

Ilocos shoots straight northward from Pangasinan along the western Luzon coast, and is probably known best as the birthplace of Ferdinand Marcos. The assorted groups of people in Ilocos are a hearty bunch, with women who smoke what must be the world's largest cigars. The terrain is a mixture of sandy plains, not especially good for agriculture, and rocky coastline.

The highlands of Luzon, following the crest of the Cordillera Central mountains, are flanked by Ilocos to the west and Cagayan to the east. Anchoring the highlands is Baguio, just a few hours north of Manila and long a cool mountain retreat from the heat of the plains to the south. Many of the indigenous people inhabiting the highlands were once coastal people – from the former headhunters of the Igorot and Dumagat people to the shy and nomadic Negrito – pushed inland by outsiders from Borneo and Malaysia.

Cagayan Valley is a long eastward descent from the highlands, a fertile valley fed by numerous rivers and long coveted by the early Spanish colonizers. The area has always been wealthy in comparison to other parts of the archipelago; the Ibanag people, for example, long traded with merchants from China, Malaysia and Japan.

Preceding pages: fishing rafts on Pangasinan river; the Mountain Trail, Luzon highlands. **Left,** highland musicians.

THE CENTRAL PLAINS OF LUZON

When Filipinos speak of Tagalog culture, they are most often referring to the culture that sprang forth on the central plains of Luzon. It was a culture nurtured in the rich alluvial soil and suckled by flowing rivers and the plentiful rains of the monsoon.

Once past the urban sprawl of Metro Manila, the scene is nothing but rice fields – black and muddy during the dry season, and green to golden during the rainy season, when up two crops are planted and harvested. Farther north, the rice gives way to vast fields of sugar cane, which, in turn, give way to corn.

The region, about the size of Israel at 18,000 square kilometers (7,000 sq mi), covers the largest contiguous lowlands in the Philippines. To the east, the Sierra Madre mountains shelter it from the fierce ocean storms, or typhoons, that whip in off the Philippine Sea. The Zambales range, to the west, cuts it off from the South China Sea. And the rugged Cordillera mountains and Pangasinan Province cap it off in the north. All three mountain ranges serve as spawning grounds for the rivers that water its fertile soil.

Officially, central Luzon is comprised of six provinces, five cities, 116 municipalities and 2,810 barangays. While the mountain provinces of Bataan and Zambales are officially included in the region, strictly speaking, they touch little of the plains. For our purposes, the central plains of Luzon are best defined by the four provinces of Bulacan, Pampanga, Tarlac and Nueva Ecija.

The main artery through the central plain's sea of rice, sugar and corn is the Pan-Philippine Friendship Highway. The tollway portion, about 85 kilometers (50 mi) long, from Manila to Dau in Pampanga Province, is known as the North Expressway. It is part of a road project covering over 2,000 kilometers (1,200 mi) throughout the whole country, from the northern tip of Luzon to southern Mindanao. Most maps refer to it, as shall we, as the **National Highway**. Older maps call it the MacArthur Highway. A secondary road, running through the eastern portion of the region from Bulacan to Nueva Ecija, rejoins the National Highway to the north.

Bulacan Province: Metro Manila gives way to **Bulacan Province** in a continuous string of industrial sprawl. The first Bulacan town of **Valenzuela**, along the National Highway, is noted for its plastic wares, factories, food-processing plants and San Miguel Brewery, a fact with which even the famed Bulacan wit may have had trouble dealing.

Fishing folk settled Bulacan sometime before the first century. They lived along the shore of Manila Bay, but soon discovered that the interior of the province had rich soil and was well drained by rivers and streams. Turning to farming, they quickly pushed inland. The *kapuk* tree, which they called *bulak*, grew profusely in the area, producing vast amounts of tradable *kapok* or Java cotton, as it is also known. The province derives its name from the tree.

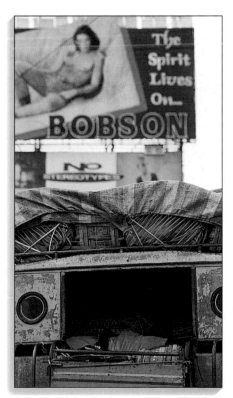

The Bulacanos sided with their long-time trading partners in Maynilad against the invading Spanish, but were soundly defeated at the Battle of Bangkusay Channel in around 1570. For the next three centuries, Bulacanos lived under Spanish rule, but not without wit.

Through the years, Bulacan writers developed a unique Spanish-Tagalog jargon that allowed them to flatter the Spanish on one hand, while slapping them in the face with the other. Francisco "Balagtas" Baltazar became a master of Bulacan wit in the late 1700s. Like other aspiring poets, Balagtas labored under strict friar supervision of his Spanish meter and metaphor, but he slipped Tagalog into his works to protest Spanish tyranny. The friars thought that his celebrated poem *Florante at Laura* was about Christians and Moors duelling in a mythical kingdom, but it was really a protest against Spanish forced labor, exorbitant taxes and the capriciousness of the friars. In the 1890s, Marcelo H. del Pilar, of Bulacan, took Balagtas a step further. He happened to

be a master satirist, with a good cartoon pen. He specialized in take-offs on the religious pamphlets regularly churned out by the friars. His sharply-turned epigrams soon became rallying cries for revolution all over the islands.

Traces of the old Tagalog culture still reside in Bulacan, but one must look in the places of yesteryear. If lucky, one might find a talkative old character who spices his speech with sly Bulacano wit, reminiscent of the days when Bulacanos made fun of friars and government.

Off the North Expressway, on the old highway, sit two and not so sweet-smelling towns, Meycauayan and Marilao. **Meycauayan**, famed for its leather craft, smells strongly of the tanneries where carabao hides are turned into bags and shoes. Just beyond, **Marilao** is noted for its piggeries and poultry production. The manure produces the smell, so hold your nose or stay on the expressway.

Bocaue: If it is the first Sunday in July, pull off the expressway into **Bocaue**; otherwise continue on. The river festival of Bocaue honors the Holy Cross of **Happy fowl vendor.**

Wawa (*Mahal na Krus sa Wawa*), said to have once saved an old women from drowning. For the festival, a giant and decorated pagoda floats down the Bocaue River on a huge boat, with all the town on board eating and singing.

Crop rotation is important in Bocaue, which marks the beginning of Luzon rice belt. The planting and harvesting of rice is a labor-intensive business. First, the germinated seeds are planted in seedbeds, while the fields are plowed, weeded and puddled. When the new plants are about three inches tall, they are transferred by hand to the flooded fields. About 120 days later, after several weedings, the fields are drained and the rice is harvested by cutting the stocks. The rice ears are then dried and winnowed from the stock. The paddy (field rice) is then bagged and taken to a mill for removal of the husk and hull. The average Philippine rice family of four produces some 100 to 120 bags of rice, with 50 or so of those bags for their own consumption. After paying fertilizer and irrigation costs, land rents, taxes, fees, and milling costs, the family will be lucky to realize US1,000 for their season's efforts.

Revolutionaries: Up the road from Bocaue, in **Balagtas** (Bigaa), is a monument to the father of Tagalog poetry, Francisco Baltazar. One of the oldest known tiled-roof houses in the province also sits here, Bahay na Tisa, built in 1849. Further on, **Malolos** is the leading historical site in the province. Here, in 1898, 52 delegates met in a revolutionary congress to ratify the Philippine declaration of independence. Know as the Malolos Congress, the delegates meet in Barasoain Church; their old printing press is displayed in nearby Casa Real. Kamistisuhan Houses in the Pariacillo typifies architecture of the times. The Hiyas Museum houses a collection of articles and documents from the revolution, while the Barasoain Museum, managed by the National Historical Institute, has a display of religious artifacts. On the last Sunday in January, a colorful Santo Niño procession parades down main street.

Rice winnowing on a bamboo platform.

On 14 and 15 May, the town of **Pulilan**, northeast of Malolos, celebrates the Carabao Festival. Like fiestas all over the region at this time of year, Pulilan's is dedicated to San Isidro Labrador, patron saint of farmers. Uniquely, though, Pulilan's festival stars the *carabao*, or water buffalo. Thousands of carabaos, adorned with summer blooms, parade to church where they kneel, as if in prayer.

Thirty kilometers (20 mi) north of Pulilan are the caves and revolutionary hideout of San Miguel – **Madlum and Aguinaldo caves**, and a mountain redoubt known as Biak-na-Bato, served as hideouts for revolutionaries in the 1890s. A nearby resort, **Sibul**, is famed for the medicinal effects of its waters.

Pampanga: Just past Pulilan on the North Expressway, a 5.3-kilometer-long (3.3 mi) viaduct threads its way into **Pampanga Province**. The heavy July-to-August floods here initiated the construction of the viaduct. It is also a favorite place for raising ducks, many of which live under the viaduct.

Pampanga may look much like the other provinces of the central plains, but it is a whole different world. The Pampango are not Tagalogo, unlike their neighbors, nor do they speak Tagalog. The first Pampanga settlers arrived in Manila Bay from Sumatra, Indonesia, around 1,700 years ago. Encountering an established population along the bay's shoreline, the Sumatrans moved up the Rio Grande de Pampanga and Rio Chico rivers to the vast open plains of central Luzon. Soon, they had established large farming communities along the river banks, becoming known as the Dwellers of the River Banks, or *Taga-Pangpang* (*Pangpang* for short). The Spanish later simplified it to Pampanga, though the people stuck to their own Pampango language.

Spanish records attest to the tight community along the river, which met them with curiosity and, among all the islands' tribes, great intelligence. The Pampango leaders were impressed with Spanish fire-power and threw the support of their kingdoms behind the new

On the street during the Carabao Festival.

178

rulers in exchange for privileges. Later, Pampango soldiers proved loyal back stops for the Spanish against the Chinese, Moros, Dutch and British.

By the 18th century, a large mestizo Chinese community was well entrenched in Pampanga. Descended of the Chinese who had fled the 1700s massacres in Manila, they fanned out through Pampanga and northward to Tarlac and Nueva Ecija. As they went, they gradually took over large tracts of sugar cane and rice lands from the Pampangao elite, who had grown fat and lazy. Pampanga's traditional sugarcane culture, as well as the opening of Manila to international trade in the 18th century, were opportunities that the Chinese community eagerly exploited.

Many of the old surnames in Pampanga today are of Chinese origin, modified by Pampangao and Spanish names. These names, very much a part of an equally old Manila social registry, are synonymous with sugar wealth. In the 18th century, the marriage of newly-rich Chinese with those of earlier aristocracy were the first wedge between rich and poor of the central plains.

Sixty-six kilometers (40 mi) from Manila is the provincial capital of **San Fernando**, footnoted in history for having once been the country's capital (along with a couple of other towns on the northward escape route of the revolutionary forces). San Fernando is today largely a commercial town, and also one of the three towns where Chinese, fleeing Manila in the 17th century, settled in large numbers. It is best visited during Christmas for the Lantern Festival.

At the San Fernando exit, one will note the colorful roofs of Paskuhan Village, or **Christmas Village**. It celebrates the Philippine tradition of having the world's longest Christmas season. The village offers a replica of a typical Philippine village celebrating Christmas, craft demonstrations by aspiring artisans, an orchidarium, and a giant maze. There is also a museum of Christmas ornaments, holding a collection of orna ments from around the world, and a basket museum displaying hundreds of

Late-night bingo.

Philippine baskets. There are also a score of local restaurants and stalls selling Betis furniture, Santo Tomas ceramics, and whatever.

Fifteen kilometers (9 mi) east of San Fernando sit swampy Candaba and mountainous Arayat. The **Candaba swamps** are noted for their scenic beauty and the hundreds of thousands of migrating ducks from China that make the swamps their winter home.

Mt. Barrio Bano (1,100 m/3,500 ft.) towers over **Arayat** and **Mount Arayat National Park**. The area has mountain trekking and bicycling trails, swimming holes, and cool breezes to beat the heat.

Angeles and Clark: Near the end of the Northern Expressway are **Angeles City** and Clark Field.

In its heyday during the Vietnam War, **Clark Field**, the former Clark Air Force Base, not only employed thousands of Filipinos, it also kept downtown Angeles alive. Once the site of Fort Stotsenburg and home of the U.S. Fifth Cavalry, assigned to control Philippine revolutionaries, it developed into a major air field and supply hub for the American military. In 1991, the eruption of Mt Pinatubo covered the base in meters of ash and it was abandoned by the Americans.

Clark, however, has arisen from the ashes as the **Clark Field Economic & Freeport Zone**. Today, a 273-room Holiday Inn sits inside the 175-hectare (430 acre) Mimosa Resort, featuring some 7,000 mimosa rain and yellow-flame trees, and a world-class 27-hole golf course. Some 30 industrial firms have set up operations, or are planning to do so soon, in the zone.

The government has big plans for Clark. It proposes to build the country's premier airport within the former base, and a railway to connect the zone with Manila. Plans have also been made to upgrade the expressway connecting Clark and Manila. However, most of these plans still linger on the drawing boards for lack of financing.

Tarlac Province: The Northern Expressway ends in Pampanga, but the National Highway continues on through **Tarlac**.

Aftermath of Pinatubo's eruptions.

The province stands as a late comer to the official organization of the central plains. It was not created until 1873, when it was carved out of the Pampanga, to the south, and Pangasinan, to the north. And like its bilateral creation, its population stands as a cross-section of peoples: Ilocanos, Pampangos, Pangasinenes and Tagalogs. No wonder it was named after a resilient weed, the *malatarlak*, or *tarlac* for short.

Death March: Tarlac is the central plains' major sugar-producing area. Unfortunately, it remains best known as the end of the infamous World War II Death March.

Three kilometers before **Capas**, near the southern border, stands the monument to the 30,000 Filipino and American soldiers who perished on the forced march by the Japanese. Twelve or so kilometers west of Capas is **Camp O'Donnel**, the concentration camp that was the ultimate destination of those who somehow survived the ordeal of the Death March. North of Capas lies **San Miguel**, where the family of former president Corazon Aquino is developing a planned community for the next century. The vast 12,000-hectare (30,000-acre) track, known as Hacienda Luisita, sits on an old sugar plantation that was said to be the last property owned by the Spanish government in the Philippines. The park-like city for industry and residents boasts a golf course and an impressive stable of Arabian horses.

Nueva Ecija is the fourth province of the central plains. Farmers migrated here from Bulacan when farm land grew scarcer in the south. Over 60 percent of the population are Tagalog; the rest are descendants of Ilocano migrants.

Four rivers irrigate the rich rice-producing lands of Nueva Ecija. As a visitor destination, Nueva Ecija has little to offer except Peñaranda, in the south near Gapan, and Minalungao Park, in the north near Pantabangan. The main importance of the province lies instead in its traditional rice-producing role and its location as a pathway to the rich Cagayan Valley.

Tending to the rice.

PANGASINAN

Three rivers flowing from the eastern mountains pour fertility into the plains and deltas of **Pangasinan Province**. The Agno River is the largest, fed by the Cordilleras. From the eastern Cordilleras come two other rivers.

These inland waters swell and overflow, claiming lives and crops during the typhoon months. But they teem with crustaceans and fish, and they prepare the soil for lush harvests of tobacco, sugar cane and rice – Pangasinan is second only to Nueva Ecija as the country's most prolific rice-growing area.

Facing the South China Sea at almost exactly the midpoint of Luzon's western coast, Pangasinan's shoreline loops around Cape Bolinao and dips sharply into the Gulf of Lingayen.

From San Fabian to Dagupan, Lingayen, Sual, Alaminos, and up to Bolinao and the small nearby islands, fishermen scoop the shoreline with hand-held nets, scour the open sea in outriggers, and harvest fish in the summer months from stocked inland ponds. So dependent are these people on Pangasinan's marine resources that, during the summer months, severe penalties have been imposed, by the locals, on fishing for or feasting on the *bangus* (milkfish) that come ashore to lay eggs. Pangasinan bangus, painstakingly cultured in inland ponds to assure a year-round harvest, are famous throughout the archipelago.

Along this coastline grew the first Pangasinan settlements thousands of years ago. From their major industry – the manufacture of salt by solar evaporation – came the name of the province: *asin* is the local word for salt, and *pang-asin-an* simply means "where salt is made". Salt from Pangasinan still has a reputation as being the finest anywhere in the country.

Lingayen Gulf stood as a regional trading center from earliest times. Tattooed Zambales, from the southern mountains, and Ygolote highlanders

Pangasinan beach.

from the north regularly descended upon Lingayen to bartered nuggets of gold for pigs, *carabaos*, and rice. The Ilocanos of the harsh northern coast came, too, with their bolos, pots and woven blankets, first to trade and gradually to settle. Ilocanos eventually became the main linguistic, cultural and economic force of Pangasinan's coastal region, at least until the Chinese arrived.

Chinese and Japanese boats carrying silk, metals, ceramics, and mirrors arrived, bartering for the riches of Pangasinan's fields and forests: indigo, fibers, sugar cane, beeswax, deerskin and civet musk.

When the Spanish came in the 16th century, Lingayen's well-organized trading culture prompted the observation that "among all the natives of these islands, the Pangasinans appear to be the most active and industrious, very energetic in producing profit and knowing how to make a scanty capital increase in all possible manner in spite of weariness." The very combination of natural wealth and human resourceful-

ness attracted outsiders to Pangasinan in the 16th century. Hardly had Juan de Salcedo reconnoitered Luzon's northern coastline when the Chinese corsair Limahong came with some 3,000 men, 64 war junks and obvious ambitions.

Unfortunately for Limahong, the Spanish already had a toehold in the region. A Chinese fort stood yet complete when 300 Spanish solders and 2,500 indigenous troops attacked and burned half the corsair's fleet, and blocked his exits to the sea. A four-month siege ensued. Limahong order his men to dig a new channel – which still can be seen today – through which he made his escape into the South China Sea. As Limahong sailed away from Luzon, several of his men remained and hid in the forest. It is not certain whether they did not want to leave or had simply been abandoned, but by the time the Spanish had the local people on their knees in prayer, the largest houses in old Lingayen town belonged to Chinese *mestizo*. To this day, there is a distinct Chinese cast to the features of many of

Bullock wagons and handicraft sellers.

the old family surnames in Lingayen.

Fighting together to expel the Chinese did not make the relationship between Spanish and Pangasinano friendly. A few of the local chieftains were impressed by Salcedo's courtesy in paying them with gold pieces for the provisions provided to him, but the greed of succeeding expeditions undid any of the goodwill that Salcedo spread. The Pangasineno, strangers to gunpowder and subjugation, were soon fleeing into the mountains. Several Spanish expeditions were mounted, with gold-greedy soldiers chasing villagers into the foothills – pillaging, raping and looting as they went. So much was the extent of damage done in Pangasinan by the soldiers that an early Augustine friar took time to write a strongly-worded letter to the king of Spain, condemning the so-called acts of "pacification".

Meanwhile, the local people continued to congregate around their woodland temples and shrines containing altars full of ceremonial vessels. Fresh off the boat, Spanish missionaries saw oils and ointments burning at the altars, while priestesses in ceremonial robes fell into trances. "It's the devil," shouted the horrified Spaniards as the priestesses rolled their eyes upward and began to speak in voices of their deities. From the mouths of the priestesses came advice on wars, undertakings and the healing of diseases.

Unknown to the missionaries, these rituals were of an ancient religion whose echo is heard in Pangasinan to this day – faith healing.

Exploring Pangasinan: The main route through Pangasinan is the **National Highway**, from Tarlac to the La Union boarder. A second route, the **Romulo Highway**, runs from Tarlac northwest past Lingayen to Alaminos. A third, much less traveled route, runs up the Zambales coast, from Olongapo to Alaminos. This third route though is not recommended for the faint at heart.

The National Highway passes through Villasis, Urdaneta, Binalonan, Pozorrbio and Sison, but there is not much to see unless looking for faith healers.

Coastal catch.

The Romulo Highway enters Pangasinan just after the Tarlac town of **San Clemente**, and passes on to Mangatarem. Near Mangatarem is the **Manleluag Springs National Park**, with its charming hot spring nestled in the foothills of the Zambales Mountains. The next towns, **Aguilar** and **Bugallon**, etch a portrait of old Pangasinan with their churches. The facade of Aguilar Church is pink from the ancient Chinese redbrick showing through the modern whitewash. A short drive on brings leads to **Sual**, where one can see Limahong's escape channel.

Lingayen: The right fork in Bugallon leads to **Lingayen**, the sprawling old capital by the sea. Lingayen has two distinct sections, architecturally and culturally different from each other. The older section, built inland by the Spanish in their particular style, has all buildings facing onto the town plaza. This is where the population center lies. Market day here is a portrait in small-town trade, with some hard bargaining among the vendors under their large *buri* fans,

used midday sun screens. The newer section, built near the sea by the American colonial government, was a choice of obvious intelligence and charm. Today, though it is a bit down-at-the-heel, its spread of wide-crowned flame trees can be a startling first sight. The provincial capital building is a model of early American colonial architecture, with marble columns and a golden eagle, stern-faced on his perch, looming down on all who enter.

Between Lingayen and **Dagupan** lie most of the World War II war memorials and beaches, where the Japanese landed in December 1941, and the Americans came ashore in January 1945. Unless you are a war buff, skip it. There are much better sights to be seen in the Hundred Islands and Cape Bolinao area.

From Lingayen, a 40-kilometer (25 mi) coast road leads west to **Alaminos**. Three kilometers along San Jose Drive, in **Lucap**, dozens of boats and ferries wait at the wharf to take travelers out to the **Hundred Islands National Recreation Area**. One hundred is a slight

Fisherman's hut, Sual.

exaggeration, but well describes the multitude of islands and islets strewn along the coast. Quezon Island has pavilions, toilets and viewing decks. Children's Island is for campers, while Governor's Island has overnight accommodations in the Philippine Tourism Authority's building. Devil's Island is rated as the best site for scuba diving. While in Lucap, stop by the Bureau of Fisheries Oceanographic Marine Laboratory to get a view of *bangu*, *siganid* and *lapu lapu* (grouper) breeding.

Cape Bolinao: Few venture beyond Alaminos to **Bolinao**, just an hour away. It is regrettable, because the old town and its surrounding *barangays* and islands are where Pangasinan's heritage still resides in ancient patterns. The **Bolinao Museum** stands as the cultural link – in backyards and along beaches some of the most important archaeological finds in the region have been made, including gold bracelets lying under coconut trees and ceramic shards washed up by floods. A lack of funds has kept museum diggings to a mini-

mum, but pot-hunters have turned up Tang, Song and Ming porcelain, as well as skeletal remains adorned with gold earrings and necklaces. All of these are considered significant links in 7th- to 15th-century Philippine history. The Bolinao Museum has only a few of the finds; most sit in private collections or have been spirited out of the country.

One Bolinao treasure that has not lent itself to cultural piracy is the venerable **Church of St James**, in the center of the old town. Built in 1609 by the Augustine Recollects, it stands in old stone grandeur. The niches on both sides of the facade still have their ancient wooden *santos*, aged by wind and sun, and their features blurred by time.

Indeed, generations of Bolinao have lived unchanged lifestyles in this quiet spot, still speaking a dialect distinct from their Pangasinan neighbors. To the port of Bolinao, as well as to the surrounding islands of Silaqui, Santiago and Dewey, have come Chinese corsairs, English and Dutch freebooters, and Moro pirates. **Santiago Island** has been home to more than its share of fugitives, many of them escaped slaves. Today, Santiago Island is a haven for scuba divers, with rich preserves of coral teeming with marine life. And off the coast of Santiago Island lies Fourteen Mile Reef, with hard and soft coral. It is considered by experts as one of the best dive spots in the Philippines. Its slope ranges from 10 to 40 meters, with an abrupt 250-meter (800 ft) drop along the western edge.

Along the South China Sea coast to the south are other interesting spots. Dendro Beach is a golden-sand beach south of the Piedra Point lighthouse. In **Agno**, Umbrella Rocks dot the mouth of the Balincaguing River; however, they look more like toadstools than umbrellas. Farther south, **Tambobong**'s White Beach is accessible through Burgos. The waters around Tambobong teem with marine life.

Bani and **Mabini**, in the center of the Cape Bolinao peninsula, offer excellent cave exploring. **Nalsoc Cave**, in Bani, has a subterranean river passing through miles of stalactites and stalagmites.

Left, pay attention. Right, cheap shelter, Pangasinan style.

ILOCOS

There is a rugged symmetry to Ilocos that sets it, and its people, apart from others in the Philippines. Perched on a narrow ledge along the rugged northwest coast of Luzon, it is a wild place, but not without its charms. The coast rises from the South China Sea to rocky bluffs and rolling sand dunes. Behind it, a slim, arable strip of land is tucked under the towering Cordillera Mountains. In this narrow confine lies the Ilocano provinces of La Union, Ilocos Sur (South), and Ilocos Norte (North).

Sometime after the first century, waves of migration swelled out of Borneo to crest along the Philippine coast. Latecomers to the archipelago, the immigrants were pushed ever northwards by those who had come earlier. By the time they reached the northwestern coast, there was no where else to go but ashore. The migrants flooded into the hundreds of coves along the jagged coast and shifted up onto the narrow plains. With superior numbers and metal weapons, the immigrants pushed the indigenous tribes, who had lived along the coast for centuries, high into the bordering mountains. The people became known for the coves (*looc*) around which they built their communities (*ylocos*).

Spanish colonizers: The conquistador Juan de Salcedo landed in Vigan, Ilocos Sur, in the late 16th century. With forceful persuasion, he convinced the Ilocanos that the presence of a Spanish garrison would be useful against the head-hunting Tingguians that the Ilocanos had earlier displaced from the coast.

Soon, the Spanish introduced corn, cocoa, tobacco and, of course, Christianity. Chapels were built alongside the garrisons, schools were organized, and soon the missions were pulling converts into the town square. The Spanish friar – an Augustinian in the Ilocos – stood as the agricultural officer, financial adviser, teacher and architect.

Compulsory native labor and hired Chinese masons and artisans soon resulted in Spain's most lasting landmarks in the Ilocos – the churches, like the grand old cathedral of Vigan. Fascinating architectural specimens, nicknamed "earthquake baroque" by Filipino historians, they were built as much to dramatize the power of the Old World god as to withstand natural disasters.

The 17th and 18th centuries saw a flowering of baroque that filtered into the Philippines. The results are marvelously alive today, if somewhat cemented over and painted sugar-land greens, yellows and pinks. A special mix of coral, limestone and sugar cane was concocted by Chinese masons for the bricks used in these churches. Vigan has a whole quarter incorporating these bricks with hardwood, capiz and intricate grill work. Called the mestizo quarter, it is where wealthy Chinese artisans built the homes in which their children, Vigan's future aristocracy, were born.

La Union Province: Leaving the flat plains of Pangasinan, the **National Highway** begins to climb over the rolling hills of southern Ilocos. The first province along the way is **La Union**. It

was carved out of Pangasinan, Ilocos Sur and the Cordilleras by royal decree in 1854. But it was not until after World War II that La Union became an administrative center of Ilocos, with San Fernando as the capital. San Fernando is 270 kilometers (170 mi) and over four hours from Manila. If taking a bus, try Pantranco or Philippine Rabbit, but be sure to request San Fernando, La Union, not San Fernando, Pampanga.

Entering La Union, the sea begins to glint behind the palms, where creamy sand beaches await. Sto. Tomas, the first coastal town encountered in La Union, is noted for the freshest and cheapest oysters in the country. The **Agoo-Damortis National Seashore Park** sits on a hooking point in Lingayen Gulf, near **Agoo**. Agoo Playa Beach Resort offers all the usual creature comforts. Further north, San Carlos and Santiago Norte beaches in Caba are becoming favorite sites for private beach homes and resorts. The sands here are nearly black because of the iron deposits. In Agoo, the Shrine of Our Lady of Char-

ity, in the basilica, is an imposing structure of Mexican Baroque architecture. The Museo de Iloko, in the old Presidencia of Agoo, houses artifacts of Ilocos culture.

Bauang Beach, with fine grayish sand, is one long strip of resorts: Cresta del Mar, Bali Hai, Cabaña, Long Beach and the Anchorage are the best. Water sports, mountain-bike races, cultural events and a water parade cap the Rambak Festival here on Easter Sunday. Along the highway, the stalls sell locally grown, sweet-green grapes. A few kilometers inland sits **Naguilian**, the *basi*-making capital of the Ilocos. Basi, the local Ilocano wine, is a fermented sugar-cane concoction, colored with *duhat* bark. It is not bad, but the taste differs from maker to maker, so sample first.

The capital of **San Fernando** produces loud bursts of sound and an array of colors on market day: loud gourd hats from up north, burnished earthenware from San Juan, and bright blankets from Bangar line the stalls and shops. Overlooking it all is a dragon-encrusted Chi-

Beach, La Union Province.

192

nese temple, Macho. During the second week of September, the Filipino-Chinese community of San Fernando travels south of Manila to Taal, in Batangas Province, to fetch the statue of the Virgin of Caysasay for their Feast of Our Lady of Caysasay.

Out on the nearby beach are quieter cottages and small resorts. While here, try some fresh sea food, including a dish known as Jumping Salad, chucks of raw fish cured in a light vinegar and spiced with garlic and chilies, and fresh shrimp cooked with a dash of lime.

Six kilometers north of San Fernando, along Monalisa Beach in San Juan, runs some of the best surf on the Ilocos coast. It has long walls, an inside bowl and a right break over the reef, from November to February. **San Juan** is a pottery town, with a century-old church and an even older Moro watchtower.

Bacnotan to Bangar: In **Bacnotan**, local silk production can be seen at the Don Mariano Marcos Memorial State University. In the mountains to the east, around **Bagulin**, trails along the Bagulin-Naguilian River offer some trekking opportunities, though one would be better served to trek in the Cordillera Region. The century-old church of St. Catherine, in **Luna**, houses an image of Our Lady of Namacpacan, the patroness of Ilocano travelers. **Bangar**, on the northern boarder of La Union, is a blanket-weaving center. Ilocano blankets are wider than most other indigenous blankets, and two people are needed to operate the age-old hand looms. The best woven blankets and handcrafted *bolos* in the region are made here.

Ilocos Sur Province twists along the coast as the narrowest province in the Ilocos. In some places, the Cordilleras reach right down to water's edge. The mountains are almost bare of timber and the soil is sandy, and rice must be imported from Ilocos Norte and Pangasinan. The principle crops are *maguey* fiber and sugar cane. Indigo was once a major crop until cheap aniline dyes were invented.

To augment the deficiencies of the soil, most people in Ilocos Sur have turned to trade and handicrafts. Each town in the region seems to have its own specialty. Those along the coast extract salt from sea water. In San Esteban, there is a quarry from which mortars and grindstones are made. San Vicente, Vigan and San Ildefonso specialize in woodcarving, importing their raw material from the mountain provinces. Skilled silversmiths work in Bantay. Other towns make saddles, harness, slippers, mats, brooms and hats. Sisal and hemp fiber extraction and weaving are household industries everywhere.

Tagudin to Narvacan: The first town in Ilocos Sur, along the National Highway, is **Tagudin**, where a sundial built by the Spanish in 1848 sits in front of the Municipal Hall. Farther up the coast in Sta. Lucia, an 18th-century, three-foot-tall image of the Virgin of Sta. Lucia can be seen in the church. Continuing north, **Candon** sports a beach complex with a huge swimming pool and other amenities. **Santiago** has a short stretch of golden sand, with amenities for picnics and water sports. The next town, **San Esteban**, has a round, stone watch tower

Spanish baroque church, Bantay.

built by the Spanish to keep lookout for Moro pirates, and Apatot Beach. The small burg of **Santa Maria** has a centuries-old church nestled atop a hill, and which served as a fortress during the 1986 revolution, and now stands as a National Landmark. Near Sta. Maria is **Pinsal Falls**, a favorite setting for many films, and where the legendary footprints of the Ilocano giant, Angalo, can be seen. **Narvacan** features rocky Sulvec Beach and the Narvacan Bagong Lipunan Lodge, operated by the Philippine Tourism Authority, but consider Vigan for overnight accommodations.

On entering **Santa**, a small picturesque church with a pure-white facade and slight greenish tint stands by the sea. Carabao wander on the beach, fishermen drag their nets in waist-deep water by the shoreline. An old woman squats in the shade to watch the timeless affair between man and sea. Nodding her approval, she lights up a foot-long cigar in satisfaction. And nearby, Imelda Park is a favorite rest stop for tired or meditative travelers.

North of Santa, **Bantay**'s Santa Maria Church stands on a vast elevated plaza, offering a good view of the surrounding area. It was recently made a UNESCO Heritage Site. The nearby belltower, like other Ilocos Sur belltowers, was built to call the faithful to prayer and to serve as a lookout for Moro pirates.

Vigan: Today, **Vigan** remains everything Manila's Intramuros would like to be. It is a living, breathing repository of Spanish architecture and Filipino culture. In 1572, it was the third Spanish city to be built in the Philippines, following the first in Cebu and the second, Intramuros, in what is now Manila. And three seems to have been a lucky number for Vigan, because it is by far the best of the old towns. If visiting nothing else in the Philippines, see Vigan.

St. Paul's Metropolitan Cathedral, built in 1641, is the center of Vigan. In 1758, a royal decree transferred the diocese of northern Luzon (Diocese of Nueva Segovia) to St. Paul's, making it the ecclesiastical center of the whole area. Built by the Augustinians, it is not

Church fiesta, Bantay.

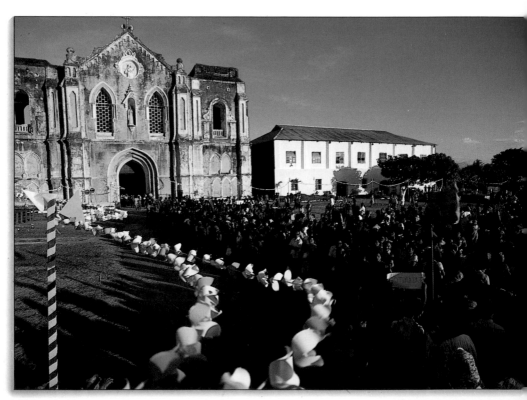

the most stunning cathedral in the archipelago, but it is one of the largest, with an 86-meter (280 ft) facade. Stretching out in front of St. Paul's is **Plaza Salcedo**, an elliptical plaza with the Salcedo Monument and a towering bell tower. Across the plaza, to the west, is the **Ayala Museum**, also called the Burgos House (open Tuesday to Sunday).

The birthplace of the martyr Father Jose Burgos, the colonial two-story house has been turned into a gem of a museum. The well-maintained house is the best repository of Ilocano culture in the whole region, featuring a fine collection of antiques, icons and a library. It includes a series of paintings depicting the heroes and heroines from the history of Ilocos.

North of Plaza Salcedo can be found the **Archbishop's Palace**, showing sliding Philippine capiz windows, floral motifs and inner-courtyard gardens. The palace also offers a priceless collection of ecclesiastical artifacts, which can be view by appointment only, from Monday to Friday.

Probably the best attraction in Vigan are the old ancestral houses in the Kamestizoan district, or Chinese Quarter, known as Heritage Village, south of St. Paul's, along Mena Crisologo Street. The Provincial Tourism Center office sits at the head of the long cobblestone street, in the Leona Florentino House. A good restaurant, Cafe Leona, is next to the tourism center. Each building in the district has been lovingly preserved, and many now house antique shops, bakeries, and craft shops. Walk through the **Kamestizoan district** in the daytime, and then take a horse-drawn carriage ride back through it in the evening. Down a side street of the district visitors will find, despite its name, the best lodgings in town, Grandpa's Inn, at 1 Bonifacio Street.

Other Vigan attractions include the Crisologo Museum, located along De los Reyes Street. The museum houses original furnishings of a typical Vigan ancestral home. Another Vigan attraction is Plaza Burgos, where local food stalls can be found. And don't miss RG

Vigan's quiet ambiance, filling a jeepney.

Pottery, where the famous Ilocano jars, or *burnay*, are made for storing vinegar and the local wine, *basi*. It is located along the southwest end of Liberation Avenue. Walk back into the kiln area and you will see one of the best examples of a Chinese dragon kiln anywhere in the world. It was built by the owner's grandfather, and attests to the Chinese influences in the Ilocos.

Viva Vigan is a cultural festival held on the first week in May, in Vigan, of course. It is a good chance to see all of Ilocano culture on parade, in song, dance and drama.

Banty to Sinait: Near Vigan, the church in **Bantay** features Philippine earthquake baroque with Gothic influences. Its belfry, a few meters away from the church, was used as a lookout for Moro pirates. Further north, in **Magsingal**, the Museum of Ilocano Culture and Artifacts has a collection of early trade porcelains, neolithic tools, weaponry, baskets, agricultural implements, and old Ilocano beadwear. A guesthouse and picnic sheds can be found along the white sands of Pug-os Beach, in **Cabugao**. The last town in Ilocos Sur, **Sinait**, has a century-old church where the Black Nazarene, found floating in a casket off the coast in the 17th century, is enshrined and feasted in early May.

Ilocos Norte Province: Unlike its poorer cousin to the south, Ilocos Norte stands rich in timber, minerals, fisheries, and agriculture. Garlic is the principle cash crop, and it gives the province its flavor and aroma. It also did not economically hurt that the Philippines longest-serving president, Ferdinand Marcos, was an Ilocano Norte, from Sarrat.

The first town in Ilocos Norte is **Badoc**. Exhibited at Luna House are reproductions of the renowned 19th-century Filipino painter, Juan Luna. The Badoc Church is also worth a visit. Past Badoc, at the kilometer 460 junction, turn left for **Currimao**. Worth stopping for are the old abandoned tobacco warehouses at the port, vestiges of the great tobacco monopoly. Close by is the D'Coral Beach Resort, with five unique *nipa* and bamboo guesthouses.

Paoay Church, blending oriental and baroque styles.

Lake Paoay: From Currimao, take the side road to **Paoay**. The church here is a real stunner and perhaps the most famous in Ilocos. It is a successful hybrid creation wedding the strong features of "earthquake baroque" (such as massive lateral buttresses) with an exotic oriental quality, reminiscent of Javanese temples. Built of coral blocks at the turn of the 18th century, its belltower served as a observation post during the Philippine revolution and was occupied by guerrillas during the Japanese occupation. Paoay Church has recently been declared an UNESCO World Heritage Site.

About half a mile from the town proper is **Lake Paoay**. Old folks will tell you it appeared after a particularly violent earthquake, submerging the now "lost town" of San Juan de Sahagun. Loom weaving is a major activity around the lake, producing textiles with ethnic Ilocano designs. Visitors to the so-called Malacañang of the North, the official Ilocos residence of former president Marcos, in *baranggay* Suba, might expect a Spanish *don* and *dona* to come out and greet them, and then be almost surprised when a sturdy Ilocano appears instead. The house is now a museum open to the public.

Marcos Country: San Nicolas, on the south bank of the Laoag River, is considered the pottery capital of the Ilocos. The first church to be built, in 1591, of stone and brick in the region stands in **San Nicolas**. There is also old Spanish house near the plaza that is a near replica of the Rizal House in Calamba, Laguna. South of San Nicolas, back down the National Highway, in **Batac** lies the **Marcos mausoleum** and the house in which he grew up.

A road leads east from San Nicolas to **Sarrat**, birthplace of Ferdinand Marcos and where the Marcos Museum houses family memorabilia, including the four-poster bed where the Great Ilocano was born; the clock beside it set to the exact minute of his delivery. Santa Monica Church and Convent, which are connected by a massive bridge-staircase across a river, are well-preserved specimens of colonial architecture. Further

Ilocos smoke.

inland, in Dingras, the adventurous can find some interesting church ruins, and an old Spanish well.

Across the **Don Mariano Marcos Bridge** (named after Marcos's father) from San Nicolas is the capital of Ilocos Norte, **Laoag**. St. William's Cathedral, dating back to the 16th century, is another notable example of earthquake baroque. Over 85 meters from the cathedral stands – or leans – the Sinking Belltower. In the center of the plaza, the Tobacco Monopoly Monument commemorates the lifting of the Spanish tobacco monopoly in 1881. The Ilocandia Museum of Traditional Costumes is housed in the old Tabacalera or Camarin de Tabaco, where tobacco was once stored before shipping to Manila. In Aurora Park, the fountain sculpture shows the Ilocano ideal of the perfect woman: she stands with her arms draped in garlic bulbs and tobacco leaves.

Fort Ilocandia: Laoag International Airport serves all of northwestern Luzon. Philippine Airlines provides direct flights to Manila, and EVA Air provides flights to Taiwan and Hong Kong. Close by the airport, the Spanish-style Fort Ilocandia Resort offers all of the expected resort amenities – great beach, golf, swimming pools, tennis, horseback riding, a duty-free shop, casino and five-star accommodations. The nearby La Paz Sand Dunes have long been a favorite film setting with Philippine directors.

Eight kilometers north of Laoag sits **Bacarra**, one of the only two places in the country still carving and playing the 17-stringed wooden harp for its town fiesta. Bacarra is also known for its leaning (quake-damaged) bell tower, a little ways from a church, whose facade has suffered from restorative zeal. You can climb up the belltower for a good view of the countryside.

Far north: The Cape Bojeador lighthouse, near **Burgos**, offers a worthwhile climb up a narrow iron spiral staircase, with a dramatic view of the northern coast. The sunset over the China Sea view is the best. A short drive north from Cape Bojeador rewards the visitor with an even loftier view from the viewing deck in **Bangui**. Here, the coves and golden sand beaches of Bangui Bay spread out on the vista, with Pagudpud in the distance.

Pagudpud on Bangui Bay has some of the best coral reefs in the archipelago. The reef off Maira-ira Beach is virtually untouched and swarms with countless species of tropical fish. The beaches here are also some of the best to be found in the Philippines, especially Ivory Beach. Villa del Mar Resort on Ivory Beach is a good places to stay, but Saud Beach Resort, a bit further on, is perhaps the better of the two. But as anywhere, resort areas have their cycles, so consider checking out both.

Balaoi is the last town in Ilocos Norte before passing into Cagayan Province. The town sits on the eastern side of Mayraira Point, the northern most point of Luzon and overlooking Paseleng Bay. Along the eastern shore of Paseleng Bay can be found what some consider one of the best hideaway resorts in the islands, Saud Beach Resort. The resort is reached from Claveria, Cagayan.

Left, barangan friends. Right, Catholic relic in wood.

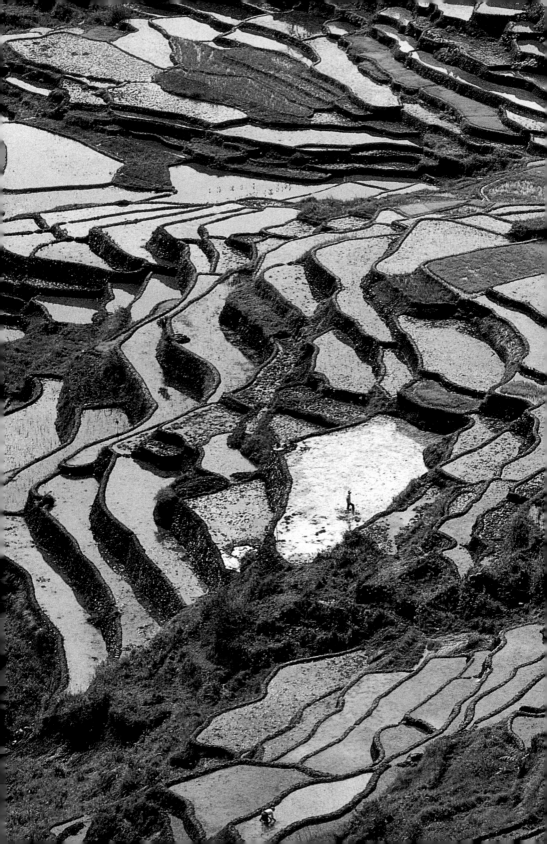

LUZON'S HIGHLANDS

A morning mist hangs low over a tightly-knit community of 30 small huts, made of *cogon* thatch and some with galvanized iron-sheet roofs. An old man winds his way through the vegetable beds tucked around the village (*ili*), stops at the council house (*ato*), where his peers are waiting for him.

Dressed scantily for the cold mountain air, the men squat around a low fire, puffing hard on their tiny pipes of carved hardwood and cast bronze. The council house is made of pine, blackened by age and soot. Its roof is a bulky, round thatch; the spirits of their forefathers, who occasionally visit, would not appreciate a tin roof that made noise when it rained. An approaching storm threatens the rice harvest. To placate the gods, a chicken has to be offered in sacrifice at the sacred tree, which, with the council house, are the twine centers of life in the highland community.

Perhaps, one day, a rare scene in the **Cordillera Administration Region**, or CAR, which encompasses all the landlocked provinces of the Cordillera Mountains. Its area accounts for over 7 percent of the total land area of the Philippines (18,300 square kilometers), but it is home to less than 2 percent of the country's population. Its topography is rugged with clay-loam soil, and over half of the region has a slope of 50 percent or more. Intended to preserve the cultural uniqueness of the highlands, the CAR is composed of five provinces: Benguet, Ifugao, Mountain, Abra and Kalinga-Apayao, and the chartered city of Baguio.

The area can be reached from several directions. Most popular is from the south, through Benguet Province from the National Highway near Sison, Pangasinan, to Baguio. Two routes also connect Baguio to La Union Province: The Marcos Highway to the National Highway in Agoo, and Naguilian Road to Naguilian.

North of Baguio is the so-called Mountain Trail, officially called the Halsema Highway, but rarely so. The **Mountain Trail** runs 110 kilometers north from Baguio to Bontoc, in Mountain Province. (Bontoc and Banaue, and the towns south to Baguio, are all reachable by bus service. Most other towns have limited, infrequent or no bus service.)

Some maps show the Mountain Trail as a principle or main highway, others show it as provincial highway. In fact, the Mountain Trail is often a rough, unpaved secondary road, and most of the spur routes are worse.

Ethnic groups: *Igorot*, literally "people of the mountains", is a blanket term invented by the Spanish. It is misused and wrong. There are several distinct ethnic groups living in the Cordilleras, including the Kankanaey and Ibaloi of Benguet Province; the Ifugao of Ifugao Province; the Kalinga and Isneg of Kalinga-Apayao Province; and the Bontoc, Balangao, Gaddang, and Bayyo of Mountain Province.

The Kankanaey and Ibaloi are regarded as the most sophisticated, with the longest exposure to lowland influ-

Preceding pages: rice terraces, Banawe. Left, Catholic church, Mountain Province. Right, tattoos, a sign of Ifugao womanhood.

ences by virtue of their geography. The Bontoc are considered the proudest, fiercest, and most warlike, whose men maintain a deep territorial imperative (*ennui*). Codes of conduct and legal matters are associated with the hard-working Ifugao, who are also known to take their rituals seriously – where others employ one or two priests, Ifugao often use as many as fifteen. For the Kalinga, the major preoccupation and basis for prestige lies in oratory skill, which has created a unique system of peace pacts, *bodong*, which culminate in grand celebrations.

The Spanish, whose occupation of the lowlands was relatively effortless, encountered stiff opposition in the mountains. Making poor headway with attempts to pacify these "restless and warlike tribes," the Spanish only governed the mountains loosely from their lowland headquarters. Missions were set up in the region, only to be sacked by "converts" reverting to their traditional customs. Head-hunting by the northern groups infuriated the Spanish, who mounted many punitive expeditions, but never pacified the tribes.

It was not until the American occupation and the opening of the northern highlands by army engineers that the tribes were finally pacified. Episcopalian missions set up by the Americans have also proven more successful than those of the Catholic Spanish.

Much of the charm of the mountain people can be found in the way they fuse Christian tradition with their own. Many people have taken Anglican first names, like Clifford and Kathleen, but retain their old tribal surnames of Kinaw-od, Tom-eg, Songgadan, and Killip. And they still cling to many of their old customs, as at a highland funeral.

Traditional funeral practices are becoming rarer due to encroachment of Christian practices. But many are still held each year in the highlands, when a feast is held for at least three days. The deceased sits strapped to a wooden chair in the center of the house, as if to survey the time-honored proceedings. Animal sacrifices are made and the meat passed

Traditional Igorot dwelling.

around to the entire gathering. Bronze gongs (*gangsas*) clang deep into the night, while the people dance in a circle with fluttering, bird-like motions. Rice wine is served from centuries-old jars, ladled with age-blackened coconut shells. Invocations are said to a pantheon of gods and spirits, including Kabunyian, the creator, and Lumawig, a folklore hero.

Baguio: The road to the highlands, for most travelers coming up from Manila, runs through **Baguio**, which is an easy four-hour drive from Manila, or 50 minutes by air on the daily flights.

Nestled aloft a 1,500-meter-high plateau in the Cordilleras, Baguio's cool climate and pine-clad hills have consistently proven lured visitors. Baguio was severely damaged by an earthquake in 1990, but little evidence of the quake is visible today. Some say, in fact, that Baguio is better now than before.

Baguio is not noted for the number of tourist "spots" enticing one to prolong a stay. Rather, a sense of leisure that comes inevitably with the first invigorating whiff of pine air is what brings both Filipinos and foreigners back. With an average mean temperature of 18°C, Baguio seduces with relatively clean parks, lovely gardens, quaint churches, winding roads, and a variety of restaurants and hotels.

Accommodations are no problem in Baguio, except during Holy Week. A list of lodgings, maps of the city, and other pertinent information are available for free at the local tourism office on Governor Pack Road. Getting around Baguio is easy, too. Jeepneys follow regular routes, but are inclined to take riders on a "short trip" to any part of the city for a set fee. Taxis can also go to any point, even out of the city to places like San Carlos Heights or down Naguilian Road for a sunset over the Ilocos coastline, or up to Mount Sto. Tomas for a view of the South China Sea.

Long walks seem to be the most popular form of recreation in Baguio, the time-honored route being up and down **Session Road**, with its gamut of bookstores, bakeries, Indian bazaars, Chi-

Baguio.

nese restaurants, coffee houses, pizza parlors, cinemas, groceries, and antique shops, all in a short distance.

At the northern end of Session Road, cross over to the **Baguio City Market** for a look around. It is an imperative for lowlanders to stop here before going home to pick up fresh strawberries, fine grass brooms, and garlands of straw flowers – three traditional items offered as gifts to friends and relatives by those returning from the mountains. In recent years, the market's attractions have multiplied, merging the produce of the highlands with that from lowland farms. Leeks, Spanish tomatoes, rutabaga, yams, blueberries, native sausages, lowland seafood and assorted delicacies all vie for attention, together with an equally rich variety of woven bags and baskets, woodcarvings, souvenir frames of pine twigs and cones, jewelry, pendants, beads, ponchos, sweaters, blankets, antiques and U.S. Army surplus junk.

Between far-flung Naguilian Road and Mt. Sto. Tomas sits **Lourdes Grotto**. Here, devotees test both zeal and heart condition by climbing the 252 steps to the grotto, which enshrines the Lady of Lourdes and offers a good view of the city. From Lourdes, head out of town to Asin Hot Springs. Along the way is the Ifugao Woodcarvers Village, about five kilometers out of town. Prices are considerably lower in the village than in town. **Asin Hot Springs** is 16 kilometers northwest of town and features a swimming pool surrounded by thermal springs, lush vegetation and hanging bridges.

North of the city center, down Bokawkan Road, is the Easter Weaving Room, where native cloth and curio items sell for bargain prices. Local weavers at work on backstrap-looms are the main attraction. Farther north, up Magsaysay Avenue and some 10 minutes drive from downtown, is the **Bell Temple**, or Bell Church, a collection of temples bedecked with dragons and Chinese ornamentation, where the monks or priests practice a blend of Buddhism, Daoism, Confucianism and Christianity. It is also a good spot to

Baguio produce market.

have one's fortune told. Five minutes away is La Trinidad, a wide valley significant for its bountiful produce.

In the northeast part of the city, down Leonard Wood Road, is the **Baguio Botanical Garden**. Interesting replicas of indigenous architecture representing the different mountain peoples can be seen here, ringed by handicraft shops, silver jewelry makers, and restaurants. Farther up is the **Mansion House**, the summer residence of Philippine presidents. Fronting it is Wright Park, featuring the Pool of the Pines, the end of which overlooks a riding field where horses can be hired.

South of Mansion House are the **Baguio Country Club** and **Club John Hay**, which was once an American military retreat. Located in the heart of Baguio, Club John Hay has fast become one of the major visitor destinations in the city. Guests can play golf on the club's 18-hole course, bowl or play a round of miniature golf. There are also various food outlets. On up Gibraltar Road and onto Torres Street is another cluster of souvenir shops. This is the **Mines View Park**, a much used scene in Baguio postcards; however, it is not much more than a promenade with a view of Benguet's mineral bowl.

North of Baguio: All points north are reached over the Mountain Trail, a rugged but gratifyingly scenic road carved out of mountains and reaching elevations of over 2,000 meters, with vistas of the Cordillera Mountains at every turn. A heavy sweater or coat is essential; it might be stifling hot in the lowlands, but it can be bitterly cold in the high elevations, especially if in an open-sided jeepney.

Benguet Province, the southernmost mountain province, surrounds Baguio. Its capital, **La Trinidad**, is the first town encountered north after leaving Baguio, and the fields around La Trinidad are a good place to load up on strawberries. Out from La Trinidad, parts of the Mountain Trail are paved, but with long stretches of unpaved road.

Kabayan, some four hours' drive from Baguio, is worth a side trip. At the

Ifugao sports at Baguio festival.

52-kilometer marker on the Mountain Trail, near the Natubleng Vegetable Terraces in Buguias, a right fork leads south to Kabayan. The town serves as the base camp for trekking **Mt. Pulog**. *Pulog* means bald in the Ibaloi dialect. The peak towers 2,930 meters, the highest on Luzon and the second highest, after Mt. Apo on Mindanao, in the country. Mt. Pulog is considered a sacred by the Ibaloi, so show respect for their hallowed land.

Trekking Mt. Pulog is best during February, March or April. The trek takes about three days and is rewarded with a stunning panoramic view of the **Cagayan Valley** and **Sierra Madre** range, with the Philippine Sea in the far distance. Pine stands give way to marvelous oak forests, then to alpine and bamboo grass-covered slopes, which thin out towards the peak. Mt. Pulog also has three mountain lakes – Tabeyo, Incolos and Bulalakaw – and several unexplored caves around its base.

Tinongchol Burial Rock awaits near Kabayan. As large as a three-story build-ing, the rock is home to the mummified remains of Ibaloi ancestors, whose coffins have been stuffed in holes bored into the solid rock. Nearby, on **Mt. Timbac**, are more burial caves, with mummies thought to be at least 500 years old. Unlike wrapped Egyptian mummies, these are naked and with tattoo marks of geometric patterns still visible. They lay in the fetal position, in wooden coffins carved out of tree trunks. The mummification process, which has long since been lost, is thought to have used indigenous herbs and oils. Some of these mummies are on display at the town hall. Opdas Cave has hundreds of skulls piled in neat rows.

Mountain Province: The Mountain Trail winds towards Bontoc, 110 kilometers and six to 12 hours from Baguio, depending on road conditions. Mountain Province was created in 1907, during American rule, and included most of what is now the CAR. Its inhabitants are mostly Bontoc, Kankanaey and Balangao, along with a few Gaddang, Ifugao, Bayyo, Ibaloi and other groups.

Kabayan's 500-year-old mummies.

All of the indigenous people practice similar planting and harvesting customs, but differ widely in their burial and wedding rituals.

Towards the 90-kilometer marker, near Sabangan, a road to the left ascends to **Bauko**, an eerily quiet logging center enshrouded in mountain mist. There is nothing much to do or see here, except for trekking through the pine forests. However, it is the best spot along the southern Mountain Trail to stop for the night. The Mt. Data Lodge, operated by the Philippine Tourism Authority, is by far the best lodge in the province. Its 22 rooms are tastefully appointed, and it has an excellent restaurant, bar and a lounge area, featuring a mammoth fireplace for cold mountain nights.

An hour on from Bauko, the road descends to the Chico River, running with it all the way to **Bontoc** and beyond. Bontoc does not offer much, but this is the only place to stock up on gas and provisions. Traveling by bus means staying the night, which can be done comfortably and cheaply at a number of lodges. Situated in a low valley, Bontoc can be quite warm in the daytime. Hikes away from town can be pleasant and provide a good survey of what goes into maintaining rice terraces. Bontoc's rice terraces are unlike the more famous ones in Banaue. Here, the walls are made from rocks instead of mud. Bontoc locals say that their terraces, though smaller than the massive spread of terraces in Banaue, are more difficult to construct, and therefore more picturesque, which can be true if you care to climb to a good vantage point.

Much of the charm and coziness lacking in Bontoc, with its harsh trading-post exterior, can be found in **Sagada**, an hour away by bus. It has become increasingly popular among travelers in recent years, and rooms can be rented here at St Joseph's Guesthouse, run by Episcopalian sisters. Pleasant hiking is the order of the day in this upland valley town, made popular by its lime and shale formations, and by its burial caves. Wooden coffins are stacked together in several caves a short walk from town.

Village along Chico River.

Others, mislabeled "hanging coffins", are stacked on rock outcroppings.

Most of the trails to the burial caves are not maintained and in fact are in poor condition; many of the stacked coffins are overgrown with vegetation and can not be easily seen.

A number of other attractions are within an hour's hike of town: an underground river, Kitongan bottomless pit that supposedly remains unfathomed, and Calvary Hill, where mushrooms edible and psychedelic are for the picking during the rainy months. Nearby is the tiny Bokong Waterfall, with its swimming hole, and Lake Danum, more of a pond than a lake, but in a pretty setting.

(In 1997, Sagada's mayor issued an order that all tourists who pass through Sagada must pay a tourist fee. Young men hang around the roads asking for a ride, and then inform travelers that they must go to the town hall and pay a fee, whether stopping or not.)

Banaue, in **Ifugao Province** 50 kilometers southeast of Bontoc, marks the usual continuation of any mountain trip. The bus leaves Bontoc in the morning for the two-hour ride over the exhilarating Mt. Polis highway. Terraced fields with spiral beds, and oak trees gnarled to perfection and laden with mountain orchids, are fascinating sidelights for travelers.

Banaue and the surrounding *barangays* remains the best sight in the Cordilleras, and one of the best in all of the Philippines. The massive expanse of rice terraces covering entire mountain sides and majestic waterfalls are bound to awe the most jaded traveler. Built some three thousand years ago, the terraces cover over 260 square kilometers of steep mountains. It is one of those places, like the Grand Canyon, that one must see in person.

Banaue sits in the heart of Ifugao country. In a way, it is the soul of these proud people. The word *ifugao* simply means hill. The Spanish changed the original spelling Ipugo to Ipugaw, and later the Americans changed it to Ifugao. And for the Ifugao people, the "hill" means everything. An extensive social

Burial cave and coffins, Sagada.

system exists among these people. Those who own the lower, larger terraces are the wealthy elite. Those who till the upper, narrower terraces are the peasants. As one Ifugao put it, "We cannot but do what our ancestors told us to do."

The Banaue Hotel and the Banaue Youth Hostel, operated by the Philippine Tourism Authority, are the best choices for accommodations. The hotel, built in the mountain lodge tradition, offers 82 superior rooms, each with its own balcony and commanding view of the rice terraces. The hotel also offers a restaurant, sun deck, swimming pool, and Ifugao dances on Saturday evenings. The Banaue Youth Hostel, across the road, offers cheaper accommodation, as do other lodges in town.

Behind the Banaue Hotel, 240 steep steps lead down to the village of **Taman**. The people here still live much as their ancestors did. Besides tending their rice terraces, they also produce woodcarvings and beadworks. For a few pesos, they will show you the bones of their ancestors, which they keep wrapped and tucked under the eves of their huts.

Reached by a climb up a series of steps from the road below Banaue Center, **Bocos** boasts some interesting sights. The huts here are adorned with heads and horns of *carabao* and wild pigs, which indicate the status of the families. The more decorations the hut has, the wealthier the family. The villagers keep their most sacred idol, Bulol, the rice god, in the granary. It only comes out at harvest time to be bathed in the blood of sacrificed animals.

A footpath leads down from the road to **Poitan**, a village that boasts a collection of richly-lined huts. Here you can get a good view of the stone post protected and idolized by the Ifugao, and the stone-lined pit where elders gather to discuss problems and affairs. Poitan also has woodcarvers and weavers.

Four kilometers from Banaue Center – about a 45-minute walk – sits an ideal spot for a picnic. A small waterfall tumbles into a natural pool in Guihob. Take a dip in the crystal-clear waters and gaze out at the surrounding rice terraces.

Playful in the highland mountains.

Hapao, 16 kilometers from Banaue, offers one of the most beautiful rice terraces in the mountains, stone-lined terraces thought to be the oldest, and the origin, of Ifugao culture. Other terraces in **Banga-an**, 14 kilometers from Banaue, are accessible up steep stone steps. Here, from March to May, rainbows flitter over the terraces just before sunset. The terraces of **Batad**, 16 kilometers from Banaue, are only accessible by a four-kilometer footpath but boast a remarkable amphitheater-like contour, where tattooed men and women work the fields. About 30 minutes on from Batad by foot cascades Tappiya Falls, with its enormous natural swimming basin. **Mayoyao**, 44 kilometers northeast from Banaue, offers a breathtaking view of rice terraces.

From Banaue, backtrack to Bontoc and Baguio, or descend to the lowlands and the National Highway through Lagawe. In Lagawe visitors can explore the Bintakan and Nah-toban caves, and a stellar museum of Ifugao culture, off the courtyard of the grade school.

Kalinga-Apayao: From Bontoc, the adventurous can a have a go at **Kalinga-Apayao Province**, to the north. The Mountain Trail runs 130 kilometers along the Chico River, from Bontoc to **Tuao** on the Cagayan-Kalinga-Apayao border. From Tuao, a spur road (210 kilometers) runs all the way to the South China Sea in Laoag, Ilocos Norte. Every kilometer of it is rough going, and not an area to drive for the unexperienced.

The province's name is derived from two local words: *kalinga* means head-hunter, while *apayao* means navigable river. The Kalinga, who make up over half the population, are subdivided into the southern and northern tribes.

The best sight in Kalinga-Apayao is its unspoiled, natural beauty. In the southern part of the province sits **Balbalasang-Balbalan National Park**, near the Abra provincial border, in Balbalan – also highly-touted for its sweet oranges, lovely women, fascinating wildlife, and 29 waterfalls. The **Apayao River** is accessible through Kabugao, 70 kilometers from Tuao, where motorized boats can be hired for a trip down the river. Apayao River is noted for its clear waters, wildlife and stands of old-growth hardwoods. The **Agamatan National Park and Wildlife Sanctuary** stands near the Ilocos Norte border, in Calansan. The province has some 67 waterfalls and spectacular terraces around **Tinglayan**.

An almost nonexistent road connects **Abra Province**, through Lagangilang and Balbalan, with the Mountain Trail; however, Abra can easily be reached through Ilocos Sur Province. It is an hour's drive from Narvacan, through the Tangadan Tunnel, to the provincial capital in Bangued. From Bangued, explore Abra's rough terrain, seldom visited by tourists. The main attractions of Abra are along the **Abra River**, which runs from Mt. Data, in Mountain Province, to Vigan, in Ilocos Sur. Once noted for the fine horses bred along the river valley, today there remains little to see except the natural landscape. At **Bangued**, one can pick up fine handicrafts, notably small bags and baskets woven from local reeds and grasses.

Left, ikat weaving. Right, village of Batad and terraces.

CAGAYAN VALLEY

Like a jagged scythe, the Cagayan Valley cuts a swath through northeastern Luzon. Geographically whole, history has divided this isolated piece of real estate into six parts: Nueva Vizcaya and Quirino provinces, in the south, stand as the hooking blade. Isabela Province, with the chartered city of Santiago, serves as the cutting edge in the middle. In the north, Cagayan Province forms the handle, with the islands of Batanes Province as a lanyard.

By a happy freak of nature, the valley is almost entirely surrounded by lofty mountain ranges. The mountains balance the monsoon with counter-monsoon, giving the valley a mild climate that allows year-round planting. In the west, the mountains of the Cordillera Central stretches for nearly 240 kilometers (150 mi), separating the Cagayan Valley from the Ilocos and the South China Sea. In the east, the Sierra Madre tower over a coastline that falls steeply into the Philippine Sea. In the south, the Caraballo Sur reach across Nueva Vizcaya to join the Sierra Madre.

Colonization: As a rule, the people of the valley saw the Spanish conquistador as a thief of their land and their freedom. When they submitted, it was often due more to force of arms than the subtler pressures of an alien perspective. For every local who succumb, a hundred more burned their own villages, fled to the mountains and never returned, except to pillage and harass the intruders.

Those who remained saw their ancestral land divided up into *ranchos* and given to "deserving" individuals, most of whom were soldiers-of-fortune who had aided the Spanish conquest. Suddenly, the inhabitants of the valley found themselves colonial subjects, obliged to pay tribute in produce or gold. Meanwhile, the missionaries were eroding the leadership of the their revered female *shaman*. Some missionaries tried to win converts by gentle example. Many more launched into persecution, by burning the shamans' wooden altars erected in spots sacred to the tribes. In turn, the locals poisoned the missionaries, and stripped and burned their chapels and altars. Whatever Spanish settlements were painstakingly established continued to be in perennial danger of attack. Sometimes it was from mountain dwellers resenting new trading patterns. At other times, years of tribute and forced labor inflamed converts to revolt.

A slow-rising crescendo of violence reached the beginnings of climax in 1780, when the Spanish imposed a tobacco monopoly. Cagayan tobacco was of extra fine quality and a lucrative export trade product. Economically drained by continuous expansion and insufficient support from Spain, the colonial government made tobacco trade its exclusive monopoly. This meant only planting of tobacco under strict government supervision. This spelled hardship for the people of the lower and middle Cagayan, and of the lower Chico River valley. When the tobacco harvest was ready, agents bought cheap and sold dear in a classic pattern familiar to all

Preceding pages: Cagayan Valley and wild cogon grass. <u>Left</u>, ricefields dotted with flowers. <u>Right</u>, Luzon's north coast.

colonial rule. All of this led up to the revolution of 1896.

Nueva Vizcaya: The present-day Nueva Vizcaya – first created in 1839 by the Spanish government, then cut in size to form Isabela in 1856, Ifugao in 1908, and Quirino in 1971 – is landlocked in the approximate center of Luzon. A significant number of the original settlers of the province – the tribes of former headhunters – still remain, living mostly in the hills along the boundaries of the province, a full 60 percent of which is still forested.

Only 40 percent of the total provincial population can be found in the three principal towns of Bayombong, Solano and Bambang. The rest reside along the main road from Santa Fe, on the southern border, to Bagabag, on the northern boundary with Ifugao Province.

At **Santa Fe**, the entry into Nueva Vizcaya is marked by a gradual ascent into the brown foothills of the Caraballo Mountains. On a zigzagging road through the 915-meter-high (3,000 ft) **Dalton Pass**, history records a long and bloody battle between Fil-American troops and the rear guard of the Japanese army, towards the end of World War II. On the lonely pass now there are only the rumblings of huge trucks hauling timber and smaller ones groaning under sacks of rice and sweet potatoes, with a memorial on a hill. Scattered all along the road are stalls selling unique woven bamboo baskets of all shapes, executed in unvarnished strips and ornamented with a few lines of earthen colors. Sold alongside are also lush sweet peppers and potatoes grown in the surrounding foothills. The baskets have caught the attention of wholesale exporters of Philippine handicrafts.

Reaching **Aritao**, St Dominic Cathedral shows vestiges of the grandeur of this old town, but there is little else to see. Beyond lies **Bambang** and one of the most interesting geographical curiosities in the country: the snow-like and white salt hill of **Salinas Salt Springs** spews salty water into the mountain air. Salinas Salt Springs sits 15 dusty kilometers (9 mi) outside **Bambang**.

Church ruins, Isabela.

218

Between Bambang and Bayombong, at the 260-kilometer marker, sits the Villa Margarita Mountain Resort with spring-fed pools set in a citrus plantation, and accommodations. **Bayombong**, the provincial capital, lies just beyond. It has a small park with some exotic plants, but little else, unless one visits during the August fiesta, when Aetas come down from the nearby mountains to dance in front of century-old church. Four kilometers from Bayombong, at the edge of a forest that holds more mysteries for the intrepid traveler, is a teasing hint of things possible in this old, little-touched landscape – a lovely waterfall provides the setting for several spiritist sects, who live and commune with nature in the manner of the vanished shamans.

Isabela: The province of Isabela, named after Queen Isabella of Spain, and the city of **Santiago** remain primarily tobacco country. The region is also known as the rice bowl of northern Luzon, a prime logging area and for its rich grazing land. Spread across its vast territory (it is the second-largest prov-

ince in the country, after Quezon) – the monotony of the road broken by low-slung bamboo huts – stand the old Spanish settlements, expanded now to accommodate larger populations (many of them Ilocano immigrants), but still converging around churches built a hundred years ago.

Unlike the churches of Cagayan Province, which were built in the earlier colonial period in baroque-style, the churches of Isabela show a simpler antique Spanish architecture. These include the distinctive unpainted and unrestored red-brick churches of Echague, Alicia, Cauayan, Tumauni and San Pablo, strung out in squat dignity all along the National Highway.

Wilderness: Even as development creeps into the plains of Isabela, it is possible to uncover wild natural beauty in the eastern highlands. **San Mariano**, 35 kilometers (20 mi) east off the National Highway at **Naguilian**, serves as the gateway to the Palanan wilderness and the Palanan rain forest. The wilderness area stands as the county's highest altitude rain forest and is home to numerous yet unclassified endemic species of flora and fauna. Highly noted for its biological diversity and sanctuary of the endangered Philippine eagle, the area remains untouched and can only be penetrated by river boat or on foot. From San Mariano, two rough mountain roads cuts over 60 kilometers (40 mi) east through the Sierra Madre range to **Palanan**, on Palanan Bay. A single road then continues 100 kilometers (60 mi) southwards along the coast to Aurora Province.

Further north on the National Highway, around **Tumauini**, sit the Fuyot National Recreation Area and Sta. Victoria Caves. A 15-kilometer (9 mi) drive from Tumauni leads to the area. The limestone outcroppings in the foothills lure spelunkers and birdwatchers.

Quirino: In the upper Cagayan River Basin, **Quirino Province** stands ringed by the peaks of the Sierra Madre and Mamparang ranges. Known for its forest lands, the area is populated by ethnic people speaking mostly Ifugao dialects. Quirino offers some of the best un-

Bamboo wares line the streets of Santa Fe.

spoiled landscapes in the Philippines and the chance to meet some of its most primitive peoples. But this rugged country is not for the faint at heart.

The only artery is the national road running across southern Isabela Province, from Cordon to San Agustin, which provides access to the Quirino towns of Diffun, Cabarroguis, Aglipay and Maddela. **Diffun** serves as the capital of Quirino, and is easily reached by a good road from Cordon, Isabela. Nagbukel Caves, 4 kilometers outside Diffun, are a good place for picnicking and hiking. The area, however, is presently being developed by the Lamplighter religious sect. **Bisangal Falls**, 35 kilometers (20 mi) from Cabarroguis and accessible from Diffun, sits in a virgin forest that serves as a wildlife sanctuary for endangered species, like the Philippine eagle.

Aglipay, accessible from Jones, Isabela, stands as a noted provincial historical site. Nearby **Aglipay Caves**, a series of 38 interlinking caves, offer good views of well-preserved stalagmites and stalactites. The rolling hills and verdant forest around Aglipay also offer good opportunities for trekking. **Maddela**, accessible from San Agustin, Isabela, offers some of the best whitewater in the archipelago. The Cagayan River tumbles down through Governor Rapids, famed for its gigantic and perpendicular limestone walls. It is also a great fishing grounds.

In southern Quirino, **Nagtipunan** is being developed as a gateway to the famed surfing beach along the Aurora coast. However, for now, it very hard to reach. One must either slug one's way down the mountain road from Maddela or take the equally hard route up from Carranglan, Nueva Vizcaya. Those who make it will find themselves surrounded by a lush rain forest, one of the last in the Philippines. Nearby **Victoria Falls** is touted as the source of the country's longest river, the Cagayan.

Cagayan Province: In this upper valley, ethnic tribes still roam the surrounding hills. Their lifestyle has been marked by their departure from the fertile plains. Never having submitted to outside domi-

Contours of the Sierra Madre range.

nation, they still live much as they have for centuries. Where missionaries earlier trudged to them with religion, anthropologists now hike miles of forest trails to record their cultures.

Originally known as the Nueva Segovia, **Cagayan** was one of the first areas on northern Luzon occupied by the Spanish. Later, it took on the name Cagayan from the *tagay* plant that grows abundantly in the area: Kayagayan (lit. a place where tagay grows), shortened to Kagayan.

At the end of World War II, the Americans bombed **Tuguegarao**, destroying much of the old Spanish capital, including the cathedral. Renovated now, St Peter's has lost its antique color, pathetically cemented over like a water tower. Layers of time flip back like flash cards as the business of the old town moves into the environs of the new, built wisely after the bombing outside Tuguegarao's old shell. In this complex lies the Cagayan Provincial Museum and Historical Research Center, one of the most distinguished in the country.

Exquisite religious artifacts, from carved wooden altars to gold-braided vestments, vie with antique porcelain tradeware and antique furniture. According to the archaeological section of the museum, most of Cagayan's prehistory stands in the Paleolithic. Fossilized remains of elephants, rhinoceros and stegodon, along with human-made stone tools that have been dug up in the valley, are displayed as evidence of life here some 40,000 years ago.

The area around Tuguegarao is a cave lover's dream. Thirty kilometers (20 mi) northeast from town are the famed caves of **Peñablanca**. Some 375 caves dot the area along the Pinacanauan River, and can be reached over a 24-kilometer back road, or by boat up the Pinacanauan River. The most famous is the **Callao Cave**, with its large opening in the roof, through which sunlight spotlights a stone altar with red velvet trim, rows of pews, and a rough earthen floor, making the place look like a latter-day catacomb. Other famed caves in the area include the Jackpot, Odessa-Tumbali and Si-

St. Peter's, Tuguegarao, and Callao Cave.

erra. Further up the river, passed the much overrated Callao Caves Resort, tens of thousands of white bats can be watched at dusk as they come out to feed in a long snaking procession.

Further up river awaits a whimsical attraction. The locals call it *maroran,* or a place of continual rain. And indeed, a fine spray immerses the boat as it catches the sunlight. It is believed that the maroran is caused by a subterranean river running along the elevated bank; the spray finds its way through rock crevices, and amidst ferns and vines that grow thick on the river banks.

Further north, there is still more forest to explore around **Gattaran**. Some 40 kilometers (25 mi) east of Gattaran sit the **Tanlangan Falls**. These three-tiered falls tumble some 100 meters (300 ft) down the mountainside. Close by are the Mapaso Hot Springs, with its black metallic beds hissing steam.

North coast: The Cagayan River, which supported the lowland tribes of the valley for countless generations, empties into the Babuyan Channel at **Aparri**, the celebrated port where the Spanish first landed. Aparri is also considered one of the best big game fishing ports for marlin and sailfish in the Philippines. Around Aparri, the coast spreads out into a run of beaches, tangled estuaries and swamps. Here ethnic tribes thrived since early times – weaving cloth, baking clay, fashioning fishing and hunting implements from the bamboo that grew thick in their forests.

Buguey, east of Aparri, is the oldest Spanish foothold on this coast. Here, one can still find old locals playing on 19th-century wooden harps, one of the last places in the Philippines where the skill still exists. To the west of Aparri, bamboo craft is also alive and well in Sanchez-Mira. Those looking for beaches will find them near Claveria, west of Sanchez-Mira and on the boarder with Ilocos Norte – great beaches and the lovely islets of **Punta Lakay Lakay** off its coast.

The best is out on **Fuga Island**, northwest of Aparri. This is a ravishing islet where stunning beaches glow pink with pulverized coral. Scuba-diving and snorkeling are the major interests of most visitors to this island. Delicious wild honey, gathered from the interior forest, and an ancient church in the old town are most rewarding fringe benefits to a visit here.

White herons flock to the rice fields on the peripheries of many of the towns along the northern coast of Cagayan. These herons keep travelers company while on the hour-and-a-half drive to the northeastern tip of the province at Port San Vicente.

On **Palaui Island** stands the old Spanish lighthouse, on **Cape Engaño** (lit. Cape Delusion). But the white beaches, steep, rugged cliffs and the surrounding deeps of the Babuyan Channel that seduce the senses are no delusion at all. Here, sea hawks fly lazily overhead on equally lazy thermals, while wild boar and carabao roam freely throughout the interior forest.

Batanes: Beyond Cape Engaño is the country's smallest province, **Batanes**, or Home of the Winds. It was first made a province (Provincia de la Concepcion) by the Spanish governor-general in 1782. Later, in 1799, it was downgraded to a territory, not to be reinstated until 1952. This collection of some 10 islands in the Luzon Strait, between Luzon and Taiwan, has long been the home of the Ivatan people. Of Malay stock, the Ivatan migrated to the islands from Taiwan sometime in the distant past.

Today, the islands of Batanes are noted for their undisturbed and unspoiled marine environment, natural beauty, and friendly Ivatan people under their all-weather headgear, known as *vakui*. Also notable here are the unique limestone block buildings and churches, with one-meter-thick walls and 30-centimeter-thick thatched *cogon* roofs.

Basco, the capital, sits on Batan Island, 55 minutes by air from Tuguegarao, Cagayan. Sabtang Island lies 14 kilometers southwest of Batan Island and can be reached by a boat ride.

Itbayat Island lies four to five hours by boat out from Batan Island. Y'ami Island stands as the northernmost island in the province, just 100 kilometers south of Taiwan.

Luzon
farmer.

SOUTH

Most excursions out of Manila lead to the provinces just south of Metro Manila – Luzon, Rizal, Cavite and Batangas – defined by the large lake of Laguna de Bay. There's much here, whether the classic rapids of Pagsanjan or the simmering Taal Volcano, in its own private lake. Too, there are the beaches of Cavite and Batangas, and some decent diving off shore. In the foothills of Mt. Banahaw, religious cults defying classification pay homage to their deities.

The Bicol region, at the southern extent of Luzon, is punctuated by still-active Mt. Mayon, perhaps the most perfectly-shaped volcano on earth. South of Bicol are the Outlying Islands, a generic grouping that includes Marinduque, home to the fabulous Moriones Festival; Mindoro, off the beaten track and lined with silky beaches and azure waters; and Palawan, one of the last refuges for endangered Philippine wildlife.

The Visayas are perhaps the Philippines' most popular islands for foreign travelers. A long and lanky island with fine diving and decent beaches, Cebu was the first island to lure sunseekers several decades ago, sporting its own an international airport. To its northeast is Samar, remote and long a holdout for anti-government rebels. Leyte, between Samar and Cebu, was the site of Gen. Douglas MacArthur's return to the Philippines, and the home of that well-shoed first lady, Imelda Marcos. Just east of Cebu is Bohol, peppered with the knobby Chocolate Hills. East of Cebu is Negros, noted for sorcerers and sugar. Then there's Panay, best known to the world for a little island off its northern tip, Boracay, with exquisite beaches and increasingly polluted waters from far too many tourists seeking the lyrical paradise.

Mindanao is the oddest shaped of the archipelago's islands, an island of superlatives and a geographical and cultural counterbalance to large Luzon in the north of the archipelago. Rich in minerals and agricultural products, the island is also rich in Islam and wild terrain. Too, it must be said, it has often been in the news because of separatist violence, which continues today. (But be not deterred, as this occurs in specific and isolated areas, leaving most of the island fine for travel.) The city of Davao, benign and safe, is towered over by Mt. Apo, laced with virgin rain forest, sulfur vents and waterfalls. Far to the west side of Mindanao is Zamboanga, whose name alone solicits fantasies of exotic chaos and remoteness. Yet Zamboanga isn't the end of the Philippines.

Extending even further south, eventually to within sight of Borneo, is the Sulu Archipelago, a string of rowdy islands challenging enough for even the most jaded adventurer. Few make it there.

Preceding pages: seashore frolic during a water festival; beach on Boracay. **Left,** Cebu is known for the quality, and quantity, of its guitars.

BICOL REGION

In a lake near the world's most perfectly-shaped volcano swim the world's tiniest fish. Steam drifts through the palm trees where geothermal power is being tapped for electricity.

Offshore are islands with some of the whitest beaches and clearest coral-reefed waters one is ever likely to see. Add those attractions to the horrible one-eyed, three-throated *ponong,* of which the curious traveler might still catch a glimpse on one of those classic dark and moonless nights... This is the Bicol region, the peninsula of diversity at the southeastern-most tip of Luzon.

Camarines Sur: The high point of the city of Naga's – in fact, all of Bicol's – year is when the great barge, or *casco,* starts its colorful voyage from the launching place near the market. This is the water parade in honor of the Virgin of Peñafrancia, patroness of the Bicol region and permanent inhabitant of **Naga**, Camarines Sur's capital. The waterborne celebration is the culmination of a nine-day festival, an event bringing tens of thousands of devotees flocking from all over the archipelago each September.

The story of this festival goes back over 300 years, to when a Spanish priest, Don Miguel de Covarrubias, arrived with a purportedly miraculous icon found on a rocky Spanish mountainside. When the priest was sent to Naga, the image came along with him, too, and was housed in a riverside shrine where, over the years, the converts of the region came to pay their respects.

Soon, the annual festival in honor of the Virgin Mary began to attract more devotees than the old shrine could handle. So it was decided that, in 1655, "the dark one" was to travel to the new cathedral for her feast day.

Since that day, the "translocation" transfer – every second Saturday of September – of the Virgin Mary has been marked with full panoply, the grandest part of the festival being the riverine return a week later.

Camarines Sur: There is far more to the city of Naga than this annual festival, of course. Founded in 1575, Naga was first called Nueva Caceres, a religious diocese ministering to the entire region, including Camarines Sur, Camarines Norte, Albay, Catanduanes and Tayabas in the Tagalog region. Within a short time the old settlement had spread across the river. By 1578, the settlement's first church had been built and was named San Francisco, after the patron saint of the Franciscan order, the major religious influence in Bicolano history.

Nowadays, after a major earthquake in 1915, only a corner tower of the original structure remains, a gaunt reminder of one of the first settlements in the country. Unfortunately, a new shell has been created out of the old remains, and it must be said that it is a most unappealing piece of architecture that all but mocks the first design.

Directly across the road from the church and in the middle of the square is the **Quince Martires monument** to 15 Filipino patriots, executed by the Span-

Left, black beach south of Legaspi. Right, carrying a shrine at fiesta, Naga.

ish during the downhill years of colonial rule. Only two years later – after a famous one-day revolt – the Spanish governor of the province surrendered to the Filipinos in the church opposite the monument. This event eventually led as well to the evacuation of the Spanish from Albay and Sorsogon provinces, and with hardly a shot fired.

For its sheer number and antiquity of early Spanish churches, Camarines Sur is believed by many to rival the Ilocos Sur region around Vigan, on Luzon's northwest coast. One of the most outstanding of these is the **Naga Cathedral**, built after the papal creation of the diocese in 1595. Like so many other churches in the country, this one has led a highly eventful life: destroyed by fire in 1768, rebuilt from 1808 to 1843, damaged by a typhoon in 1856, restored again between 1862 and 1879, once more damaged by an earthquake in 1887, and rebuilt in 1890.

It is a short bus ride from Naga to **Iriga**, sheltering in the shadow of Mt Asog, also known as Mt Iriga. On nearby **Lake Buhi**, the fishermen's nets have a fine mesh – exactly what is needed when fishing for tiny fish. *Tabios* and *simarapan*, the principal catch in Lake Buhi, are claimed to be the smallest fish in the world. Whether this claim still holds true or not is doubtful; the lake, like so many other fishing grounds in the Philippines, has sadly been exploited and over-fished.

Albay: Beautiful it's called and truly the mountain is such – with a threatening, deadly beauty. **Mayon** – from *magayon*, or beautiful in the Bicolano dialect – first erupted for European eyes in 1616, when a passing Dutch ship witnessed its explosive abilities. Since then, Mayon has erupted no less than 45 times – in this century, on 3 February 1993. And a wisp of smoke continually plays around the cone's top, suggesting that this mountain is really only a sleeping beauty.

In 1814, Mayon erupted with brief but massive violence, and a bombardment of red-hot boulders drove local inhabitants to take shelter in the Cagsawa

Mayon, and Lake Buhi.

Church. Any escape was blocked when a mighty tide of lava flowed down right into the church. Following that tragic day in February, **Cagsawa** found itself 40 meters (130 ft) lower. Even worse, at least 1,200 persons had perished. Today, only the church steeple and the remnants of the pediments are visible above ground. The rest of the structure lays under 10 to 12 meters of *lahar*.

The survivors sensibly rebuilt their church a few miles away at **Daraga**, on a hilltop overlooking the town. The Daraga church today is blackened and weathered by age. Among the stone carvings, tufts of greenery sprout from unlikely places, and already the church is taking on the half-ruined look of so many of the Spanish churches in the Philippines. In a delightfully incongruous touch, which one soon realizes is intrinsically Filipino, a neon cross tops the ancient tower.

Down below, Daraga is a center for Filipino handicrafts, particularly *abaca*. Shops are filled with abaca place mats, abaca bags, abaca floor mats, abaca

Altar boys, Daraga Church.

you-name-it-and-it's-here. It is interesting, but really only a pale reminder of how, in the early 1800s, hemp for ship cordage was an international commodity and the source of old Bicolano wealth. A century later, wire rope and other hemp sources had conspired to undercut the thriving trade. Today, abaca is used mostly for cottage industry products. Other popular buys in the area include woodcarvings and bowls, pottery, and the local delicacy, *pili* nuts.

Mayon towers over the whole Albay area, but right beside Legazpi airport is a small offspring with an interesting legend. **Lingyon Hill** is actually the result of volcanic magma escaping from the main cone in a new direction, but the story is far more picturesque, doubtlessly invented by an astute observer of local sociology.

Once upon a time, as all good legends start, the giant Kulakog lived here – or rather, he lazed here while his long-suffering wife, Tilmag, did all the hard work. The harder that poor Tilmag slaved, the lazier, fatter and more unpleasant Kulakog became. The most he would do was stretch out his arm for her to walk along – out to Mayon, for instance, to bring back fire for cooking his food. One day, as Tilmag staggered, exhausted, back from another fire-collecting mission, she tripped and dropped a hot ember on her giant husband's arm. Kulakog flinched, causing Tilmag to fall to her death. In time, the hill arose over her grave.

Limestone caves: About 11 kilometers (7 mi) outside Camalig, or 15 kilometers (9 mi) from Legazpi, are the **Hoyop-Hoyopan Caves** – blow-blow in the local dialect and derived from the sound of the wind whistling through the main entrance. The caves are part of an extensive series of limestone caves in the region. Carrying a smoky flare, the guide (accompanied by a half dozen children and an assortment of dogs) leads visitors down a twisting subterranean path that eventually ends on the other side of the mountain.

A steep climb up the hill arrives at another entrance and then dives back underground. A fourth access point offers a magnificent vista of green coconut plantations, with Mayon towering above them. Finally, the hike re-emerges at the original entry point.

The **Calabidong Caves**, about two kilometers further away, have a small underground stream and a dense population of bats. Altogether, over a dozen caves have been discovered within an eight-kilometer (5 mi) radius of the main caves. The guide will no doubt claim to have followed a series of tunnels along a route so long it took a whole day.

These caves have a scientific interest. In 1972, an American priest from nearby Camalig, assisted by some of the young locals, excavated one of the chambers and found pottery, bones in burial pots, beadwork and other artifacts believed to be 4,000 years old. Pieces of pottery can still be seen embedded in the stalactites, but you can inspect the first artifacts discovered in a small museum room found at the Camalig Church.

The caves also served as a shelter even long after prehistoric Filipinos used them as a homes. During World War II, Filipino guerrillas took advantage of the multiplicity of entrances and exits to elude the Japanese. Today, in the face of severe typhoons, they still serve as a stout hideaway, and they are even used as a disco by youngsters from the local village – one of the large chambers makes a good dance hall.

After inspecting the archaeological finds in **Camalig Church**, look around the old building itself. On the right hand side of the church interior is a memorial stone, in Spanish, to a Camalig resident who died in 1912 – aged 115 years. It's worth climbing up to the top of the old tower to see the massive church bells and admire the view over the surrounding countryside.

During the last days of World War II, American forces kept watch from this tower over Japanese stragglers hiding in caves in the hills on the other side of town. The Americans noticed with horror that the huge central bell, suspended just above their heads, was tied only with lengths of vine. They tied it more securely with steel wire, but now, 50

Harbor at Legaspi.

234

years later, the steel has rusted through, but the vines remain.

As a symbol of the region's liberation, the American forces provided yet another bell – modeled on their own Liberty Bell – that now stands outside the city hall in the provincial capital. An inscription reads, "Individually or collectively, if oppression ever knocks at your door, feel free to ring this bell."

Some 45 kilometers (30 mi) north of Legazpi lies **Tiwi**, an active thermal area. Visitors are welcome at the Tiwi geothermal power plant and also at the geothermal salt-making plant, where natural steam heat is used to produce various grades of salt from sea water.

It is possible, and recommended, for those on a scenic-drive ramble to veer off the main highway from Pili, past Naga, and take the road to Tigaon. From here, it is a fine drive south to **Legazpi**, capital of Albay, by way of a coastal cliffside road that loops up and down across mountain ridges plummeting straight to the sea. The motoring continues from Legazpi to the southernmost province in Bicol, **Sorsogon**, noted for its natural attractions.

Seven kilometers (4 mi) from the capital town of Sorsogon is a white-sand beach in **Bacon**, where cottages and picnic huts are available. Twenty kilometers (12 mi) from here is the famous **Rizal Beach** in **Gubat**, which is a long, crescent-shaped beach of white sand. A few miles south is the town of **Barcelona**, interesting for its church and fortress ruins, and for those who pursue such, its good beach.

Farther south is **Lake Bulusan**, 600 meters (2,000 ft) above sea level, at the foot of **Bulusan Volcano**, in the town of Bulusan. The crater lake is set in a forest rimmed with lush vegetation, abundant ferns, orchids and other wild flowers. A one-mile (two-km) hiking trail winds around the lake.

Catanduanes and Masbate: Way off the beaten track, yet only a few minutes' flight northeast from Legazpi, is the island of **Catanduanes**. A huge mountain mass with thick forests of hardwoods, it is one of the main sources

Mutya Pilipina beauty pageant.

of Philippine mahogany. Lying east of Luzon, Catanduanes bears the first impact of the typhoons that regularly strike the area, and has been called The Land of the Howling Winds. But during the warm and dry months, it's a pleasant place to visit. From Legazpi, a flight lifts up over the black-sand beaches extending up the coast. The small islands in the Albay Gulf, fringed with a whole series of white sandy beaches, disappear below and for a few minutes the plane skims over the wave tops before Catanduanes comes into view.

Virac airport is only a two-kilometer "tricey" ride from the town, where there are a couple of hotels, a few restaurants and from there a whole selection of beaches and waterfalls wait to be explored by the adventurous. When it is time to head back to the mainland, the boat return could be more interesting.

The other major island of the Bicol region is also accessible by air or sea. A ferry departs from **Bulan**, south of Sorsogon, to cross to **Masbate**, the cattle island of the Philippines. Masbate

has much more than just cattle, to say the least. There are some spectacular caves, waterfalls and fine beaches (particularly on the nearby island of Ticao), and a pottery excavation site in Kalanay.

Like Catanduanes, Masbate (and its lesser islands of Burias and Ticao) lies in the direct path of typhoons. Its isolation is part of its singular attraction to travelers, having been a haunt of the world-weary as early as the 16th century, when Spanish settlers came to escape the tedium of day-to-day management of the nearby Cebu colony.

Those visits were well worth it. This was especially so when the Spanish found relatively rich veins of gold bearing quartz in the area. Earlier, it was a similar find in Paracale, Camarines Norte, that propelled Spanish exploration of the Bicol region. There were hardwoods to be found here as well, which were used in the building of galleons; historical documents often mentions the island for its shipyards.

South from Bulan is the town of **Matnog**, marking Luzon's southern extremity. In this portion of Sorsogon, one can hear the musical blend of the Bicolano, Tagalog and Visayan dialects: Hiligaynon, Cebuano and Waray. As with Masbate and its two offshore islands, this place is one of the traditional transition points for travel between Luzon and the Visayas.

Bicol's Express: A final word on the region: Bicol's former isolation from the rest of Luzon is now all but a thing of the past. With television, radio and Tagalog movies, it now follows right along with the rest of the Philippines' largest island. There are, however, certain unique cultural strains that literally spice up a visit.

One that should not be missed is the local pepper, which rejoices in the nickname Bicol Express, after the train that once ran between Manila and the region. The moniker is meant to describe the speed with which you may reach for a glass of water after an accidental nibble. These tiny chilies liberally lace almost all Bicol dishes, awash with coconut milk and bits of pork, fish, crab, fat and gabi leaves.

Left, horse-drawn *calesa*. **Right**, member of a wedding party.

OUTLYING ISLANDS

Despite a wealth of natural attractions, the islands of Marinduque, Mindoro, Lubang and Palawan, including the Calamian group, usually rate no more than a brief mention in travelers' tales of the Philippines. But these islands offer some of the best adventure travel to be found anywhere.

Marinduque: An isolated volcanic mass surrounded by coral reefs, **Marinduque** lies between Mindoro Island and Quezon Province's Bondoc Peninsula. Legend would have the heart-shaped island rising from the seas as a consequence of a tragic love story. A powerful southern Luzon king named Datu Batumbacal prevented his daughter Marin from accepting the love of a fisherman-poet, Garduke. When the pair persisted in meeting secretly, the king ordered the beheading of Garduke, but the lovers sailed out to sea and drowned themselves instead. At that instant, an island rose from the sea, Marinduque.

Once a year, a beheading occurs in the island when its famed Moriones Festival grabs the limelight during Holy Week. Residents don masks as Roman soldiers to enact a Lenten spectacle, a vivid and uniquely Philippine rendition of the Passion of Christ. The ritual centers on Longinus, the one-eyed Roman centurion who regains full sight when blood spurts from the crucified Jesus into his blind eye. While guarding Jesus's body, he witnesses the resurrection and is converted to Christianity. Longinus is pronounced guilty by the Romans after a trial and is beheaded – or during this reenactment, his wooden mask is chopped off.

The colorful festival is celebrated in the towns of Boac, Gasan and Mogpog. On the morning of Good Friday, a masked Jesus emerges from **Boac**'s fortress-church and is led in a mournful procession up a hill to be crucified. Similar re-enactments, known as *kalbaryuhan* (for calvary), are held in **Gasan** and **Mogpog**, where the crucifixion is intoned in poetic Tagalog.

Three o'clock in the afternoon signals the hour of Jesus's death. Black-veiled women wearing leafy wreaths on their heads walk mournfully about. Flagellants – for the most part young men in their teens, clad in gaudy basketball shorts – whip themselves with fervor. Their naked backs, incised beforehand by friends and spectators, soon become gory red pools made brilliant by the afternoon sun.

Saturday then passes as a quiet day of mourning. Come Sunday, the festival reaches its high point with the aggressive beheading.

On an elevated stage by the Boac River, with loudspeakers blaring the proceedings for the benefit of the thousands of spectators milling about, Pontius Pilate and his prelates pronounce the sentence on Longinus. Twice Longinus escapes to lead the morion-clad soldiers on a merry chase across the river and up several hillocks. But in the end he winds up on the chopping block. A wooden sword flashes down. There is a spurt of make-believe blood. Longinus'

mask is held aloft, as his "headless" body is borne aloft on a bamboo pallet to the church.

The Moriones is said to have originated in the 1580s when Spanish sailors, who used the Marinduque coast as a repair station for the galleon trade, introduced the first masked soldiers, something they had seen in an old town in Mexico. In fact, the word *morion* is Spanish for helmet, and all festival soldiers are supposed to wear something similar to the traditional Spanish helmets of the 16th and 17th century.

Some of the masks worn by the participants are sold to tourists right after the beheading, but most are stored for the next festival. These traditional masks are carved from a local wood called *dapdap*, with harsh, angry expressions and fiercely-painted eyes. The helmets are decorated with colored paper and tinsel flowers, and while most the festival solders look authentic enough with their plumed helmets, leather jerkins, and thong sandals, others make do with cloth vests or display their ingenuity with outlandish costumes fashioned out of feathers and shells, coconut husks, broomsticks, and even seeds strung together to form a mask.

Like the famed Ati-Atihan festival on Panay Island, Marinduque's Moriones Festival attracts a great number of Manileños and foreign visitors. (The 40-minute plane flights from Manila to Boac Airport are booked well in advance. Ships from Manila and ferryboats from Lucena City, Quezon Province, to Balanacan, Marinduque (4 hrs) and to Santa Cruz harbor (Buyabod, 5 hrs) also take passengers. Another ferry runs between Gasan and Pinamalayan on Mindoro.)

Boac, the provincial capital and commercial center, is situated on Marinduque's west coast. The Lady of Biglang Awa (Sudden Mercy), reputedly miraculous, may be seen at the old citadel-church of Boac. Thirteen kilometers (8 mi) south of here is **Gasan**, from where one can take a 30-minute ride by motorized outrigger to Tres Reyes (Three Kings) Islands. The larg-

**Boac,
Marinduque.**

242

est of the three, and closest to Marinduque's southwest coast, is **Gaspar Island**, with Melchor Island and Baltazar Island beyond. These islands are ideal for fishing, swimming, and snorkeling, with their precipitous shore cliffs and wonderful underwater caves and reefs. A short distance south of Gasan is Malbog Sulfur Springs, not far from Buenavista town. Also near Buenavista are two nice beaches.

Sta. Cruz town, on the north coast, has several white-sand beaches and natural caves, the more prominent being **Bathala Cave**. Probably the best beach on Marinduque is White Beach, near the town of Torrijos, on the southeast coast. The ringing reef is great for snorkelling, and there is a good view of 1,160-meter-high (3,800 ft) Mt. Malindig.

Mindoro: West of Marinduque is the large island of **Mindoro**. Its name comes from Spanish, *mina de oro,* meaning gold mine, though no gold seems to have ever been found there. Geographically and politically, it's divided by the Mindoro Mountains into Mindoro Ori-

ental, on the east side, and Mindoro Occidental, on the west side. A three-hour ferry ride from Batangas delivers travelers to Puerto Galera, on the island's north coast. A one-hour flight from Manila can whisk visitors to Mamburao or San Jose, both on Mindoro's Occidental coast.

Puerto Galera: In a sheltered inlet, where the scenic harbor seems perfect for those with the a little sea-gypsy in their soul, sits **Puerto Galera**. Today, the place marks its days with the comings and goings of the ever increasing number of visitors as it has become developed – some would say overdeveloped – into a resort area.

Although **Sabang Beach** has been described as Little Ermita, owing to the proliferation of bars and the like, there are still a few peaceful, pleasant spots to be found along the coast. Try Small Lalaguna with its fine diving, **White Beach** or **Tamaraw Beach**. While Puerto Galera might be a busy place these days, a deeply-tanned would-be Hemingway from California, who

Tamaraw Beach.

camped for several months on White Beach, put it: "I'll stay here until I grow fins or wings."

Mamburao: It is possible, though difficult because of the condition of the roads, especially during the rainy season, to cross over to Abra de Ilog in Occidental Mindoro. From there, one can take the proverbial rickety bus down to the capital town of **Mamburao**, on the west coast. On an idyllic spot of land near Mamburao, an enterprising Manileño, Anthony Lehman, and his family have built an unusual and luxurious back-to-nature style resort, simply named Mamburao.

Off the northeastern tip of Mindoro lies **Lubang Island**, with its exceptional array of beaches and coves. The waters around Lubang are a favorite fishing ground for anglers who cross over the narrow channel from Manila and Nasugbu, Batangas. Lubang was in the limelight several years back with the discovery and subsequent surrender of a Japanese straggler from World War II, Lt Hiroo Onoda. And the barren rock island of Cabra has become a Catholic pilgrimage site since the early 1960s, when the Virgin allegedly appeared in a religious miracle *á la* Fatima.

Lake Naujan: Mindoro Oriental's capital city, **Calapan**, is about 45 kilometers (28 mi) south of Puerto Galera. Several beaches may be found around Calapan, with the better ones on Aganahaw Island and Silonay Island, about a kilometer off the mainland.

Forty kilometers (25 mi) south of Calapan sits **Lake Naujan**, a wildlife sanctuary where hunting and fishing are supervised and regulated by the national park personnel.

A boat ride to **Bulalacao**, near Mindoro's southern tip, leads to a Hanunoo Mangyan settlement – fascinating for a close look at Mindoro's original settlers. The Hanunoo pride themselves as the real Mangyans, a tribal title that has carelessly been applied to all seven different ethnic groups found on the island.

The Hanunoo, having a pre-Spanish syllabary of Indic origin, inscribe po-

Coral beach, Mindoro.

ems called *ambahan* on bamboo tubes, employing the favored Philippine native meter of seven syllables with rhymed endings. These allegorical verses are often chanted or recited without the accompaniment of musical instruments, which the Hanunoo reserve for their other verse forms.

A poetic language highly distinct from their everyday vocabulary is used in the traditional ambahan, the wealth of which is still being added to by present-day composers. The Hanunoo make music with guitars and a three-stringed violin called *git-git*, which is carved out of wood and uses human hair for both the strings and the bow.

The Hanunoo also excel in weaving baskets and purses from bamboo splints, and *buri* and *nito* strips. Their soft-strip baskets with striking geometric designs are of excellent quality, and rank among the best of the Philippine's traditional indigenous handicrafts.

Like most of Mindoro's other ethnic minorities, the Hanunoo now live in government-protected settlements. A few still roam the hinterlands practicing slash-and-burn agriculture, producing rice, corn, and various root crops. These tribes have all been pushed to the hills, and to some extent still suffer the needless bullying of their Christian brothers, who have been known to pull surprises with land-title grabs.

San Jose: On the far southwestern coast of Occidental Mindoro is **San Jose**, the largest and most progressive town in the province. San Jose will appeal to those visitors who want to get off the beaten track. The offshore waters are still fairly rich with tuna, marlin, sailfish, and swordfish, despite considerable dynamite fishing in the area.

From San Jose, a guide can take travelers to the **Mt Iglit-Mt Baco National Wildlife Sanctuary**, one of Mindoro's reservation areas for the *tamaraw*, a rare buffalo species found nowhere else in the world. Like the monkey-eating eagle, which is also found only in the Philippines, the tamaraw has been threatened by extinction. Hunting is now totally banned, and one would be lucky to spot one for "shooting" with a camera – there are only 200 tamaraw in the sanctuary.

The tamaraw, said to be related to the *anoa* of Sulawesi, bears a close resemblance to the more familiar *carabao*, or Philippine water buffalo. But the tamaraw is smaller and with horns growing straight upwards in a V instead of curving in a wide arc. The tamaraw's ferocity also distinguishes it from the docile carabao. No full-grown tamaraw has ever been captured live. They are prone to wild rampages when hunted, and attack anything in their path.

To reach the national wildlife sanctuary for a possible sighting of this rare creature, take a rough two-hour jeepney ride north from San Jose to the small *barangay* of **Puy-Puy**, from where an eight-hour hike through secondary forest and shoulder-high grass winds its way to the tamaraw's grazing areas.

Two other tamaraw reserves are found in Occidental Mindoro: one in Sablayan northwest of Mt Iglit, and another in the Mt Calavite National Recreation Area, on the island's northwest tip.

Church, Batanes.

San Jose is also the jumping off place for the Philippines' most famous reef and diving spot, **Apo**. The island and the massive reef nearby in the Mindoro Strait sits in the **Apo Reef National Park**. Apo itself is less than a kilometer long, but the extensive reef holds enough underwater interest to keep divers busy for a week. Shark Ridge presents the best underwater adventure on the reef. The best time to visit Apo is from March to early June, between the monsoons and when seas are calmer.

A slow boat makes the weekly trip from Manila to Palawan, stopping halfway at **Coron**, on **Busuanga Island**, in the Calamian group north of Palawan. (Coron is also accessible by three flights a week from Manila.) While in Coron, find out how long the ship will stay docked for cargo. Chances are you'll have enough time to wander about the old town for some good handicraft buys, a gallon of pure wild honey for as low as 30 pesos, and dried sea cucumbers sunning on some pavement fronting a Chinese store.

Alternatively, hire a pumpboat to **Maquinit Hot Springs**, where one can bathe in hot sulfuric water in twin waist-deep pools set on a picturesque beach corner, in front of a grotto for the Virgin Mary. This is probably the best hot spring site in the country. Unfrequented and easily accessible, it is highly recommended, especially for those who develop kinks with third-class boat travel. If the medicinal water becomes unbearably hot, bathers can always jump out and run the five kilometers (3 mi) of beach to the cool sea. Where else can you combine such pleasures with the chance to make a spontaneous offering of a piece of naturally-sculpted mangrove to the Virgin Mary?

Off the northern tip of Busuanga Island sits the unique **Calauit National Wildlife Sanctuary**, on Calauit Island. Giraffes, elands, zebras, bushbacks, impalas, gazelles and waterbucks were shipped here in 1977. To get there, take Conservation and Resource Management Foundation (CRMF) outrigger from Baluang for the crossing to Calauit.

An offshore oil rig, Palawan.

Palawan: Southwest of Mindoro lay the elongated island-province of **Palawan**, pointing like a *kris* (Malay for a type of short sword) towards northern Borneo. Some 25 percent of the Philippine archipelago's islands are found in the Palawan group, but their geography has resulted in virtual isolation until recently. As in Mindoro's case, interest in the province's development is rapid and irreversible.

Several oil companies are presently drilling in Palawan's offshore areas, and most of Palawan's residents say that it is simply a matter of time before oil of commercial quantity is discovered. The notion of black gold certainly was not in Pigafetta's mind when, early in the 16th century, he cited Palawan as the "land of promise". But Magellan's chronicler must have deduced from what he saw of the island's immense wealth and sparse population that it would be just a matter of time before this lucrative afterthought to the rest of the archipelago would be exploited.

When the Spanish arrived, the island was controlled by the sultans of Jolo and Borneo, and it wasn't until the 19th century that Spain managed to gain a foothold in the town that was later to be called Puerto Princesa and is now the provincial capital.

Ten centuries earlier, this same settlement on the eastern coast had moved the Chinese to call the island Palao-Yu, or "land of beautiful safe harbor". The island was then inhabited by settlers of proto-Malay stock, whose descendants still exist today as the Batak, Palawanon, and Tagbanua. Their migration from the Indonesian islands is popularly believed to have been by way of the land bridges that then attached the Philippine archipelago to the Asian subcontinent. The theory finds great evidence in the distinctive fauna and flora of Palawan, which, like those of Mindanao, are uncommon to the rest of the country.

In the 13th century, more settlers filtered in from the Majapahit empire of Java. Today, despite continuing migration, Palawan remains underpopulated. Even as migrants from Luzon and the

Palawan's still-pristine water.

Visayas respond to a government call for resettlement, they do so only in small numbers. Palawan is still considered too remote by most Filipinos.

Improvement of the infrastructure will certainly change this, but until then, roads remain atrocious and travel even within the main island is done mostly by boat. But for the adventurous seeking fringe locations – explorer, naturalist or beach mandarin – Palawan's rough going yields rewards of considerable merit.

The waters off the entire east coast abound with game fish. Exotic wildlife roams the interior, including the Palawan peacock pheasant, which is the smallest of its kind in the bird world; foot-high mousedeer or chevrotain, which is the smallest of Asiatic hoofed animals; monkey-eating eagle; *tabon* bird, whose large eggs are collected from beach burrows to make a prized omelet; Palawan mongoose, hornbill, bear cat, civet, stink badger, scaly anteater, porcupine, flying squirrel and the giant sea turtle, which lays eggs on certain beaches at the end of the year.

Visitors might watch the birds' nest gatherers at work, intrepidly scaling the cliffs for the prized nest of swiftlets that will make their way to some Chinese restaurant in Manila. It's possible to motor up a subterranean river to marvel at natural cathedrals, visit a cave complex containing some of the country's most important archaeological finds, take the pick of souvenir handicrafts from a unique farm prison, savor the fabulous sunsets off the west coast, or watch more than a hundred thousand birds darken the skies as they come home to roost in their island sanctuary.

There are daily Philippine Air flights from Manila to **Puerto Princesa**, and the weekly steamer from Manila to the same port. Puerto Princesa sits near the middle of Palawan Island's eastern coast. It is the capital and serves as the hub of travel in the Palawan group.

Roads, not all of them decent enough to be called such, branch out from Puerto Princesa only to stop at certain points, from where further travel is done by coast-hugging boats.

St. Paul's Subterranean National Park.

From Puerto Princesa, travel overland to **Baheli** town close to the western coast, 60 kilometers (40 mi) away, then proceed by boat for an additional two hours to get to Palawan's famous Underground River in **St. Paul's Subterranean National Park**.

Tabon Caves: Six hours' overland travel southwest from Puerto Princesa leads to the town of **Quezon** on the west coast, from where there is a half-hour boat ride to **Tabon Caves**.

This is a huge and fascinating complex of some 200 caves, of which only 30 or so have been explored; less than a dozen caves around Lipuun Point have been excavated by archaeologists since their discovery in 1962. Here, human fossils were found and carbon-dated 22,000 to 24,000 years ago, the oldest traces so far of *Homo sapiens* in the Philippines archipelago.

With the Tabon relics were found Stone Age implements and relics of later eras, including burial jars and kitchen utensils. Overlooking a bay studded with small islands, the entrance to Tabon Caves is situated about 30 meters (20 ft) above sea level, on a promontory facing the South China Sea. The large mouth leads to an equally imposing dome-shaped chamber, beyond which are numerous sections where archaeological work is still patiently, and literally, being carved out.

Close by Quezon, along Kanalong Bay in **Tarampitao**, runs a 10-kilometer (6 mi) stretch of white beach where the swimming is good and the viewing fine for majestic sunsets.

Penal colony: Closer to Puerto Princesa, 16 kilometers (10 mi) south, is the **Iwahig Penal Colony**. Most of the prisoners here roam freely within the reservation's 37,000 hectares (90,000 acres) of beautiful undulating rice fields and orchards. Handcarved items of *kamagong* (mahogany) and mother-of-pearl inlay work are among the best of the various handicrafts turned out by the inmates to supplement their income from agriculture. Two river resorts within the colony are favorite excursion retreats for Puerto Princesa residents.

On the road south from Puerto Princesa, at kilometer 69, is the town of **Abovlan**, near Narra. This is an agricultural town where a reservation has been set aside for the Tagbanua people. One-hundred-fifty kilometers (90 mi) farther south and over very rough roads is **Brooke's Point**, another progressive municipality. Still farther south, more easily reached by sea, are the Muslim communities of Bataraza and Rio Tuba.

Nearby islands: Five kilometers (3 mi) off Rio Tuba sits the **Ursula Island National Wildlife Sanctuary**. This bird sanctuary was severely hit by a rat plague several years ago, and most of the birds moved to far off Tubbataha Reef.

Now, with the establishment of the sanctuary, some of the birds are starting to return. Some migratory birds from China and Siberia also roost here from November to February. The Ursula Island National Wildlife Sanctuary can most easily be reached by a five-hour pumpboat ride from Brooke's Point.

Off the southern tip of Palawan Island is **Balabac Island**, famous for its rare seashells. Much further on, at the Ma-

Boring beach.

laysia boarder, sits **Turtle Island National Park** in – where else? – the Turtle Islands. Philippine territory ends on this southwest corner, where motorized Muslim *vinta* and *kumpit* make frequent runs across the border to the Malaysian islands off Borneo's northern coast. (Don't even consider it because of the pirates that frequent this southern part of the archipelago, unless armed to the teeth and there are many of you.)

The world's largest pearl, the "Pearl of Lao-tze", was found in the shell of a giant clam off Palawan, in 1934. It weighed in at 6.6 kilograms (15 lb) and measured 24.2 centimeters (9.5 in) long and 14 centimeters (5.5 in) in diameter. It is valued at more than US$5 million dollars and spends most of its time in a San Francisco bank vault.

Taytay: Close to the northern tip of Palawan is the old town of **Taytay**, one of the first Spanish fortifications to be built on Palawan. Founded in 1622, Taytay was once the Spanish capital of the province that the early Spanish colonizers had renamed Paragua. Close

by is the island of **Paly**, with its waterfalls and white beaches, where giant sea turtles lay their eggs in November and December. Off Taytay is Malampaya Sound, an angler's paradise that has been dubbed, rather tediously, the "fish bowl" of the Philippine archipelago.

El Nido: Northwest of Taytay, 50 kilometers (30 mi) away, is **El Nido**, where towering black marble cliffs provide swiftlets with enough nooks and crannies in which to build their nests so popular in soups throughout the Chinese world.

Gatherers clamber up rickety bamboo scaffolding to collect the nests from crags and deep caves up in the cliffs. About one kilogram (2 lb) of these prized nests may net a professional cliff-scaler hundreds of pesos, a minimal sum compared to what they will fetch in Manila or elsewhere in Asia, where a traditional Chinese meal often starts with delicately flavored El Nido soup.

A bonus of visiting these islands is as stay at one of the superior and far-flung resorts, like Club Noah Isabelle or El Nido Ten Knots, on **Miniloc Island**. These are havens for divers, along with snorkeling, windsurfing and the whole gamut of aquatic sports all readily available. The area is especially popular with Japanese divers, who appreciate El Nido's fabled shrimp and lobster dinners. (The resorts are Japanese-owned.)

Some 40 minutes by pumpboat from El Nido village lies Jock Gordon's Pangulasian Island Resort, on a real Robinson Crusoe-type island. Jock, a Scotsman as the name would suggest, was washed up on these shores some years ago when sailing around the world. A romantic resort, well-known to cognoscenti who sail down from Manila, Hong Kong and Singapore, **Pangalusian Island** has surprising British touches, such as the formality of the resort's meal service.

And when not lounging like a sloth, eating seafood or downing an ice-cold San Miguel beer from a tall bottle, the traveler can stroll along the remote hibiscus-lined trails, windsurf, dive a superb reef or island hop. Or simply bask like a lizard in the seducing sun.

Left, Pangalusian Island. Right, Batak hunter.

THE VISAYAS

"Islands of now in a sea of yesteryear," enthused one visitor. Hanging like a necklace of uneven beads strung together by varying geographies of seas, straits, channels and gulfs, the Visayas lend themselves readily to such wistful opinions. The six major land masses and fringe groups of isles parade together in a series of idyllic images – calm waters, shimmering coves, rocky coasts and palm-fringed beaches.

The soft and burnished appearance of Visayans comes from slow play and a lingering that is nearly a blessing. The fishermen sew up their nets during the lazy part of the day. The young boys shimmy up the trees to gather fresh coconuts. The women tend a slow fire for the noonday meal. Late afternoon finds a fleet of outriggers pushing off into sunset, where soon a line of flickering lights will outlast the night.

People from Luzon, when asked about the southern islands, generally point out this slower pace, the seductive lilt to the Visayans' speech, and the loving reputation of the women. As an afterthought, they might cite the fresh seafood of amberjacks, blue-finned tuna, red snappers, crabs, lobsters and giant prawns.

Magellan's landfall: On 16 March 1521, a Portuguese sailor – Fernao de Magalhaes, who had renounced his citizenship and taken up the Spanish flag under the name Hernando de Magallanes, which the English-speaking world later came to know as Ferdinand Magellan – anchored off the tiny island of Homonhon in Leyte Gulf. He named the new-found place the Isles of St Lazarus, after the saint on whose blessed day he first sighted it. (The Philippines would not get its present name until 1542, when Ruy Lopez de Villalobos named it *Filipinas* after the infant who later, in 1556, became King Philip II of Spain.

Two days after dropping anchor for the first time, Magellan sailed on through the Gulf of Leyte and the Surigao Strait to the island of Limasawa. While Magellan stands credited with the discovery and Villalobos with the naming, it was a Malay slave that uttered the first greeting between Spaniard and Filipino. Enrique de Molucca, Magellan's Moluccan slave, hailed – on the captain's orders – a small boat of eight natives from the rail of the *Trinidad*. The natives understood him perfectly; the world had been circled linguistically, and Enrique de Molucca became the first known person to circumnavigate the globe, though he has never been credited with the deed.

Six weeks later, Magellan was dead. From Limasawa, he had sailed up through the Canigao Channel to the island of Cebu, where he Christianized the rajah and 500 of his followers. A minor rajah of Mactan – a flat, muddy island where Cebu's international airport now stands – stood in rebellion to the rajah of Cebu and his new foreign guests. Now known to all Filipinos as Lapu Lapu, Rajah Cilapulapu (the *ci* simply means, the) defended his island with some 2,000 warriors against 48

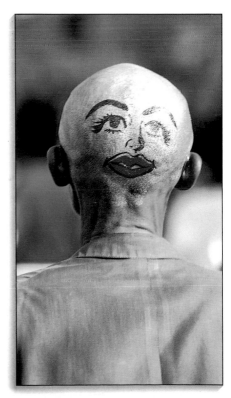

Preceding pages: disappearing sunset, Boracay. Left, Boracay surfing instructor. Right, face of Ati-Atihan.

armor-clad Spaniards, in April of 1521. During the battle that raged for over an hour, Magellan was slain.

Today, a tall white obelisk stands on Mactan Island marking the spot where Magellan fell. The dedication on its eastern side, facing Spain, records the event as a tragedy: "Here on 27th April 1521 the great Portuguese navigator Hernando de Magallanes. In the service of the King of Spain, was slain by native Filipino..." On the western side, facing the Philippines, it records a triumph: "Here on this spot the great chieftain Lapu Lapu repelled an attack by Ferdinand Magellan, killing him and sending his forces away..." The latter version is most preferred by Filipinos.

Visayans: *Bisaya*, or Visayan, is the term generally accorded a fifth of the population of the Visayas Islands, although there are actually three distinct cultural and linguistic groups, with not much love lost amongst them. The Waray of Samar and Leyte belong to one of the least-developed regions in the country. The two islands, Samar and Leyte, are separated by the San Bernardino Strait and lie directly in the path of typhoons roaring in from the northwest. The Cebuano is the most aggressive among the Bisaya. They are well aware that they have to try harder than Manila's brash cosmopolitans, but their attempts to keep up are done mostly on a scale compatible with the Visayan's traditional good humor. The Ilonggos, particularly those of western Negros and southern Panay, are considered the most decadent of the Southerners. In a sense, they bring the Bisaya's essence to a lofty distillation, marked by genteel pursuits and a disdainful regard for the harsher facets of living. Sugar is the key word to the Ilonggo's lifestyle.

Broad lowland plains on the western part of Negros Island, with its rich volcanic soil, supports extensive commercial sugar production, which accounts for more than two-thirds of the national sugar export. *Hacenderos* – landowners, most of whom can trace their lineage to early Spanish settlers – have long been looked upon as an idle and profli-

Fiesta reveler, Cebu.

gate group who have long seemed to possess effective political clout. Until recently, that is.

Commercial sugar production on Negros Island had its beginnings in the late 19th century, when some enterprising European settlers assisted the Spanish mestizos in modernizing the industry. Since then, migrant workers called *sacadas* have streamed seasonally into Negros from the rest of the Visayas.

In around 1250, as a history heavily laced with popular folklore would have it, 10 Bornean *datu* (chiefs), fleeing the collapse of the once-mighty Srivijayan empire, sailed northwards with their followers and landed on the island of Panay. They bought the coastal lands from the native Negrito inhabitants with gold, pearls and other ornaments.

This legendary barter between Malays and native inhabitants is commemorated yearly in what is the most popular and colorful festival in the whole country. On the third weekend of January, the small coastal town of Kalibo, in Aklan Province, plays host to thousands of Filipinos and foreign visitors who join the three-day revelry and fiesta known as Ati-Atihan.

Exploring the Visayas: The best way to travel the Visayas is by boat. Only then will one experience the islanders' disdain for the dubious benefits of speed. Jets whisk travelers from Manila to Cebu and most other Visayan capitals in less than an hour. There are times when flying becomes necessary, but speed dose not leave time to savor the subtleties of transition.

It takes some 20 hours to sail from Manila to the Visayas. The passage from Manila Bay compensates for the chaotic pier bustle and the likely delays before departure. But as the Manila skyline recedes, one feels like slapping one's self on the back for having given metropolitan clutches the slip.

Samar: Overland travel into the eastern Visayas is via the **National Highway** (sometimes called the Pan-Philippine or Maharlika Highway), which passes through Samar and Leyte from the southern tip of Luzon's Bicol Penin-

Ati-Atihan, Kalibo.

sula. Ferries depart from Matnog, in Sorsogon Province, for **Allen** on northern Samar. The National Highway winds along the western coast of Samar, from Allen to Tacloban (about 250 kilometers/ 150 mi), on the Leyte boarder. From Tacloban, the National Highway continues south on Leyte, to Maasin (about 160 kilometers/100 mi), where ferries depart for Surigao City on Mindanao.

Close to Allen is **Rosario Hot Springs**. Several interesting waterfalls are found in northern Samar, among them Victoria, Veriato, Hingarog, and Pinipisican. The last one is particularly pretty, but like the rest, it requires considerable hiking in roadless territory. Allen and Laoang, a town off the northeastern coast, have resthouses, while **Catarman**, the provincial capital, has small hotels.

Calbayog, 65 kilometers (40 mi) south of Allen in western Samar, is serviced by air from Manila and Cebu. Further south is **Catbalogan**, the provincial capital, and accessible by ship from Manila and Tacloban, in Leyte Province. Halfway between Calbayog and Catbalogan is the town of **Gandara**, with its Blanca Aurora Falls. The road continues southward from Catbalogan, circling the rich fishing grounds of Maqueda Bay, until it hits the **San Juanico Bridge** linking Samar to Leyte.

South on the Samar side of the San Juanico Bridge sits **Basey**, site of the Sohotan Caves, Sohotan Natural Bridge, and **Sohotan National Park**. Basey is also the home of mat weavers, whose designs have become popular items in the markets of Tacloban across the San Juanico Bridge.

Leyte: The capital of Leyte Province is the port of **Tacloban**. It is also the trading center of the eastern Visayas. Its provincial capitol building features the scene of Gen. Douglas MacArthur's historic landing on Leyte, in 1945. In the center of town is an attractive Spanish-style museum and shrine, the Santo Niño Shrine, housing Imelda Marcos' collection of statues of the infant Jesus. (Leyte is Imelda's home province.) One can stay at the Leyte Park Hotel while in

San Juanico Bridge, between Leyte and Samar.

Tacloban. Built by Imelda, the hotel's most striking feature is a heart-shaped swimming pool.

The Leyte Landing Marker is found on Red Beach at **Palo**, a town a few kilometers south of the city. Palo is the site of yet another Imelda Marcos-inspired monument – the MacArthur Park Beach Resort, worth a brief stopover.

From Palo, a road leads west to the coastal towns of Carigara Bay before turning south to **Ormoc**, on Leyte's southwestern coast, some three hours' drive. Across Carigara Bay lies **Biliran Island**, easily reached by motorized *banca*. The island has several fine beaches on its western coast, notably Agta Beach in Almeria and Banderrahan Beach in Naval. The town of **Caibiran**, on the eastern coast, has the spring-fed San Bernardo Swimming Pool and Tumalistis Falls, once claimed as having the sweetest water in the world. Off Caibiran are the hot sulfur springs of Mainit and Libtong. The smaller islands of Maripipi and Higatanga have many secluded white-sand beaches, if those found on Biliran do not suffice.

From Tacloban, the National Highway follows the eastern coastline southwards past Palo and **Tolosa**, the hometown of former First Lady Imelda Marcos. Don't miss a visit to her former grand residence, Olot House, if you can get past the guards at the entrance. Although the residence was opened by the Department of Tourism (DOT) to the public after Ferdinand and Imelda fled the country, there appears to be confusion about whether it is still open or not. In any case, it has fallen into a state of unpresidential disrepair.

Past **Abuyog**, the road veers west and crosses Leyte's Central Cordillera Mountains to the town of **Baybay**. The road then follows the western coastline to Southern Leyte's provincial capital of **Maasin**, about 160 kilometers from Tacloban. Ferries cross the Surigao Strait from Maasin southeasterly to Lipanta Point, in Surigao del Norte, from where the highway proceeds across Mindanao.

Off the southern tip of Leyte is historic **Limasawa Island**, where a marker

MacArthur's return on a wall relief, Leyte's provincial capitol building.

commemorates the first Catholic mass celebrated on Philippine soil. Motorized bancas, more popularly known as pumpboats, provide a 30-minute ferrying service to Limasawa from the small town of Padre Burgos, south of Maasin.

Southern Leyte's proximity to Bohol and Cebu has given it a predominantly Cebuano-speaking population. Ships regularly cross the Canigao Channel and Camotes Sea separating Leyte from the Central Visayas, either from Maasin or Ormoc City, the latter is also on the Visayas air routes.

Bohol: For its relatively small size, **Bohol Island** has much to offer in history and natural attractions. Miguel Lopez de Legazpi (c. 1510-72), the Spanish conqueror and colonizer of the Philippines, anchored briefly on the island in 1563 and is said to have sealed a blood pact with a chieftain, Sikatuna.

Boholanos are known to be an extremely industrious lot, and possibly for this reason are often pointed out as bogeymen in a region more familiar with lassitude. The province is one of the largest coconut-growing areas in the country, while cottage industries continue their impressive production of delicacies and various handicrafts, which flood the Manila markets.

Notable among the Boholano weaver's products are mats and sacks made of *saguran* fibers, antequera baskets combining bamboo and *nito*, and items woven out of local grasses and reeds.

A good road system traverses the island. The coastline is marked by picturesque coves and clean, white-sand beaches, most of them a short ride from **Tagbilaran**, the provincial capital. Tagbilaran is Bohol's main port of entry. Ferries also cross over from Cebu to Tubigon town on the northwestern coast. It is a 20-minute plane flight from Tagbilaran to Cebu. A bridge connects Tagbilaran with tiny **Panglao Island**, where a luxury resort, the Bohol Beach Club, sits on Alona Beach. Another resort popular with scuba divers is Bohol Divers' Lodge.

Seven kilometers (4 mi) from Tagbilaran is **Baclayon Church**, one of

Chocolate Hills, Bohol.

the country's oldest and built in 1595. Also known as the Church of La Purisima Concepcion (Immaculate Conception), it has an interesting museum housing a rich collection of religious relics, ecclesiastical vestments, and old librettos of church music in Latin on animal skins.

Ten kilometers (6 mi) from the capital is the town of **Dauis**, on Panglao Island and where the **Hinagdanan Cave** offers an underground bathing pool with an eerie atmosphere: sunlight streams in through a pair of natural skylights, casting an ethereal glow on the cool waters.

Also worth visiting are the Punta Cruz Watch Towers in **Maribojoc**, a short distance north of Tagbilaran, and Calape Church, with its famous and reputedly miraculous Virgin Mary image.

But what remains Bohol's most famous attraction, with which in fact the island has become synonymous, is a unique panorama in the vicinity of **Carmen**, a town 55 kilometers (34 mi) northeast of Tagbilaran in Bohol's central regions. Here, several hundred haycock hills – formed by limestone, shale, and sandstone – rise some 30 meters (100 ft) above the flat terrain. These are the **Chocolate Hills**, so-called for the confectionery-like spectacle they present at the height of summer, when their sparse grass cover turns dry and brown. Two of the highest hills have been developed, replete with a hostel, restaurant, swimming pool and observation deck.

Cebu Island: Recently, the city of Cebu, not without considerable help from its strong Chinese community, has become a model for independent industrial development. With its splendid deep-water port, and attractive beaches and resorts, the city and province of the same name are magnets for investment, both Filipino and foreign, especially with its international airport and seaport.

Cebu is the oldest city in the Philippines, the commercial and education center of the Visayas, and the hub of air and sea travel throughout the South.

A 30-minute drive takes visitors from **Mactan International Airport** into Cebu, passing through Lapulapu on

Cebu.

Mactan Island and Mandaue on the mainland. Jeepneys ply regular routes connecting the three cities. Metered taxicabs and non-metered ones called PUs (public utilities), which charge a flat rate for short trips, are readily available. Also available for short distances is the *tartanilla*, a low-slung version of the horse-drawn rig that looks less precarious than the Luzon *carretelas*.

Cebu is a busy capital, second in commercial activity only to Manila. The original settlement of Zubu was already an important trading community even before the arrival of the Spanish; ships from the East Indies, Siam and China paid tribute to the local chief for the right to berth here and barter. Legazpi successfully started colonization in 1565, making Cebu the capital until the takeover of Manila six years later.

A large wooden crucifix that was left by Magellan in 1521 commemorates the archipelago's first encounter with the West. **Magellan's cross** is Cebu's most important historical landmark. Its remnants are encased by a black cross of *tindalo* wood and housed in a kiosk at upper Magallanes Street. It comprises a shrine commemorating the conversion of the first Filipinos to Christianity.

Close by, on Juan Luna Street, is the **San Agustin Church**, built in 1565 to house the country's oldest religious relic, the Image of the Holy Child Jesus, presented by Magellan to Queen Juana of Cebu on her conversion to Christianity. One of Legazpi's men found the image intact some 40 years later, when Spain resumed its colonization of the Philippines. The church is now known as Basilica of Santo Niño, its conversion ordered by the Vatican in 1965 in recognition of its importance as the cradle of Christianity in Asia.

As the oldest Spanish settlement in the country, Cebu has plenty of spots that depict its rich colonial heritage. The foremost is **Fort San Pedro**, a Spanish fort built in the early 1700s to repel the attacks of the Muslim raiders. The main building of the fort now serves as the Cebu office of the Department of Tourism (DOT).

Fort San Pedro.

The **Osmena Residence** is an important visitor destination that houses some important artifacts in Philippine history, including some of Gen. Douglas MacArthur's personal memorabilia and personal mementos of Sergio Osmena, the first president of the Philippines.

Close to the fort runs **Colon Street**, the oldest street in the country, situated within the Parian district, which was Cebu's original Chinatown. The Chinese community is much in evidence in Cebu, and is largely responsible for its continued growth as an industrial and commercial center.

For many visitors, Cebu means handcrafted guitars and ukeleles of soft jackfruit wood. The guitar-making industry is centered in Abuno and Maribago, on Mactan, where a day's production includes at least a hundred assorted instruments – guitars, ukeleles, mandolins, banjos and string basses.

On top of Beverly Hills in the Lahug district is Cebu's Daoist temple, while a short drive up north to Mandaue leads to the Chapel of the Last Supper, which features life-sized statues of Jesus and the apostles handcarved during the Spanish times.

The **Magellan Monument**, erected in 1886, marks the spot where he was slain on Mactan's shore, while the **Lapulapu Monument** stands at the plaza fronting the Lapulapu City Hall.

Cebu is well-known for its pristine, sun-drenched white beaches and year-round tropical climate. The coastal waters off Cebu offer fantastic scuba-diving sites.

Among them are **Mactan Island**, the Olango Islands and Moalboal, all of which have complete facilities and international-standard accommodations. Off Olango Island (Sta. Rosa), near Mactan Island, is a bird sanctuary that's best visited in October – take the short boat ride from the Maribago Resort to reach the sanctuary.

Among Mactan's better beach resorts are Tambuli, Costabella, Balibago Blue Water Bay and Coral Reef. Plantation Bay Resort on Mactan looks like a plantation and offers both fresh- and saltwa-

A large cross encloses a piece of Magellan's cross.

ter pools. The Delta Philippines Dream Boat, anchored off Mactan offers a hotel and a casino.

Resorts further afield boast far superior beaches. Cebu Club Pacific Hotel lies past the town of **Sogod**, some 60 kilometers (40 mi) north of the city, and has its own private stretch of white sand, cottage accommodations, and restaurant facilities.

On the southwest coast, **Moalboal** is a haven for scuba diving enthusiasts as well as budget travelers, while nearby Badian Island Resort is one of better resorts in the province.

Island-hopping from Cebu to Negros Island may be done by ship, taking from six to eight hours, or by land down Cebu Island to Bato and then by ferry across Tanon Strait to Tampi, south of Amlan. Buses make the trip from Cebu in six hours. A flight from Cebu to Dumaguete or Bacolod takes less than 30 minutes.

Negros: The capital of Negros Oriental (Eastern Negros) Province, **Dumaguete** is a small university town built around the prestigious Protestant-run **Silliman University**. Some fine swimming and snorkeling beaches dot the coastline north and south of Dumaguete. A short way from any part of the city leads to Silliman Farm Beach. From Amlan you can hike up to the twin crater lakes of Balinsasayao and Danao. Another possible route up is through the San Antonio Golf Course.

A little way south is the pretty town of **Valencia**, which may be reached by bus or motorized tricycle. *Suman* (rice cakes wrapped in banana leaves) and hot thick chocolate is an inexpensive treat at the Valencia market, after which another tricycle ride heads up to **Camp Lookout** in the foothills of Mt Talinis, also known as Cuernos de Negros (Horns of Negros) for its twin peaks. At Camp Look-out, there is a good view of Negros' southern portion, Siquijor Island across the channel, and the tip of Cebu Island.

Siquijor Island is accessible by pumpboat from Dumaguete. This small island has long been considered the center of sorcery in the south. The Spanish called it Isla del Fuego, or Fire

Daoist temple, Cebu.

Island, which seems to tally with the Siquijodnons' story of their island having risen from the sea amid the crash and flare of thunder and lightning. Some 50 or so of the 75,000 islanders are *mananambals*, or folk healer-sorcerers. They are classified as "white" or "black" sorcerers, depending on the nature of their abilities, some having better talents as healers than as agents of harm.

The town of **Siquijor** stands as the center for shamanistic activities. Here, mananambals from all over the Visayas and Mindanao gather every Holy Week for a ritual called *tang-alap*. Medicinal plants and various elements from the surrounding forests, caves, and cemeteries are gathered, after which the adepts, laughing and joking, form a circle and chip off a piece of each ingredient to make several piles.

The final, exclusively dawn ritual, is held in one of the caves found on the island. Some of the exotic paraphernalia used by the Siquijor mananambals are found in Silliman University's anthropology museum.

Church mural of Filipino saints.

Further south of Dumaguete are several coastal towns with secluded coves and beaches. It is possible to round Negros Island's southern end by bus, and follow the western coastline all the way north to Bacolod, in Negros Occidental, but the road can be quite a disappointment.

Another regular, eight-hour route by express bus (meaning it stops only at a number of towns and not at every one) follows the eastern coast north and goes all the way up to round the northern end before turning south on the western side towards Bacolod. The regular route weaves through vast tracts of sugar cane while occasionally providing glimpses of the sea.

Negros Occidental: The capital of Negros Occidental (Western Negros) Province, **Bacolod**, is a relatively new city on the west coast that has flourished somewhat haphazardly from sugar production. Attempts to diversify the economy into prawns, corn, rice and native crafts have regressed owing to a recent resurgence in the sugar industry.

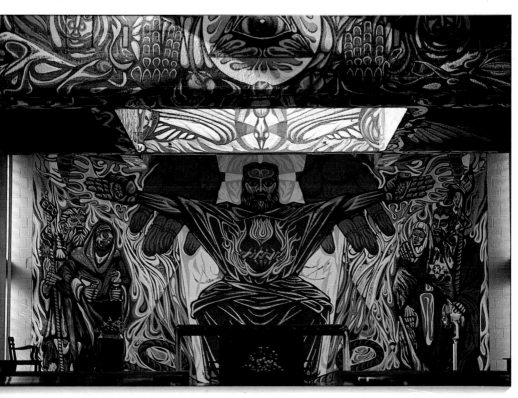

In Bacolod, treat yourself to some chicken *inasal* (barbecued chicken with lemon grass), which can be found in sidewalk stalls all over the city. Or try La Paz *batchoy*, a soupy noodle dish found in most restaurants. *Dulce gatas* (sweetened carabao milk cooked to a rough consistency) rounds off the better attractions in this city caught in an awkward stage of modernization.

Bacolod has its fair share of large hotels, restaurants, cinemas and shopping malls. But its points of interest do not go beyond several fine antique collections, ceramic shops, and weaving centers producing principally *hablon*, a fabric originally developed in Bacolod and much in vogue in the 1960s.

North of Bacolod: A few minutes' drive north is **Silay**, small and sleepy, but with several interesting old houses recalling the Castilian past, when Silay was the proud cultural center of the region. A bit further north is Victorias Milling Company, reputedly the largest sugar-cane mill and refinery in the world.

Within the Vicmico compound is St Joseph, the workers' chapel, with its psychedelic mural and mosaic of pop bottles depicting an angry Jesus with the saints as Filipinos in native dress. Close to **Cadiz**, some 50 kilometers (30 mi) north of Bacolod, is **Llacaon Island**, with beaches and coral reefs.

South of Bacolod: Some 45 minutes' drive southeast of Bacolod, through the town of **Murcia**, is Mambucal Summer Resort, with a tourist lodge, several cottages, camping grounds, swimming pools, and seven waterfalls, three of which are easily accessible along concrete pathways. The best feature is a hot bathhouse, where for a minimal fee one can soak in hot sulfuric water.

Mountain climbers might try the **volcano of Kanlaon**, which rises 2,470 meters (8,100 ft) to a summit of twin craters, one extinct and the other active. The usual starting point for the climb is Kanlaon, 100 kilometers (60 mi) from Bacolod and 170 kilometers (100 mi) from Dumaguete.

Some of the Negros Occidental towns at the volcano's foothills also serve as jump-off bases. One trail starts near Ara-al, a *barangay* of **La Carlota**, while another one that is better-marked and easier to follow ascends the southwest side, starting near the barangay of Biak-na-Bato. **Hacienda Montealegre** has become the starting point for an organized trek led by the local guides.

A night is usually spent halfway up at a surprising 2-hectare (5-acre) stretch of white sand called **Margaha Valley**. A second night may be spent by leisurely climbers at the volcano's shoulder some 600 meters (1,970 ft) below the craters. From the top of the summit, one can peer into the 100-meter-wide (330-ft) active crater, which descends to a depth of 250 meters (820 ft).

The coastline south of Bacolod is dotted with a number of inconsequential beach resorts. But further down in the towns of Cauayan, Sipalay and Hinoba-an are unfrequented beaches that are among the most beautiful in the country. **Sipalay**, 180 kilometers (110 mi) from Bacolod, has a major lure in **Tinagong Dagat** (Hidden Sea), accessible through a narrow channel between

Negros chapel.

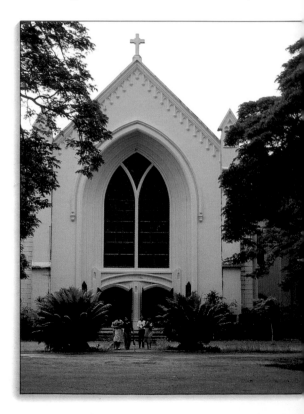

Dinosaur Island and the mainland. Corals and tropical fish teem in this seaside lake. Nearby, **Maricalum Bay** boasts of a similarly abundant marine life, and is particularly attractive for deep-sea anglers with its varieties of mackerel, barracuda, grouper and tuna.

Panay: From Bacolod, it is a leisurely two-hour ride across Guimaras Strait to **Iloilo**. Negros Navigation provides daily ferry services to Iloilo. A cheap but comfortable cruise, it can be most pleasant at sundown. Past Guimaras Strait, the ferry turns into Iloilo Strait separating Panay and Guimaras Islands, then wends its way up the Iloilo River into the city's excellent protected harbor.

Iloilo, the capital of Iloilo Province on the southeast coast of **Panay Island**, is considered a culturally older Ilonggo center that has retained much of the distinctive charm of its Castilian heritage. It lies just across the Guimaras Strait from Bacolod, and has remained the most important port in the region since it was opened to international shipping in 1855.

Hearing of Iloilo's excellent harbor, Legazpi moved there from Cebu in 1569, and subsequently made Iloilo his base for explorations northwards to Manila.

By the river's mouth is **Fort San Pedro**, built to defend the city against the Muslims, British and Dutch, who made repeated incursions into the Visayas at the turn of the 17th century. The fort is now a popular promenade area in the early evening hours.

Iloilo's colorful jeepneys, bulkier versions with chrome rear ends jutting out for an indestructible look, crowd the wharf area together with the PUs (minicabs with set fares), themselves gaudily painted and sporting such names as Paradise For Two and Lover Man. J. M. Basa Street is the main artery, and together with Guanco, Iznart and Ledesma streets, comprises Iloilo's commercial center. It would be a mistake to expect a flurry of activity here. There is no rushing the Ilonggo resident; even commercial activities submit to langor.

Some good Chinese restaurants may be found on J. M. Basa, as well as

Iloilo architecture.

department stores and movie houses that have taken over the old shells of art deco buildings.

The **Museo ng Iloilo** (**Iloilo Museum**) on Bonifacio Drive showcases prehistoric artifacts from the many burial sites dug up on Panay Island, including gold-leaf masks for the dead, seashell jewelry, and other ornaments worn by pre-Spanish islanders. Also of note is an exhibit of the cargo recovered from a British ship that sank off Guimaras Island, in the 19th century; Victorian chinaware, port wine and Glasgow beer are among the shipwreck's treasures.

Molo district, three kilometers from the city center, has a Gothic-Renaissance church completed in the 1800s, and the Asilo de Molo, an orphanage where little girls hand-embroider church vestments. Molo has become famous outside Panay for a noodle dish called *pancit Molo*, just as La Paz, another Iloilo district, is the home of the original (although restaurants from Manila to Bacolod will claim this popular adjective) *La Paz batchoy*. Both are variations of the Chinese *mee* (noodles), and are regular fare in most restaurants in the western Visayas.

Panaderia de Molo (Molo Bakery), the oldest bakery in the south, is a favorite stop among travelers. Biscuits, breads, and assorted delicacies are pre-packed in round tins for convenient *pasalubong*, or take-home gifts.

Jaro, another district two kilometers from Iloilo proper, also has a Gothic cathedral. The ruined belfry of Jaro church is found at the edge of the town plaza. Jaro has been the traditional center for loom-weaving and hand embroidery of *piña* and *jusi*, delicate fabrics used for the Filipino *barong tagalog*.

Arevalo district, six kilometers (4 mi) from the city center, is called the Flower Village for its traditional production of lei, bouquets, corsages and wreaths. In the 16th century, Arevalo was a shipbuilding center and served as a supply base for Spanish expeditions to Muslim Mindanao and the Moluccas.

Guimaras Island: Fifteen minutes by pumpboat from Iloilo is **Guimaras Island**, known among Visayans as the site of the much-admired Roca Encantada (Enchanted Rock), summer house of the distinguished Lopez family of Iloilo. The house is perched on a promontory overlooking Guimaras Strait, and is visible on the ferry ride to or from Bacolod.

Across the promontory is **Siete Pecados** (Isles of Seven Sins), a curious counterpoint to the attractions of spiritual value found in Guimaras. Its capital town is **Jordan**. Nearby is a Trappist monastery, the only one in the country. Bala-an Bukid atop Bundulan Point is a favorite Catholic pilgrimage site.

And in the town of **Nueva Valencia** is **Catilaran Cave**, from where Ming jars have been unearthed and where, on Good Friday, the *pangalap* ritual similar to that of Siquijor is held. Hundreds of devotees recite Latin prayers while at the same time crawling through the 550-yard cave, believing they will acquire supernatural powers, especially useful against evil spirits.

Some 45 minutes by pumpboat from Iloilo's Fort San Pedro pier, Isla Naburot Resort has been lovingly created by the **Church in Molo.**

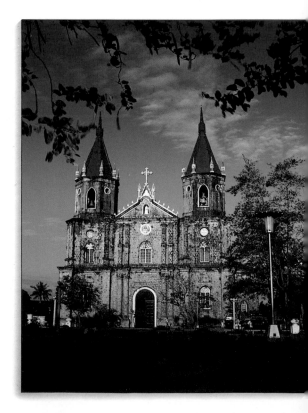

268

Saldaña family of Iloilo. It is crammed with unusual features such as antique wooden doors that double as windows, *patadyongs* (similar to a Muslim *malong*) for comfortable island dress, and a cuisine based on fruits plucked from the resort's trees and fresh seafood from the emerald waters surrounding Isla. Respectable roads branch out from Iloilo, but tend to deteriorate the further one goes.

The presence of many old churches underscores the high regard the Spanish colonizers had for Iloilo province as a religious and commercial center for the region. Thirteen kilometers (8 mi) north is **Pavia Church**, with red brick walls and window frames of coral rock. Construction reportedly began in 1886, but somehow the church was never finished. Two kilometers further up is the neoclassical Sta. Barbara Church, where Ilonggos first gathered to declare the revolution against the Spanish rulers.

At kilometer 25 on the same northward road is **Cabatuan Church**, which is also of neoclassic style and built in the early 1880s. Nearby is Cabatuan Cemetery, walled in with coral rock and sandstone, and built in 1886 with a central chapel also of coral rock.

More untapped islands lie off the northeastern coast of Panay amid the rich fishing grounds of the Visayan sea. From **Ajuy**, one can proceed northward to **Estancia**, a fishing town dubbed by local geography books as the Alaska of the Philippines.

A 20-minute pumpboat ride from Estancia leads to **Sicogon**, an island which has been developed into a classy resort. Covering most of the mountainous 1,000-hectare (2,500-acre) island is virgin forest, where wild boar can be found. White-sand beaches slope down to 100 meters (300 ft) beyond the shoreline, the waters crystal-clear to that distance. Handsome cottages have been built on parts of the island, along with a restaurant, swimming pools, tennis courts, a golf course and other facilities.

Westward from Iloilo along the southern coast runs a more frequented road past several beach resorts and the more

Naburot, Guimaras.

distinctive of Iloilo's old churches. At kilometer 22 is the coastal town of **Tigbauan**, worth a stop for its old baroque church, unfortunately ruined by an earthquake, like so many of the country's churches, in 1948.

At kilometer 40 is the **Miagao Fortress Church**, built nearly 200 years ago as a place of worship, as well as a fortress against Muslim pirates.

Past kilometer 53 is **San Joaquin**, the southernmost town of Iloilo. San Joaquin Church, dating back to 1869, is of gleaming white coral, and has another unusual facade depicting the historic Battle of Tetuan, where Spanish forces routed the Moors in Morocco in 1859.

From here, the road continues northward through rolling terrain to **Antique Province**, which hugs the western coast of Panay. A high and rugged range of mountains runs parallel to this coast, thus lending the province an isolated character underscored by the poor roads.

San Jose de Buenavista, the capital, is 100 kilometers (60 mi) from Iloilo. Several beach resorts are found in the

barangay of San Jose. An hour's drive south will leads to Anini-y, on the southern tip of Panay. Off Anini-y is **Nogas Island**, which has a white-sand beach and is ideal for scuba diving and snorkeling. Located in Barangay Dapog of Anini-y is Sira-an Hot Springs, close to a fairly good swimming beach.

Aklan to Boracay: North of **Culasi**, you cross over into **Aklan Province**, near Panay's northwestern tip. World-famous **Boracay Island** lays just off shore here. Southwest from Ibajay is **Kalibo**, the oldest town in Aklan and home of the famous Ati-Atihan festival.

The nearby port town of **New Washington** handles interisland shipping connections. Those who failed to make early plane or ship reservations can fly or take the ship to Roxas instead, then travel by bus to Kalibo.

Capiz Province: Roxas is the capital of Capiz, Panay's northeast province. Anglers will find the Capiz coastline a rich fishing ground. Napti Island, off nearby Pan-ay town, offers great varieties of fish, in addition to giant lobsters, coral reefs, and pretty beaches.

Panay Church has a marble floor and three-meter-thick (10-ft) walls of white coral. The interior is decorated with *retablos* (altar-pieces) of silver and hardwood. The Panay Cemetery also has walls and a chapel made of coral.

Romblon: Lying due north of Ibajay, between the Mindoro and Masbate islands, **Romblon Province** consists of 20 islands and islets noted for marble production in the Philippines.

The capital town on Romblon Island is also called **Romblon**. It's a short walk from the dock to Romblon Cathedral, which features a Byzantine altar and several distinctive icons and paintings. A 250-step climb up a hill leads to the ruins of **Fort San Andres**, now converted into a weather station. Bonbon Beach is the most accessible of the many lovely beaches in the islands.

Romblon is accessible by ship or ferry from either New Washington or Roxas. Moreover, a boat leaves Manila several times a week for the 14-hour trip. Alternatively, flights from Manila take just under an hour and land on Tablas Island.

Left, beach artist. Right, Boracay.

BORACAY

In an archipelago of 7,107 islands, there's bound to be one island that really stands out. Boracay, in the Visayas off Panay Island, is shaped like a slender butterfly drawn in sugar-fine white sand.

It was first "discovered" back in the 1960s, when beachcombers went looking for its rare *puka* shells. By the 1970s, Boracay was on the must list of every intrepid adventurer in Asia. They came in small numbers at first, staying in the *nipa* huts along White Beach, for a couple of dollars a night.

But like every other magical spot — with a pristine environment and an increasing cachet amongst backpack travelers — the word spread. By the 1980s, the adventurers had become the hoards, and boutique resorts sprang up all along White Beach. It was still a journey to reach, as it remains today, but that was part of the draw.

Today, Boracay has moved way up-market. Since the mid 1980s, it has attracted the well heeled of Europe, America and Asia, who rush to Boracay to get an off-the-beaten-track feeling. But not without just cause. The sight greeting arrivals is nothing but spectacular: a gentle sea, the whitest of white beaches, and tall palms swaying in the breeze.

But not all is well in paradise. The resorts, restaurants and bars that have sprung up to serve the hordes of tourists have been dumping their sewage and garbage into that sugar-fine sand that made Boracay so famous, which, in turn, has acted like an aqua-filter back into the sea. In 1997, the Philippine Department of Health declared the once-pristine beaches and waters around Boracay to be severely polluted.

New arrivals stake out a stretch of white sand and bath in Boracay's special sun, mostly topless for non-Filipino women. Meanwhile, the locals in *maong* pants and T-shirts quietly serve the outsiders' needs.

Visitors can hire sailboats and windsurfers, and an instructor, if needed, at any of the score of rental shops that have sprung up along White Beach. Pathetic little horses wait above the beach for those who have always dreamed of riding along the sands. Further back, the courts of tennis await, and of course, snorkel or scuba boats bob everywhere.

For those who still feel the need for exploration, bicycles are available to explore the tiny island, eight kilometers long by three kilometers wide. Thirty minutes of pedaling leads through the corn and cassava fields to the two fishing villages that have been there for, well, nearly forever. Yap-ak village on the northern end is where everyone heads for puka shells.

Accommodations can be found everywhere nowadays. There's still some basic nipa huts, but it's mostly resorts that splatter the beach now. These include the Pearl of the Pacific, Fridays, Sandcastles and Lorenzo Village, along with a couple of dozen others. It's has gotten so crowded that resorts are even springing up along the eastern coast.

Boracay dining, which was once simple and good island fare, now ranges from haute Filipino to haute French, with Indonesian, Thai, Italian, Chinese, Swiss, and even bloody English available. The island's undressed code (bare feet and bikini) is acceptable even in the smarter joints, whether of French, Thai, and or Mexican cuisine. Some offer dancing on the beach beneath the stars.

Getting there is not quite the adventure it once was. Fly from Manila to Caticlan and take the 15-minute boat ride to Boracay, or fly to Kalibo, take a jeepney (2-3 hrs) to Caticlan, and then make the crossing. ■

MINDANAO

Mindanao is a land of superlatives: the world's largest eagle, the monkey-eating *haribon*; the world's most expensive shells, the Gloria Maris; and the world's richest nickel deposits.

Mindanao stands as the second-largest island in the Philippines, after Luzon, and it's the southernmost of the country's 11 main islands. Of irregular shape, Mindanao is punctuated by five major peninsulas and five major mountain ranges, some volcanic in origin. The peninsulas, with several sizable gulfs and bays, give the island an extremely long coastline. It is prevented from being two islands by a 16-kilometer (10-mi) waist between Iligan and Illana bays. Mountains, valleys, rivers, lakes, waterfalls, forests, mangrove swamps, lowlands and marshland make up Mindanao's varied topography.

The island has an abundance of minerals, containing about 80 percent of the country's iron reserves and, in the province of Surigao del Norte, all of the country's nickel. Also found are copper, silver, gold, coal and limestone.

In agriculture, Mindanao produces over half the nation's pineapple, corn, coffee, copra, cocoa and *abaca* (hemp). And the waters that surround the island teem not only with a wide variety of shellfish and corals, but with giant fish.

The Moros: Although Mindanao and the Sulu Archipelago originally served as a haven for those fleeing from the militant spread of Islam in Indonesia, by the end of the 14th century the crescent flew over the Sulus, and by the time Miguel de Legazpi arrived in 1565, the entire southern region was bowing to Allah. Indeed, only the arrival of the *conquistadors* halted the northern movement of Islam throughout the Philippine archipelago. The Islam encountered by Legazpi and even that practiced today must raise eyebrows in Al Azhar. Nevertheless, none will bow lower than the Moros, to use their Spanish name.

The Moro Wars started in the 1700s, but lasted, intermittently, for three cen-

turies. It ended only when the Spanish regime in the Philippines collapsed. Even with the coming of the Americans, the Muslims of Mindanao did not give up their struggle to maintain their way of life. Not until 1915 was an uneasy peace signed. As a result of educational, economical, cultural and political reforms, the Moros were brought within the framework of the government centered at Manila.

The fragile peace, however, collapsed in the early 1970s, mainly because large-scale migrations, since World War II, of Christians from the neighboring Visayas made the two million-plus Muslims a minority in their own homeland. Predictably, in a 1977 referendum, the Moros were thunderously defeated on the question of autonomy. In any case, the plebiscite was said to have been "fixed" by Marcos.

A 1989 referendum saw most southern provinces choosing to stay outside the Autonomous Region of Muslim Mindanao. Only Maguindanao, Tawi Tawi, Sulu and Lanao del Sur, domi-

Preceding pages: boys in Lake Sebu; stilt village in southern Mindanao. Left, Muslim boy in shop. Right, Badjao youth in his canoe.

nated by three rival Muslim groups – the Maguindanaos, Tausugs and Maranaos – voted yes to autonomy. The Moro National Liberation Front (MNLF), the amalgamation of several armed guerrilla groups which appeared in the early 1970s, has negotiated a peace with the government of Fidel Ramos, with most of the guerillas now integrated into the government's armed forces, but radical splinter groups continue their fight for autonomy, often reverting to terrorism.

In addition to the Muslims, many cultural minorities live in Mindanao, ranging from the Tasaday to the Kulaman to the T'bolis. Indeed, nearly half of the 60 or so minority groups in the Philippines live in Mindanao. Many of these groups still hold animist beliefs, while others have been converted to Christianity.

Like the Moros, many are losing their land by decimation and depredation, but lacking the unity of the Moros, they are unable to protect themselves because of small numbers and lack of outside assistance.

Exploring Mindanao: Much of what Mindanao has to offer the traveler can readily be seen, like the Badjaos (sea gypsies), coconut plantations and Mt Apo. Some can be seen with difficulty, like the T'bolis, pineapple plantations and the Maria Christina Falls. And a few are practically impossible to see, like the Tasaday, the monkey-eating eagle and Gloria Maris shells.

The largest city in Mindanao and the starting point of most Mindanao adventures is **Davao**. The city sits at the head of Davao Gulf in the island's southeast quadrant. At the airport, a brightly painted statue in tribal attire, holding a durian, welcomes the visitor. Davaoeños say the figure is of a Manobo native, the true aborigine of Davao; others claim that it is Pinnochio. (A settlement of Manobos can be visited in Wangan, Calinan, 50 minutes from Davao, but rarely do they wear their ethnic costumes or play their unusual musical instruments.

Midway between the airport and the city is the Insular Hotel, possibly **Philippine eagle.**

Davao's major focus of relaxation. Relax over a glass of *tuba,* or fresh palm wine, in the immaculately-kept ground. Sixteen men who tap palm trees for tuba (*mananguets*) make this the largest tuba-producing area in Davao. The tapping of trees prevents coconuts from forming and falling on guests' heads.

Of intellectual interest in Davao are the 18 colleges and two universities, which testify to the fact that no country – other than the United States – has as many persons of college age attending college as the Philippines. The city is also noted as the base of Alsa Masa, an anti-Communist vigilante movement founded in 1986. Since then, the influence of the communist New People's Liberation Army (NPLA) has decreased.

The **Aldevinco Shopping Center**, immediately off Claro M. Recto Avenue, the city's principal thoroughfare, has several shops with good selections of Muslim brass and tribal artifacts – baskets, weaving and musical instruments – and also Chinese wares. In fact, Davao has the largest Chinese popula-

tion in Mindanao. The beautiful Buddhist temple on Leon Garcia Street is in stark contrast to the squatter quarters and slums in the area of **Magsaysay Park** and Santa Anna Harbor.

Sasa, Davao's harbor and where there is a factory for extracting oil from copra, is about eight kilometers (5 mi) further up the gulf. Several small restaurants in this area serve the popular *kilawin* (raw fish), which is usually eaten with soya sauce or other marinates.

Outside Davao: Leaving central Davao, cross the **Davao River** and travel southeast. Immediately on the left, side roads lead to a series of beaches. **Times Beach**, two kilometers from the city, is unattractive, but over the next 15 kilometers (9 mi), the black-sand beaches of Talomo, Talisay, Salokot and Guino-o, to name a few, are pleasant and made interesting by their proximity to fishing villages. **Talomo** was the scene of the Japanese landing in 1942, and the American landing in 1945.

Instead of turning left to the beaches, turn right four kilometers out of town. A

Davao girl and dolls of the Yakan.

two-kilometer-long road twists, turns and climbs past the Stations of the Cross to end at the **Shrine of the Holy Infant Jesus of Prague**. Much can be learned about Philippine Catholicism by visiting this sanctuary.

Further along the main road, on the right, is the **Apo Golf and Country Club,** 11 kilometers (7 mi) from town and boasting an excellent 18-hole golf course. A bit further, a road on the right leads in a few hundred yards to **Caroland Resort**. This is a beautiful and unspoiled savanna, rich in fruit trees and teeming with wild ducks. Horseback riding and fishing in a lagoon for *gourami*, *dalag* (mudfish), *tilapia* and *hito* (catfish) can be enjoyed. Another pond is stocked with carp. Put a piece of bread in your mouth, and bend over the water – the fish will take bread out of your mouth.

Mt. Apo: Of great interest to conservationists is the **Philippine Eagle Breeding Station**, near Calinan. To get there, board a Calinan jeepney in Davao and alight at the terminus. Take a tricycle for the 15-minute ride to the camp.

Located in Davao is the country's highest peak, **Mt Apo**, which rises 2,956 meters (9,698 ft) in height. The inactive volcano is peppered with waterfalls, river rapids, lakes and geysers. Its forests are home to the Philippine eagle and other endangered plant and animal species. The local office of the Department of Tourism (DOT) at the Apo View Hotel organizes regular treks and climbs to Mt Apo.

The Davao coastline enjoys a year-round, mild tropical climate and has white-sand beaches. The most popular beach resort is the Davao Pearl Farm, while the beaches of **Samal Island** are renowned for their fine white sand and coral reefs.

To the north: Governmental seat of Misamis Oriental Province, **Cagayan de Oro** is the normal jumping-off point for adventures in northern Mindanao. This boom town has sprouted a number of heavy-industries that process steel, ferrochrome, sintered iron, cement, flour and coconut oil. Nowhere is the expansion more evident than at **Phividec In-**

Mt. Apo, and sulfur crater formations.

dustrial Estate, one of the largest in Southeast Asia and the most successful of its type in the Philippines.

An unusual mode of transport in Cagayan is the *motorola*, a six-person motor scooter in front of a chassis.

The city itself boasts innumerable banks, government offices, shopping malls and department stores. Cagayan sits astride, more or less at mid-point, the National Highway. It has space in which to grow, a superb harbor, and draws electrical power from the Maria Cristina Falls, in Iligan.

This large and sprawling city is bisected by the Cagayan River. On the west side of the river, where it is spanned by a bridge, Gaston Park surrounds San Agustin Cathedral, with its unusual water tower and Lourdes College.

A few hundred meters further, an attractive mall runs from the river through the town to Xavier University. The university boasts an excellent small museum with archaeological findings, Hispanic antiquities, tribal artifacts and a shell collection.

The best beach in the area is at Opol, nine kilometers (6 mi) west of the city. A road inland at Cugman leads to the small but attractive Catanico Falls, which plunge into a swimming hole, with large boulders serving as picnic tables. Seven kilometers (4 mi) past Cugman is the town of Bugo, which is the site of the canning factory of the Philippine Packing Corporation. Guided tours to see pineapples canned – by special arrangement – take place between 8am and 2pm.

From Bugo, a steep twisting highway strikes inland and immediately offers superb views of Macajalar Bay, with its 175-kilometer-long (110 mi) shoreline. As the bay is below the typhoon belt, the Americans considered carrying out their 1944 landing here. However, Leyte was preferred; five days after the landing, a typhoon hit Leyte.

The road continues for 21 kilometers (13 mi) until, at an altitude of 650 meters (2,132 ft), it comes to an end at Camp Philips, the headquarters of the 9,000-hectare (22,200-acre) Del Monte

Pineapple fields, Camp Philips.

Philippines. This is maybe the largest pineapple plantation in the world, has its own airstrip from where Gen. MacArthur left for Australia after being secreted off Corregidor. Visitors may or may not be welcome – it varies. The estate has a moderately-difficult 18-hole golf course.

An interesting and exciting half-day excursion from Cagayan is to the **Huluga Caves**, where material was unearthed – now in the Xavier University Museum – which may date from the late neolithic times, around 4,500 years ago. Six kilometers southwest of the city, on the bank of a tributary of the Cagayan River, is **Barangay Balulang**. (Best to look for a guide here.) The river is crossed by a cable boat, and after an easy two-kilometer stroll through pleasant farmland, you reach the east bank of the Cagayan River. The river is 100 meters wide, the current swift and the cable boat crossing not for the timid. A further kilometer to the north is the granddaddy of all trees, no longer freestanding but partially buried in a 50-meter-high (160-ft) embankment. The athletic can scramble up its roots and branches to reach, about 25 meters (80 ft) above ground, three tiny caves. A simpler, quicker, yet less exciting way to reach the caves is to drive to the Roxas Timber Mill. Then walk 400 meters to the river and, exactly opposite, is the old tree and its caves. At high tide it might be possible to reach the caves by renting a pumpboat at the bridge at Gaston Park; however, the voyage is against the current.

Less interesting archaeologically, but much larger, is the **Macahambus Cave** 14 kilometers (9 mi) southeast of the city. Here, a vastly outnumbered and ill-equipped group of Filipino revolutionaries scored a major upset over American forces. Walk through the cave and emerge among gigantic rocks and savage trees overlooking Cagayan River.

Those interested in archaeology or ecclesiastical history might wish to visit **Butuan**, 200 kilometers (120 mi) east of Cagayan de Oro. Archaeological artifacts were accidentally uncovered in 1974 during the digging of drainage **Pineapple plantation worker.**

canals. Sustan, the most interesting site, is five kilometers (3 mi) northeast of the city, towards Masao Port. Findings, mostly burial, are pre-Hispanic. Many are in Xavier University's museum.

Back in Cagayan de Oro and a 90-minute drive westward along the National Highway and past Opol Beach, **Iligan** is where the highway begins – or ends. Iligan is an uninteresting yet prosperous town which owes its wealth to hydroelectric power, but it remains unremarkable because of its topography and poor harbor.

Nine kilometers (6 mi) south of the town are the **Maria Christina Falls**. (A visitor's pass must be obtained from the Philippine constabulary in Iligan.) From the checkpoint, it is a two-kilometer road along a brooding, verdant canyon to the observation platform at the hydroelectric station. The falls, one of the tallest in the country, are 60 meters (200ft) high and nearly as wide, plummeting straight down.

A couple of kilometers before the entrance to the falls, a good road turns left and starts climbing inland. Short of 20 miles on the left is the airport, which serves Iligan and Marawi. Two kilometers beyond is the small town of **Boloi**. The traveler is now in the land of the crescent rather than the cross.

Here, on the left of the road, is the first of innumerable mosques, brilliantly painted in reds, yellows and greens. The trucks are blazoned on their bumpers with *Trust in Allah* rather than *Trust in Jesus*, and the girls are dressed in tubular step-in *malongs*, rather than skirts.

Lake Lanao: Eleven kilometers (7 mi) further along Ambush Road, so called because of the high incidents of holdups enroute, Lanao Del Norte is left behind as one enters Lanao Del Sur. The countryside is lush and green, and corn abounds and horses are nearly as common as jeepneys. Forty kilometers (25 mi) after leaving Iligan, **Lake Lanao** – the second-largest and deepest lake in the Philippines – comes into view. The road descends and a couple of kilometers later is **Marawi**, at an altitude of 780 meters (2,559 ft).

Central Mindanao landscape.

Life, especially on Sundays and Thursdays – market days – centers on the lake. Wave after wave of long, low, sleek boats arrive, switching off their motors and poling to the shore, to literally debouch – for nearly all are hidden from view below deck – countless passengers coming from the villages all around the lake.

Most emerge topside from the stern. The boats' flat decks become catwalks as malong-clad women walk to the shore. Violets, purples and mauves, greens, reds and yellows abound. Floral patterns outnumber geometric ones. Rich indigo malongs with emerald scarfs are worn around the head, like a turban, with the loose end slung nonchalantly over the left shoulder. All women wear earrings, and bracelets dangle on many wrists. The colors are equaled, if not surpassed, by the painted hulls of the boats – greens, yellows, blues and red, some of which are fancifully decorated with sinuous arabesques.

The dress of the men, if not drab, is mundane, apart from their headgear, the *kepiah*, a kind of army forage cap, or a turban. The former is usually of cloth but sometimes of fur, usually black but sometimes fawn. The latter is invariably white, signifying that the wearer has made the *hajj* to Mecca. About a quarter of the men and many of the women have made the hajj at least once.

From the lake, several small streets constituting the market stretch the couple hundred of meters to the main road. Close by, the sound of hammers beating on metal announces the place to purchase Maranao brassware, gongs and drums, betel boxes and kettles, and *malongs*, *banigs* and *lakobs*. The latter are attractive bamboo-tube containers impregnated with red, green, yellow and purple colors, for holding tobacco.

Turning north from Quezon Boulevard is a road passing Dansalan College where, at its community shop, one can place orders for Maranao textiles. A further 400 meters and to the right is the headquarters of the **Equifilibricum Society**, recognized by a plaster statue of the society's founder, Hilario Camino

Maranao brassware, Marawi.

Moncado, dressed in academic gown and mortar board. Behind this is a simple white building, not recognizable as a church except that painted on it are the words *Church* and *Equifilibricum World Religion Inc.* Alongside is a large plaster bowl representing the Ark, and within it, in various stages of decay, are plaster models of pairs of giraffes, lions and other animals.

The story of the founder and of the society is inscribed on the pedestal supporting Moncado. His title of doctor was not lightly earned, and one learns that he held nearly a dozen degrees. Some, like A.B., are familiar, but others – K.PH.D., N.PH.D., HN.PH.D. – are not. These, it transpired, stood respectively for Doctor of Philosophy in Kabala; Doctor of Philosophy in Numerology and Doctor of Philosophy in Human Nature. Dr. Moncado had earned these when "at the age of only six years, he was sent by his father to India to attend the College of Mystery and Psychics (sic), known as the Indian College of Mystery in Calcutta. He graduated (sic)

with honor at the age of nine." There are only about a dozen families belonging to this society, whose religion is founded on the trinity of equality, fraternity and liberty, but it is claimed that there are more than 15,000 members in the Philippines, and active groups in America.

West of Quezon Boulevard and across the bridge spanning the Agus River is an insignificant 40-meter (130-ft) hill. When the Philippines was an American colony, signals were sent from here, **Signal Hill**, to Camp Vicars at the south end of the lake, and to Camp Overton in Iligan. During World War II, the Japanese executed American prisoners on this hill. A few hundred meters further on is a branch in the road. The right leads to the zero-kilometers stone, from which all distances in Mindanao are measured. This is not the Euclidian, but rather the American center of the island. Here, during the American-Filipino wars, stood Camp Keithley.

About two kilometers beyond is the **Mindanao State University**, founded in 1962. It serves not only as an educa-

tional institute but also as a center of social and cultural integration. More than half of its students are Christians.

The handsome **King Faisal Mosque** and **Institute of Islamic and Arabic Studies** stand just within the university gates. (There is no church on campus, nor, for that matter, in Marawi.) The road then climbs through the sprawling 1,000-hectare (2,500-acre) campus, probably the most beautiful in the country, passing the golf course below with the Marawi Resort Hotel and ending at the crest of the hill. The vista across the lake is superb and claimed by many to be the most splendid in the Philippines.

The **Aga Khan Museum** at the crown of the campus is a repository for Maranao and other Moro artifacts. Attention should be paid to the symbolic *sarimanok* bird. Were it not for the name (*manok* means chicken or rooster), the creature could be mistaken for those eagles, hawks and kingfishers often seen picking up fish from the lake. The figure of the bird is executed in patterns that are characteristic of *okir*, as the art of the

Maranao is called. An analysis of okir reveals that Maranao art is extremely systematized, and specific design patterns carry specific names. The motifs are combined into ever-increasing complicated designs and are used ubiquitously. Several examples will be seen in the museums, which also contains some tribal textiles, Chinese pottery and a natural-science section.

Visible from the university campus and reached from the Iligan–Marawi road is the 150-meter-high (490-ft) **Sacred Mountain**, with a pond at its summit. The visitor is warned against climbing this hill, and there are many horror stories told about people who have, but that is exactly what they are – stories.

Continuing on around the lake leads to **Tugaya**. Nearly every item of Maranao brass seen in the Philippines is made at Tugaya. Practically every family has a bellows in the area below their home where the metal is smelted and, using the *cire perdue* or lost-wax technique, made into cannons and gongs, betelnut boxes and rice pots.

North of Zamboanga City, some 40 minutes by air, is **Dipolog**, provincial capital of Zamboanga del Norte. Some 26 kilometers (16 mi) away by tricycle (a motorcycle with sidecar) lies the sleepy town of **Dapitan**, where Jose Rizal was exiled from 1892 to 1896.

Dapitan is said by some to be the prettiest town in the Philippines. A short banca ride leads to the Dakak Beach Resort, which has a short sandy beaches, swimming-pool jacuzzis, Spanish galleon-style bar, mango trees and air-conditioning as well as a bowling alley.

To the west: The normal jumping-off point for exploring western Mindanao, **Zamboanga** sits on the southern tip of the most western of Mindanao's arms. The wharf is all hustle and bustle. Passenger and cargo vessels from all over the archipelago tie up alongside naval craft. Ferry boats, which serve different ports on Mindanao and the islands of the Sulu Sea, fight for space with *kumpits* (long, deep, enclosed motorboats), which carry cargo between Zamboanga and Borneo. These cargoes stock the barter trade, and the black market, too.

King Faisal Mosque.

286

Not so long ago, kumpits made their way clandestinely, as smuggling had for centuries been a way of life in this part of the world. The only customs these people know was tribal law (*adat*) rather than taxes. To them, permeable watery frontiers meant nothing – why worry if an island belongs to the Philippines or to Malaysia? All efforts to eradicate smuggling failed, so the Philippine government decided to legalize the trade. The result is the barter trade with goods from Borneo.

Sotanghon is a kind of noodle fairly representative of what is found in the barter market – food, toiletries and batiks. Visit the terrace fronting the sea and become a lotus-eater. Also try eating *curacha*, Zamboanga's culinary specialty. It's a kind of half-crab, half-lobster. Do not be surprised at the dialect heard. It is Chabacano, a part of Zamboanga's Castilian heritage consisting of a mixture of Spanish nouns and unconjugated verbs, dosed by a dozen local dialects.

Immediately behind the wharf lies **Plaza Pershing**, named in honor of the general who was the first American governor of Moro country. The quasi-baroque city hall, completed in 1907, stands at the southeast corner of the plaza and houses the post office. Walk from here along Valderros Street to the Lantaka Hotel, where the Department of Tourism (DOT) offices are located.

A dozen or so *vintas* are tied up at the hotel's sea wall. Aboard them are Badjaos (sea gypsies) and Samals – mostly children. The vintas and the sea wall are showcases for brush and brain corals, cowrie and cone, conch and clam, *tambuli* and turban shells. Small mounds of red, white and black coral necklaces and black coral bracelets occupy the gaps between large turtle shells.

(This shell and coral trade, however, is destroying the coral reefs of the Philippines – dynamite is used.)

Aboard some vintas are also bundles of pandanus mats (*banigs*). Mauve, purples and violets are the predominant colors, but greens and yellows also feature in the geometric patterns. It is easy

Wharf market, Zamboanga.

to see why Badjao women have earned the reputation of being the finest mat weavers in the archipelago.

Tiny dugout canoes, some no more than one meter long, putter around the vintas. Toss a coin into the water and immediately, three or four children jump into to retrieve it. It's said amongst the Badjaos that when a child is born, he's thrown into the water and if he cannot swim, he's left to drown as not worthy.

Out in the bay are a score of otherworld *basligs* whose brilliant colors repeat and complement those of the banigs. The Visayas are the home of these long, slim Viking-like fishing craft with high pointed prow and stern, and huge outriggers. The vast web of rigging stretching from a mast rising exactly amid ships evokes mizzens and jibs, foresails and stays, yet these crafts are motorized. The countless ropes serve merely to support the outriggers – nothing more.

Arrangements can be made at Lantaka landing to rent a pumpboat for the 25-minute voyage to **Great Santa Cruz Island**. The Samals have a graveyard

here and the beach is fine for swimming and sunbathing. But take care: tourists have been robbed there.

Just past the Lantaka Hotel is **Fort Pilar**, its one-meter-thick coral walls overgrown with green moss. A bronze plaque at the eastern gate tells not only its dramatic story, but much of the history of Mindanao. Built in 1635, abandoned in 1663, rebuilt in 1718, it has been a bastion through the centuries against Muslim, Dutch, British and Portuguese attacks. Then, with the arrival of the Americans in 1898, it became Pettit Barracks. Built into the eastern wall is the open-air shrine of the patron saint of Zamboanga, the Lady of Del Pilar. Here, especially on Saturday evenings and Sundays, the faithful light their candles and make their vows.

A few hundred yards to the east is the large Samal water village of **Rio Hondo** which, fortunately for the residents, sadly for the tourists, is losing much of its ethnic charm. Urban renewal is making its mark, and gone are the crazily-tilted *nipa* huts, each different, and gone

Shrine to Zamboaga's patroness, Fort Pilar.

288

are the zig-zag walkways with many missing planks. Now all the neat wooden tiled-roof houses are identical and the walkways made of perfect two-by-fours. However, urban renewal or not, Rio Hondo will always have, especially where the bridge joins the water village to the mainland, glistening naked children calling out *Hi Joe!* and *Gimme one!* (Take one photo of me).

Taluksangay is a quieter, more sedate village on stilts, 20 kilometers (12 mi) east of the city. Its mosque, with silvery dome and turrets, is most photogenic. Taluksangay is a Samal village, but at the south end there are always some Badjaos; the village, on occasion, is a haven for Yakans and other Moros. About one kilometer before the village and 100 meters) to the north is a small Badjao cemetery.

Westward from Zamboanga, the road immediately enters the two-kilometer-long **Cawa Cawa Boulevard**. This pocket-sized edition of Manila's Roxas Boulevard, lined by old acacia trees, is the favorite swimming place for the locals. At the far end are several beer parlors, and on occasion, basligs anchor in this area. Soon after **Campo Islam**, a predominantly Tausug water village, there are two large oil-processing factories. However, it is white coconut (copra) rather than black gold that is processed. Zamboanga is probably the largest coconut-oil port in the world.

Along the road is a small colony of Yakan families, who will demonstrate their weaving and sell the cloth. Beyond is **Yellow Beach**, where the American forces landed in March 1945.

At 22 kilometers (14 mi) is the **San Ramon Prison and Penal Farm**. Souvenirs, mainly in the form of wood carvings, can be purchased here. At this 19th-century Spanish-built prison farm, the salesman will probably be an old man who is in prison for some crime, which he will tell you he did not commit. One trustees said his imprisonment had been profitable: he learned woodwork and fathered nine children.

The Philippines has an enlightened policy towards prisoners, and after an initial period of incarceration, they are permitted to build their own nipa huts near the jail and have their families live with them. Some, when discharged, remain rather than face the difficulties of the outside world.

Seven kilometers (4 mi) north of Zamboanga City is Zamboanga's pride and joy, **Pasonanca Park**. Most travelers will find it more interesting for its unintentional humor than its scout camp, swimming pools and tree house. An official brochure tells of a "swimming pool for children with concrete slides (wee-wee pool) and a tree house, ideal for honeymooners, where both foreign and domestic tourists are invited to stay at no charge. Check with the city hall to arrange your reservation.

Basilan Island: A two-hour voyage on a decent enough ferry, south from Zamboanga City across the 25-kilometer (16-mi) Straits of Basilan, takes travelers to **Basilan Island**. Enroute, the boat skirts Great Santa Cruz Island. The last part of the voyage, before reaching **Isabela**, the capital and port, is through a one-kilometer-wide mangrove chan-

Textiles from Basilan Island.

nel backed by palm trees and adorned with nipa huts on stilts.

The town of Isabela has little to offer. However, pumpboats from alongside the quay cross the channel to a busy fascinating Samal water village. Here is the tottering topsy-turvyness now missed at Rio Hondo. Arrangements can be made with the boat owners to tour the village by water.

A rough road southward from Isabela through rubber, palm-oil and coconut plantations, and past stands of coffee, lanzones and pepper, leads after 32 kilometers (20 mi) to the small fishing village of **Maluso**. A look round one of the few rubber processing plant in the Philippines, Menzi's is worthwhile.

A similar road to the northeast passes citrus groves and the plants already mentioned. After 30 kilometers (20 mi), it arrives at the village of **Lamitan** where on market days, the Yakans, indigens of Basilan, can be seen in their colorful clothing. The Yakans are justly renowned as the best of all Moro weavers on Mindanao.

The Sulu Sea: Beyond Basilan, an infinite number of stepping stones – the far flung islands of the Sulu archipelago – lead to Borneo. But note that travel in this region can be hazardous – there is much piracy, banditry and confrontation between rebels and Philippine military forces.

Forty minutes by air from Zamboanga lies **Jolo**, capital of **Sulu Province** and the only place in the region where the Spanish managed to hoist their flag (some 300 years after they reached the Philippines). In 1974, Jolo was burned to the ground when fighting broke out between rebeling Muslims and government troops.

Things to do in Jolo include visiting the fish market, Barter Trade Market (smuggled goods from Borneo – there are plans to move Zamboanga's market here) and swimming at Quezon Beach, three kilometers northeast of town.

Every morning, a flight departs Zamboanga for **Sanga Sanga**, some 12 kilometers (7 mi) from the Tawi Tawi capital of **Bongao**. The sight that greets arriving passengers is pure Arabian Nights: a silver dome capping a mosque with graceful minarets towering above a water village on stilts; tall people with dazzling smiles feasting on *curachas* (coconut crabs) and children frolicking in the water.

But the island is hardly organized for tourism. The town's only hotel, The Southern, lacks baths and electricity in the rooms (and just about everything else). But the wanderlustful traveler would not have it any other way.

The Celebes Sea: Further out into the Celebes Sea is **Sibutu**, of wild boar fame. The wild boars swim over from Malaysia and are occasionally hunted by shooting parties from Manila.

Finally, almost at the border with Malaysia is the Venice of the East, **Sitangkai**, a town built on stilts over crystal-clear waters and a reef.

Be sure to try *kalawa* and *baulo* cakes while sitting out over the water at sunset, watching the sun go down at the western end of the Philippine world. One doesn't find a place more representative of the archipelago than here. **Maranao man.**

INSIGHT GUIDES
Travel Tips

Insight Guides *portray destinations in depth, providing the complete picture and the top photography*

Insight Pocket Guides *focus on the best choices for places to see and things to do and include large fold-out maps*

Insight Compact Guides *portability makes them the perfect books to carry with you for on-the-spot reference*

Three types of guide for all types of travel

INSIGHT GUIDES Different people need different kinds of information. Some want *background information* to help them prepare for the trip. Others seek *personal recommendations* from someone who knows the destination well. And others look for *compactly presented data* for on-the-spot reference. With three carefully designed series, Insight Guides offer readers the perfect choice. Insight Guides will turn your visit into an experience.

The world's largest collection of visual travel guides

Getting Acquainted

The Place

The Philippine archipelago spreads over 7,107 islands. The Philippine Sea in the east, the South China Sea and Luzon Sea in the west, and the Sulu Sea and Celebes Sea in the south surround it all in azure waters. Eleven main islands account for over 95 percent of the total land area of 300,000 sq. kilometers (116,000 sq. mi). Only some 2,000 islands are inhabited, and some 2,500 others have yet to be named. Most islands have white sand beaches and lush tropical vegetation with small lakes and rivers. From north to south the islands stretch for 1,840 kilometers (1,140 mi) and east to west for 1,100 kilometers (700 mi). The highest peak is Mt Apo, in Davao province on Mindanao, at 2,950 meters (9,690 ft). The second highest is Mt Pulog, near Baguio in northern Luzon, at 2,930 meters (9,610 ft). The islands are capped by over 200 volcanoes, 22 of which are classified as active. The best known are Mayon Volcano in southern Luzon near Legaspi, Taal Volcano south of Manila, and Mt Pinatubo north of Manila.

There are four distinct geographical regions: 1) **Luzon**, the largest and northernmost island, is where the capital Manila is located. 2) In the center are the tightly-packed **Visayas**: Negros, Cebu, Bohol, Panay, Samar and Leyte islands. 3) To the south is **Mindanao**, the second-largest island and where Davao, Zamboanga, Marawi City and Cagayan de Oro can be found. From the southwestern tip of Mindanao, the islands of the Sulu Archipelago, including Basilan, Jolo and Tawi Tawi, run down to Borneo. 4) To the west of the Visayas lies **Palawan**, with some 1,700 islands.

Land use is varied, much of it determined by climate and geography. It includes arable land (26 percent); permanent crops (11 percent); meadows and pastures (4 percent); forest and woodland (40 percent); and other use (19 percent). About 18 percent of the land is irrigated (16,500 sq. kilometers – 6,400 sq. miles).

Time Zones

The Philippines is 8 hours ahead of Greenwich Mean Time (GMT). Lying near the equator, sunrise and sunset are nearly equally spread at about 6am and 6pm, give or take 30 minutes.

Climate

There is no one best time to visit the Philippines. It depends on where you plan to go within the archipelago, though December to May, the so called 'dry season', is usually the best pick.

Rainfall is the most significant factor affecting Philippine climate. The distribution of rainfall over a given area is classified by four types:

Type 1: These areas have two pronounced seasons, dry from December to May and wet from June to November. Type 1 areas are mainly found along the western half of Luzon, Palawan, Coron, Cuyo, lower part of Antique, Iloilo, and Negros.

Type 2: These areas have no dry season with a very pronounced maximum rain period during December to February. Type 2 areas include the eastern parts of the Bicol region, eastern Mindanao, northern and eastern Samar, and southern Leyte.

Type 3: These areas do not have a very pronounced maximum rain period and a short (one to three month) dry season. Type 3 areas include the mid-part of central Luzon, Visayas, and western Mindanao.

Type 4: These areas have a more or less even rainfall throughout the year. Includes the eastern coast of Luzon, the islands of Leyte and Bohol, and the central provinces of Mindanao.

The whole archipelago is affected by the southwest monsoon (winds from the southwest) from June to September, and by the northeast monsoon from mid-November to mid-March. The rest of the year are transition months, when the prevailing winds shift direction.

The annual mean temperature is 27°C. January is the coolest month with a mean of 26°C. May is the warmest month with a mean of 28°C. Minimum temperatures during the year range from 13°C in Baguio in February to 26°C in Manila. Maximum temperatures vary from 23°C in Baguio in January to 35°C in Cabanatuan in May. Humidity is high, ranging from a low of 79 percent during March to May to a high of 84 percent during July to October. The annual mean humidity stands at 83 percent.

Typhoons take their toll in the Philippines, where they are also called *baguios*. Sitting astride the typhoon belt, the archipelago is affected by an average of 20 typhoons each year, with eight to nine of them passing directly over the islands. Typhoon season runs from June to November, with most in July to September, coinciding with the peak of the southwest monsoon. The period from December to May, however is not entirely typhoon free.

The People

The country has a population of just under 70 million people, of whom 11 million live in the greater Metro Manila area. Filipinos are basically of Malay stock, though there is evidence of Indian, Chinese, Spanish, Arab and North American stock. The population increases annually at about 1.5 million or at about two percent. Attempts to implement family planning programs have met with strong opposition from the Catholic Church.

The primary religion is Christianity: 83 percent of all Filipinos are Roman Catholic, 9 percent Protestant, 5 percent Muslim, and 3 percent Buddhist or fall into another category.

Life expectancy averages 69.5 years, and the functional literacy rate is 84 percent. Pilipino and English are the official languages, with Pilipino (derived from Tagalog) the primary.

The Economy

Political stability and major economic reforms under the administration of President Fidel Ramos have triggered a remarkable economic turnaround for the Philippines. Anchored on Ramos's vision of the Philippines, which aims to transform the country into a newly industrializing country by the year 2000, the economy has posted steady growth since 1992. Gross National Product (GNP) has averaged 7 percent annually.

Protectionism and state intervention have finally given way to economic liberalization and industry deregulation during the past years. With the privatization of major state-owned companies almost completed, plans for the next wave of privatization covers the sale of public utilities and some basic social services. This, it is hoped, will put the country in a good position to exploit its traditional strengths: a good strategic location; abundant natural resources; a working democracy; a high standard of living; and a highly westernized business environment with a large pool of highly educated, English-speaking workers.

Although much of the economic activity remains concentrated in Metro Manila, there are a number of dynamic growth centers in other areas of the archipelago. One of the most notable is the Subic Bay Freeport Zone, a former American naval base which has been transformed into a successful commercial-industrial-tourism center with a new international airport.

A property boom is currently in full swing, particularly in Metro Manila. Two new central business districts – one adjacent to the financial district of Makati and another in southern Metro Manila – are on the drawing board.

That the country has regained the confidence of the international business community is best shown by the continued strength of the stock market, one of the best performers in Asia and the third best in the world. Long term market prospects for investors remain bullish.

The agricultural sector employs more than 40 percent of the population and contributes 20 percent of GNP. The country is, however, moving away from agricultural and mineral product exports, and has begun to diversify into higher value manufactured goods. So while coconut oil and sugar remain major exports, the top dollar earners now include electronics, apparel and clothing accessories, and computer related products.

Major export markets are the US, Japan, Netherlands, Singapore, and the UK. In the last two years, however, trade with other Asian countries has increased significantly, particularly with Taiwan, Thailand, China and South Korea. More importantly, the coming years will see the member-countries of the Association of Southeast Asian Nations (ASEAN) move closer to their goal of establishing a free-trade area in the region. A company operating in the Philippines will thus have access to a huge potential market of over 400 million consumers.

The country has a strong balance of payments position and because of this, the International Monetary Fund (IMF) has removed the Philippines from the list of member-countries eligible for a special loan facility designed for countries experiencing foreign exchange difficulties.

Despite the expanding economy, domestic inflation has been kept under control and has been cut from 18.7 percent in 1991 to an approximate 4.8 percent in 1997.

Visitors who have been to overcrowded malls in Metro Manila and Cebu City may wonder where people's purchasing power comes from, given official statistics on poverty (35 percent of total families live in poverty) and unemployment. The answer lies in the fact that there are two important facets of the Philippine economy: the informal economy and the number of Filipinos working overseas. Estimates on the size of the informal sector ranges from 25 percent to 40 percent of GNP. In addition, over a million Filipinos live or work abroad and dollar remittances reached US$4.7 billion in 1995. In the next five years, per capita income is projected to double to almost US$2,000, a development which should translate into substantially higher discretionary spending.

As President Ramos approaches the end of his term in May 1998, the question of his succession has arisen. Looking at the list of the possible presidential contenders, practically all are expected to continue the same set of free-market policies.

Government

The official name of the country is the Republic of the Philippines, but most common name used in tourist promotions and by most Filipinos is the Philippine Islands.

A 1935 constitution, modeled on that of the United States, was suspended by the then-President Ferdinand Marcos in 1972, when he declared martial law. A new constitution was ratified the following year, but over time, Marcos meddled with the constitution until he had complete power and authority. After the February 1986 "People Power" uprising that ousted Marcos, the country reverted to a democratic form of government.

In a February 1987 plebiscite, the country ratified a new constitution, providing for a democratic republican state and a presidential form of government. This paved the way for reestablishment of an elected bicameral legislative body. Following the experience of Marcos' two decades of rule, the president is now limited to a single six-year term.

For administrative purposes, the republic is divided into 16 regions, 77 provinces, 67 officially-chartered cities, 1,540 municipalities, and 41,935 barangays. Provinces consist of several municipalities centered on a provincial capital. Municipalities are subdivided into barangays, the smallest socio-political unit, headed by a barangay captain.

The legal system is based on Spanish and Anglo-American law.

The National Flag

The Philippine flag shows a white triangle with a yellow sunburst and three stars over horizontal fields of blue and red. In times of peace, the blue is over the red field, while in war the red field is over the blue.

The eight rays of the Philippine sun, in the middle of the triangle, represent the first eight provinces that revolted against Spanish domination. The three stars at the triangle's corners indicate the three major groups of the Philippine islands: Luzon, the Visayas and Mindanao.

Planning the Trip

What To Bring

Apart from your own special personal requirements, there is no need to bring any equipment other than possibly a travel plug adaptor and photographic supplies. Medications are available at drug stores in major cities and film processing is available everywhere. Any Tourist Information Center can advise you as to where you can go to buy your special requirements.

Electricity

The standard voltage in the Philippines is 220 volts AC, 60 cycles. Many areas also have 110 volts capability.

What To Wear

Light and loose clothes are most practical. Pack a sweater, especially if planning to go to the mountains even during the hottest months. At formal gatherings older Filipino men usually wear the *barong tagalog* (Tagalog shirt). This is a long-sleeved shirt with side slits worn outside the pants. Traditionally it is made in white or pastels out of a very fine silk called *jusi*. The shirt is so transparent that a T-shirt is always worn underneath. The front and cuffs, and sometimes the sleeves, are ornately embroidered. The style is from the 19th century, when only Spaniards were allowed to tuck their shirts inside their pants. Wearing the *barong* therefore distinguished a Filipino male from a Spaniard and became a declaration of patriotism.

Older Filipino women often wear the *terno* for formal occasions. This is a long gown with huge "butterfly" sleeves, and which has elaborate embroidery on the skirt and bodice.

The young wear much the same as the rest of the world wears.

If visiting churches and mosques, it is well for visitors to remember that shorts and scanty or provocative dress will be inappropriate.

Entry Regulations

Visas & Passports

All tourists must have valid passports. Except tourists from countries with which the Philippines has no diplomatic relations, stateless persons and nationals from restricted countries, everyone may enter without visas and stay for 21 days, provided they hold onward or return tickets.

Extensions of Stay

Visitors who wish to extend their stay from 21 to 59 days should contact the Bureau of Immigration and Deportation. Fees range from P1,000 to P2,000 depending on whether the visitor filed an application for extension before or after the 21 limit.

Customs

Tourists may bring in duty-free cigarettes, alcohol and vehicles within the following stipulations. Each passenger is allowed 400 cigarettes (20 packs) or 100 cigars or 500 grams of pipe tobacco, or an assortment of these. Two regular-sized bottles of alcoholic beverages are allowed per person, and cars and other vehicles are allowed duty-free entry provided they have *Carnets de Passages in Douanes* and a letter from the Philippine Motor Association guaranteeing the exportation of the vehicle within 1 year from the date of arrival or else the payment of duties and tax.

Porter Services

You will never want for a porter anywhere in the Philippines. The problem is usually quite the reverse as several porters will compete to carry your bags. About P10 per bag is appropriate, more for heavy packages.

Health

Yellow fever vaccination is necessary for those arriving from an infected area, except for children under 1 year old, who may be subject to isolation when necessary. When traveling in remote areas of the country it is advisable to take anti-malarial drugs.

Drinking water is generally safe in Metro Manila, although it is wise to drink mineral or bottled water which is radially available everywhere, especially when in the provinces.

Money Matters

The monetary unit of the Philippines is the peso (P). There are 100 centavos to a peso. The US dollar, pound sterling, Swiss franc, French franc, Deutsche mark, Canadian dollar, Italian lira, Australian dollar and the Japanese yen are all easily convertible. Outside Manila, generally, the US dollar is widely acceptable after the peso.

Traveler's checks can be easily cashed in Manila and with a bit of work and fees in the provinces. Major credit cards are widely accepted in Manila while they are limited to major establishments in other cities. Avoid street money changers.

Public Holidays

The Gregorian calendar is used in the Philippines. The principal public and religious holidays are listed below.

Note: Travel during the Easter and Christmas holiday seasons can be extremely difficult not to mention chaotic. Make reservations far in advance, or else don't travel during these periods.

January 1: New Year's Day. Pyrotechnics greet the coming of the new year on the eve of December 31st.

Maundy Thursday: Flagellants in the streets, processions and "*Cenaculos*" (passion plays).

Good Friday: processions.

Easter Sunday: morning processions.

April 9: *Araw ng Kagitingan* (Day of Valor). Celebrations at Fort Santiago in Manila to commemorate the bravery of the Filipinos who fought during World War II.

May 1: Labor Day. A day of tribute to the Filipino worker.

June 12: Independence Day. Parades at Rizal Park in Manila.

June 24: Manila Day (Manila only). Parade, film festivals and cultural presentations to celebrate the founding of Manila, the capital of the Philippines.

November 1: All Saints Day. A day to honor the dead.

November 30: Bonifacio Day. Celebration of the birth of the country's great commoner, Andres Bonifacio.

December 25: Christmas Day. Nine days of pre-dawn masses called *Misa de Gallo*, culminating in a midnight mass on Christmas eve, which is immediately followed by a *Noche Buena* or midnight repast.

December 30: Rizal Day. Wreath laying ceremony at the National Hero's Monument in Rizal Park (Manila) in honor of Dr Jose Rizal, the country's national hero.

Getting There

By Air

The majority of visitors arrive in and depart from Manila by air, with over 420 international flights arriving weekly. Ninoy Aquino International Airport and the domestic terminal are centrally located, 7 kilometers (4 mi) from the city center. Several international flights also land weekly at Cebu's Mactan International Airport, as well as Subic, Zamboanga, and Davao International Airports.

By Sea

Many freighters and cruise ships stop in Manila Bay, although most travelers arrive by air.

Note: The government is adamant about protecting tourists from endangering themselves by traveling on small craft between East Malaysia (Borneo) and the Philippines's southernmost islands. The Moro rebels and continuing piracy make this exotic route unadvisable.

Special Facilities

Doing Business

Philippine Chamber of Commerce and Industry, ground floor, Philippine International Convention Center, Cultural Center of the Philippines Complex, Roxas Boulevard, Pasay City, Metro Manila, Tel: 833-8591, Fax: 833-8595.
American Chamber of Commerce of the Philippines, 2nd floor, Corinthian Plaza, Paseo de Roxas, Makati City, Metro Manila, Tel: 818-7911, Fax: 811-3081.
Australia-New Zealand Chamber of Commerce (Philippines), Penthouse, YL Holdings Bldg., Herrera corner Salcedo streets, Legaspi Village, Makati City, Tel: 816-3836, Fax: 893-8208.
Canadian Chamber of Commerce of the Philippines, Penthouse, YL Holdings Bldg., Herrera corner Salcedo streets, Legaspi Village, Makati City, Tel: 812-8568, Fax: 812-8569.
European Chamber of Commerce of the Philippines, 5th floor, King's Court

II, Pasong Tamo, Makati City, Metro Manila, Tel: 811-2234, Fax: 815-2688.
Federation of Filipino-Chinese Chamber of Commerce, 6th floor, Federation Center Bldg., Muelle de Binondo, Manila, Tel: 241-9201, Fax: 242-2361.
Indian Chamber of Commerce, Room 1803, Cityland 10 Tower, H.V. dela Costa St., Salcedo Vill., Makati City, Tel: 844-7222.
Spanish Chamber of Commerce, Room 42 Zeta Bldg., 191 Salcedo Street, Legaspi Village, Makati City, Metro Manila, Tel: 893-5966, Fax: 892-6215.
Philippine Convention and Visitors Corp., 4th floor, Suites 5,7,1017, Legaspi Towers, 300 Roxas Blvd., Metro Manila, Tel: 525-9318, Fax: 521-6165.
Board of Investments, 385 Sen. Gil Puyat Avenue, Makati City, Metro Manila, Tel: 897-6682, Fax: 895-3521.
Bureau of Customs, Customs Bldg., Port Area, Manila, Tel: 527-8401.
Center for International Trade Exhibitions & Missions Inc., Philtrade Complex, Roxas Blvd., Pasay City, Metro Manila, Tel: 832-3956.
Department of Trade & Industry, 361 Sen. Gil Puyat Avenue, Makati City, Metro Manila, Tel: 890-4901, Fax: 818 0892.
National Economic Development Authority, Ortigas Complex, Pasig, Metro Manila, Tel: 631-0945, Fax: 631-3747.

Useful Addresses

Tourist Information

Department of Tourism (DOT), Dept. of Tourism Bldg., T.M. Kalaw Street, Ermita, Manila, Tel: 523-8411, Fax: 521-7374.

24-Hour Tourist Assistance Hotlines: 524-1660 and 524-1728.

DOT REGIONAL OFFICES

Metro Manila
Department of Tourism (DOT), Dept. of Tourism Bldg., Room 207, T.M. Kalaw Street, Ermita, Tel: 524-2345, Fax: 524-8321, Email: dotncr@mnl.sequel.net

Luzon Highlands
Department of Tourism, DOT-Complex, Gov. Pack Road, Baguio City, Tel: (074) 442-6708, Fax: (074) 442-8848.

Northwestern Luzon
DOT, Mabanag Justice Hall, San

Fernando, La Union, Tel/Fax: (072) 412-098.
DOT, Ilocano Heroes Memorial Hall, Laoag City, Tel: (077) 772-0467.

Northeastern Luzon
DOT, 2nd floor, Tuguegarao Supermarket, Tuguegarao, Cagayan, Tel/Fax: (078) 844-1621.

Central Luzon Plain
DOT, Paskuhan Village, San Fernando, Pampanga, Tel: (045) 961-2665.
DOT, Corporate Office Bldg. 1584, Civil Aviation Complex, Clark Special Eco-Zone, Clark Field, Pampanga, Tel: (045) 599-2843.

Southwestern Luzon
DOT, Dept. of Tourism Bldg., Room 206, T.M. Kalaw Street, Ermita, Manila, Tel: 524-1969, Fax: 526-7656, Email: dotr4@mnl.sequel.net

Southeastern Luzon
DOT, 3F, Meliton Dy Bldg., Rizal Street, Legazpi, Tel: (05221) 243-215, Fax: 243-266.

Visayas
DOT, Western Visayas Tourism Center, Capitol Ground, Bonifacio Drive, Iloilo, Tel: (033) 337-5411, Fax: 335-0245.
Bacolod Field Office, DOT, Bacolod Plaza, Bacolod, Tel: (034) 290-21.
Boracay Field Office, DOT, Balabag, Boracay, Malay, Aklan, Tel/Fax: (036) 288-3689.

Cebu
DOT, 3rd floor, GMC Plaza Bldg., Legaspi Extension, Cebu, Tel: (032) 254-2811, Fax: 254-2711, Airport Office Tel: 340-8229.

Leyte
DOT, Children's Park, Sen. Enage Street, Tacloban, Tel: (053) 321-2048, Fax: 325-5279.

Western Mindanao
DOT, Lantaka Hotel By the Sea, Valderosa Street, Zamboanga, Tel: (062) 991-0218, Fax: 991-0217.

Northern Mindanao
DOT, A. Velez Street, Cagayan de Oro, Tel: (08822) 726-394, Fax: 723-696.

Southern Mindanao
DOT, Door No. 7, Magsaysay Park

Complex, Sta. Ana District, Davao, Tel: (082) 221-6798, Fax: 221-0070.

Southwestern Mindanao
DOT, Elizabeth Tan Bldg., De Mazenod Ave., Cotabato, Tel: (064) 421-1110, Fax: 421-7868.

Northeastern Mindanao
DOT, Tourism Assistance Center, City Hall Compound, Butuan, Tel: (08522) 557-12, Fax: 644-97.

OVERSEAS OFFICES
ASIA-PACIFIC
Australia, Philippines Dept of Tourism, Consulate General of the Philippines, Wynyard House, Suite 703, Level 7, 301 George Street, Sydney, 2000, Tel: (612) 299-6815, 299-6899, Fax: 283-1862, Email: ptsydney@ozmail.com.au
Hong Kong, Philippine Consulate General, 6th Floor, Room 602, United Centre, 95 Queensway, Hong Kong, Tel: (852) 2866-6471, Fax: 2866-6521.
Singapore, Embassy of the Philippines, Office of the Marketing Representative, 20 Nassim Road, Singapore 258395, Tel: (65) 235-2154, Fax: 235-2548.
Taiwan, Manila Economic & Cultural Office, Dept. of Tourism, Tourism Center, 4F Metrobank Plaza, 107 Chung Hsiao East Road, Section 4, Taipei, ROC, Tel: (886-2) 778-6511, Fax: 745-994.

EUROPE
France, Service de Tourisme, Ambassade des Philippines, Dept. of Tourism, Batiment B, 3 Faubourg, Saint Honore 75008 Paris, Tel: (331) 4265-0234, Fax: 4265-0238.
Germany, Philippine Department of Tourism, Kaiserhof Strasse 7, 60313 Frankfurt Am Main 1, Tel: (4969) 208-93, Fax: 285-127.
Germany, Philippine Department of Tourism, Whistlermeg 20, 81479 Munich, Tel: (4989) 749-9262, Fax: 749-9241.
Israel, Philippine Department of Tourism, 4 Ben Gurion Street, Ness Ziona 70400, Tel: (972-8) 940-1789, Fax: 930-1769.
Italy, Philippine Department of Tourism, G.S. Air S.R.L. Rome, Via Cassis, 901-A00187 Rome, Tel: (396) 474-4062, Fax: 474-3780.
Spain, Philippine Department of Tourism, Torre de Madrid Planta, Oficina 7, Plaza de Espana, 28008 Madrid, Tel: (341) 542-3711, Fax: 217-9268.

Sweden, Philippine Department of Tourism, Airtyler Ab, Skiylinsgrand 5, 183 38 Taby/Stockholm, Fax: (468) 758-8915.
U.K., Embassy of the Philippine, Department of Tourism, 17 Albermarle Street, London WIX 4LX, Tel: (44171) 499-5443, Fax: 499-5772.

UNITED STATES
Los Angeles, Philippine Consulate General, 900 Suite 825, 3660 Wilshire Boulevard, Los Angeles, California 90010, USA, Tel: (213) 487-4527, Fax: 386-4063.
New York, Philippine Center, 556 Fifth Avenue, New York, New York 10036, USA, Tel: (212) 575-7915, Fax: 302-6758.
San Francisco, Philippine Consulate General, Suite 507, 447 Sutter Street, San Francisco, California 94108, USA, Tel: (415) 956-4060, Fax: 956-2093.

Diplomatic Missions
Argentina, 6th floor, ACT Tower, 135 Sen. Gil Puyat Avenue, Salcedo Village, Makati City, Metro Manila, Tel: 810-8301, Fax: 893-6091.
Australia, Doqa Salustiana D. Ty Bldg., Paseo de Roxas corner Perea street, Makati City, Metro Manila, Tel: 817-7911, Fax: 754-6268.
Austria, 4th floor, Prince Bldg., 117 Rada street. Legaspi Village, Makati City, Metro Manila, Tel: 817-9191, Fax: 813-4238.
Belgium, 9/F, Multinational Bancorporation Center, 6805 Ayala Ave., Makati, Metro Manila, Tel: 845-1869, Fax: 845-2076.
Brazil, 6th floor, RCI Bldg., 105 Rada Street, Legaspi Village, Makati City, Metro Manila, Tel: 892-8181/82, Fax: 818-2622.
Canada, 9 & 11th floors, Allied Bank Center, 6754 Ayala Avenue, Makati City, Metro Manila, Tel: 810-8861, Fax: 810-8839.
Chile, 6th floor, Doqa Salustiana D. Ty Bldg., Paseo de Roxas corner Perea Street, Makati City, Metro Manila, Tel: 810-3149, Fax: 815-0795.
China, 4896 Pasay Road, Dasmariqas Village, Makati, Metro Manila, Tel: 810-8597, Fax: 892-5181.
Colombia, 18th floor, Aurora Tower, Araneta Center, Cubao, Quezon City, Tel: 911-3101, Fax: 911-2846.
Cuba, 11th floor, Heart Tower Condominium, 108 Valero Street, Salcedo

Village, Makati City, Metro Manila, Tel: 817-1192, Fax: 916-4094.
Czech Republic, 1267 Acacia Road, Dasmarinas Village, Makati, Metro Manila, Tel: 812-9254.
Denmark, 6th floor, Doqa Salustiana D. Ty Bldg., Paseo de Roxas corner Perea Street, Makati City, Metro Manila, Tel: 894-0086, Fax: 817-5729.
Finland, 21F, Far East Bank Center, Sen. Gil Puyat Ave., Makati, Metro Manila, Tel: 891-5011.
France, 16th floor, Pacific Star Bldg., Sen. Gil Puyat corner Makati avenues, Makati City, Metro Manila, Tel: 810-1981 to 88, Fax: 813-1908.
Germany, 6th floor, Solidbank Bldg., Paseo de Roxas, Makati City, Metro Manila, Tel: 892-4906/1001, Fax: 810-4703.
India, 2190 Paraiso Street, Dasmariqas Village, Makati City, Metro Manila, Tel: 843-0101.
Indonesia, Indonesian Embassy Bldg., 185 Salcedo Street, Legaspi Village, Makati City, Metro Manila, Tel: 892-5061 to 68, Fax: 818-4441.
Israel, 23F Trafalgar Plaza, H.V. de la Costa Street, Salcedo Village, Makati, Metro Manila, Tel: 892-5329.
Italy, 6th floor, Zeta Bldg., 191 Salcedo Street, Legaspi Village, Makati City, Metro Manila, Tel: 892-4531, Fax: 817-1436.
Malaysia, 107 Tordesillas Street, Salcedo Village, Makati City, Metro Manila, Tel: 817-4581 to 85, Fax: 816-3158.
Mexico, 18F Ramon Magsaysay Center, 1680 Roxas Blvd., Pasay, Metro Manila, Tel: 526-7461.
Myanmar, 4F Basic Petroleum Condominium, 104 Carlos Palanca Jr. Street, Legaspi Village, Makati, Metro Manila, Tel: 817-2373, Fax: 817-5895.
Netherlands, 9th floor, King's Court Bldg. I, 2129 Pasong Tamo Street, Salcedo Village, Makati, Metro Manila, Tel: 812-5981 to 83, Fax: 815-4579.
New Zealand, 23F Far East Bank Bldg., Sen. Gil Puyat Ave., Makati, Metro Manila, Tel: 891-5358.
Norway, 69 Paseo de Roxas, Urdaneta Village, Makati, Metro Manila, Tel: 893-9866.
Peru, 7F Country Space One Bldg., Sen. Gil Puyat Ave., Makati, Metro Manila, Tel: 813-8731.
Singapore, 6th floor, ODC International Plaza Building, 219 Salcedo Street, Legaspi Village, Makati, Metro Manila,

Tel: 816-1764/65, Fax: 818-4687.
Spain, 5th floor, ACT Tower, 135 Sen. Gil Puyat Avenue, Salcedo Village, Makati City, Metro Manila, Tel: 818-3581/61, Fax: 810-2885.
Sri Lanka, 1143 Pasong Tamo, Makati, Metro Manila, Tel: 899-5533.
Sweden, 16th floor, PCI Bank Tower II, Makati Avenue corner Dela Costa Street, Salcedo Village, Makati City, Metro Manila, Tel: 819-1951, Fax: 815-3002.
Switzerland, 18th floor, Solidbank Bldg., 777 Paseo de Roxas, Makati City, Metro Manila, Tel: 819-0202, Fax: 815-0381.
Thailand, 107 Rada Street, Legaspi Village, Makati, Metro Manila, Tel: 816-0696/97, Fax: 815-4221.
United Kingdom, L.V. Locsin Bldg., 6752 Ayala Ave., corner Makati Avenue, Makati, Metro Manila, Tel: 816-7116, Fax: 819-7206.
United States, 1201 Roxas Boulevard, Ermita, Manila, Tel: 521-7116, Fax: 522-1361.
Vietnam, 554 Vito Cruz, Malate, Metro Manila, Tel: 524-0364.

Practical Tips

Emergencies

Security & Crime
The **Tourist Assistance Unit** (TAU) is open 24 hours to assist visitors in trouble. Telephone 524-1660, 524-1728 or 523-8411 and ask for TAU. The **Department of Tourism** (DOT) is at T.M. Kalaw Street, Rizal Park, Manila.

The **Philippine National Police Headquarters** is at Camp Crame, EDSA, Metro Manila, Tel: 723-0401.
> **Police (Manila):** 166
> **Ambulance/fire:** 160

Travelers should be aware of sporadic problems with both communist guerrillas (NPA/New People's Army) and Muslim separatists. The government has engaged in negotiations with both groups, and the situation has, for the most part, improved significantly over the past few years. But radical splinter groups continue.

Parts of Mindanao remain dubious areas for foreign travelers. Similarly, the remote islands of the Sulu archipelago can be dangerous; there have been several kidnappings of foreigners in Sulu and Basilan.

Before traveling in the countryside, check with your embassy for updates on the situation.

Loss of Belongings
Lost credit cards should be reported immediately to:
American Express, Tel: Manila 815-9366.
Diners Club, Tel: Manila 890-5421.

Valuables: Most larger hotels have a safe or a safe box where your valuables may be deposited. When traveling, conceal such valuables as cameras. Always lock your car.

Medical Services
It is advisable to have medical insurance when visiting the Philippines as payment must usually be guaranteed before treatment. Major Manila hospitals are located at:

Cardinal Santos Medical Center, Wilson Street, San Juan, Metro Manila, Tel: 727 0001.
Makati Medical Center, 2 Amorsolo corner de la Rosa streets, Makati City, Metro Manila, Tel: 815-9911.
Manila Doctor's Hospital, 667 United Nations Avenue, Ermita, Manila, Tel: 524-3011.
St Luke's Medical Center, 279 Rodriguez Boulevard, Quezon City, Metro Manila, Tel: 723-0301.
Medical Center Manila, 1122 General Luna Street, Ermita, City of Manila, Tel: 523-8131.

There is a risk of malaria year-round below 600 meters (2,000 ft) in elevation, except in urban areas; the malignant falciparum strain is present, said to be highly resistant to chloroquine.

Rabies is present. If bitten by any mammal, seek medical treatment immediately. Bilharzia (schistosomiasis) is present, so avoid swimming in fresh water. Swimming pools that are chlorinated are quite safe.

Note: As far as possible, avoid medical treatment in the Philippines outside of Manila, as many travelers and expatriates have reported unpleasant experiences.

Business Hours
Shops open Monday–Saturday, 9 or 10am–7pm. Most shopping centers, department stores, and supermarkets are open from 10am–7pm daily. The Philippine attitude of *Bahala na* (whatever happens) prevails outside Manila, so shops don't usually stick to any kind of schedule.

Government and business hours are Monday–Friday, 8am–5pm and workers break for lunch from noon–1pm. Some private offices are open on Saturdays, 8am–noon. Banks are open Monday–Friday, 9am–3pm.

Tipping
Most major restaurants and hotels add 10 percent service charge automatically. Smaller establishments leave tipping to discretion, but even if service charge is levied, it is better to leave something. Taxi drivers, beauticians, bellboys, pool attendants in fact anyone who performs a service for you expects a small gratuity.

Religious Services
Historically, the Filipinos have embraced two of the great religions of the world Islam and Christianity. Islam was introduced during the 14th century, shortly after the expansion of Arab commercial ventures in Southeast Asia. By the 16th century, it was extending its influence northward when the Spaniards came to curb its spread and introduced Catholicism to the islands. Today, Islam is mostly limited to the southern region of the country.

Locally, two Filipino independent churches were organized at the turn of the 20th century and are prominent today. These are the *Aglipay* (Philippine Independent Church) and the *Iglesia Ni Kristo* (Church of Christ), founded in 1902 and 1914, respectively. The *Iglesia Ni Kristo* has expanded its membership considerably. In fact, the *Iglesia Ni Kristo* church, with its unique towering architecture, is a prodigious sight in almost all important towns, provincial capitals and major cities.

Most Christian church services are held on Sunday morning and evening while Friday is the Muslim holy day. Details of these and other services are usually available at hotel reception desks and Tourist Information Centers. (Manila, Tel: 524-1703).

Media

Newspapers & Magazines

Manila must have the galaxy's largest selection of local newspapers per capita. And, in fact, a vigorous, even rambunctious, group they can be. Numerous morning and evening English-language daily newspapers are published in Manila. These include the *Philippine Daily Inquirer*, *Philippine Star*, *Manila Bulletin*, *Manila Times*, *Malaya*, *Today*, *Manila Standard* and *Manila Chronicle*. For business and economic news, there is the *Businessworld* and the *Business Star*.

The *Fookien Times* is published in both, English and Chinese. There are also a number of local magazines published in English, for example: *Mr & Ms*, *Lifestyle Asia*, *Taipan*, *Metro*, *Computer Times*, *What's on in Manila*, *Expat*, *Mod* and *Panorama*.

A fairly large selection of foreign magazines and newspaper are available, for example: *Newsweek*, *Time*, *Asiaweek*, *Far Eastern Economic Review*, *Asian Business*, *Business Traveller*, *The Economist*, *Reader's Digest*, *Vogue*, *Yazhou Zhoukan*, plus the *Asian Wall Street Journal* and the *International Herald Tribune*. All the above are sold either in major hotels or at bookstores, supermarkets and news-stands throughout the city.

TV & Radio

People's Television (Channel 4) broadcasts a variety of programs in color which includes the latest national and foreign news, sports events, live coverages, variety shows, foreign serials and shows, and soap operas.

There are also a number of independent television stations serving Manila: Radio Philippine Network (RPN) channel 9; Greater Manila Area TV (GMA) channel 7; Intercontinental Broadcasting Network (IBC) channel 13; Alto Broadcasting System/Chronicle Broadcasting Network (ABS/CBN) channel 2, ABC channel 5, RJTV channel 21, and channel 23. Most hotels have cable television for international news and programs.

Most radio stations are privately owned. They broadcast music ranging from classical to hard rock, inter-spersed with news bulletins, commercials and entertainment talk.

Postal Services

Post offices are open from 8am–5pm on weekdays and 8am–1pm on Saturday and holiday. The Philippine Postal Corporation is located at Plaza Lawton, (Liwasang Bonifacio), Manila.

There are private agencies in Manila which deliver express mail within city boundaries. For general letter posting, there are plenty of mail boxes at the post offices, street posts and in some commercial establishments. At Ninoy Aquino International Airport, the post office is located at the arrival area. Stamps can be bought at post offices and in some government offices, hotels and commercial establishments.

Alternatives such as Federal Express and DHL are available for domestic and international mails.

Speed Mail

Same-Day Delivery: First-class letters mailed on or before 9am on any working day at the following post offices are delivered the same day. The addresses must be within their respective delivery areas.

There is also express mail to most parts of the world.
Manila Post Office, Liwasang Bonifacio, Manila
Makati Post Office, G. Puyat (Buendia Avenue)
Pasay Post Office, F.B. Harrison, Pasay
San Juan Central Post Office, Pinaglabanan, San Juan

Telephone & Telex

There are nine telecommunication firms operating international, domestic and cellular phone services in the country. Most telephone services are operated by Philippine Long Distance Telephone Company (PLDT). There is a minimum charge of P2.00 (whole coin or two one peso coins) from public pay phones. Prepaid telephone cards are available in the Metro Manila area for use in pay phones. As public telephones are still inadequate, it is a common practice to use the phones of small businesses and shops for a minimum charge of P3.00. Be warned that using the telephone will prove frustrating to anyone accustomed to Western-style efficiency.

Most of the larger Philippine hotels have telex and fax facilities available to guests at a small charge.

International access code: 00
Philippines country code: 63
Domestic calls, operator: 109
International calls, operator: 108
Dialing assistance: 112
Directory assistance: 114

City codes:
Angeles: 045
Bacolod: 034
Baguio: 074
Batangas: 043
Cagayan de Oro: 08822
Clark: 045
Cebu: 032
Davao: 082
General Santos City: 083
Iloilo: 033
Manila: 02
Subic: 047

Note: Refer to the local phone director for other city and province area codes. All operators speak English.

Tour Companies

For official tour operators and guides registered with the Department of Tourism (DOT), telephone Manila: 524-1703. Over 60 tour operators are listed in the Directory of Philippine Tour Operators, all of whom are members of the Philippine Tour Operators Association. The directory is available from any DOT office.

Getting Around

Domestic Travel

Transportation around the archipelago normally begins and ends in the country's hub, Manila. Flying is quick and cheap and Philippine Airlines, Grand Air, Cebu Air, Air Philippines, and Aerolift, the country's domestic carriers, cover the country with their routes. For those with time to spare transportation possibilities include bus, train, car and boat.

Philippine Airlines is the major domestic (and international) carrier operating to over 40 domestic points. Grand Air International, the second national carrier, flies to Cebu, Davao, Iloilo, Cagayan de Oro and Tacloban. Up-and-coming airlines competing with the flag carriers include Cebu Pacific Air, which flies twice a day to Cebu, Davao, Tacloban, Iloilo and Cagayan de Oro City; Air Philippines, which flies daily to Subic, Iloilo, Zamboanga and Puerto Princesa; and Aerolift, which covers Daet, Cebu, Boracay, Bohol, Dipolog, Lubang and Busuanga. Listed below are the telephone numbers of the airlines.

Aerolift, Tel: 812-6711
Air Philippines, Tel: 843-7011
Cebu Pacific Air, Tel: 636-4938
Grand International, Tel: 893-9768
Philippine Airlines, Tel: 816-6691

Other domestic carriers include **Air Ads**, serving Busuanga, Caticlan and Lubang (Tel: 833-3264); **Asian Spirit**, serving Calbayog, Catarman, San Jose, Virac and other destinations (Tel: 840-3811). As of mid-'97, **Pacific Airways Corp.** has suspended operations.

Note: Travel during the Easter and Christmas holiday seasons can be extremely difficult not to mention chaotic and nerve-wracking. Buses and ferries are always overloaded, sometimes dangerously, and flight reservations impossible to find. Make reservations far in advance, or don't travel during these periods.

Water Transport

Manila and Cebu are the two centers of shipping. Be advised that interisland boat travel will only suit those prepared to rough it. The effort is rewarding, however, as some of the ports served by the steamers have hardly changed in decades and the bonus is that seemingly half the local populace greets arriving boats at the wharf. Tickets on major lines (eg Manila – Cebu) can be booked through travel agencies.

Public Transport

In Metro Manila, the bus and jeepney rates are P2.00 for the first 4 kilometers (2 mi) plus 50 centavos for every kilometer thereafter.

Tricycles (motorcycle with a side-car attached) are sometimes available for short trips on the side streets.

There are also air-conditioned buses plying major thoroughfares such as EDSA, Ayala Avenue, Sen. Gil Puyat Avenue, Taft Avenue and the South and North expressways. Air-conditioned bus terminals are located in Escolta, in Binondo, Manila, The Center Makati and Ali Mall in Cubao, Quezon City.

Taxis can be found almost everywhere, especially near hotels, shopping centers and cinemas. Always have small change available and pay in pesos. Air-conditioned taxis are more expensive, but worth it.

LRT, the elevated light-rail system in Manila, charges a flat rate of P10.00 at any point along Taft and Rizal Avenue, from Baclaran to Monumento in Caloocan City. There are 16 stations, about one per kilometer, and the entire route takes half an hour.

Trains

Train travel is only for the very brave with lots of time to spare. Only one line operates through Manila. The train from Manila's Tutuban Station in Tondo runs south to Legaspi City, from where you can visit Mayon Volcano in the Bicol region, and north to San Fernando, La Union.

Buses

The central Luzon region near Manila and areas surrounding provincial capitals have a reasonable road system. Dozens of bus companies operate services to the main tourist centers of Luzon and fares are low by Western standards; the 5-hour journey from Manila to Baguio costs P120 on ordinary buses and P160 on air conditioned buses.

Private Transport

You can rent station wagons, bantams, coasters, buses, jeepneys and air-conditioned limousines. Cars may be rented with or without a driver. Charges vary according to type of vehicle.

Hourly rates are available, charges at one-sixth the daily rate. A valid foreign or international driver's license is acceptable.

Car Rental

Avis Rent-A-Car, G & S Transport Corp., 3F ASA Bldg., Delbros Ave., Paranaque, Manila, Tel: 526-2847, Fax: 551-4361.
Budget Rent-A-Car, Peninsula Manila Hotel, Ayala Avenue, Makati City, Tel: 818-7363, Fax: 816-2211.
Carlines Transportation, Makati Tuscany Condominium, 6751 Ayala Ave., Makati City, Tel: 844-2479, Fax: 810-3466.
Dollar Rent-A-Car, Motorcity Complex, Pasong Tamo, Makati, Tel: 896-9251, Fax: 896-9256.
Executive Transport & Cars, Casa Blanca, 1447 M. Adriatico Street, Ermita, Manila, Tel: 523-5595, Fax: 526-0717.
First Imperial Rent-A-Car, Suite 109, State Condominium IV, Ortigas Ave., Greenhills, San Juan, Metro Manila, Tel: 724-9306, Fax: 721-4009.
Filcar Transport Services, G/F, Torre de Salcedo Bldg., Salcedo Street, Makati City, Metro Manila, Tel: 843-3530, Fax: 819-2502.
Grayline Philippines, 7737 St. Paul St., San Antonio Village, Makati, Manila, Tel: 890-3965, Fax: 563-2537.
Hertz Rent-A-Car, Roxas Blvd., Paranaque, Metro Manila, Tel: 832-5325.
Island Rent-A-Car, 3rd Floor, Maripola Bldg., 109 Perea Street, Legaspi Village, Makati City, Metro Manila, Tel: 819-1379, Fax: 815-6628.
Mancars Rental Services, 3514A Hilario Street, Palanan, Makati City, Tel: 833-0564.
Metropolitan Car Charter Services, Milom Bldg., Amorsolo St., Makati, Metro Manila, Tel: 893-6150.
National Car Rental Philippines, P. Burgos Street, Makati City, Metro Manila, Tel: 897-9023, Fax: 810-1889.
Pacific Rent-A-Car, Shangri-La Manila Hotel Arcade, Makati, Manila, Tel: 894-1191, Fax: 813-5039.
Safari Rent-A-Car, 1943 Flordeliz Street, La Paz Village, Makati City, Tel: 890-3606, Fax: 899-2304.
Sandeco Rent-A-Car, 5446-48 South Superhighway corner Gen. Lucban Street, Makati, Tel: 818-1360 or 817-2208.
Silver Star Rent-A-Car, 2436 Iba cor-

ner Chico streets, UPS 1, Paraqaque, Metro Manila, Tel: 823-7034 or 805-8291.
Suburban Car Rental Services, 5077-D P. Burgos Street, Makati City, Tel: 896-3885 or 896-7581.
Transport 2000, 72 Apo Street, Mandaluyong City, Metro Manila, Tel: 531-0213.
Tropical Transport Service, G/F Marvin Plaza Bldg., 2153 Pasong Tamo, Makati City, Tel: 816-7719 or 892-3859.

Where To Stay

Hotels

The Philippines offers a wide range of accommodations for every budget from beach resorts and pension houses to apartments and luxury hotels.

Manila boasts numerous deluxe hotels. The city has been well organized for tourism and conventions. The Department of Tourism and the Philippine Convention and Visitors Corporation have an excellent network of promotion offices all over the world to provide information, and, in some cases, make hotel reservations. For information contact the Tourist Information Center, Department of Tourism (DOT), 2nd floor, T.M. Kalaw Street, Rizal Park, Manila, Tel: 524-1703.

Manila

EXPENSIVE
Century Park Hotel, Vito Cruz, Tel: 522-1011, Fax: 521-3413.
Grand Boulevard Hotel, 1990 Roxas Blvd., Tel: 521-0004, Fax: 536-0111.
Holiday Inn Manila Pavilion, UN Ave. corner Orosa Street, Ermita, Manila, Tel: 522-2911, Fax: 522-3531.
Hotel Intercontinental, Ayala Center, Makati, Tel: 815-9711, Fax: 817-1330.
Dusit Hotel Nikko, Ayala Center, Makati, Tel: 810-4101, Fax: 817-1862.
Hyatt Regency, 2702 Roxas Blvd., Pasay City, Tel: 833-1234, Fax: 833-5913.
Mandarin Oriental Manila, Paseo de Roxas Triangle Makati, Tel: 893-3601, Fax: 817-2472.

Manila Diamond Hotel, Roxas Blvd., Ermita, Manila, Tel: 526-2211, Fax: 526-2255.
Manila Galleria Suites, ADB Ave., Ortigas Center, Pasig, Tel: 633-7111, Fax: 633-2824.
Manila Hotel, Rizal Park, Tel: 247-0011, Fax: 530-0325.
Manila Peninsula, Ayala Avenue corner Makati Ave., Makati, Tel: 844-2566.
New World Hotel, Pasay Road corner Makati Ave., Makati, Tel: 811-6888, Fax: 811-6777.
Shangri-La Hotel Manila, Ayala Avenue corner Makati Ave., Makati, Tel: 813-8888, Fax: 813-5499.
Shangri-La's Edsa Plaza, 1 Garden Way, Ortigas Center, Mandaluyong, Tel: 633-8888, Fax: 631-1067.
Hotel Sofitel Grand Boulevard Manila, 1990 Roxas Blvd., Ermita, Tel: 526-8588, Fax: 526-0111.
The Heritage Hotel, Roxas Blvd. corner EDSA, Pasay City, Tel: 891-8888, Fax: 8918808.
The Westin Philippine Plaza, Cultural Center Complex, Roxas Blvd., Tel: 832-0701, Fax: 832-3485.

MODERATE
Admiral Hotel, 2138 Roxas Blvd., Ermita, Tel: 521-0905, Fax: 522-2018.
Adriatico Arms Hotel, 561 J. Nakpil Street, Ermita, Manila, Tel: 521-0736.
Aloha Hotel, 2150 Roxas Blvd., Tel: 523-8441.
Ambassador Hotel, 2021 A. Mabini Street, Malate, Tel: 524-6011.
Bayview Park Hotel, 1118 Roxas Blvd., Tel: 526-1555, Fax: 522-3040.
Hotel Aurelio, Roxas Blvd. corner Padre Faura Street, Ermita, Tel: 524-9061.
Hotel Las Palmas, 1616 A. Mabini Street, Malate, Tel: 524-5602.
Hotel La Corona, 439 Arquiza Street, M.H. del Pilar, Ermita, Tel: 524-2631, Fax: 521-3909.
Manila Midtown Hotel, P. Gil corner Adriatico streets, Ermita, Tel: 521-7001, Fax: 522-2629.
Mercure Philippine Village Airport Hotel, MIA Road, Pasay City, Tel: 833-8081.
Rothman Inn Hotel, 1633 M. Adriatico Street, Ermita, Tel: 521-9251, Fax: 522-2606.
Sundowner Hotel, 1430 A. Mabini Street, Ermita, Tel: 521-2751.
Traders Hotel Manila, 3001 Roxas Blvd., near CCP, Tel: 523-6745.

INEXPENSIVE
Hotel MacArthur, 2120 A. Mabini Street, Malate, Tel: 521-3911.
Hotel Soriente, 1123 Bocobo Flores Street, Ermita, Tel: 523-7139.
Iseya Hotel, 1241 M.H. del Pilar Street, Ermita, Tel: 592-016.
BUDGET
Malate Pension, 1771, M. Adriatico, Malate, Tel: 593-489.
Rich & Famous Pension House, 1655, L. Guinto, Ermita, Tel: 506-437.

BEACH RESORTS NEAR MANILA
Anilao Seaport Center, Mabini, Batangas, Tel: 801-1850.
Aqua Tropical Resort, Mabini, Batangas, Tel: 583-289.
Maya Maya Reef Club, Nasugbu, Batangas, Tel: 810-6865.
Montemar Beach Club, Bagac, Bataan, Tel: 815-3490.
Puerto Azul Beach Hotel, Ternate, Cavite, Tel: 526-1781.
Punta Baluarte, Calatagan, Batangas, Tel: 894-5793.
Vistamar, Mabini, Batangas, Tel: 525-1812.

LAGUNA
Hidden Valley Resort, Alaminos, Laguna, Manila Tel: 524-9903.
Pagsanjan Rapids Hotel, General Taino Street, Pagsanjan, Manila Tel: 834-0403.
Villa Escudero Resort, San Pablo, Laguna, Manila Tel: 523-0392.

BAUANG LA UNION
Bali Hai Beach Resort, Bauang, La Union, Tel: 412-504.
Cabaqa Beach Resort, Bauang, La Union, Tel: 412-824.
Cresta Del Mar, Bauang, La Union, Tel: 413-297.

AGOO LA UNION
Agoo Playa Hotel, San Nicolas West, Agoo, Tel: 631-2861.
Burnham Hotel, 21, Calderon Street, Tel: 442-2331.

BAGUIO CITY
Club John Hay, Baguio City, Tel: 442-7902, Fax: 442-5782.
Mount Crest Hotel, Corner Urbano & Legarda Road, Tel: 442-3324.
Hotel Monticello, Maryheights, Kennon Road, Tel: 442-6566.
Venus Parkview Resort Hotel, Kisad Road, Tel: 442-5597.

Mountain Lodge, Leonard Wood Road, Tel: 442-4544.
Safari Lodge, 191, Leonard Wood Road, Tel: 442-2419.

BANAWE
Banawe Hotel and Youth Hostel, Ifugao, Tel: 588-191.

BONTOC
Happy Times, Bontoc, Mt Province.
Mount Data Lodge, Halsema Highway, Tel: 599-031.
Pines Kitchenette & Inn, Bontoc, Mt Province.

LAOAG
Fort Ilocandia Resort Hotel, Calayab, Laoag City, Tel: 221-166.
Playa Blanca Resort, Victoria, Currimao, Tel: 220-784.

BUDGET
Modern Hotel, Nolasco Street, Tel: 23-48.
Texicano Hotel, Rizal Street, Tel: 220-606.

BATANES
Lily's Lodge, Washington, Basco.

ZAMBALES
Subic International Hotel, Sta. Rita Road, Subic Bay Free Port Zone, Tel: 888-2288, Fax: 894-5549.

The Outlying Islands

PUERTO GALERA
Capt'n Gregg's, Sabang Beach, Puerta Galera.
Coco Beach Resort, Coco Beach, Puerto Galera, Manila Tel: 521-5260.
Terraces Garden Resort, Sabang Beach, Puerto Galera.

BUDGET
Apples Huts, Balete Beach, Puerto Galera.
Outrigger, Hondura Beach, Puerto Galera.

MAMBURAO
Mamburao Beach Resort, Mamburao, Manila Tel: 815-3454.

PALAWAN HOTELS
Badjao Hotel, 182 Rizal Avenue Extension, Puerto Princesa, Tel: 27-61.
Rafols Hotel, National Highway, Puerto Princesa, Tel: 357.

BUDGET
Abelardo's Pension, Demangga Street, Puerto Princesa, Tel: 20-68.
Yayen's Pension, Manalo Ext, Puerto Princesa, Tel: 22-61.

PALAWAN RESORTS
Club Paradise, Dimakya Island, Manila Tel: 832-3372.
El Nido Resort, Miniloc Island, Manila Tel: 818-2640.
El Nido Pangalusian Resort, Pangalusian Island.
Legaspi CityAl-Bay, Peqaranda Street, Tel: 22-18.
Kagayonan Beach Resort, Padang, Tel: 23-98.
La Trinidad, Rizal Street, Tel: 29-51.

BUDGET
Ritz Pension, Peqaranda Street, Tel: 26-70.
Xandra Hotel, Peqaranda Street, Tel: 40-88.

The Visayas

BACOLOD CITY
Bascon Hotel, Gonzaga Street, Tel: 231-41.
Sea Breeze Hotel, St Juan Street, Tel: 245-71.
Sugarland Hotel, Singcang, Tel: 224-62.

BUDGET
Best Inn, Bonifacio Street, Tel: 233-12.
Halili Inn, Locsin Street, Tel: 815-49.

CEBU CITY
Cebu Acropolis Hotel, V. Rama corner Singson streets, Guadalupe, Tel: 211-911, Fax: 212-305.
Cebu Midtown Hotel, Fuente Osmeqa, Cebu City, Tel: 219-711.
Cebu Plaza Hotel, Nivel Hills, Lahug, Tel: 311-231, Fax: 312-061.
Hallmark Hotel, Colon Street, Cebu City, Tel: 776-71, Fax: 537-33.
Hotel Esperanza, Manalili Street, Tel: 917-11, Fax: 537-33.
Hotel La Nivel, Lahug, Cebu City, Tel: 731-71, Fax: 314-597.
Hotel de Mercedes, Pelaez Street, Tel: 976-31, Fax: 213-880.
Magellan International, Gorordo Avenue, Lahug, Tel: 746-21, Fax: 216-417.
Montebello Villa International, Banilad, Tel: 313-861, Fax: 314-455.
Park Place Hotel, Fuente Osmeqa,

Cebu City, Tel: 211-131, Fax: 210-118.
Rajah Hotel, Fuente Osmeqa, Tel: 962-31.
Shangri-La's Mactan Island Resort, Punta Engano Road, P.O. Box 86, Lapu-Lapu City, Cebu, Tel: 310-2888.
Sky View, Corner Plaridel and Juan Luna streets, Luym Bldg., Tel: 730-51.
St Moritz Hotel, Gorordo Avenue, Lahug, Tel: 743-71, Fax: 312-485.
Sundowner Centrepoint Hotel, Juan Luna corner Plaridel streets, Cebu City, Tel: 211-831.

BUDGET
Tagalog Hotel, Sanciangko Street, Tel: 725-31.
Town & Country Hotel, Osmeqa Blvd., Tel: 781-90.

CEBU PROVINCE RESORTS
Alegre Beach Resort, Sogod, Cebu, Tel: 311-231, Fax: 214-345.
Argao Beach Club, Dalaguete, Cebu, Tel: 314-365, Fax: 314-365.
Badian Island Beach Hotel, Badian Island, Cebu, Tel: 613-06, Fax: 213-85.
Cebu Club Pacific, Sogod, Cebu, Tel: 791-47, Fax: 314-621.

BUDGET
Cora's Palm Court, Moalboal, Cebu.

RESORTS NEAR CEBU CITY
Coral Reef, Agus, Mactan Island, Cebu, Tel: 211-191, Fax: 211-192.
Costabella, Buyong, Mactan Island, Cebu, Tel: 210-828.
Hadsan Beach Resort, Buyong, Mactan Island, Tel: 726-79.
Kota Beach Resort, Bantayan Island, Cebu, Tel: 751-01.
Mary Cielo Beach, Mactan Island, Cebu, Tel: 212-232, Fax: 501-1268.
Maribago, Blue Water Bay, Mactan Island, Tel: 211-620, Fax: 310-437.
Sunshine Beach Club, Argao, Cebu, Tel: 948-03, Fax: 217-925.
Tambuli, Buyong, Mactan Island, Cebu, Tel: 211-543/522-23-01 (Manila), Fax: 530-97.

BOHOL
Bohol Beach Club, Bohol, Manila Tel: 522-2301, Fax: 522-2304.

BUDGET
Its Lodge, 27, Garcia Ave, Tagbilaran, Tel: 33-10.
Clifftop Hotel, Grupo Street, Tagbilaran, Tel: 31-62.

ILOILO

Amigo Terrace Hotel, Iznart-Delgado streets, Iloilo City, Tel: 748-11.
Del Rio Hotel, M.H. Del Pilar Street, Molo, Iloilo City, Tel: 755-85.
Isla Naburot, Iloilo, Tel: 761-12.
Sarabia Manor Hotel, Gen. Luna Street, Iloilo City, Tel: 727-31.
Sicogon Resort, Carles, Iloilo, Tel: 792-91.

BUDGET
Family Pension House, Gen. Luna Street, Iloilo City, Tel: 20-47.
Iloilo Lodging House, Aldeguer Street, Iloilo City, Tel: 723-84.

KALIBO
Glowmoon, S. Martelino Street, Kalibo, Tel: 31-93.

BORACAY
Boracay Beach & Yacht Club, Manila Tel: 819-0282.
Club Panoly, Manila Tel: 536-0682.
Friday's, Manila Tel: 521-2283.
Lorenzo's, Malay, Aklan, Manila Tel: 990-719.
Sand Castles, Manila Tel: 823-2725.

BUDGET
Tito's Place, White Beach.
Summer Place, White Beach.

LEYTE
Leyte Park Hotel, Palo, Tacloban City, Manila Tel: 924-5851.
MacArthur Park Beach Resort Hotel, Tacloban, Leyte, Manila Tel: 810-4741.

BUDGET
Primrose Hotel, Salazar cor Zamora Streets, Tacloban.
Manabo Lodge, Zamora Street, Tacloban, Tel: 37-27.

Mindanao

CAGAYAN DE ORO
Hotel Caprice, Gusa District, Tel: 48-80.
Pryce Plaza, Carmen Hill, Tel: 726-464.
VIP Hotel, Apolinar/Velez Street, Tel: 36-29.

BUDGET
Golden Star Inn, Borja Street, Tel: 40-79.
A & E Pension, Pacana Street, Tel: 46-52.

CAMIGUIN

Camiguin Seaside Resort, Agoho, Mambajao.
Caves Resort, Agoho, Mambajao.

DAPITAN
Dakak Beach Resort, Dapitan City, Zamboanga del Norte, Manila Tel: 721-0447.

DAVAO CITY
Apo View Hotel, J. Camus Street, Tel: 221-6430, Fax: 221-0748.
Davao Insular Intercontinental Inn, Lanang, Tel: 234-3050, Fax: 62-959.
Durian Hotel, JP Laurel Ave., Tel: 72-725.
Evergreen Hotel, Magsaysay Ave., Tel: 221-3860.
Hotel Maguindanao, C.M. Recto Ave., Tel: 221-2894.

BUDGET
D' Fabulous Venee's Hotel, MacArthur Highway, Matina, Tel: 78-934.
Meng Seng Hotel, San Pedro Street, Tel: 75-185.
Yncierto's Hotel, Digos, Davao del Sur, Tel: 23-57.
Al-jem's Inn, A. Pichon Street, Tel: 221-3061.
Aveflor Inn, CM Recto Ave., Tel: 78-512.
B.S. Inn, Monteverde corner Gempesaw streets, Tel: 221-3980.
Carpel's Emerald Inn, J. Camus Extension, Tel: 73-707.
Davao Fortune Inn, Magsaysay Ave., Tel: 76-703.
Kadayawan Inn, Palma Gil Street, Tel: 74-881.
Midland Inn, Vicente Compiund, Anda Street, Tel: 221-1775.
Park Square Inn, Sandawa Plaza, Quimpo Blvd., Tel: 297-2005.
Royal House, 34 CM Recto Ave., Tel: 221-8105.
Saroma Tourist Inn, Digos, Davao del Sur, Tel: 29-03.
Southern Tourist Inn, Villa Abrille Street, Tel: 74-875.
Sunview Inn, Lizalda St, Tel: 78-859.
The Manor Inn, A. Pichon Street, Tel: 221-5674.
Traders' Inn, Dela Cruz Street, Tel: 73-578.
Villa Margarita, JP Laurel Avenue, Tel: 221-5674.

ZAMBOANGA

Lantaka Hotel By The Sea, Valderrosa Street, Tel: 991-2033.
New Astoria Hotel, Mayor Jaldon Street, Tel: 20-75.
Zamboanga Hermosa Hotel, Mayor Jaldon Street, Tel: 20-71.

BUDGET
Fortune Inn, Claudio Street, Tel: 32-42.
Hotel Pasonanca, Claudio Street, Tel: 45-79.

BASILAN
Basilan Hotel, J.S. Alano Street.

JOLO
Helen's Lodge, Buyon Street.

TAWI TAWI
New Southern Hotel, Datu Halun Street, Bongao.

Eating Out
What To Eat

Nowhere else is the Philippines' long history of outside influences more evident than in its food, which is remarkably varied. Philippine cuisine, an intriguing blend of Malay, Spanish, and Chinese influences, is noted for the use of fruits, local spices and seafoods. Food, to the Filipino, is an integral part of local art and culture, and the result is a tribute to the Pinoy's ingenuity in concocting culinary treats from eastern and western ingredients.

Filipinos eat rice three times a day. It is a "must" to sample a Filipino breakfast of fried rice, *longaniza* (native sausage) and fish, which is normally salted and dried, accompanied by tomatoes and *patis* (fish sauce) on the side.

When ordering, it's best to watch the Filipinos. Even before the food arrives, sauce dishes are brought in and people automatically reach for the vinegar bottle with hot chili, or the soy sauce, which they mix with *kalamansi* (small lemons). Grilled items are good with crushed garlic, vinegar and chili. It's a good idea to start a meal with sinigang, a clear broth slightly soured with small nature fruit and prepared with bangus (milkfish) or shrimp.

Some typical Philippine dishes worth trying are tinola, which is made with chicken and pancit molo, dumplings of pork, chicken and mushrooms cooked in chicken or meat broth. Adobo is pork in small pieces, cooked for a long time in a light vinegar with other ingredients such as chicken, garlic and spices and then with rice.

A typical feast dish, lechon is suckling pig stuffed with tamarind leaves and roasted on lighted coals until the skin is crackling and the meat tender. It is generally served with liver sauce. Sinanglay, another festive dish, is fish or piquant crabs with hot pepper wrapped in leaves of Chinese cabbage, and then cooked in coconut milk.

Other Filipino favorites include lumpia a salad of heart-of-palm and small pieces of pork and shrimp wrapped in a crepe and served with garlic and soya sauce, and kare-kare, which is a rich mixture of oxtail, knuckles and tripe, stewed with vegetables in peanut sauce and served with bagoong, an anchovy based sauce.

Puddings are generally made with coconut rice or coconut milk. Among the most famous is bibingka, which consists of ground rice, sugar and coconut milk, baked in a clay oven and topped with fresh and salted duck eggs. Guinatan is a coco-pudding, served with lashings of coconut cream. Ice creams are made in several fruit flavors such as nangka (jackfruit), ube and mango, as well as the more usual vanilla, chocolate and strawberry.

Where To Eat

The following selection of non-hotel restaurants covers the wide range of cuisines of Manila restaurants. Those serving Filipino food are marked with an asterisk (*).

The Aristocrat*, 432 San Andres St., Malate, Manila, Tel: 521-8147.

Barrio Fiesta*, Cor. EDSA & Rochester Sts., Mandaluyong, Tel: 701-513.

Cafe Adriatico*, Cor. Adriatico and Remedios Sts., Malate, Manila, Tel: 521-6682 or 524-3779.

Cafe Ysabel, Gino's & Gine's Bisro*, 455 P. Guevarra St. Cor. C.M. Recto St., 1500 San Juan, Manila, Tel: 722-

0349 or 726-9326.

Gourmet's Cafe, Suite 504, Nat'l Life Bldg., Ayala Ave., Makati, Manila, Tel: 818-7661.

Guernica's, 1326 M.H. Del Pilar St., Ermita, Manila, Tel: 500-936 or 582-225.

Illustrado*, 744 Calla Real del Palacio, Intramuros, Manila, Tel: 527-3674.

Kamayan Sa Nayong Pilino*, Nayong Pilipino Complex, Pasay, Manila, Tel: 833-7674.

La Primavera Ristorante Italiano, Garden Square Bldg., Cor. Greenbelt Drive & Lagaspi Sts., Makati, Tel: 818-1945.

Le Souffle, 2F, Josephine's Bldg., Greenbelt, Makati, Tel: 812-3247.

Marco Polo, 867 EDSA corner Times St., Quezon, Tel: 928-2302.

Max's, Greenbelt Park, Ayala Center, Makati, Tel: 819-5156

Nandau*, Delton Center, Legaspi Street, Makati, Metro Manila, Tel: 816-0621 or 818-3388.

New Orleans, 2F La Tasca Bldg., Legaspi St., Ayala Center, Makati, Metro Manila, Tel: 817-2956.

Prince of Wales Pub & Restaurant, Basement, New Plaza Bldg., Ayala Center, Makati, Metro Manila, Tel: 815-4273 or 885-694.

Schwarzwalder German Restaurant, The Parkway Bldg., Makati Avenue, Ayala Center, Makati, Metro Manila, Tel: 865-179 or 875-220.

Sugi, Greenbelt Mall, Ayala Center, Makati, Tel: 812-8519.

Zamboanga, 1619 M. Adriatico St., Malate, Manila, Tel. 572-835 or 521-9836.

Hotel Restaurants

The Champagne Room, Manila Hotel, Rizal Park, Manila, Tel: 247-0011.

Cowrie Grill, Manila Hotel, Rizal Park, Manila, Tel: 247-0011.

Maynila, Manila Hotel, Rizal Park, Manila, Tel: 247-0011.

Old Manila, Manila Peninsula Hotel, Ayala Avenue Makati, Metro Manila, Tel: 844-2566.

Bahia Rooftop Restaurant, Hotel Intercontinental Manila, Ayala Ave., Makati, Metro Manila, Tel: 815-9711.

Prince Albert Rotisserie, Hotel Intercontinental Manila, Ayala Ave., Makati, Metro Manila, Tel: 815-9711.

Rotisserie, Holiday Inn Manila Pavilion, United Nations Ave., Manila, Tel: 522-2911.

The Tivoli Grill, Mandarin Oriental Hotel,

Makati Ave., Makati, Tel: 893-3601.

Tin Hau, Mandarin Oriental Hotel, Makati Ave., Makati, Tel: 893-3601.

Abelardo's, The Westin Philippine Plaza, Cultural Center Complex, Roxas Blvd., Manila, Tel: 832-0701.

Attractions

Country

The Philippines is renowned for its beaches. Choose from Boracay, Cebu, Puerto Galera, Camiguin, Bauang La Union, Sicogon, Batangas, Laoag and hundreds more.

If you tire of sun and sand, try heading for the hills of Baguio, and for the fabled rice terraces of Banawe, visiting Bontoc en route, but skip Sagada.

Visitors looking for something different might consider climbing Davao's Mt Apo, diving in Palawan, golfing in Batangas, walking on Camiguin, visiting the tribal people in Zamboanga and Sulu hopping around the islands.

Having "done" Manila, anyone with time to spare would do well to check out the following day trips: Corregidor, Tagaytay and Taal Volcano, Villa Escudero, Sarao Jeepney Factory, Las Piqas Bamboo Organ, Hidden Valley Springs, Pagsanjan Falls and Batangas Philippine Experience.

Culture

Museums

Manila is quite a city for the museum lover, with some 17 at the last count. Around the islands museums worth visiting include those of Villa Escudero, Corregidor, Vigan, Laoag, Bontoc, Baguio, Cebu, Davao and Zamboanga. Also considered as museums are the palatial former Marcos mansions: the Coconut Palace in Manila, the Bamboo House in Puerto Azul, Malacaqang ti Amianan in Barrio Suba Pady, Ilocos Norte, Canlubang House in Laguna and the Santo Niqo shrine plus Olot House in Leyte. To visit to these luxurious mini-palaces, contact the Coconut Palace, Manila, Tel: 832-0223.

Ayala Museum of Philippine History and Iconographic Archives, Makati Avenue, Makati, Metro Manila. 60-odd diorama windows portraying Philippine history; iconographic exhibits; and ship models of ancient vessels. Open Thursday–Sunday, 9am–6pm.

Casa Manila, General Luna Street, Intramuros, Manila. Open Tuesday–Sunday, 9am–noon; 1–6pm.

Lopez Memorial Museum, Chronicle Building, Meralco Avenue, Pasig, Metro Manila. Painting of two classical Philippine artists of 19th century, Felix Resurreccion Hidalgo and Juan Luna; extensive collection of excavated pottery from Calatagan, Batangas diggings. Open Monday–Friday, 8.30am–noon; 1–4pm.

Malacañang Palace, Malacañang, Manila. Open Monday and Tuesday, 1–3pm (guided tour for P200); Thursday–Friday, 9–11am; Saturday, 1–3pm.

Museo Ng Buhay Pilipino, (Museum of Philippine Life). Central Bank Security Printing Bluding. East Avenue, Quezon City, Metro Manila. House-museum display; showcasing the traditional lifestyle of lowland Christian Filipinos, in furnishings, tools, costumes and ambiance. Open Monday–Friday, 9am–4pm.

Museo Ng Kalinangang Pilipino, 3F Cultural Center of the Philippines, Roxas Boulevard, Manila. Potenciano Badillo ceramics, one of the world's largest grouping of export ceramics, Chinese, Annamese, Siamese; excavated beads and gold jewelry; Maranao and Maguindanao artifacts. Open daily, 9am–6pm.

Philippine Museum of Ethnology, Nayong Pilipino Complex, Ninoy Aquino Int'l Airport Road, Pasay. Comprehensive showcase of cultural artifacts of the Philippines' major ethnic minority groups. Open 9am–6pm.

National Museum of the Philippines, P. Burgos Street, Manila. Proto-historical collection of excavated pottery ware. Open Monday–Saturday, 8.30am–noon; 1– 5pm.

San Augustin Museum, San Agustin Monastery, General Luna Street, Intramuros, Manila. Open Monday–Sunday, 8am–noon; 1–5pm.

Art Galleries

Few visitors to Manila realize that one of the best collections of turn-of-the-century Philippine masters including Luna, Hidalgo, Guerrero and Flores can be found in the Lopez Memorial Museum, Chronical Bluding, Tektite Road, Pasig, Manila (Monday–Friday, 8.30am–noon; 1–4.30pm). For art lovers, other galleries worth visiting are:

Ateneo Art Gallery, Rizal Library Bluding, Ateneo de Manila University, Loyola Heights, Quezon City, Metro Manila. Permanent collection of selective works by Philippine contemporary artists. Open Monday–Friday, 8am–5pm; Saturday, 8am–noon.

Galeria De Las Islas, 744 Calle Real del Palacio, Intramuros, Manila. Open 9am–5pm.

Metropolitan Museum of the Philippines, Central Bank Complex, Roxas Boulevard, Manila. A variety of visiting exhibitions of classical and contemporary painting and prints from Europe and the Americas; slide shows and films almost daily. Open Tuesday–Saturday, 9am–6pm.

Concerts & Theaters

Plays, ballet and concerts are performed regularly at the Cultural Center of the Philippines. Other popular theaters include the Metropolitan Theater, Meralco Theater, Insular Life Auditorium, William J. Shaw Theater, and at the Shangri-La Plaza. Open air concerts are held in Puerta Real, Rizal Park and Paco Park on weekends. Experimental theater performances are at the University of the Philippines.

Dance & Ballet

Ballet Philippines is the country's foremost company, based at the Cultural Center of the Philippines. In cultural dance the Bayanihan Dance Company typically excels.

Cultural Center of the Philippines (CCP)

The sprawling Cultural Center of the Philippines on Roxas Boulevard houses several theaters, a museum, a library, restaurants, galleries and exhibition rooms. Built as the pride and joy of former first lady Imelda Marcos, the CCP was an attempt to give cultural life a boost, with the hope of presenting the arts Filipino style to the world stage. Regrettably the past cultural policy restricted free development of both the visual and performing arts. Today the focus of the center's cultural policy is to support free expression in the hope that the local arts will reach their apogie.

Cultural Center of the Philippines, Roxas Boulevard, Manila, Tel: 832-1125.

Movies

Moviegoing in the Philippines is as popular as ever. It is also one of the best bargains in entertainment, since tickets cost just P45. American films are most popular, particularly those with romance, action-adventure or science-fiction themes. The drawback is that foreign movies are screened at Manila cinemas somewhat later than their release in the United States and they are rarely shown at the times scheduled outside the theater.

Tagalog cinema is big in the Philippines; the industry almost rivals that of Bombay, but many of the films are of doubtful artistic merit. The movie business is dramatized in the entertainment and gossip columns of the local press to the extent that many Filipino youngsters dream of becoming film star.

Nightlife

Manila by night is a swinging town with its own distinctive color, flavor and style. Manileños love their nightlife and it is really after dark that the capital rouses itself, stirs and sparkles. Manila, in fact, can be quite a place for a holiday, especially if you sleep during the day and save your energy for the nightlife. There is entertainment to suit every taste ranging from discos, jazz clubs, theaters, movies to a wide variety of bars and restaurants.

At sunset the cocktail shakers of the big hotels echo like the angelus. Later crowds are drawn to the elegant supper clubs and throbbing discos of the 5-star establishments. Along nightclub row at the Southern end of Roxas Boulevard, dozens of night spots vie with each other with patronage. However, the new hot-spot in town is the strip in Makati.

As a guide to dress, the Philippines has not succumbed entirely to casual dress for evening wear, so its advisable to check beforehand when planning a night on some of the more elegant tiles.

Bars & Discos

70's Bistro, 46 Anonas St., Quezon, Manila, Tel: 922-0492.

RJ Bistro, Olympia Towers, Makati Ave., Makati, Metro Manila, Tel: 818-8484. One of Makati's best known live music spots.

Chatterbox, 41 West Ave., Quezon, Manila, Tel: 928-7539.

Club Dredd, Km. 19 EDSA, Quezon, Manila, Tel: 912-8464.

Endangered Species Cafe Bar, 1834 M.H. del Pilar, Ermita, Manila, Tel: 524-0167.

Euphoria, Hotel Intercontinental Manila, Ayala Ave., Makati, Metro Manila, Tel: 815-9711. This ranks as one of the city's top discos.

Freedom Bar Cafe, 2F Anonas Commercial Complex, Anonas St., Project 3, Quezon, Manila, Tel: 433-3884.

Giraffe, 6750 Ayala Ave., Makati, Tel: 815-3232.

Hard Rock Cafe, Quad 3, Ayala Center, Makati. Good food, drinks and rock-and-roll music.

Hobbit House, 1801 A. Mabini, Ermita, Manila, Tel: 521-7604. A folk music house run by dwarfs. Folk singer Freddy Aguilar performs here on a regular basis.

Jazzbox, 1903 M. Adriatico St., Malate, Manila, Tel: 524-5526.

Jazz Rythms, 126 Jupiter St., Makati, Tel: 896-5232.

Jools, 5043 P. Burgos Street, Makati, Metro Manila, Tel: 897-9060. Nightly variety show at 9.30pm. Tastefully done.

Kampo, West Ave., Quezon, Manila, Tel: 964-207.

Mayrics, 1320 Espana Ave., Manila, Tel: 732-3021.

Moulin Rouge, U.N. Ave., Manila. Manila's answer to the Paris establishment of the same name. Several shows nightly from 8.30pm onwards with disco dancing in between.

Music Museum, Greenhills Shopping Center, San Juan, Metro Manila, Tel: 721-6726. As the name suggests, this is the place for music fans to head to in Asia's music capital.

Strumm's, Greenbelt, Makati Ave., Makati, Tel: 812-2345.

Studebaker's, Quad 3, Ayala Center, Makati, Tel: 811-4041. A fast-rising music bar, wine bar and a discotheque all rolled into one.

Ten Years After, 1786 M. Adriatico Street, Malate, Manila, Tel: 523-4975.

Zu, Shangri-la Hotel Manila, Ayala corner Makati Ave., Makati, Tel: 813-8888. A one-stop entertainment center where disco and live band music give life to an African setting.

Gambling

High rollers can feed the slot machines or "hungry tigers" as they are locally known at Manila's three casinos, located at the Holiday Inn, the Heritage Hotel and the Hotel Sofitel Grand Boulevard. Also offered are baccarat, black jack, craps and roulette as well as the oriental game of hi-lo. Around the archipelago casinos are found in Angeles, Olongapo, Baguio, Subic, Cebu, Bacolod and Davao. Semi-formal dress code applies.

Festivals

Fiestas

January

January 1: Nationwide; New Year's Day, a national holiday.

January 6: Santa Cruz and Gasan in Marinduque; Three Kings' Pageant.

January 9: Quiapo, Metro Manila; Feast of the Black Nazarene.

Third weekend: Cebu City and in Tondo, Manila; Feast of the Holy Child (*Fiesta de Santo Nino*).

2nd weekend: Kalibo, Aklan; Ati-Atihan (landing of 10 Bornean datus).

variable: Bontoc, Mt Province; Appey (Harvest Festival).

variable: San Jose, Antique; Binirayan (landing of 10 Bornean datus).

variable: Bontoc, Mt Province; *Manerway* (rain dance festival).

3rd Weekend: Cebu City; Sto. Niqo de Cebu (week-long festival).

4th weekend: Dinagyang restioal, Iloits.

February

February 17: Laguna de Bay; *Armadahan* Regatta.

February 2: Jaro, Iloilo; Feast of Our Lady of Candelaria.

February 11: Kanlaon, Quezon City; Feast of Our Lady of the Rosary.

February 22–25: Metro Manila; People Power Anniversary/*Fiesta sa EDSA*.

variable: Muslim communities and provinces; *Hari Raya Hadji*.

variable: Chinatown, Metro Manila; Chinese New Year.

February 24–25: Zamboanga; Bale Zamboanga Festival (cultural shows).

March

March 10–16: Davao City; *Araw ng Dabaw* (6 days of gaiety to celebrate Davao's founding).

variable: Nationwide; Holy Week.

Lenten Week: Boac, Marinduque; *Moriones* Festival.

variable: Baguio City; Baguio Summer Festival.

March 25: Ilog, Negros Occidental; Sinulog Festival (tribal dance festival).

April

April 9: Nationwide; Bataan Day (commemorates "Death March" and fall of Bataan).

variable: Manila; Jeepney King Festival.

variable: Pakil, Laguna; Feast of *Virgen de Turumba* (followers leap, fall and revel in this religious procession).

May

May 1: Nationwide; Labor Day.

May 14–15: Pulilan, Bulacan; Carabao Festival.

May 15: Sariaya, Quezon, Lucban; Feast of San Isidro Labrador (*Pahiyas*).

May 15–17: Obando, Bulacan; Obando Festival (fertility rites).

May 1–31: various places; *Santacruzan* (procession of St Helena Constantinople).

May 1–31: various places; *Flores de Mayo* (flower processions).

May 1–31: Antipolo, Rizal; Pilgrimage to the Shrine of Our Lady of Peace and Good Voyage.

variable: San Dionisio, Paraqaque, Metro Manila; *Moro-moros* (plays or comedies on based on traditional story-lines, mainly battles between Christians and Moors).

variable: Manila; *La Bella Filipina*, Carnival Queen Festival.

May 27–June 2: Makati, Metro Manila; Makati, Makati Festival.

June

June 12: Nationwide; Philippine Independence Day.
June 24: San Juan, Metro Manila; San *Juan Bautista* (water-dousing festival).
June 24: Manila; *Araw ng Maynila*.
June 24: Balayan, Batangas; *Parada ng Lechon*.
June 27: Baclaran, Metro Manila; Our Lady of Perpetual Help.
June 29: Apalit, Pampanga; Fluvial Parade in honor of St Peter.
variable: Muslim communities and provinces; *Maolod En Nabi* (birthday of Mohammed).
June 28–30: Tacloban, Leyte; Tacloban Festival.
Last Friday in June: Luban, Quezon; Feast of the Sacred Heart (*Gigantes* Festival).

July

July 1–30: Mt Provinces; Harvest Festival.
July 4: Nationwide; Fil-American Friendship Day.
First Sunday in July: Bocaue, Bulacan: Fluvial Procession (*Pagoda sa Wawa*).
July 29: Pateros, Metro Manila; Fluvial Festival for St Martha.
July 30: Butuan, Agusan del Norte; Santa Ana Kahimonan Abayan Festival.

August

August 19: Lucban, Quezon; Lucban Town Fiesta (another *gigantes* festival).
variable: Bontoc, Mt Province; Lesles Festival (planting rites).
variable: Bontoc, Mt Province; *Fagfagto* Festival (planting rites).
variable: Bayombong, Nueva Vizcaya; *Sumbali* (Aeta Festival)
August 18–31: Davao City; *Kadayawan sa Dabaw* (orchid, food, fruit and tribal festival).
August 27–28: Cagayan de Oro; *Cagayan de Oro Fiesta*.
August 28–September 3: Baguio City; Baguio Foundation Day.

September

variable: Paraqaque, Metro Manila; *Sunduan* (procession of the town's marriageable lads and ladies).
Third Saturday in September: Naga City, Camarines Sur; *Peqafrancia* Festival (fluvial procession).
September 29: Iligan, Lanao del Norte; Seqor San Miguel.

variable: Quezon City; *La Naval*, Quezon City Foundation Day.

October

October 7–8: Roxas City, Capiz; Halaran Festival.
October 7–12: Zamboanga City; Zamboanga Hermosa.
October 19: Pakil, Laguna; *Turumba* (fertility rites dedicated to Mary).
October 21–22: Bacolod City; *Masskara* (festival of Smiling Masks).
Last Sunday in October: Metro Manila; Feast of Christ the King (procession).
October 26–31: Mambajao, Camiguin; *Lanzones* Festival.
October 28–31: Olongapo City; *Oktoberfest*.

November

November 1: Nationwide; All Saints' Day (Catholic feast).
November 2: Nationwide; All Souls' Day.
variable: Muslim communities and provinces; *Hari Raya Puasa*.
November 30: Zambales; *Binabayani*.

December

December 1–14: Manila; *Fiesta Intramuros*.
December 16: Catholic towns and cities; Start of *Misa de Gallo* (nine dawn masses preparatory to the Christmas celebration).
December 16–25: Nationwide; *Simbang Gabi* (Midnight Mass).
December 23–24: San Fernando, Pampanga; Lantern Festival.
Last Sunday in December: Ermita, Manila; *Bota de Flores* (procession for Our Lady of the Way).

Shopping

What To Buy

The Philippines is an old Asian shopping emporium, dating back to the days when its coastal towns sold pearls, beeswax and tortoise shells to trading vessels all the way from Arabia. Today, the emphasis is on handicraft, woodcarving and the gifts of the sea. Almost all major cities are worth a shopping trip, but even a limited schedule that takes you to Manila, Cebu, Baguio and Zamboanga yields sufficient reward.

Basketry

Philippine baskets are now found in many fashion capitals of the world, thanks to enterprising Pinoys who have at last seen their export potential after years of having taking them for granted. With all of their varying regional designs and recent streamlining, Philippine baskets are both the scholar's and the plain old shopper's delight. Made out of a range of natural fibers bamboo, rattan, nipa, various palms these baskets come in a whole range of sizes and purposes, both functional and decorative.

They are everywhere in the tourist shops but a special joy accompanies seeing them in bazaar-like display under the Quiapo Bridge, in the heart of Metro Manila. The Baguio market up in the mountain province is also worth a visit, because it is where the antique designs of the mountain province converge with baskets from all over the Philippines, from Bicol through the Visayas and Mindanao.

Note also that there is a special line of baskets that have lately caused collection fever among the more knowledgeable Philippine-watchers. These are the smoked fish traps and locust baskets, as well as the lunch containers bought from the huts of Northern Luzon, where they are considered family heirlooms. So popular are these antique baskets that a line of endeavor has sprung up in the north "cooking" new baskets woven in the old design to look as though they have stood beside a smokey Igorot hearth for decades.

Mats

First cousin to the baskets, Philippine mats are fascinating bits of local color adapted for lining the walls of hotels. They range from the natural-colored pandan mats of most of Luzon to the playfully designed ones of Leyte and Samar in the Visayas and the dramatic geometries of Basilan and Sulu in Mindanao. What you find in Manila can be severely limited, with the exception of the Quiapo Bridge market, but finding yourself in Cebu, Davao or Zamboanga is the perfect opportunity to stock up on these inexpensive bits of folk art.

Handicrafts

Abaca hats, placemats, coasters, bamboo trays, shell windchimes, ceramic pots and gewgaws are ubiquitous in the tourist shops around the airport, Makati commercial center and the Ermita tourist belt. The macrami fever is also in full blush in these places, in shirts, blouses, bags and dresses, planters and wall hangings.

Shoes & Bags

The former First Lady, Imelda Marcos, put shoes on the map. Marikina, Rizal, is the traditional bag-and-shoe capital of the country, churning out footwear and matching bags with impeccable fashion consciousness. Shoes in the Philippines are a better buy than any other place in the world if what you want is to keep up with styles in the least expensive way. If you're staying longer, it might be worth your while to order custom-made shoes.

Embroidery

Very few guests, in the country for the first time, can resist the attractions of Philippine embroidery. The barong tagalog is now internationally famous and has many versions from the thou-

sand-peso Pierre Cardin type to the humbler *polo barongs* (short-sleeved) much beloved by casual tourists. Depending on your tastes, you can choose the translucent pineapple fiber, *piqa*, for your material with the finest hand-embroidery, or else the less expensive ramie with machine-embroidery (though you sometimes can hardly tell). Go to the better known houses to shop.

There is no lack of embroidered clothes for women, either the barong dress shaped like the *barong tagalog* but longer, the embroidered kaftans and jelabas with matching scarves, bags and handkerchiefs.

Jewelry

The most typically Philippine lines are shell and silver jewelry. Mother-of-pearl is perhaps the most popular, although coral and tortoise shell are also coming into their own.

Note: Visitors are strongly urged not to buy items made from coral and tortoise shells, however. The coral reefs of the Philippines are rapidly becoming damaged irreversibly and purchasing these items simply encourages further destruction of both these species (coral is a living thing) and the surrounding habitats.

The best silver jewelry is to be found in Baguio, where the guild-like training from St Louis University has today engendered fine craftmanship.

You can also find many examples of wood and vine jewelry in the specialty shops of Ermita and Makati, as well as beadwork from the tribes, notably the necklaces, earrings and ornamental hair pieces of the T'boli, the Mangyan and the Igorot tribes.

Shells

The collector is invariably fascinated with Philippine shell shops. The golden cowrie, abundant in the southern seas, can be found in the middle of the Ermita tourist belt.

Note: As with coral, the trade in shells results in considerable damage to coral reef ecosystems.

Furniture

Wicker and rattan has come a long way in the country where a sense of the contemporary is combined with tradition. It is also light enough to ship without spending large amounts of money.

Antiques

Since the country was right on the Chinese trade route, there are a number of porcelain finds in the shops of Manila. However, know what you're buying. There is some piquant charm to be had in roadside antique stalls in the province of Laguna.

There are also a number of interesting santos in the antique shops of Ermita and Makati, as well as smaller shops in the older towns of the country, such as Vigan in Ilocos Sur.

Brassware

The first smiths of the Philippines are recorded in Mindanao. To this day, they continue to manufacture gongs, jewel boxes, betel nut boxes, brass beds and cannon replicas. They're all over the tourist belt but if someone tries to sell you an 'antique', check it out first with a knowledgeable shopping guide. There are also ceremonial canopies embroidered and sequined to celebrate royal Muslim weddings and feasts in these shops. They make lovely buys.

Woodcarving

Giant hardwood carvings of the Igorot tribe were among the first items of Filipiniana brought home by the Americans. What they did not see were other more fascinating things, like the rice granary god carvings and the animal totems from Palawan that can now be found in the Ermita tourist belt.

Shopping malls abound in Metro Manila. There is the **Ayala Town Center** in Alabang adjacent to the **SM South Mall**. In Makati, there is the **Ayala Center**, where famous department stores such as Shoemart, Rustan's and Landmark are housed. In Mandaluyong, there is the **SM Megamall** right along edsa and the **Shangri-la Plaza**. A few minutes away to the north is the **Robinson's Galleria** at the right portion of Ortigas Avenue and the **Greenhills Shopping Center**. Further down north of edsa is **Araneta Shopping Complex** in Cubao and the **SM North Mall**. Shopping hours are 10am–8pm in general.

Sports

Golf

For many visitors to the Philippines, golf is a big attraction, as the country has some of the finest courses in the world including several championship courses. Teeing off amid lush tropical vegetation and water-laced inland resorts gives any golfer enjoyment of the game. Also, because of the climate, golf is an ideal year-round sport.

The Club Intramuros, operated by the Dept. of Tourism, winds around the stone walls of the old Spanish fort in central Manila. Its 18 holes are open to the public daily.

To date there are more than 60 golf courses in the archipelago. Most are in Luzon, although there are some fine courses in the large cities of the Visayas and Mindanao. From its humble beginnings of a few thousand golfers in the 1920s, Philippine golf has become an increasingly popular sport with the advent of international golf tournaments and the development of well-appointed country clubs.

Green fees vary from link to link and are often slightly higher on weekends. Caddies, carts, golf clubs and shoes are available for hire hourly.

Diving

The archipelago is a diver's paradise. In general the islands offer steep drop-offs, huge coral heads, large and small inlets, warm waters and fairly easy to obtain diving gear. Underwater photographers will have a heyday among the multicolored feather star, colorful coral gardens, clouds of tropical aquarium fish and schools of pelagic jacks.

Submarine cliff *aficionados* can experience the pulse-pounding thrill of swimming with schools of 30-pound garoupas, napoleon wrass and snappers, or witness the sinuous grace of a shark and the capacity of a 5-foot barracuda. The best diving season in the Philippines is March through early June. During this period, seas all around are calm, rainfall low and waters are crystal clear.

On the island of Luzon, the main dive area is Batangas, two hours' drive south of Manila. The most popular dive site is Sombrero Marine Park, a hat-shaped island surrounded by a fringe reef: black coral, jacks, snappers, turtles, rays, shells, gorgonians, soft corals are all here. Diving is shallow along the top rim, and a 30-meter (90 ft) drop-off to the west offers more extensive deep-diving thrills.

The Cathedral, a giant rock formation looking like a roofless underwater amphitheater, has been seeded with corals and hand-fed fish. A spectacular subject for photographers are the shoals of fish awaiting their supper. For a change of pace, there is diving off Bonete Island, Lipgo, Mainit Point, Layag-Layag, Culebra Island or Shark Reef. Top dive resorts in the area include Punta Baluarte, Maya Maya, Anilao and Aqua Tropical.

Apo Reef in Mindoro Strait is one of the country's best-known dive sites. Divers tackling this 34 sq. kilometers (13 sq. mi) atoll-like reef can charter live-aboard dive boats, and find enough of underwater interest to last at least 10 days.

The jumping-off point for Apo Island is San Jose, a 30-minute flight from Manila. From the reef drop-off, a sheer wall plunges to 50 meters (150 ft). The walls, covered with corals, are the breeding ground of tuna, barracuda, manta rays and marine turtles. Shark's Ridge to the north of Apo Reef, which is still largely unexplored, offers some spectacular drop-off diving. Mantas and black-and white-tip sharks are a common sight. And nearby Hunter Island is a sea snake rookery.

Puerto Galera in Mindoro Oriental is blessed with some of the most rewarding diving. A lot of the dive sites have a moderate-to-strong current, encouraging tremendous coral growth but requiring careful planning and experienced guides. Bottom composition is rock, sand and coral. At Verde Island, divers can find a Spanish galleon that ran aground in 1620 lying offshore in 3 meters (10 ft) of water. Plates, cups and cannonballs recovered by local divers are on display in local dive shops.

In the Visayas' Balicasag Island, a round and flat islet surrounded by submarine cliffs is inhabited by reef and pelagic fishes. It's Bohol's best-known dive site. The north side features exceptional wall diving, with drop-offs seeming to fall to infinity and a visibility of 30 meters (100 ft).

A guide is needed to locate the best underwater caves off Cabilao Island in Bohol Strait. Near the northwestern tip, the drop-off falls to a sand ledge with corals growing on it at 30 meters, from which the drop-off plunges vertically into the darkness many hundreds of feet down. Schools of jacks and walls of butterfly fish feed in the strong currents. Cabilao and other dives around Bohol are served by Cebu's Argao resort, and by Bohol Beach Club and Cie Garden resort on Bohol Island.

Six World War II wrecks lying off Coron Bay are the star attraction of northern Palawan's Calamianes Island. The wrecks are part of the fleet of supply ships for Admiral Kurita of the Japanese navy. During the 1944 battle off Leyte Gulf, these vessels were ambushed and torpedoed by American carrier aircraft.

Calamianes Island is for dedicated enthusiasts. It does not offer the luxury and amenities of Cebu or Batangas. Divers may have to rough it sleeping on the beach, rationing water and bringing tanks and compressors. Local boatmen can tell visitors where to fish, the direction and time of the tides, and warn if there is a 8-meter (25-ft) white shark lurking in the depths. Calamianes Island is accessible by hired dive or other boats from San Jose, Mindoro.

Climbing

MOUNT APO

From the depths of the island of Mindanao soars Mount Apo – a mountain surrounded by mystery and legend. Bagobo tribes people living on its slopes believe that it had its beginning in the rain forest around Lake Venato. The Bagobo are practicing Christians or Muslims, but they quietly respect the forest spirits that inhabit and protect the sanctity of Mount Apo.

Today, Mount Apo National Park is a wide tract of virgin tropical rain forest, boiling mineral springs, sulfur vents and waterfalls. At 2,956 meters

(9,698 ft), it is the Philippines' highest peak. Now classified as a dormant volcano, it had only one recorded eruption, in 1640, yet it still smolders. Geothermal activity presents occasional tremors and releases sulfurous gases and steam into the air.

Mt Apo is easily accessible from Davao City, with well-marked trails to follow. Porters can prove to be indispensable not only to ease the weight off climbers' shoulders, but, with their knowledge of wilderness survival, can also ensure safety.

The journey begins with an early morning bus ride from Davao City to the North Cotabato town of Kidapawan, where climbers should register with the municipality. A jeepney ride follows to Barangay Ilomavis, where porters can be hired. The first stop is Blue Lake, known locally as Lake Agko. Surrounded by a lush jungle of tree ferns, bananas and bushes, it appears to leap out of the underbrush. A large lake of turquoise-blue water that lives up to its name, Agko steams hot with a smell of sulfur in the air.

A strong hiker can bypass Blue Lake to reach a campsite 2.5 hours away along the Marbel River. This entails going over and along two ridges and walking down slippery, almost vertical footpaths. Camp is made in a natural clearing next to the foot of the mountain at 1,800 meters (5,900 ft) above sea level.

Midway at the 2,100 meter (6,900 ft) level lies a hot spring and twin waterfalls. Another two hours' trek leads to Lake Venado. The lake is shallow and rain-fed, its clear waters mirroring the peaks of Mount Apo. Cool and quiet, it is a good spot for camping before the final ascent. The altitude here is 2,400 meters (7,870 ft).

The trail to the summit is much steeper and trickier, but it takes only three hours to scale the final 550 meters (1,800 ft). A forest of stunted trees encircles this side of the slope, marking the edge of the treeline. Leaving this behind, the peak appears suddenly stretching up into the sky. From the top, look into the crater of sulfur vents spewing fumes into the air.

MOUNT MAYON

Since a Spanish priest first climbed to the crater of Mt. Mayon in 1852, many have made the climb and a few have died in the attempt. Mayon is not a difficult mountain to climb – no particular expertise is required – but towards the top, it is perilously steep over loose, crumbling stones and volcanic ash.

Climbing takes a day and a half to the top, at 2,462 meters (8,077 ft) above sea level, then half a day back down to Legazpi. The first stage is a gradual climb along foot trails through dense vegetation to a steep bed of solid lava, which leads to the overnight camp. Early the next morning, you set out on the hardest, most tiring part to the top. The climb can be made from either side of the volcano – the northern route from the Mayon Resthouse starts at a higher altitude, but getting from Legazpi to the resthouse and back after the climb is difficult unless a car is waiting. The southern route starts much closer to sea level, but the starting point is easily reached from Legazpi.

The rewards for all this effort? Well, the feeling of conquering the world's most perfect volcano cone may be part of it, but it's the other-worldly view that wins. Nothing impinges on the sight line, since the slopes fall away in one continuous, graceful sweep, right down to the sea. The impression of sheer height is simply stunning.

If time or energy (or plain good sense) precludes you from actually climbing to Mayon's top, one of the closest approaches can be made at the Mayon Resthouse on the north slope. From Tabaco, the road skirts the edge of Mayon for 20 km (12 mi) before a sign marks the small access road to the resthouse. The road winds uphill past abaca plantations. The resthouse stands about 800 meters (2,625 ft), and Mayon towers so close above it that it seems impossible to think you are less than a third of the way to the summit.

The views of the brooding, lava-covered cone, as well as the sweep of mountains and volcanoes to the north, are worth even a short trip up. From the west, you can see several of the peaks of the other volcanoes forming the rigid backbone of this volatile, fertile region – Iriga, Isarog and Malinao sloping down to the ocean, with the town of Tiwi at its feet.

Horse Racing

Horse racing is generally held on Tuesdays, Wednesdays, Saturdays and Sundays at San Lazaro Hippodrome and Santa Ana Race Track. Betting on horses is a big-time operation. Major races include the Gran Copa, National Grand Derby, the Founder's Cup and the Presidential Cup.

Language

General

Pilipino and English are the national languages. Much of Pilipino is derived from Tagalog, the language spoken in Manila and nearby provinces. Other major languages are Ilocano and Pangasinan, spoken in Northern Luzon; Waray in Samar and Leyte; Cebuano in Cebu, Bohol, Negros Oriental and most of Christian Mindanao in the Lanao area; Maguindanao in Cotobato and Tausug in the Sulu and Tawi-Tawi group. (All languages and dialects spoken in the Philippines belong to the Malayo-Polynesian family.)

English is widely spoken and Spanish is still used by a small minority. Listed below are some basic and useful Filipino (Tagalog) expressions.

Numbers

One/*isa*
Two/*dalawa*
Three/*tatlo*
Four/*apat*
Five/*lima*
Six/*anim*
Seven/*pito*
Eight/*walo*
Nine/*siyam*
Ten/*sampu*
Eleven/*labing-isa*
Twelve/*labing dalawa*
Thirteen/*labing-tatlo*
Nineteen/*labing-siyam*
Twenty/*dalawampu*
Twenty-one/*dalawampu't isa*
Twenty-two/*dalawampu't dalawa*

Twenty-nine/*dalawampu't siyam*
Thirty/*tatlumpu*
Thirty-one/*tatlumpu't isa*
Forty/*apatnapu*
Forty-one/*apatnapu't isa*
Fifty/*limampu*
One hundred/*isang daan*
One hundred and one /*isang daan at isa*
Four hundred/*apat na raan*
Five hundred/*limang daan*
Six hundred/*anim na raan*
Seven hundred/*pitong daan*
Eight hundred/*walong daan*
Nine hundred/*siyam na raan*
One thousand/*isang libo*
Ten thousand/*sampung libo*

Days of the Week

Sunday/*Linggo*
Monday/*Lunes*
Tuesday/*Martes*
Wednesday/*Miyerkoles*
Thursday/*Huwebes*
Friday/*Biyernes*
Saturday/*Sabado*
yesterday/*kahapon*
today/*ngayon*
tomorrow/*bukas*
everyday/*araw araw*
some day/*balang araw*
anytime/*maski kailan*
when?/*kailan?*
now/*ngayon*

Greetings & Civilities

How are you?/*kumusta po sila?*
Good morning./*magandang umaga po.*
Good afternoon./*magandang hapon po.*
Good evening./*magandang gabi po.*
Good-bye./*paalam na po.*
Please come in./*tuloy po kayo.*
Please sit down./*maupo ho kayo.*
I'm well, thank you./*mabuti po naman.*
Thank you./*salamat.*
Please drive slowly./*dahan-dahan lang po.*
May I take a photo?/*maari po bakayong kunan ng retrato?*
I cannot speak Tagalog./*hindi po ako nagsasalita ng Tagalog.*
What do you call this in Tagalog?/*ano pong tawag dito sa Tagalog?*
Where do you live?/*saan po kayo nakatira?*
no/*hindi po.*
yes/*opo.*

Directions & Travel

where/*saan*
left/*kaliwa*
right/*kanan*
straight/*derecho*
slow down/*dahan-dahan*
stop here/*dito lang*
drive/*maneho*
be careful/*konting ingat lang*
fast/*bilis*
What town is this?/*Anong bayan ito?*
How many kilometres to...?/*Ilang kilometro hanggang...?*
Wait a few minutes/*Hintay lang po sandali.*
I want to go to.../*Gusto kong pumuntasa...*
entrance/*pasukan*
exit/*labasan*
bus station/*istasyon ng bus*
railway station/*istasyon ng tren*
airport/*airport*
gas station/*istasyon ng gas*
hotel/*otel*
police station/*istasyon ng pulis*
embassy/*embasi*
taxi/*taksi*
motorized pedicab/*traysikel*
street/*kalye*
village/*barrio*
town/*bayan*
city/*lungsod or syudad*
island/*isla*
beach/*beach*
mountain/*bundok*

Ordering & Bargaining

Do you have...?/*Meron ba kayong...?*
I want.../*Gusto ko ng...*
I want more.../*Gusto ko pa ng...*
How much is this?/*Magkano ito?*
How much per meter?/*Magkanong metro?*
I want to buy four meters./*Apat na metro nga po.*
How much of a discount?/*Magkanong tawad?*
Do you have something cheaper?/*Meron bang mas mura?*
Do you have a smaller size?/*Meron bang mas malliit?*
O.K. wrap it up./*Pakibalot nga.*
Bill, please./*Ang bill nga.*

Other Useful Phrases

enough/*tama na*
a lot/*marami*
too much/*masyadong marami*
who/*sino*
what/*ano*
when/*kailan*
where/*saan*
how old?/*gano katanda?*
yes, right/*oo, tama*

no, not right/*hindi, hindi tama*
well, comfortable/*mabuti*
not well, sick/*may sakit*
cold weather/*malamig*
cold temperature/*malamig*
hot/*mainit*
water/*tubig*
delicious/*masarap*
sweet/*matamis*
sour/*maasim*
hungry/*nagugutom*
thirsty/*nauuhaw*
sleepy/*inaantok*
old (age)/*matanda*
young/*bata*
new/*bago*
old/*luma*
big/*malaki*
small/*maliit*
to like/*magustuhan*

Further Reading

General

Adventures of a Frenchman in the Philippines, by Paul P. de la Gironiere. Good local color from a French doctor who settled in Manila and subsequently, the fringes of Laguna Lake in the 1800s.

Adventures in Rizaliana, by Paz Policarpio Mendez. A good cross-section of a mountain of Rizal lore.

Almanac for Manileños, by Nick Joaquin. A non-fiction memory trip touching on city lore, lives of saints, the Hispanic past.

The Culinary Culture of the Philippines, by Gilda Cordero Fernando. Cuisine as culture and history is the interesting thesis of this well-written, well-illustrated hardbound volume.

Ermita: The First Nine. Bound volume of nine of the 10 issues of a short-lived "underground" paper put out from Ermita, Manila's bohemian enclave, four years after Martial Law.

Dialogue for Development. Edited by S.J. Francisco Demetrio. A good collection of research papers on the subject of Filipino folklore.

Faces of Manila, by Marilies Von Brevern. Oral history of 30 authentic Filipino life stories.

Fiesta, by Alfredo Roces. Another fine coffee-table book with sparkling text and photos.

Filipino Heritage Volumes I-X. A 10-volume encyclopedia with full-color illustrations and many entertaining tidbits on history and culture.

German Travelers on the Cordillera; by Semper *et al*; *Travel Accounts of the Islands*; by Pires *et al*; *Travel Accounts of the Islands*, by Goncharov *et al*. Part of the series of the Filipiniana Book Guild series dedicated to rescuing forgotten manuscripts of observers (mostly European) of the Philippine scene before and during the Spaniards.

History on the Cordillera and Discovery of the Igorot and Hollow Ships on a Wine-Dark Sea, by William Henry Scott. This scholar-missionary distinguished himself in Philippine scholarship with his thoroughness, elegance and sympathy for the peoples of the Philippine north.

Manila Trade Pottery Seminar Introductory Notes, by Abaya and Locsin Addis. A set of nine pamphlets with good advise on starting a collection Filipino antique jars.

Noli Me Tangere and *El Filibusterismo*, by Jose Rizal. The two novels, written in the Victorian mould of the time, led to the execution by the Spanish authorities of the country's greatest hero.

A Past Revisited – The Continuing Past, by Renato Constantino. A ranging commentary on Philippine history by a "nationalist" thinker.

The Philippines, by Onofre D. Corpuz. A political scientist's balanced analysis of the forces which have a bearing on Philippine history.

A Question of Heroes, by Nick Joaquin. Essays on selected Philippine heroes written with the casual erudition of National Artist Joaquin.

A Question of Identity, by Carmen G. Nakpil. A tongue-in-cheek history by one of the Philippines' most formidable writers.

Readings in Philippine History, by Horacio S.J. de la Costa. Far and away the best intuitive guide to Philippine history for the browsers who are weary of formal histories.

The Rise and Fall of Imelda Marcos, by Carmen Navarro Pedrosa.

A Short History of the Philippines, by Teodoro Agoncillo. This pocketbook is a charming, if at times slightly too personal, account of Filipino history.

Spain in the Philippines, by Nicholas S.J. Cushner. A very readable account of the circumstances and historical ambience of Spain's adventure in the Philippines.

The Streets of Manila, by Luning B. Ira and Isagani R. Medina. A handsome volume on the origins of the place-names as well as the lore of the avenues, streets and "callejons" of a very old City.

T'boli Art, by Gabriel S. Casal, o.s.b. An analysis of the art of the T'boli, a minority tribe of amazing grace living in the hills of Cotabato in Mindanao.

Treasure of a Minority, by Antoon Pastma. Poems by the Hanunoo Mangyan, an ethnic minority of Mindoro Island.

Tropical Gothic: Prose & Poems, by Nick Joaquin. Short stories, plays and poetry by the Philippines' most revered living writer.

Turn of the Century. Edited by Gilda Cordero Fernando. A lavishly illustrated book on the Philippines' entry into the 20th century.

Index

A
B
C
D
E
F
G
H
I

a
b
c
d
e

g
h
i
j
k
l

The Insight Approach

The book you are holding is part of the world's largest range of guidebooks. Its purpose is to help you have the most valuable travel experience possible, and we try to achieve this by providing not only information about countries, regions and cities but also genuine insight into their history, culture, institutions and people.

Since the first Insight Guide – to Bali – was published in 1970, the series has been dedicated to the proposition that, with insight into a country's people and culture, visitors can both enhance their own experience and be accepted more easily by their hosts. Now, in a world where ethnic hostilities and nationalist conflicts are all too common, such attempts to increase understanding between peoples are more important than ever.

Insight Guides:
Essentials for understanding
Because a nation's past holds the key to its present, each Insight Guide kicks off with lively history chapters. These are followed by magazine-style essays on culture and daily life. This essential background information gives readers the necessary context for using the main Places section, with its comprehensive run-down on things worth seeing and doing.

Finally, a listings section contains all the information you'll need on travel, hotels, restaurants and opening times.

As far as possible, we rely on local writers and specialists to ensure that information is authoritative. The pictures, for which Insight Guides have become so celebrated, are just as important. Our photojournalistic approach aims not only to illustrate a destination but also to communicate visually and directly to readers life as it is lived by the locals. The series has grown to almost 200 titles.

Compact Guides:
The "great little guides"
As invaluable as such background information is, it isn't always fun to carry an Insight Guide through a crowded souk or up a church tower. Could we, readers asked, distil the key reference material into a slim volume for on-the-spot use?

Our response was to design Compact Guides as an entirely new series, with original text carefully cross-referenced to detailed maps and more than 200 photographs. In essence, they're miniature encyclopedias, concise and comprehensive, displaying reliable and up-to-date information in an accessible way. There are almost 100 titles.

Pocket Guides:
A local host in book form
However wide-ranging the information in a book, human beings still value the personal touch. Our editors are often asked the same questions. Where do *you* go to eat? What do *you* think is the best beach? What would *you* recommend if I have only three days? We invited our local correspondents to act as "substitute hosts" by revealing their preferred walks and trips, listing the restaurants they go to and structuring a visit into a series of timed itineraries.

The result: our Pocket Guides, complete with full-size fold-out maps. These 100-plus titles help readers plan a trip precisely, particularly if their time is short.

Exploring with Insight:
A valuable travel experience
In conjunction with co-publishers all over the world, we print in up to 10 languages, from German to Chinese, from Danish to Russian. But our aim remains simple: to enhance your travel experience by combining our expertise in guidebook publishing with the on-the-spot knowledge of our correspondents.

> **I was first drawn to the Insight Guides by the excellent "Nepal" volume. I can think of no book which so effectively captures the essence of a country. Out of these pages leaped the Nepal I know – the captivating charm of a people and their culture. I've since discovered and enjoyed the entire Insight Guide series. Each volume deals with a country in the same sensitive depth, which is nowhere more evident than in the superb photography.**

Sir Edmund Hillary

The World of Insight Guides

400 books in three complementary series cover every major destination in every continent.

Insight Guides

Alaska
Alsace
Amazon Wildlife
American Southwest
Amsterdam
Argentina
Atlanta
Athens
Australia
Austria
Bahamas
Bali
Baltic States
Bangkok
Barbados
Barcelona
Bay of Naples
Beijing
Belgium
Belize
Berlin
Bermuda
Boston
Brazil
Brittany
Brussels
Budapest
Buenos Aires
Burgundy
Burma (Myanmar)
Cairo
Calcutta
California
Canada
Caribbean
Catalonia
Channel Islands
Chicago
Chile
China
Cologne
Continental Europe
Corsica
Costa Rica
Crete
Crossing America
Cuba
Cyprus
Czech & Slovak Republics
Delhi, Jaipur, Agra
Denmark
Dresden
Dublin
Düsseldorf
East African Wildlife
East Asia
Eastern Europe
Ecuador
Edinburgh
Egypt
Finland
Florence
Florida
France
Frankfurt
French Riviera
Gambia & Senegal
Germany
Glasgow

Gran Canaria
Great Barrier Reef
Great Britain
Greece
Greek Islands
Hamburg
Hawaii
Hong Kong
Hungary
Iceland
India
India's Western Himalaya
Indian Wildlife
Indonesia
Ireland
Israel
Istanbul
Italy
Jamaica
Japan
Java
Jerusalem
Jordan
Kathmandu
Kenya
Korea
Lisbon
Loire Valley
London
Los Angeles
Madeira
Madrid
Malaysia
Mallorca & Ibiza
Malta
Marine Life in the South
  China Sea
Melbourne
Mexico
Mexico City
Miami
Montreal
Morocco
Moscow
Munich
Namibia
Native America
Nepal
Netherlands
New England
New Orleans
New York City
New York State
New Zealand
Nile
Normandy
Northern California
Northern Spain
Norway
Oman & the UAE
Oxford
Old South
Pacific Northwest
Pakistan
Paris
Peru
Philadelphia
Philippines
Poland
Portugal
Prague

Provence
Puerto Rico
Rajasthan
Rhine
Rio de Janeiro
Rockies
Rome
Russia
St Petersburg
San Francisco
Sardinia
Scotland
Seattle
Sicily
Singapore
South Africa
South America
South Asia
South India
South Tyrol
Southeast Asia
Southeast Asia Wildlife
Southern California
Southern Spain
Spain
Sri Lanka
Sweden
Switzerland
Sydney
Taiwan
Tenerife
Texas
Thailand
Tokyo
Trinidad & Tobago
Tunisia
Turkey
Turkish Coast
Tuscany
Umbria
US National Parks East
US National Parks West
Vancouver
Venezuela
Venice
Vienna
Vietnam
Wales
Washington DC
Waterways of Europe
Wild West
Yemen

Insight Pocket Guides

Aegean Islands★
Algarve★
Alsace
Amsterdam★
Athens★
Atlanta★
Bahamas★
Baja Peninsula★
Bali★
Bali *Bird Walks*
Bangkok★
Barbados★
Barcelona★
Bavaria★
Beijing★
Berlin★

Bermuda★
Bhutan★
Boston★
British Columbia★
Brittany★
Brussels★
Budapest &
  Surroundings★
Canton★
Chiang Mai★
Chicago★
Corsica★
Costa Blanca★
Costa Brava★
Costa del Sol/Marbella★
Costa Rica★
Crete★
Denmark★
Fiji★
Florence★
Florida★
Florida Keys★
French Riviera★
Gran Canaria★
Hawaii★
Hong Kong★
Hungary
Ibiza★
Ireland★
Ireland's Southwest★
Israel★
Istanbul★
Jakarta★
Jamaica★
Kathmandu *Bikes &
  Hikes*★
Kenya★
Kuala Lumpur★
Lisbon★
Loire Valley★
London★
Macau
Madrid★
Malacca
Maldives
Mallorca★
Malta★
Mexico City★
Miami★
Milan★
Montreal★
Morocco★
Moscow
Munich★
Nepal★
New Delhi
New Orleans★
New York City★
New Zealand★
Northern California★
Oslo/Bergen★
Paris★
Penang★
Phuket★
Prague★
Provence★
Puerto Rico★
Quebec★
Rhodes★
Rome★
Sabah★

St Petersburg★
San Francisco★
Sardinia
Scotland★
Seville★
Seychelles★
Sicily★
Sikkim
Singapore★
Southeast England
Southern California★
Southern Spain★
Sri Lanka★
Sydney★
Tenerife★
Thailand★
Tibet★
Toronto★
Tunisia★
Turkish Coast★
Tuscany★
Venice★
Vienna★
Vietnam★
Yogyakarta
Yucatan Peninsula★

★ = *Insight Pocket Guides*
with Pull out Maps

Insight Compact Guides

Algarve
Amsterdam
Bahamas
Bali
Bangkok
Barbados
Barcelona
Beijing
Belgium
Berlin
Brittany
Brussels
Budapest
Burgundy
Copenhagen
Costa Brava
Costa Rica
Crete
Cyprus
Czech Republic
Denmark
Dominican Republic
Dublin
Egypt
Finland
Florence
Gran Canaria
Greece
Holland
Hong Kong
Ireland
Israel
Italian Lakes
Italian Riviera
Jamaica
Jerusalem
Lisbon
Madeira
Mallorca
Malta

Milan
Moscow
Munich
Normandy
Norway
Paris
Poland
Portugal
Prague
Provence
Rhodes
Rome
St Petersburg
Salzburg
Singapore
Switzerland
Sydney
Tenerife
Thailand
Turkey
Turkish Coast
Tuscany
UK regional titles:
  Bath & Surroundings
  Cambridge & East
    Anglia
  Cornwall
  Cotswolds
  Devon & Exmoor
  Edinburgh
  Lake District
  London
  New Forest
  North York Moors
  Northumbria
  Oxford
  Peak District
  Scotland
  Scottish Highlands
  Shakespeare Country
  Snowdonia
  South Downs
  York
  Yorkshire Dales
USA regional titles:
  Boston
  Cape Cod
  Chicago
  Florida
  Florida Keys
  Hawaii: Maui
  Hawaii: Oahu
  Las Vegas
  Los Angeles
  Martha's Vineyard &
    Nantucket
  New York
  San Francisco
  Washington D.C.
  Venice
  Vienna
  West of Ireland